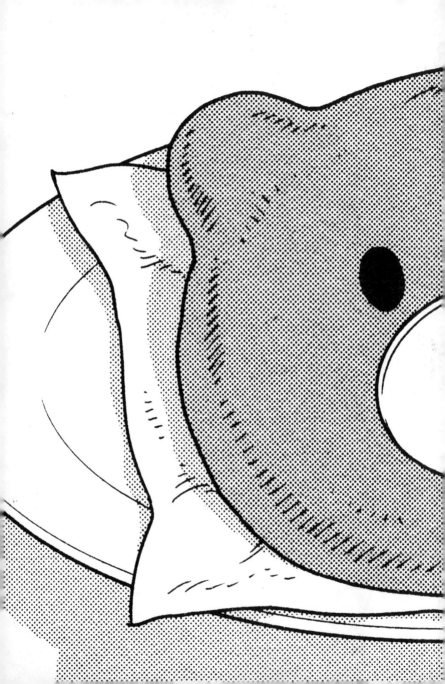

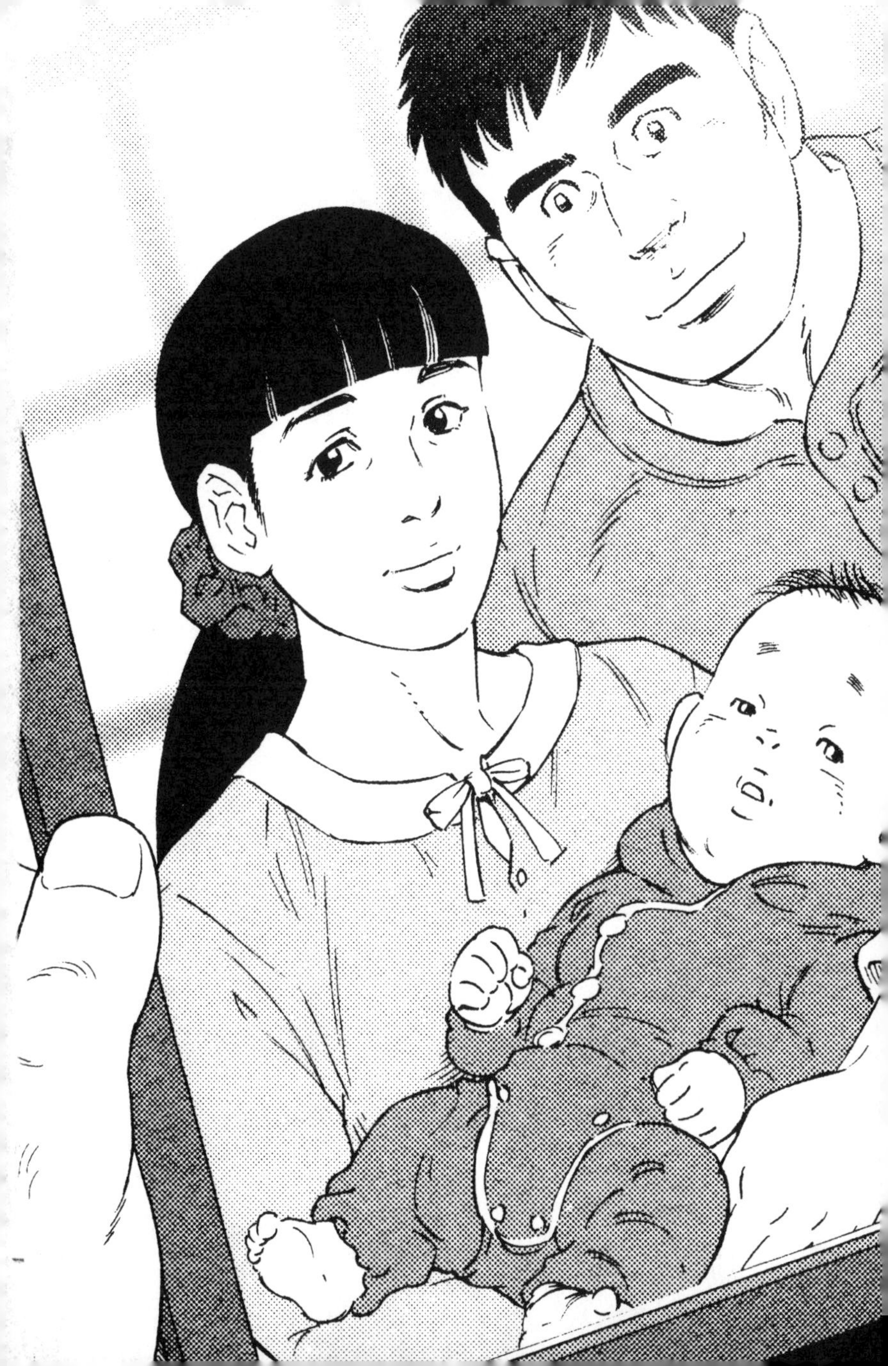

MY BROTHER'S HUSBAND

VOLUME 1

GENGOROH TAGAME

TRANSLATED FROM THE JAPANESE BY ANNE ISHII

PANTHEON BOOKS, NEW YORK

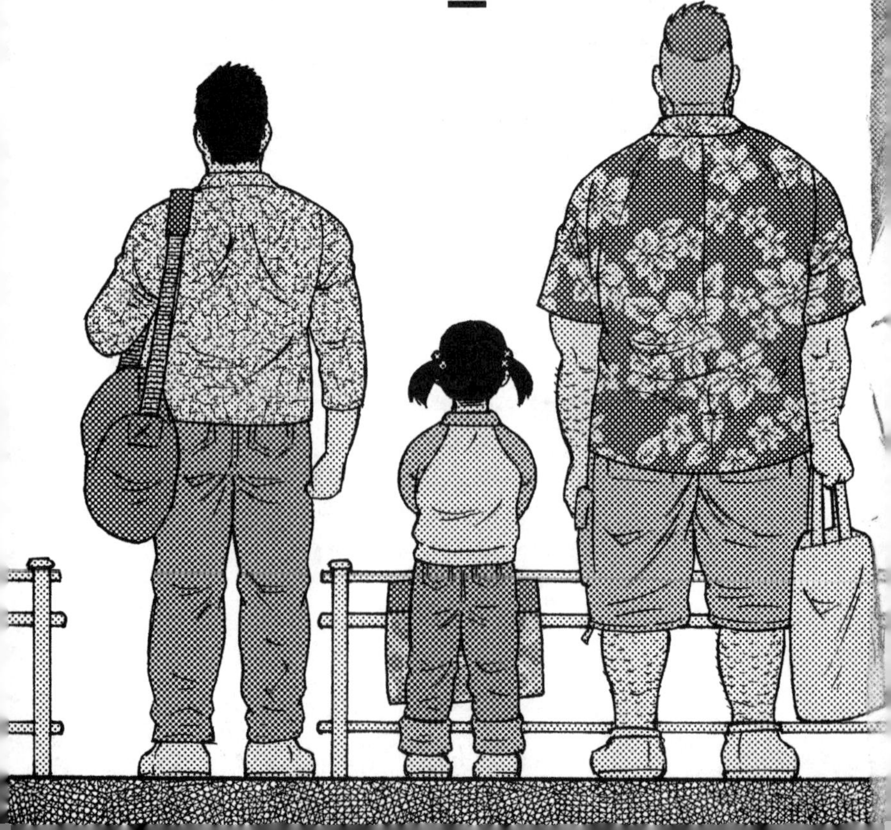

TRANSLATION COPYRIGHT © 2017 BY ANNE ISHII

ALL RIGHTS RESERVED. PUBLISHED IN THE UNITED STATES BY PANTHEON BOOKS, A DIVISION
OF PENGUIN RANDOM HOUSE LLC, NEW YORK, AND DISTRIBUTED IN CANADA BY RANDOM HOUSE
OF CANADA, A DIVISION OF PENGUIN RANDOM HOUSE CANADA LIMITED, TORONTO. ORIGINALLY
PUBLISHED IN JAPAN AS *OTŌTO NO OTTO* BY FUTABASHA PUBLISHERS LTD., TOKYO, IN 2014.
COPYRIGHT © 2014 BY GENGOROH TAGAME. THIS ENGLISH-LANGUAGE EDITION PUBLISHED
BY ARRANGEMENT WITH FUTABASHA PUBLISHERS LTD., TOKYO.

PANTHEON BOOKS AND COLOPHON ARE REGISTERED TRADEMARKS OF
PENGUIN RANDOM HOUSE LLC.

LIBRARY OF CONGRESS CATALOGING-IN-PUBLICATION DATA
NAMES: TAGAME, GENGOROH, [DATE] AUTHOR, ARTIST. ISHII, ANNE, TRANSLATOR.
TITLE: MY BROTHER'S HUSBAND / GENGOROH TAGAME ; TRANSLATED BY ANNE ISHII.
OTHER TITLES: OTOUTO NO OTTO. ENGLISH.
DESCRIPTION: FIRST AMERICAN EDITION. NEW YORK : PANTHEON, 2017.
IDENTIFIERS: LCCN 2016047082 (PRINT). LCCN 2016050241 (EBOOK).
ISBN 9781101871515 (V. 1 : HARDCOVER). ISBN 9781101871522 (EBOOK).
SUBJECTS: LCSH: GAY MEN--JAPAN--COMIC BOOKS, STRIPS, ETC. GRAPHIC NOVELS.
BISAC: FICTION/FAMILY LIFE. COMICS & GRAPHIC NOVELS/LITERARY.
COMICS & GRAPHIC NOVELS/MANGA/GAY & LESBIAN.
CLASSIFICATION: LCC PN6790.J33 T255613 2017 (PRINT).
LCC PN6790.J33 (EBOOK). DDC 741.5/952--DC23
LC RECORD AVAILABLE AT LCCN.LOC.GOV/2016047082

WWW.PANTHEONBOOKS.COM

JACKET AND CASE ILLUSTRATION BY GENGOROH TAGAME
JACKET AND CASE DESIGN BY CHIP KIDD
PRODUCTION ASSISTANCE BY JOHN KURAMOTO

PRINTED IN THE UNITED STATES OF AMERICA
FIRST AMERICAN EDITION

9 8 7 6 5 4 3 2 1

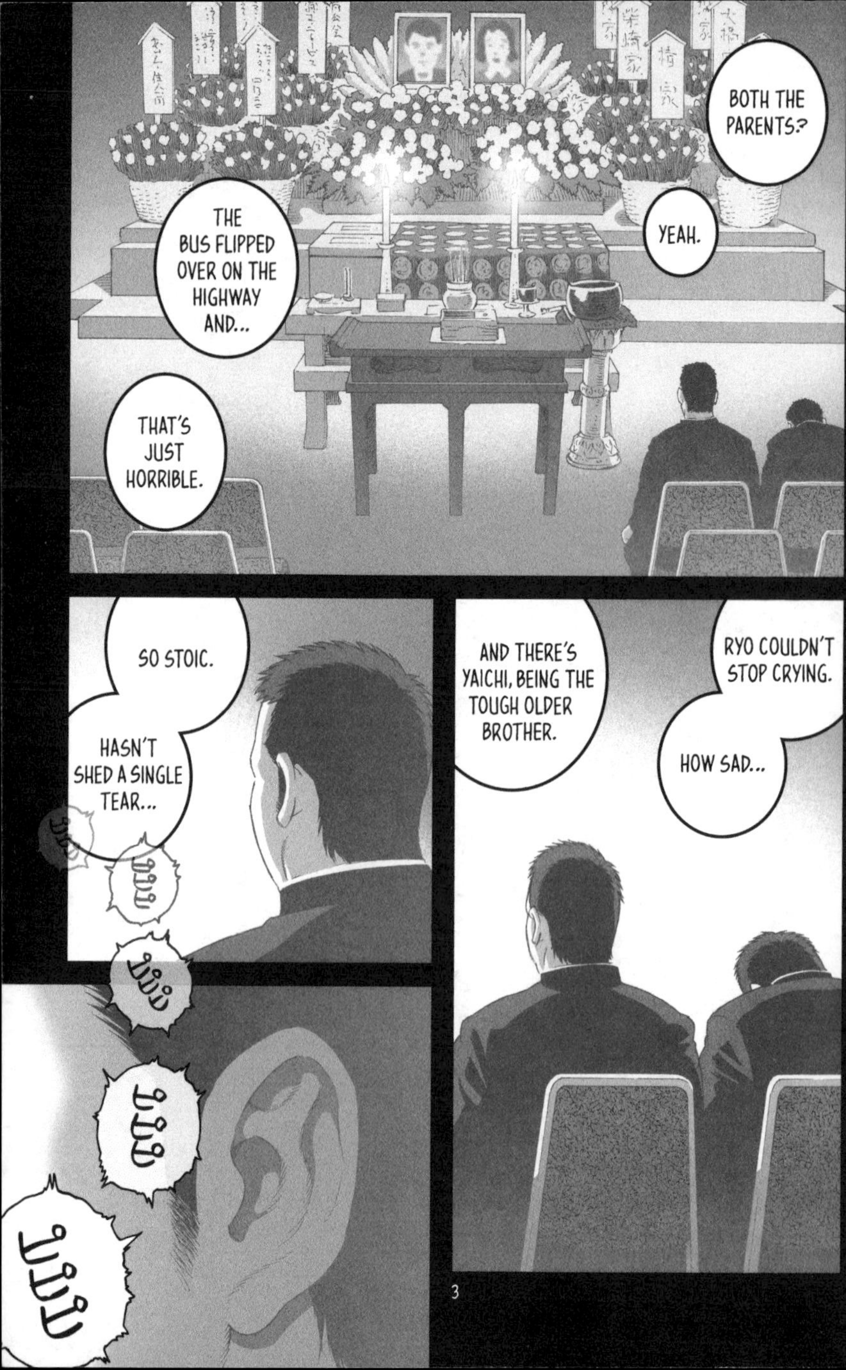
BOTH THE PARENTS?
YEAH.
THE BUS FLIPPED OVER ON THE HIGHWAY AND...
THAT'S JUST HORRIBLE.
RYO COULDN'T STOP CRYING.
HOW SAD...
AND THERE'S YAICHI, BEING THE TOUGH OLDER BROTHER.
SO STOIC.
HASN'T SHED A SINGLE TEAR...

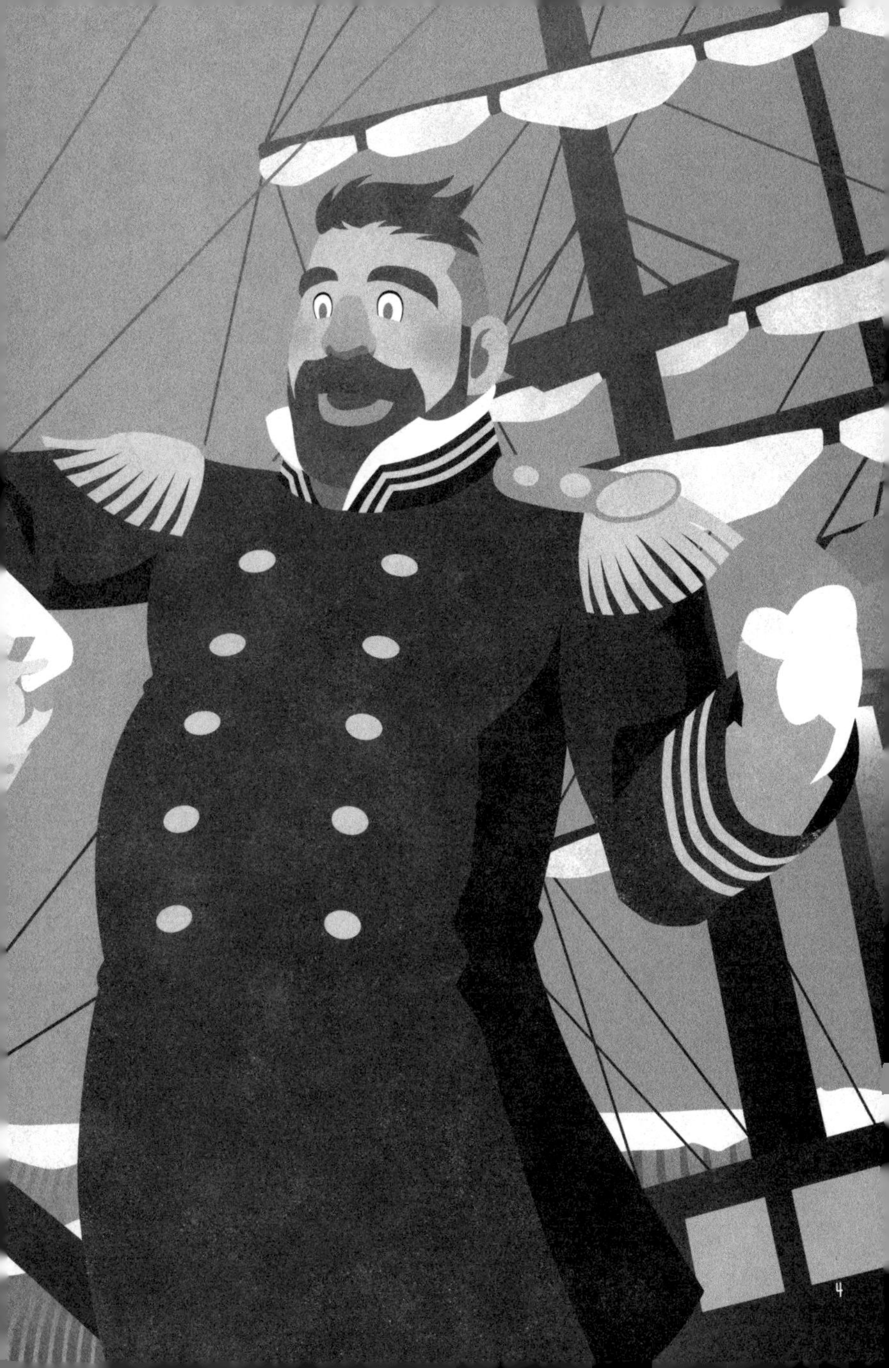

CHAPTER ONE

THE BLACK SHIPS ARRIVE

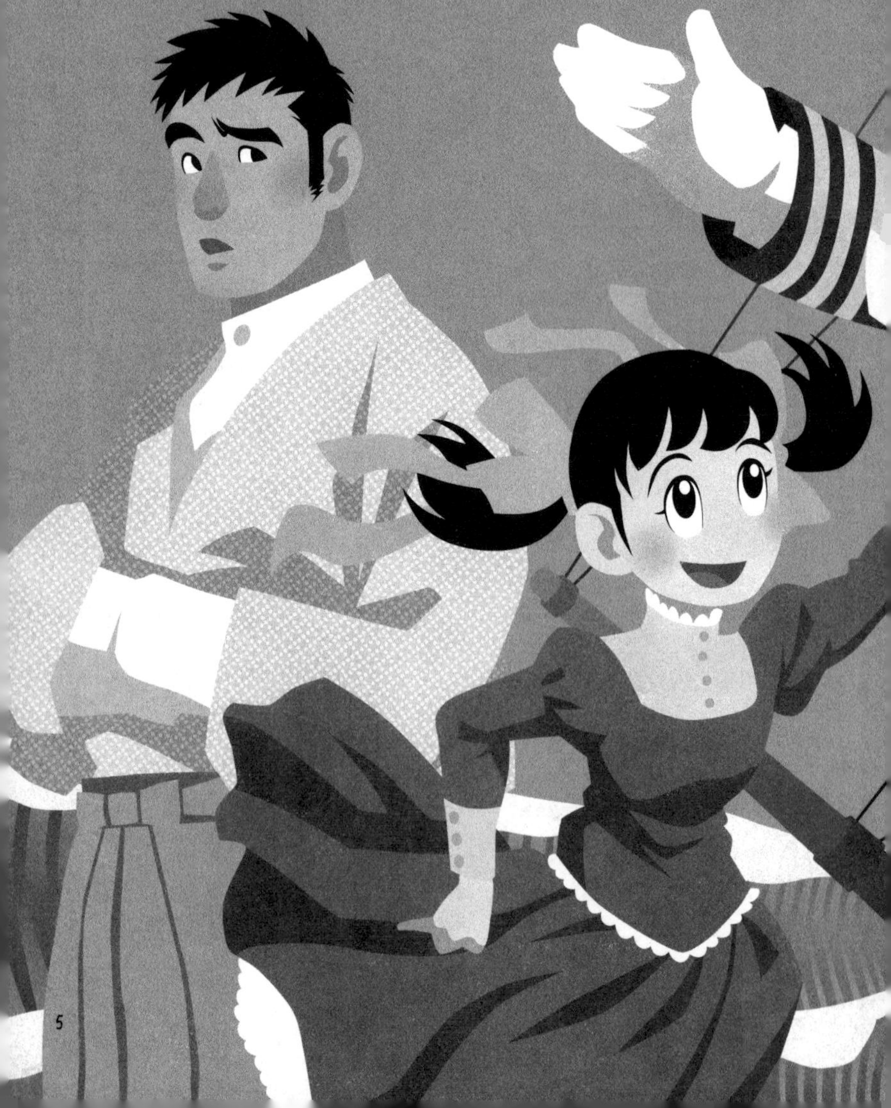

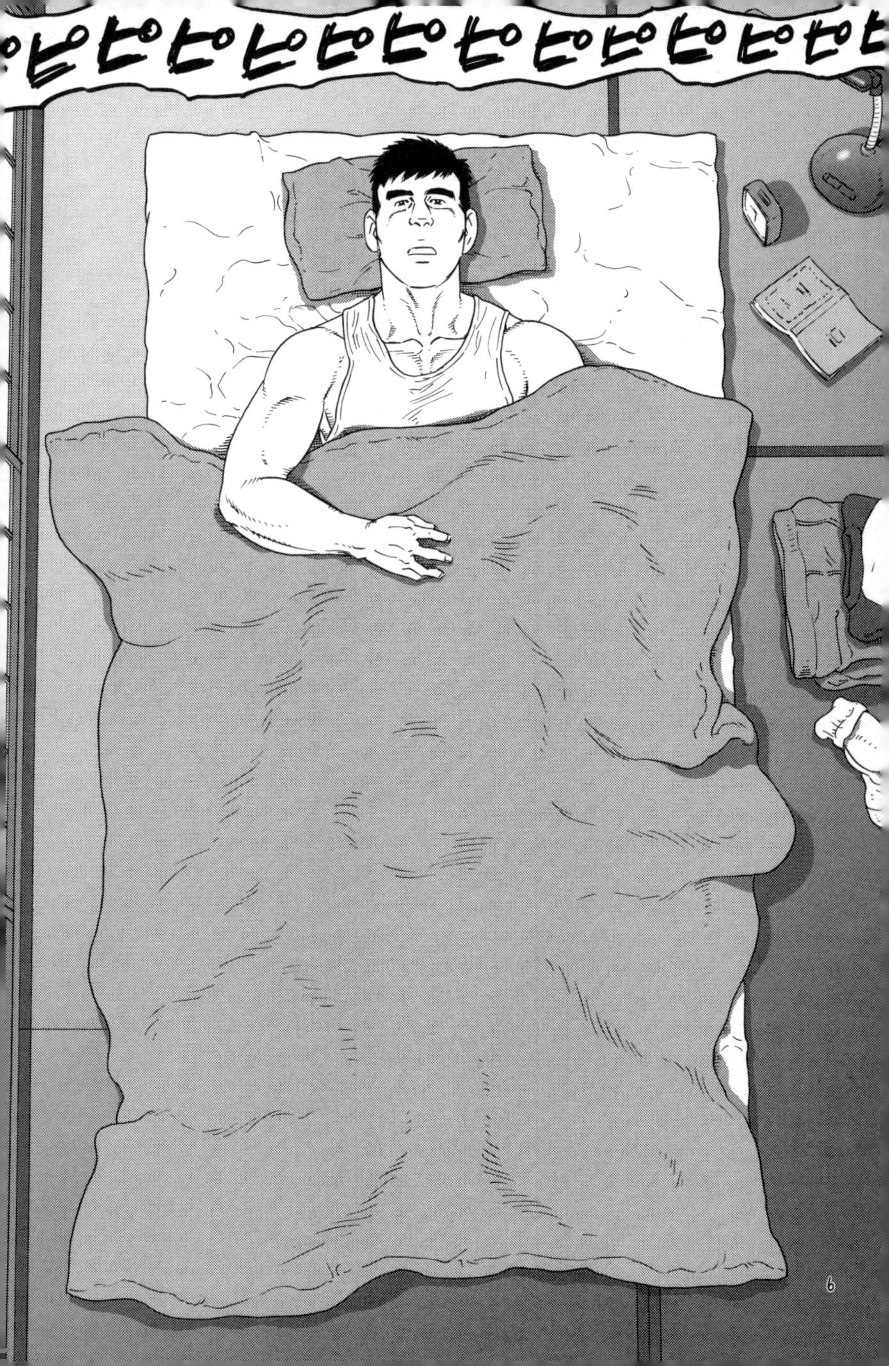
ピピピピピピピピピピピピ

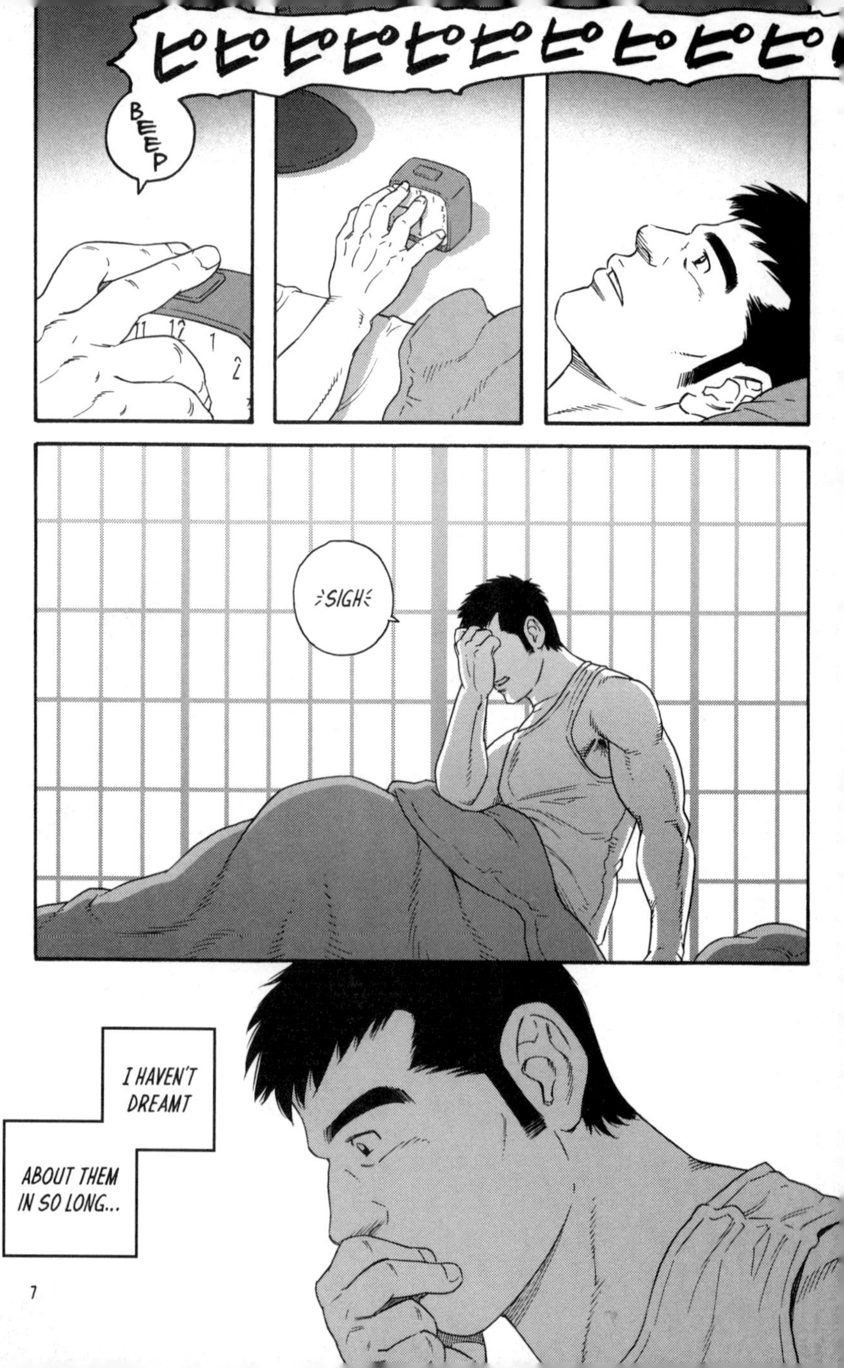
ピピピピピピピピピピ
BEEP
SIGH
I HAVEN'T DREAMT
ABOUT THEM IN SO LONG...

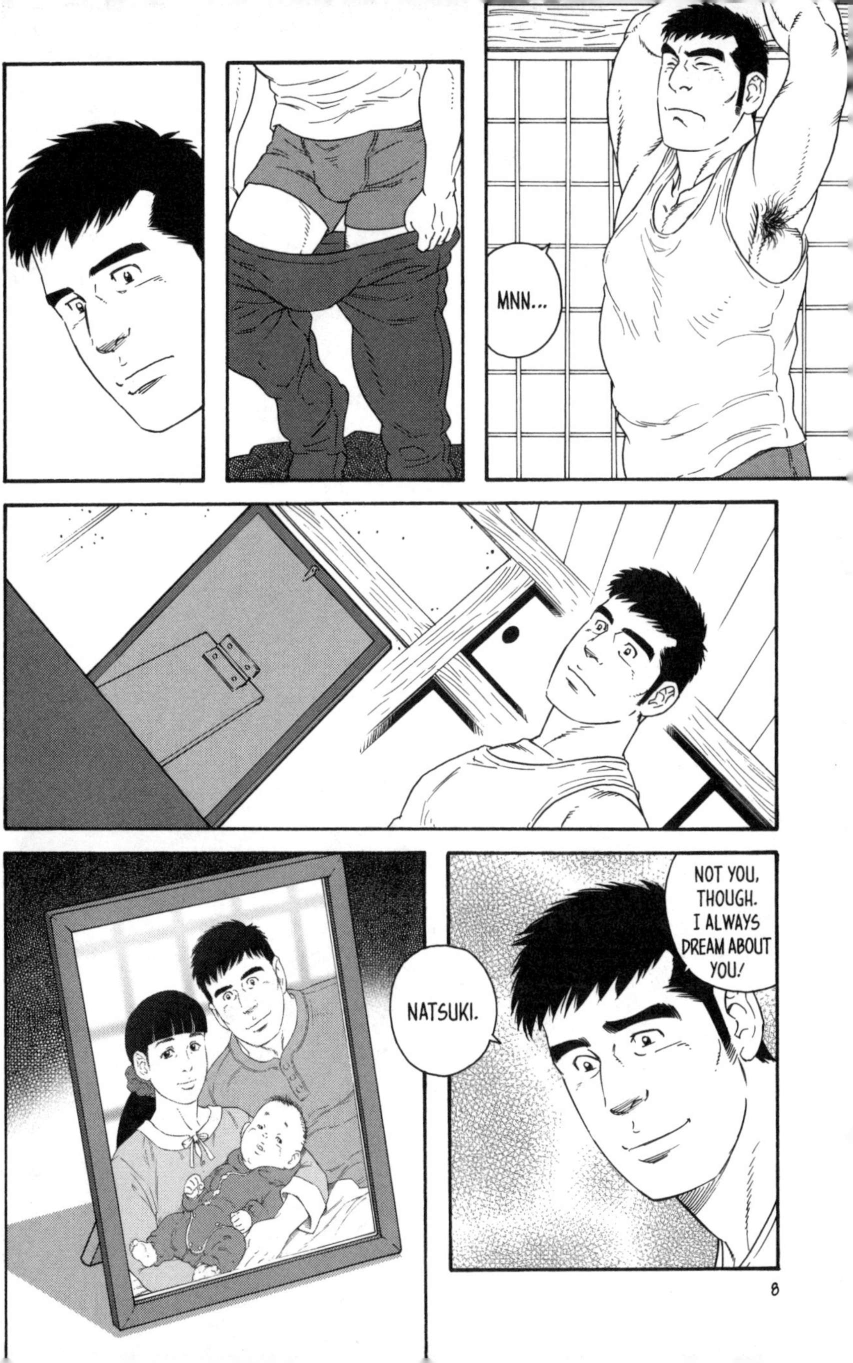
MNN...
NOT YOU, THOUGH. I ALWAYS DREAM ABOUT YOU!
NATSUKI.

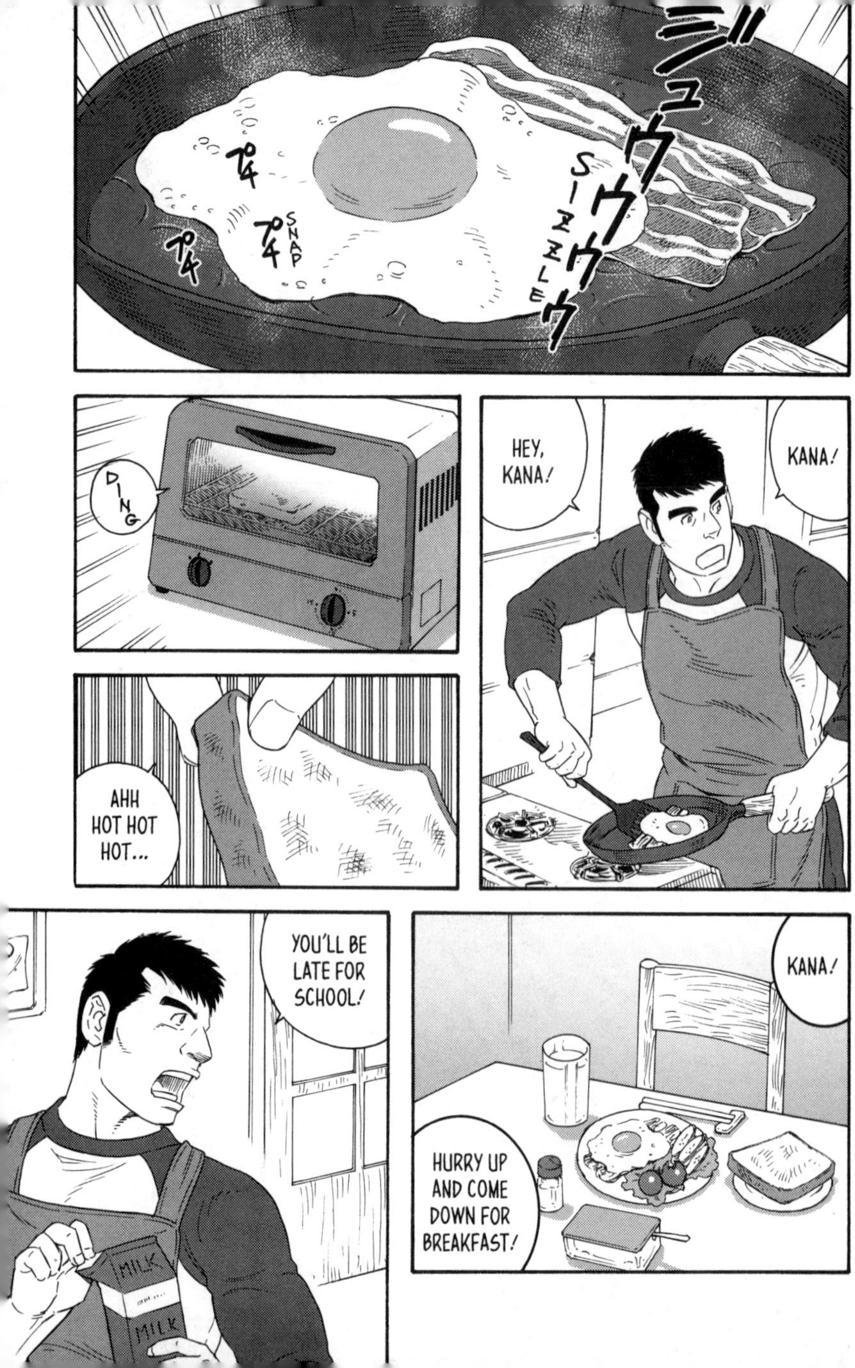
ジュウウウウ
SIZZLE
プチ
プチ
SNAP
プチ
KANA!
HEY, KANA!
DING
AHH HOT HOT HOT...
KANA!
HURRY UP AND COME DOWN FOR BREAKFAST!
YOU'LL BE LATE FOR SCHOOL!
MILK
MILK

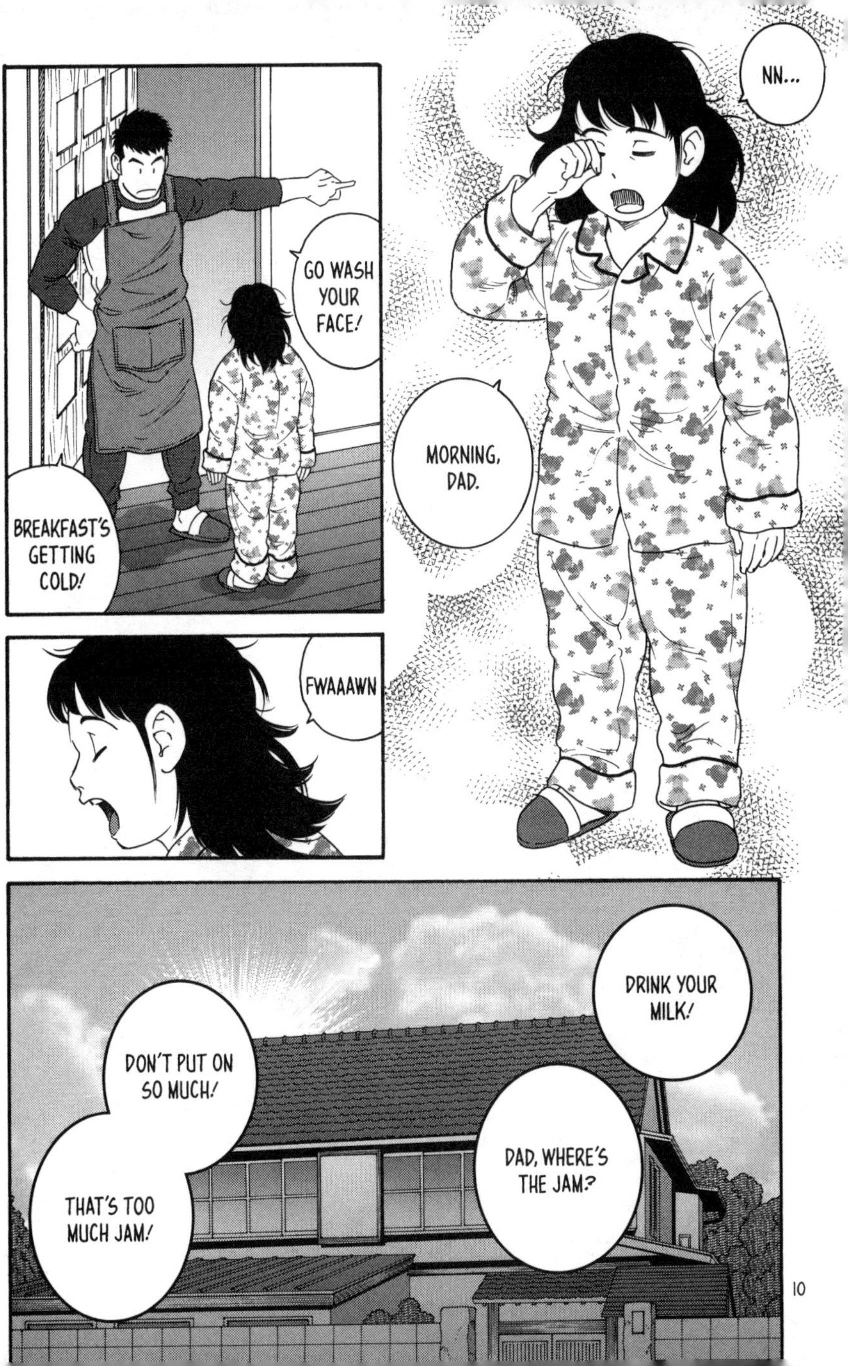
NN...
MORNING, DAD.
GO WASH YOUR FACE!
BREAKFAST'S GETTING COLD!
FWAAAWN
DRINK YOUR MILK!
DAD, WHERE'S THE JAM?
DON'T PUT ON SO MUCH!
THAT'S TOO MUCH JAM!

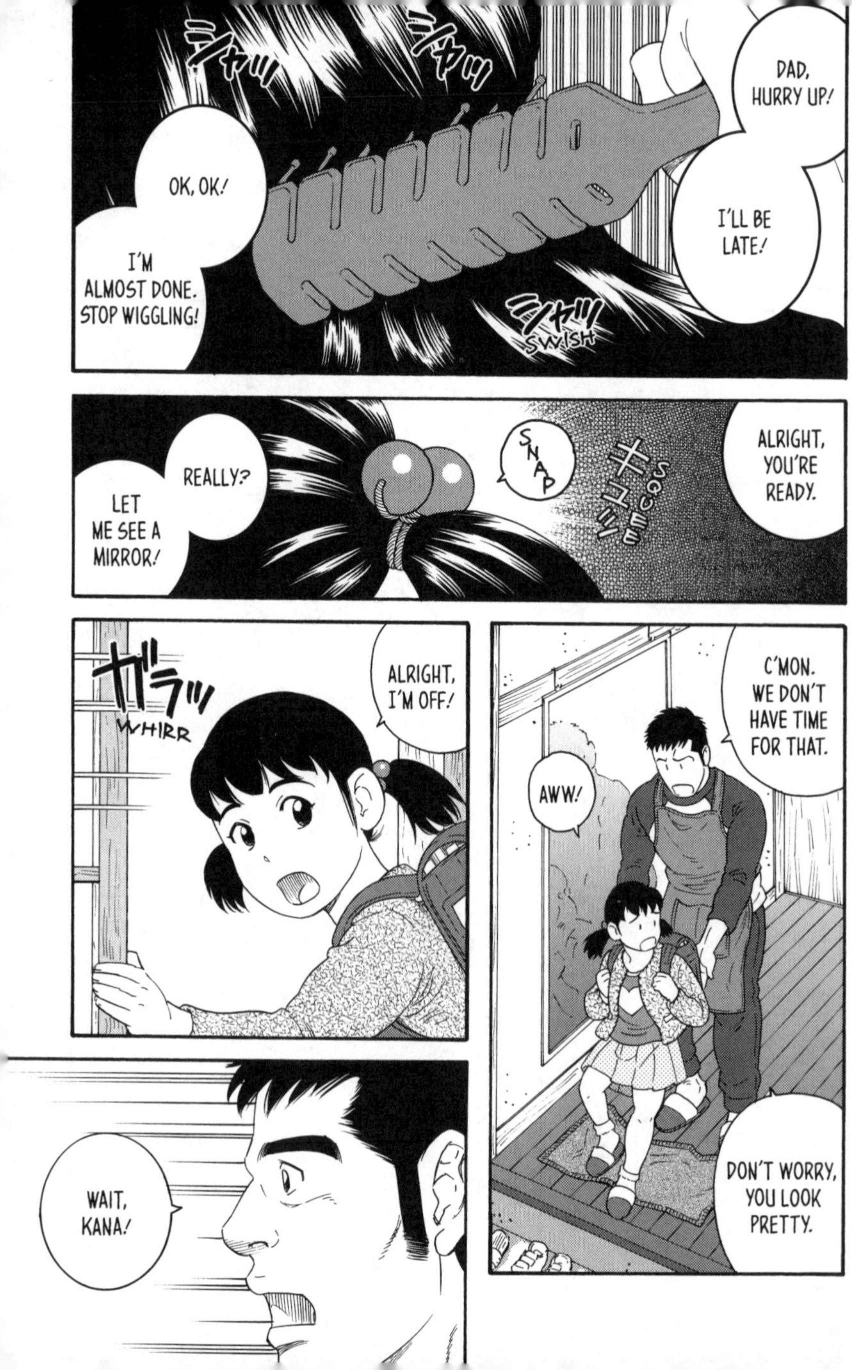
DAD, HURRY UP!
I'LL BE LATE!
シャッ
シャッ
OK, OK!
I'M ALMOST DONE. STOP WIGGLING!
シャッ SWISH
ALRIGHT, YOU'RE READY.
キュッ SQUEE
SNAP
REALLY?
LET ME SEE A MIRROR!
C'MON. WE DON'T HAVE TIME FOR THAT.
AWW!
DON'T WORRY, YOU LOOK PRETTY.
ALRIGHT, I'M OFF!
ガラッ WHIRR
WAIT, KANA!

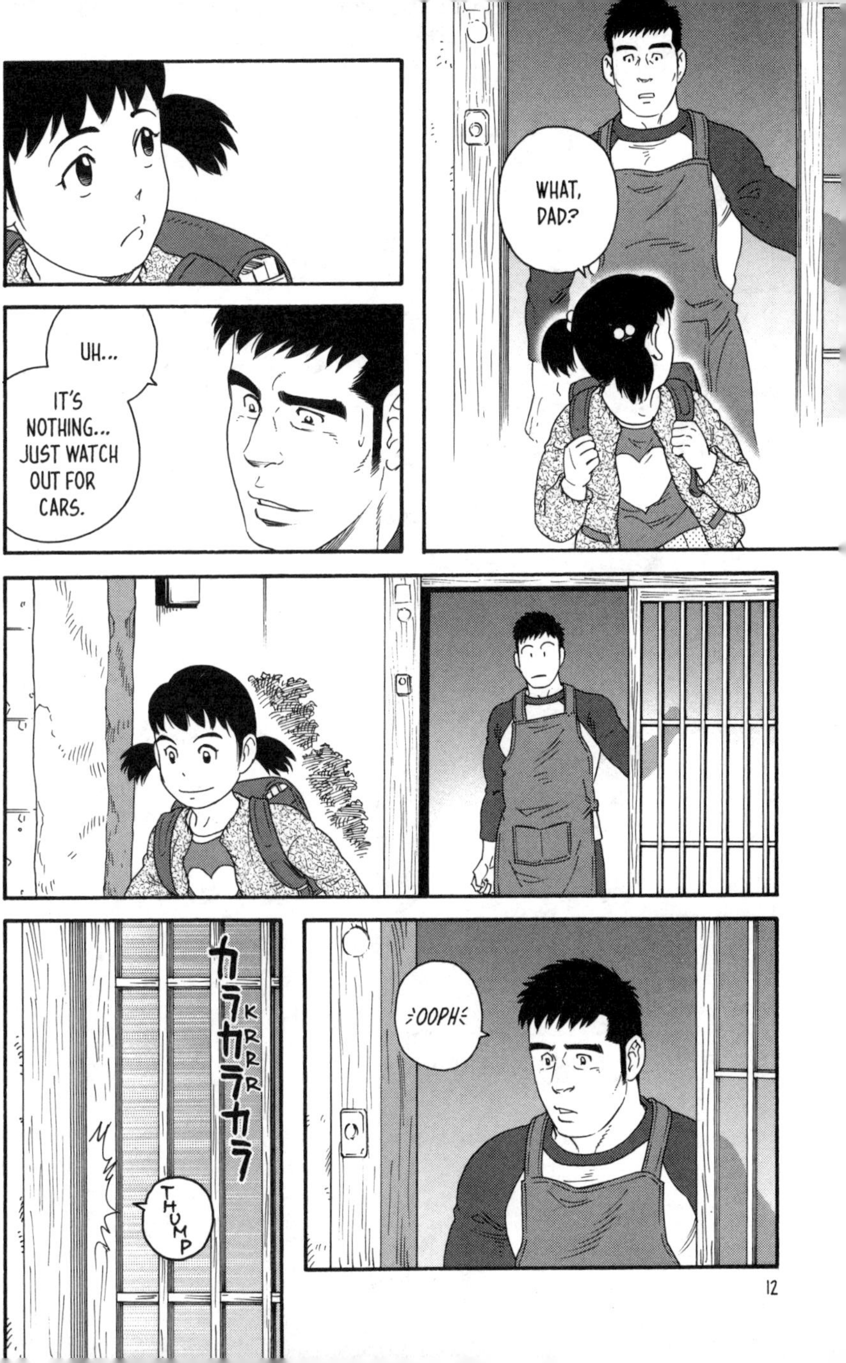
WHAT, DAD?
UH...
IT'S NOTHING... JUST WATCH OUT FOR CARS.
OOPH
カラカラカラ
KRRR
THUMP

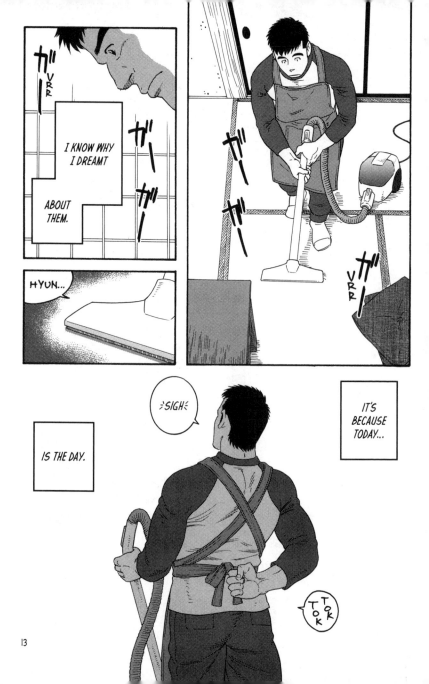

GA VRR

I KNOW WHY I DREAMT

GA

ABOUT THEM.

GA

GA

HYUN...

GA VRR

≶SIGH≶

IT'S BECAUSE TODAY...

IS THE DAY.

TOK TOK

13

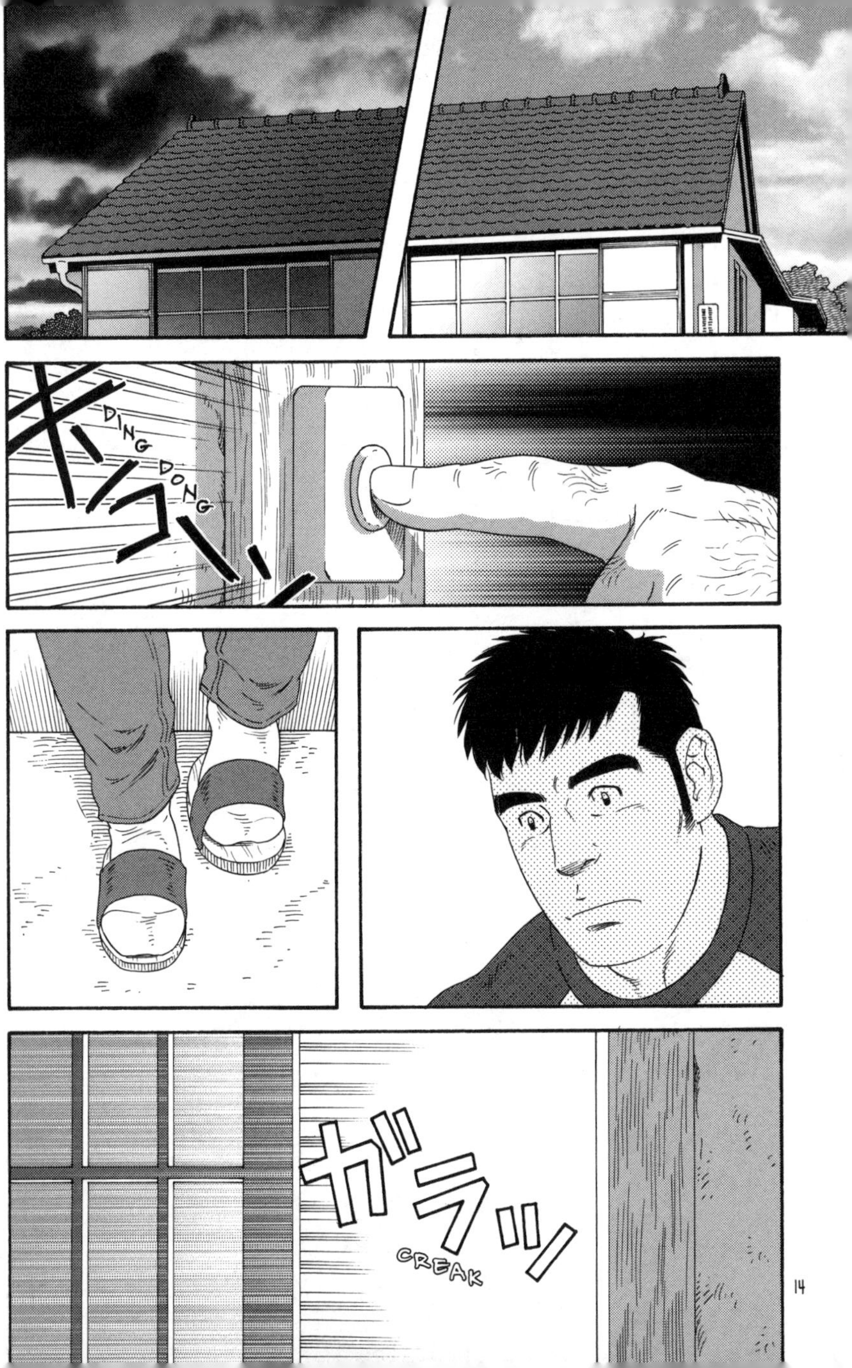
キンコーン
DING DONG
ガラッ
CREAK

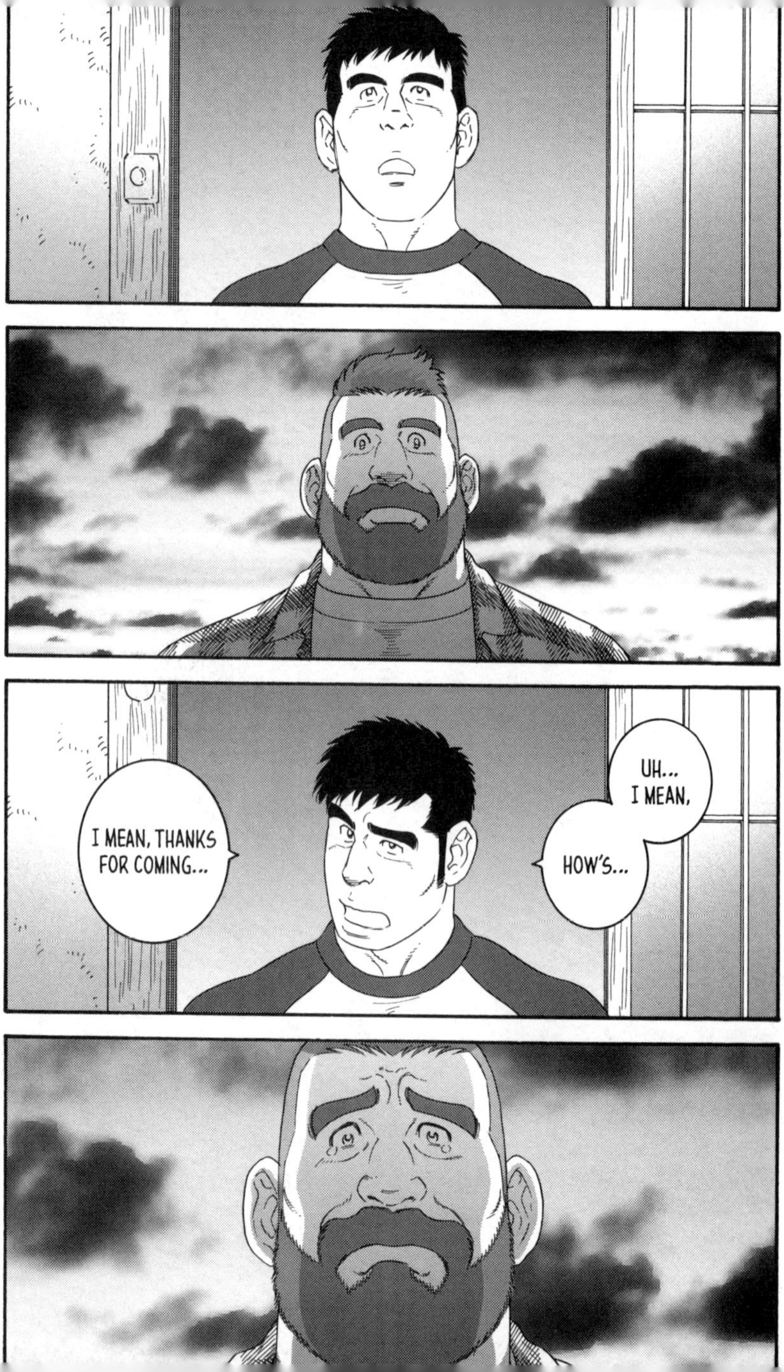
UH... I MEAN,
HOW'S...
I MEAN, THANKS FOR COMING...

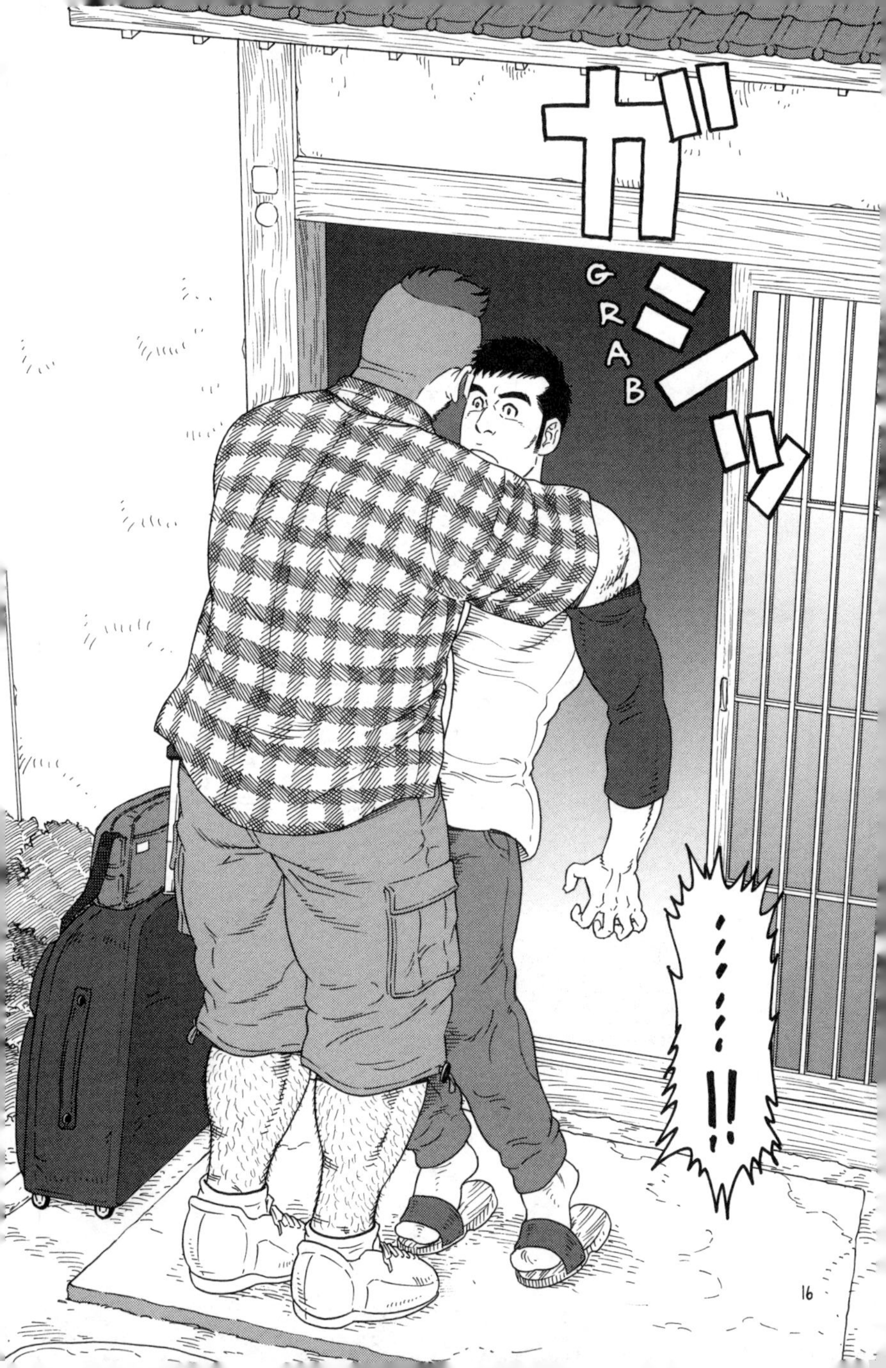
ガシッ
GRAB
……!!

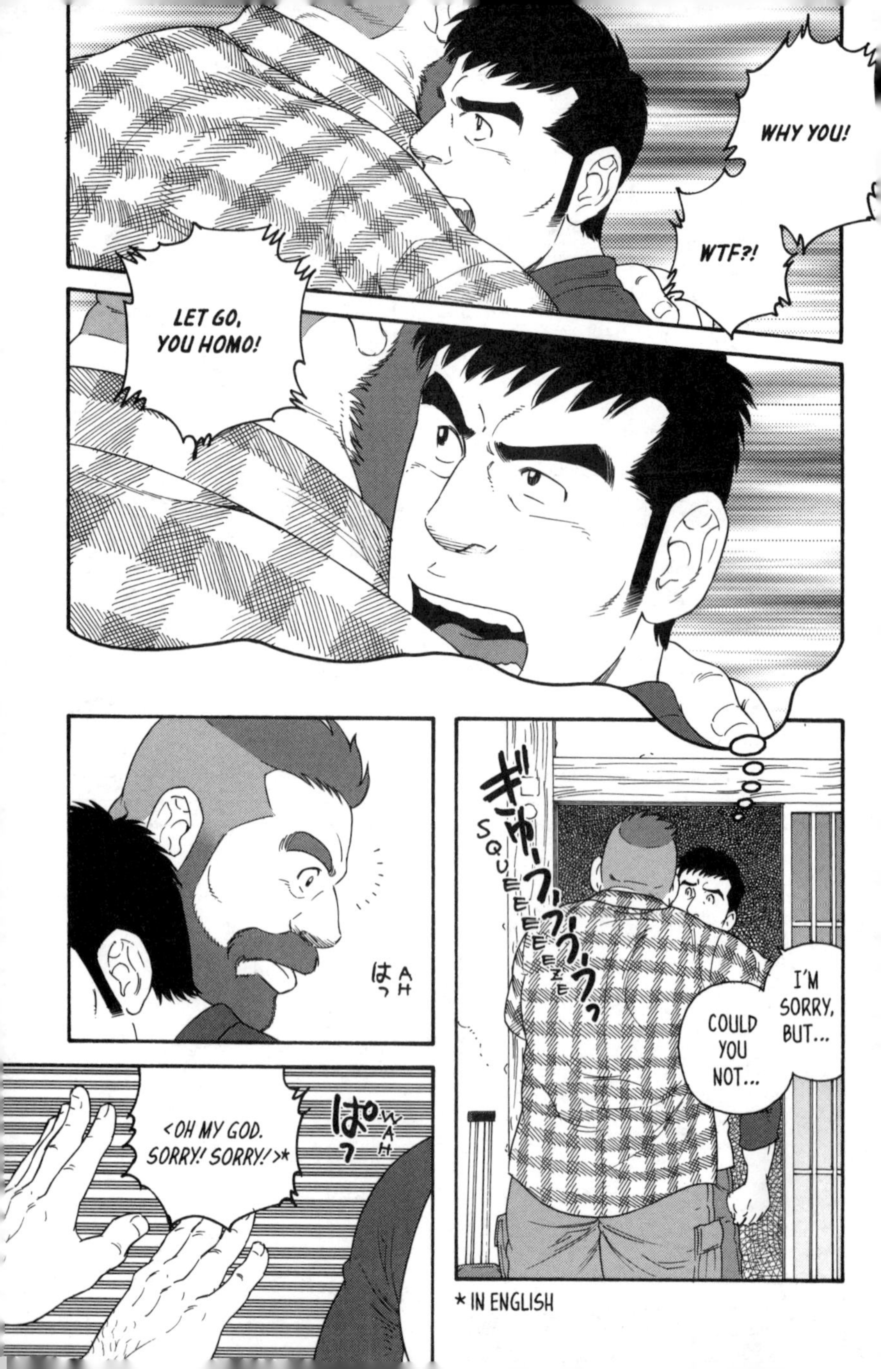
WHY YOU!
WTF?!
LET GO, YOU HOMO!
ぎゅううう
SQUEEEEEZE
I'M SORRY, BUT...
COULD YOU NOT...
はっ
AH
ぱっ
WAH
<OH MY GOD. SORRY! SORRY!>*

* IN ENGLISH

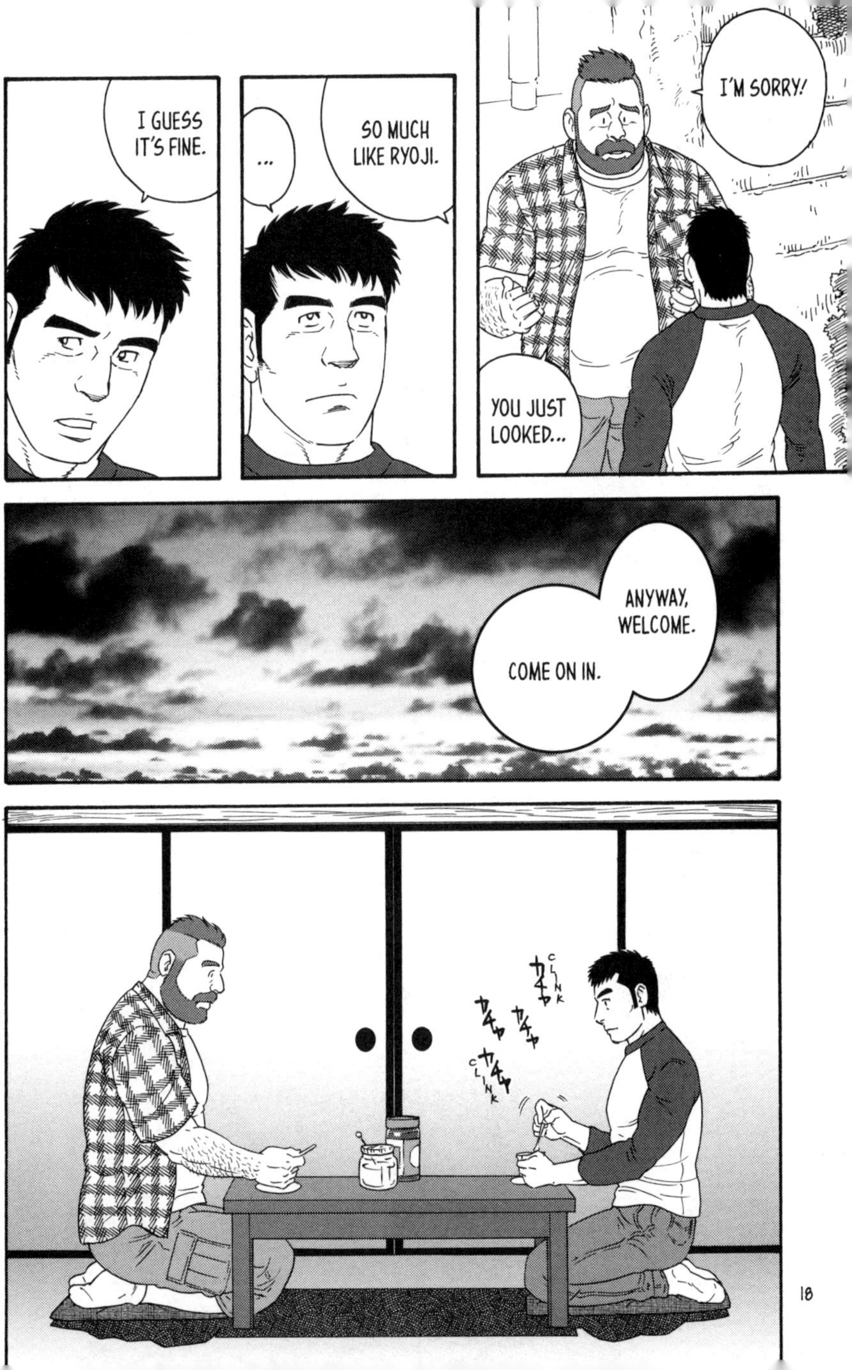
I'M SORRY!
YOU JUST LOOKED...
SO MUCH LIKE RYOJI.
...
I GUESS IT'S FINE.
ANYWAY, WELCOME.
COME ON IN.
カチャ CLINK
カチャ
カチャ
カチャ CLINK

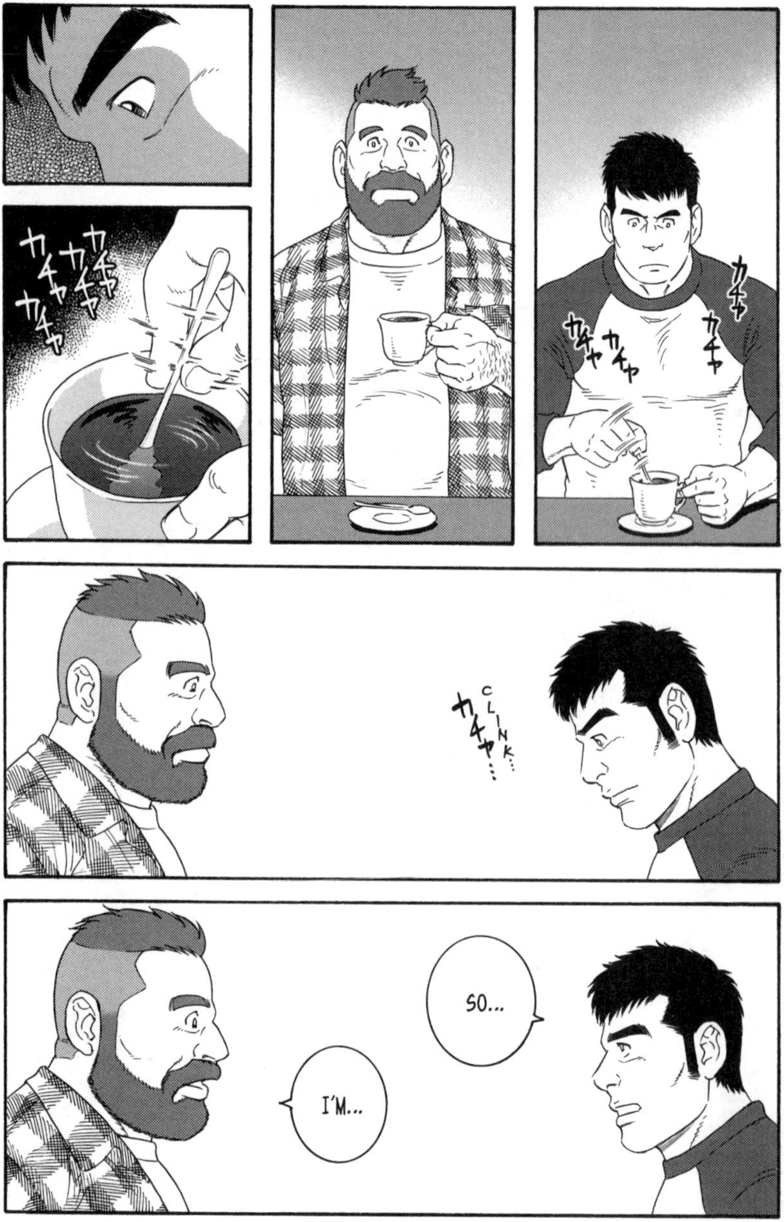
カチャ
カチャ
カチャ
カチャ
カチャ
カチャ
カチャ
カチャ…
CLINK…
SO...
I'M...

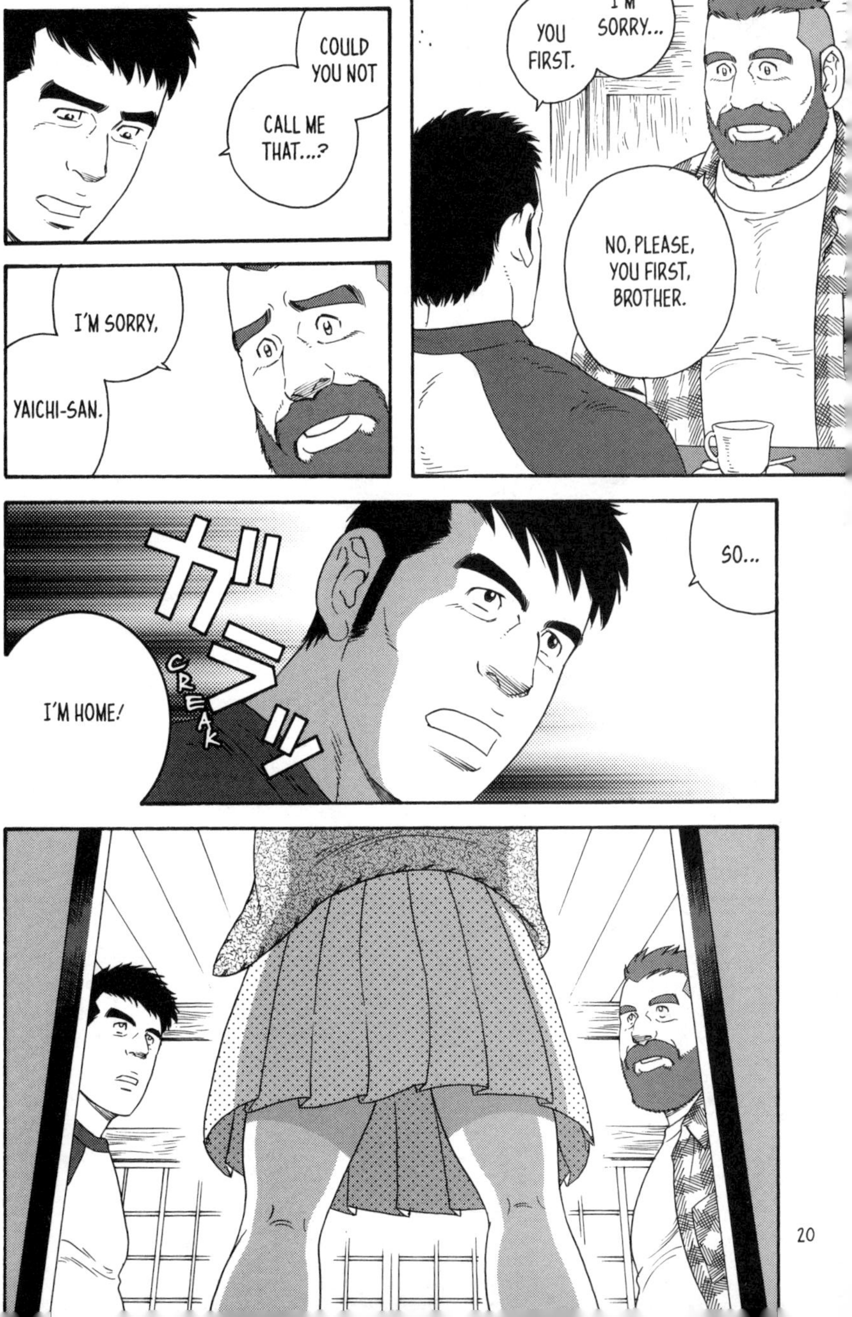

I'M SORRY...
YOU FIRST.
NO, PLEASE, YOU FIRST, BROTHER.
COULD YOU NOT CALL ME THAT...?
I'M SORRY, YAICHI-SAN.
SO...
ガラッ
CREAK
I'M HOME!

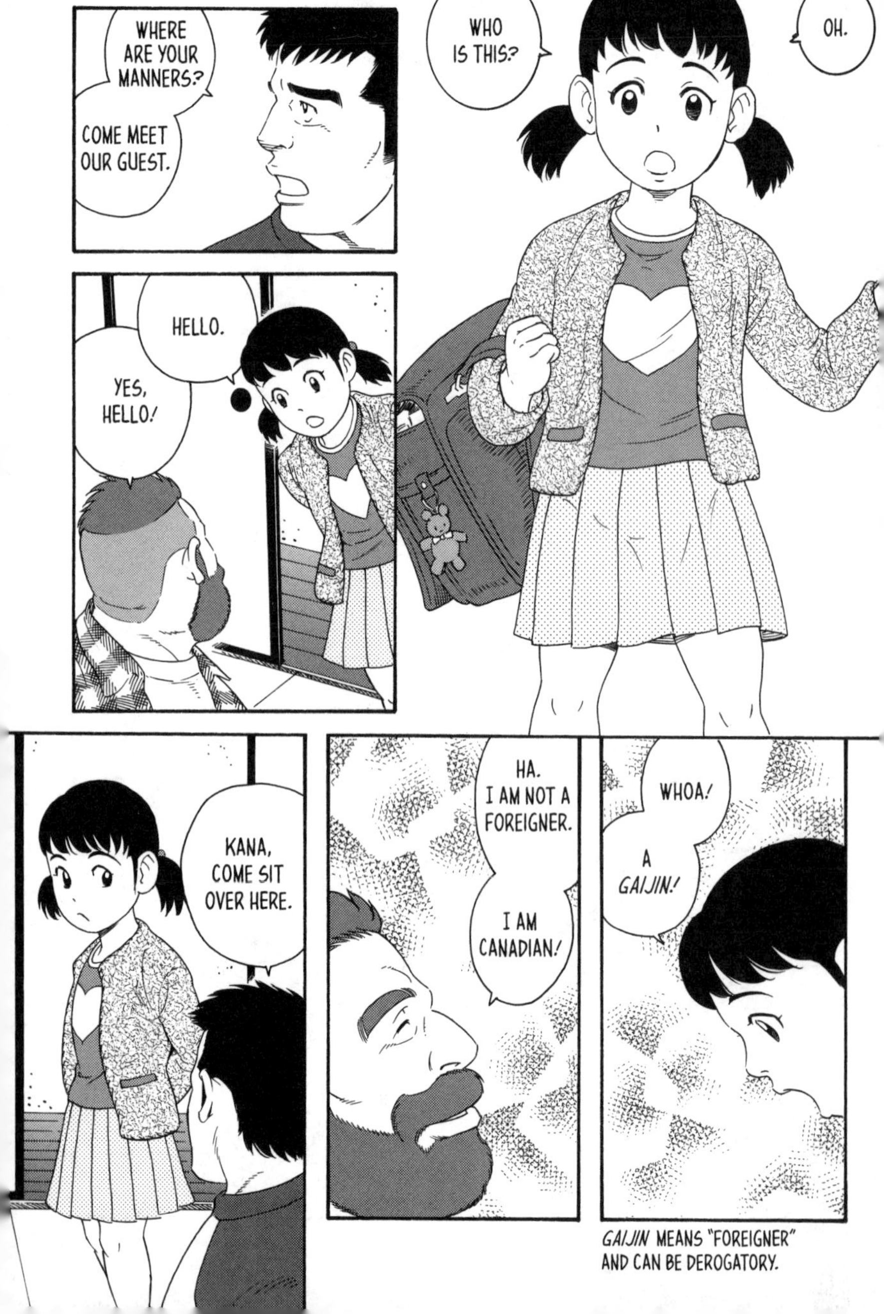
OH.
WHO IS THIS?
WHERE ARE YOUR MANNERS?
COME MEET OUR GUEST.
HELLO.
YES, HELLO!
WHOA!
A *GAIJIN!*
HA. I AM NOT A FOREIGNER.
I AM CANADIAN!
KANA, COME SIT OVER HERE.

GAIJIN MEANS "FOREIGNER" AND CAN BE DEROGATORY.

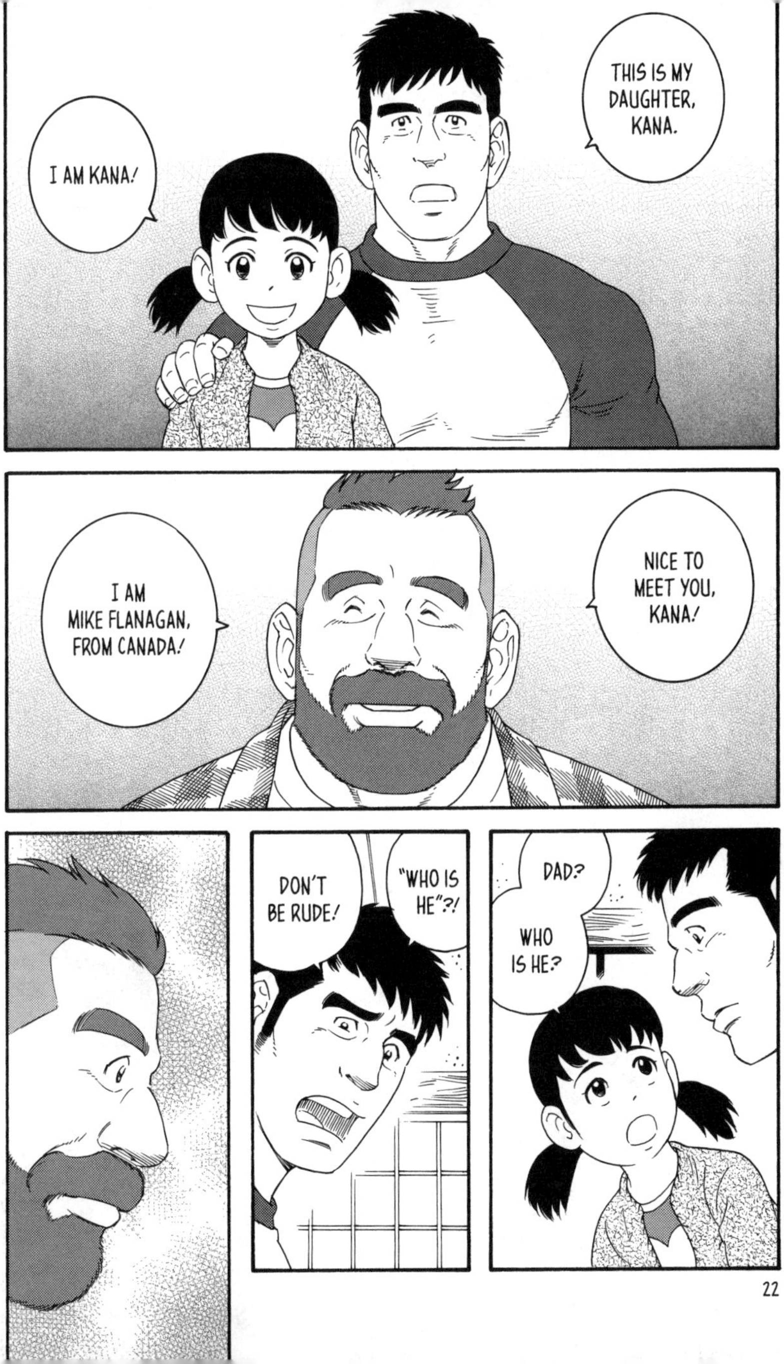
THIS IS MY DAUGHTER, KANA.
I AM KANA!
NICE TO MEET YOU, KANA!
I AM MIKE FLANAGAN, FROM CANADA!
DAD?
WHO IS HE?
"WHO IS HE"?!
DON'T BE RUDE!

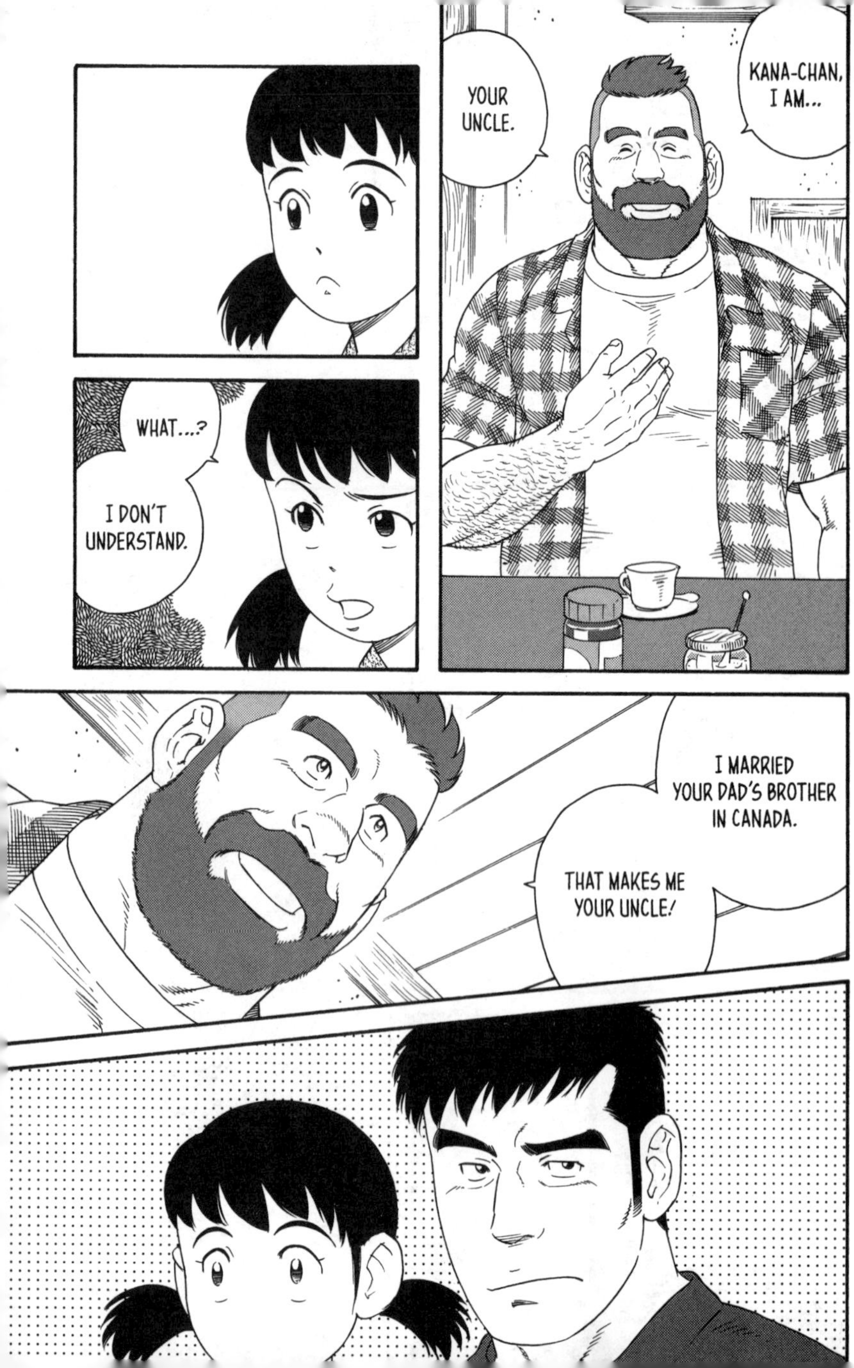
KANA-CHAN, I AM...
YOUR UNCLE.
WHAT...?
I DON'T UNDERSTAND.
I MARRIED YOUR DAD'S BROTHER IN CANADA.
THAT MAKES ME YOUR UNCLE!

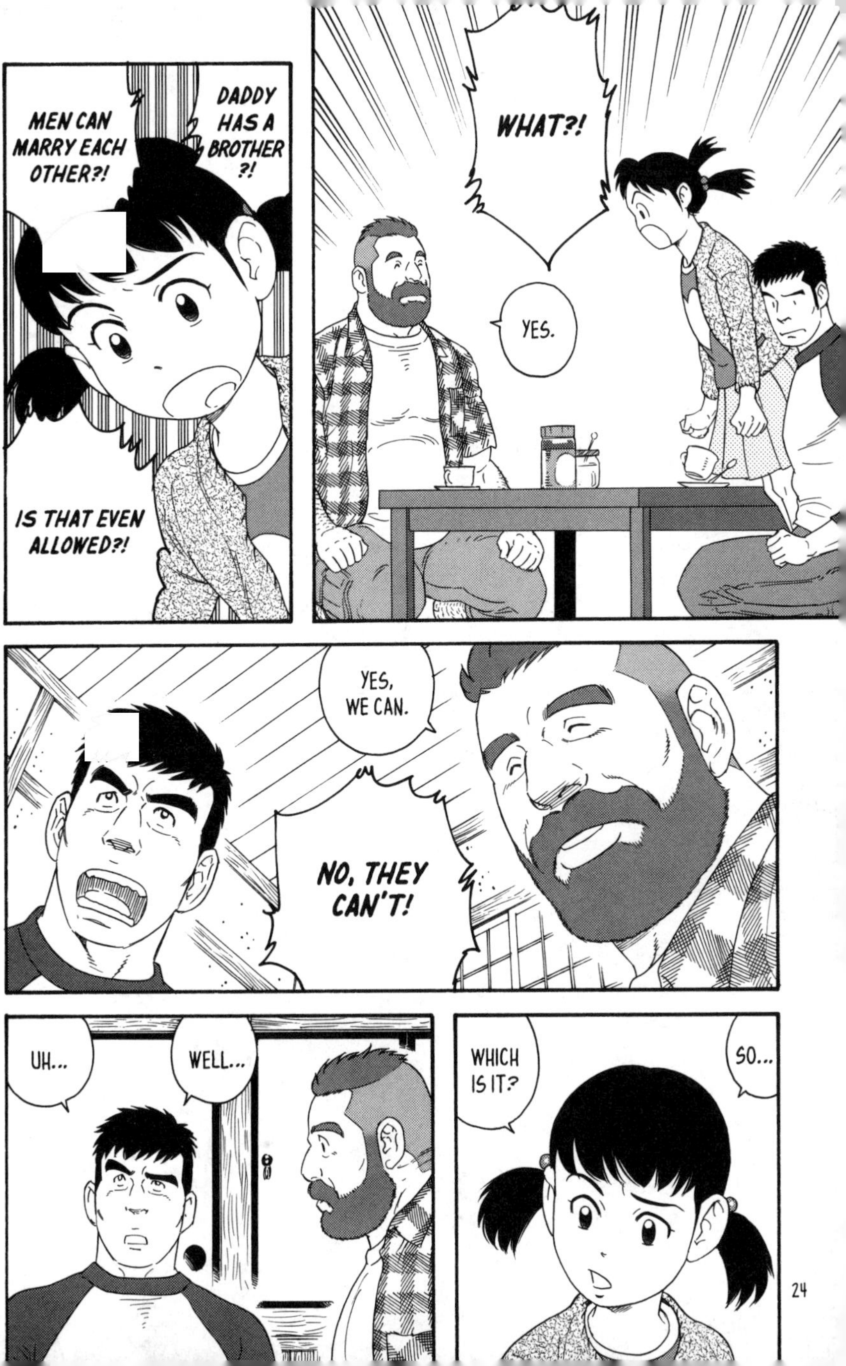
WHAT?!
YES.
DADDY HAS A BROTHER ?!
MEN CAN MARRY EACH OTHER?!
IS THAT EVEN ALLOWED?!
YES, WE CAN.
NO, THEY CAN'T!
SO...
WHICH IS IT?
WELL...
UH...

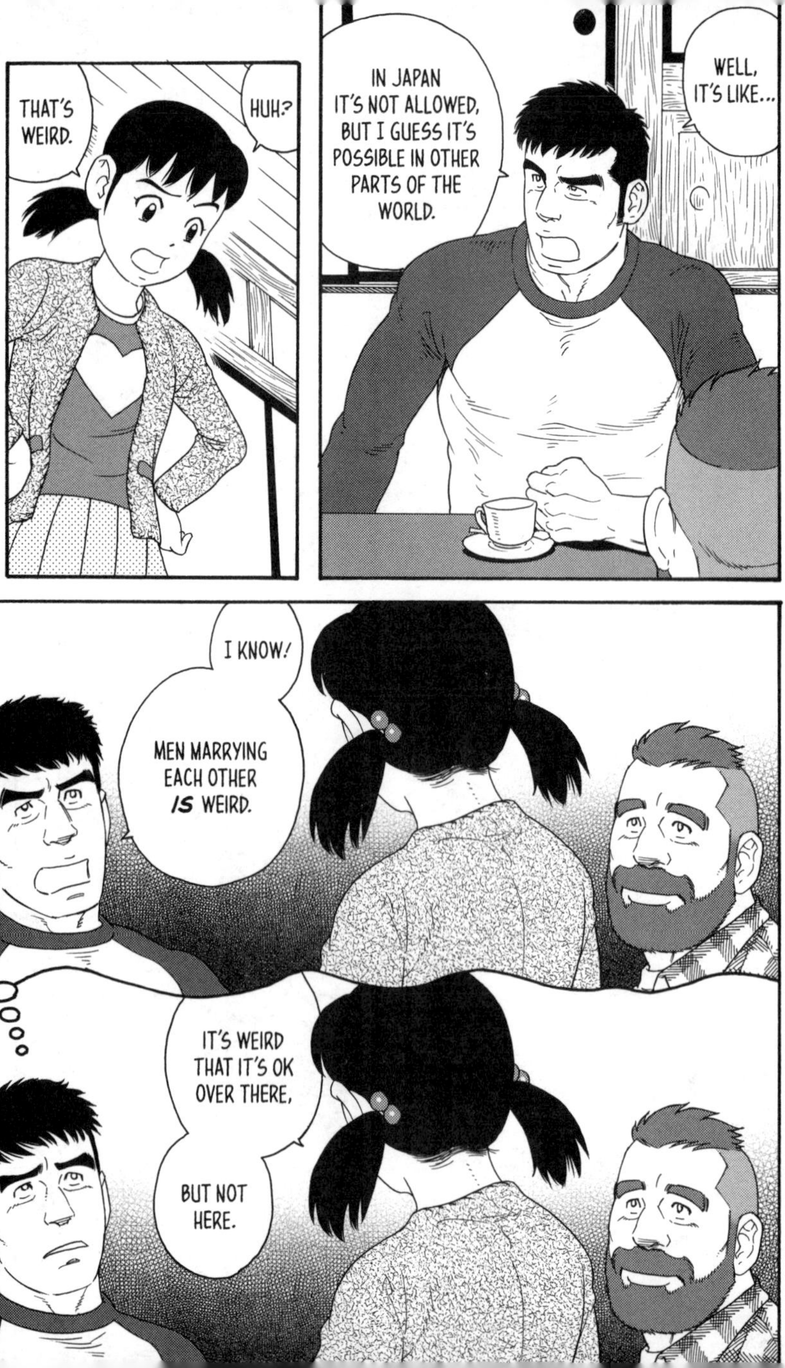
WELL, IT'S LIKE...
IN JAPAN IT'S NOT ALLOWED, BUT I GUESS IT'S POSSIBLE IN OTHER PARTS OF THE WORLD.
HUH?
THAT'S WEIRD.
I KNOW!
MEN MARRYING EACH OTHER *IS* WEIRD.
IT'S WEIRD THAT IT'S OK OVER THERE,
BUT NOT HERE.

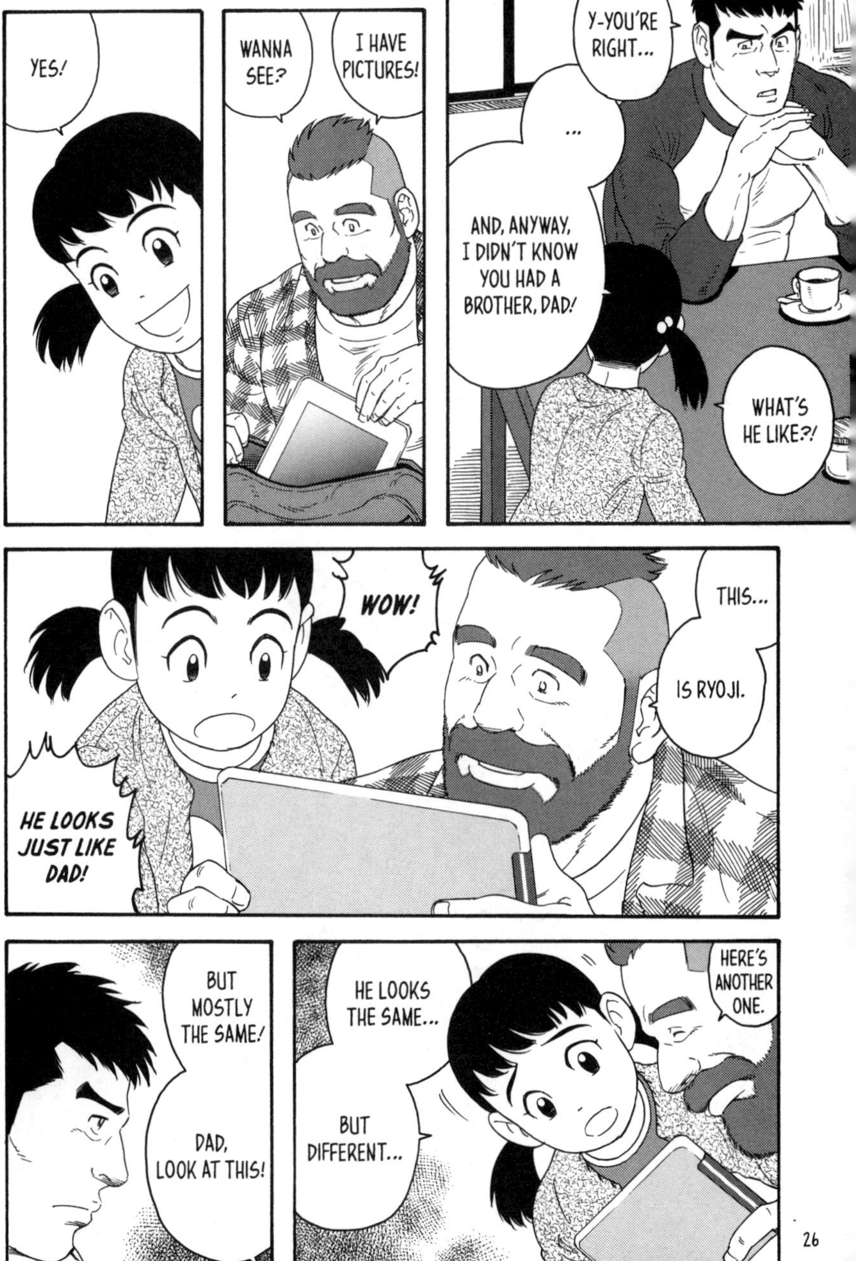
Y-YOU'RE RIGHT...
...
AND, ANYWAY, I DIDN'T KNOW YOU HAD A BROTHER, DAD!
WHAT'S HE LIKE?!
I HAVE PICTURES!
WANNA SEE?
YES!
THIS...
IS RYOJI.
WOW!
HE LOOKS JUST LIKE DAD!
HERE'S ANOTHER ONE.
HE LOOKS THE SAME...
BUT DIFFERENT...
BUT MOSTLY THE SAME!
DAD, LOOK AT THIS!

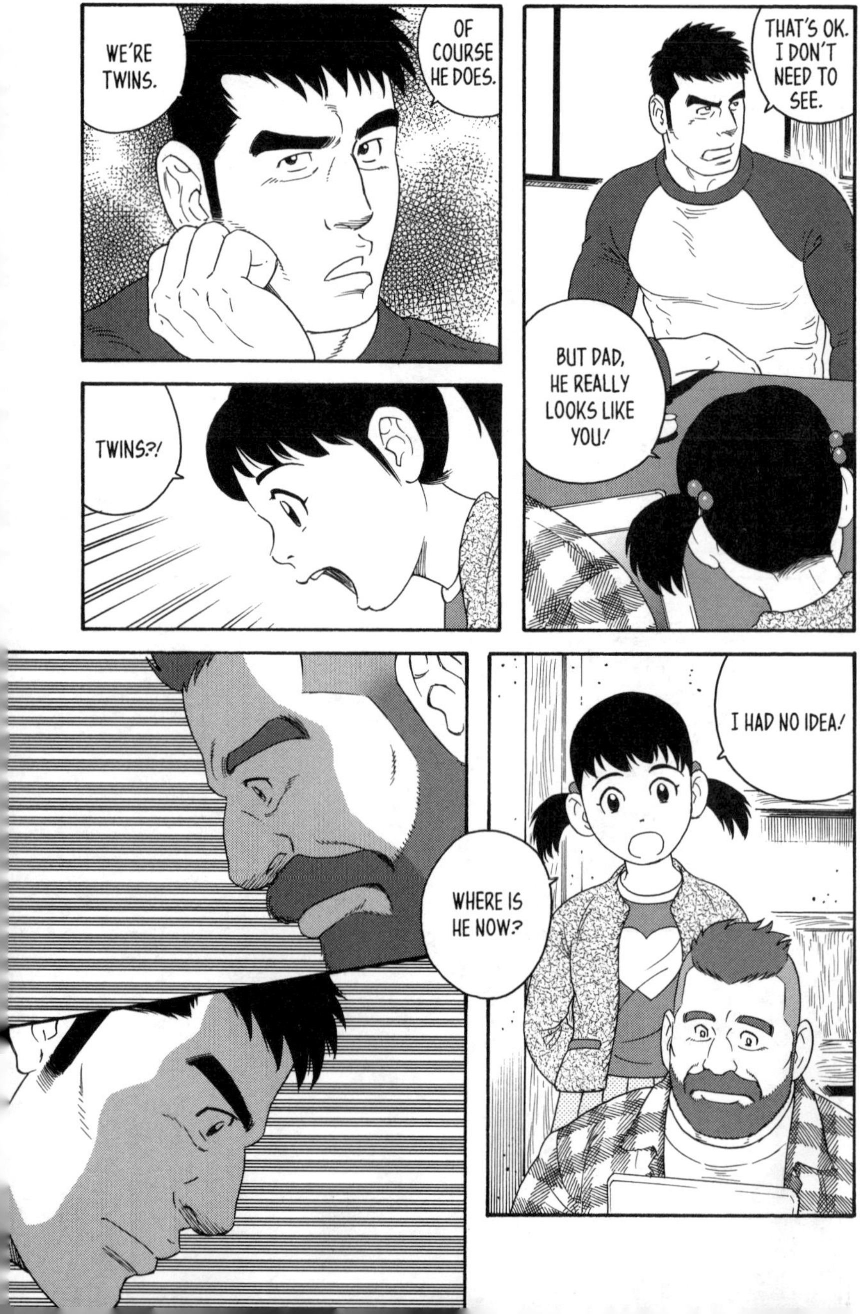
THAT'S OK. I DON'T NEED TO SEE.
BUT DAD, HE REALLY LOOKS LIKE YOU!
OF COURSE HE DOES.
WE'RE TWINS.
TWINS?!
I HAD NO IDEA!
WHERE IS HE NOW?

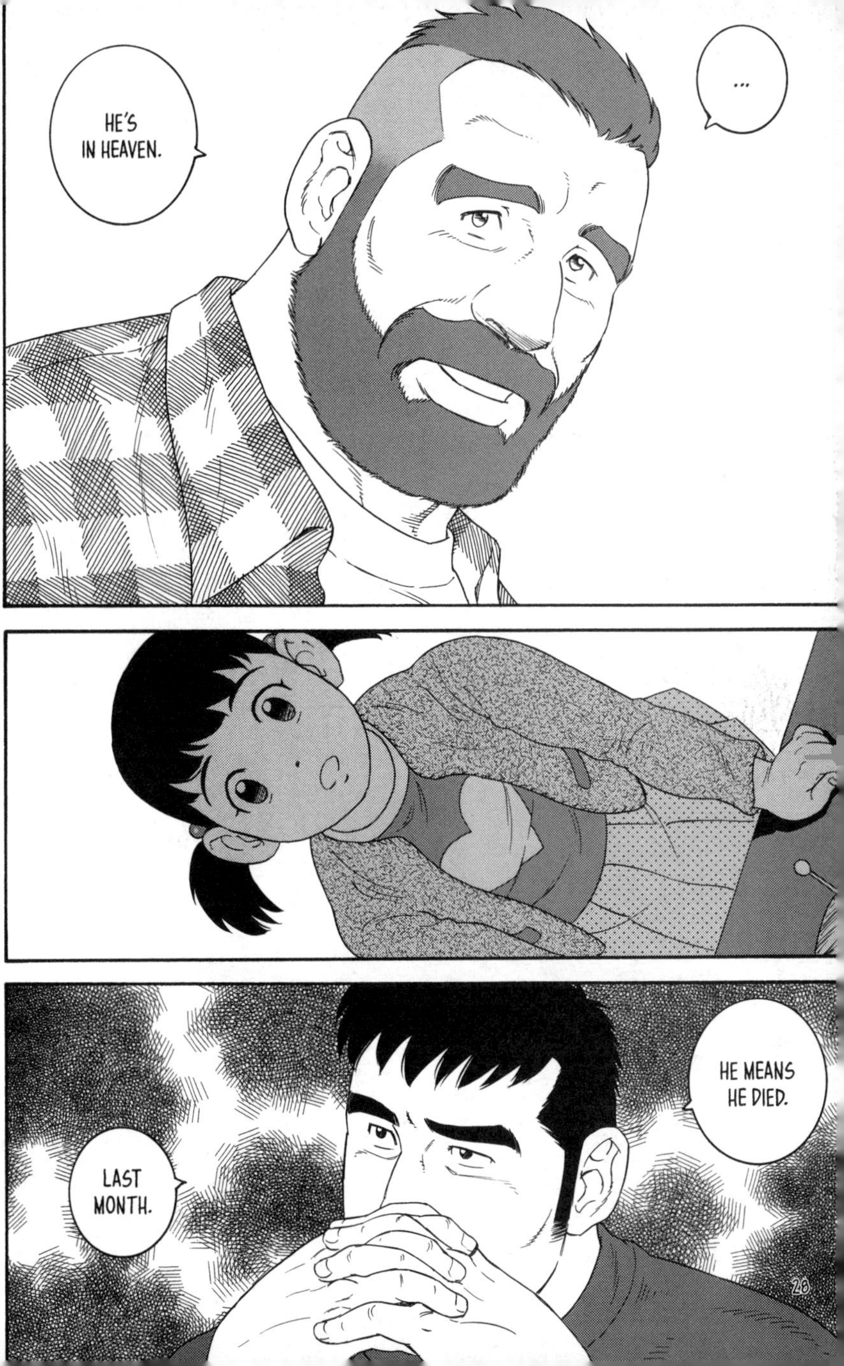
...
HE'S IN HEAVEN.
HE MEANS HE DIED.
LAST MONTH.

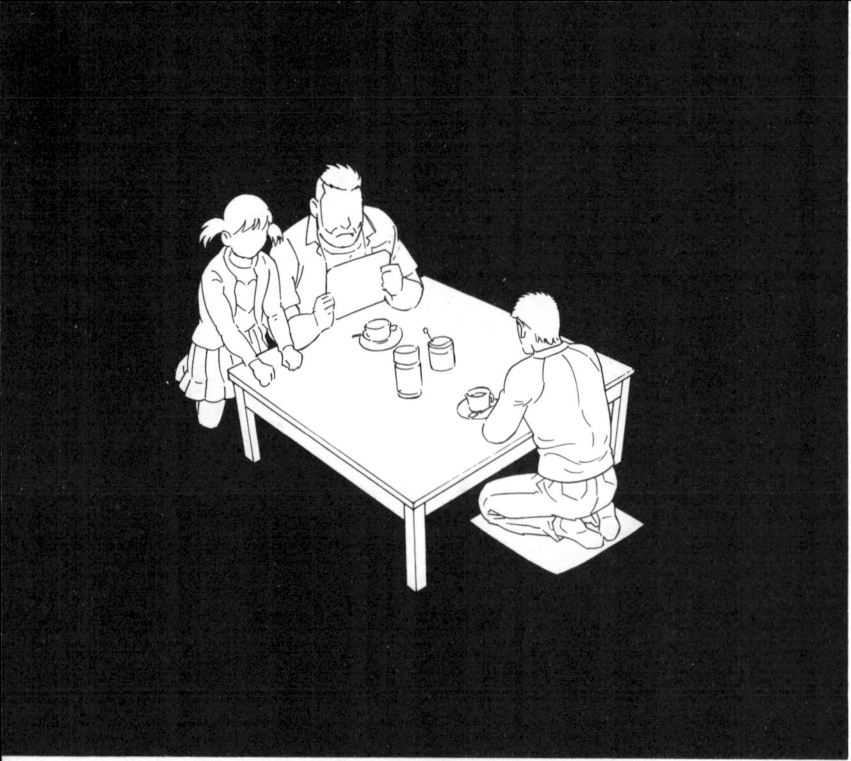

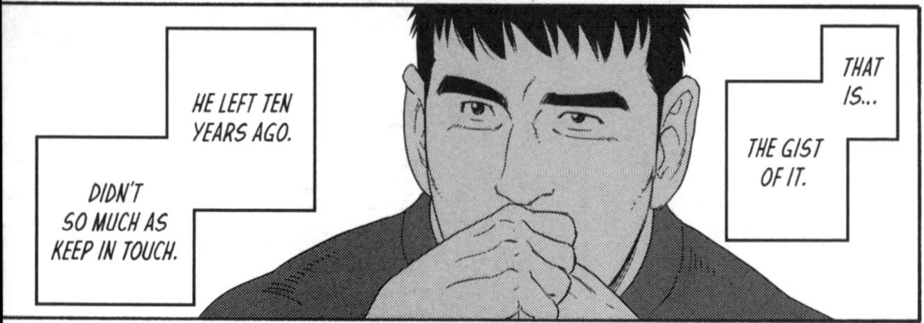
THAT IS...
THE GIST OF IT.
HE LEFT TEN YEARS AGO.
DIDN'T SO MUCH AS KEEP IN TOUCH.

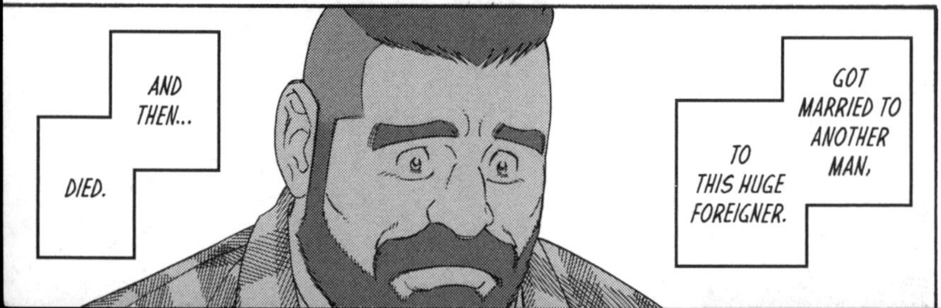
GOT MARRIED TO ANOTHER MAN,
TO THIS HUGE FOREIGNER.
AND THEN...
DIED.

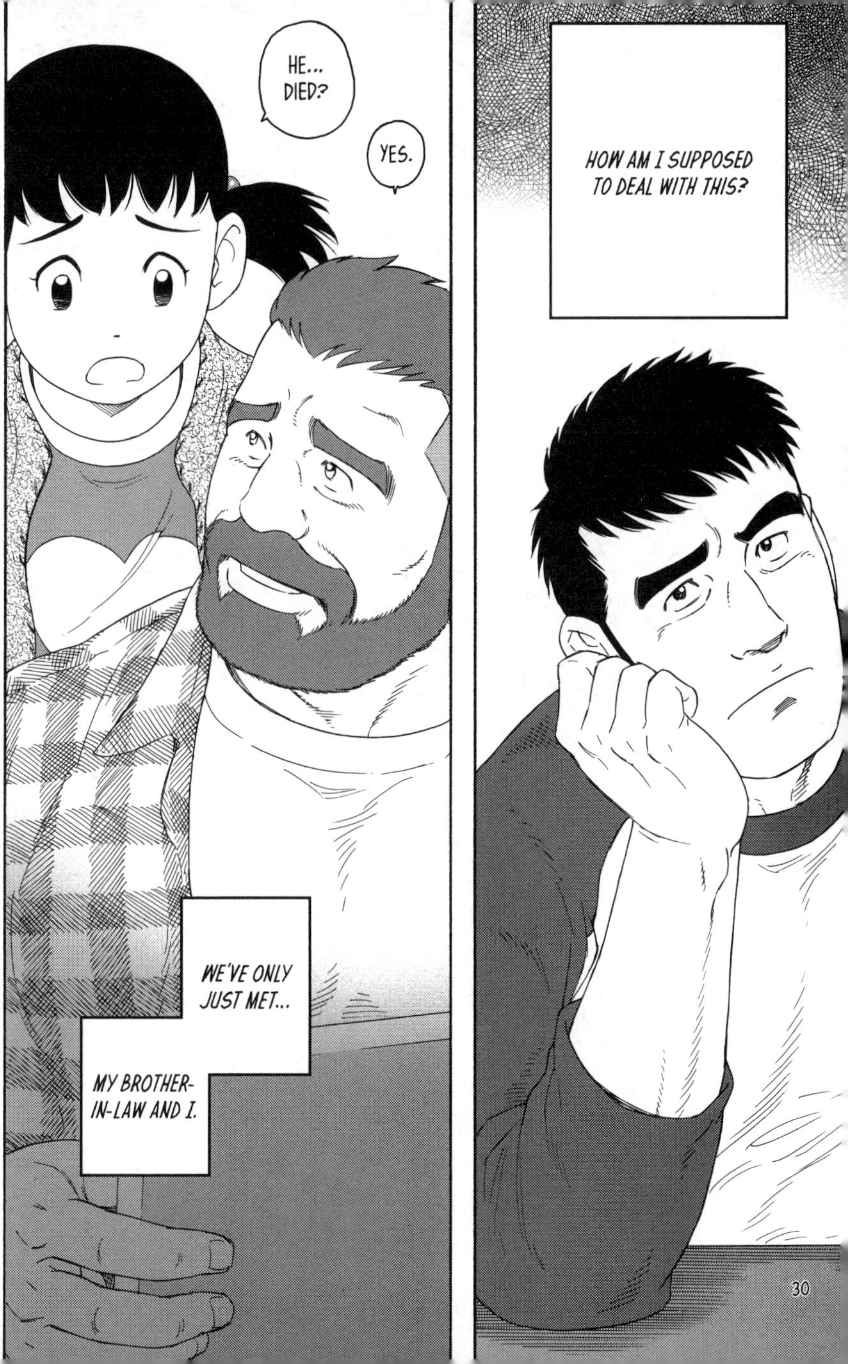
HOW AM I SUPPOSED TO DEAL WITH THIS?
HE... DIED?
YES.
WE'VE ONLY JUST MET...
MY BROTHER-IN-LAW AND I.

CHAPTER TWO

TEMPURA SUSHI

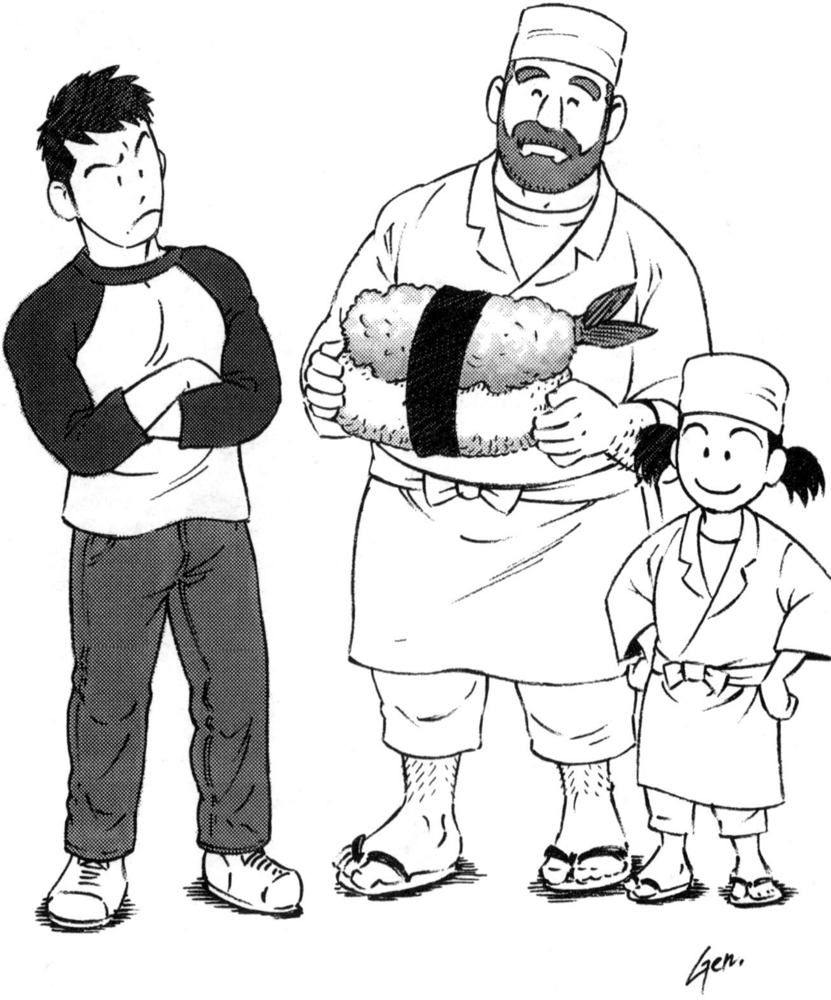
Gen.

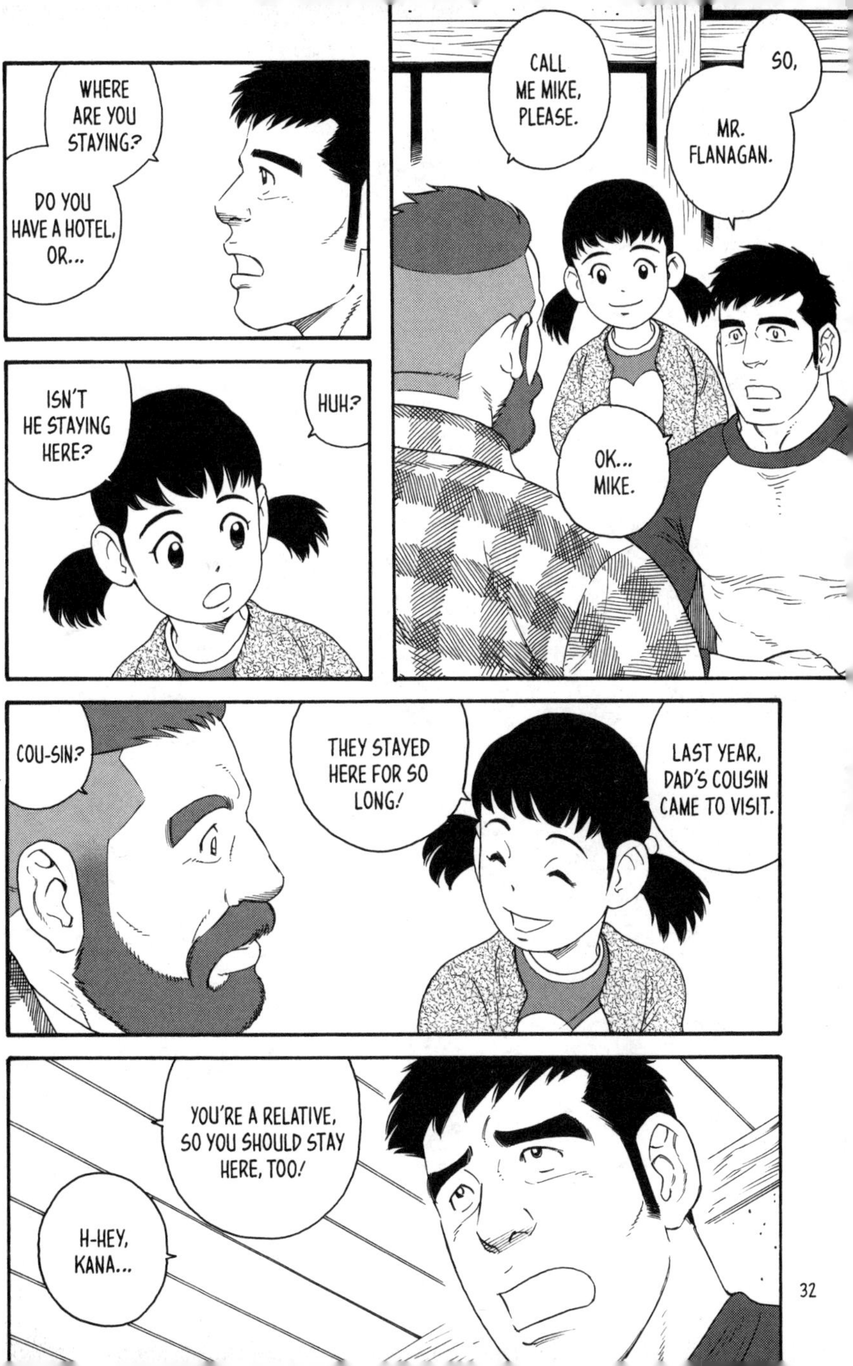
SO, MR. FLANAGAN.
CALL ME MIKE, PLEASE.
OK... MIKE.
WHERE ARE YOU STAYING?
DO YOU HAVE A HOTEL, OR...
HUH?
ISN'T HE STAYING HERE?
LAST YEAR, DAD'S COUSIN CAME TO VISIT.
THEY STAYED HERE FOR SO LONG!
COU-SIN?
YOU'RE A RELATIVE, SO YOU SHOULD STAY HERE, TOO!
H-HEY, KANA...

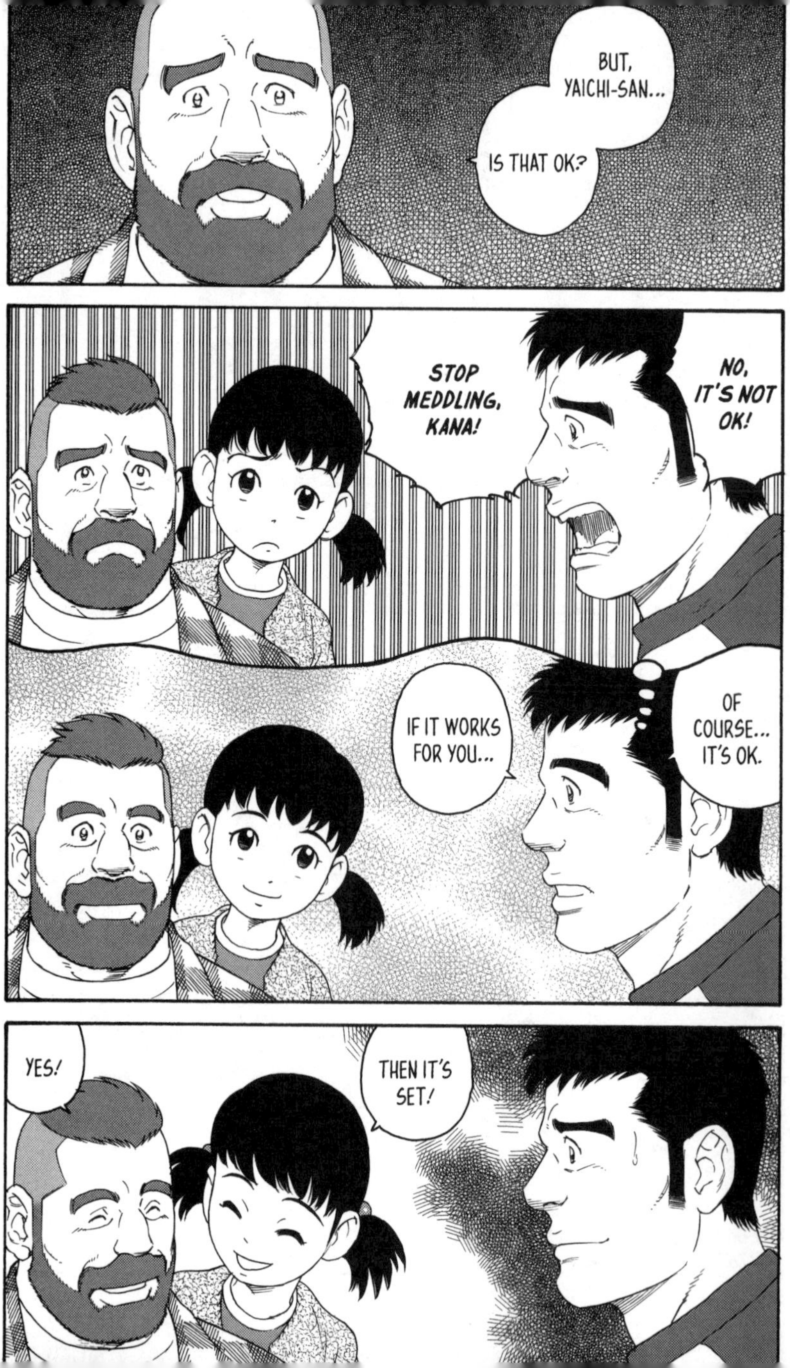
BUT, YAICHI-SAN...
IS THAT OK?
NO, IT'S NOT OK!
STOP MEDDLING, KANA!
OF COURSE... IT'S OK.
IF IT WORKS FOR YOU...
THEN IT'S SET!
YES!

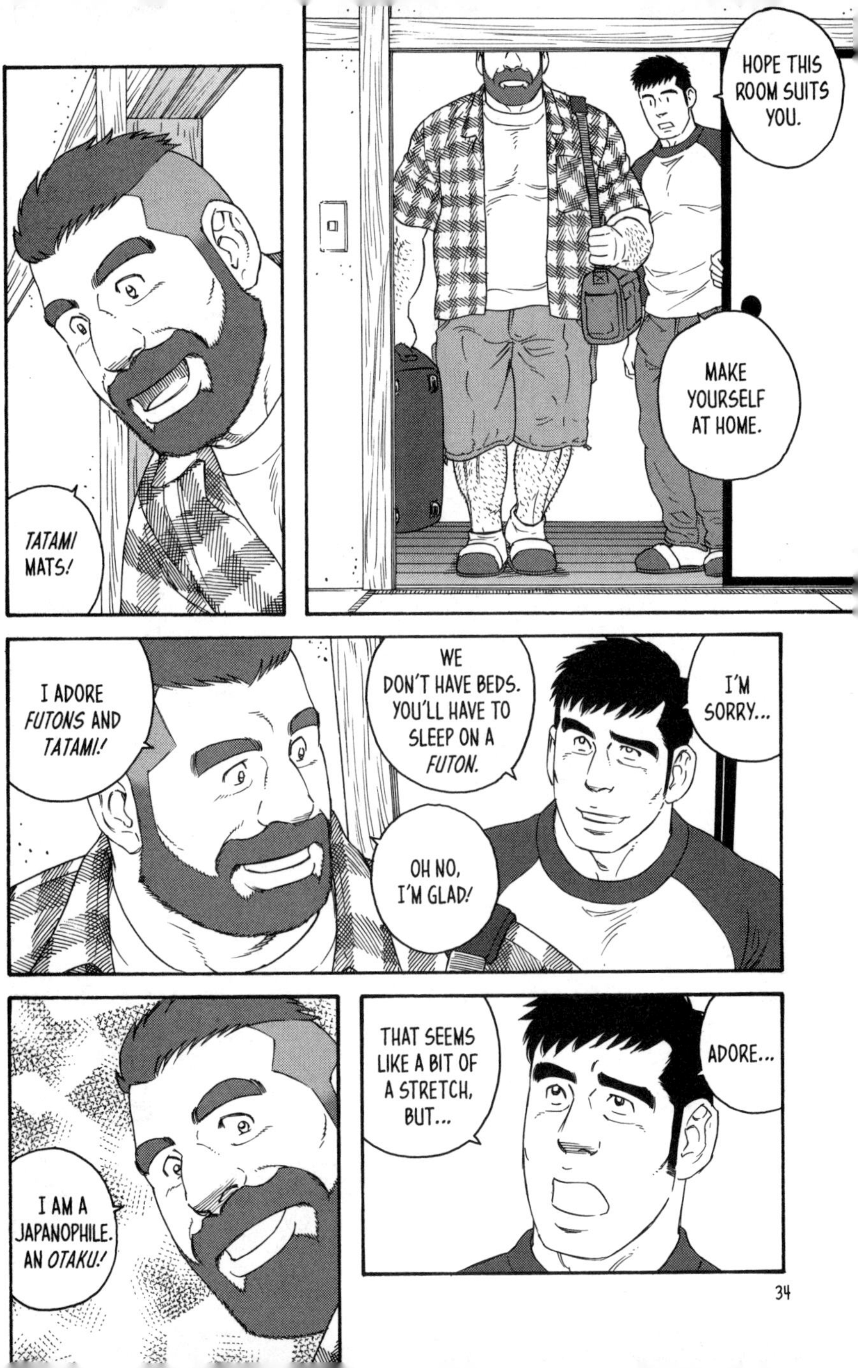
HOPE THIS ROOM SUITS YOU.
MAKE YOURSELF AT HOME.
TATAMI MATS!
I'M SORRY...
WE DON'T HAVE BEDS. YOU'LL HAVE TO SLEEP ON A *FUTON*.
OH NO, I'M GLAD!
I ADORE *FUTONS* AND *TATAMI*!
ADORE...
THAT SEEMS LIKE A BIT OF A STRETCH, BUT...
I AM A JAPANOPHILE. AN *OTAKU*!

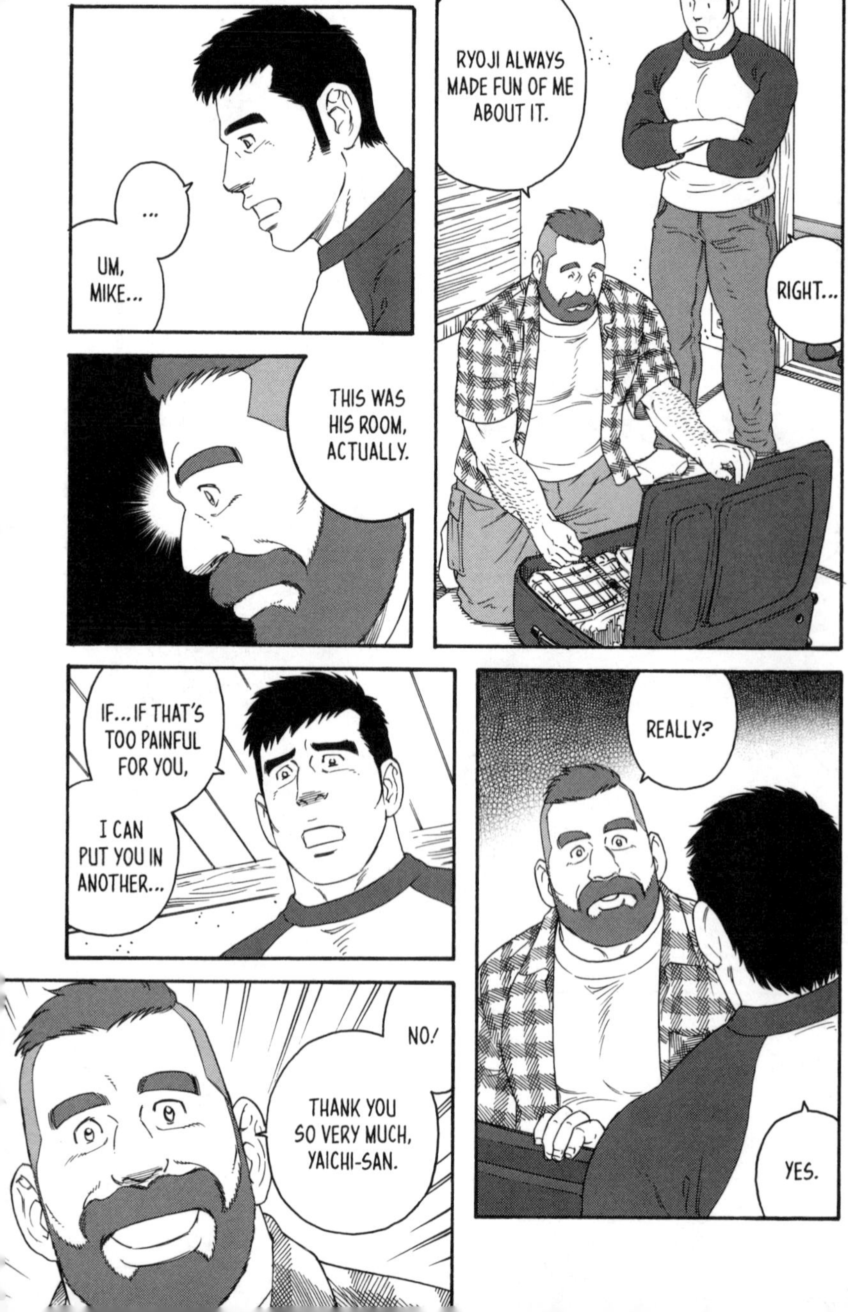
RYOJI ALWAYS MADE FUN OF ME ABOUT IT.
RIGHT...
...
UM, MIKE...
THIS WAS HIS ROOM, ACTUALLY.
REALLY?
YES.
IF... IF THAT'S TOO PAINFUL FOR YOU,
I CAN PUT YOU IN ANOTHER...
NO!
THANK YOU SO VERY MUCH, YAICHI-SAN.

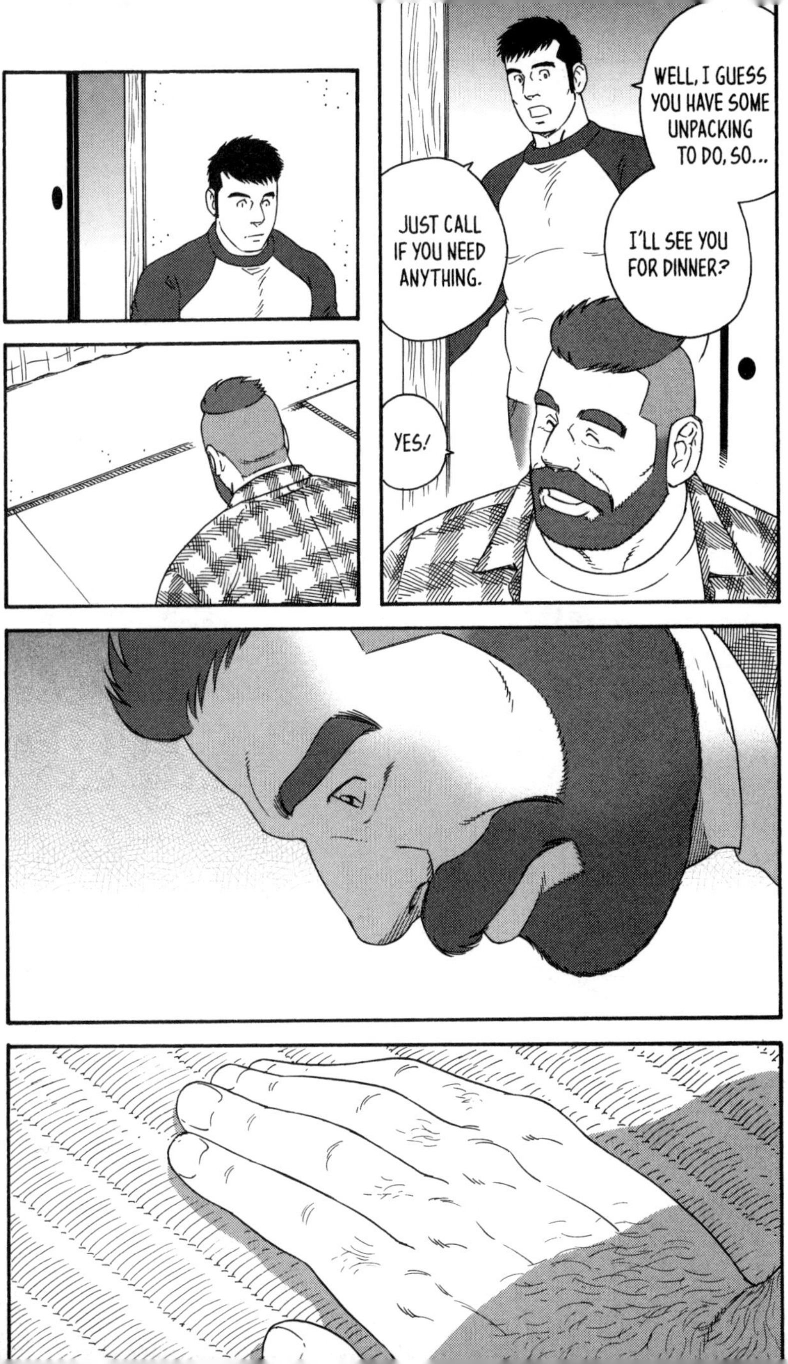
WELL, I GUESS YOU HAVE SOME UNPACKING TO DO, SO...
I'LL SEE YOU FOR DINNER?
JUST CALL IF YOU NEED ANYTHING.
YES!

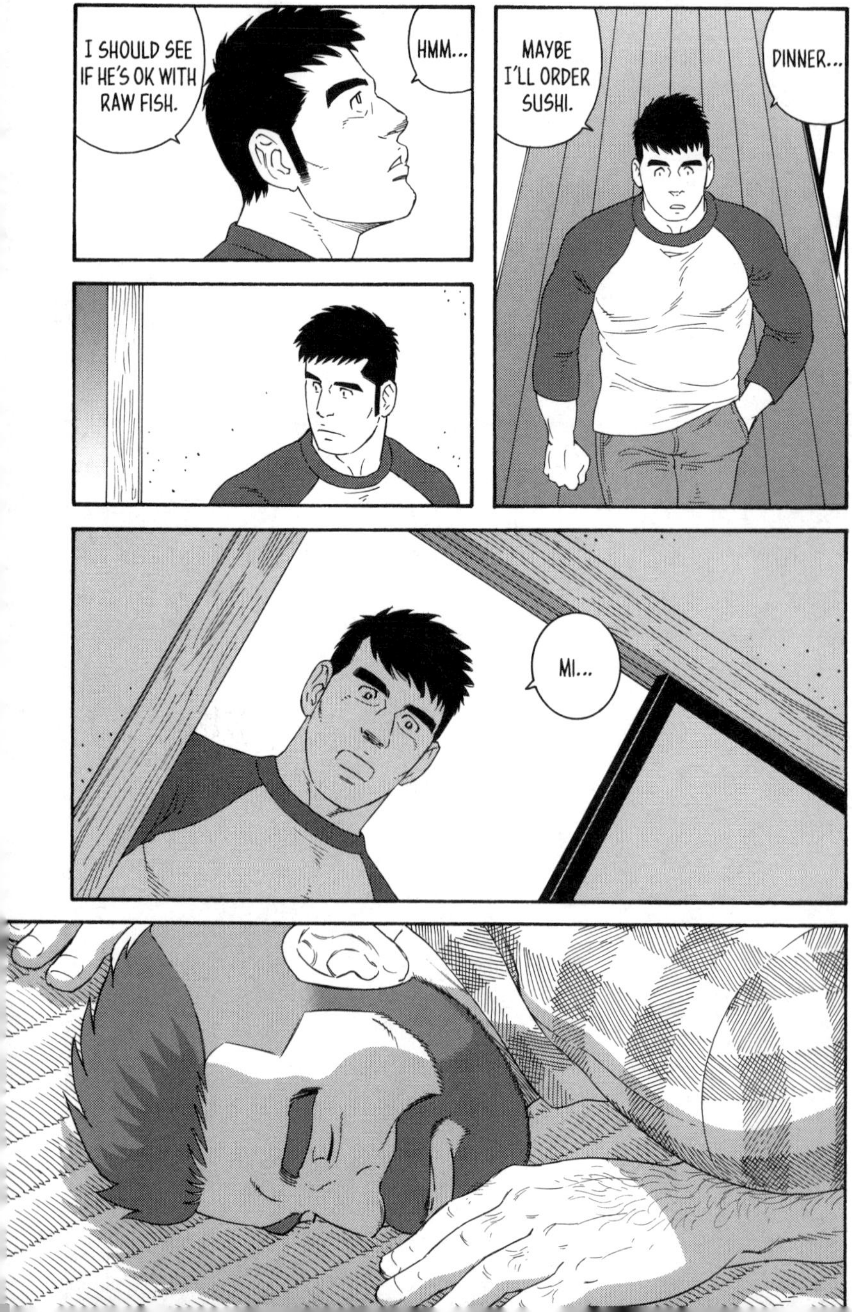
DINNER...
MAYBE I'LL ORDER SUSHI.
HMM...
I SHOULD SEE IF HE'S OK WITH RAW FISH.
MI...

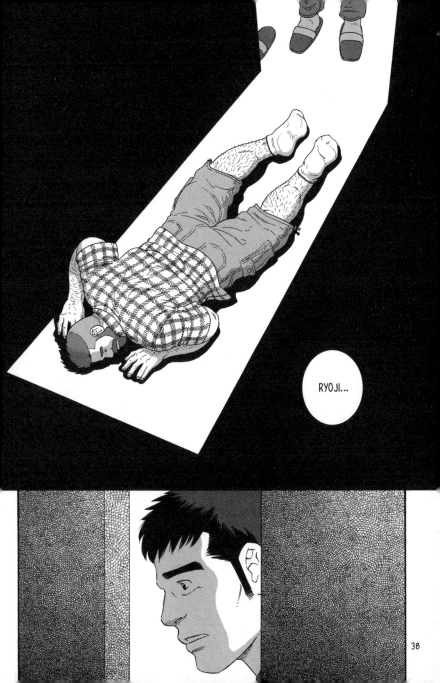

RYOJI...

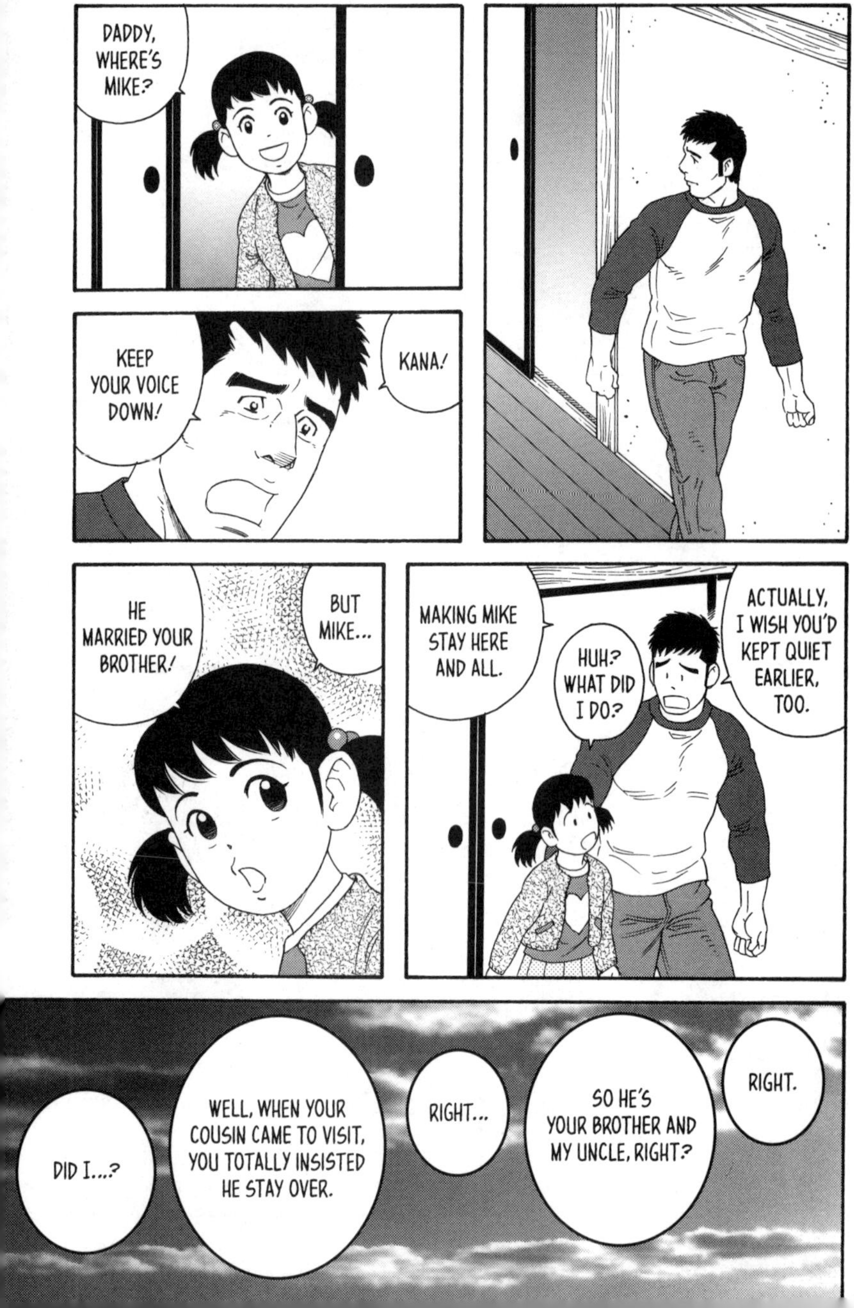
DADDY, WHERE'S MIKE?
KANA!
KEEP YOUR VOICE DOWN!
ACTUALLY, I WISH YOU'D KEPT QUIET EARLIER, TOO.
HUH? WHAT DID I DO?
MAKING MIKE STAY HERE AND ALL.
BUT MIKE...
HE MARRIED YOUR BROTHER!
RIGHT.
SO HE'S YOUR BROTHER AND MY UNCLE, RIGHT?
RIGHT...
WELL, WHEN YOUR COUSIN CAME TO VISIT, YOU TOTALLY INSISTED HE STAY OVER.
DID I...?

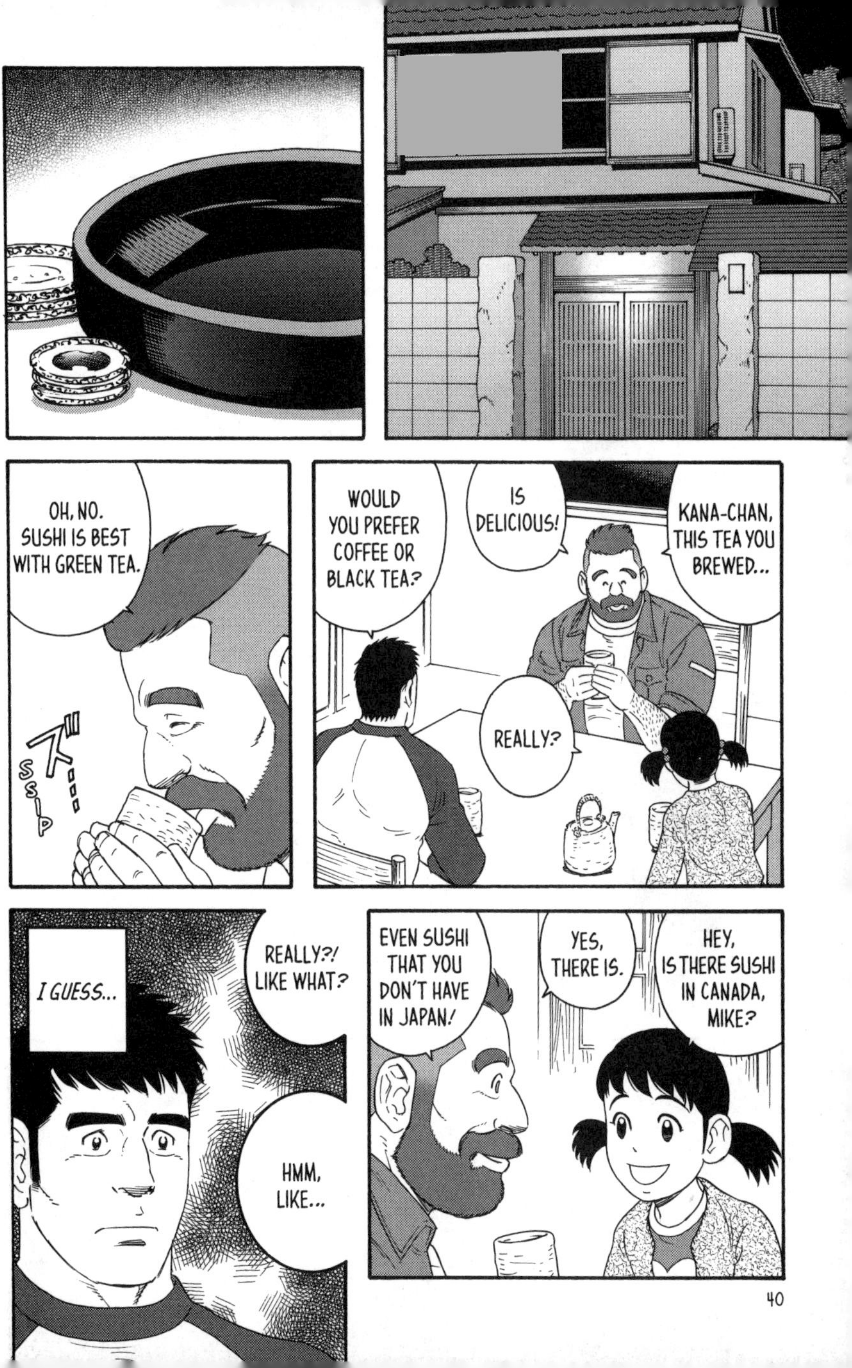
KANA-CHAN, THIS TEA YOU BREWED...
IS DELICIOUS!
REALLY?
WOULD YOU PREFER COFFEE OR BLACK TEA?
OH, NO. SUSHI IS BEST WITH GREEN TEA.
SSIP
HEY, IS THERE SUSHI IN CANADA, MIKE?
YES, THERE IS.
EVEN SUSHI THAT YOU DON'T HAVE IN JAPAN!
REALLY?! LIKE WHAT?
HMM, LIKE...
I GUESS...

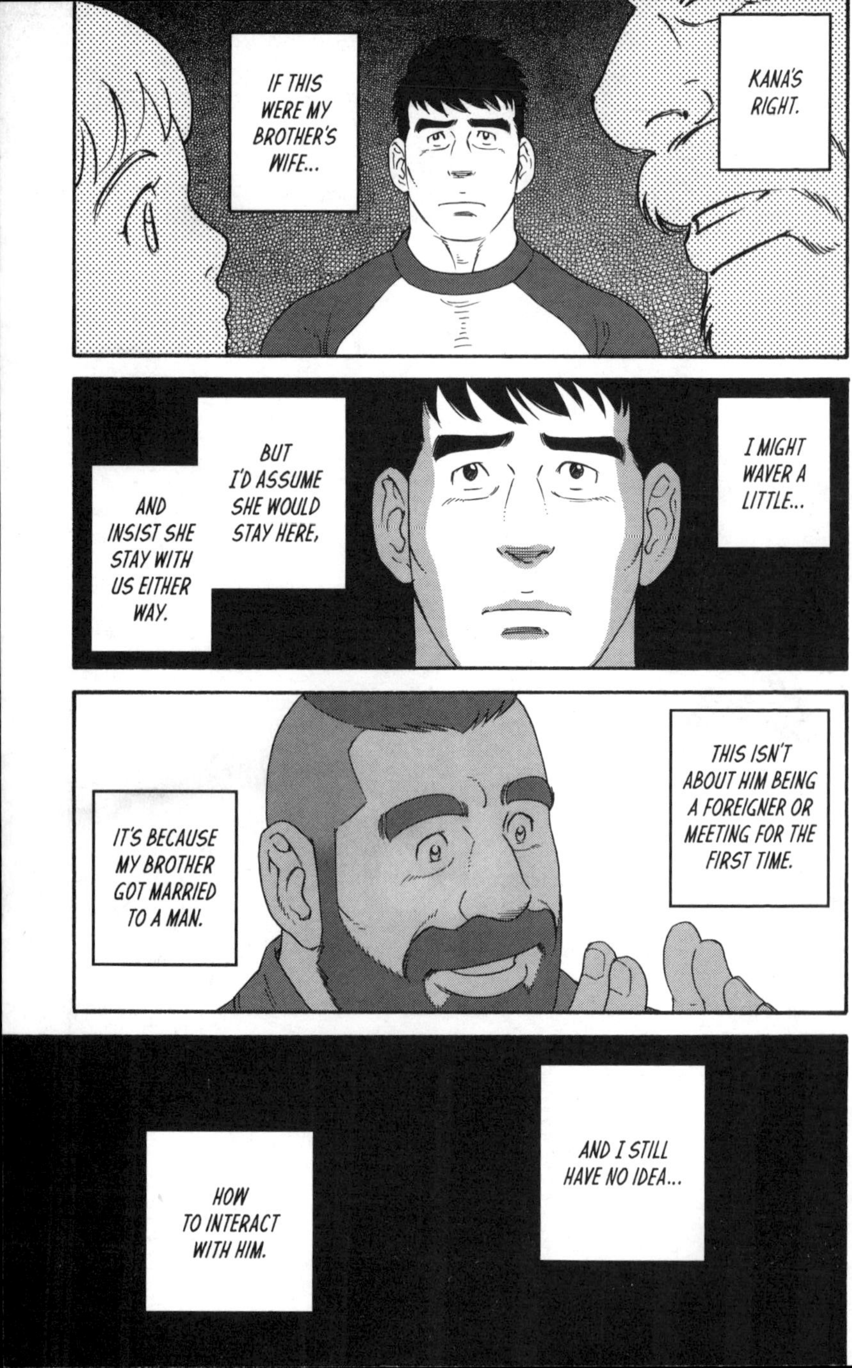
KANA'S RIGHT.
IF THIS WERE MY BROTHER'S WIFE...
I MIGHT WAVER A LITTLE...
BUT I'D ASSUME SHE WOULD STAY HERE,
AND INSIST SHE STAY WITH US EITHER WAY.
THIS ISN'T ABOUT HIM BEING A FOREIGNER OR MEETING FOR THE FIRST TIME.
IT'S BECAUSE MY BROTHER GOT MARRIED TO A MAN.
AND I STILL HAVE NO IDEA...
HOW TO INTERACT WITH HIM.

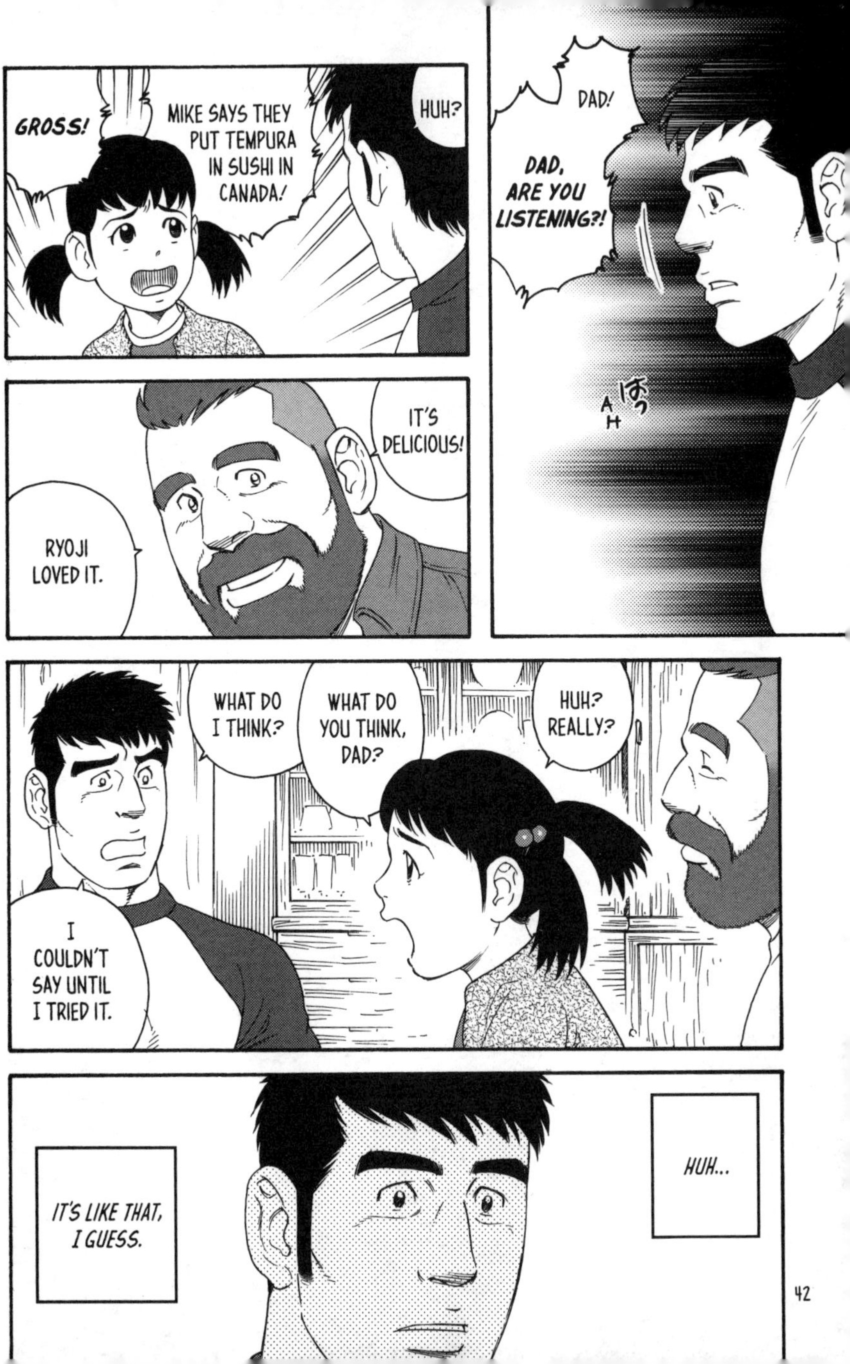
DAD!
DAD, ARE YOU LISTENING?!
はっ
AH
HUH?
MIKE SAYS THEY PUT TEMPURA IN SUSHI IN CANADA!
GROSS!
IT'S DELICIOUS!
RYOJI LOVED IT.
HUH? REALLY?
WHAT DO YOU THINK, DAD?
WHAT DO I THINK?
I COULDN'T SAY UNTIL I TRIED IT.
HUH...
IT'S LIKE THAT, I GUESS.

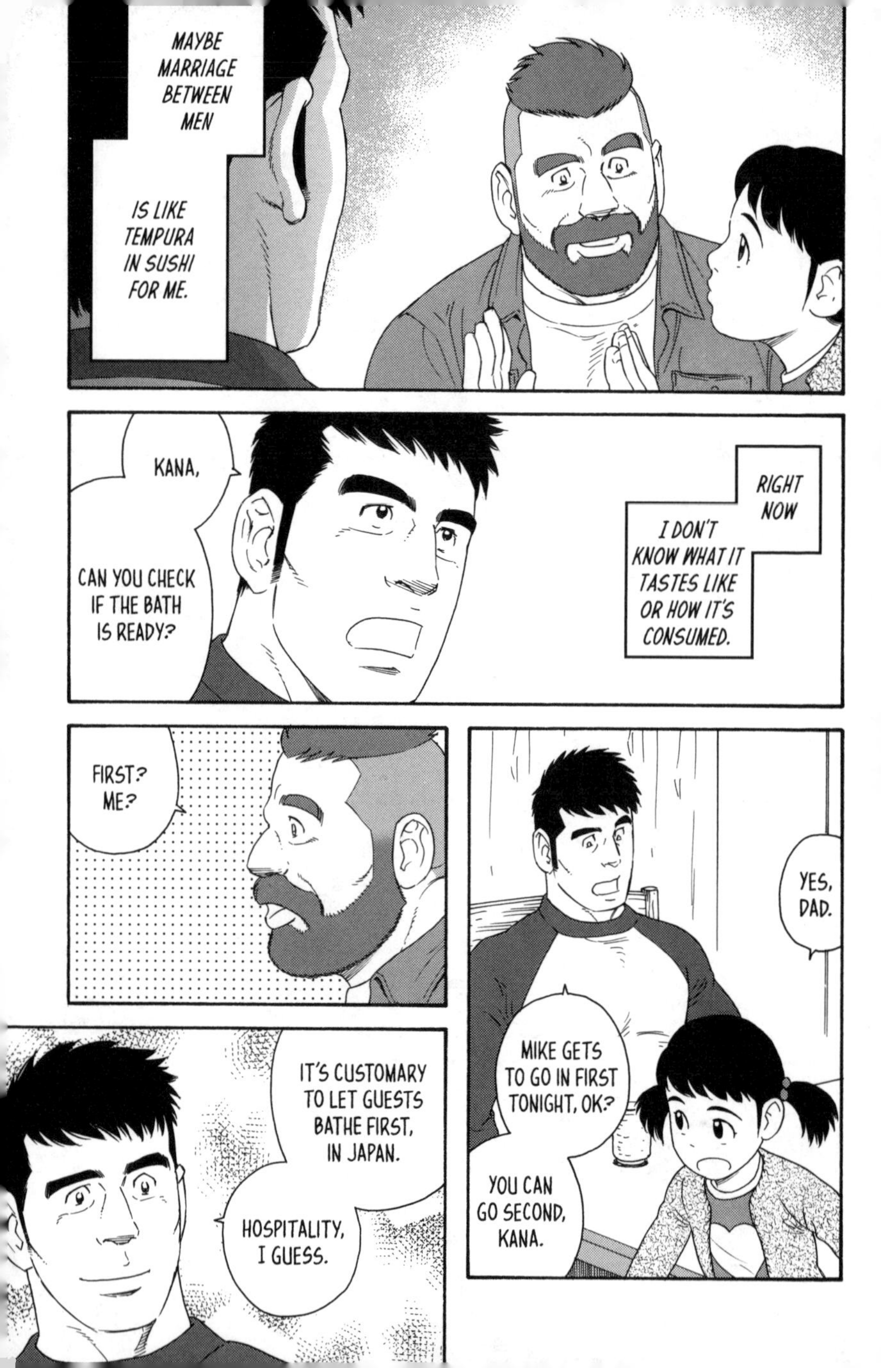
MAYBE MARRIAGE BETWEEN MEN
IS LIKE TEMPURA IN SUSHI FOR ME.
RIGHT NOW I DON'T KNOW WHAT IT TASTES LIKE OR HOW IT'S CONSUMED.
KANA,
CAN YOU CHECK IF THE BATH IS READY?
YES, DAD.
MIKE GETS TO GO IN FIRST TONIGHT, OK?
YOU CAN GO SECOND, KANA.
FIRST? ME?
IT'S CUSTOMARY TO LET GUESTS BATHE FIRST, IN JAPAN.
HOSPITALITY, I GUESS.

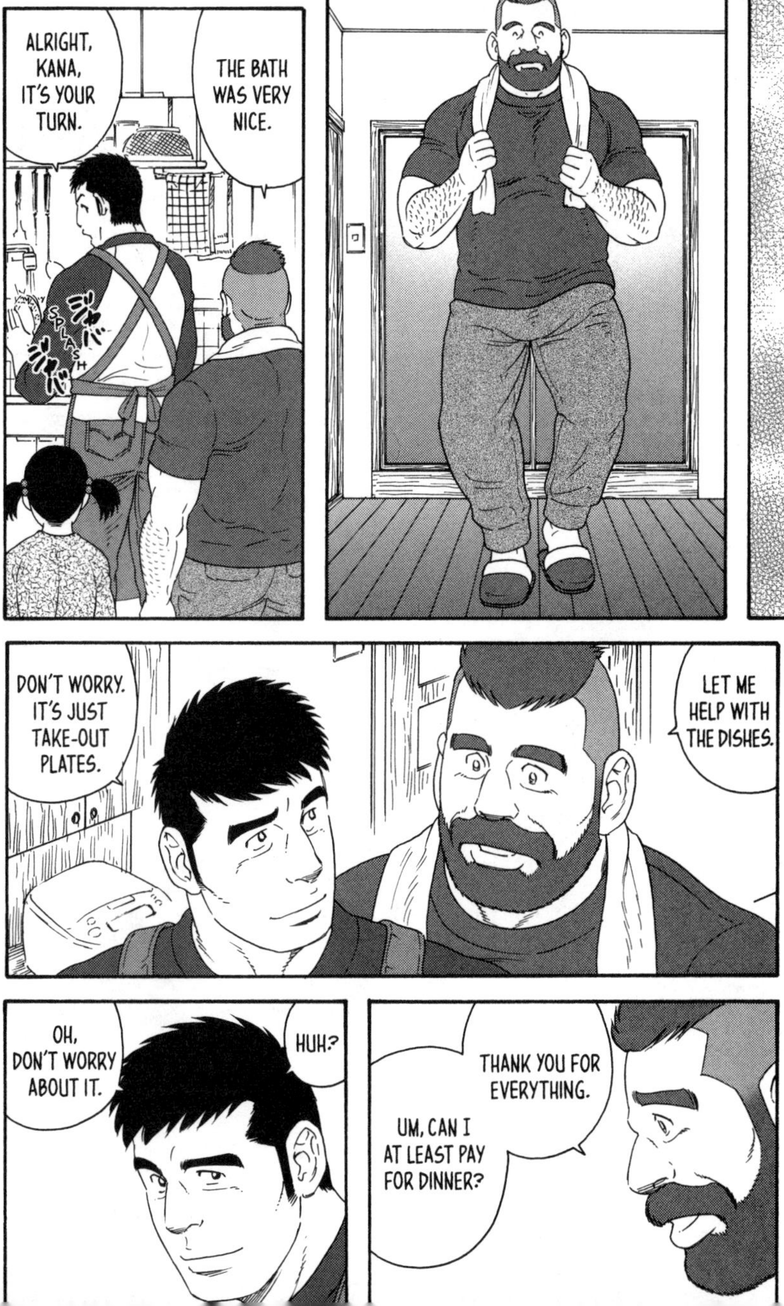
THE BATH WAS VERY NICE.
ALRIGHT, KANA, IT'S YOUR TURN.
ジャバジャバ
SPLASH
LET ME HELP WITH THE DISHES.
DON'T WORRY. IT'S JUST TAKE-OUT PLATES.
THANK YOU FOR EVERYTHING.
UM, CAN I AT LEAST PAY FOR DINNER?
HUH?
OH, DON'T WORRY ABOUT IT.

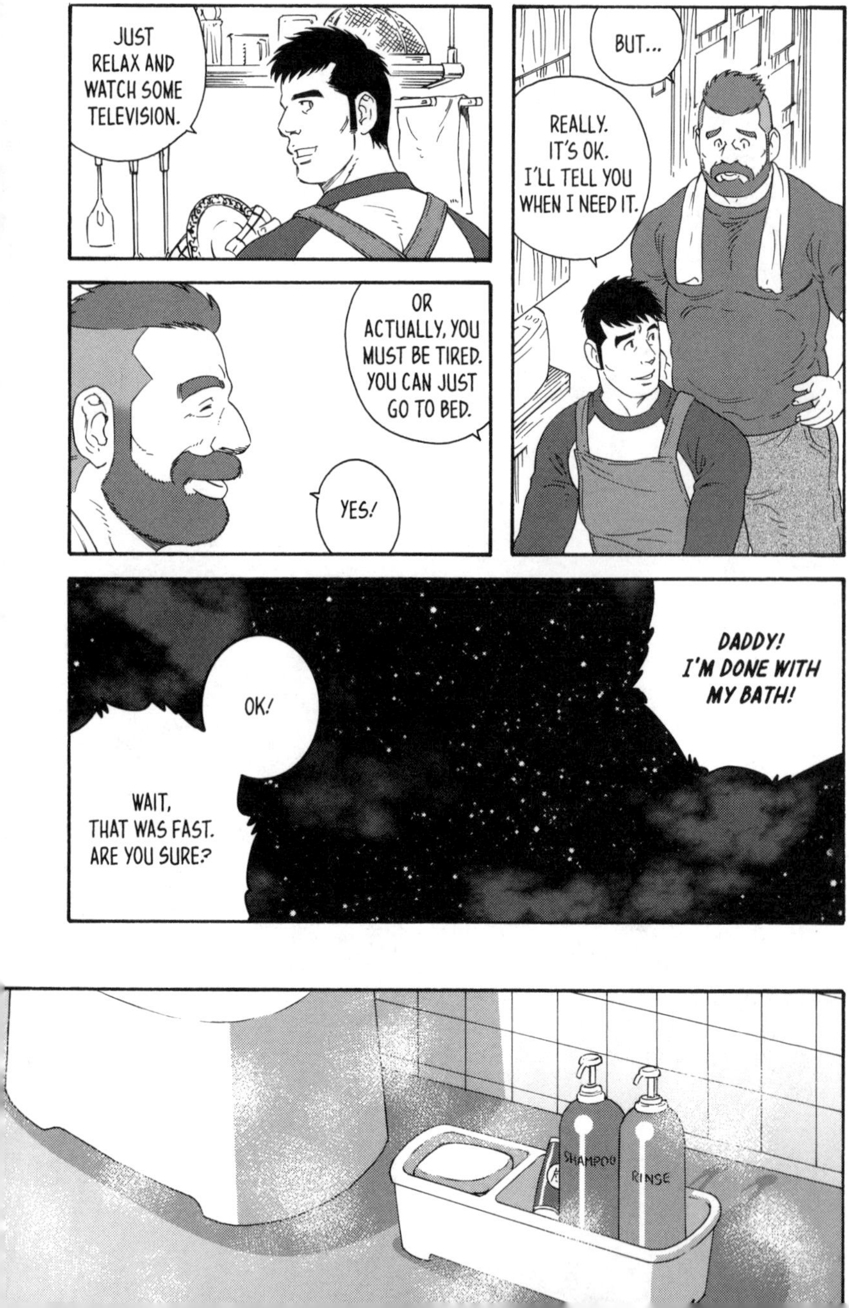
BUT...
REALLY. IT'S OK. I'LL TELL YOU WHEN I NEED IT.
JUST RELAX AND WATCH SOME TELEVISION.
OR ACTUALLY, YOU MUST BE TIRED. YOU CAN JUST GO TO BED.
YES!
DADDY! I'M DONE WITH MY BATH!
OK!
WAIT, THAT WAS FAST. ARE YOU SURE?
SHAMPOO
RINSE

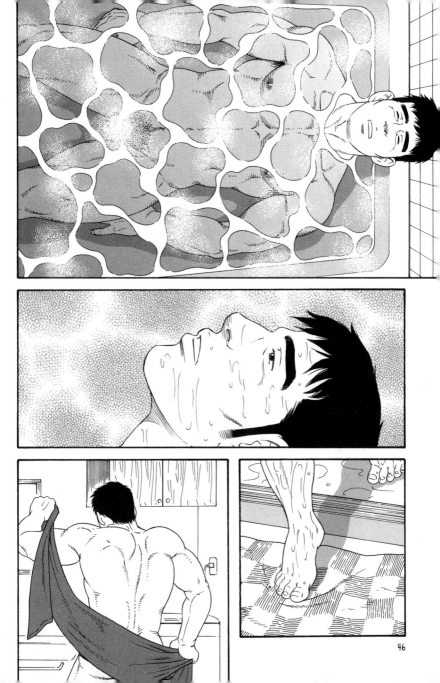

46

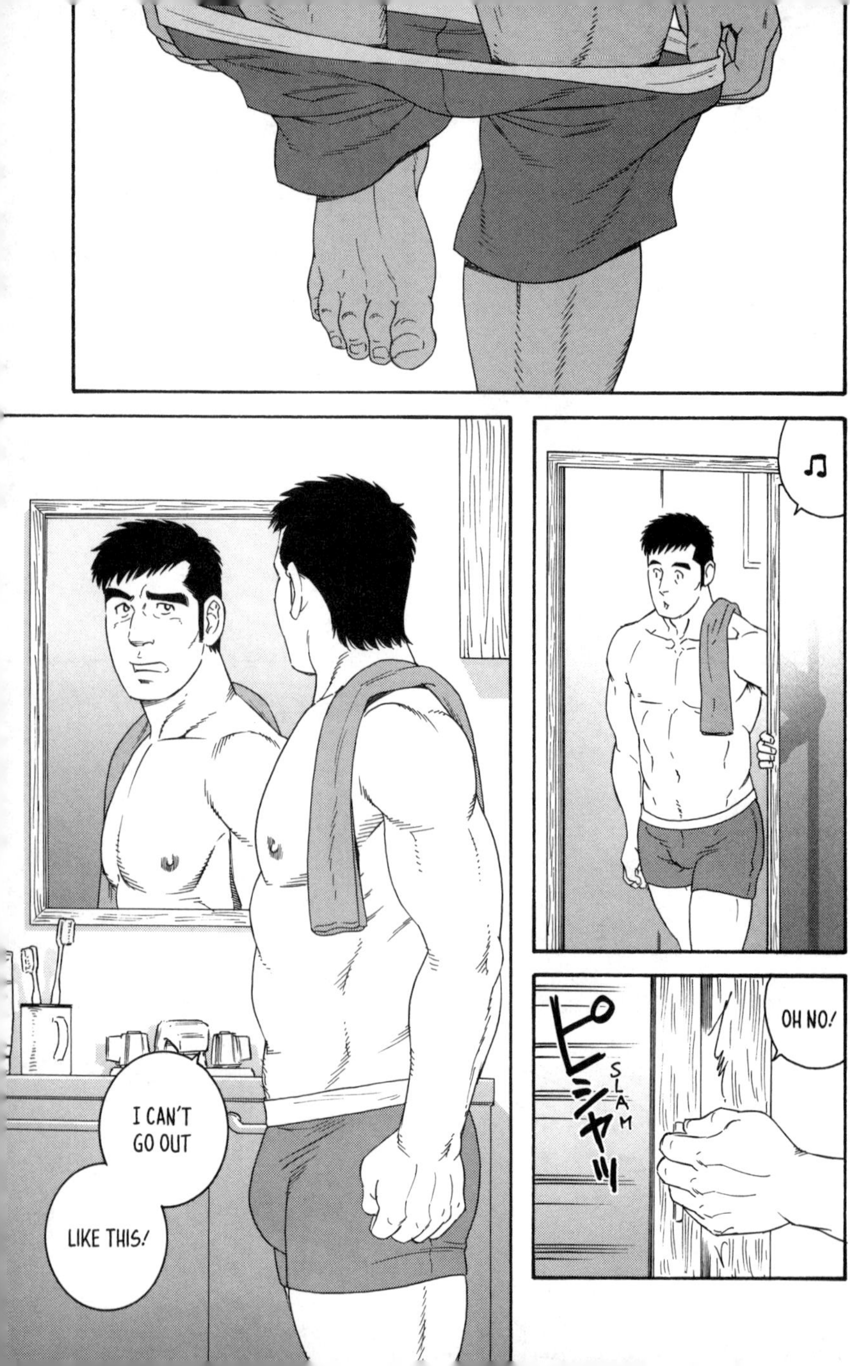
♫
OH NO!
ピシャッ
SLAM
I CAN'T GO OUT
LIKE THIS!

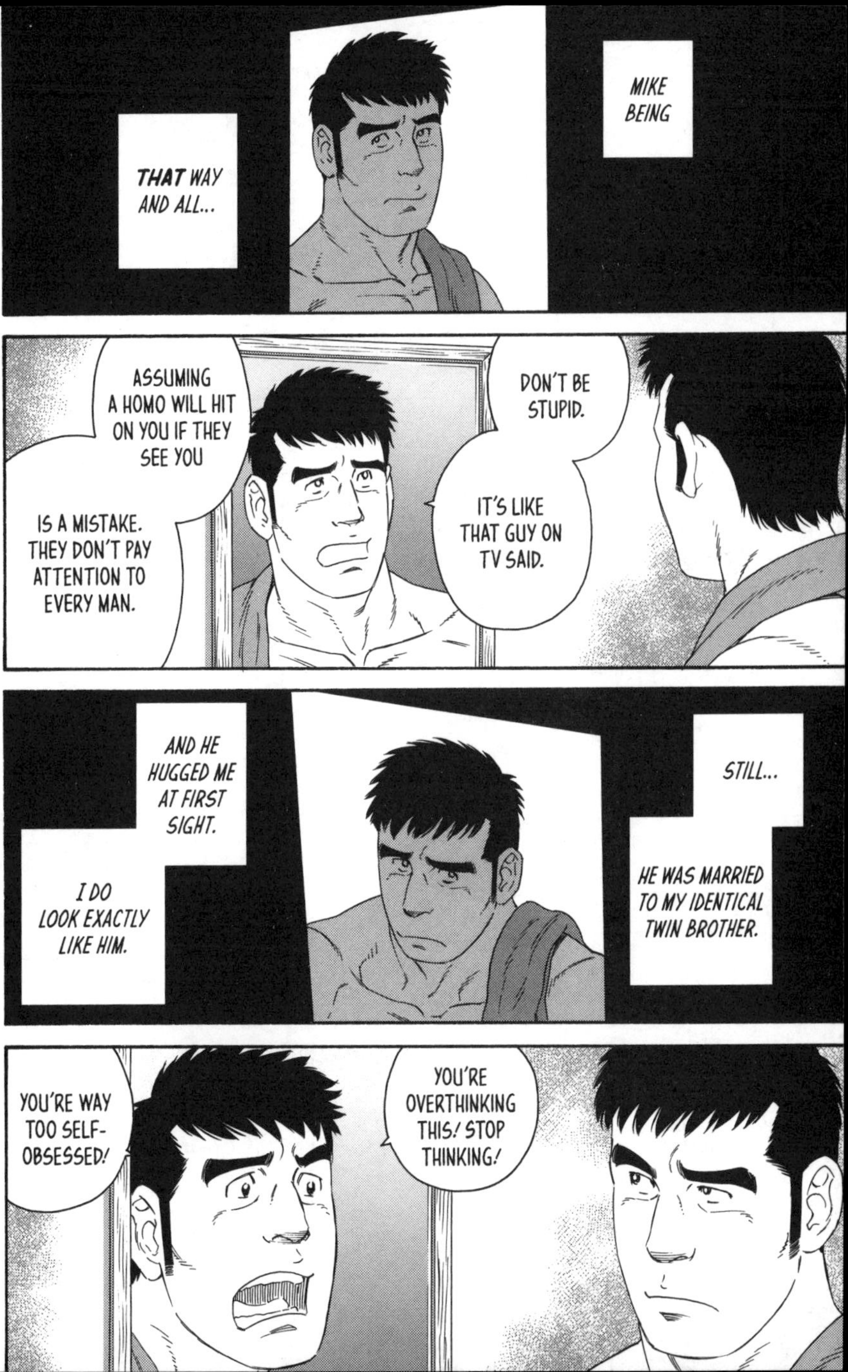
MIKE BEING
THAT WAY AND ALL...
DON'T BE STUPID.
IT'S LIKE THAT GUY ON TV SAID.
ASSUMING A HOMO WILL HIT ON YOU IF THEY SEE YOU
IS A MISTAKE. THEY DON'T PAY ATTENTION TO EVERY MAN.
STILL...
HE WAS MARRIED TO MY IDENTICAL TWIN BROTHER.
AND HE HUGGED ME AT FIRST SIGHT.
I DO LOOK EXACTLY LIKE HIM.
YOU'RE OVERTHINKING THIS! STOP THINKING!
YOU'RE WAY TOO SELF-OBSESSED!

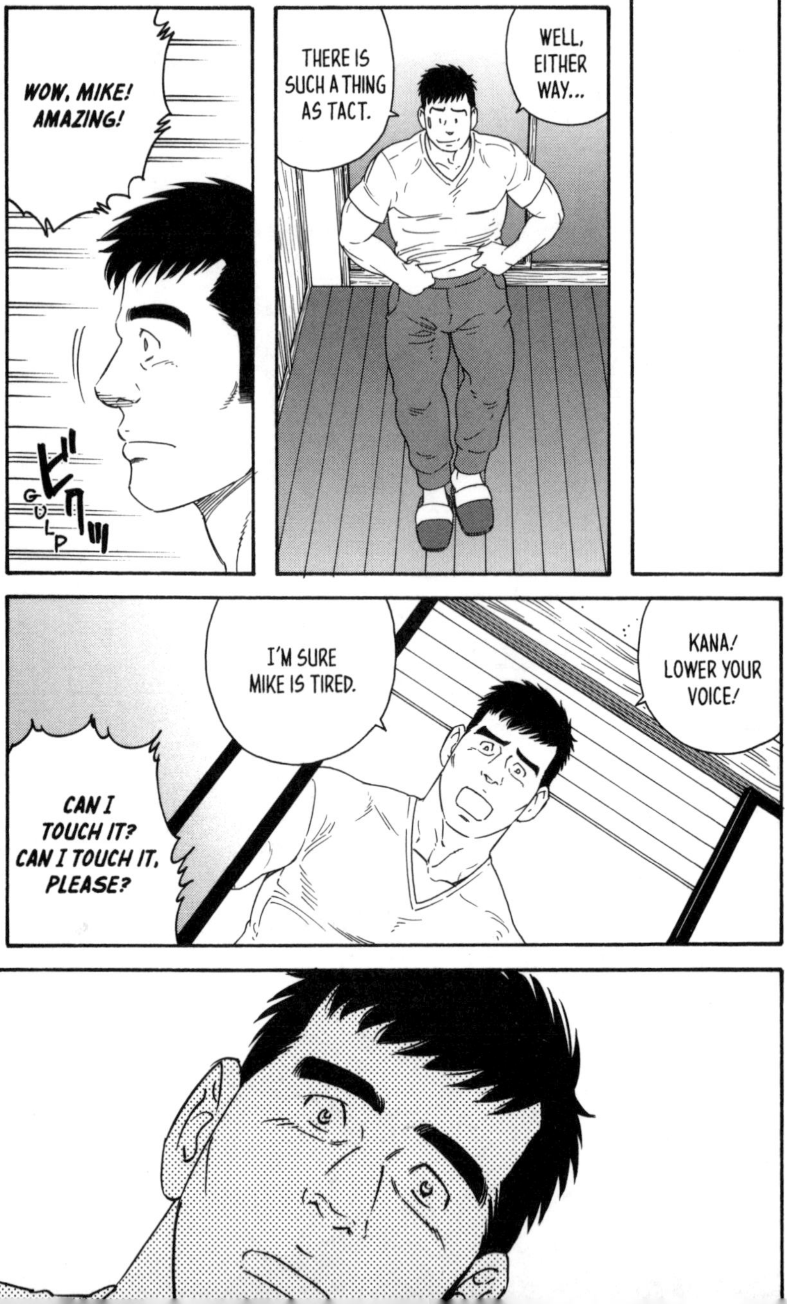
WELL, EITHER WAY...
THERE IS SUCH A THING AS TACT.
WOW, MIKE! AMAZING!
ビクッ
GULP
KANA! LOWER YOUR VOICE!
I'M SURE MIKE IS TIRED.
CAN I TOUCH IT? CAN I TOUCH IT, PLEASE?

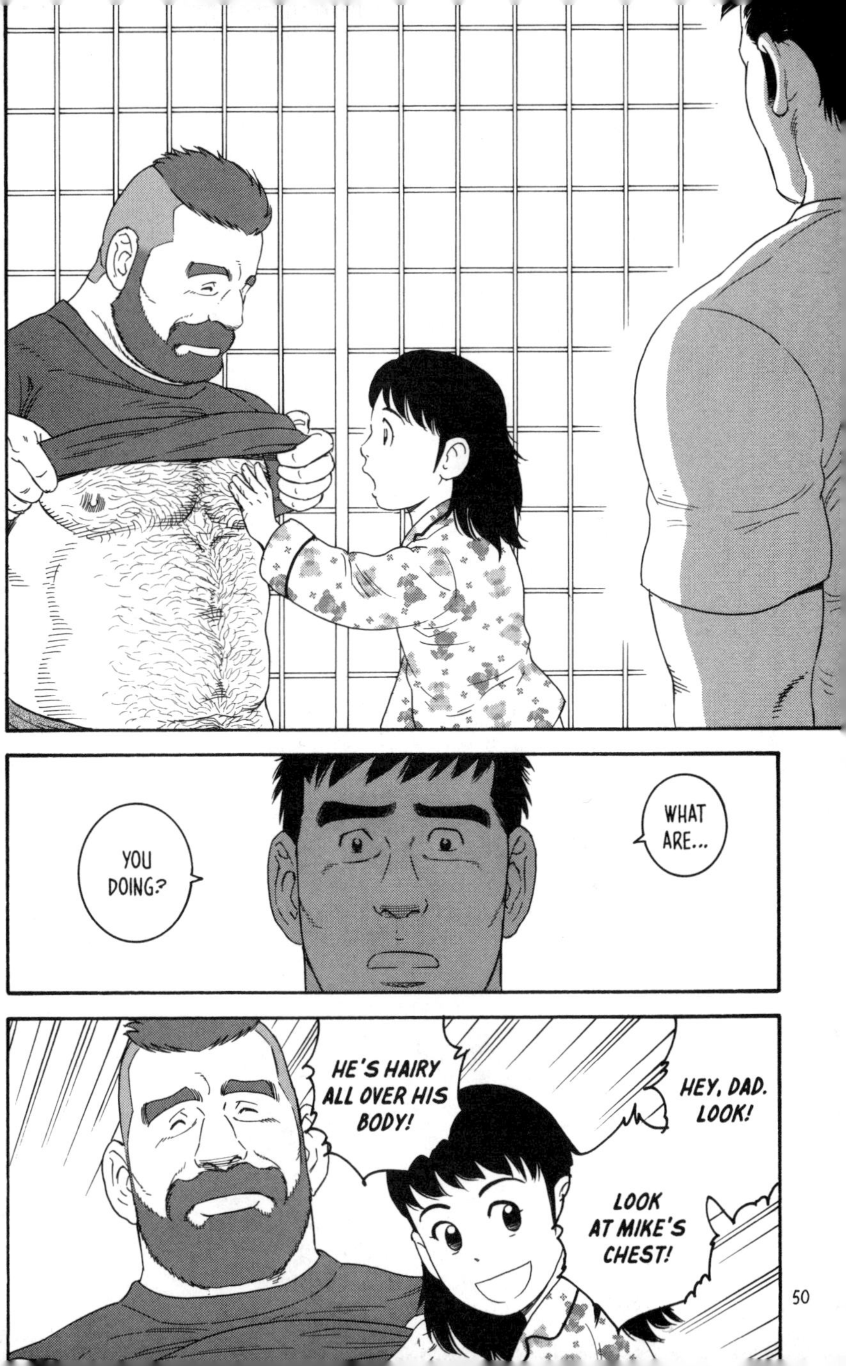
WHAT ARE...
YOU DOING?
HEY, DAD. LOOK!
LOOK AT MIKE'S CHEST!
HE'S HAIRY ALL OVER HIS BODY!

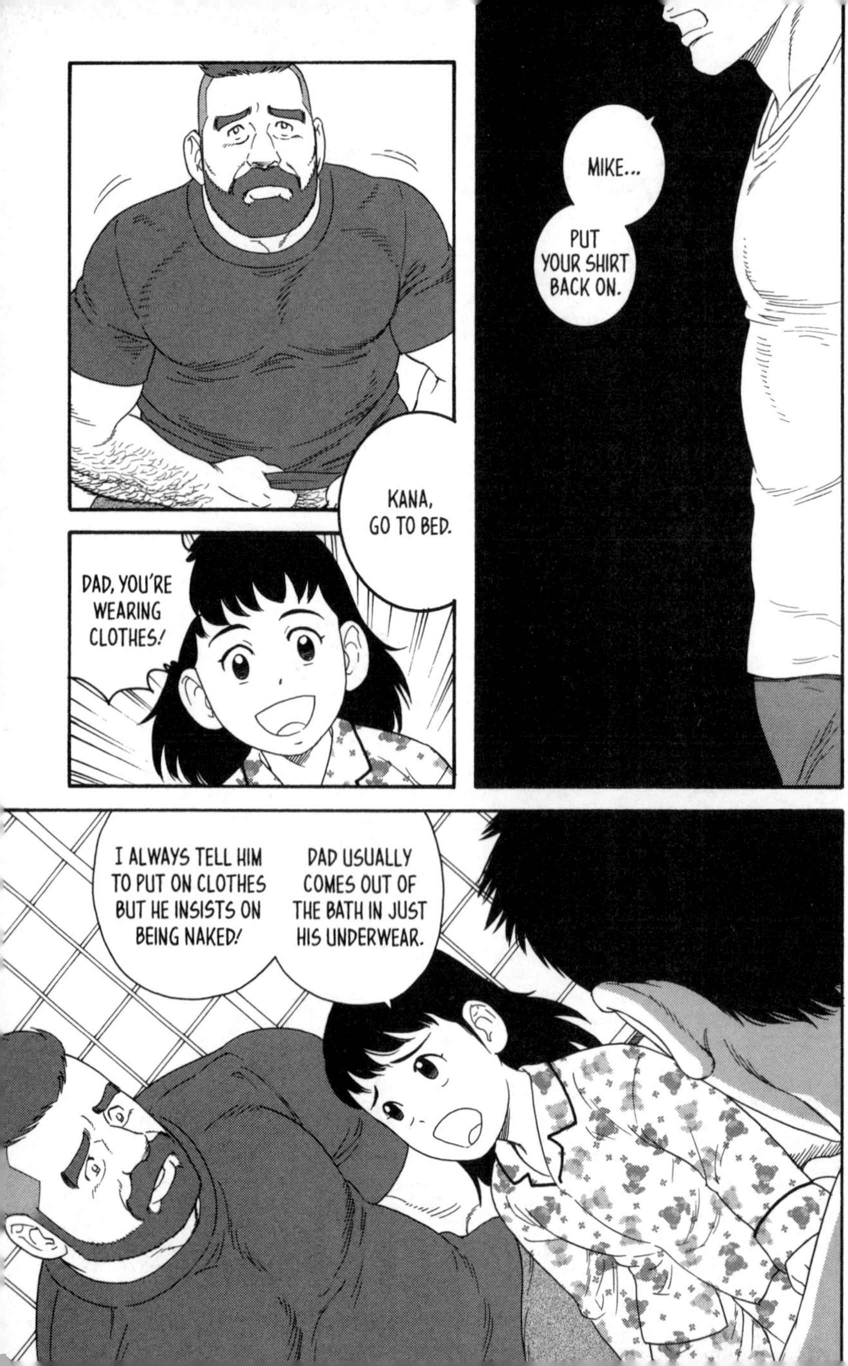
MIKE...
PUT YOUR SHIRT BACK ON.
KANA, GO TO BED.
DAD, YOU'RE WEARING CLOTHES!
DAD USUALLY COMES OUT OF THE BATH IN JUST HIS UNDERWEAR.
I ALWAYS TELL HIM TO PUT ON CLOTHES BUT HE INSISTS ON BEING NAKED!

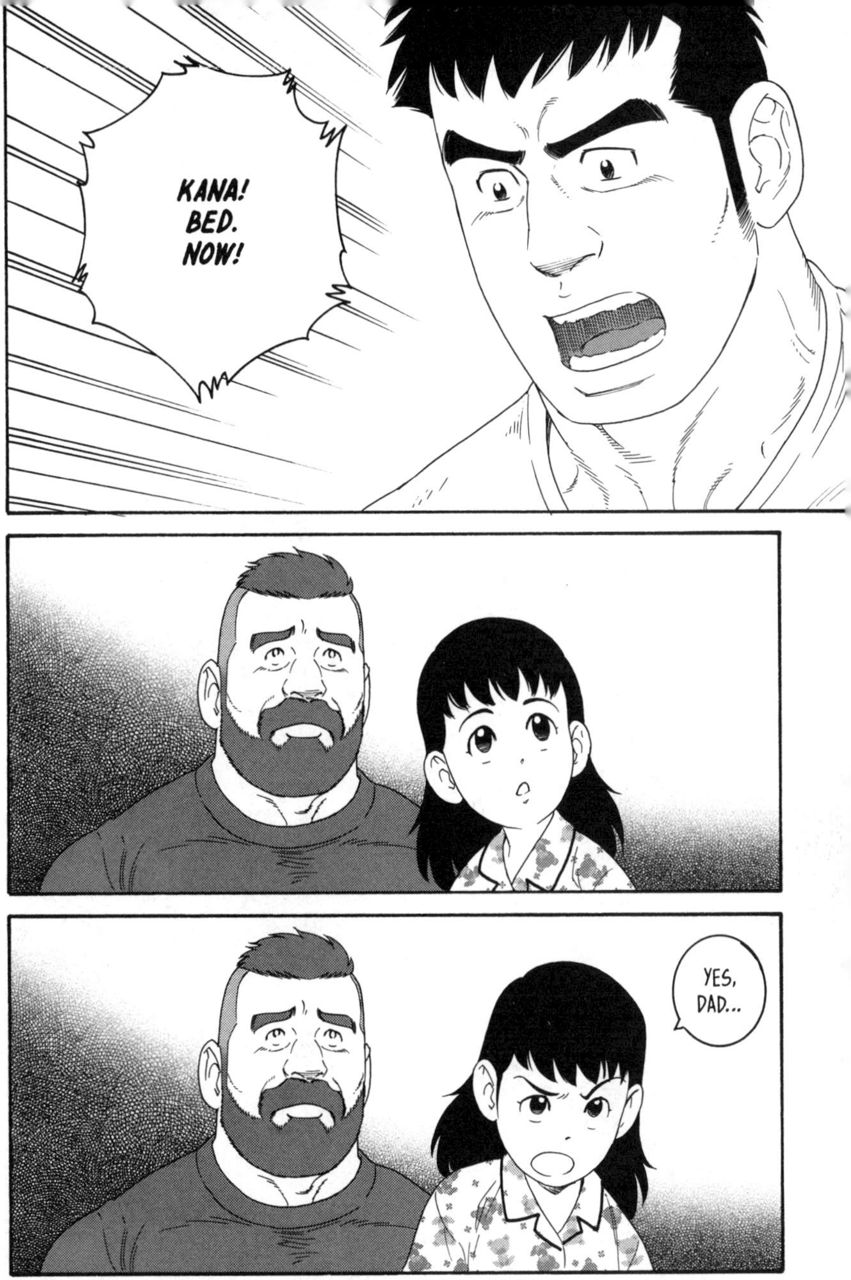
KANA! BED. NOW!
YES, DAD...

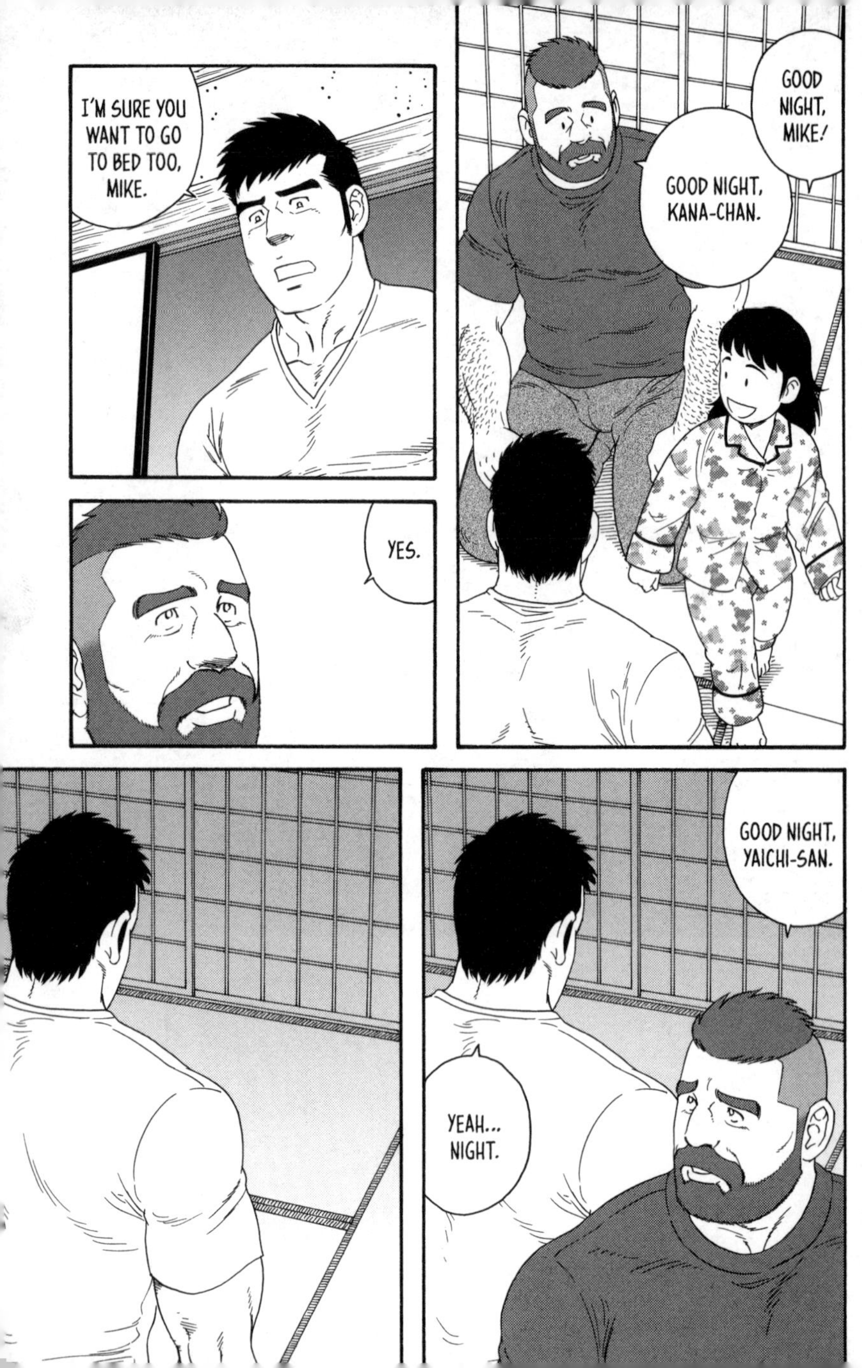
GOOD NIGHT, MIKE!
GOOD NIGHT, KANA-CHAN.
I'M SURE YOU WANT TO GO TO BED TOO, MIKE.
YES.
GOOD NIGHT, YAICHI-SAN.
YEAH... NIGHT.

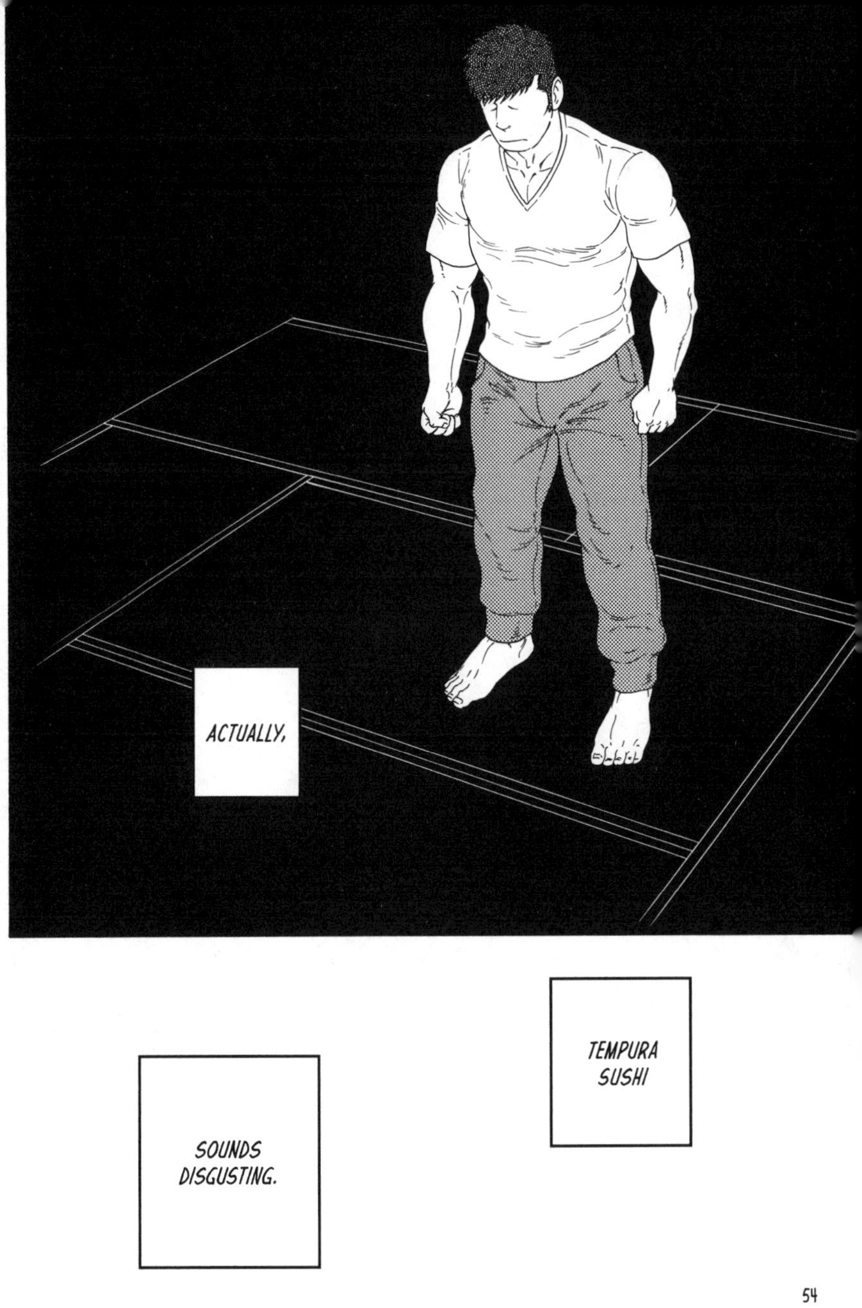
ACTUALLY,

TEMPURA
SUSHI

SOUNDS
DISGUSTING.

CHAPTER THREE

MEMORIES

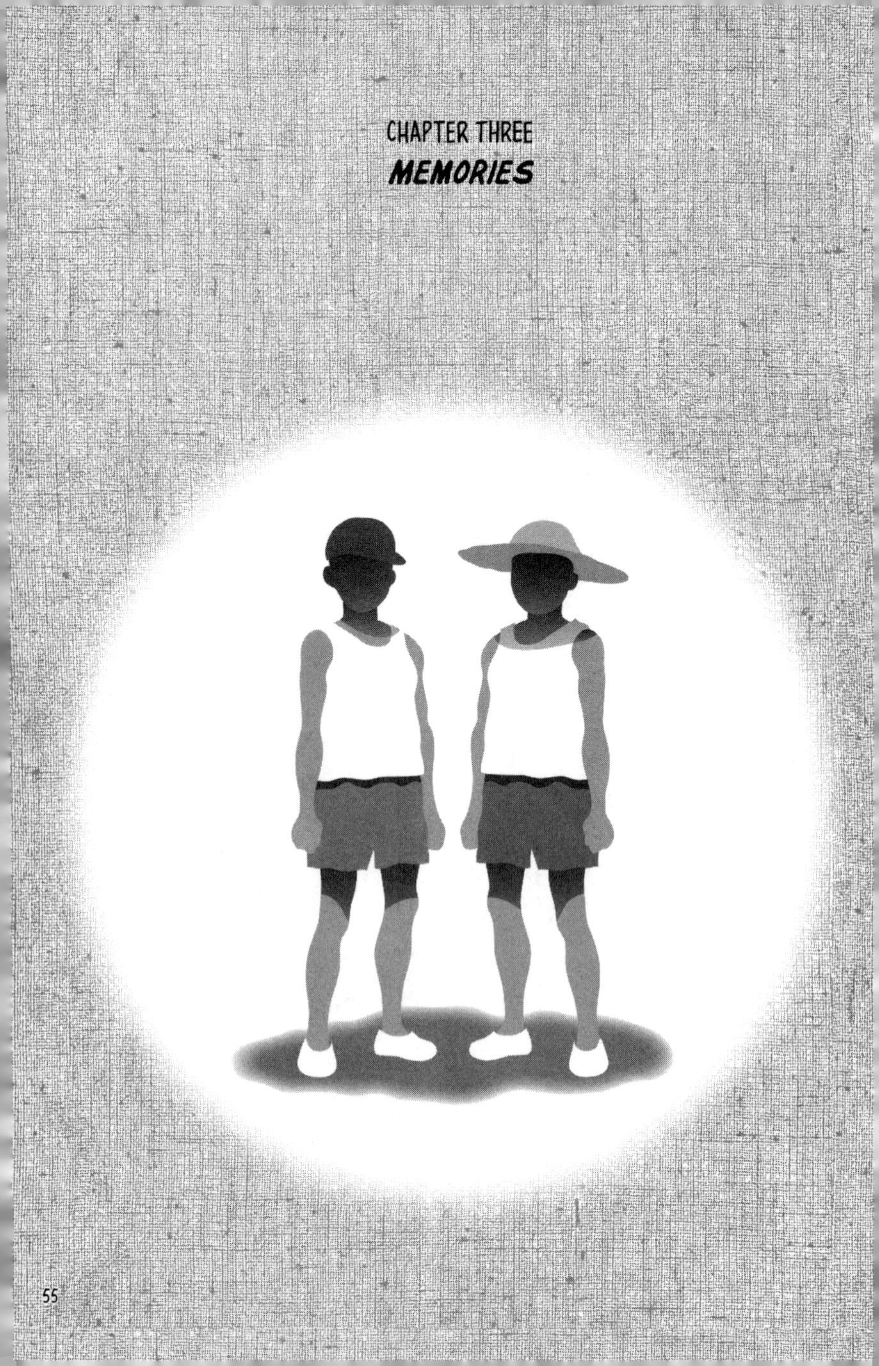

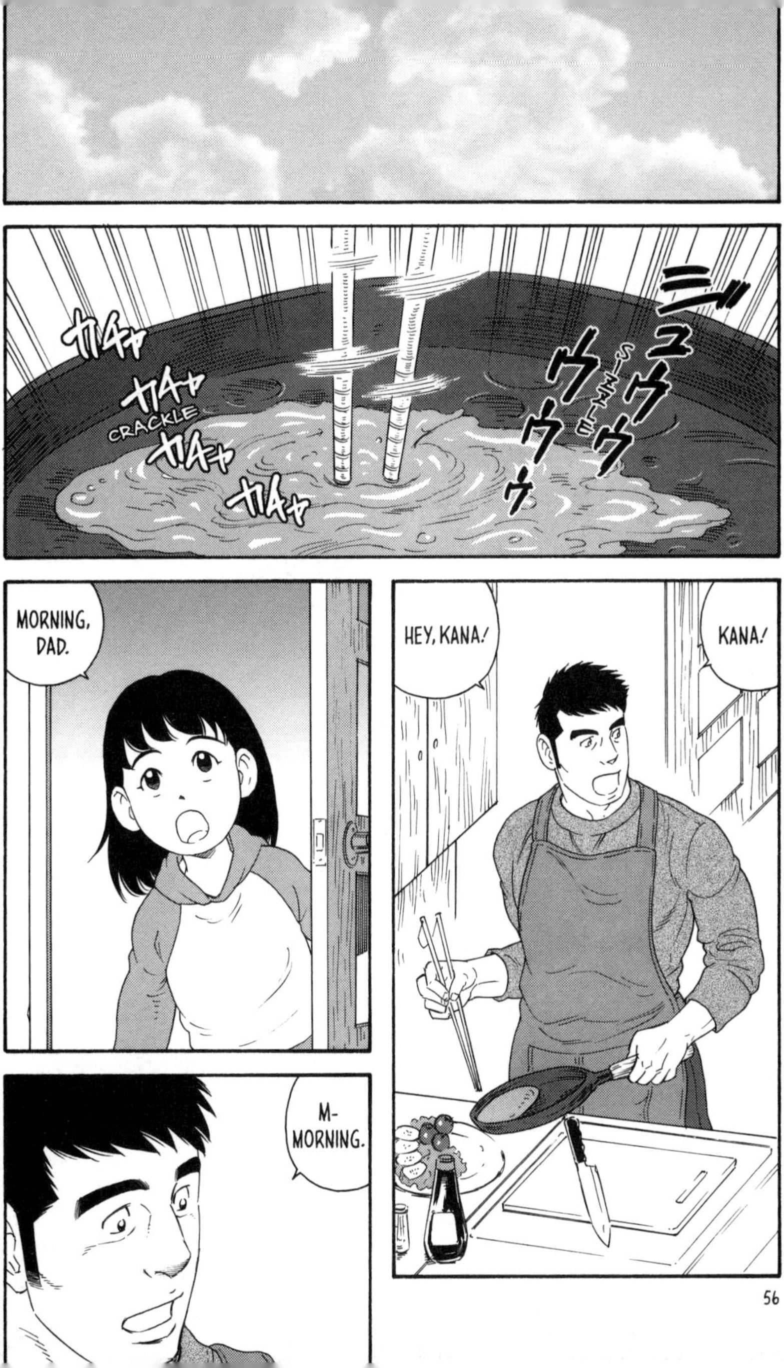

ジュウウウウウ
S-SIZZLE
カチャ
カチャ
CRACKLE
カチャ
カチャ
KANA!
HEY, KANA!
MORNING, DAD.
M-MORNING.

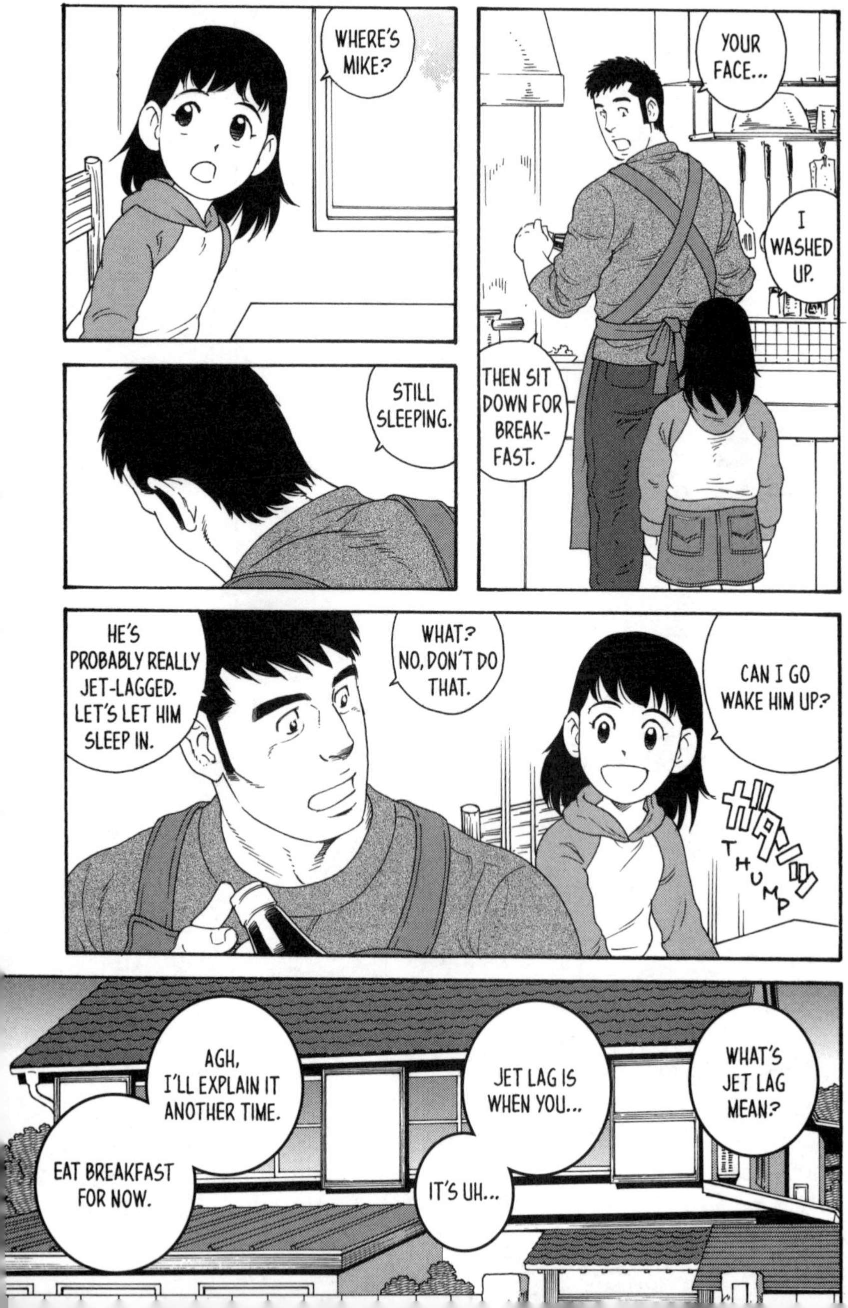
YOUR FACE...
I WASHED UP.
THEN SIT DOWN FOR BREAK-FAST.
WHERE'S MIKE?
STILL SLEEPING.
CAN I GO WAKE HIM UP?
ガタンッ
THUMP
WHAT? NO, DON'T DO THAT.
HE'S PROBABLY REALLY JET-LAGGED. LET'S LET HIM SLEEP IN.
WHAT'S JET LAG MEAN?
JET LAG IS WHEN YOU...
IT'S UH...
AGH, I'LL EXPLAIN IT ANOTHER TIME.
EAT BREAKFAST FOR NOW.

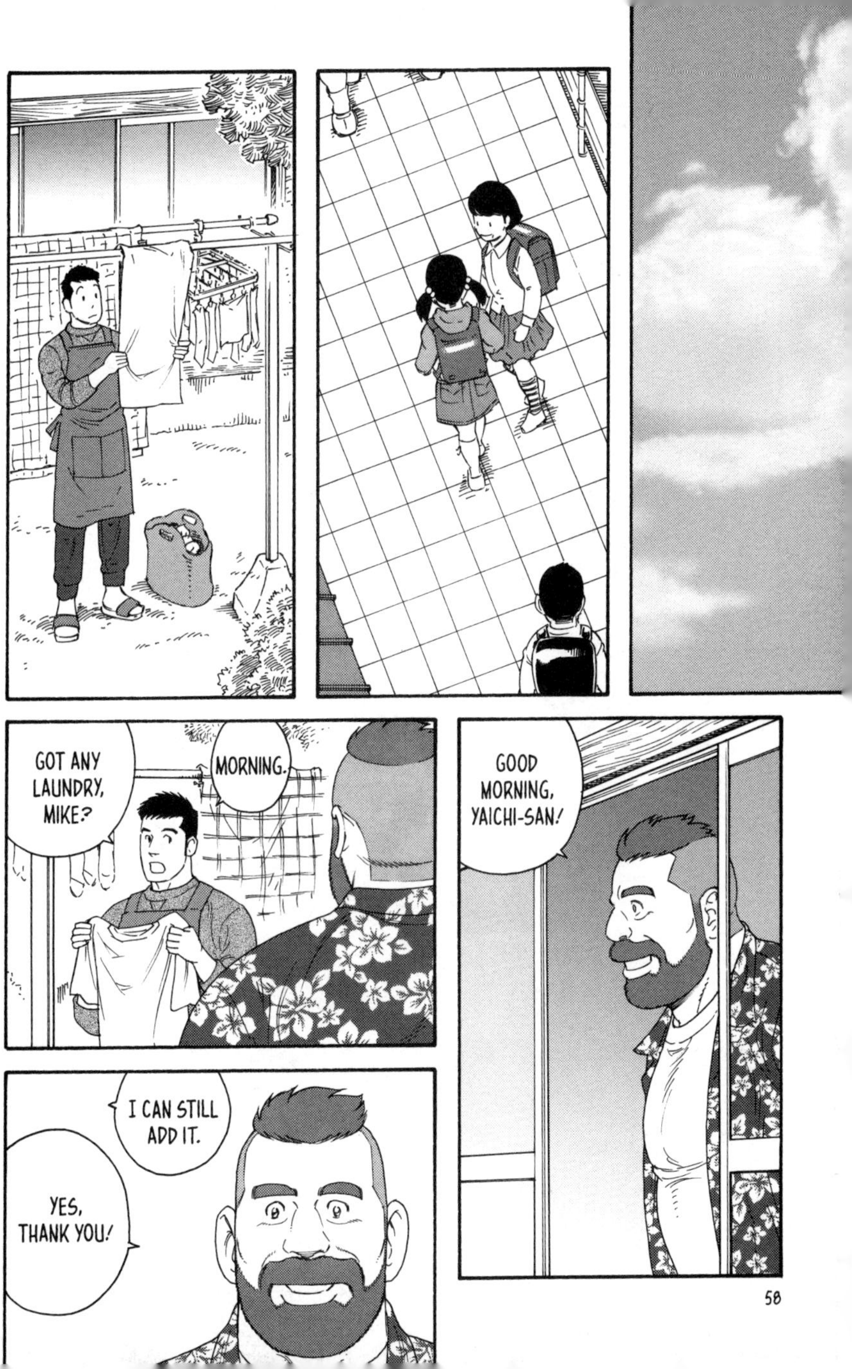
GOOD MORNING, YAICHI-SAN!
MORNING.
GOT ANY LAUNDRY, MIKE?
I CAN STILL ADD IT.
YES, THANK YOU!

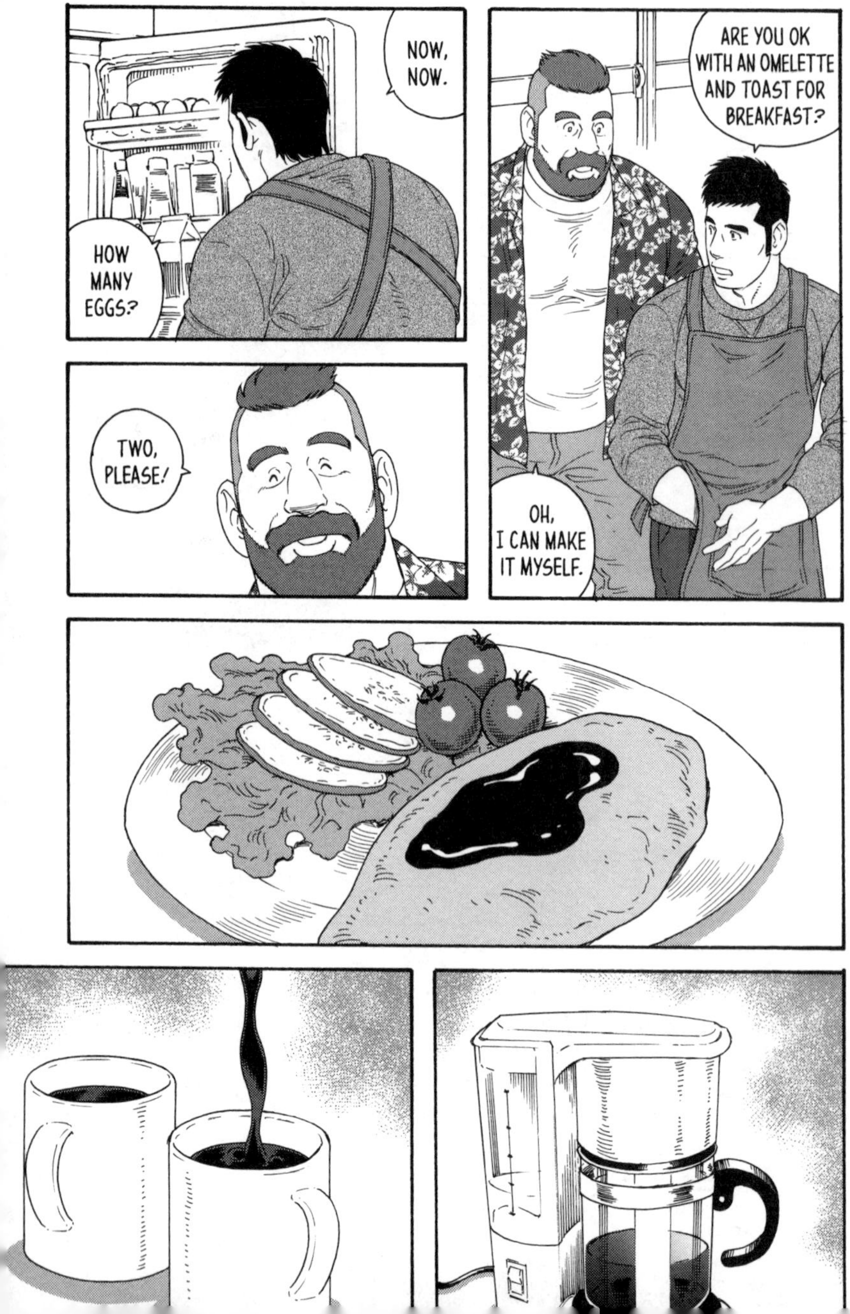
ARE YOU OK WITH AN OMELETTE AND TOAST FOR BREAKFAST?
OH, I CAN MAKE IT MYSELF.
NOW, NOW.
HOW MANY EGGS?
TWO, PLEASE!

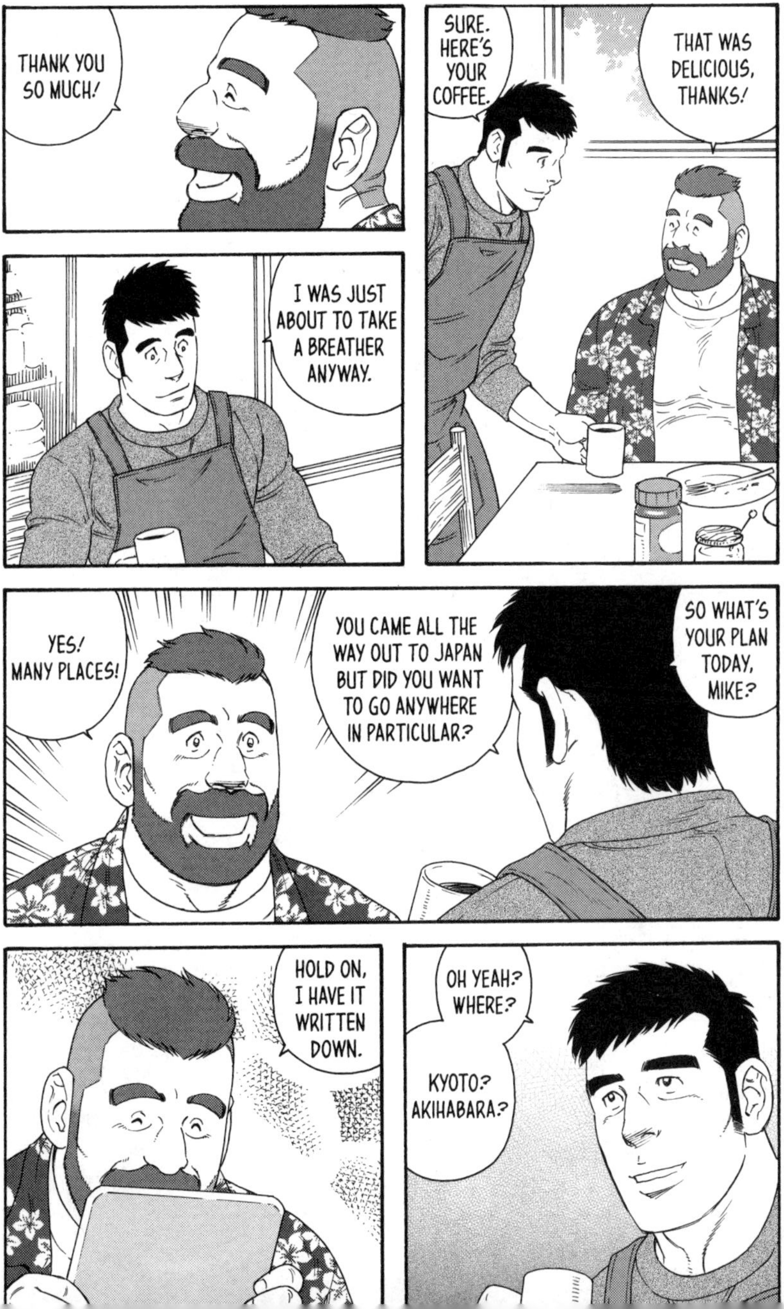
THAT WAS DELICIOUS, THANKS!
SURE. HERE'S YOUR COFFEE.
THANK YOU SO MUCH!
I WAS JUST ABOUT TO TAKE A BREATHER ANYWAY.
SO WHAT'S YOUR PLAN TODAY, MIKE?
YOU CAME ALL THE WAY OUT TO JAPAN BUT DID YOU WANT TO GO ANYWHERE IN PARTICULAR?
YES! MANY PLACES!
OH YEAH? WHERE?
KYOTO? AKIHABARA?
HOLD ON, I HAVE IT WRITTEN DOWN.

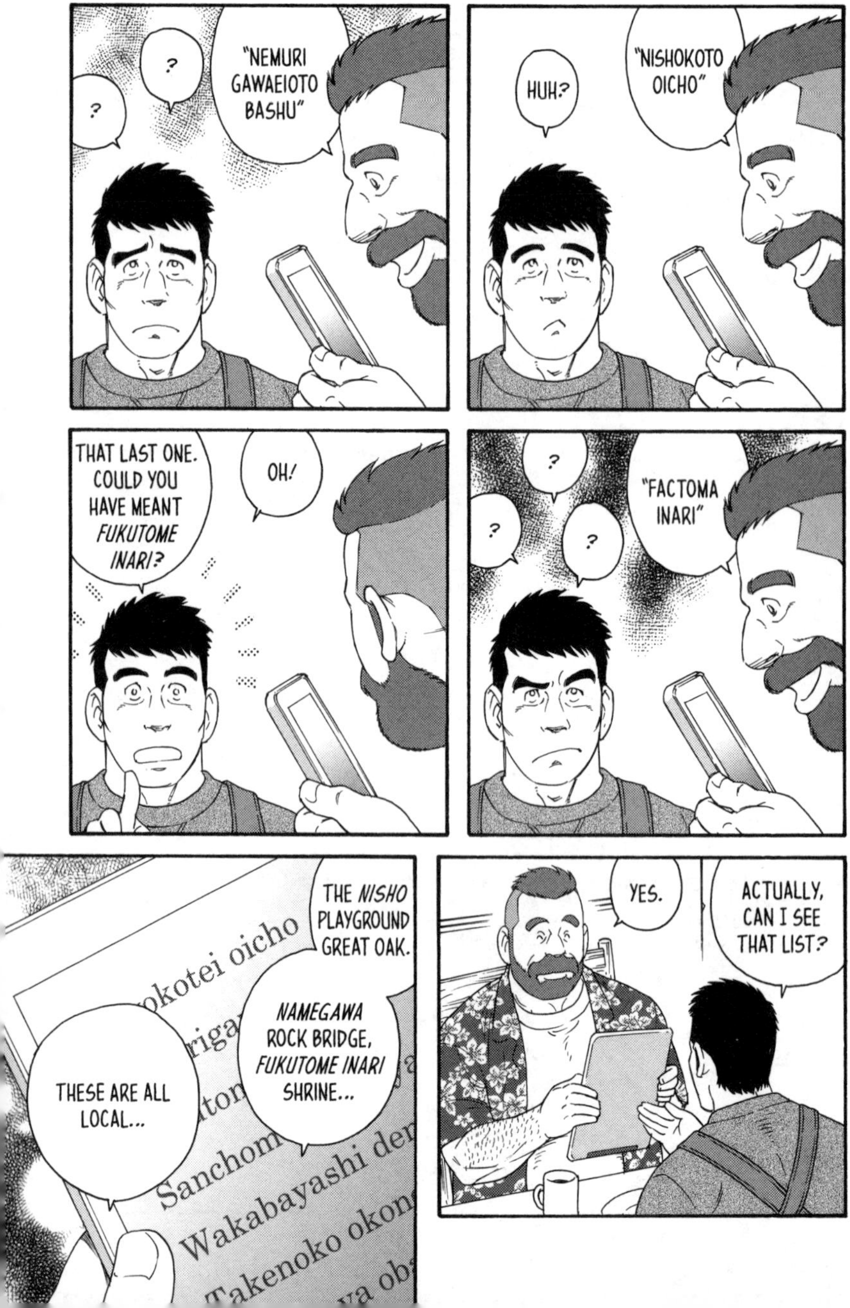
"NISHOKOTO OICHO"
HUH?
"NEMURI GAWAEIOTO BASHU"
?
?
"FACTOMA INARI"
?
?
?
OH!
THAT LAST ONE. COULD YOU HAVE MEANT *FUKUTOME INARI*?
ACTUALLY, CAN I SEE THAT LIST?
YES.
THE *NISHO* PLAYGROUND GREAT OAK.
NAMEGAWA ROCK BRIDGE, *FUKUTOME INARI* SHRINE...
THESE ARE ALL LOCAL...

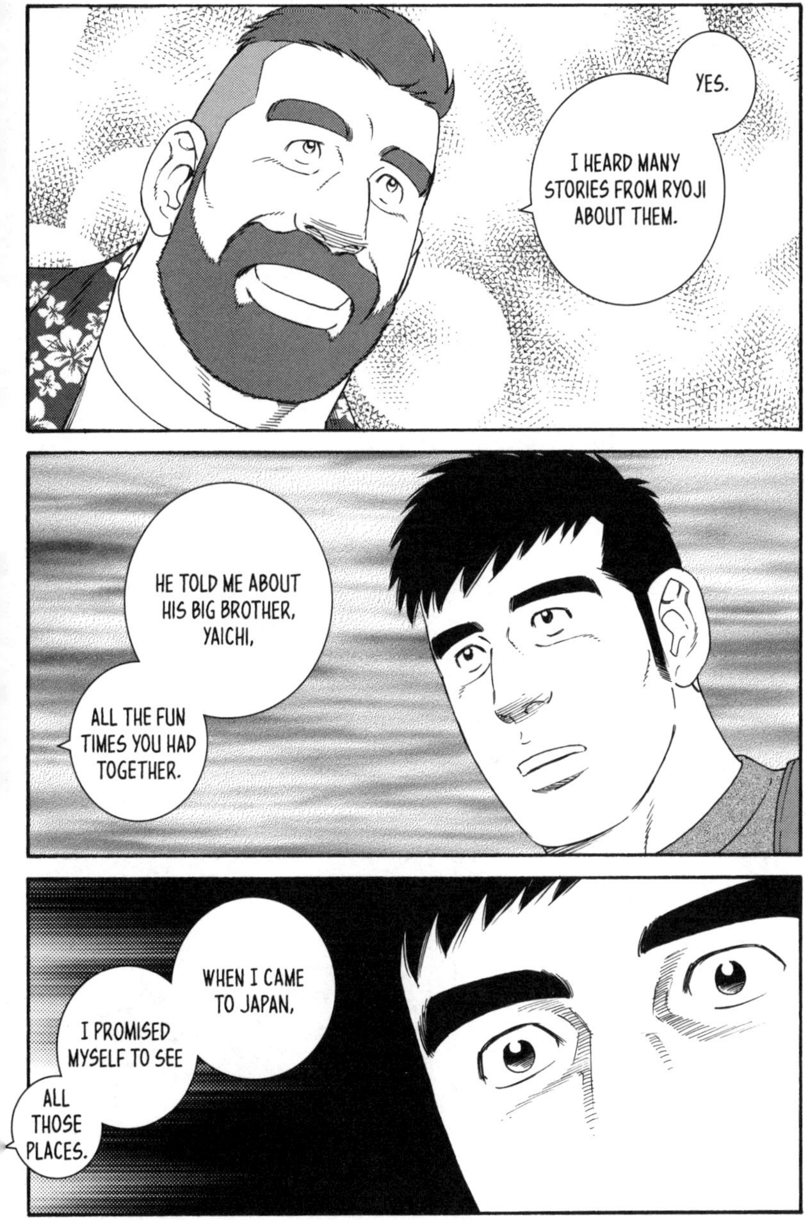
YES.
I HEARD MANY STORIES FROM RYOJI ABOUT THEM.
HE TOLD ME ABOUT HIS BIG BROTHER, YAICHI,
ALL THE FUN TIMES YOU HAD TOGETHER.
WHEN I CAME TO JAPAN,
I PROMISED MYSELF TO SEE
ALL THOSE PLACES.

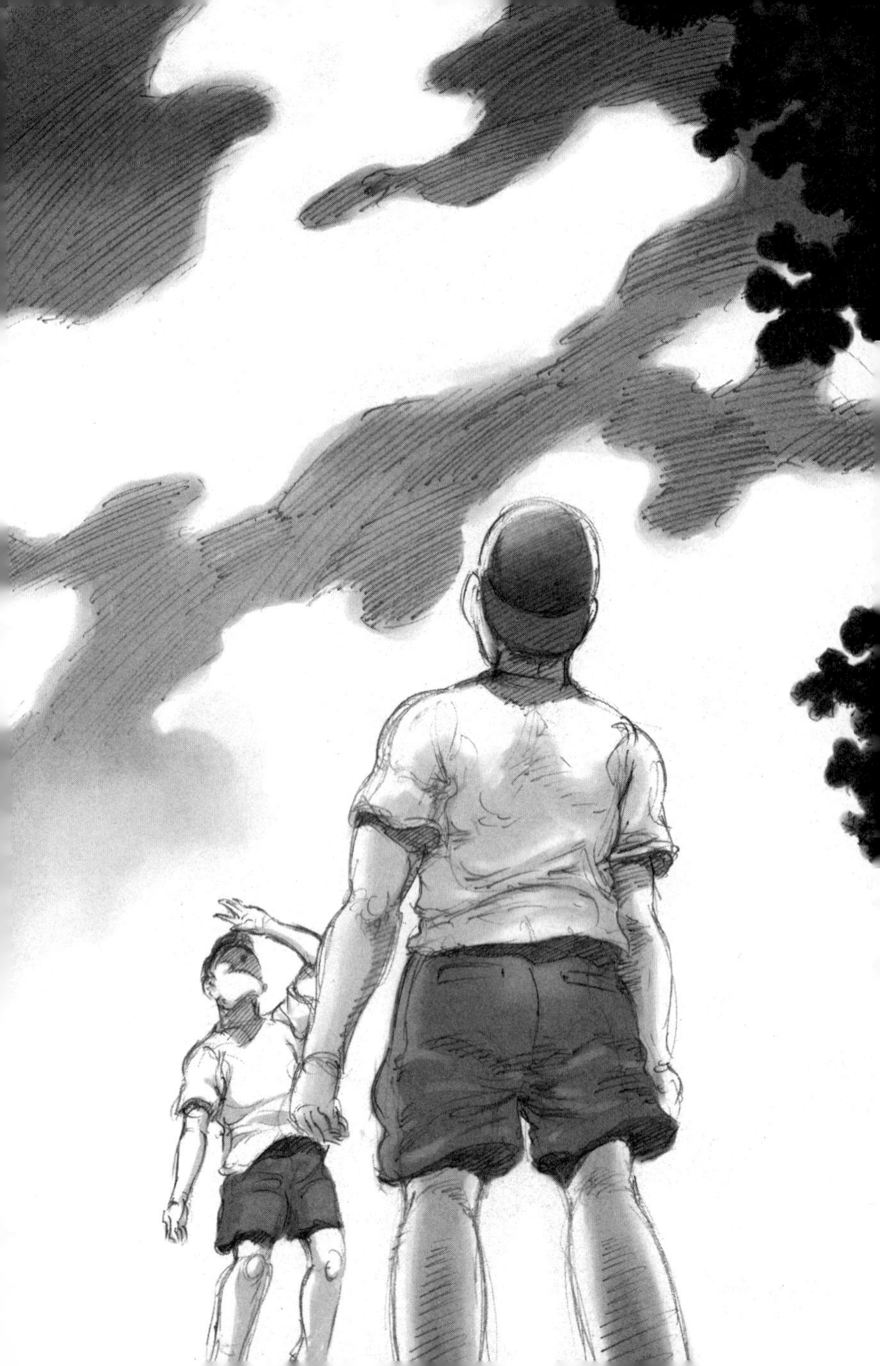

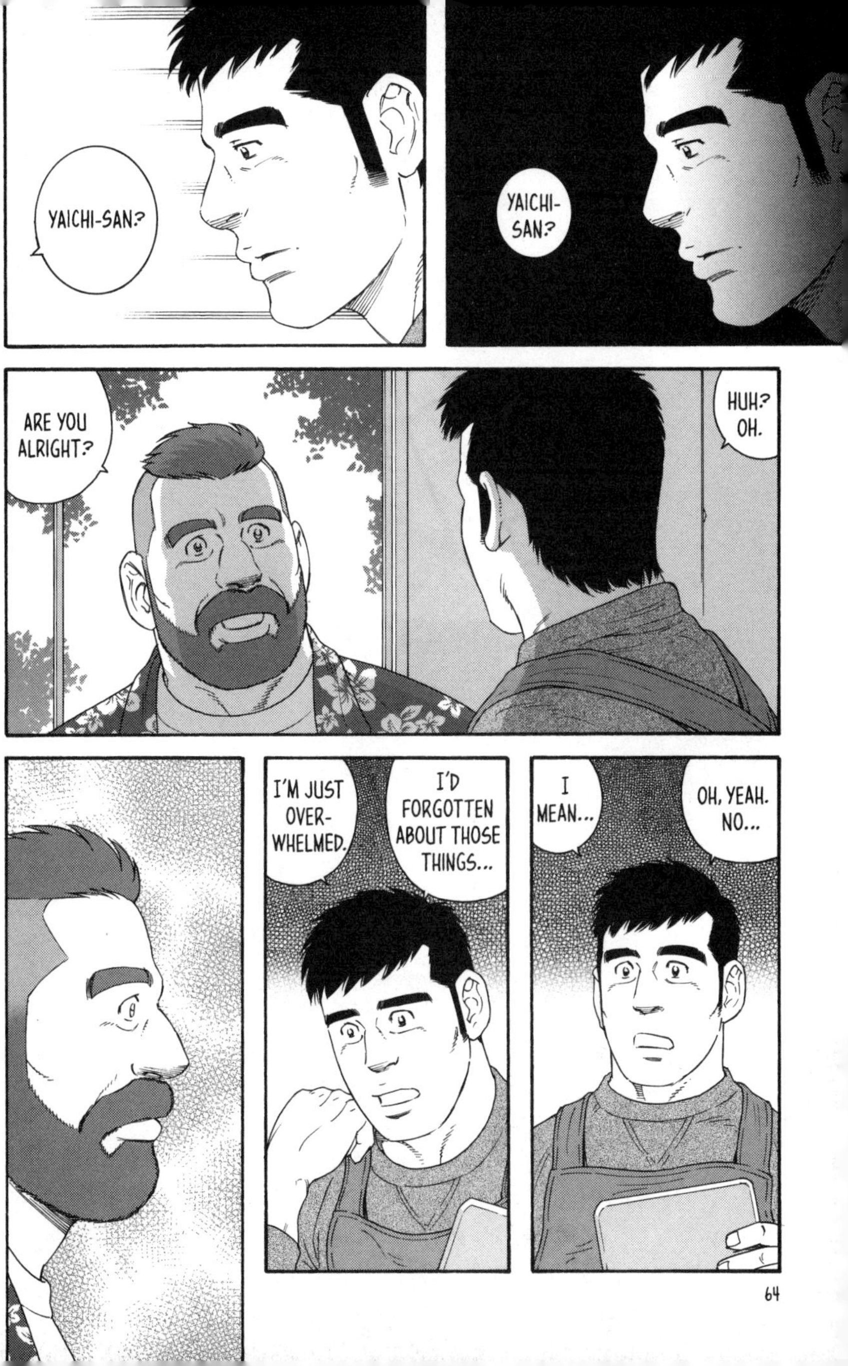

YAICHI-SAN?
YAICHI-SAN?
HUH? OH.
ARE YOU ALRIGHT?
OH, YEAH. NO...
I MEAN...
I'D FORGOTTEN ABOUT THOSE THINGS...
I'M JUST OVER-WHELMED.

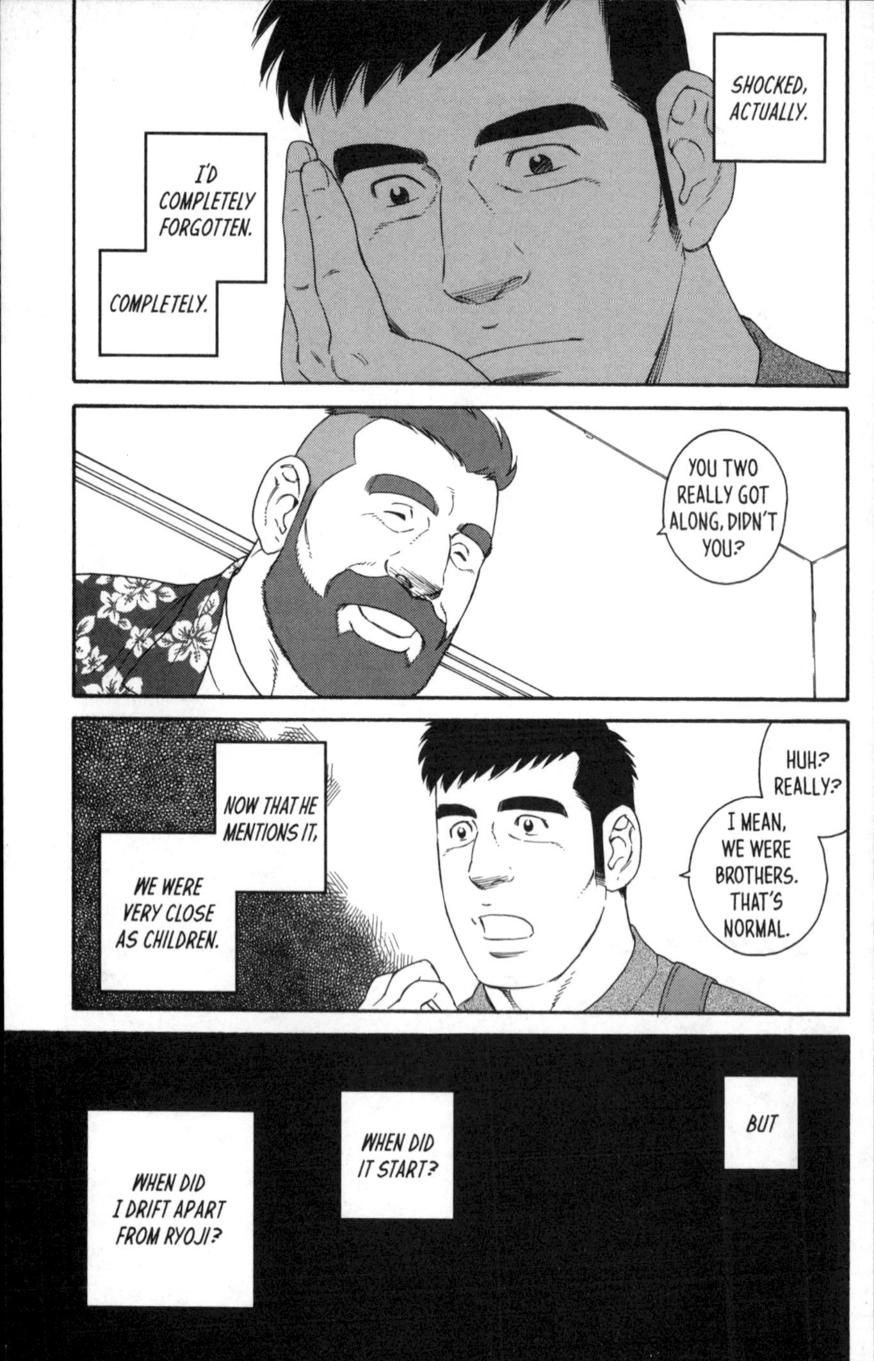
SHOCKED, ACTUALLY.
I'D COMPLETELY FORGOTTEN.
COMPLETELY.
YOU TWO REALLY GOT ALONG, DIDN'T YOU?
HUH? REALLY?
I MEAN, WE WERE BROTHERS. THAT'S NORMAL.
NOW THAT HE MENTIONS IT,
WE WERE VERY CLOSE AS CHILDREN.
BUT
WHEN DID IT START?
WHEN DID I DRIFT APART FROM RYOJI?

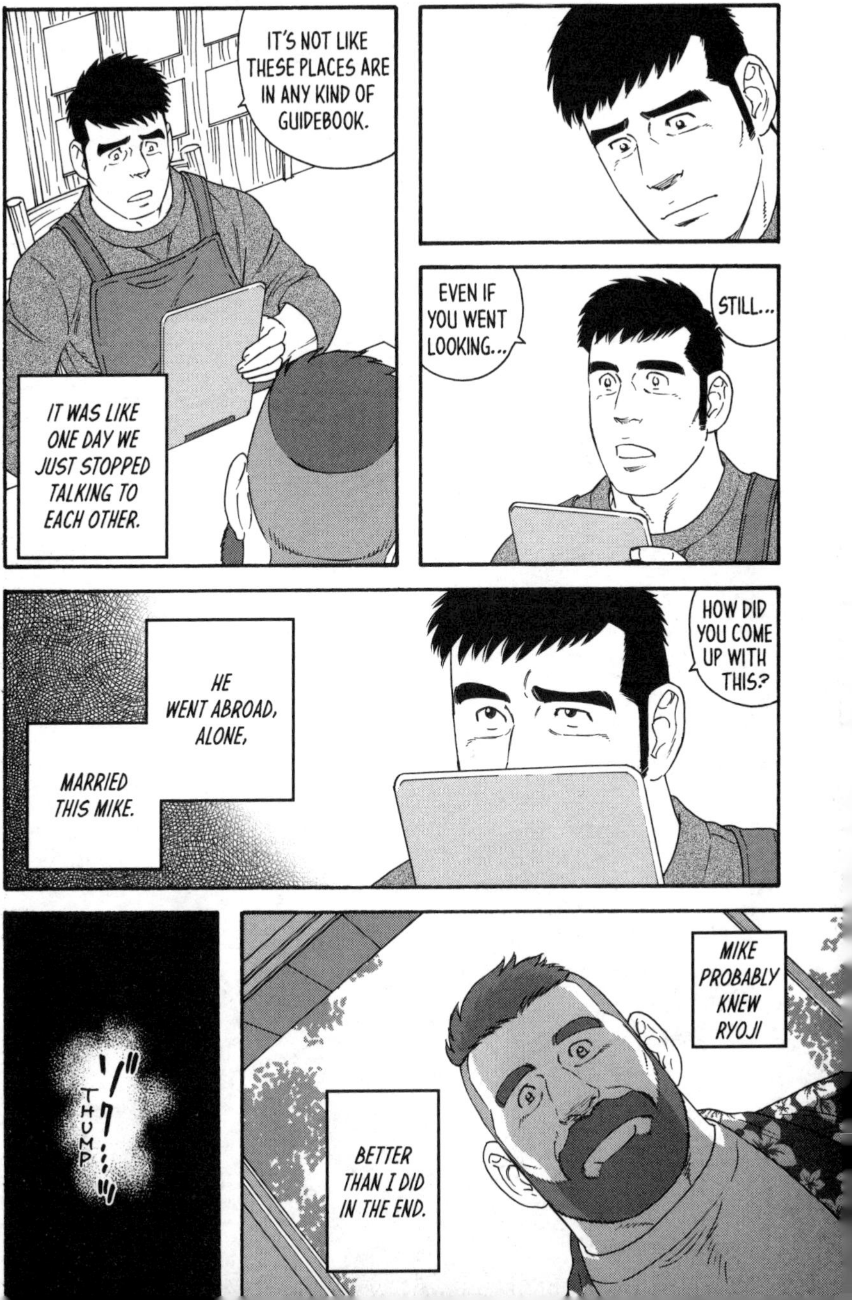
STILL...
EVEN IF YOU WENT LOOKING...
IT'S NOT LIKE THESE PLACES ARE IN ANY KIND OF GUIDEBOOK.
IT WAS LIKE ONE DAY WE JUST STOPPED TALKING TO EACH OTHER.
HOW DID YOU COME UP WITH THIS?
HE WENT ABROAD, ALONE,
MARRIED THIS MIKE.
MIKE PROBABLY KNEW RYOJI
BETTER THAN I DID IN THE END.
THUMP

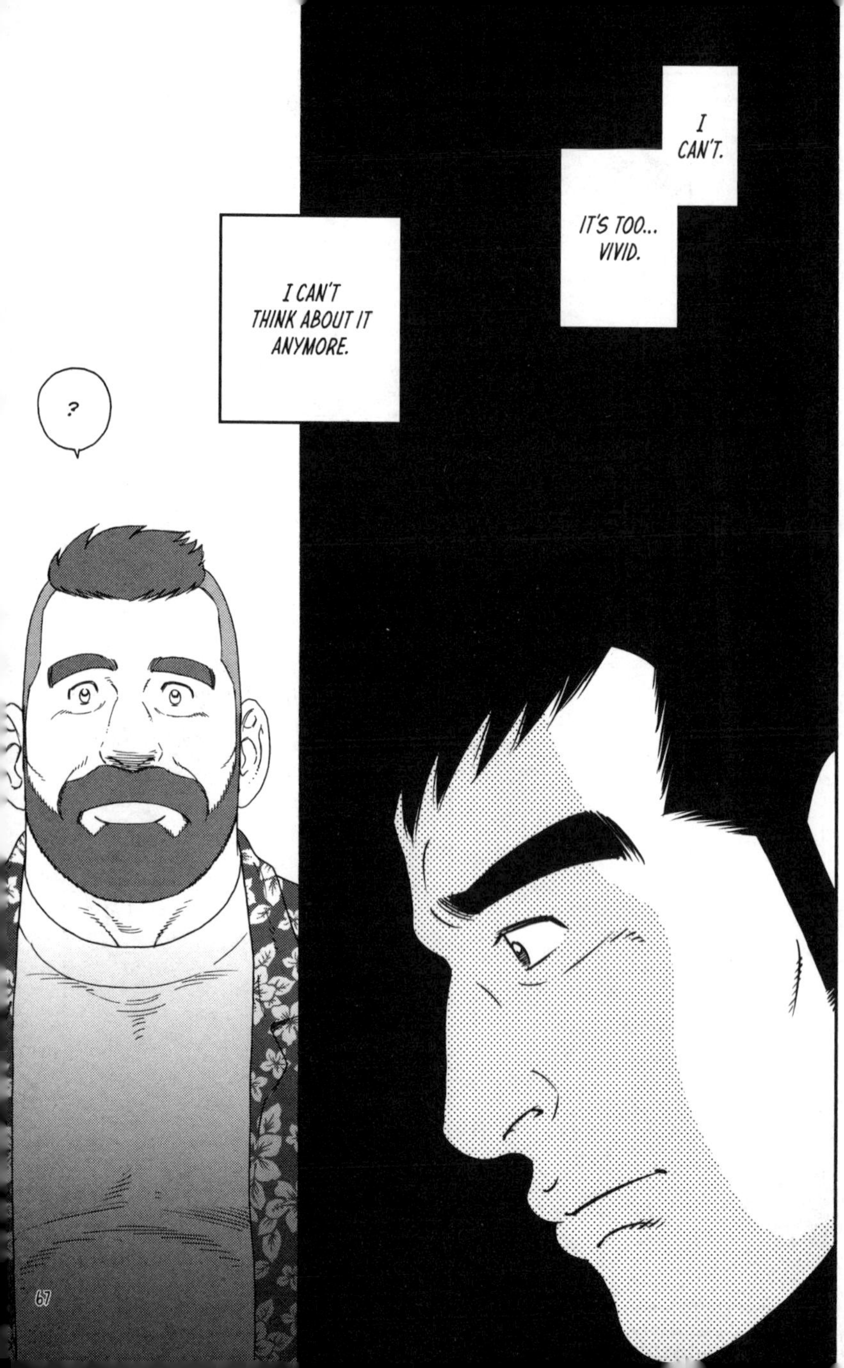
I CAN'T.
IT'S TOO... VIVID.
I CAN'T THINK ABOUT IT ANYMORE.
?

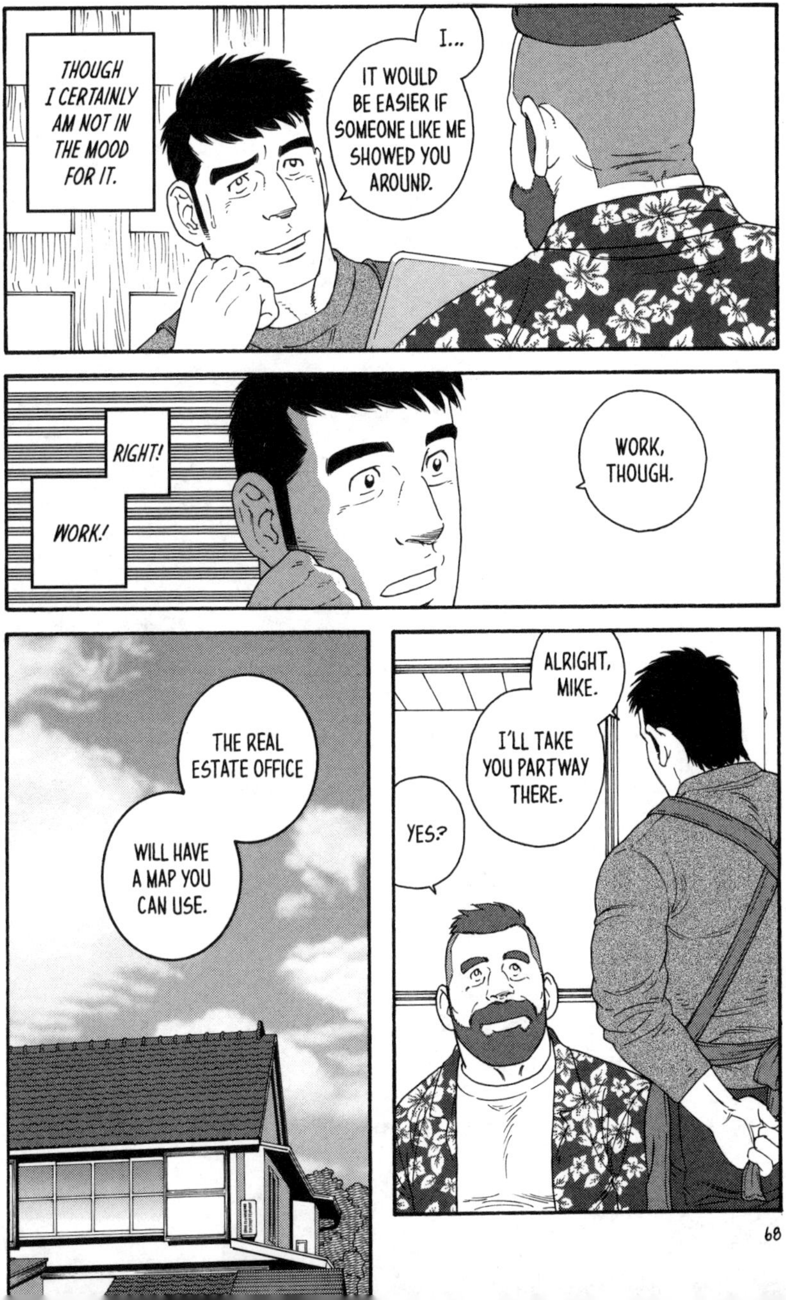
I...
IT WOULD BE EASIER IF SOMEONE LIKE ME SHOWED YOU AROUND.
THOUGH I CERTAINLY AM NOT IN THE MOOD FOR IT.
WORK, THOUGH.
RIGHT!
WORK!
ALRIGHT, MIKE.
I'LL TAKE YOU PARTWAY THERE.
YES?
THE REAL ESTATE OFFICE
WILL HAVE A MAP YOU CAN USE.

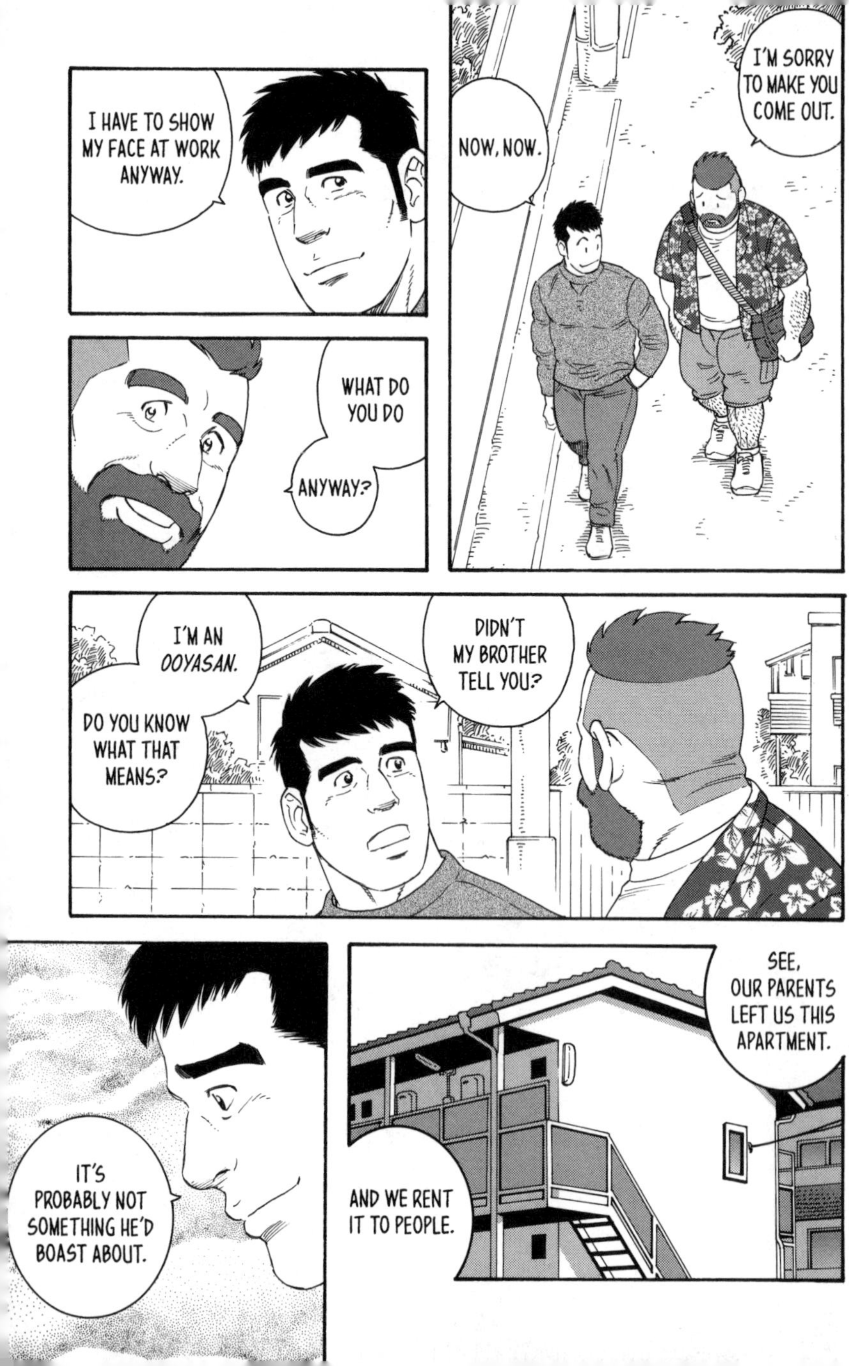
I'M SORRY TO MAKE YOU COME OUT.
NOW, NOW.
I HAVE TO SHOW MY FACE AT WORK ANYWAY.
WHAT DO YOU DO
ANYWAY?
DIDN'T MY BROTHER TELL YOU?
I'M AN *OOYASAN.*
DO YOU KNOW WHAT THAT MEANS?
SEE, OUR PARENTS LEFT US THIS APARTMENT.
AND WE RENT IT TO PEOPLE.
IT'S PROBABLY NOT SOMETHING HE'D BOAST ABOUT.

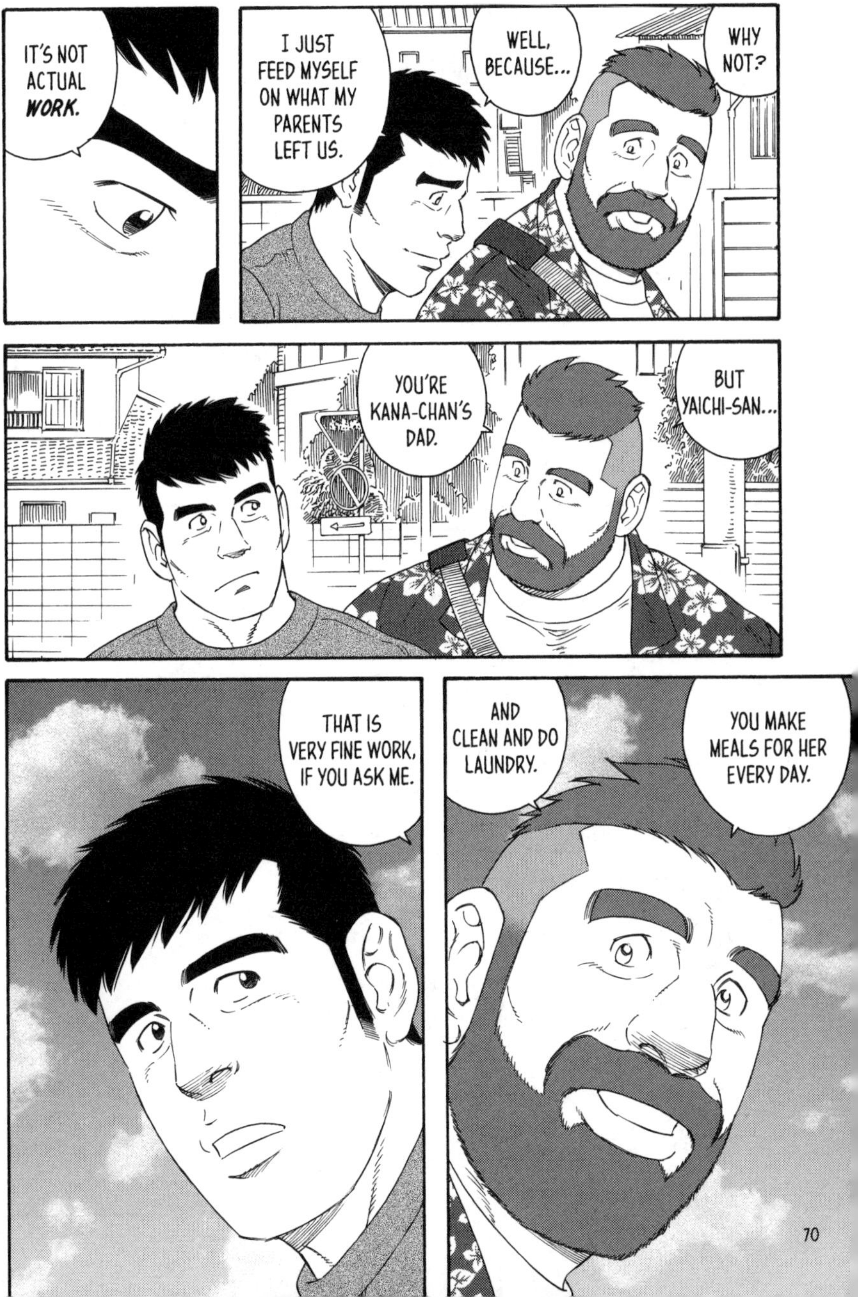
WHY NOT?
WELL, BECAUSE...
I JUST FEED MYSELF ON WHAT MY PARENTS LEFT US.
IT'S NOT ACTUAL **WORK.**
BUT YAICHI-SAN...
YOU'RE KANA-CHAN'S DAD.
YOU MAKE MEALS FOR HER EVERY DAY.
AND CLEAN AND DO LAUNDRY.
THAT IS VERY FINE WORK, IF YOU ASK ME.

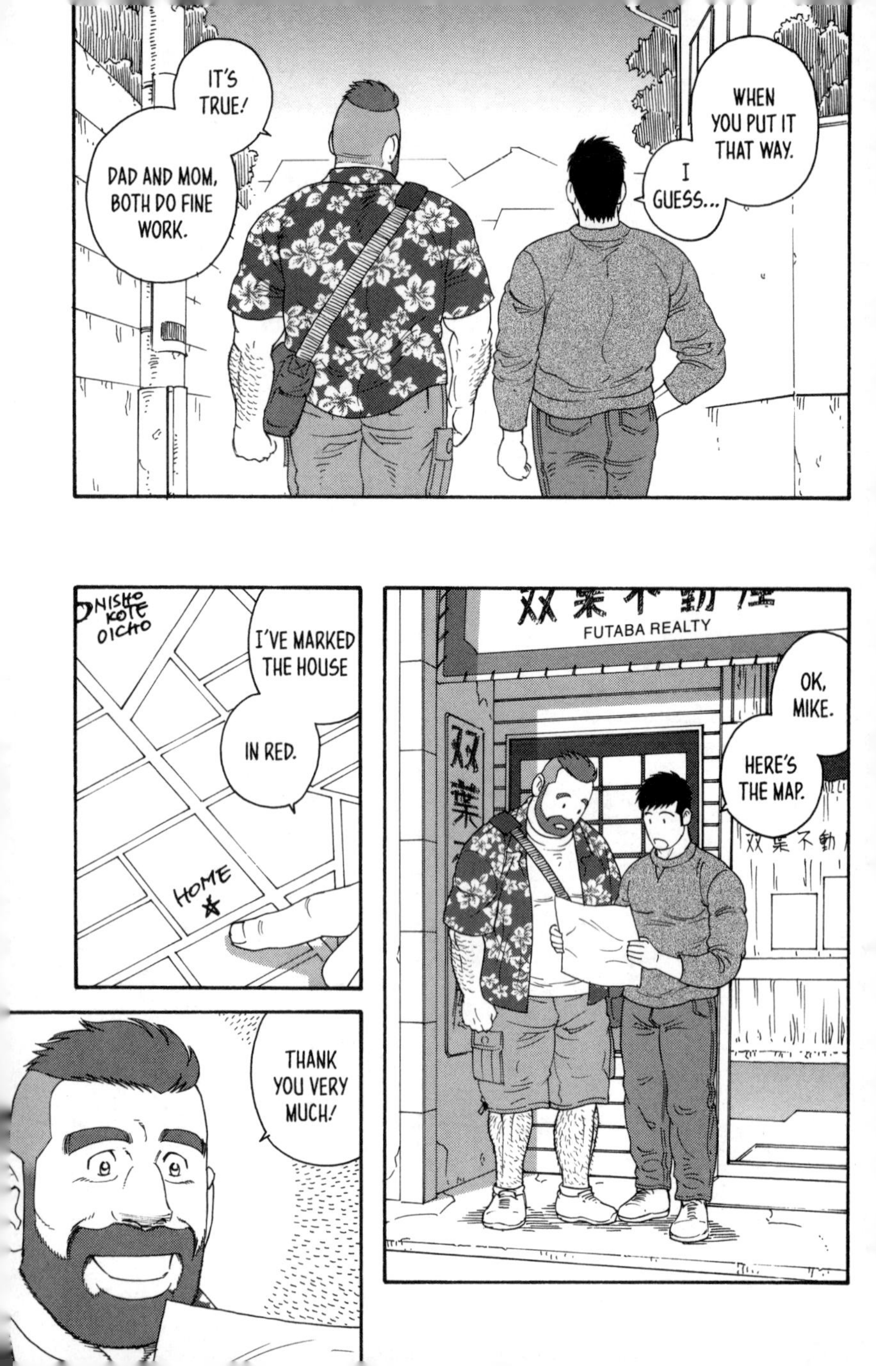
WHEN YOU PUT IT THAT WAY.
I GUESS...
IT'S TRUE!
DAD AND MOM, BOTH DO FINE WORK.
双葉不動産
FUTABA REALTY
OK, MIKE.
HERE'S THE MAP.
I'VE MARKED THE HOUSE
IN RED.
NISHO KOTE OICHO
HOME
THANK YOU VERY MUCH!

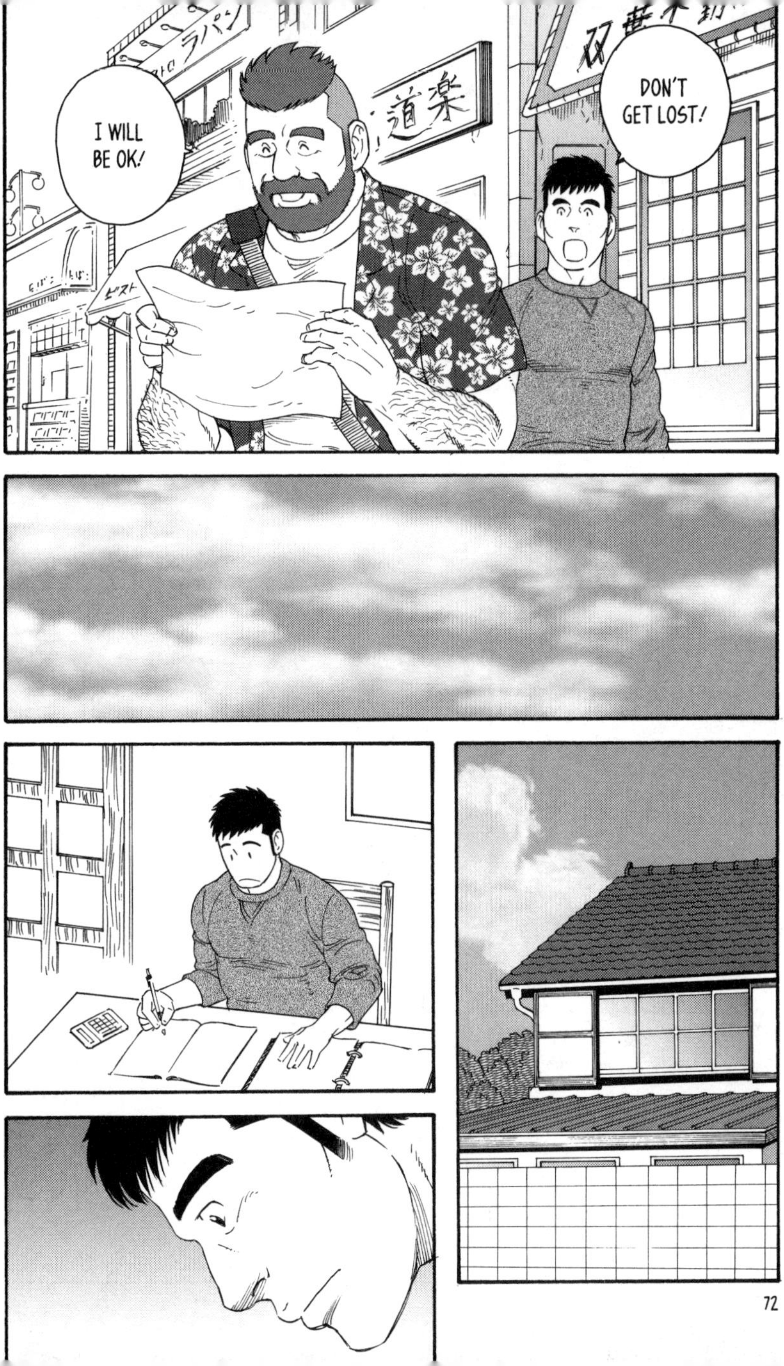
DON'T GET LOST!
I WILL BE OK!

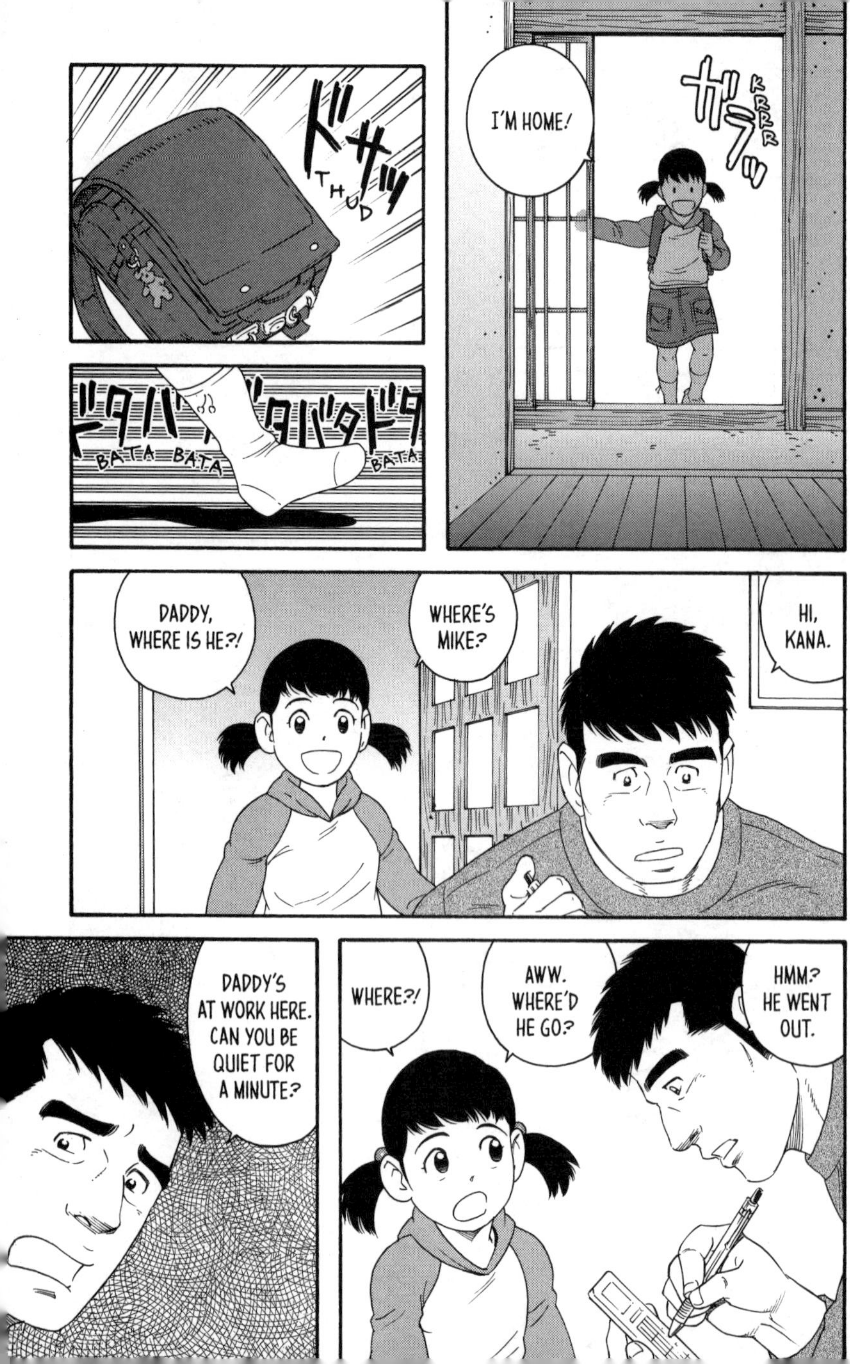
I'M HOME!
ガラッ
KRRRR
ドサッ
THUD
BATA BATA
BATA
HI, KANA.
WHERE'S MIKE?
DADDY, WHERE IS HE?!
HMM? HE WENT OUT.
AWW. WHERE'D HE GO?
WHERE?!
DADDY'S AT WORK HERE. CAN YOU BE QUIET FOR A MINUTE?

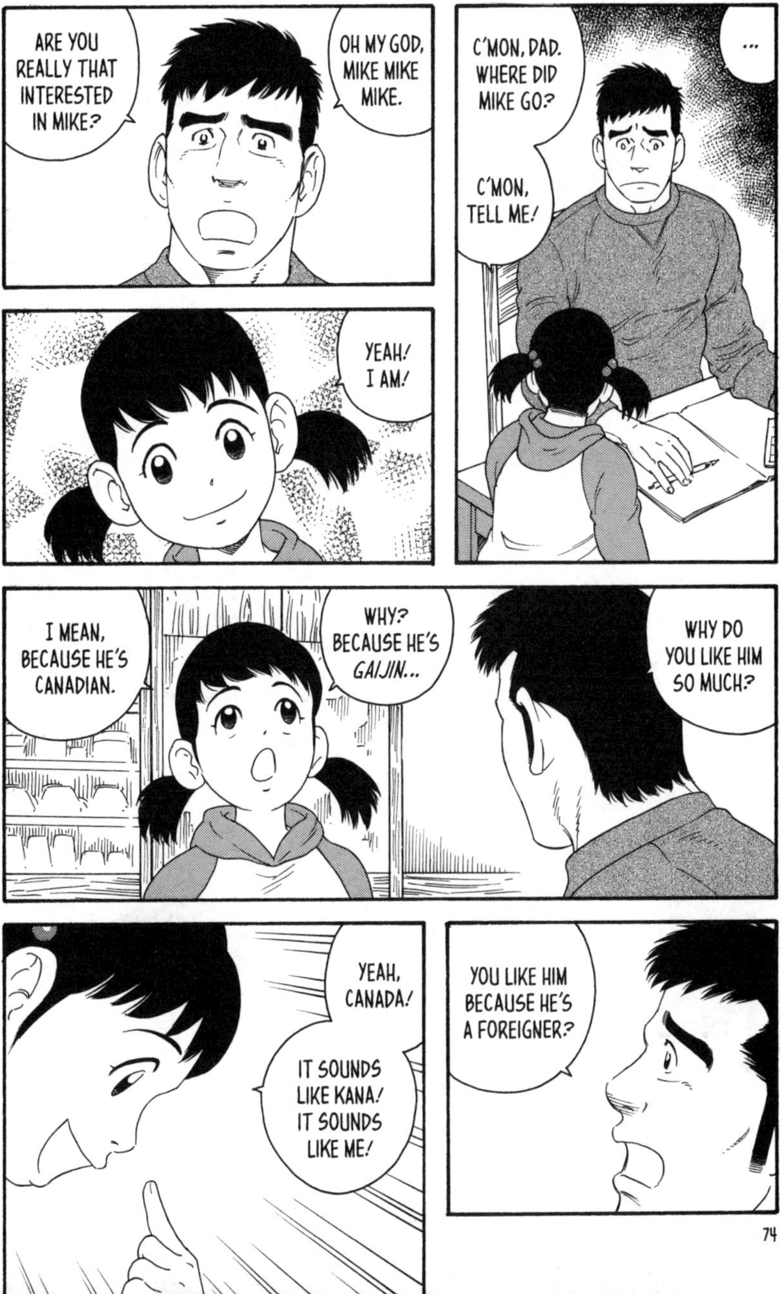
...
C'MON, DAD. WHERE DID MIKE GO?
C'MON, TELL ME!
OH MY GOD, MIKE MIKE MIKE.
ARE YOU REALLY THAT INTERESTED IN MIKE?
YEAH! I AM!
WHY DO YOU LIKE HIM SO MUCH?
WHY? BECAUSE HE'S *GAIJIN*...
I MEAN, BECAUSE HE'S CANADIAN.
YOU LIKE HIM BECAUSE HE'S A FOREIGNER?
YEAH, CANADA!
IT SOUNDS LIKE KANA! IT SOUNDS LIKE ME!

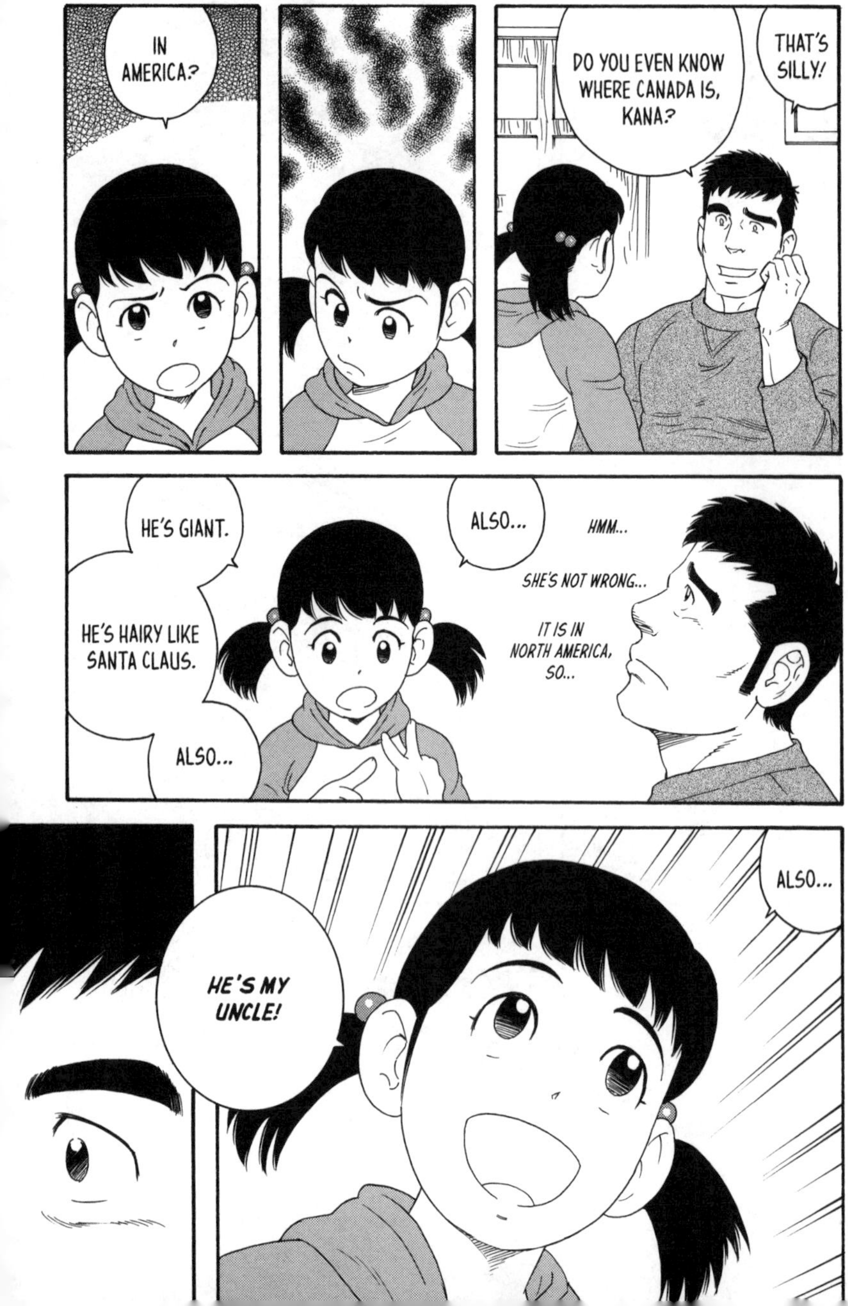
THAT'S SILLY!
DO YOU EVEN KNOW WHERE CANADA IS, KANA?
IN AMERICA?
ALSO...
HMM...
SHE'S NOT WRONG...
IT IS IN NORTH AMERICA, SO...
HE'S GIANT.
HE'S HAIRY LIKE SANTA CLAUS.
ALSO...
ALSO...
HE'S MY UNCLE!

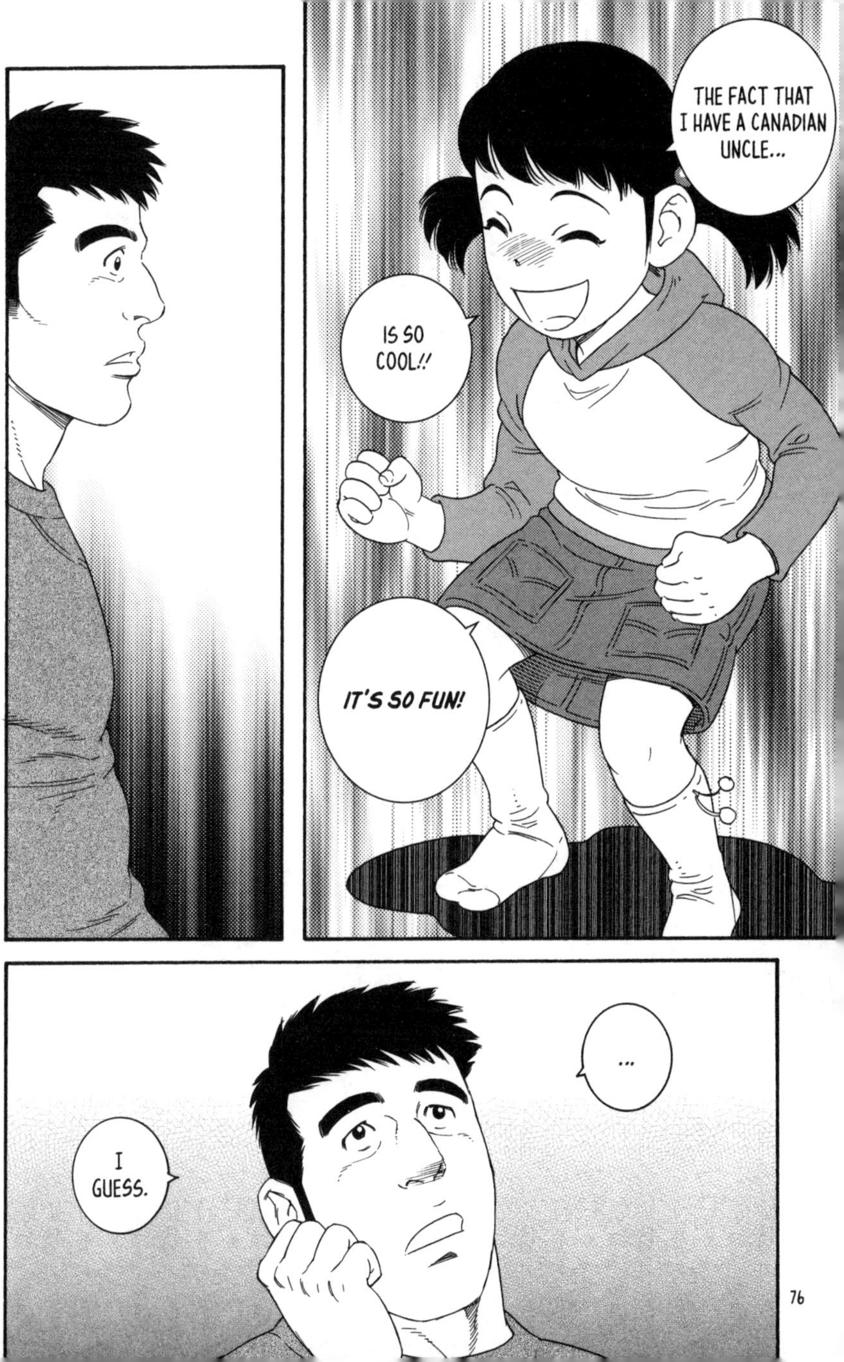
THE FACT THAT I HAVE A CANADIAN UNCLE...
IS SO COOL!!
IT'S SO FUN!
...
I GUESS.

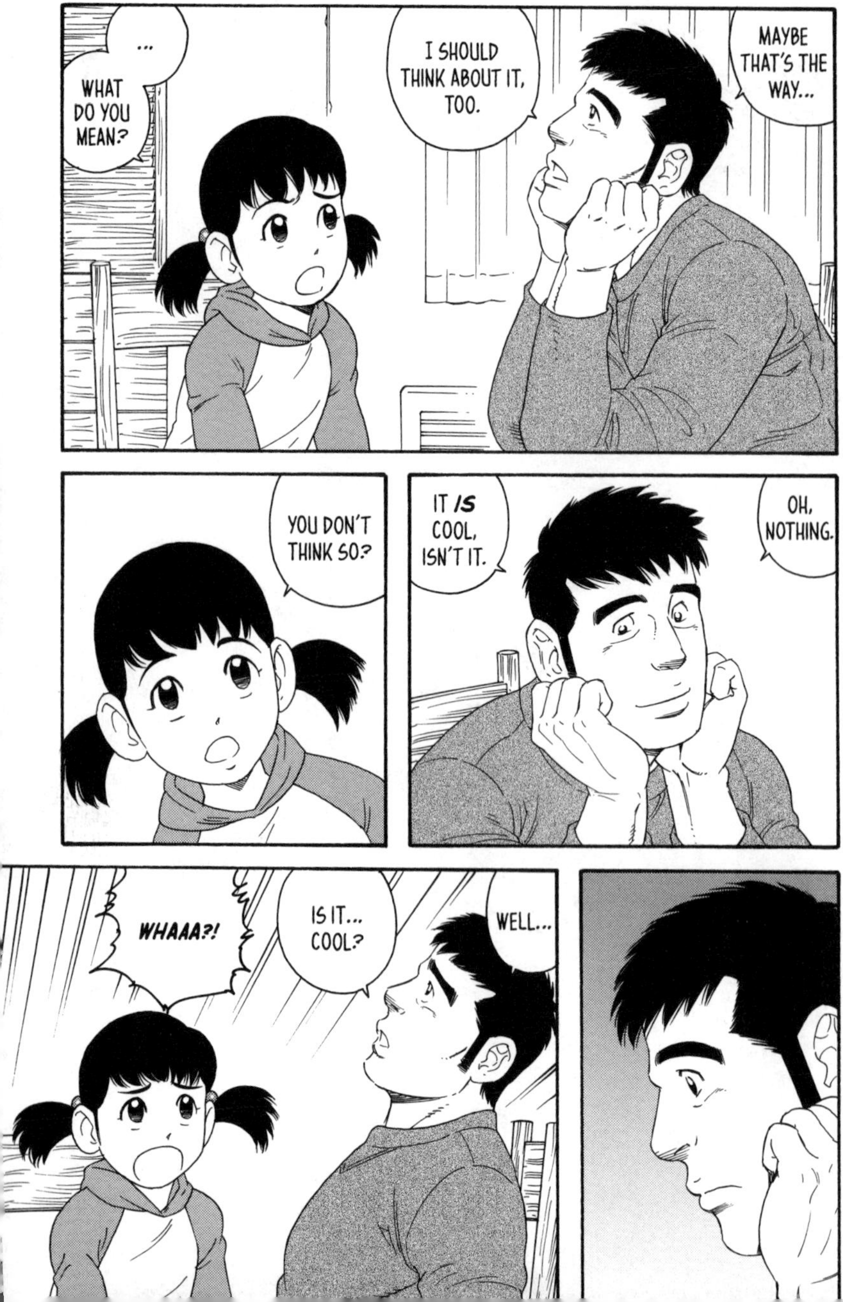
MAYBE THAT'S THE WAY...
I SHOULD THINK ABOUT IT, TOO.
...
WHAT DO YOU MEAN?
OH, NOTHING.
IT *IS* COOL, ISN'T IT.
YOU DON'T THINK SO?
WELL...
IS IT... COOL?
WHAAA?!

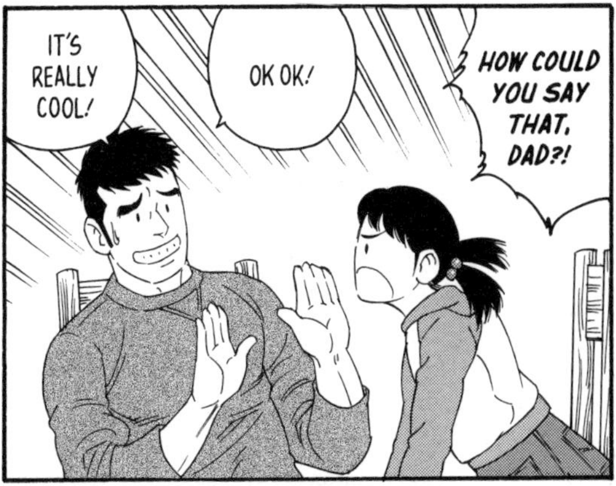
HOW COULD YOU SAY THAT, DAD?!
OK OK!
IT'S REALLY COOL!
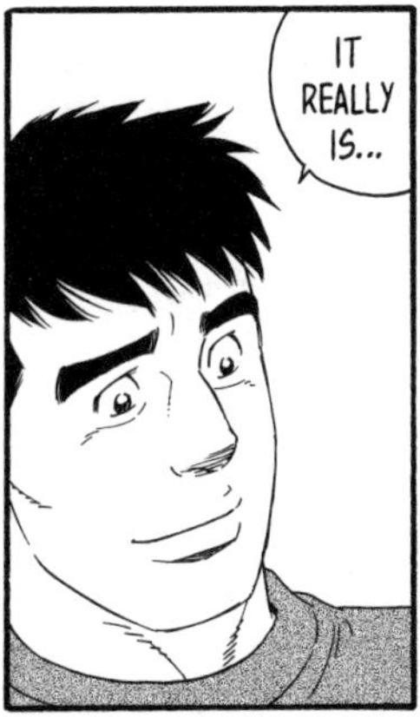
IT REALLY IS...
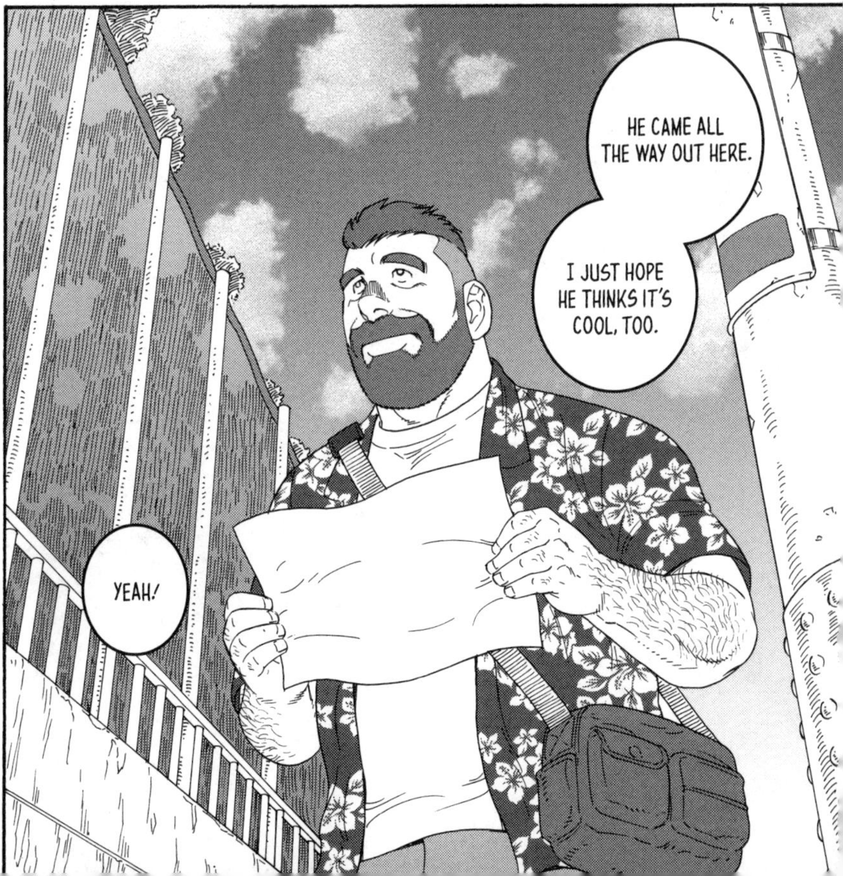
HE CAME ALL THE WAY OUT HERE.
I JUST HOPE HE THINKS IT'S COOL, TOO.
YEAH!

CHAPTER FOUR

MACARONI AND CHEESE

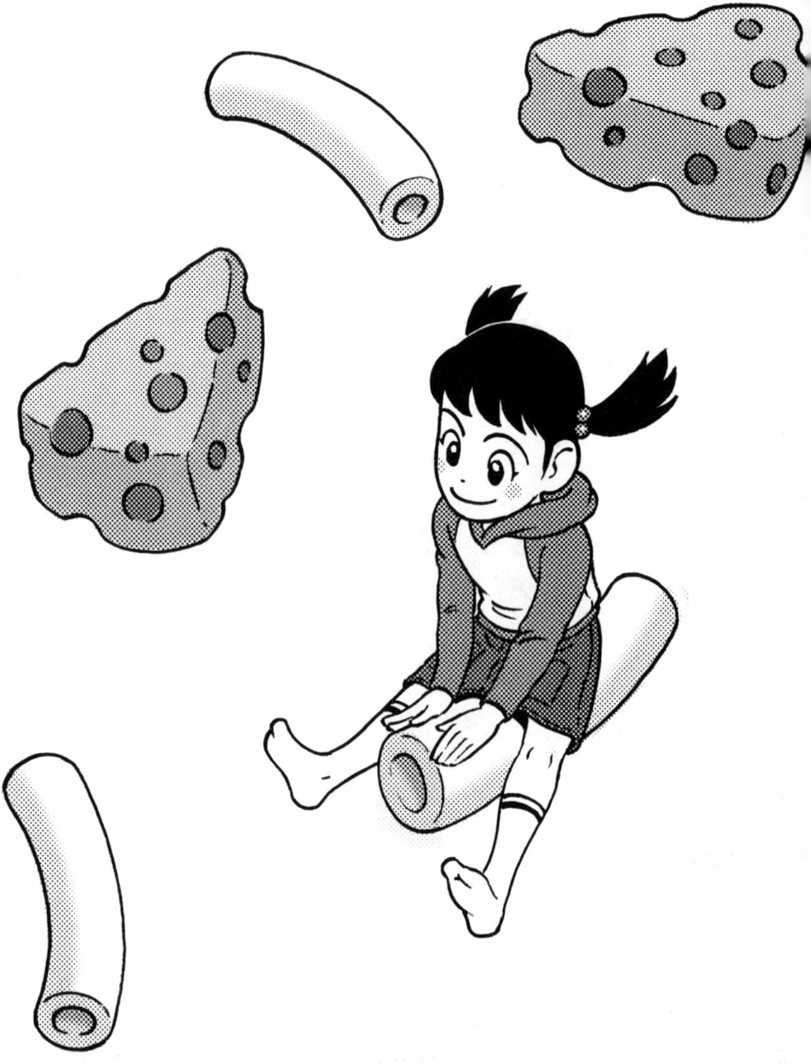

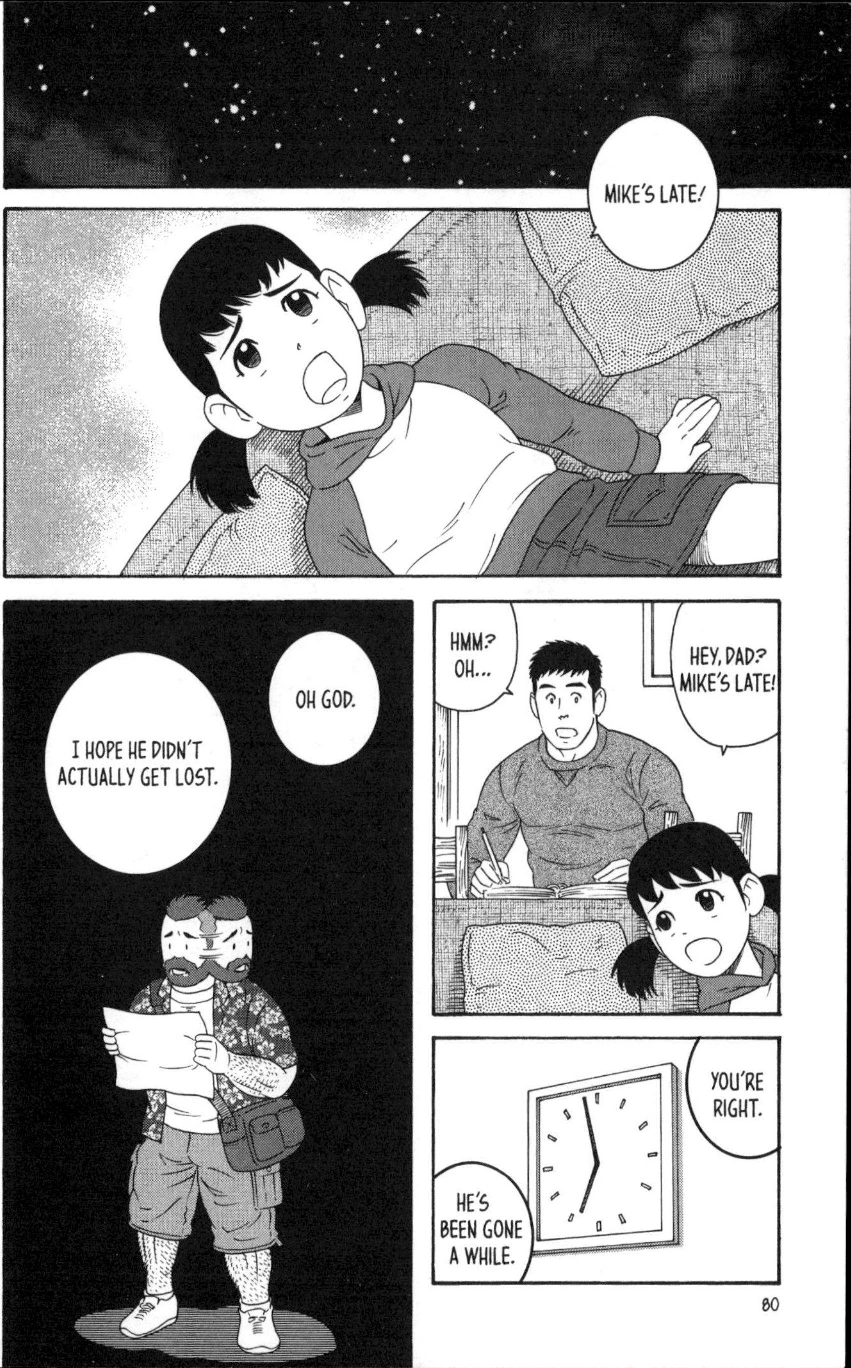
MIKE'S LATE!
HEY, DAD? MIKE'S LATE!
HMM? OH...
YOU'RE RIGHT.
HE'S BEEN GONE A WHILE.
OH GOD.
I HOPE HE DIDN'T ACTUALLY GET LOST.

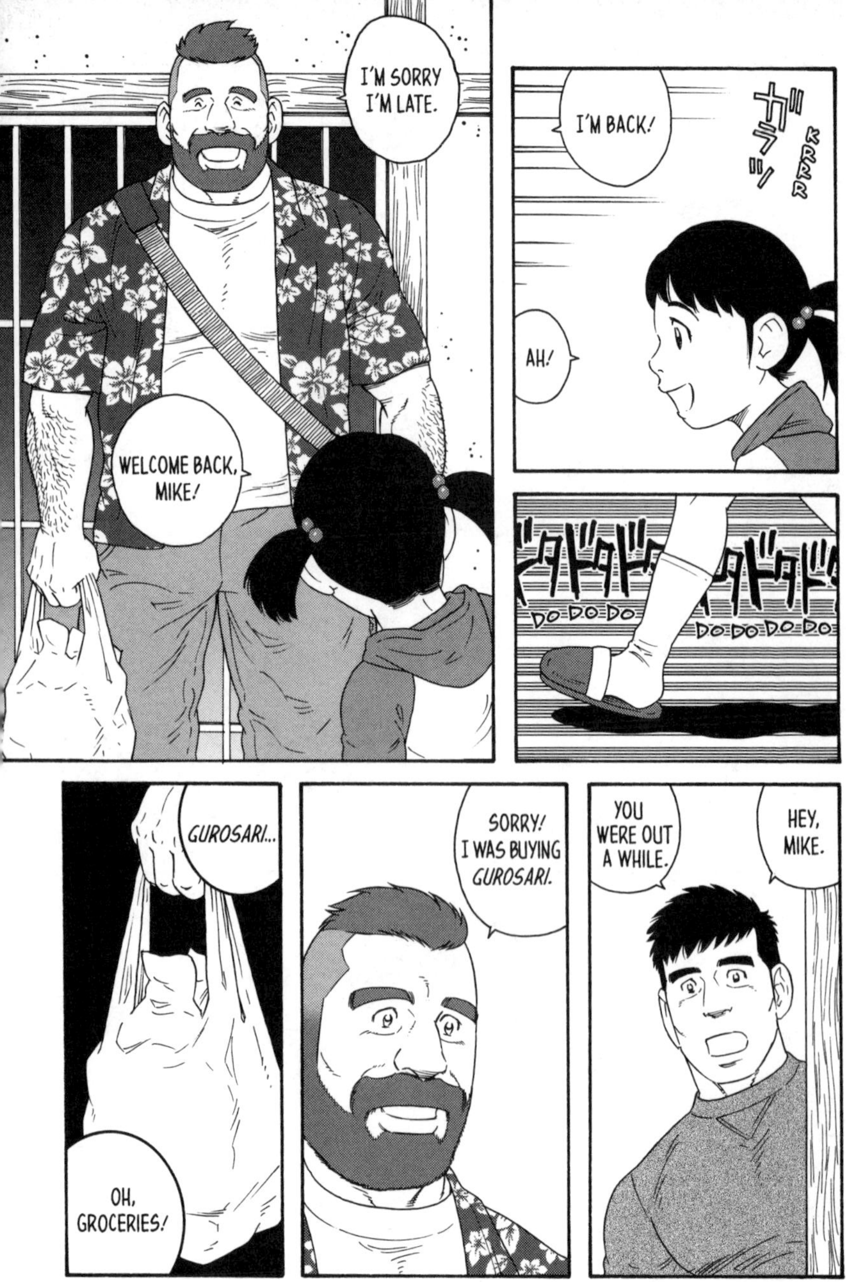
ガラッ
KRRR
I'M BACK!
AH!
DO DO DO
DO DO DO DO
I'M SORRY I'M LATE.
WELCOME BACK, MIKE!
HEY, MIKE.
YOU WERE OUT A WHILE.
SORRY! I WAS BUYING *GUROSARI*.
GUROSARI...
OH, GROCERIES!

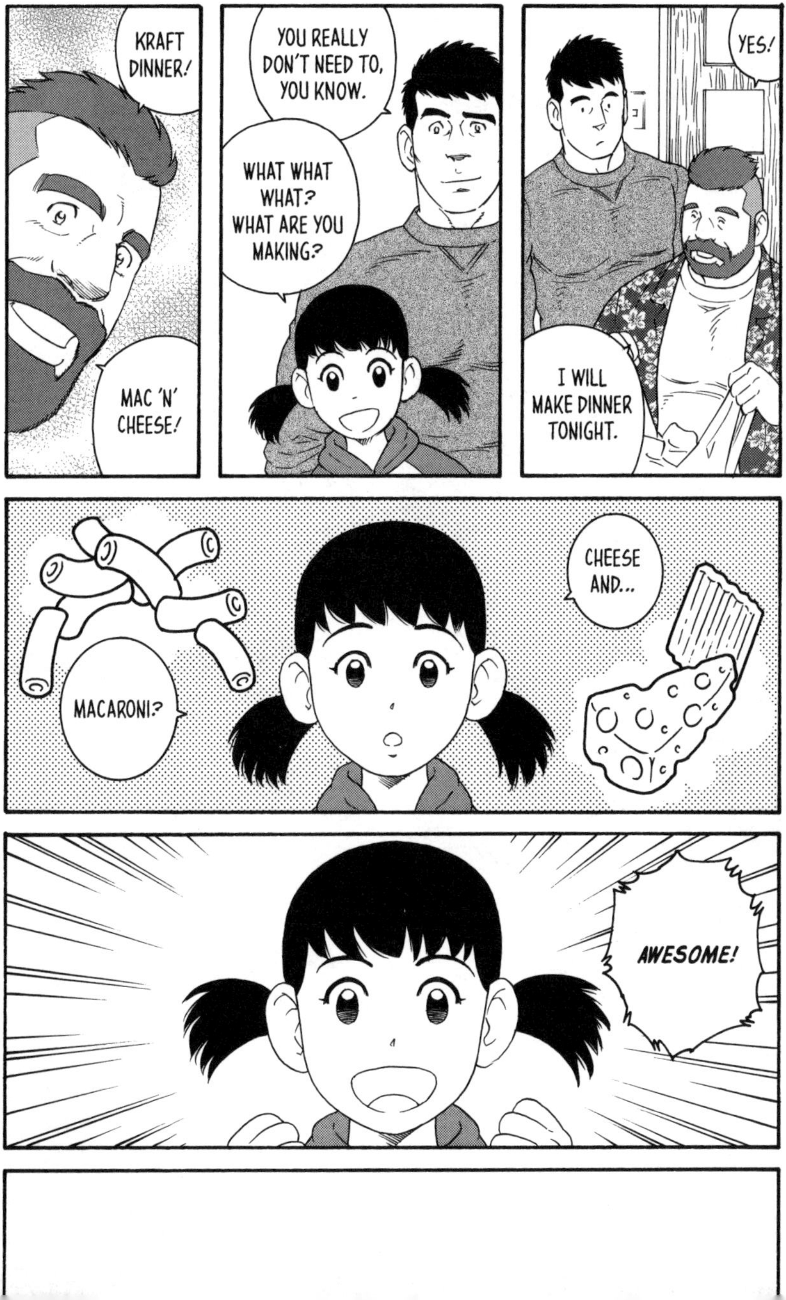
YES!
I WILL MAKE DINNER TONIGHT.
YOU REALLY DON'T NEED TO, YOU KNOW.
WHAT WHAT WHAT? WHAT ARE YOU MAKING?
KRAFT DINNER!
MAC 'N' CHEESE!
CHEESE AND...
MACARONI?
AWESOME!

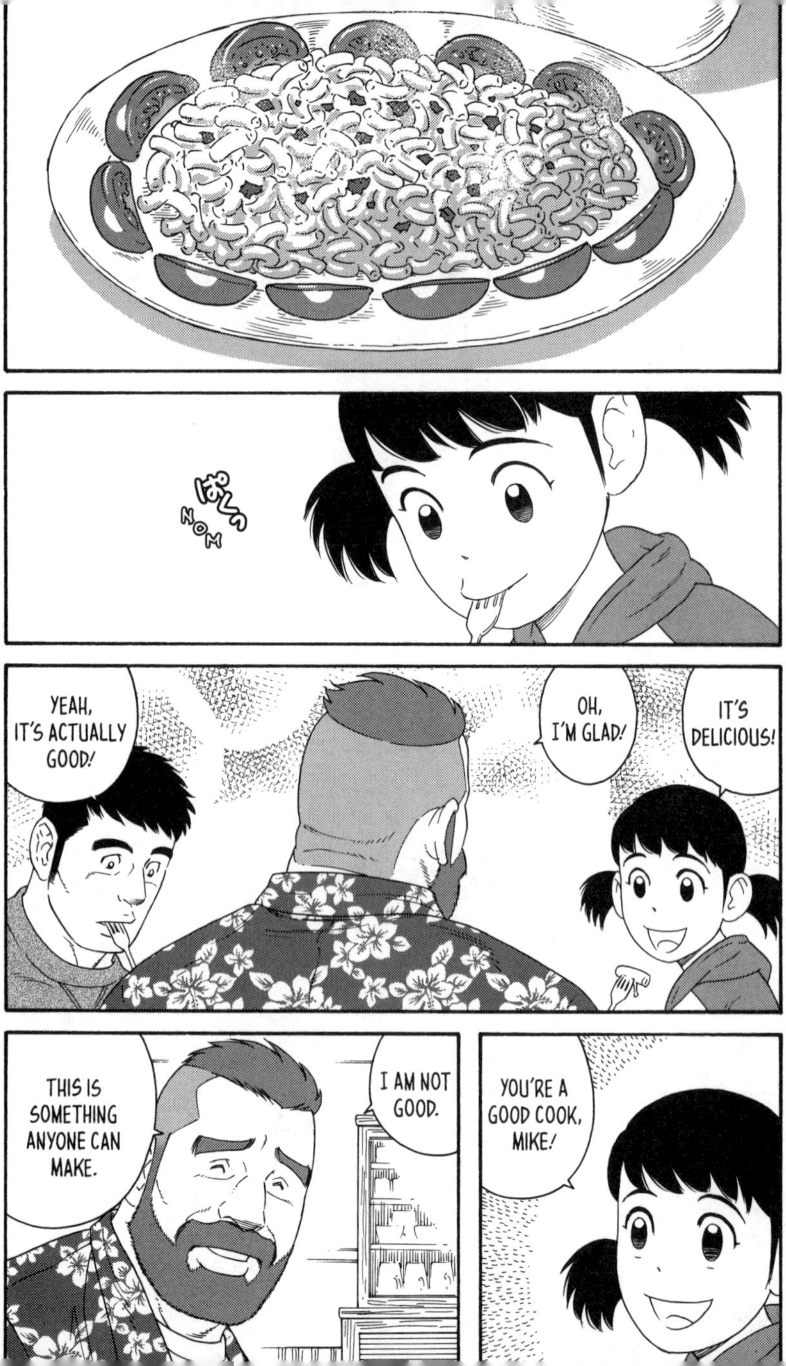
ぱくっ
NOM
IT'S DELICIOUS!
OH, I'M GLAD!
YEAH, IT'S ACTUALLY GOOD!
YOU'RE A GOOD COOK, MIKE!
I AM NOT GOOD.
THIS IS SOMETHING ANYONE CAN MAKE.

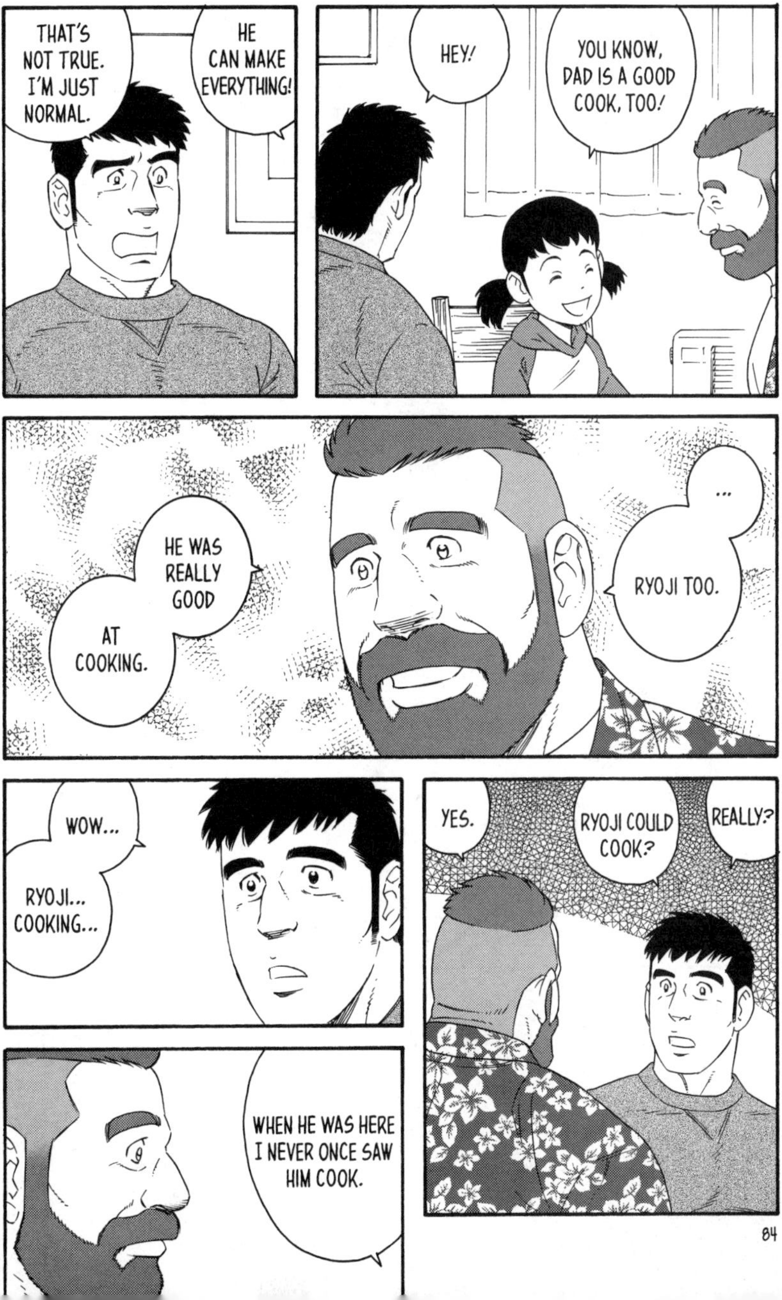
YOU KNOW, DAD IS A GOOD COOK, TOO!
HEY!
HE CAN MAKE EVERYTHING!
THAT'S NOT TRUE. I'M JUST NORMAL.
...
RYOJI TOO.
HE WAS REALLY GOOD
AT COOKING.
REALLY?
RYOJI COULD COOK?
YES.
WOW...
RYOJI... COOKING...
WHEN HE WAS HERE I NEVER ONCE SAW HIM COOK.

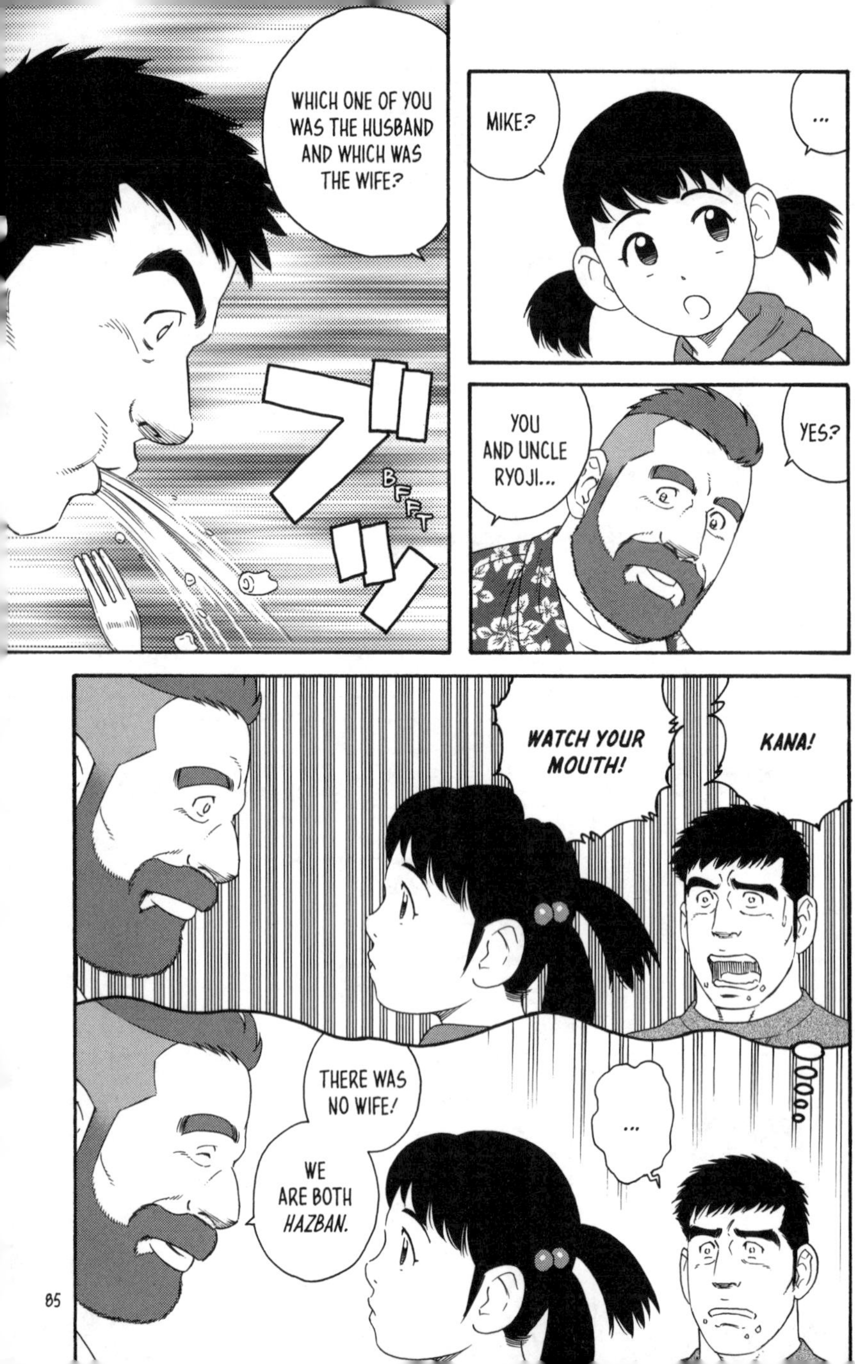
...
MIKE?
YES?
YOU AND UNCLE RYOJI...
WHICH ONE OF YOU WAS THE HUSBAND AND WHICH WAS THE WIFE?
BFFT
KANA!
WATCH YOUR MOUTH!
...
THERE WAS NO WIFE!
WE ARE BOTH *HAZBAN.*

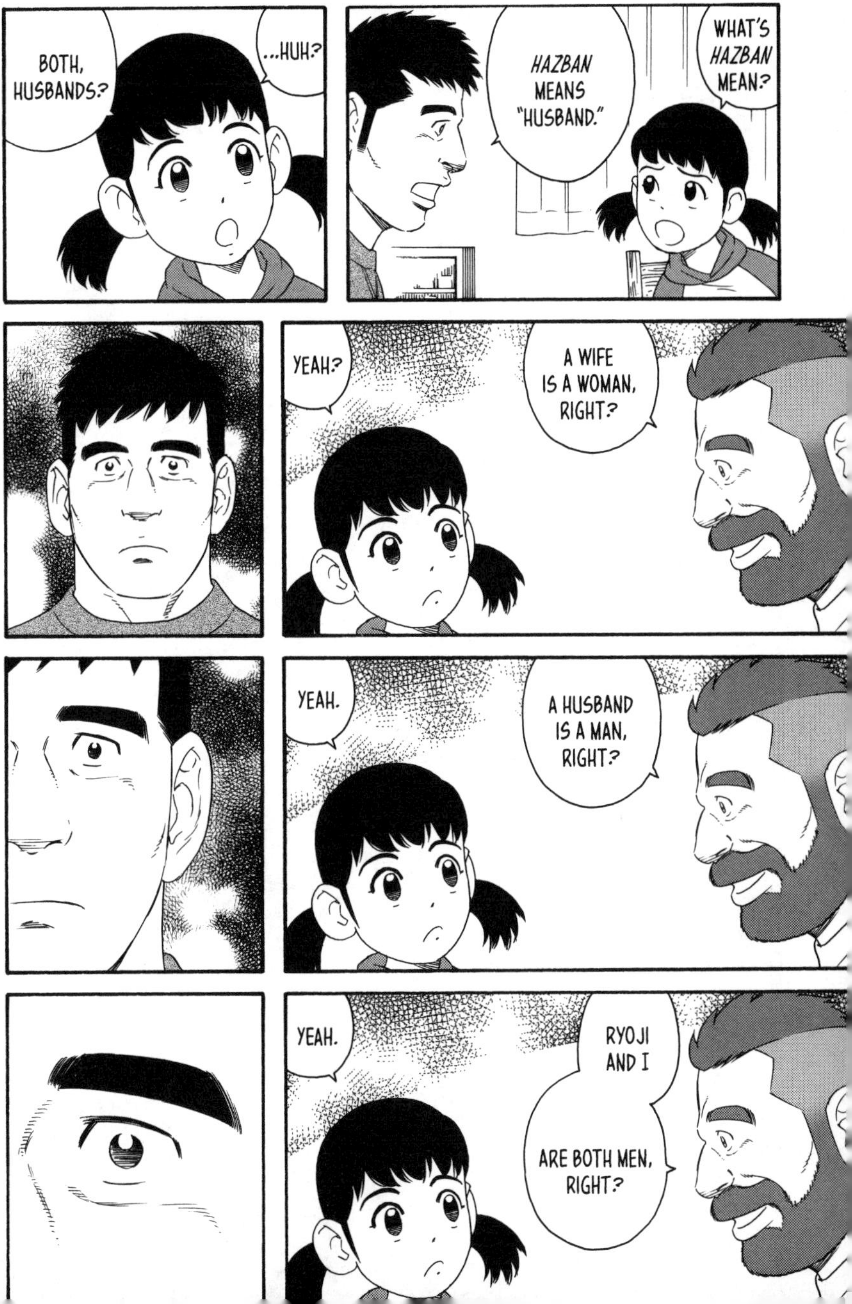
WHAT'S *HAZBAN* MEAN?
HAZBAN MEANS "HUSBAND."
...HUH?
BOTH, HUSBANDS?
A WIFE IS A WOMAN, RIGHT?
YEAH?
A HUSBAND IS A MAN, RIGHT?
YEAH.
RYOJI AND I
ARE BOTH MEN, RIGHT?
YEAH.

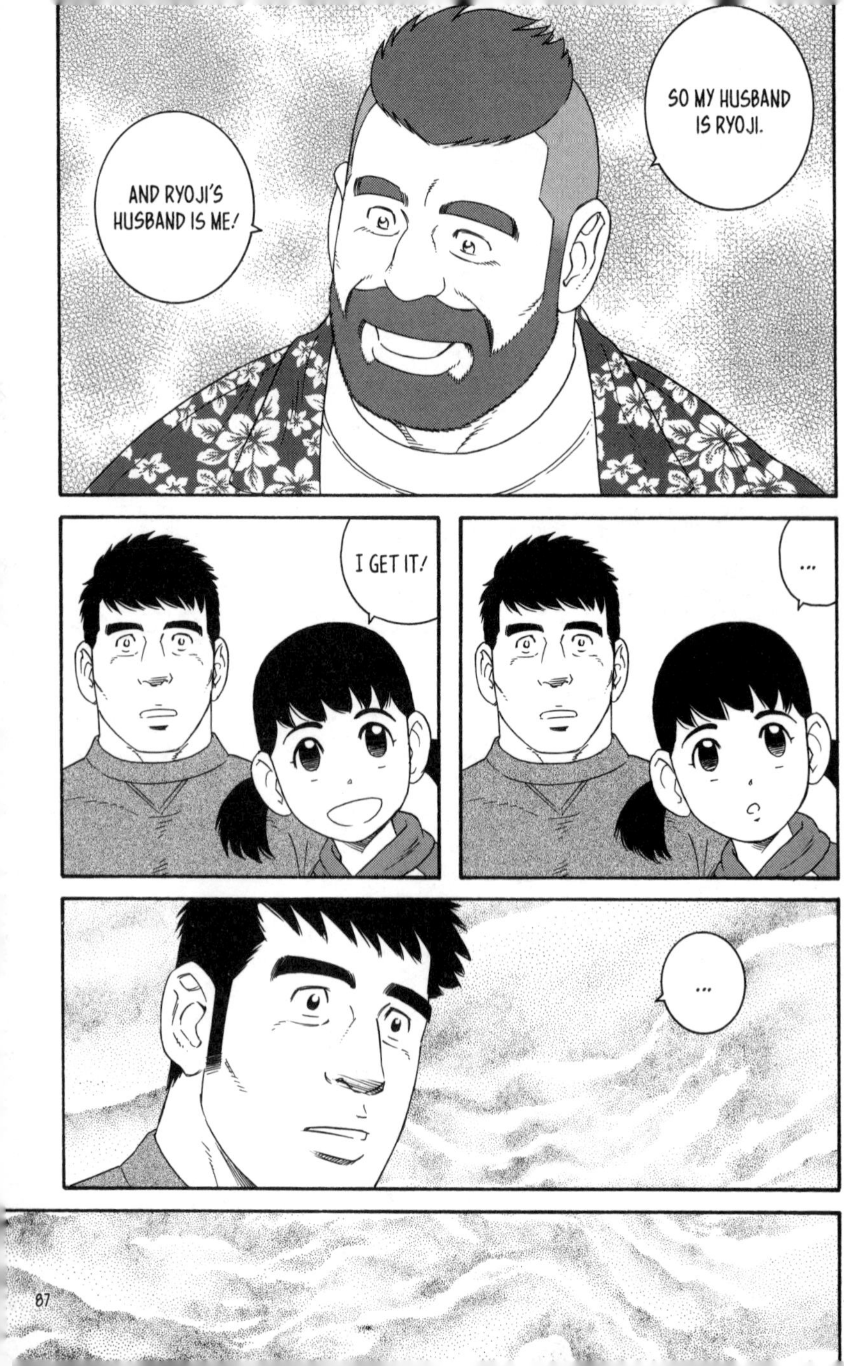
SO MY HUSBAND IS RYOJI.
AND RYOJI'S HUSBAND IS ME!
...
I GET IT!
...

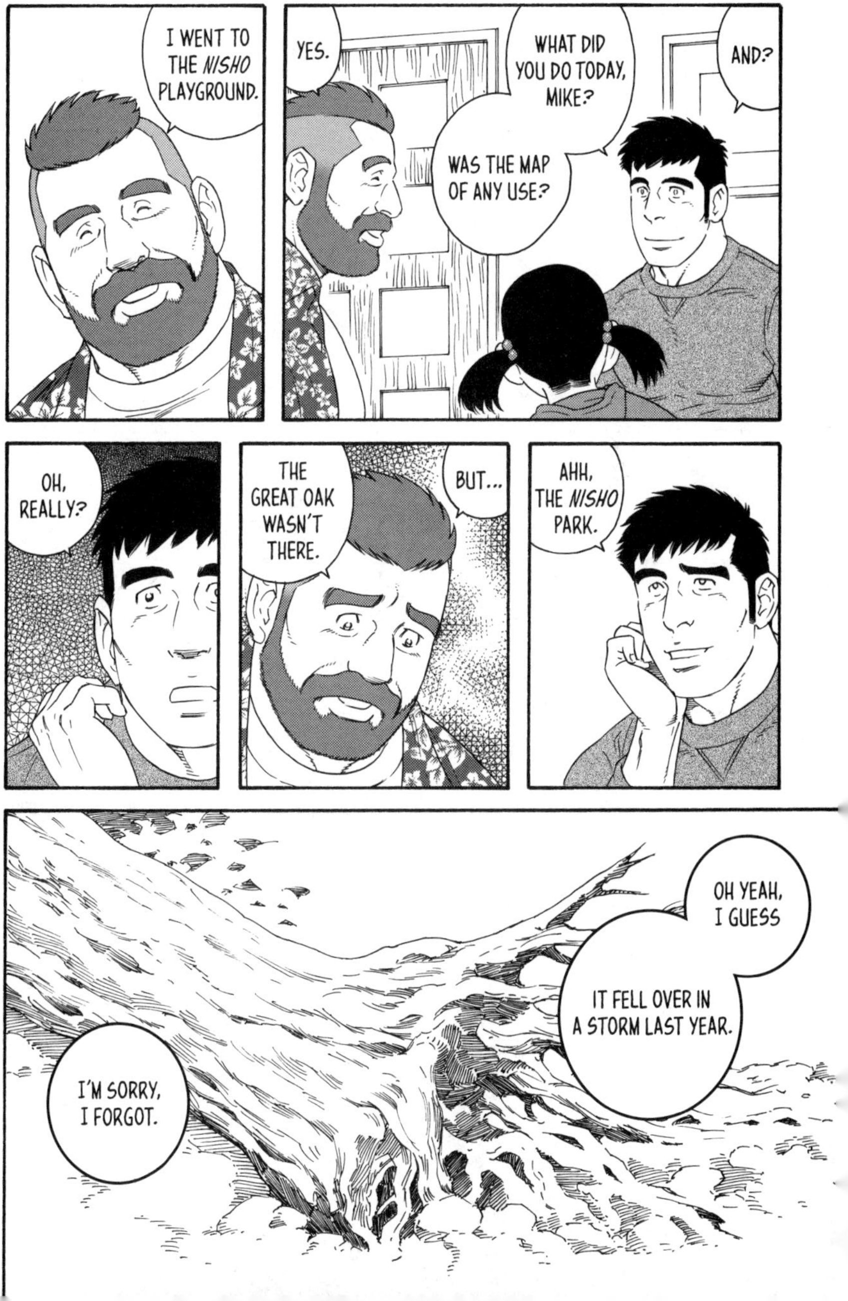
AND?
WHAT DID YOU DO TODAY, MIKE?
WAS THE MAP OF ANY USE?
YES.
I WENT TO THE *NISHO* PLAYGROUND.
AHH, THE *NISHO* PARK.
BUT...
THE GREAT OAK WASN'T THERE.
OH, REALLY?
OH YEAH, I GUESS
IT FELL OVER IN A STORM LAST YEAR.
I'M SORRY, I FORGOT.

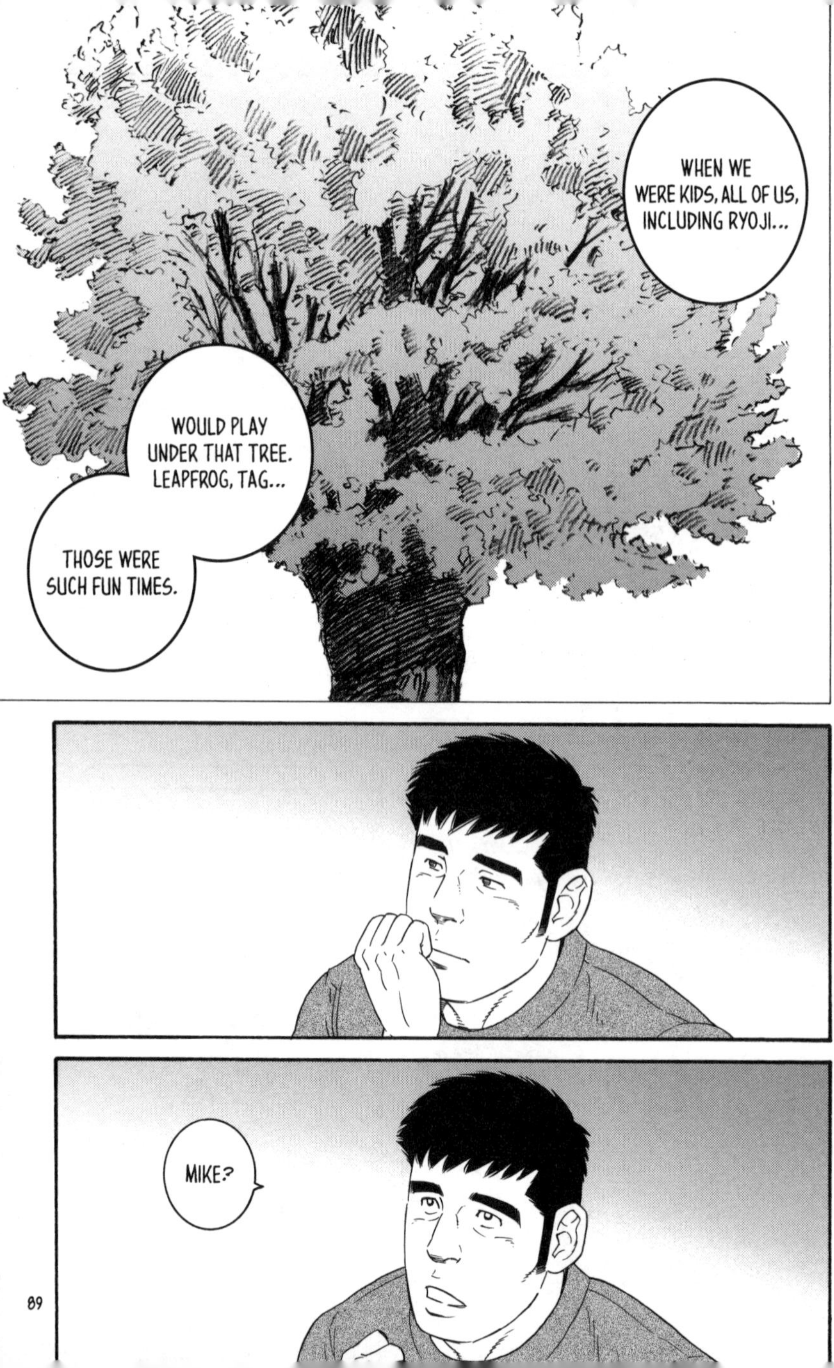
WHEN WE WERE KIDS, ALL OF US, INCLUDING RYOJI...
WOULD PLAY UNDER THAT TREE. LEAPFROG, TAG...
THOSE WERE SUCH FUN TIMES.
MIKE?

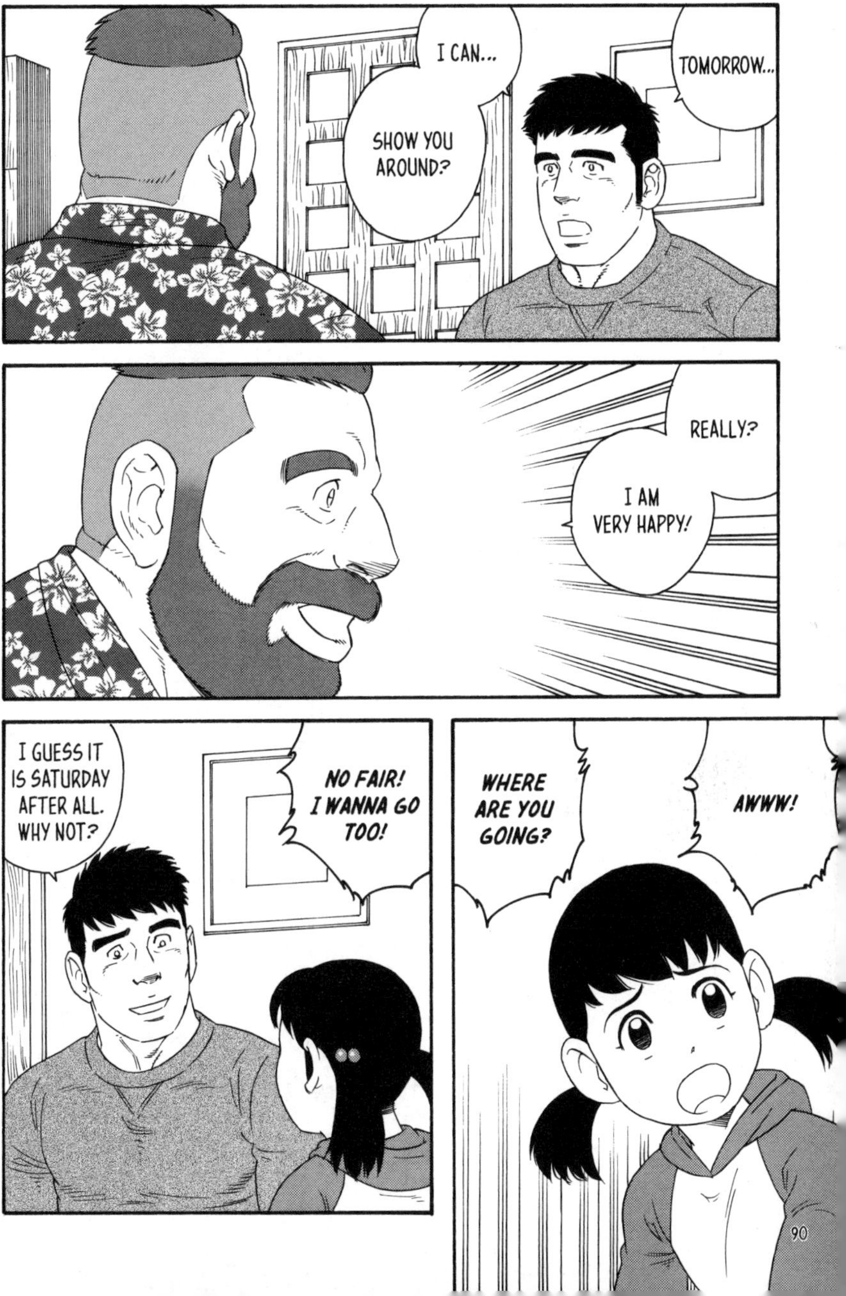
TOMORROW...
I CAN...
SHOW YOU AROUND?
REALLY?
I AM VERY HAPPY!
AWWW!
WHERE ARE YOU GOING?
NO FAIR! I WANNA GO TOO!
I GUESS IT IS SATURDAY AFTER ALL. WHY NOT?

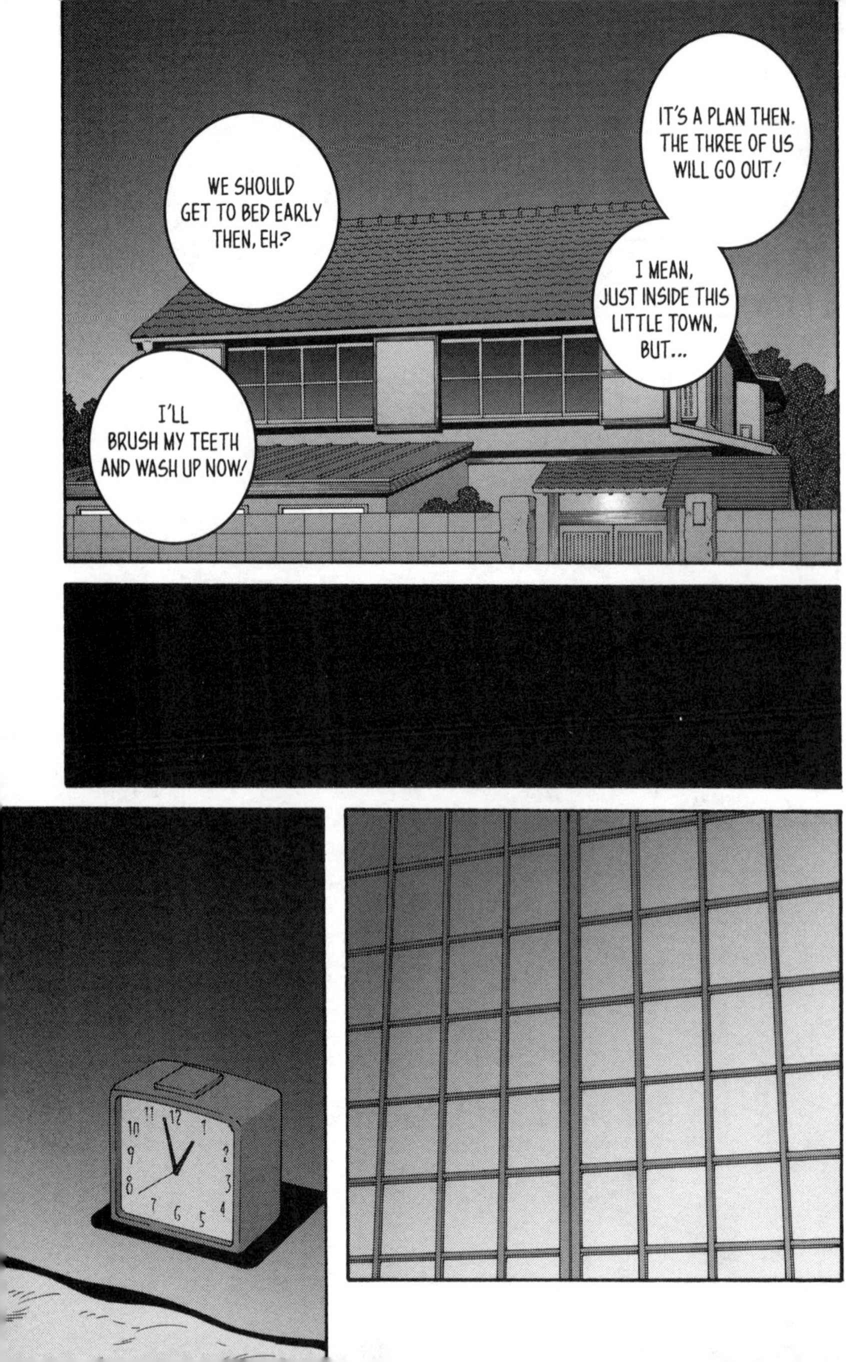
IT'S A PLAN THEN. THE THREE OF US WILL GO OUT!
WE SHOULD GET TO BED EARLY THEN, EH?
I MEAN, JUST INSIDE THIS LITTLE TOWN, BUT...
I'LL BRUSH MY TEETH AND WASH UP NOW!

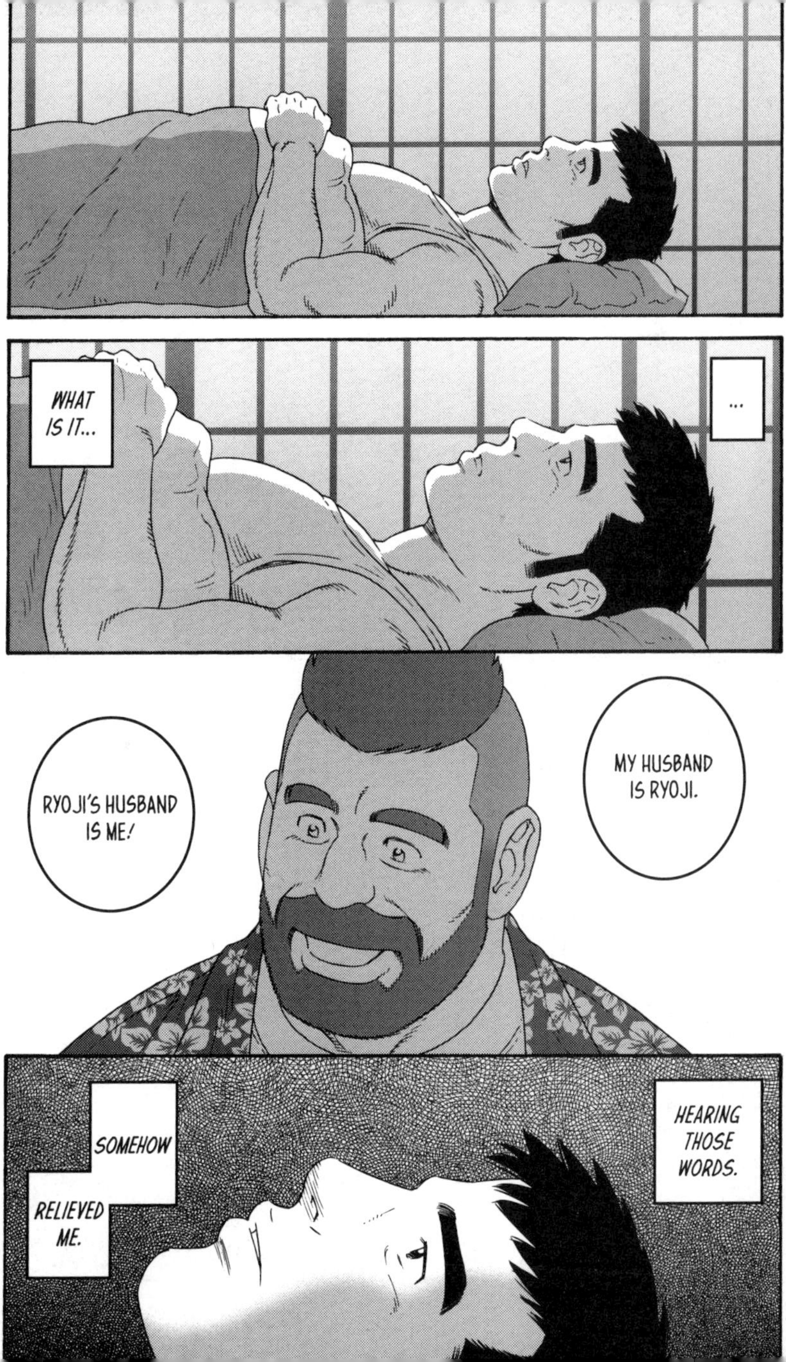
...
WHAT IS IT...
MY HUSBAND IS RYOJI.
RYOJI'S HUSBAND IS ME!
HEARING THOSE WORDS.
SOMEHOW
RELIEVED ME.

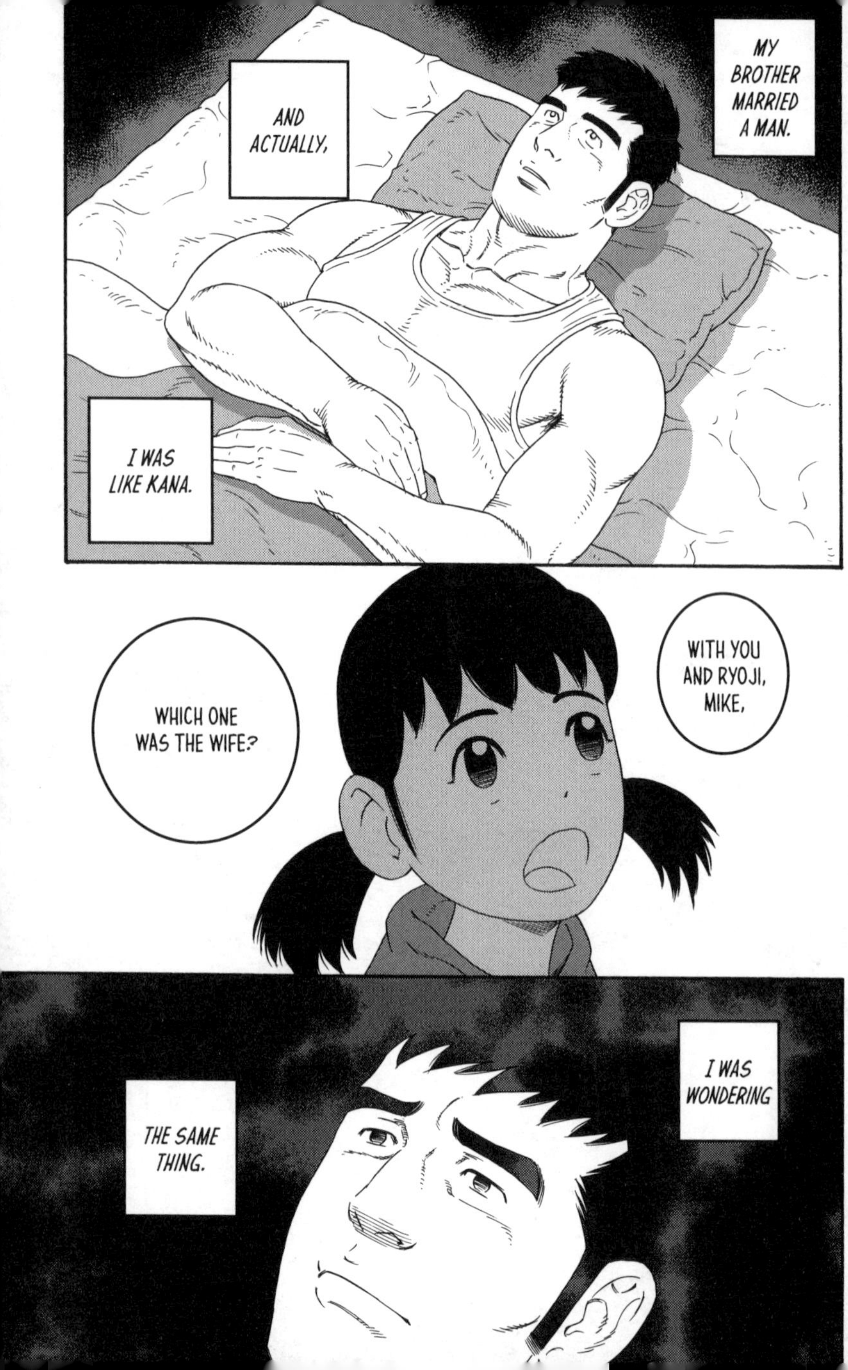
MY BROTHER MARRIED A MAN.
AND ACTUALLY,
I WAS LIKE KANA.
WITH YOU AND RYOJI, MIKE,
WHICH ONE WAS THE WIFE?
I WAS WONDERING
THE SAME THING.

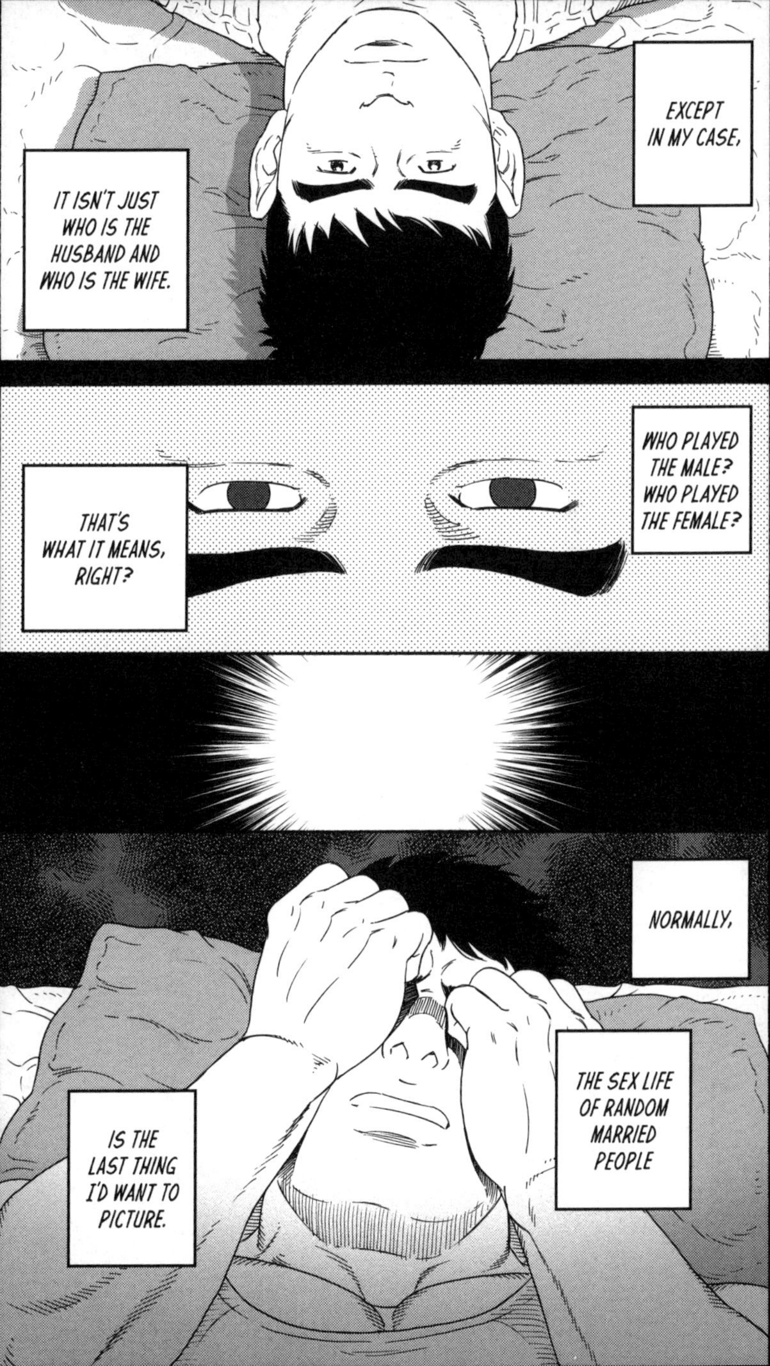
EXCEPT IN MY CASE,
IT ISN'T JUST WHO IS THE HUSBAND AND WHO IS THE WIFE.
WHO PLAYED THE MALE? WHO PLAYED THE FEMALE?
THAT'S WHAT IT MEANS, RIGHT?
NORMALLY,
THE SEX LIFE OF RANDOM MARRIED PEOPLE
IS THE LAST THING I'D WANT TO PICTURE.

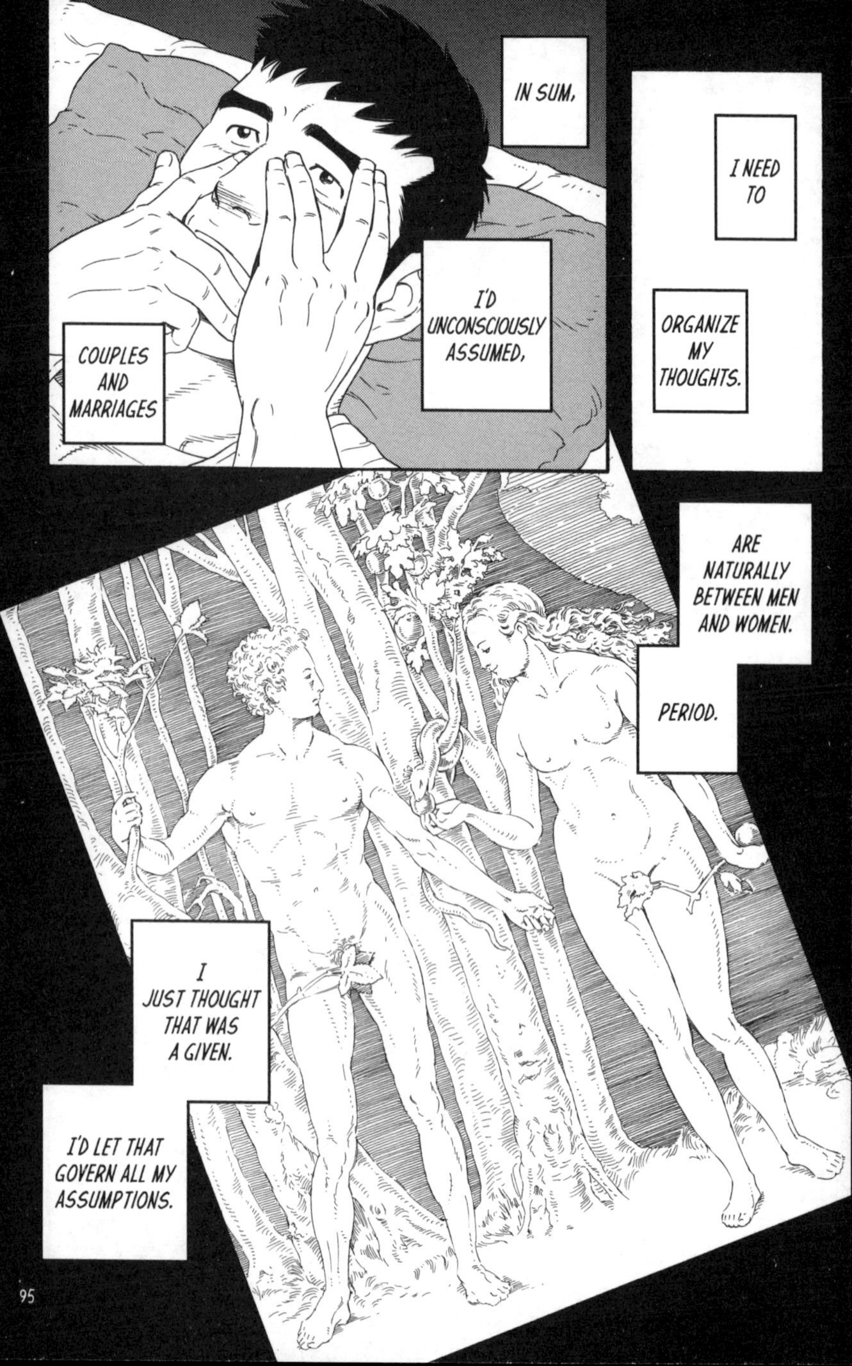
I NEED TO
ORGANIZE MY THOUGHTS.
IN SUM,
I'D UNCONSCIOUSLY ASSUMED,
COUPLES AND MARRIAGES
ARE NATURALLY BETWEEN MEN AND WOMEN.
PERIOD.
I JUST THOUGHT THAT WAS A GIVEN.
I'D LET THAT GOVERN ALL MY ASSUMPTIONS.

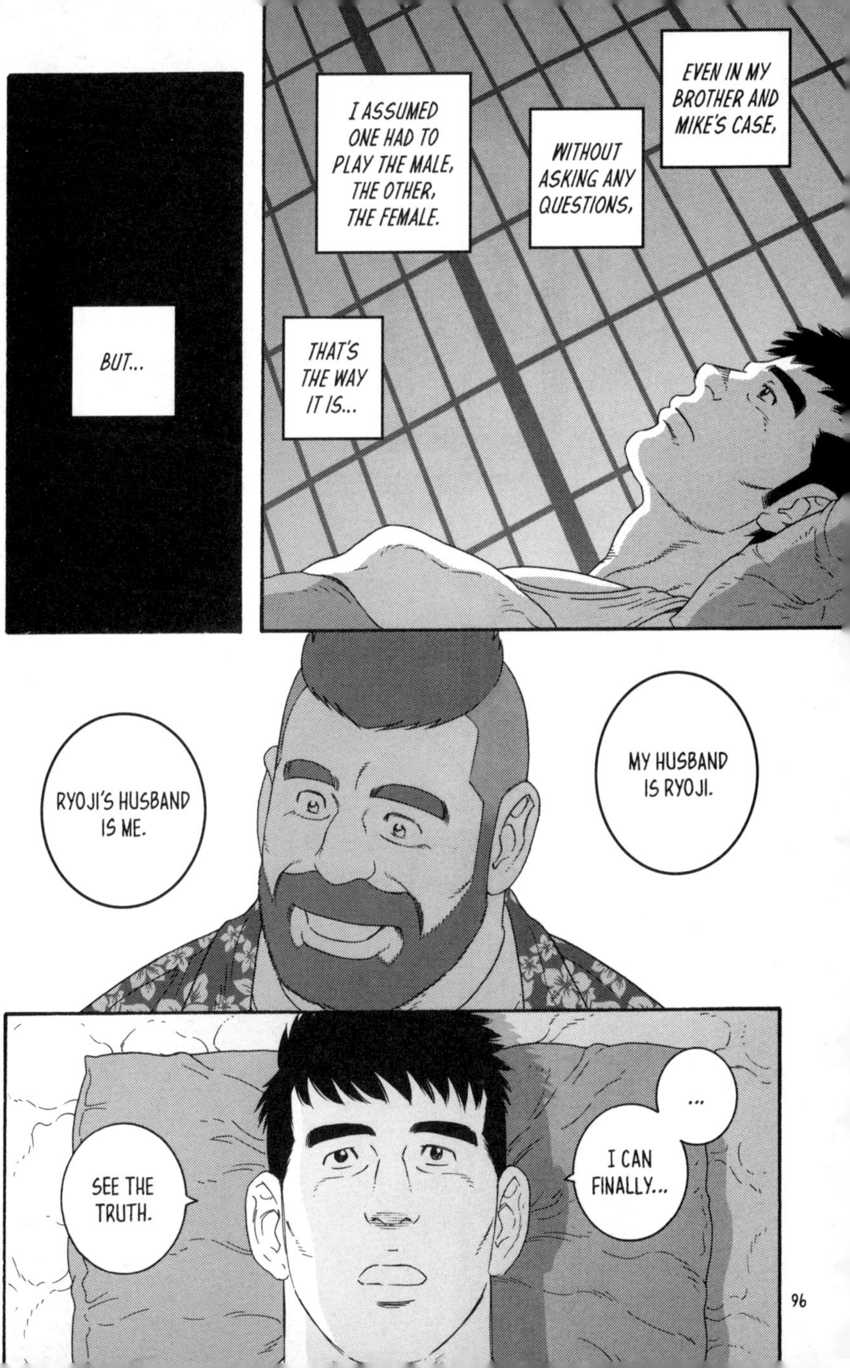
EVEN IN MY BROTHER AND MIKE'S CASE,
WITHOUT ASKING ANY QUESTIONS,
I ASSUMED ONE HAD TO PLAY THE MALE, THE OTHER, THE FEMALE.
THAT'S THE WAY IT IS...
BUT...
MY HUSBAND IS RYOJI.
RYOJI'S HUSBAND IS ME.
...
I CAN FINALLY...
SEE THE TRUTH.

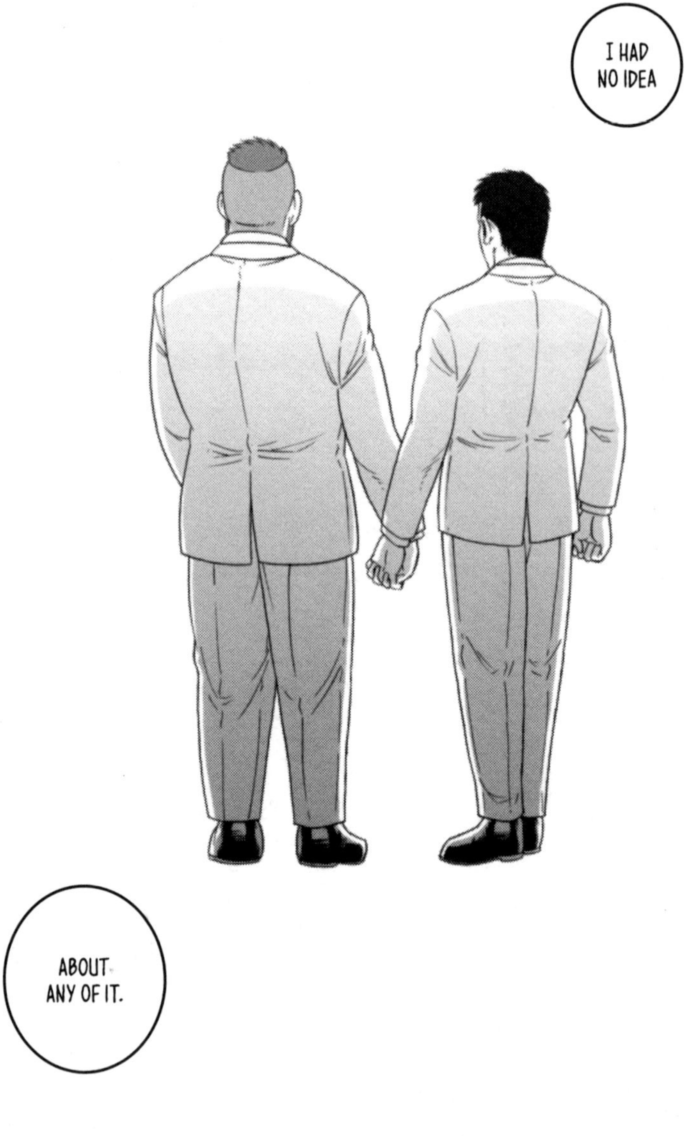
I HAD NO IDEA
ABOUT ANY OF IT.

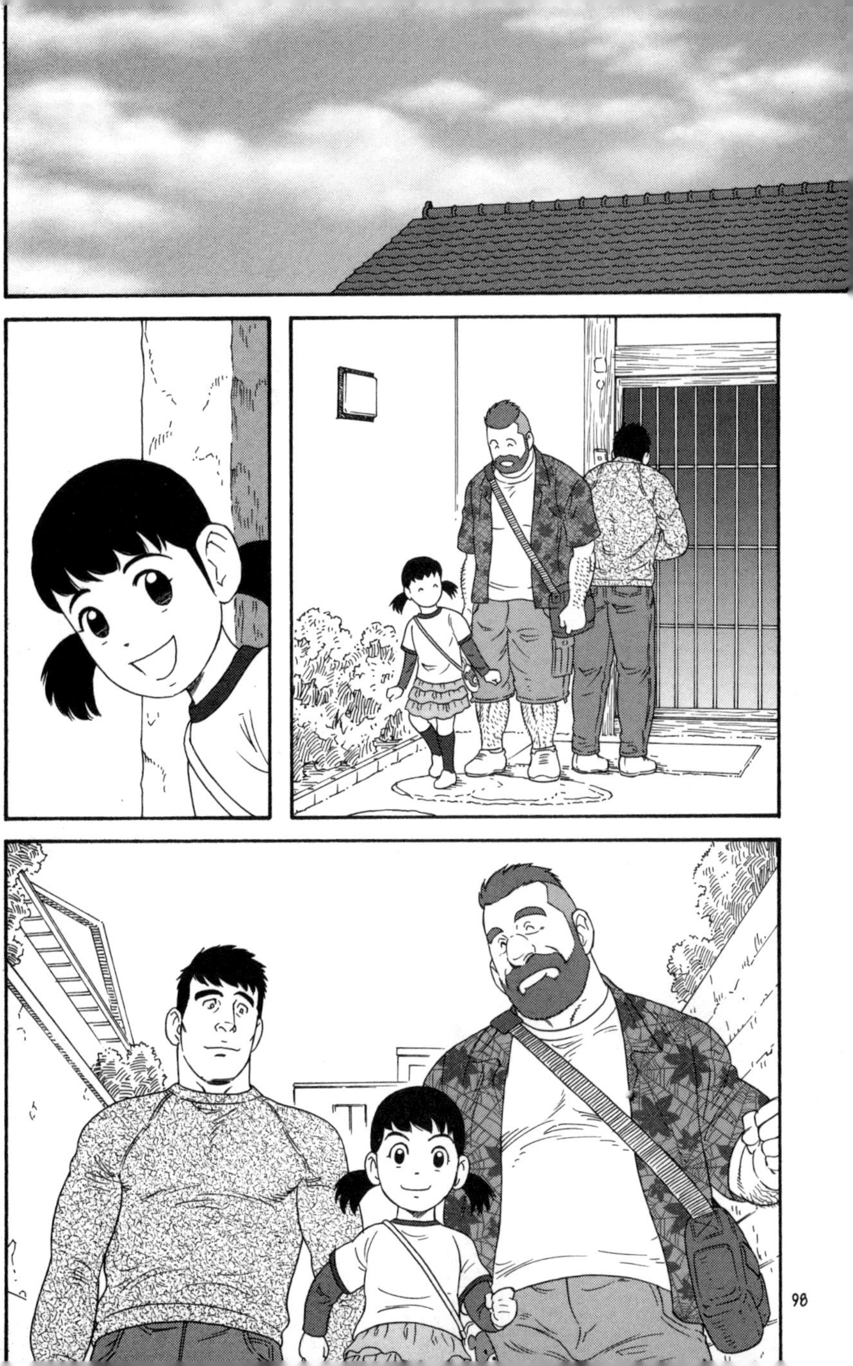

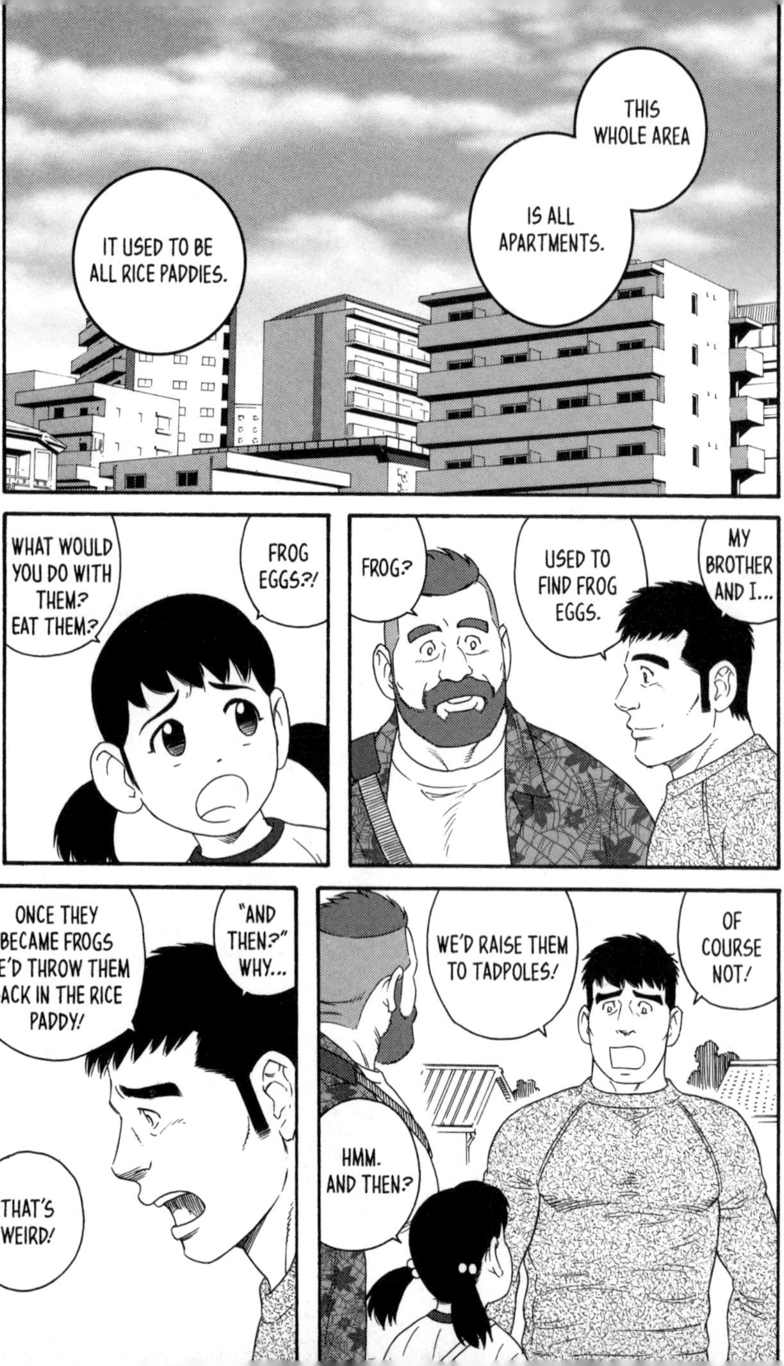
THIS WHOLE AREA
IS ALL APARTMENTS.
IT USED TO BE ALL RICE PADDIES.
MY BROTHER AND I...
USED TO FIND FROG EGGS.
FROG?
FROG EGGS?!
WHAT WOULD YOU DO WITH THEM? EAT THEM?
OF COURSE NOT!
WE'D RAISE THEM TO TADPOLES!
HMM. AND THEN?
"AND THEN?" WHY...
ONCE THEY BECAME FROGS WE'D THROW THEM BACK IN THE RICE PADDY!
THAT'S WEIRD!

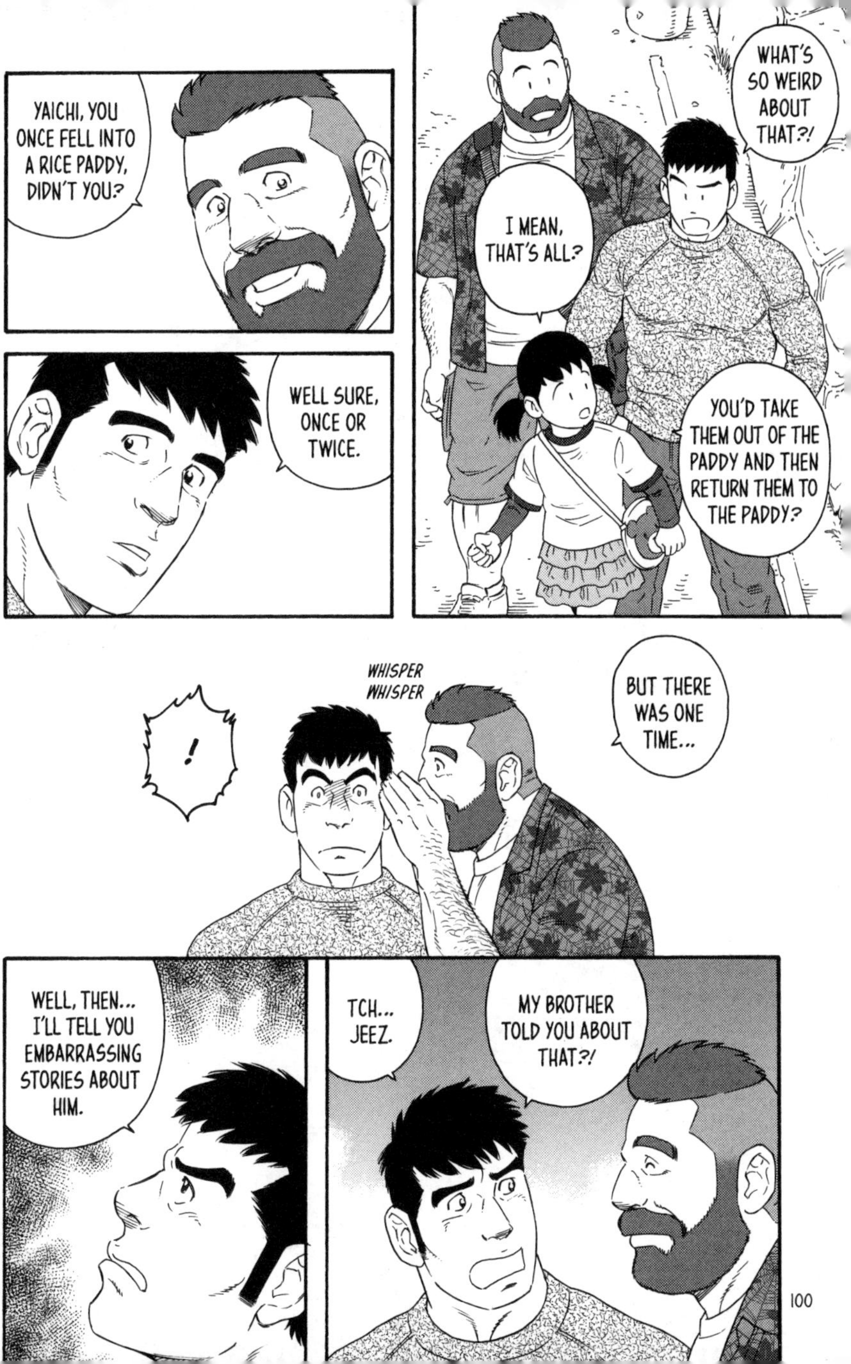
WHAT'S SO WEIRD ABOUT THAT?!
I MEAN, THAT'S ALL?
YOU'D TAKE THEM OUT OF THE PADDY AND THEN RETURN THEM TO THE PADDY?
YAICHI, YOU ONCE FELL INTO A RICE PADDY, DIDN'T YOU?
WELL SURE, ONCE OR TWICE.
BUT THERE WAS ONE TIME...
WHISPER WHISPER
!
MY BROTHER TOLD YOU ABOUT THAT?!
TCH... JEEZ.
WELL, THEN... I'LL TELL YOU EMBARRASSING STORIES ABOUT HIM.

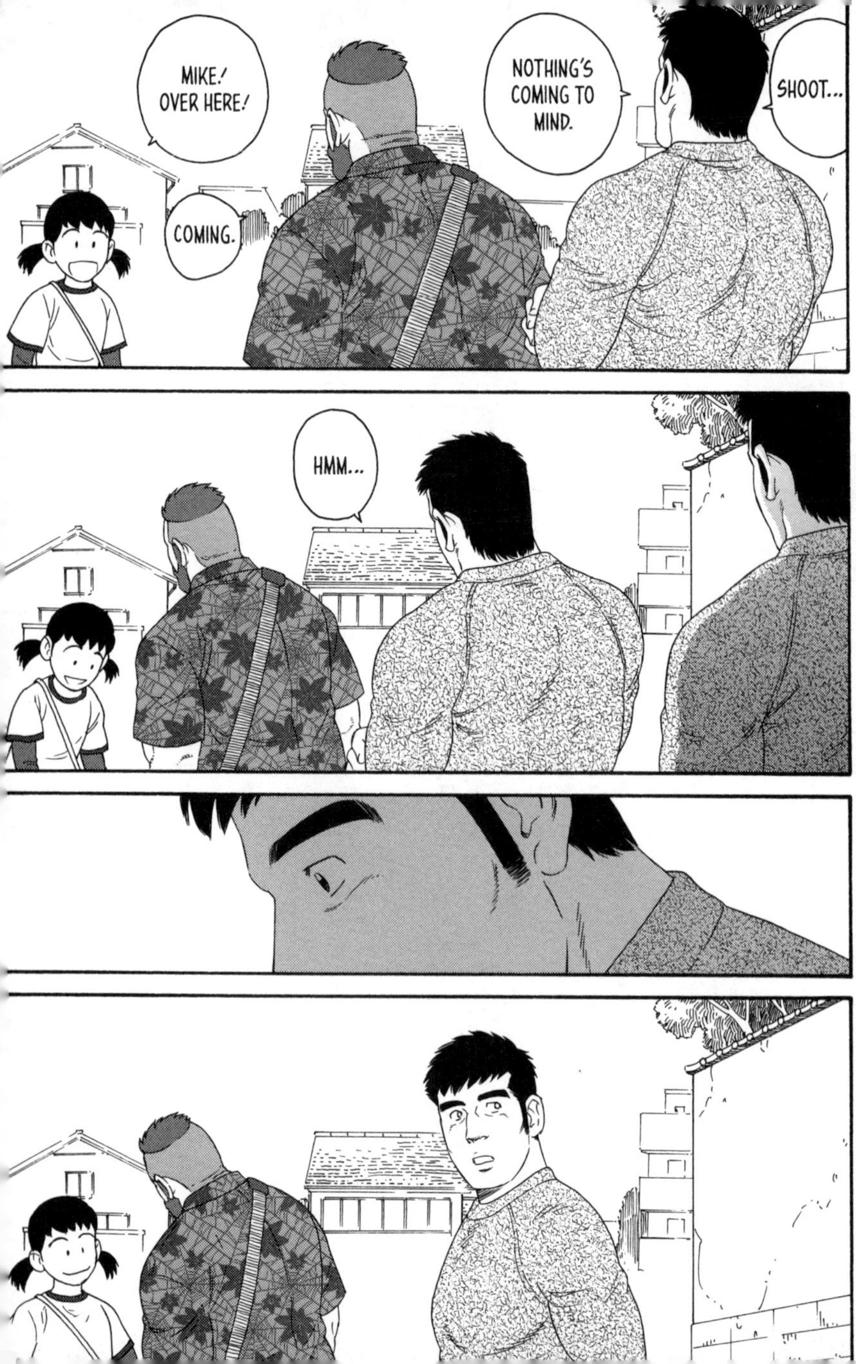
SHOOT...
NOTHING'S COMING TO MIND.
MIKE! OVER HERE!
COMING.
HMM...

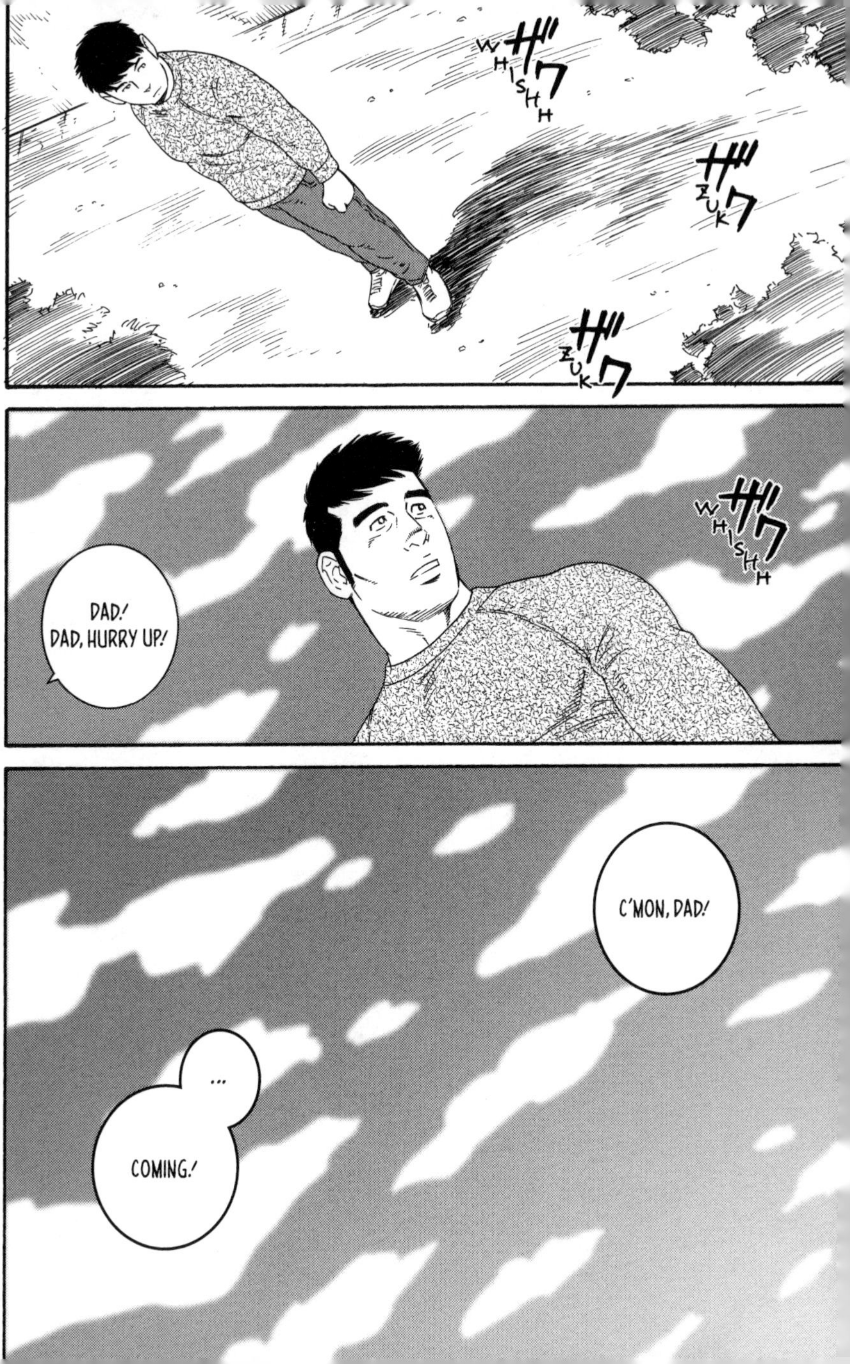
ザク WHISHH
ザク ZUKK
ザク ZUKK
ザク WHISHH
DAD! DAD, HURRY UP!
C'MON, DAD!
...
COMING!

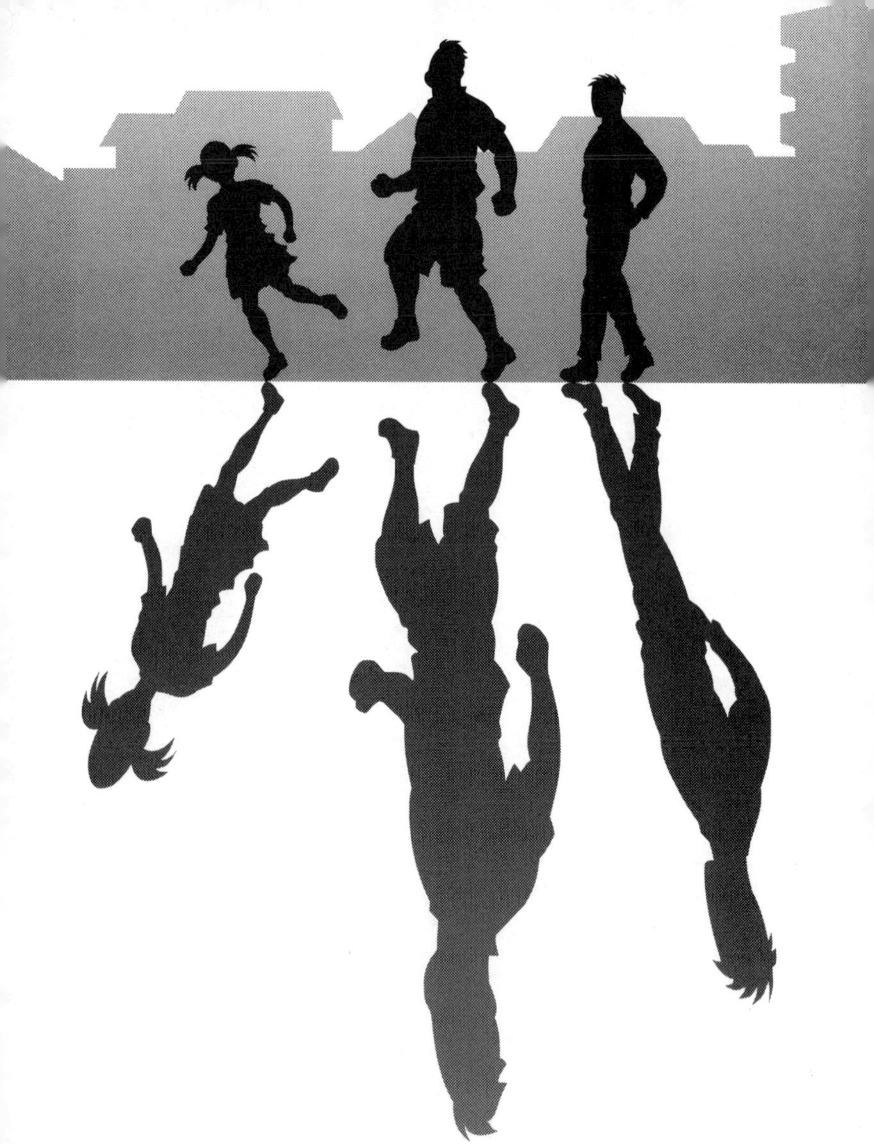

CHAPTER FIVE

SILHOUETTE

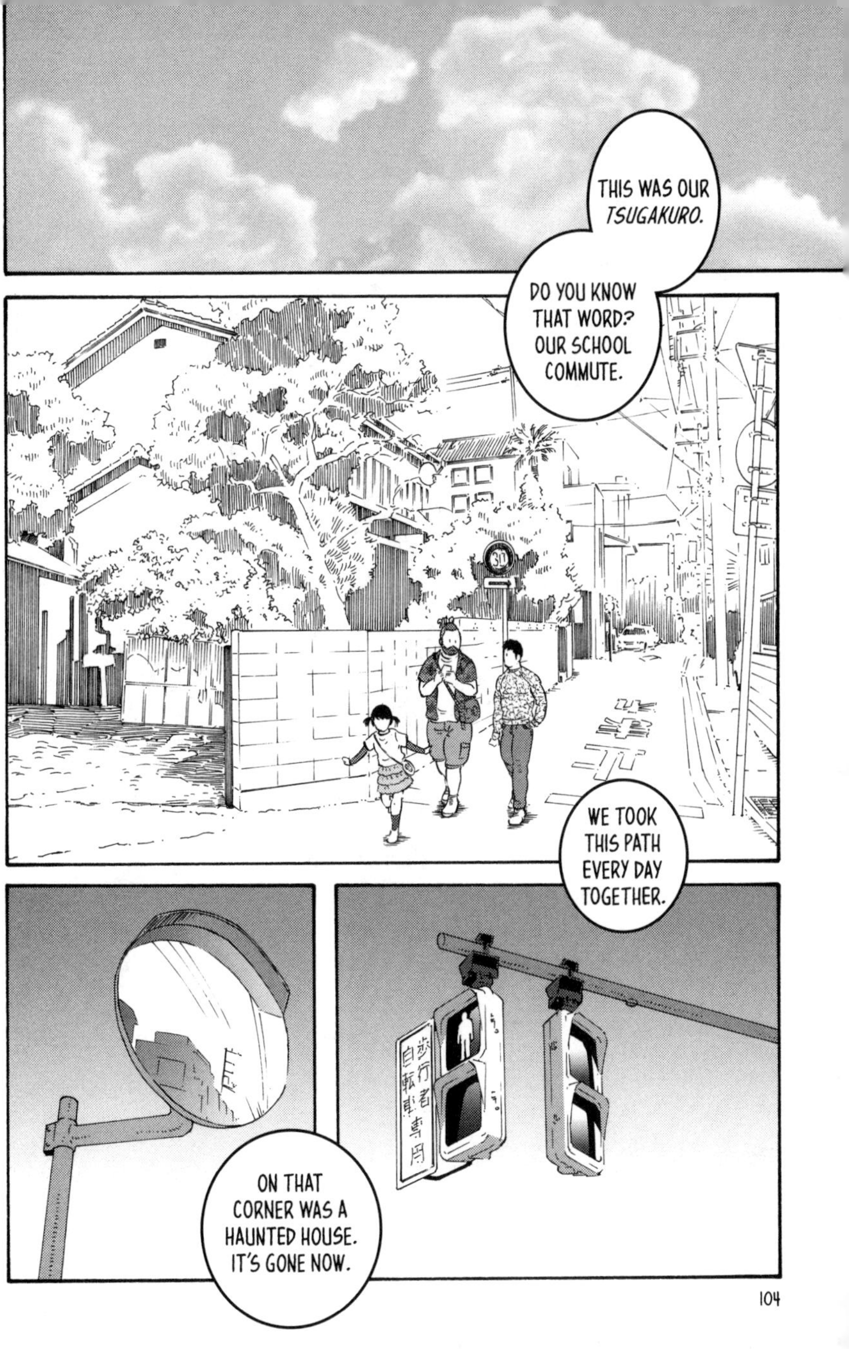
THIS WAS OUR *TSUGAKURO.*
DO YOU KNOW THAT WORD? OUR SCHOOL COMMUTE.
30
WE TOOK THIS PATH EVERY DAY TOGETHER.
歩行者
自転車専用
ON THAT CORNER WAS A HAUNTED HOUSE. IT'S GONE NOW.

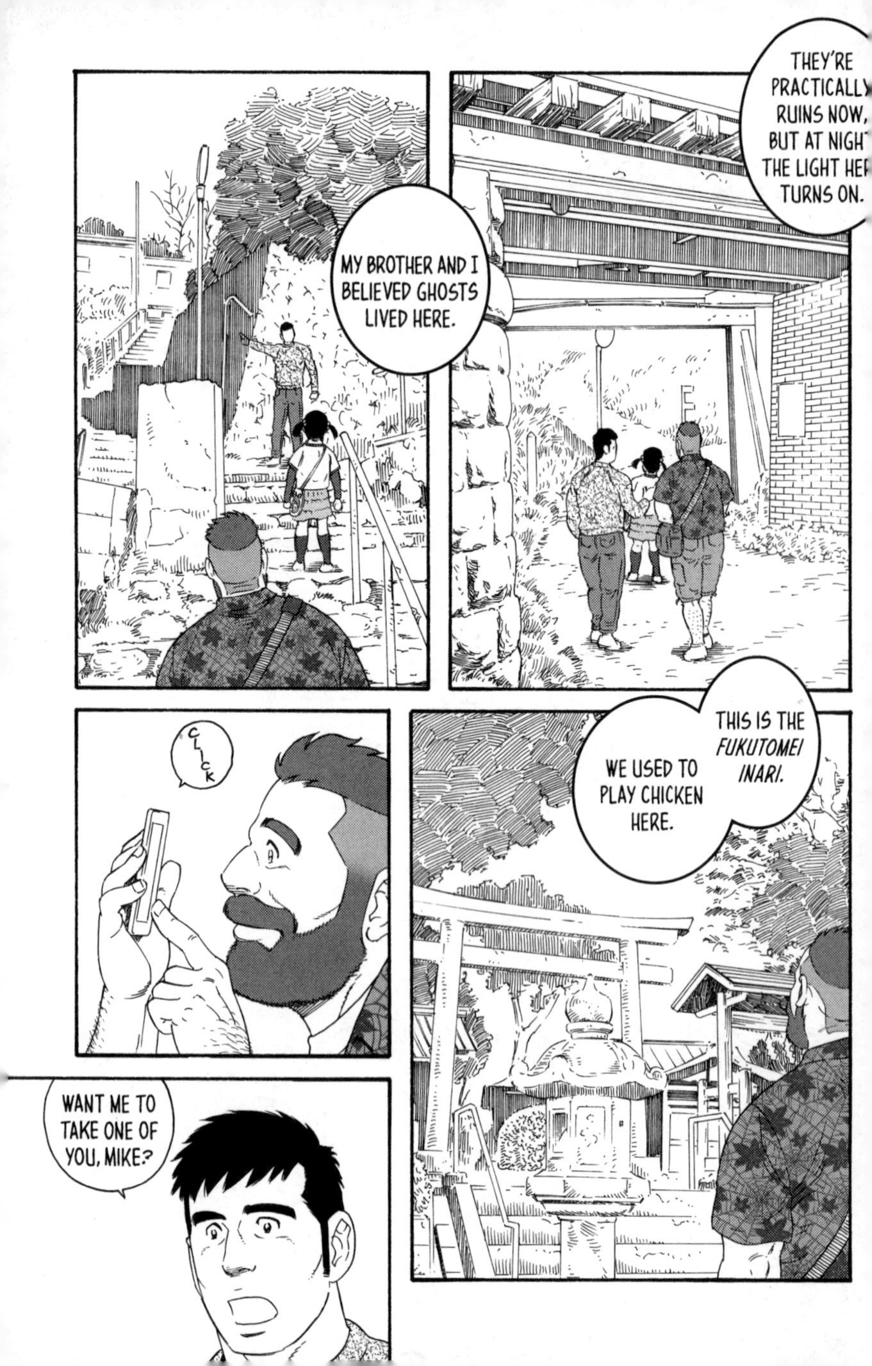
THEY'RE PRACTICALLY RUINS NOW, BUT AT NIGHT THE LIGHT HER TURNS ON.
MY BROTHER AND I BELIEVED GHOSTS LIVED HERE.
THIS IS THE *FUKUTOMEI INARI.*
WE USED TO PLAY CHICKEN HERE.
CLICK
WANT ME TO TAKE ONE OF YOU, MIKE?

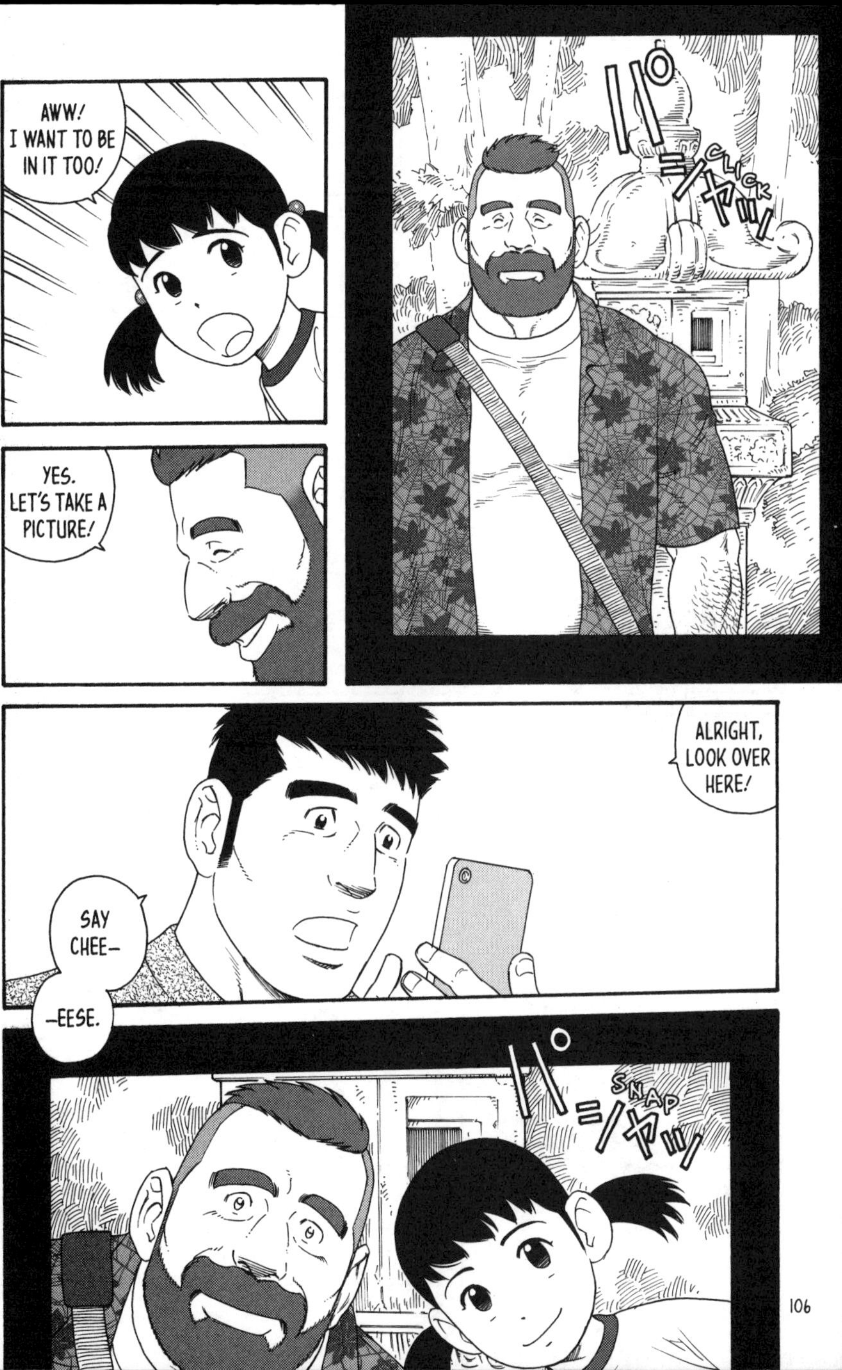
パシャッ
CLICK
AWW! I WANT TO BE IN IT TOO!
YES. LET'S TAKE A PICTURE!
ALRIGHT, LOOK OVER HERE!
SAY CHEE-
-EESE.
パシャッ
SNAP

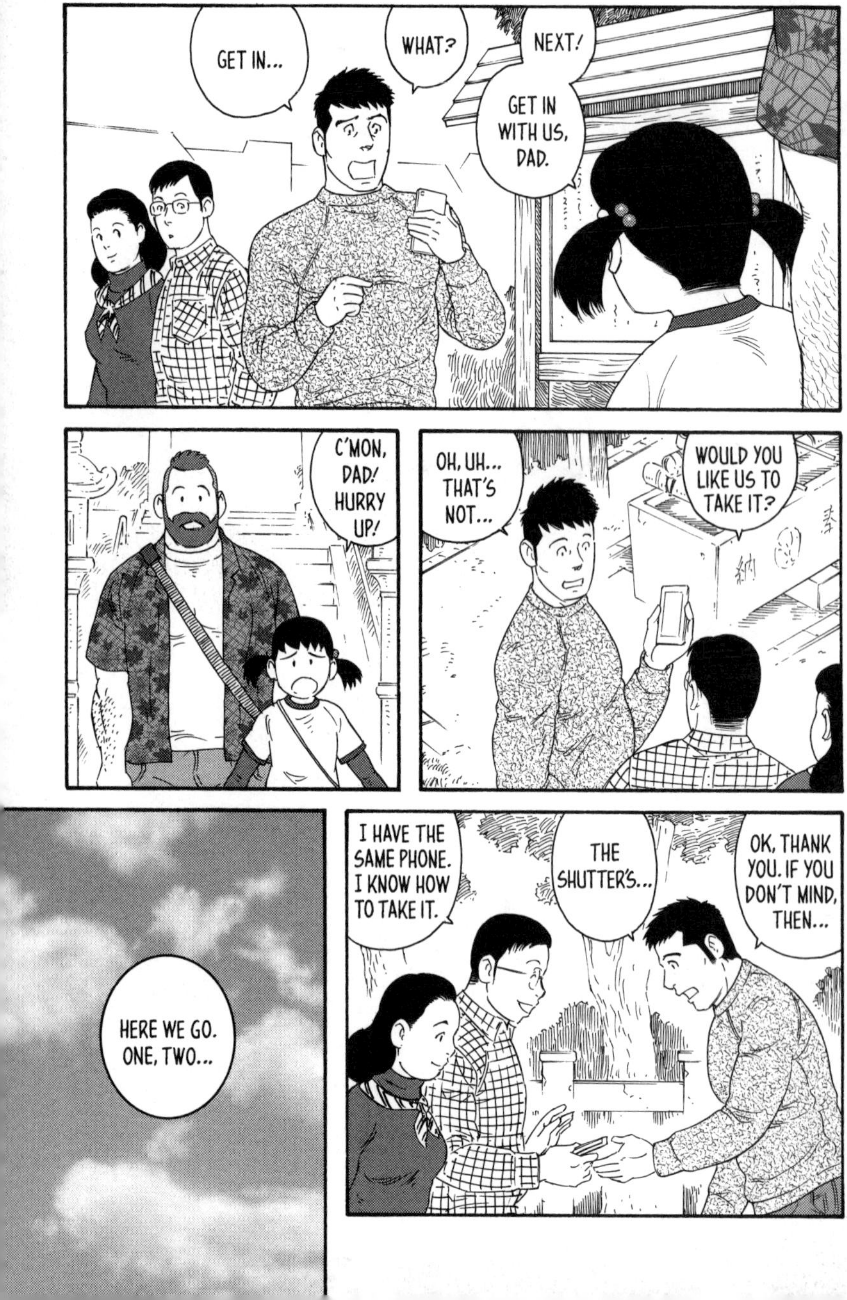
NEXT!
GET IN WITH US, DAD.
WHAT?
GET IN...
WOULD YOU LIKE US TO TAKE IT?
OH, UH... THAT'S NOT...
C'MON, DAD! HURRY UP!
OK, THANK YOU. IF YOU DON'T MIND, THEN...
THE SHUTTER'S...
I HAVE THE SAME PHONE. I KNOW HOW TO TAKE IT.
HERE WE GO. ONE, TWO...

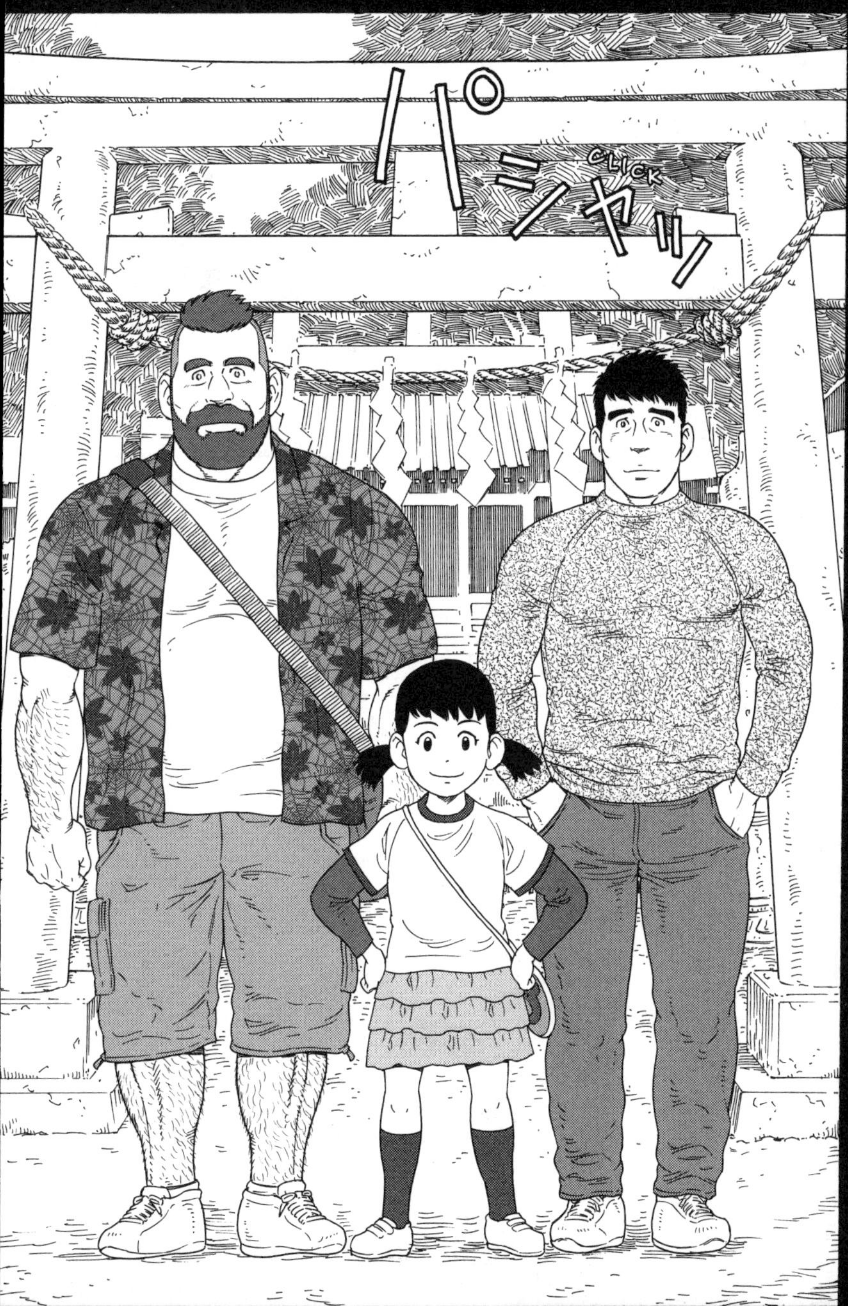
パシャッ
CLICK

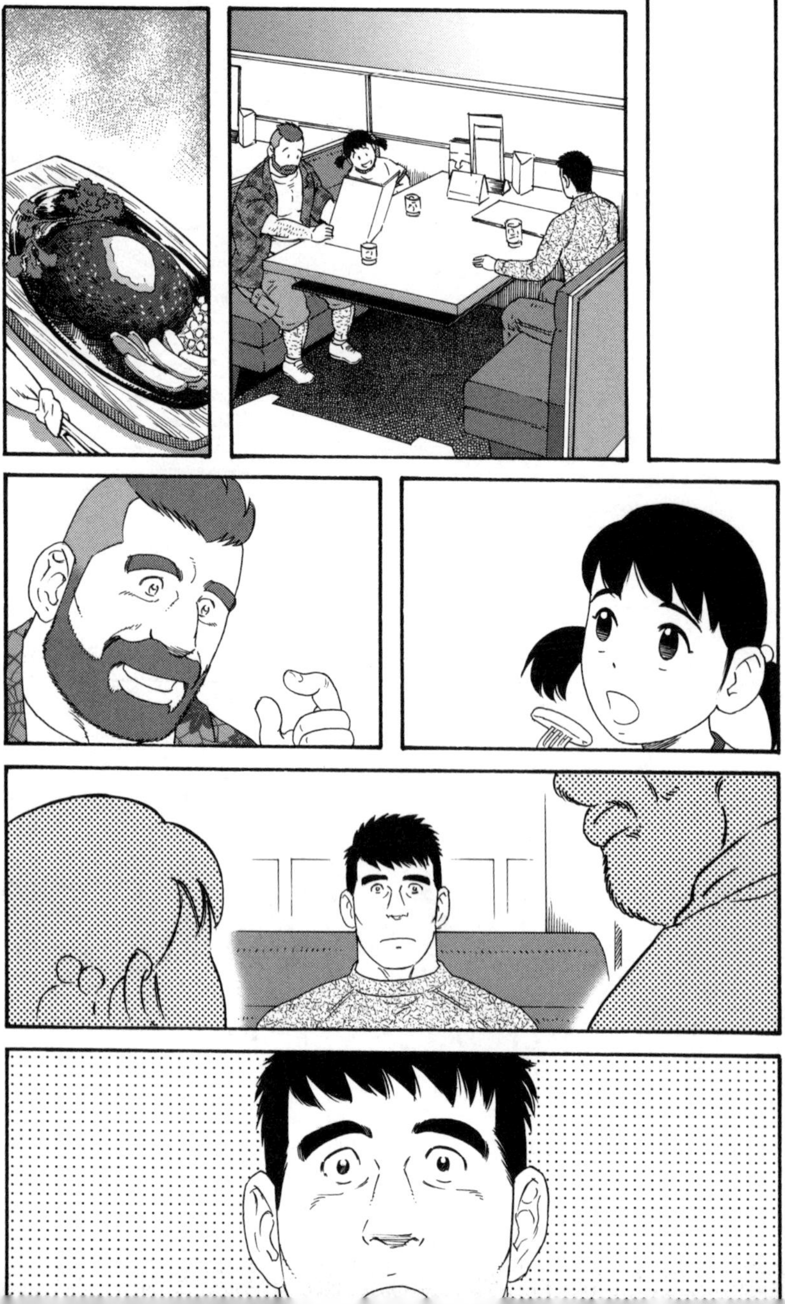

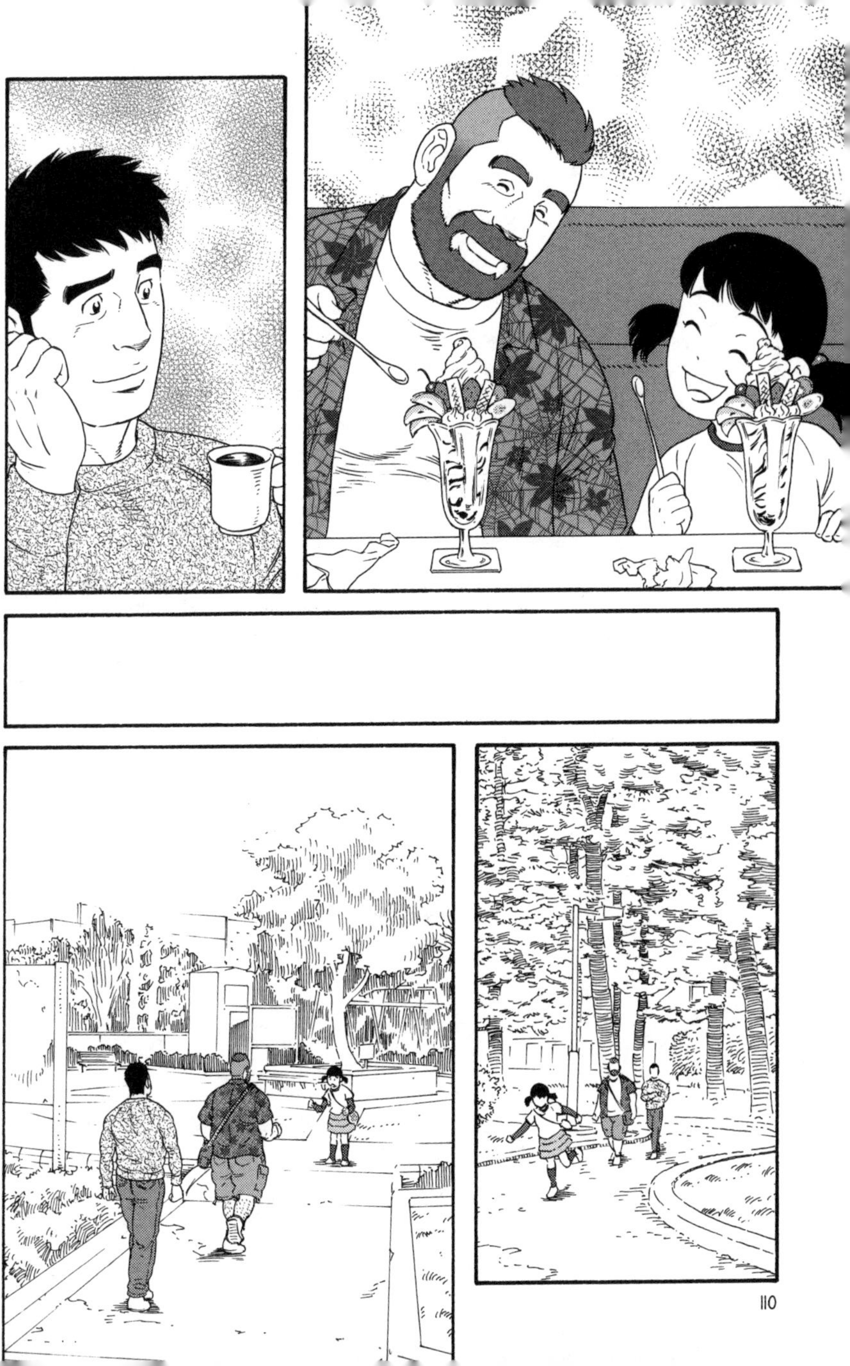

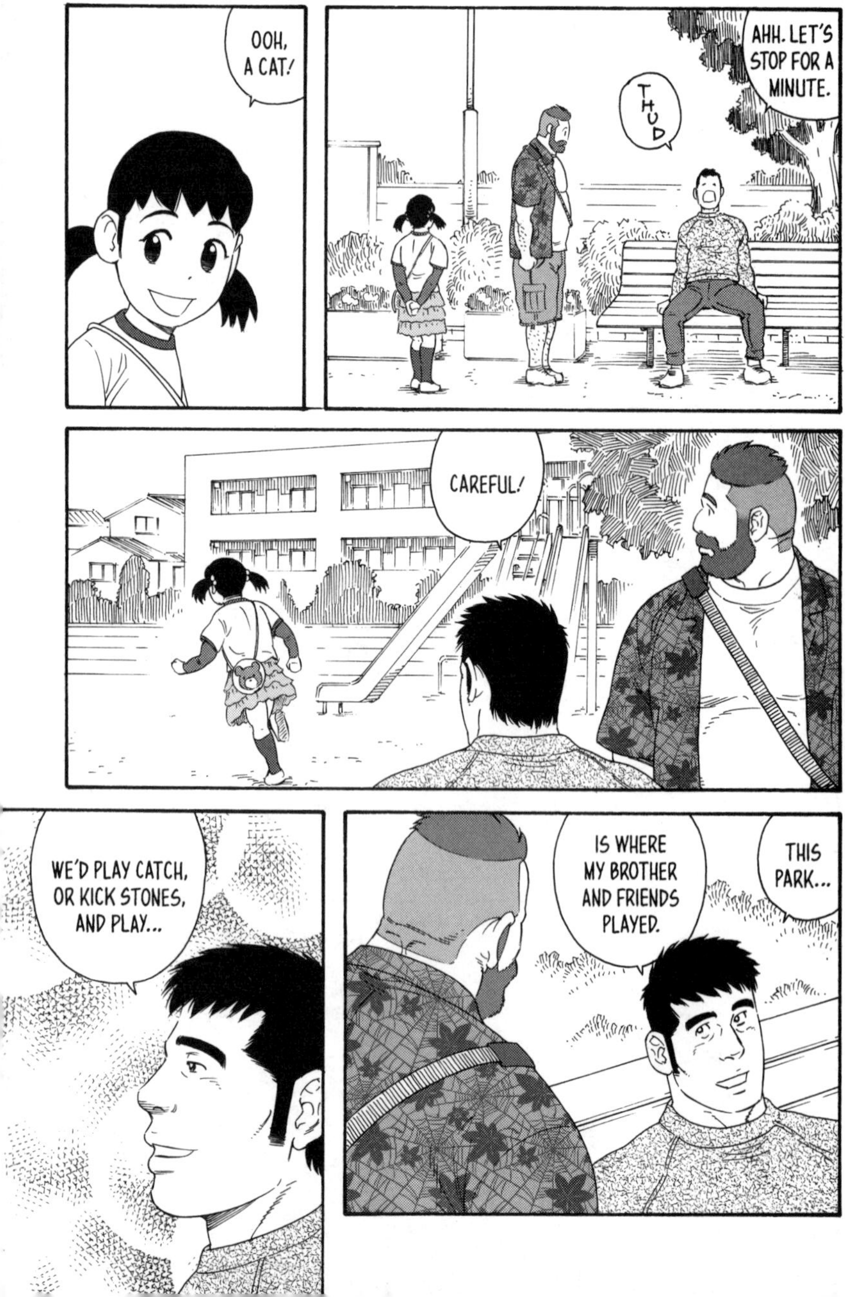
AHH. LET'S STOP FOR A MINUTE.
THUD
OOH, A CAT!
CAREFUL!
THIS PARK...
IS WHERE MY BROTHER AND FRIENDS PLAYED.
WE'D PLAY CATCH, OR KICK STONES, AND PLAY...

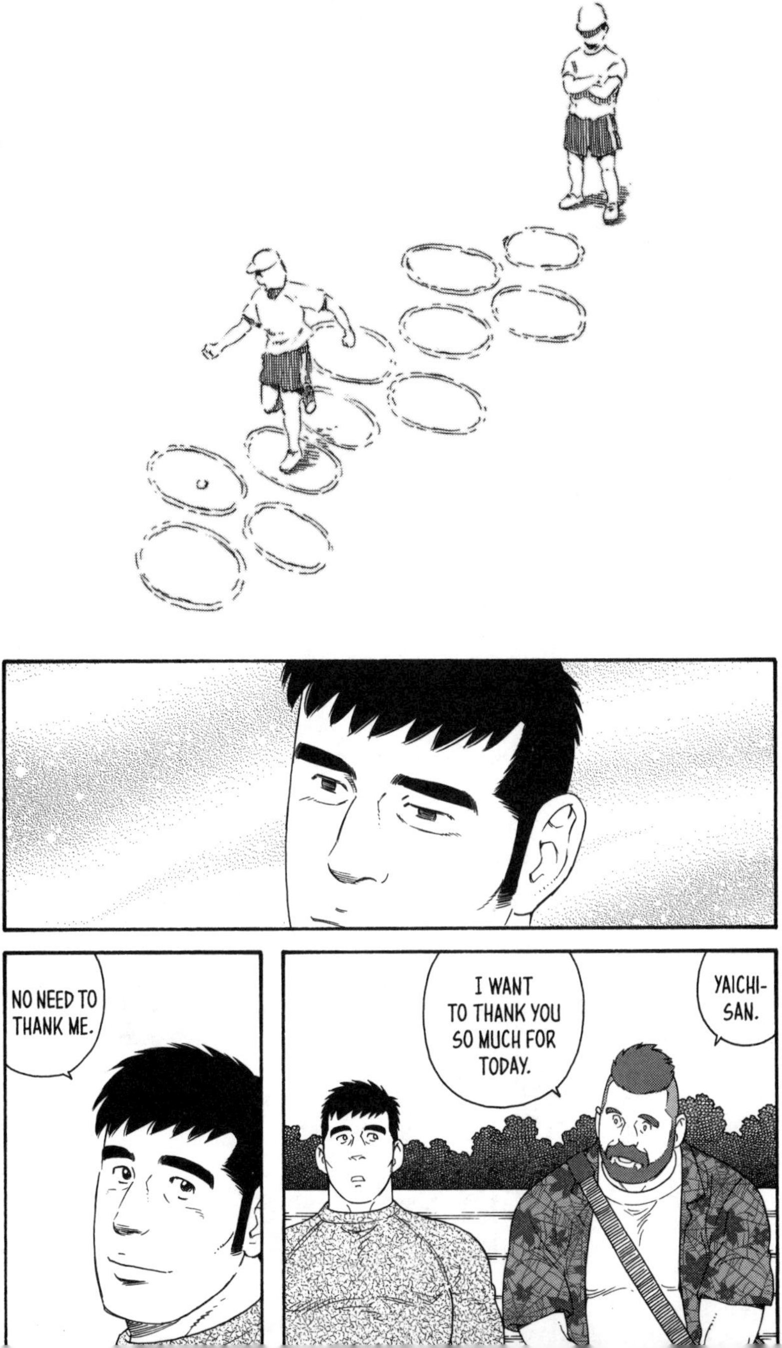
YAICHI-SAN.
I WANT TO THANK YOU SO MUCH FOR TODAY.
NO NEED TO THANK ME.

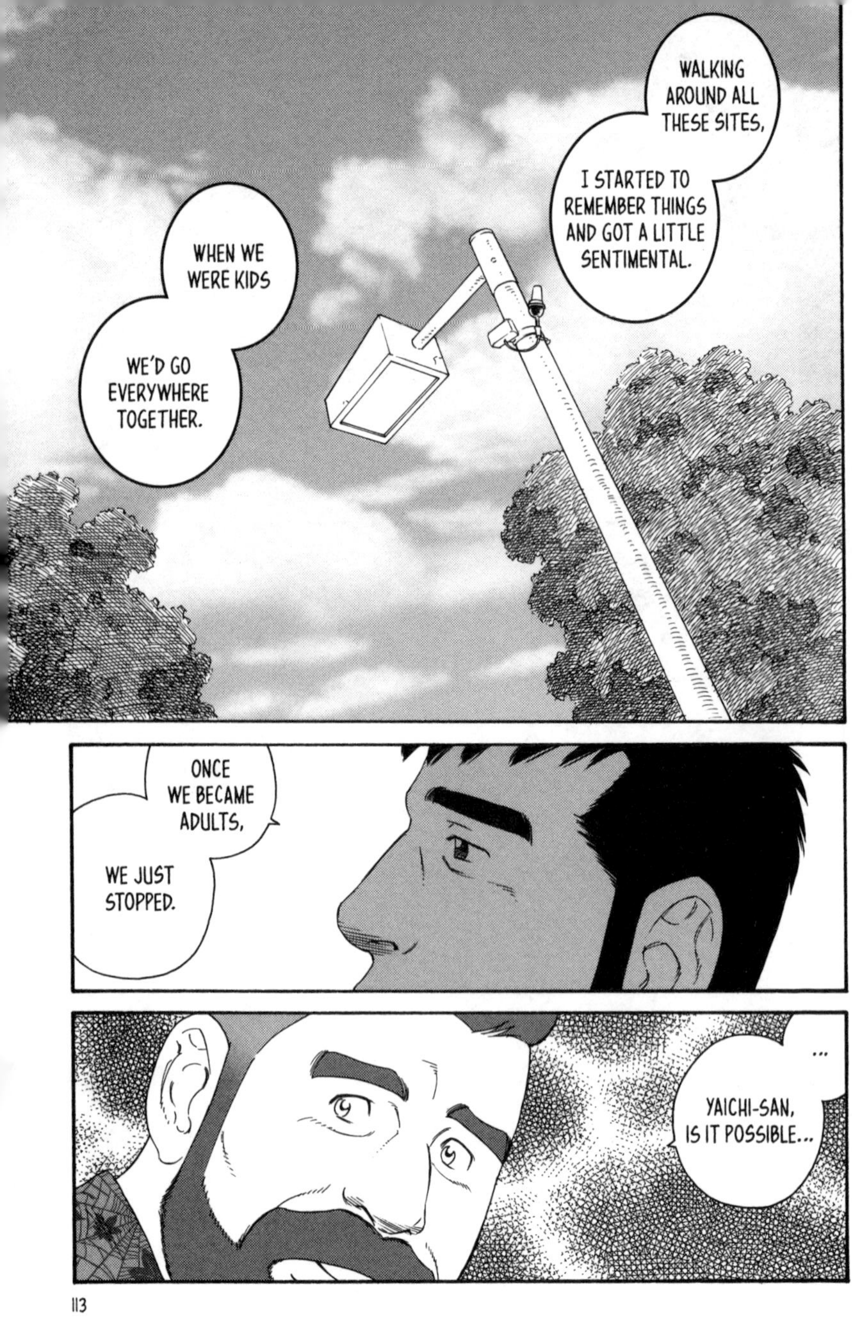
WALKING AROUND ALL THESE SITES,
I STARTED TO REMEMBER THINGS AND GOT A LITTLE SENTIMENTAL.
WHEN WE WERE KIDS
WE'D GO EVERYWHERE TOGETHER.
ONCE WE BECAME ADULTS,
WE JUST STOPPED.
...
YAICHI-SAN, IS IT POSSIBLE...

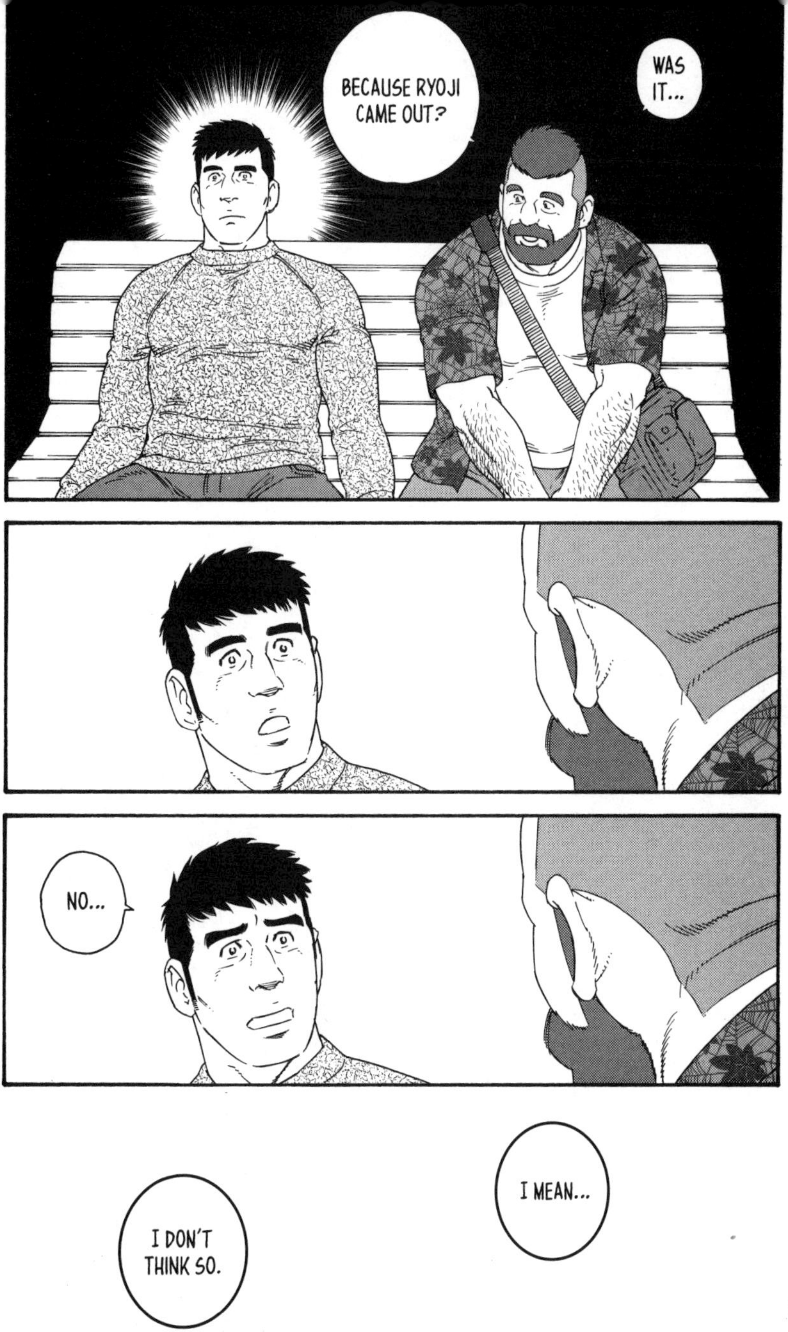
WAS IT...
BECAUSE RYOJI CAME OUT?
NO...
I MEAN...
I DON'T THINK SO.

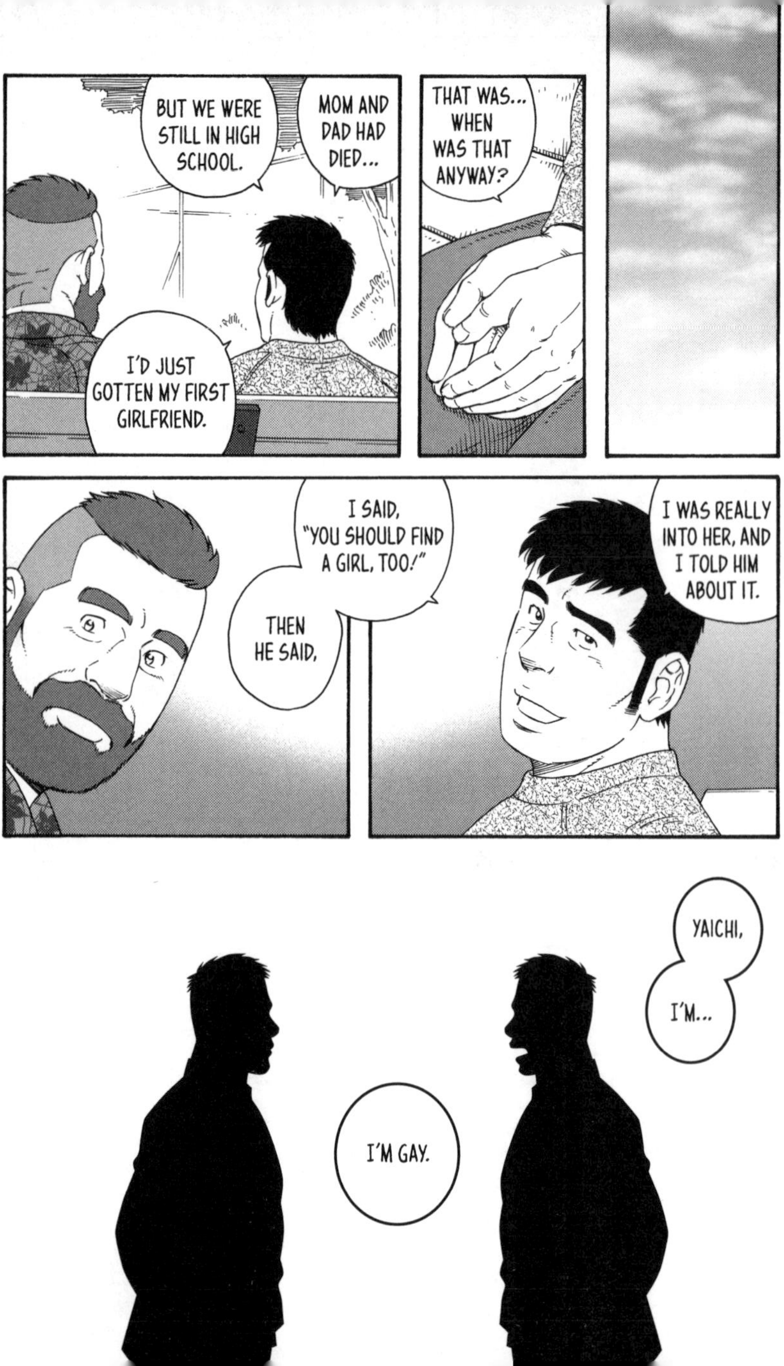
THAT WAS... WHEN WAS THAT ANYWAY?
MOM AND DAD HAD DIED...
BUT WE WERE STILL IN HIGH SCHOOL.
I'D JUST GOTTEN MY FIRST GIRLFRIEND.
I WAS REALLY INTO HER, AND I TOLD HIM ABOUT IT.
I SAID, "YOU SHOULD FIND A GIRL, TOO!"
THEN HE SAID,
YAICHI,
I'M...
I'M GAY.

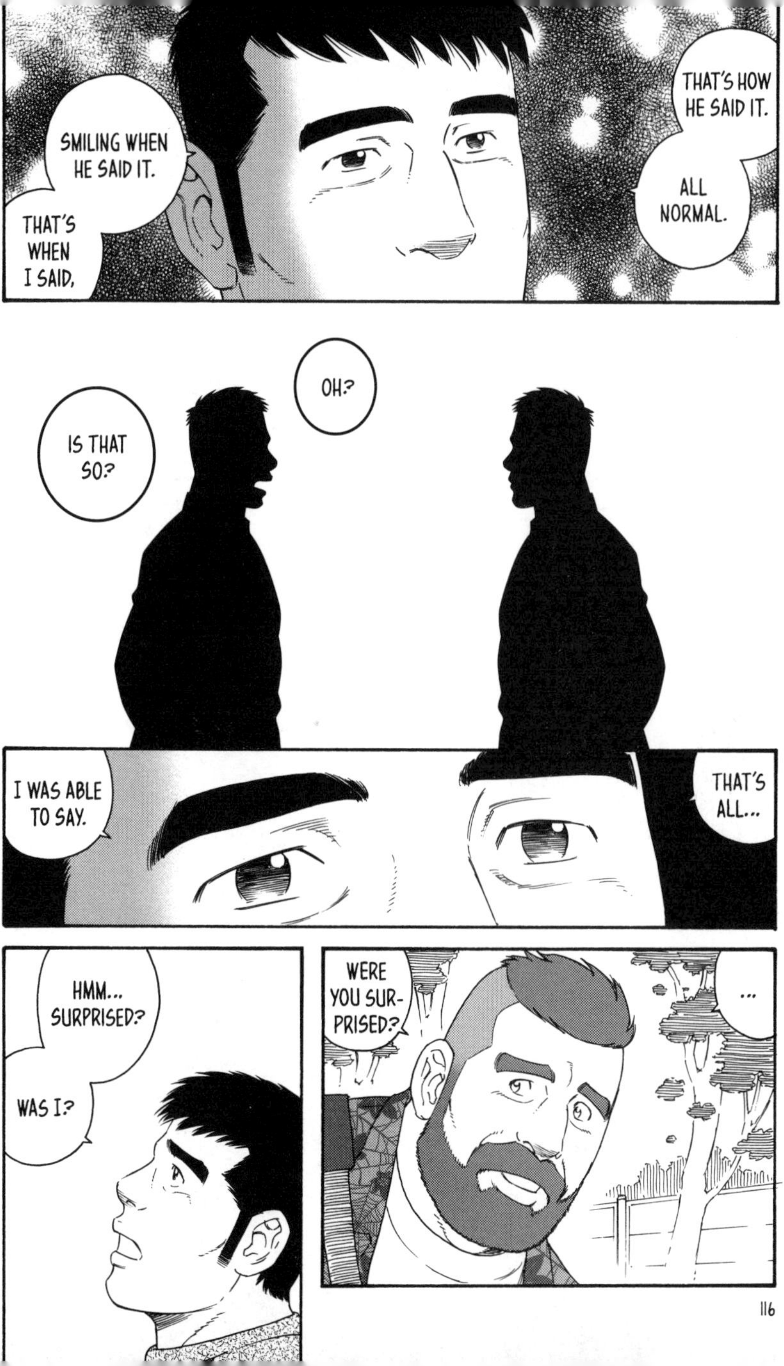
THAT'S HOW HE SAID IT.
ALL NORMAL.
SMILING WHEN HE SAID IT.
THAT'S WHEN I SAID,
OH?
IS THAT SO?
THAT'S ALL...
I WAS ABLE TO SAY.
...
WERE YOU SUR-PRISED?
HMM... SURPRISED?
WAS I?

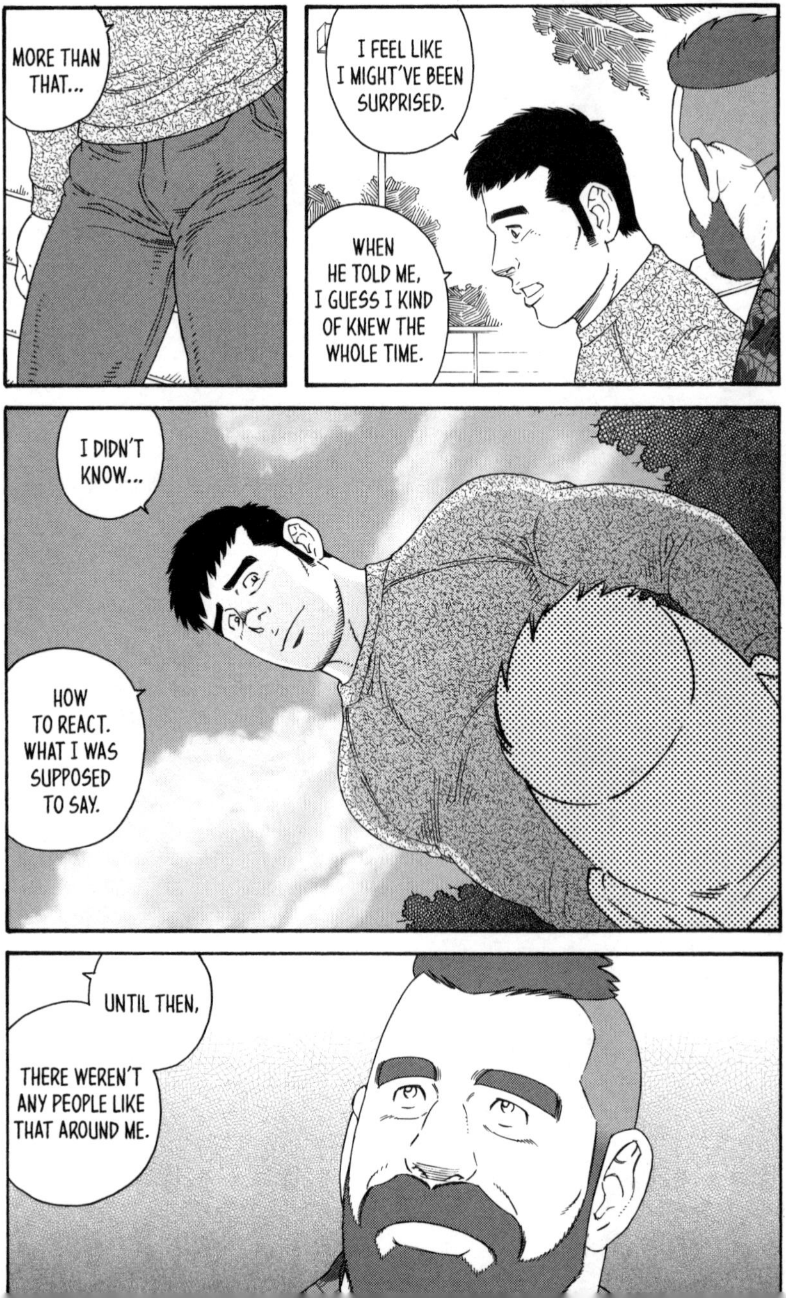
I FEEL LIKE I MIGHT'VE BEEN SURPRISED.
WHEN HE TOLD ME, I GUESS I KIND OF KNEW THE WHOLE TIME.
MORE THAN THAT...
I DIDN'T KNOW...
HOW TO REACT. WHAT I WAS SUPPOSED TO SAY.
UNTIL THEN,
THERE WEREN'T ANY PEOPLE LIKE THAT AROUND ME.

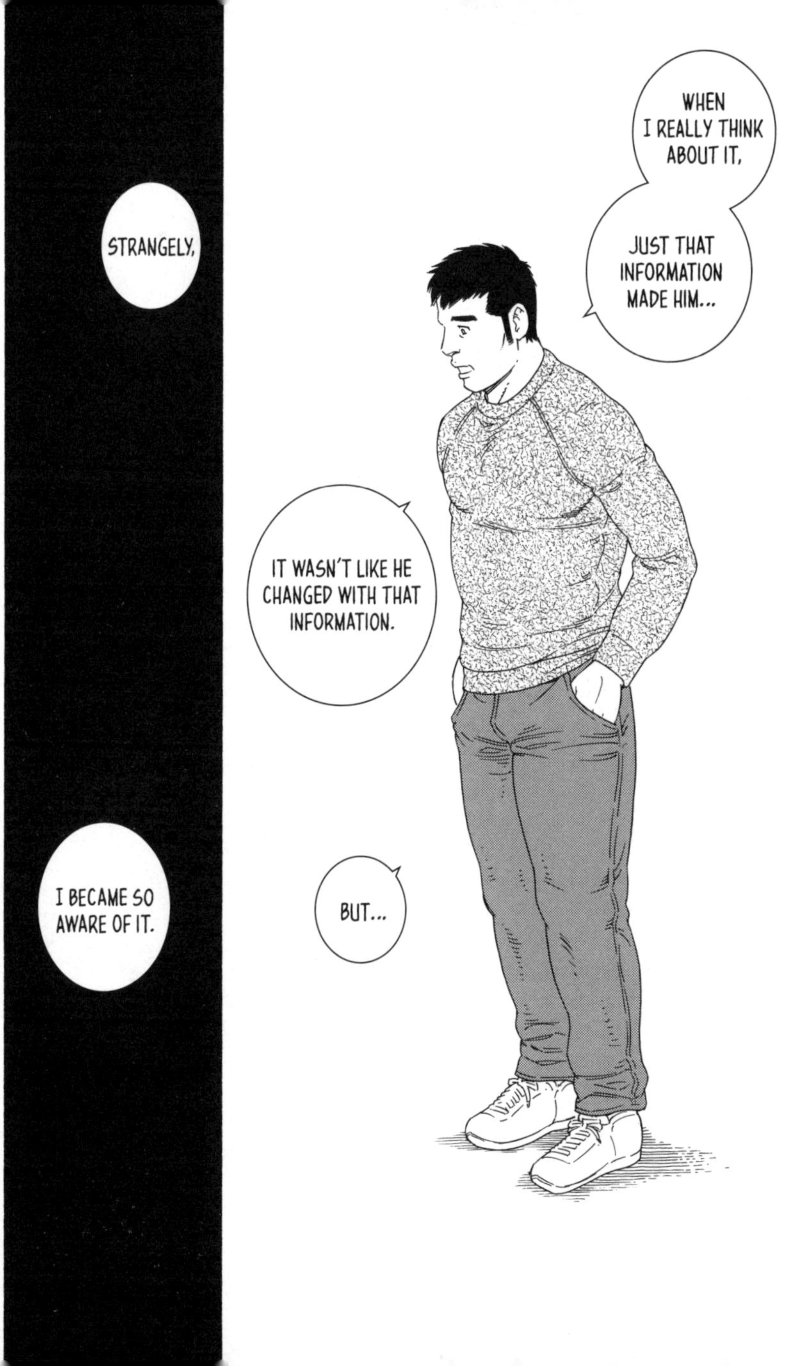
WHEN I REALLY THINK ABOUT IT,
JUST THAT INFORMATION MADE HIM...
IT WASN'T LIKE HE CHANGED WITH THAT INFORMATION.
BUT...
STRANGELY,
I BECAME SO AWARE OF IT.

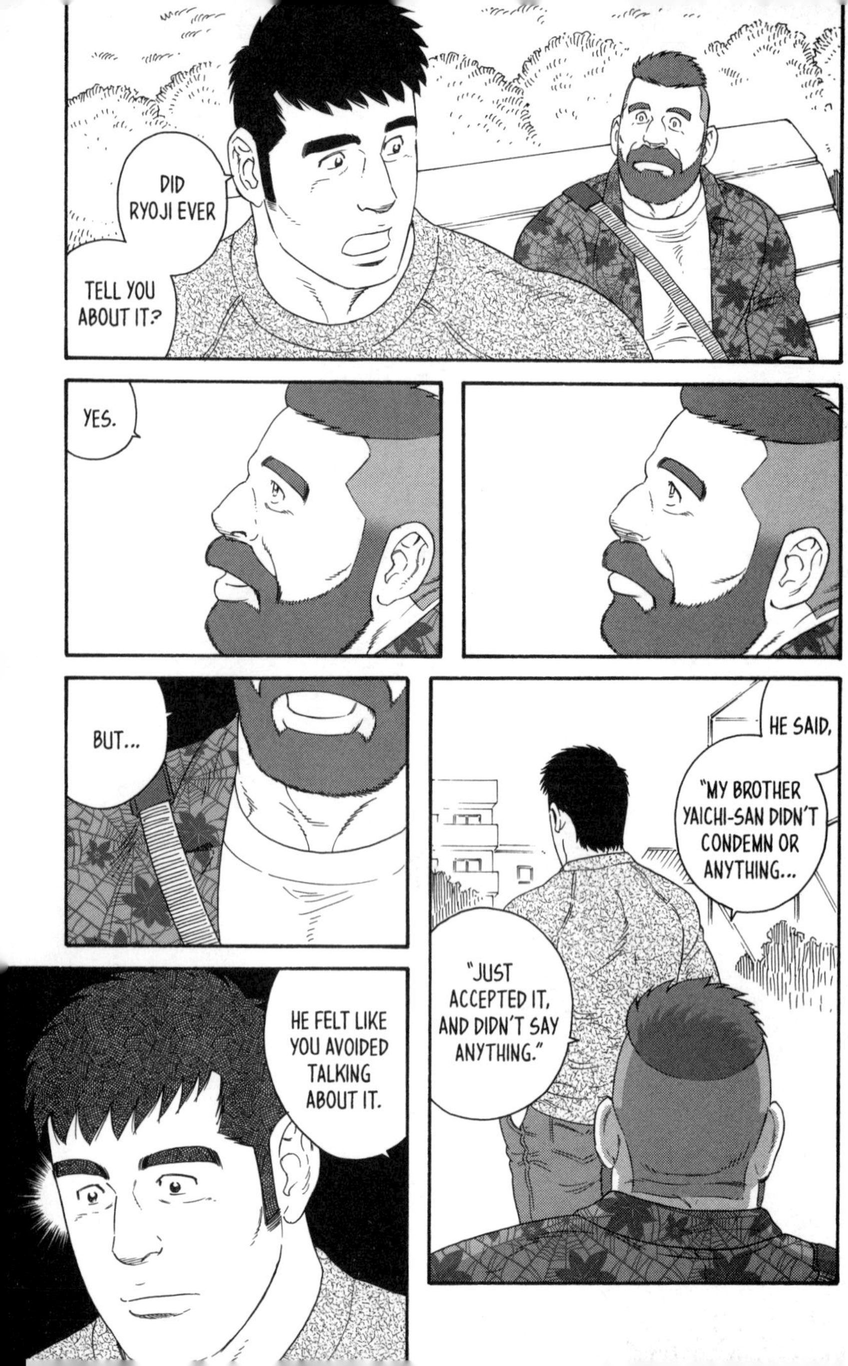
DID RYOJI EVER
TELL YOU ABOUT IT?
YES.
HE SAID,
"MY BROTHER YAICHI-SAN DIDN'T CONDEMN OR ANYTHING...
"JUST ACCEPTED IT, AND DIDN'T SAY ANYTHING."
BUT...
HE FELT LIKE YOU AVOIDED TALKING ABOUT IT.

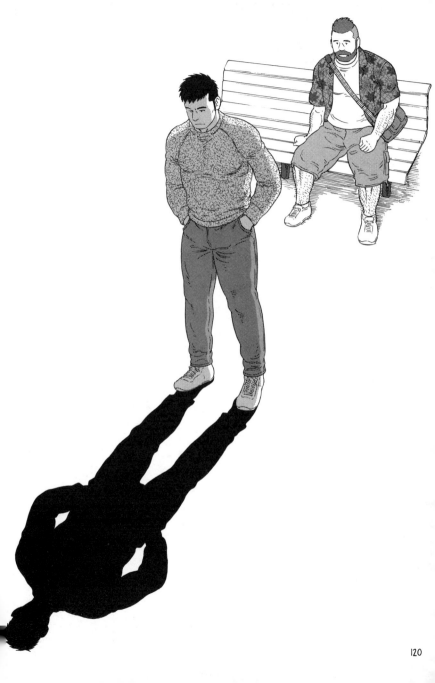

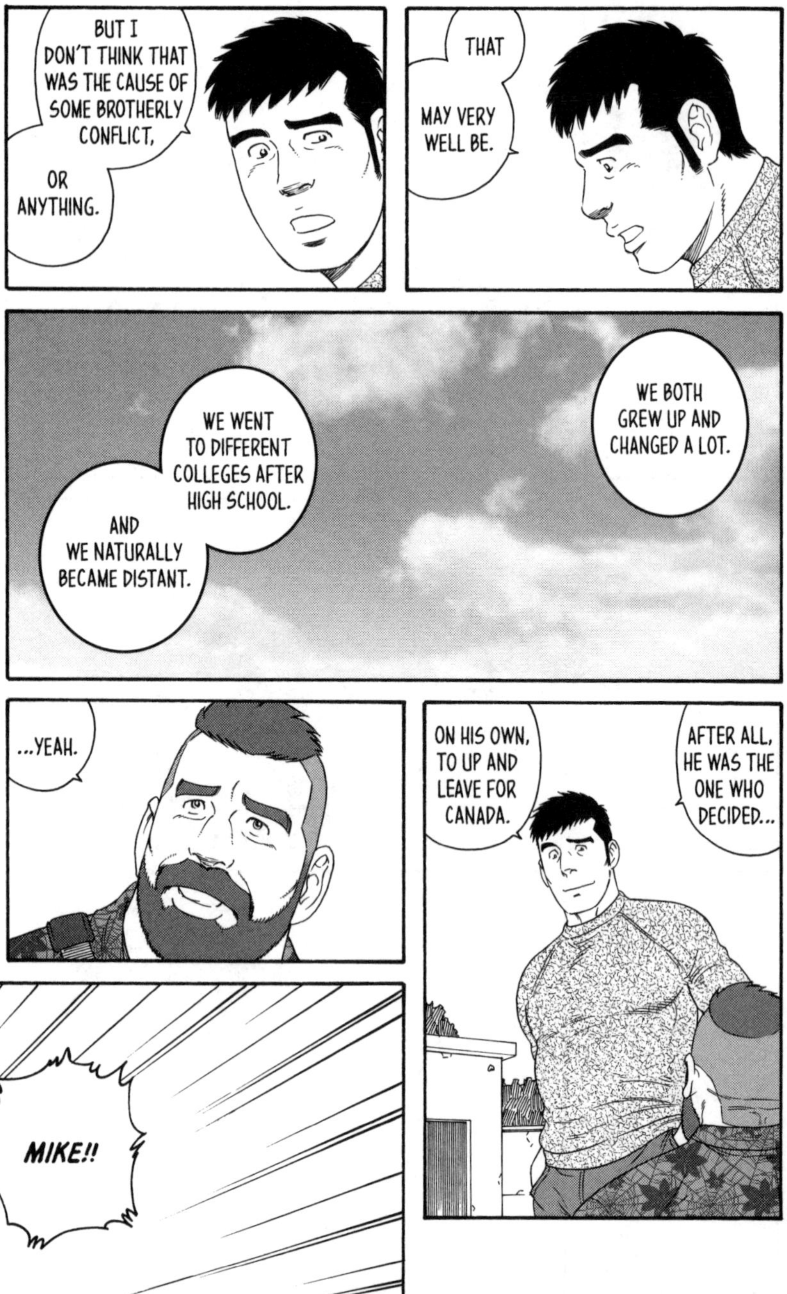
THAT
MAY VERY WELL BE.
BUT I DON'T THINK THAT WAS THE CAUSE OF SOME BROTHERLY CONFLICT,
OR ANYTHING.
WE BOTH GREW UP AND CHANGED A LOT.
WE WENT TO DIFFERENT COLLEGES AFTER HIGH SCHOOL.
AND WE NATURALLY BECAME DISTANT.
AFTER ALL, HE WAS THE ONE WHO DECIDED...
ON HIS OWN, TO UP AND LEAVE FOR CANADA.
...YEAH.
MIKE!!

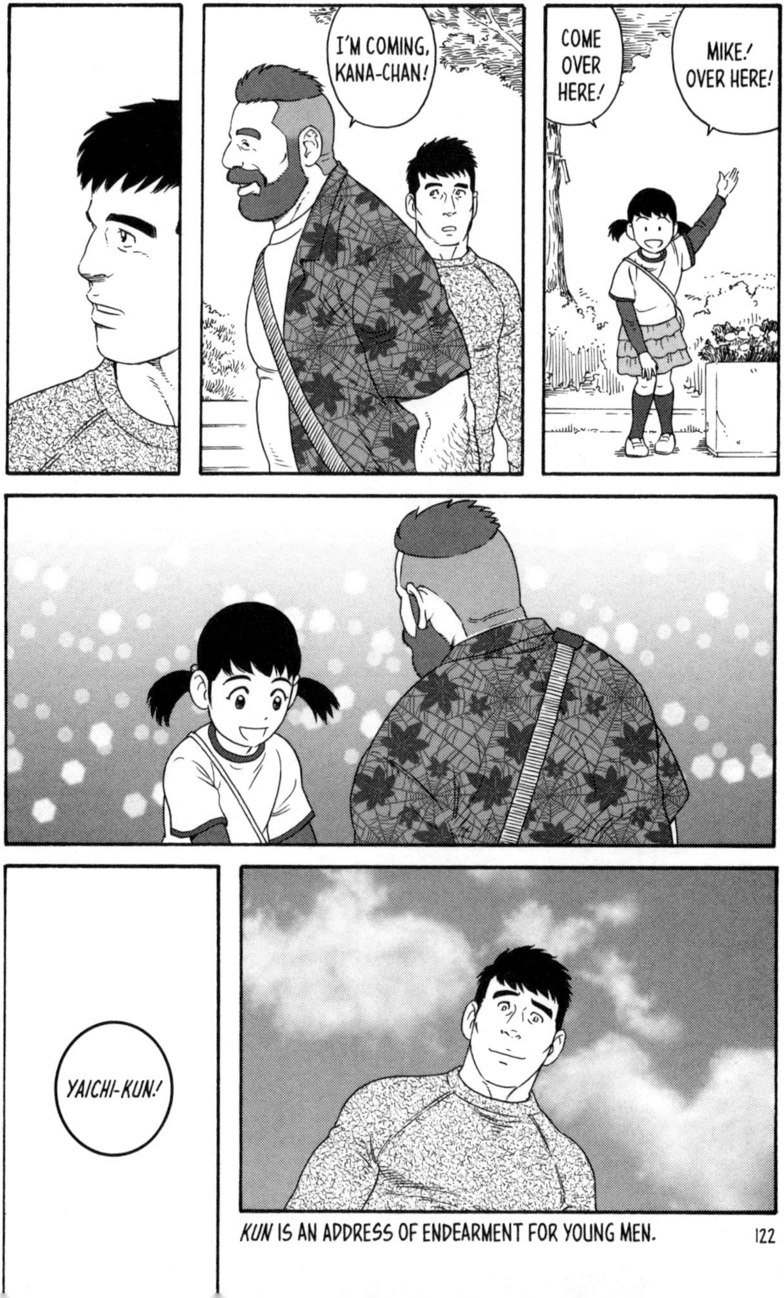
MIKE! OVER HERE!
COME OVER HERE!
I'M COMING, KANA-CHAN!
YAICHI-KUN!

KUN IS AN ADDRESS OF ENDEARMENT FOR YOUNG MEN.

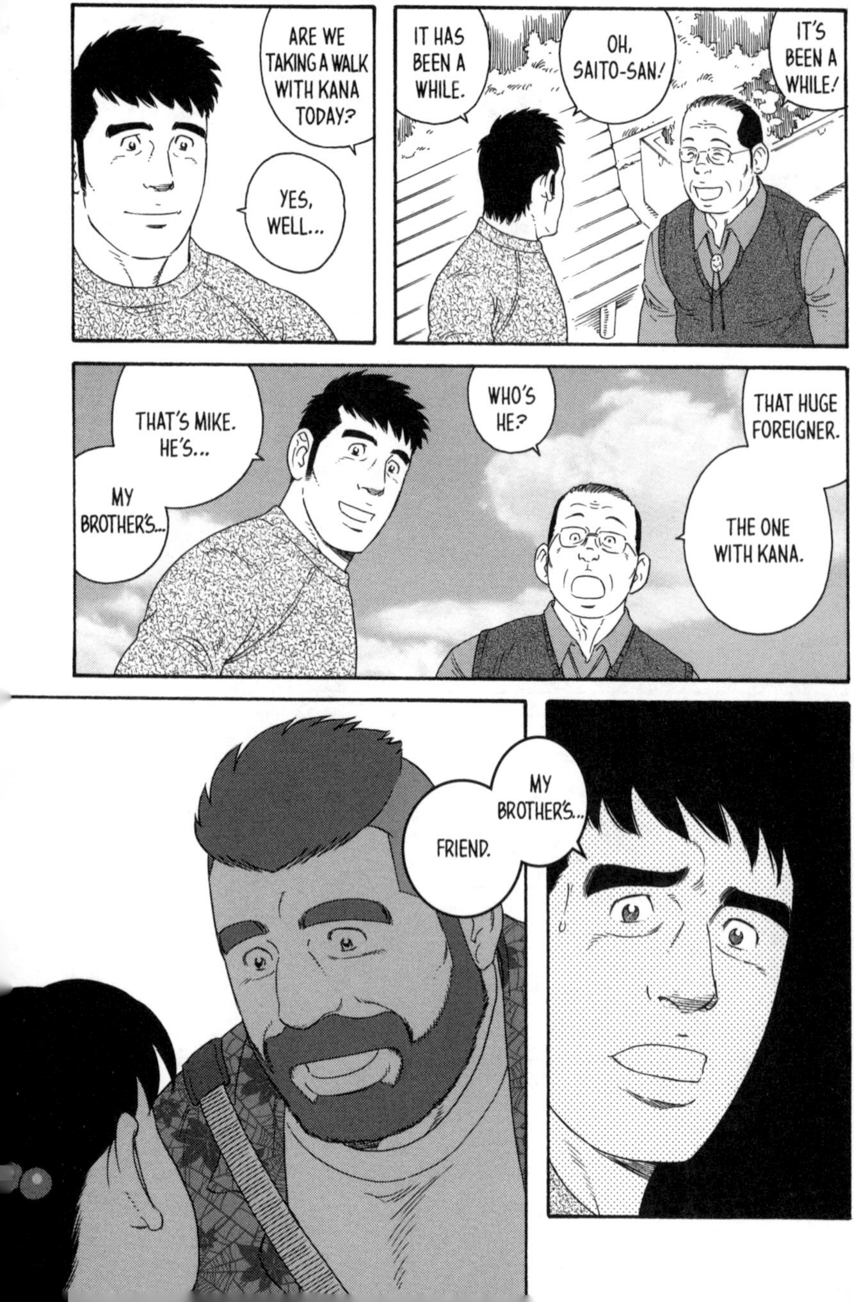
IT'S BEEN A WHILE!
OH, SAITO-SAN!
IT HAS BEEN A WHILE.
ARE WE TAKING A WALK WITH KANA TODAY?
YES, WELL...
THAT HUGE FOREIGNER.
THE ONE WITH KANA.
WHO'S HE?
THAT'S MIKE. HE'S...
MY BROTHER'S...
MY BROTHER'S...
FRIEND.

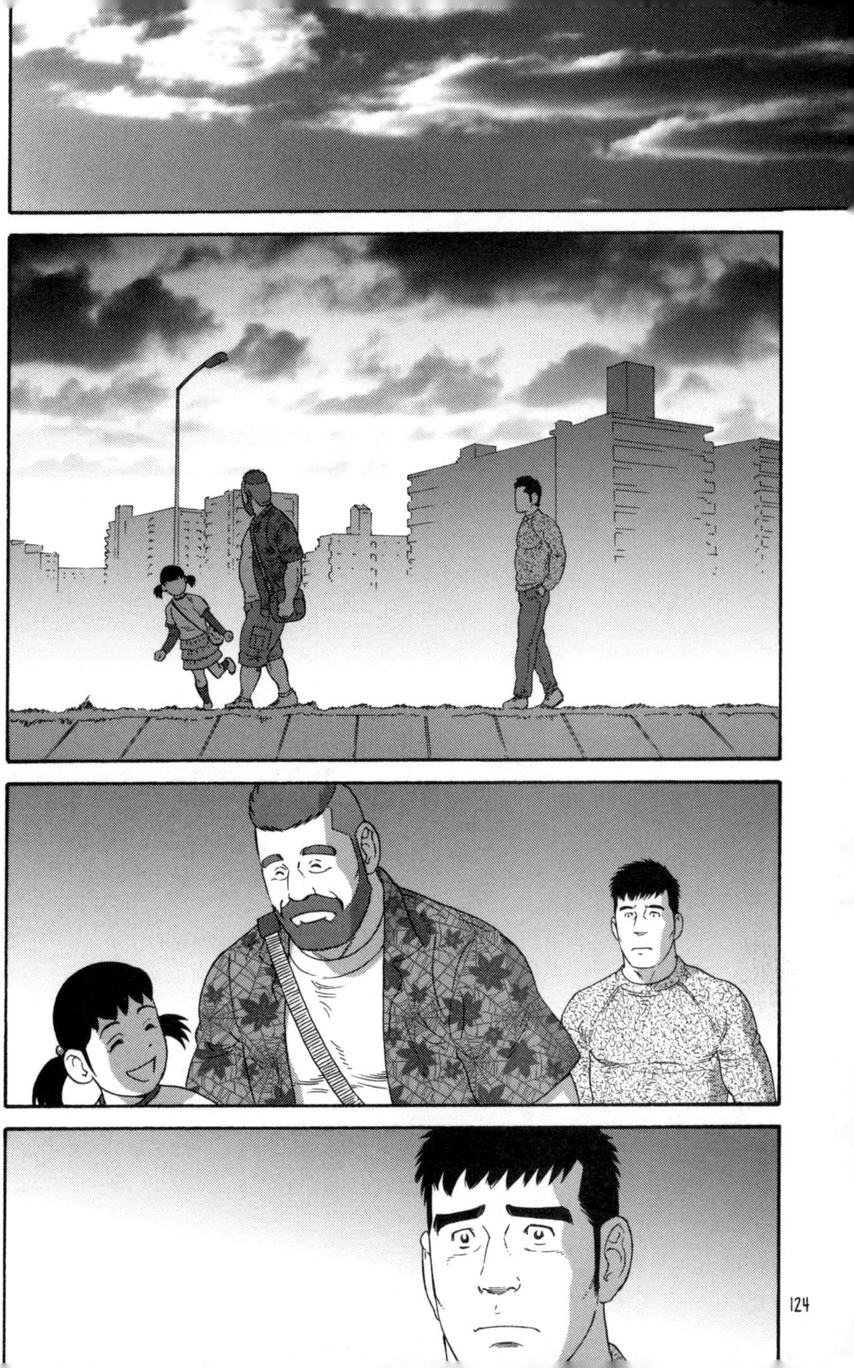

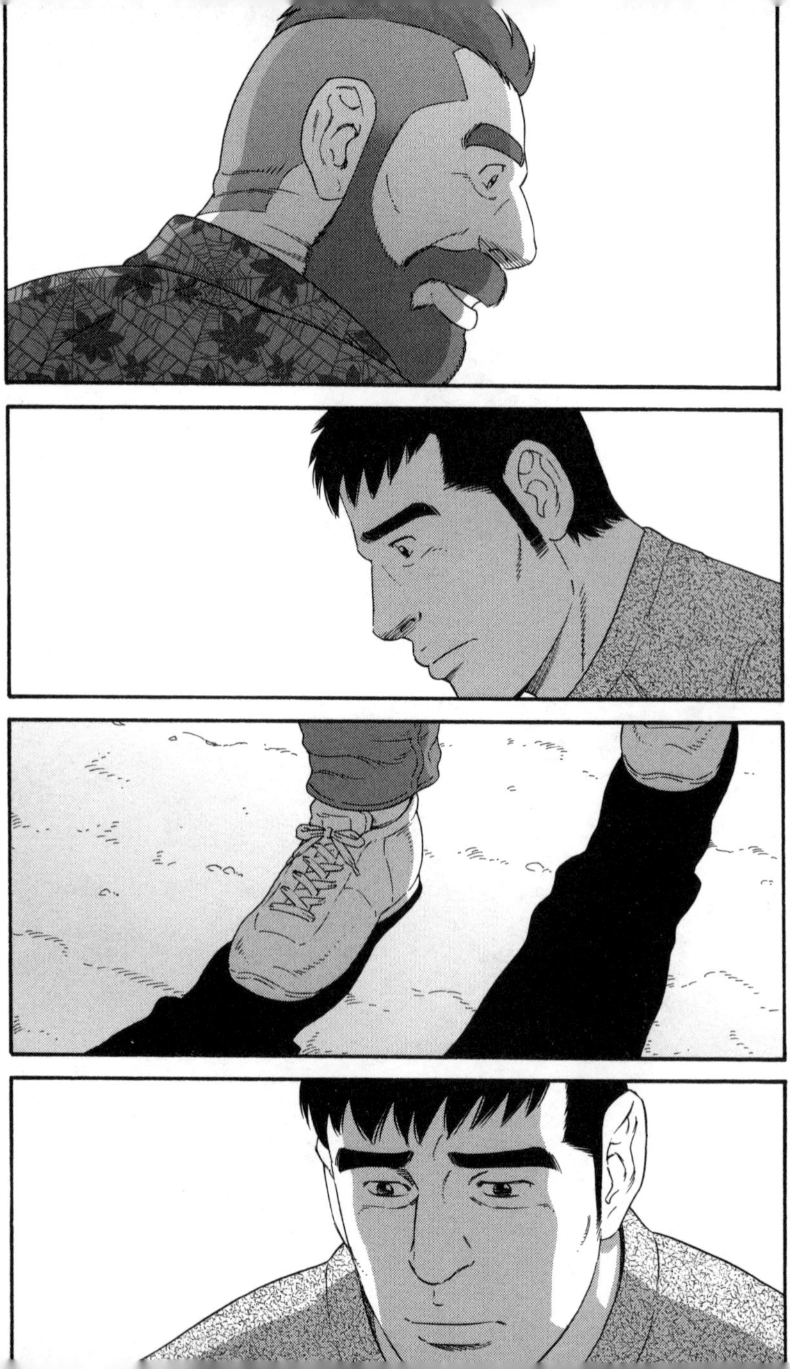

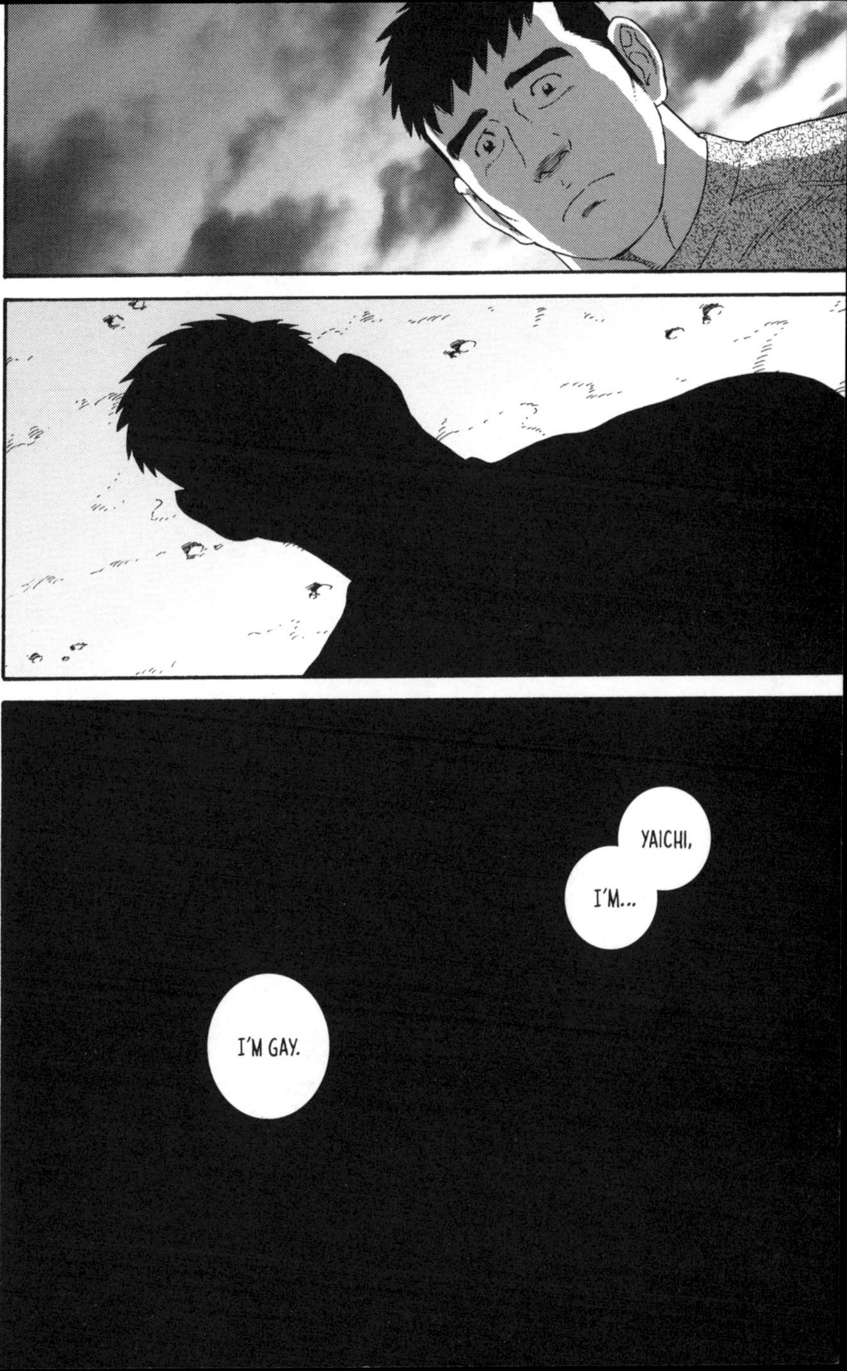
YAICHI,
I'M...
I'M GAY.

CHAPTER SIX
TEARS

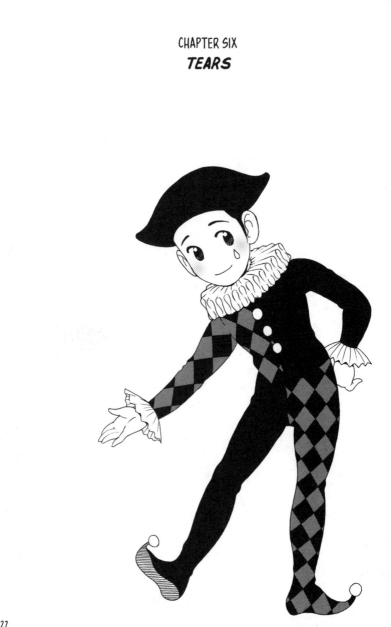

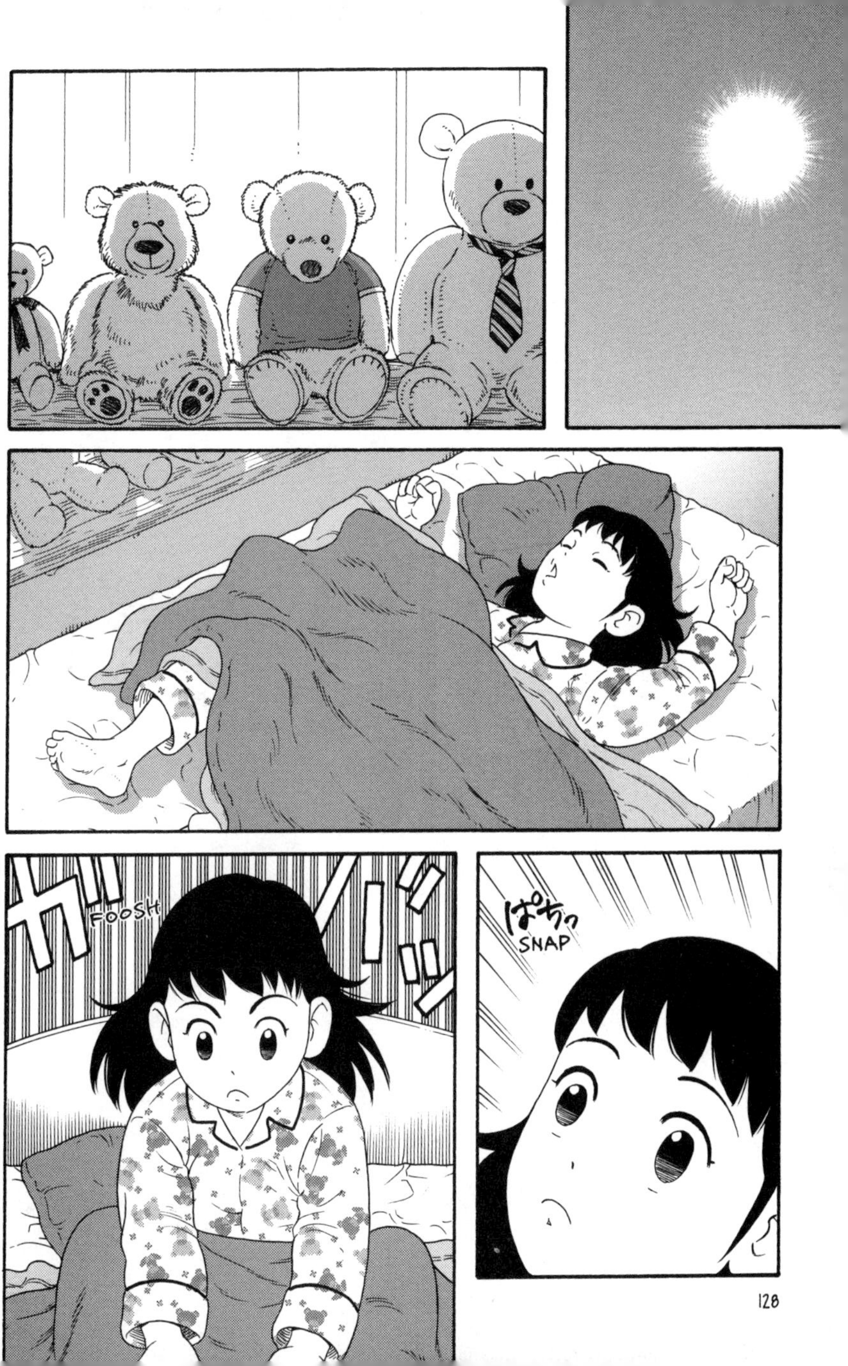
ぱちっ
SNAP
FOOSH

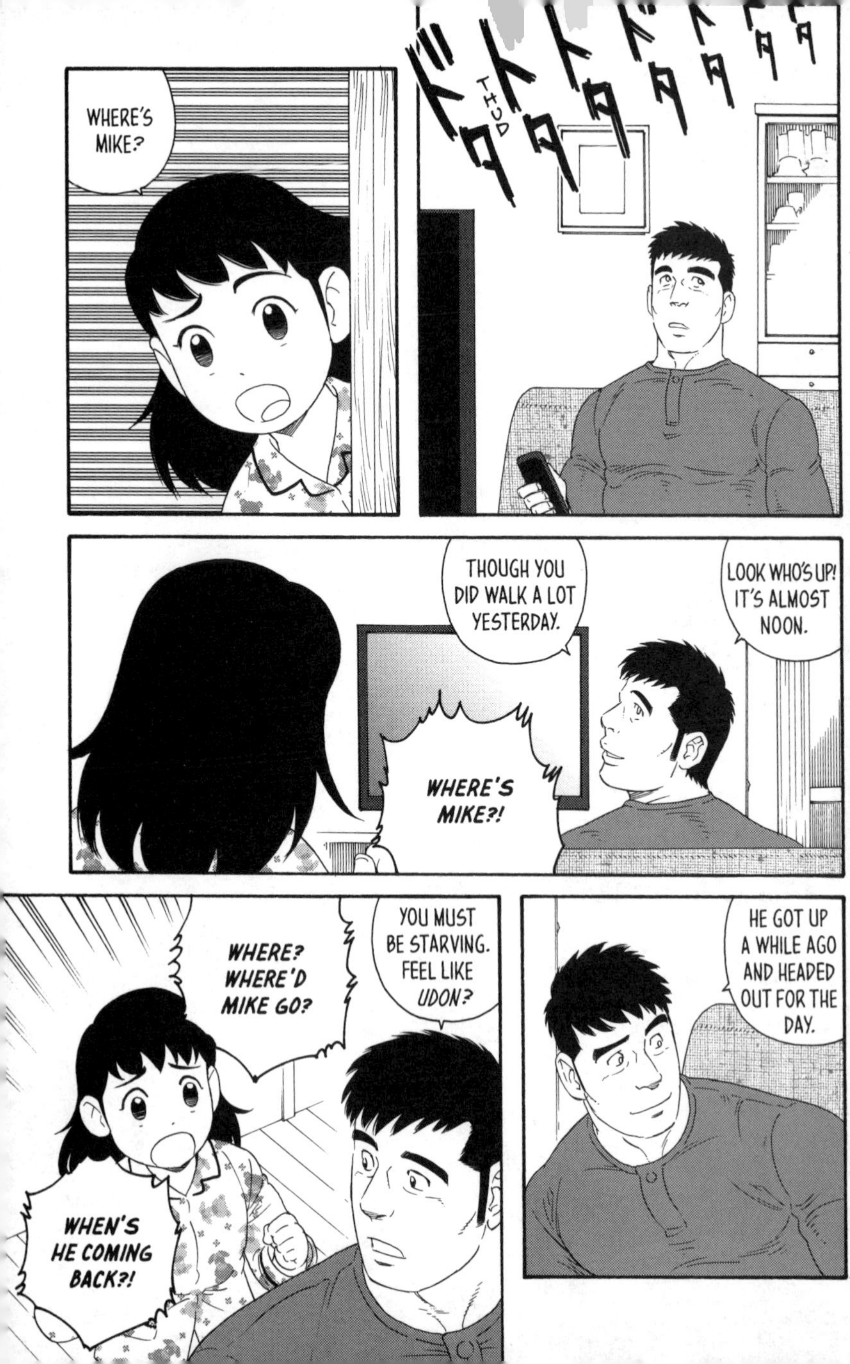
THUD
WHERE'S MIKE?
LOOK WHO'S UP! IT'S ALMOST NOON.
THOUGH YOU DID WALK A LOT YESTERDAY.
WHERE'S MIKE?!
HE GOT UP A WHILE AGO AND HEADED OUT FOR THE DAY.
YOU MUST BE STARVING. FEEL LIKE *UDON?*
WHERE? WHERE'D MIKE GO?
WHEN'S HE COMING BACK?!

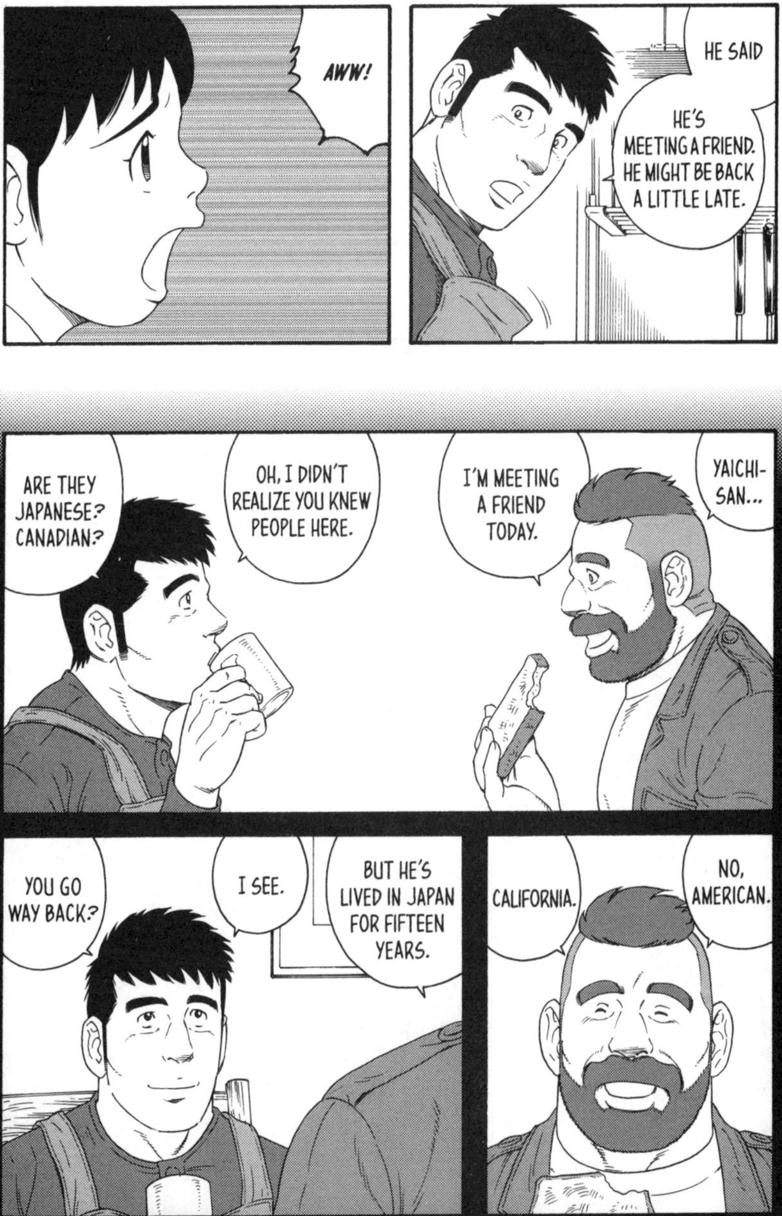
HE SAID
HE'S MEETING A FRIEND. HE MIGHT BE BACK A LITTLE LATE.
AWW!
YAICHI-SAN...
I'M MEETING A FRIEND TODAY.
OH, I DIDN'T REALIZE YOU KNEW PEOPLE HERE.
ARE THEY JAPANESE? CANADIAN?
NO, AMERICAN.
CALIFORNIA.
BUT HE'S LIVED IN JAPAN FOR FIFTEEN YEARS.
I SEE.
YOU GO WAY BACK?

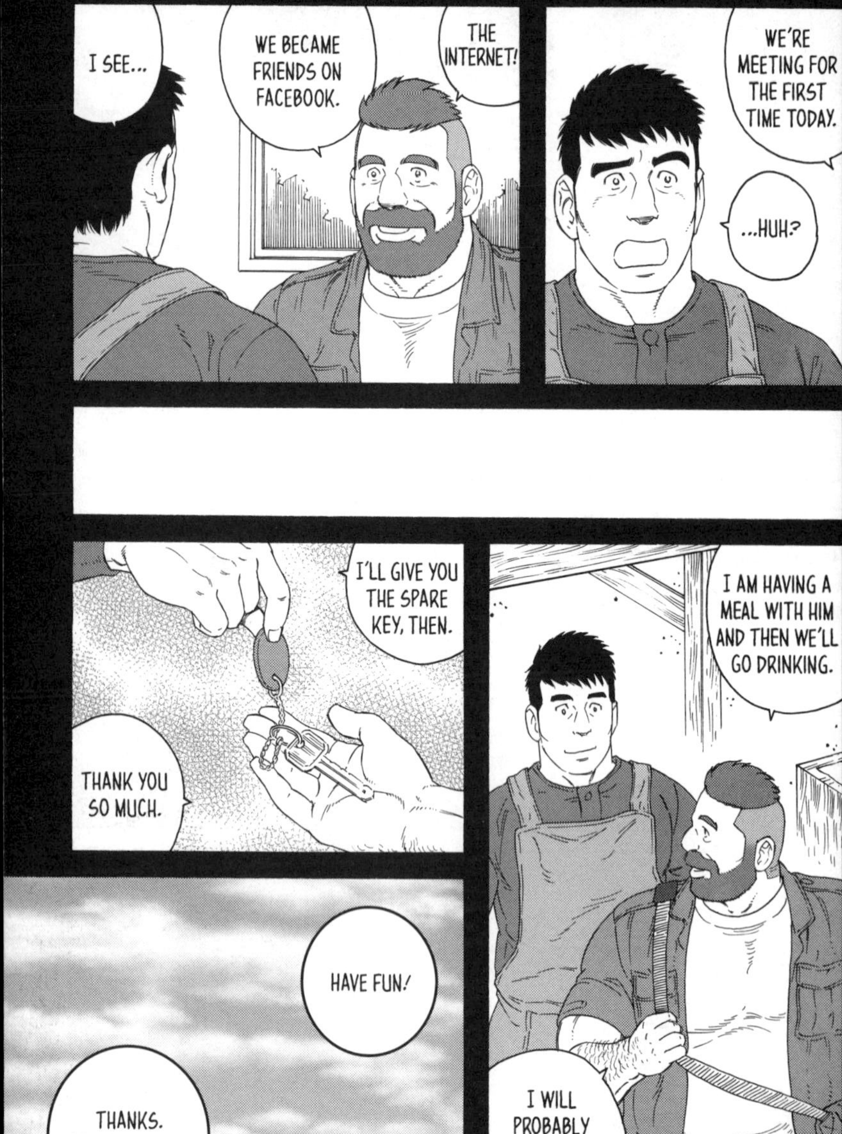
WE'RE MEETING FOR THE FIRST TIME TODAY.
...HUH?
THE INTERNET!
WE BECAME FRIENDS ON FACEBOOK.
I SEE...
I AM HAVING A MEAL WITH HIM AND THEN WE'LL GO DRINKING.
I WILL PROBABLY COME HOME LATE.
I'LL GIVE YOU THE SPARE KEY, THEN.
THANK YOU SO MUCH.
HAVE FUN!
THANKS. SEE YOU LATER!

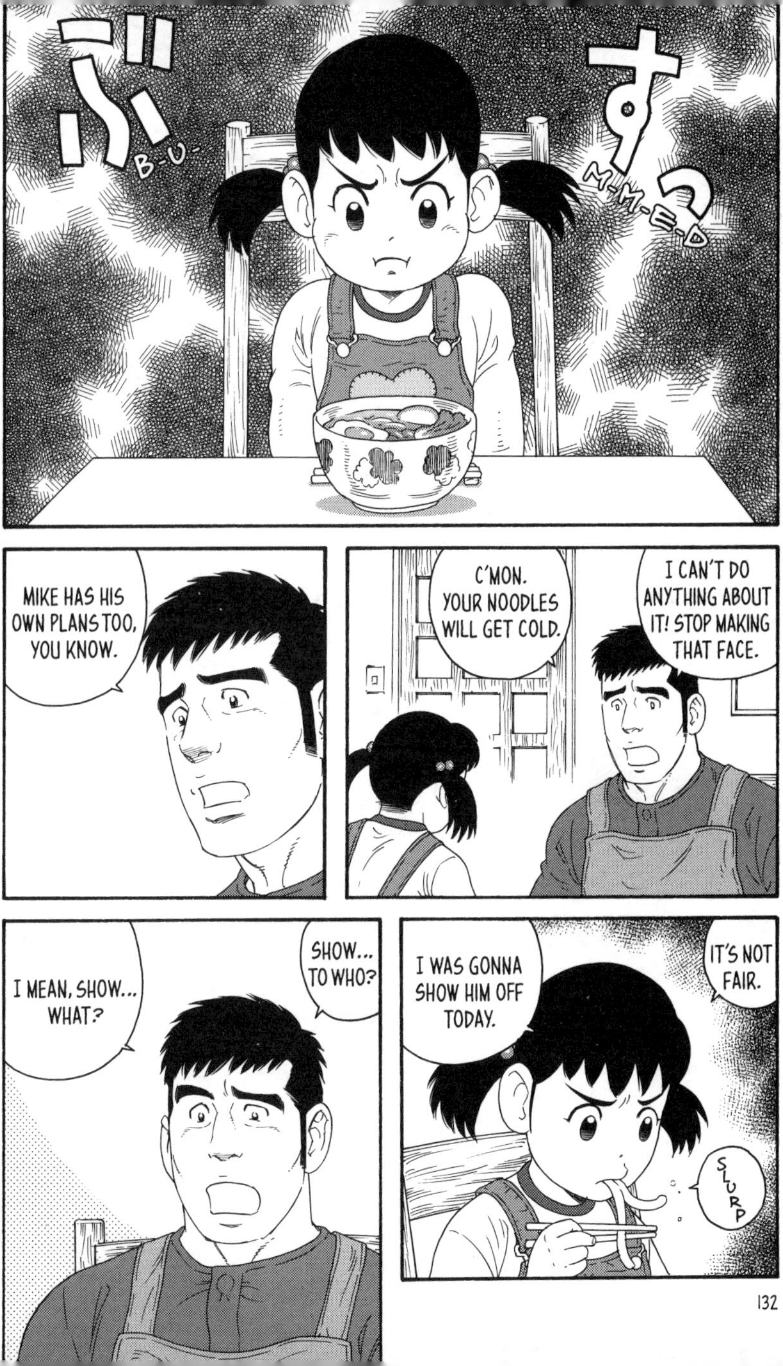
すっ
M-M-E-D
ぶー
B-U-
I CAN'T DO ANYTHING ABOUT IT! STOP MAKING THAT FACE.
C'MON. YOUR NOODLES WILL GET COLD.
MIKE HAS HIS OWN PLANS TOO, YOU KNOW.
IT'S NOT FAIR.
I WAS GONNA SHOW HIM OFF TODAY.
SLURP
SHOW... TO WHO?
I MEAN, SHOW... WHAT?

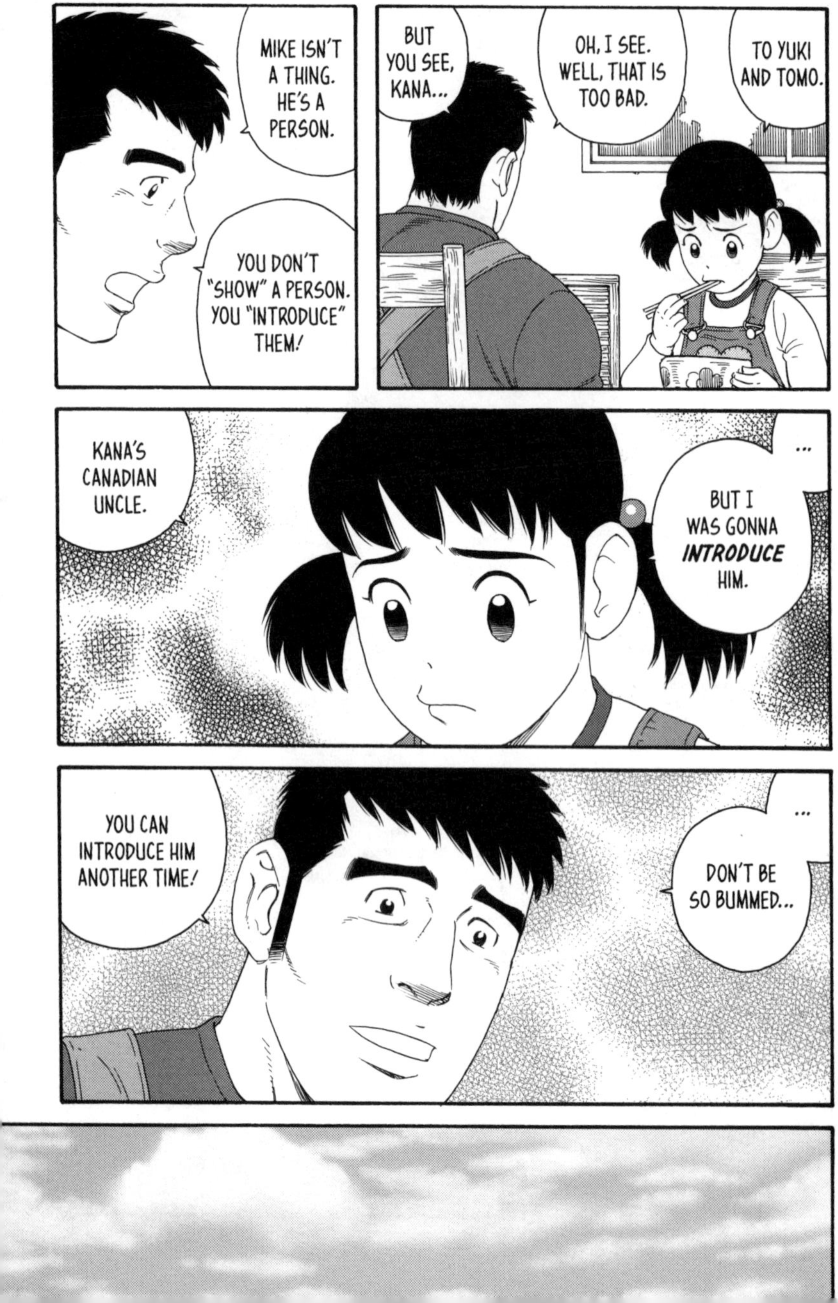
TO YUKI AND TOMO.
OH, I SEE. WELL, THAT IS TOO BAD.
BUT YOU SEE, KANA...
MIKE ISN'T A THING. HE'S A PERSON.
YOU DON'T "SHOW" A PERSON. YOU "INTRODUCE" THEM!
...
BUT I WAS GONNA ***INTRODUCE*** HIM.
KANA'S CANADIAN UNCLE.
...
DON'T BE SO BUMMED...
YOU CAN INTRODUCE HIM ANOTHER TIME!

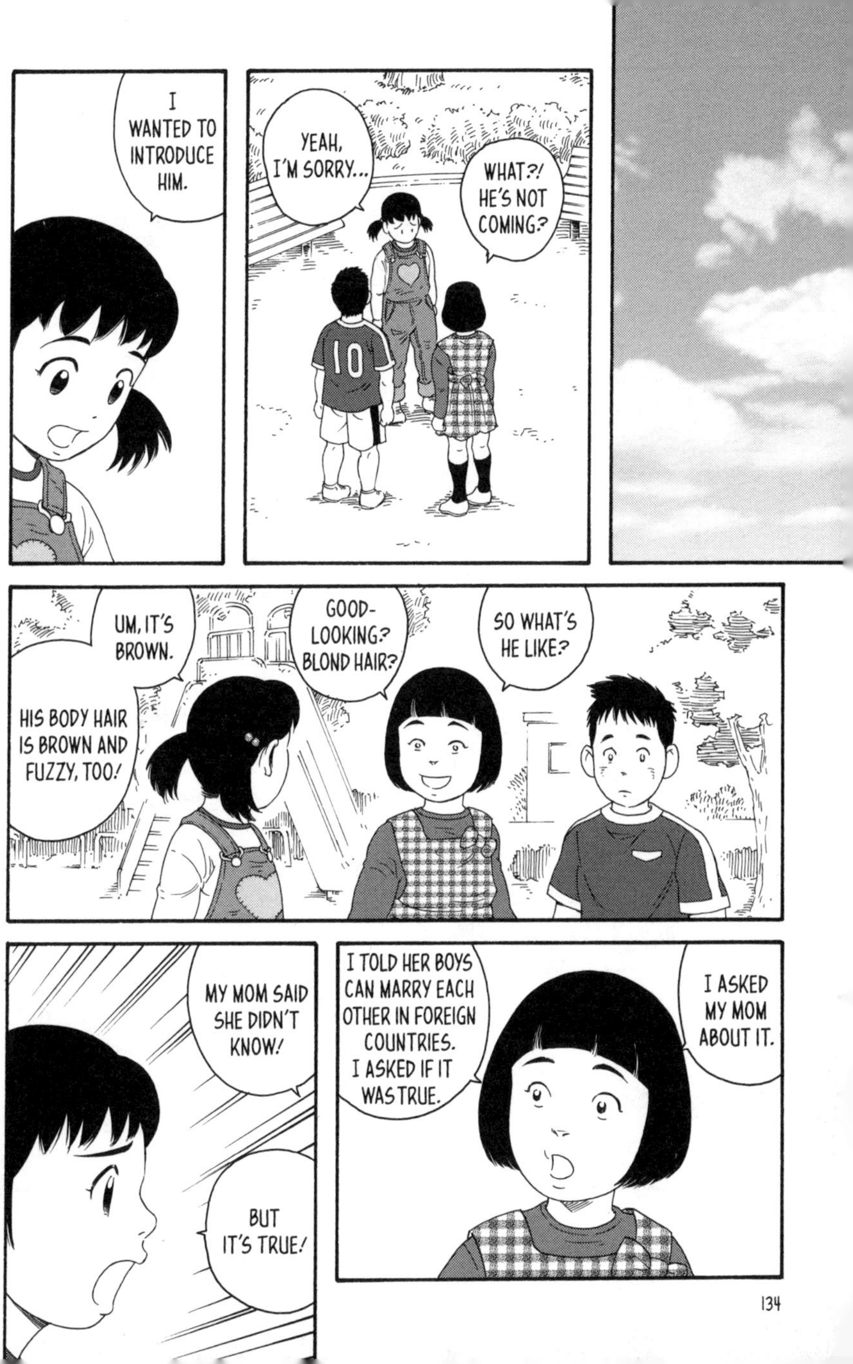
WHAT?! HE'S NOT COMING?
YEAH, I'M SORRY...
I WANTED TO INTRODUCE HIM.
SO WHAT'S HE LIKE?
GOOD-LOOKING? BLOND HAIR?
UM, IT'S BROWN.
HIS BODY HAIR IS BROWN AND FUZZY, TOO!
I ASKED MY MOM ABOUT IT.
I TOLD HER BOYS CAN MARRY EACH OTHER IN FOREIGN COUNTRIES. I ASKED IF IT WAS TRUE.
MY MOM SAID SHE DIDN'T KNOW!
BUT IT'S TRUE!

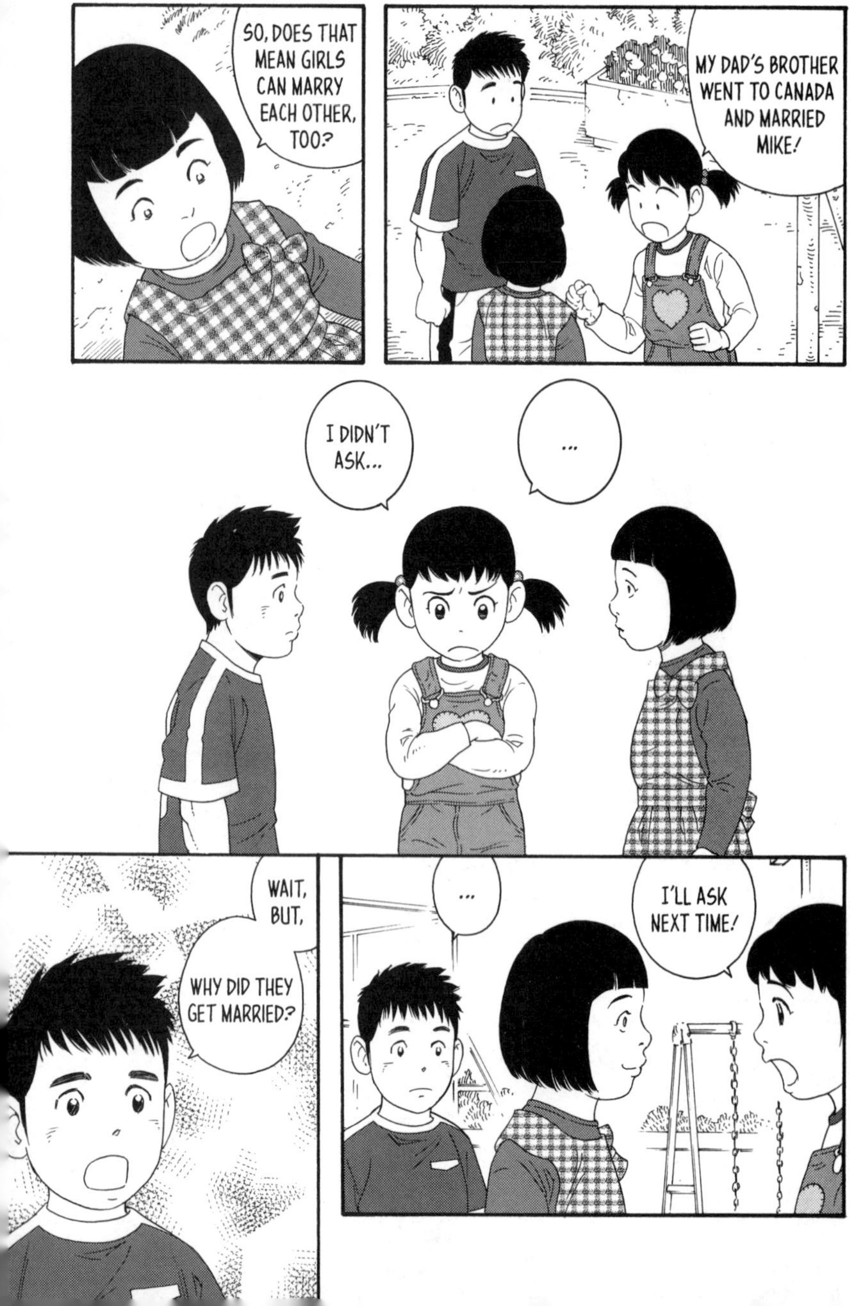
MY DAD'S BROTHER WENT TO CANADA AND MARRIED MIKE!
SO, DOES THAT MEAN GIRLS CAN MARRY EACH OTHER, TOO?
...
I DIDN'T ASK...
I'LL ASK NEXT TIME!
...
WAIT, BUT,
WHY DID THEY GET MARRIED?

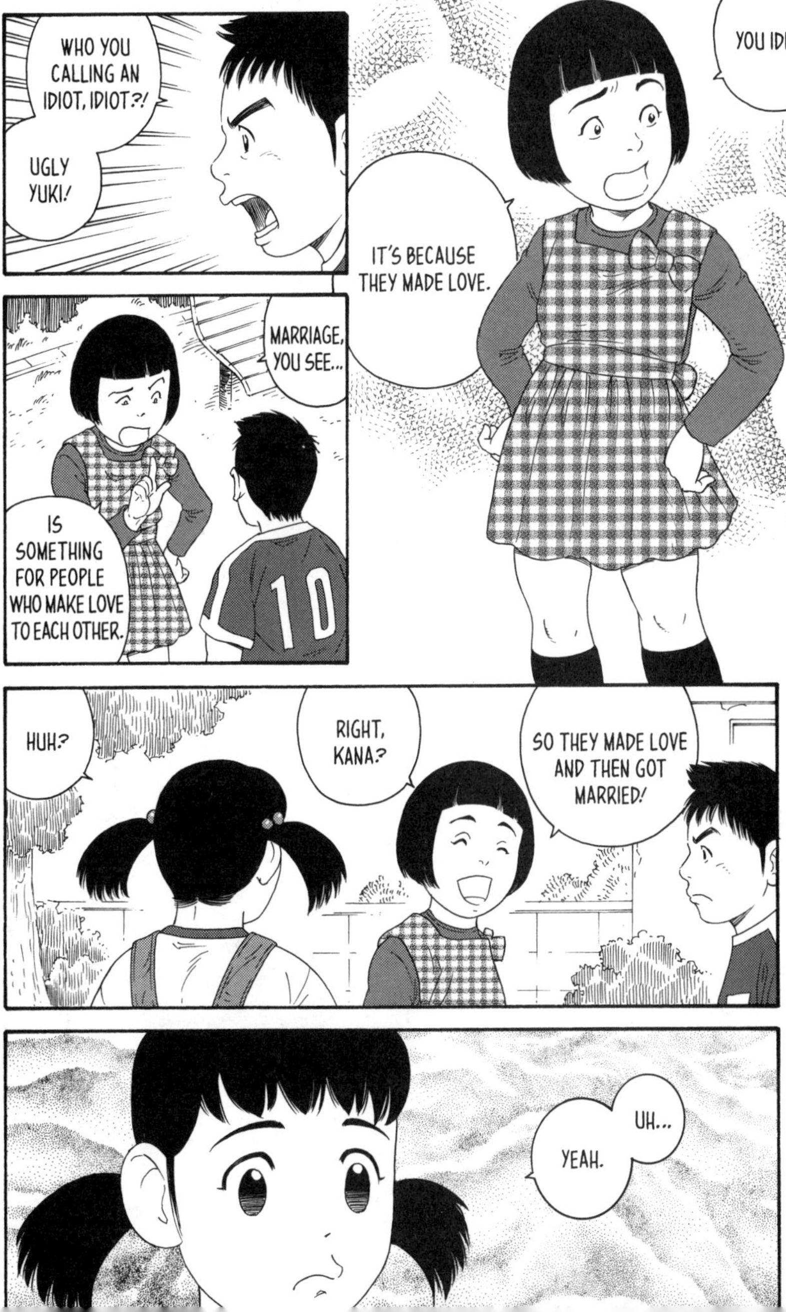
YOU IDIOT.
IT'S BECAUSE THEY MADE LOVE.
WHO YOU CALLING AN IDIOT, IDIOT?!
UGLY YUKI!
MARRIAGE, YOU SEE...
IS SOMETHING FOR PEOPLE WHO MAKE LOVE TO EACH OTHER.
SO THEY MADE LOVE AND THEN GOT MARRIED!
RIGHT, KANA?
HUH?
UH...
YEAH.

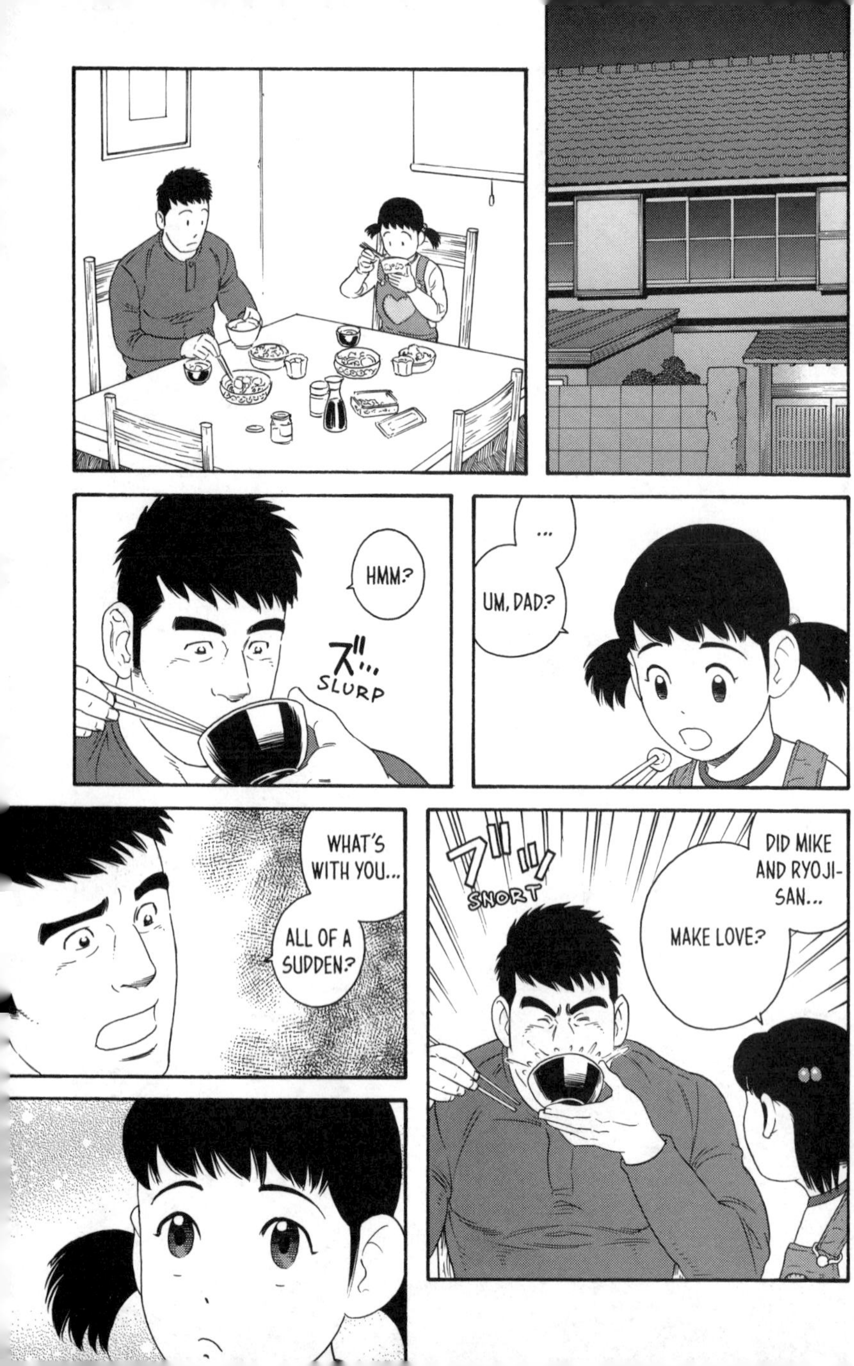
...
UM, DAD?
HMM?
ズ...
SLURP
DID MIKE AND RYOJI-SAN...
MAKE LOVE?
ブッ
SNORT
WHAT'S WITH YOU...
ALL OF A SUDDEN?

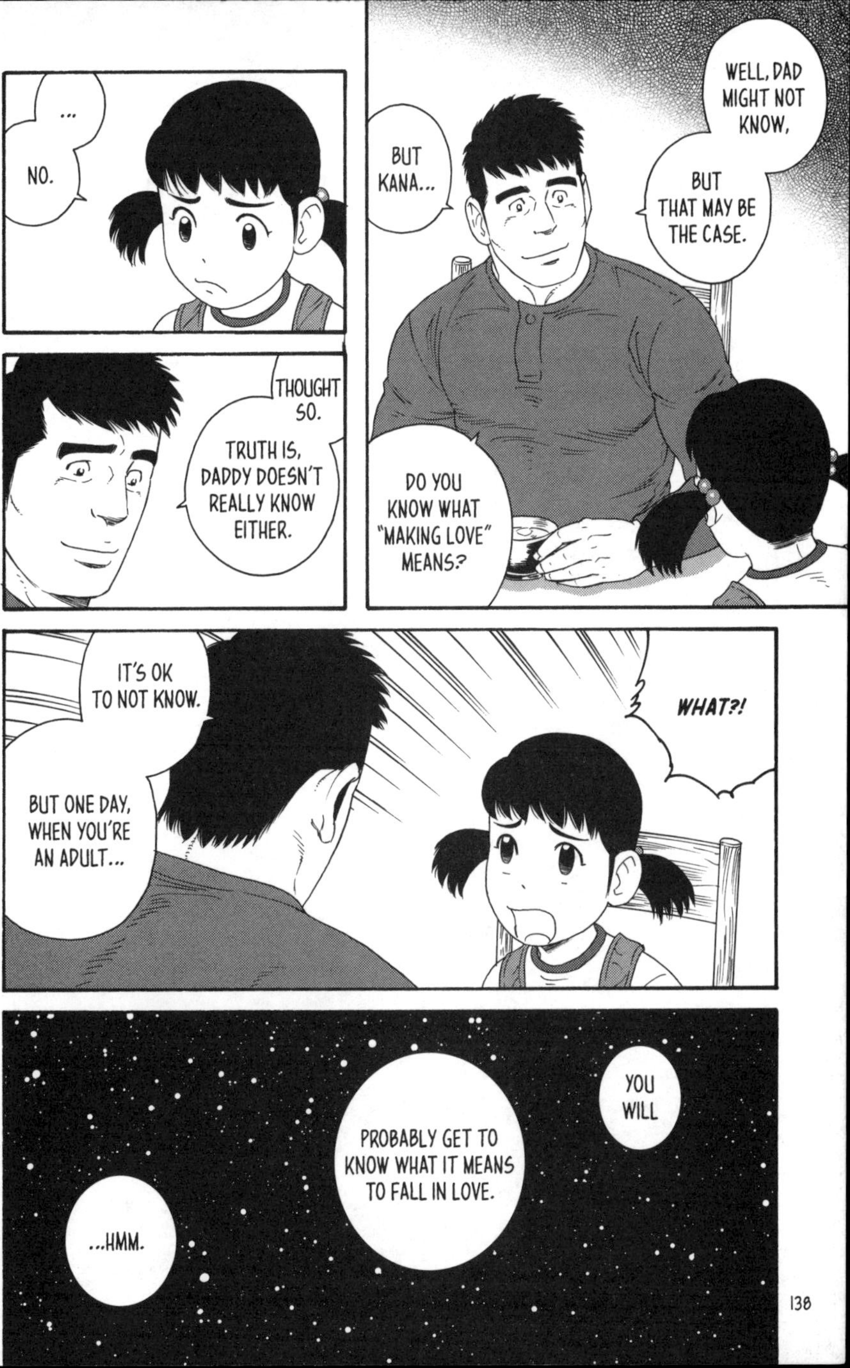
WELL, DAD MIGHT NOT KNOW,
BUT THAT MAY BE THE CASE.
BUT KANA...
DO YOU KNOW WHAT "MAKING LOVE" MEANS?
...
NO.
THOUGHT SO.
TRUTH IS, DADDY DOESN'T REALLY KNOW EITHER.
WHAT?!
IT'S OK TO NOT KNOW.
BUT ONE DAY, WHEN YOU'RE AN ADULT...
YOU WILL
PROBABLY GET TO KNOW WHAT IT MEANS TO FALL IN LOVE.
...HMM.

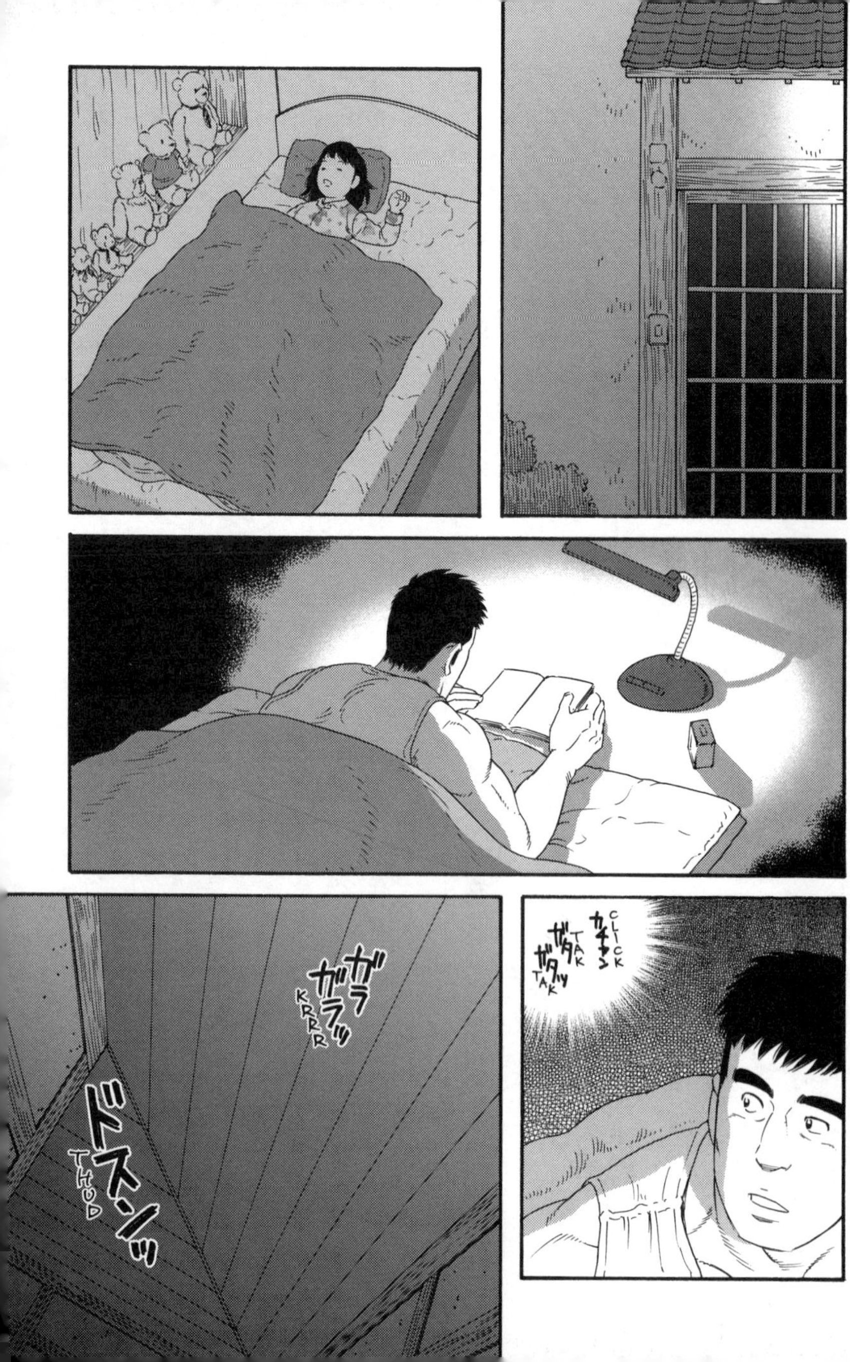
カチャン
CLICK
ガタ
TAK
ガタッ
TAK
ガラ
ガラッ
KRRRR
ドスンッ
THUD

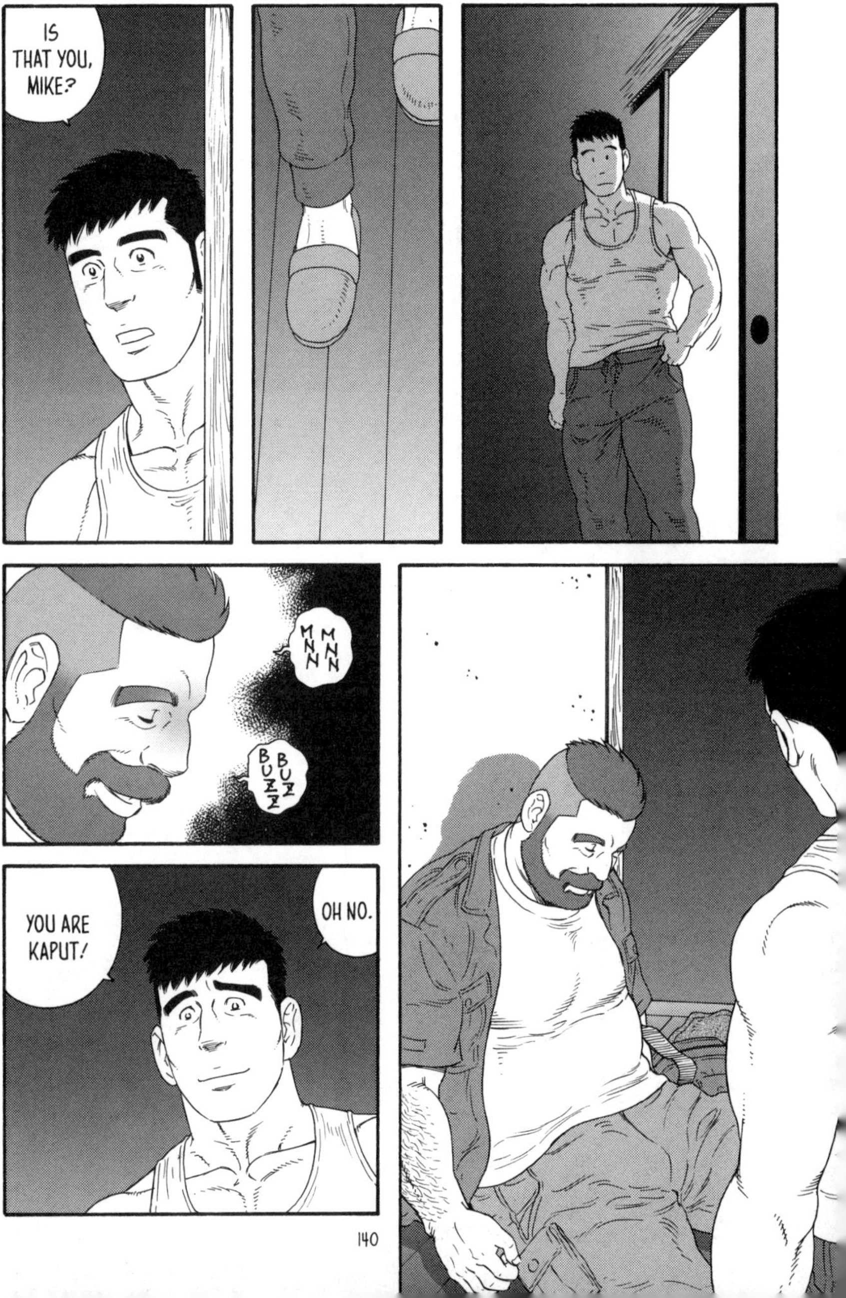
IS THAT YOU, MIKE?
MNN MNN
BUZZ BUZZ
OH NO.
YOU ARE KAPUT!

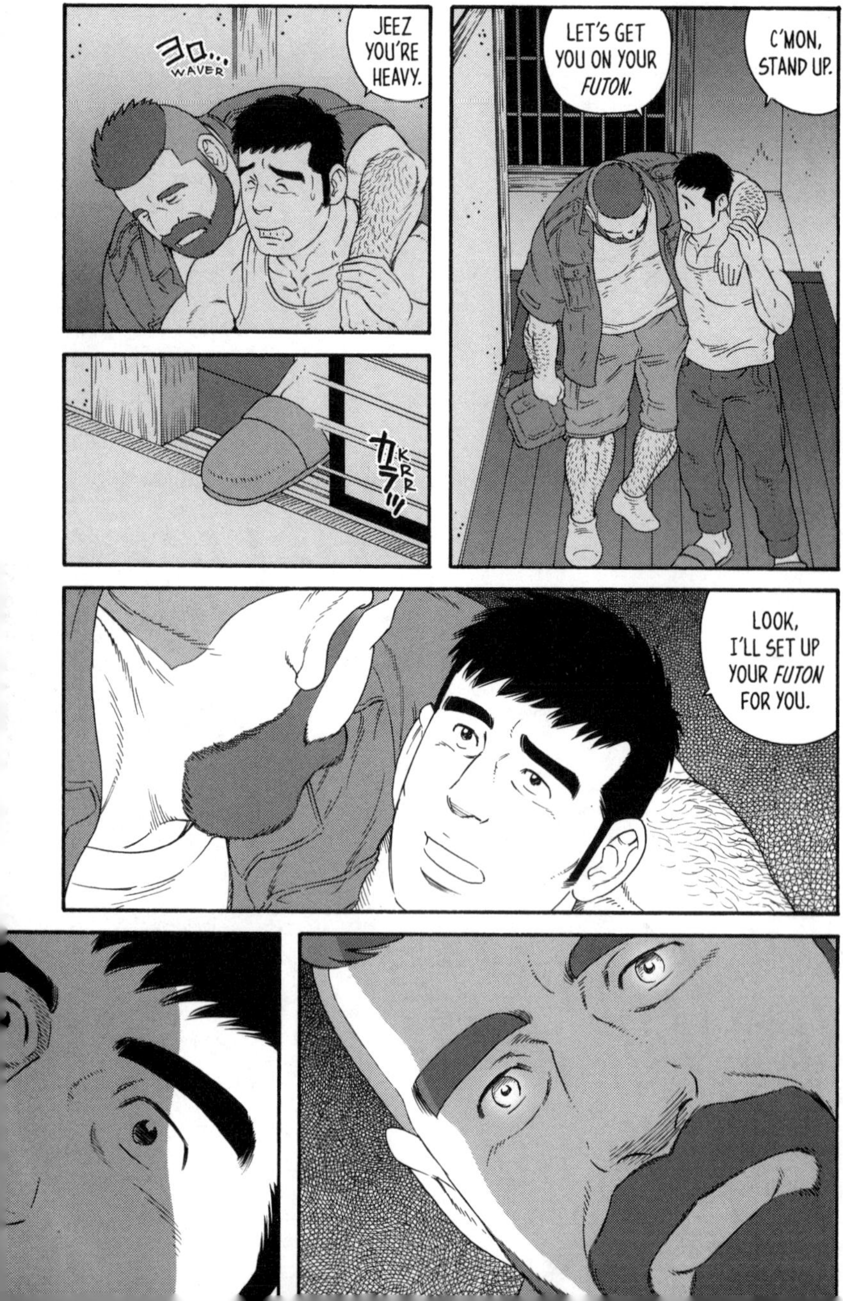
C'MON, STAND UP.
LET'S GET YOU ON YOUR *FUTON.*
JEEZ YOU'RE HEAVY.
ヨロ… WAVER
カラッ KRR
LOOK, I'LL SET UP YOUR *FUTON* FOR YOU.

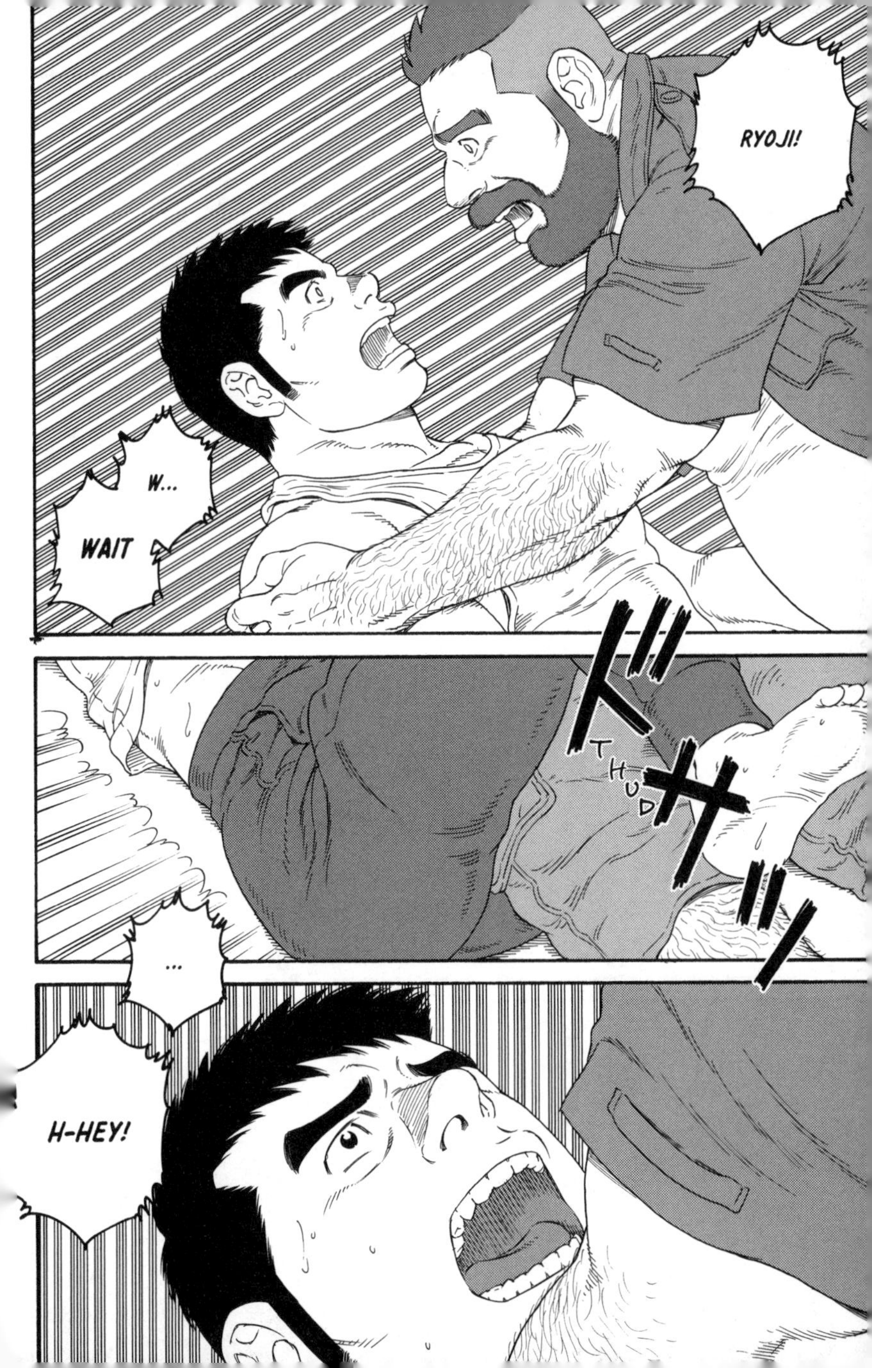
RYOJI!
W...
WAIT
ドサッ
THUD
...
H-HEY!

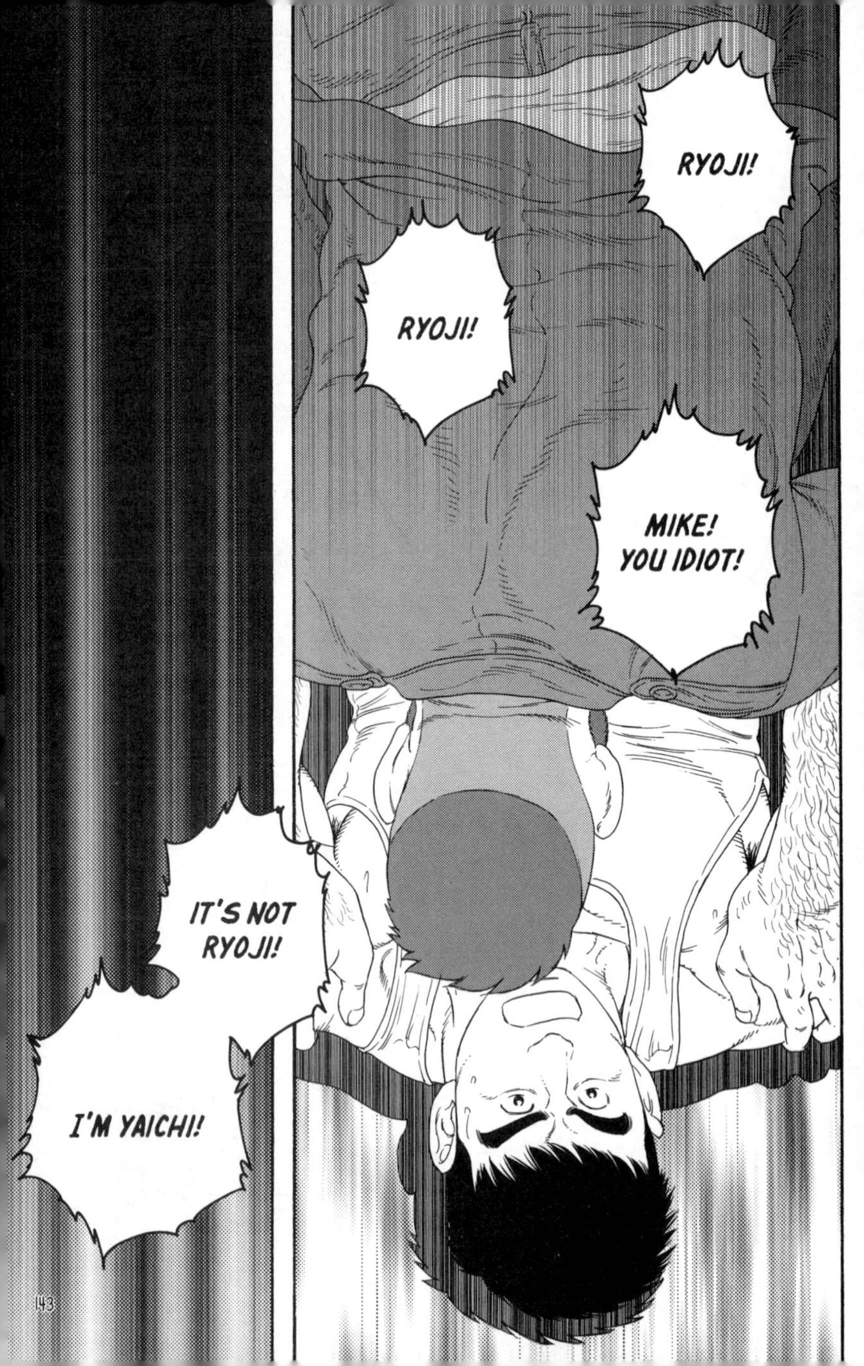
RYOJI!
RYOJI!
MIKE! YOU IDIOT!
IT'S NOT RYOJI!
I'M YAICHI!

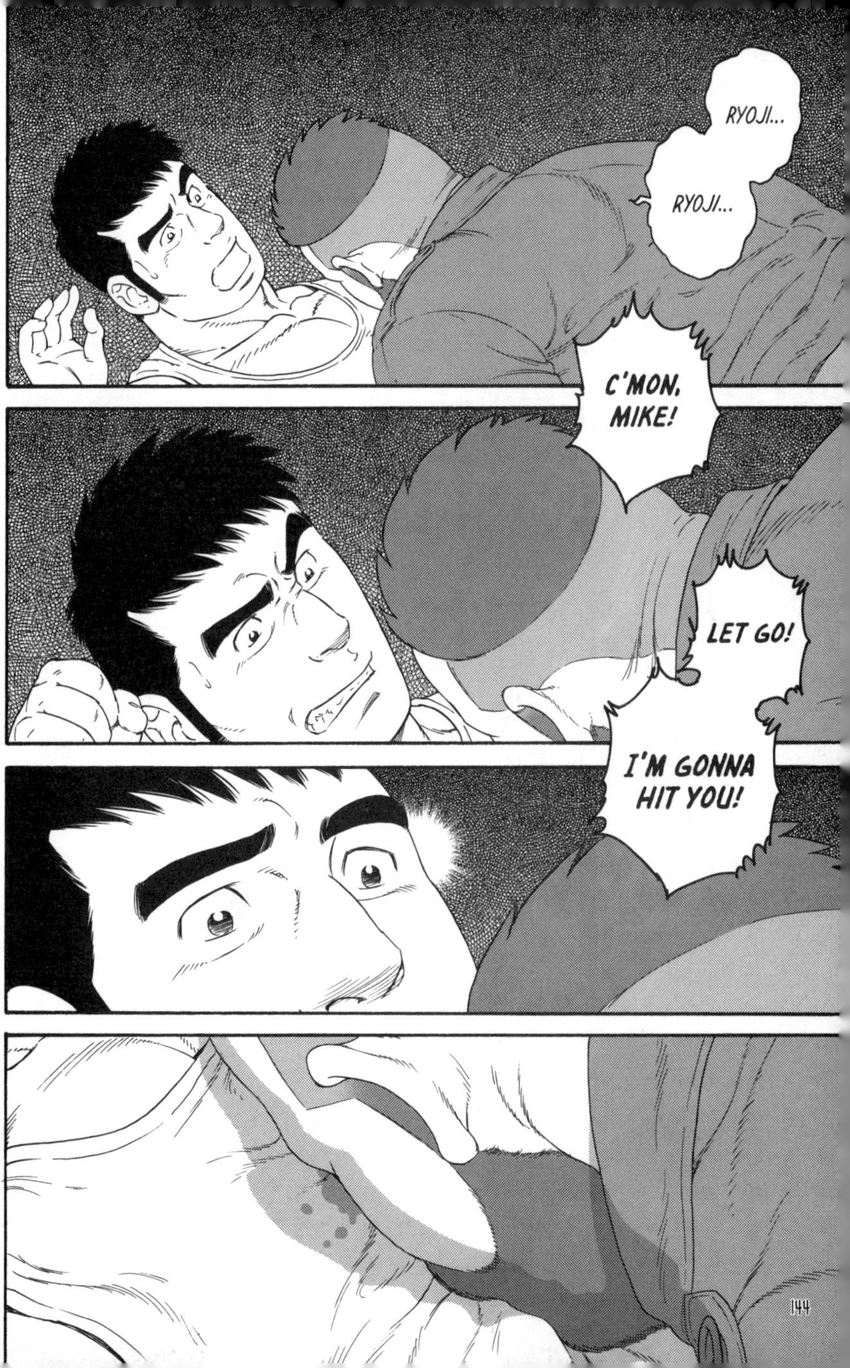
RYOJI...
RYOJI...
C'MON, MIKE!
LET GO!
I'M GONNA HIT YOU!

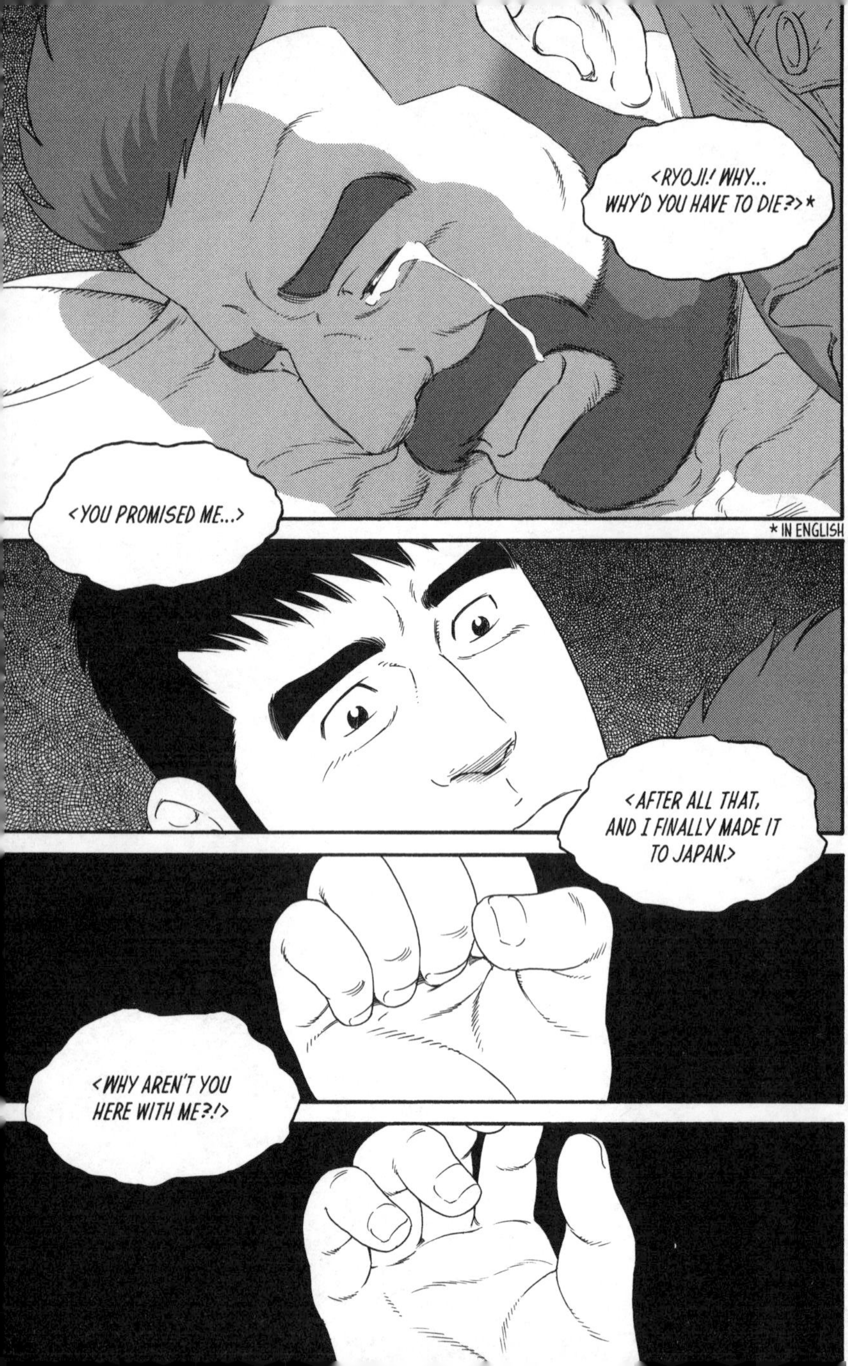
<RYOJI! WHY... WHY'D YOU HAVE TO DIE?>*
<YOU PROMISED ME...>
* IN ENGLISH
<AFTER ALL THAT, AND I FINALLY MADE IT TO JAPAN.>
<WHY AREN'T YOU HERE WITH ME?!>

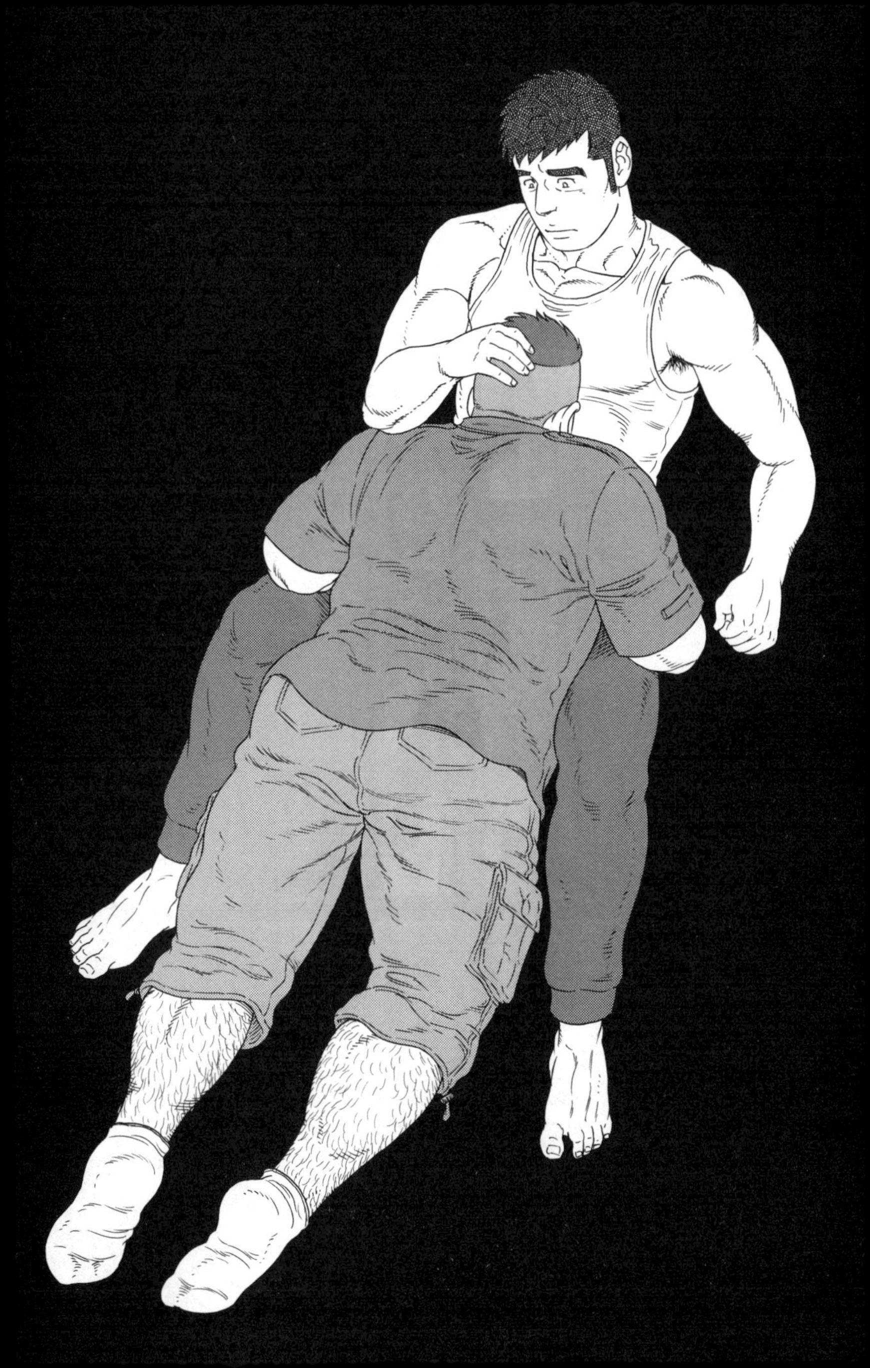

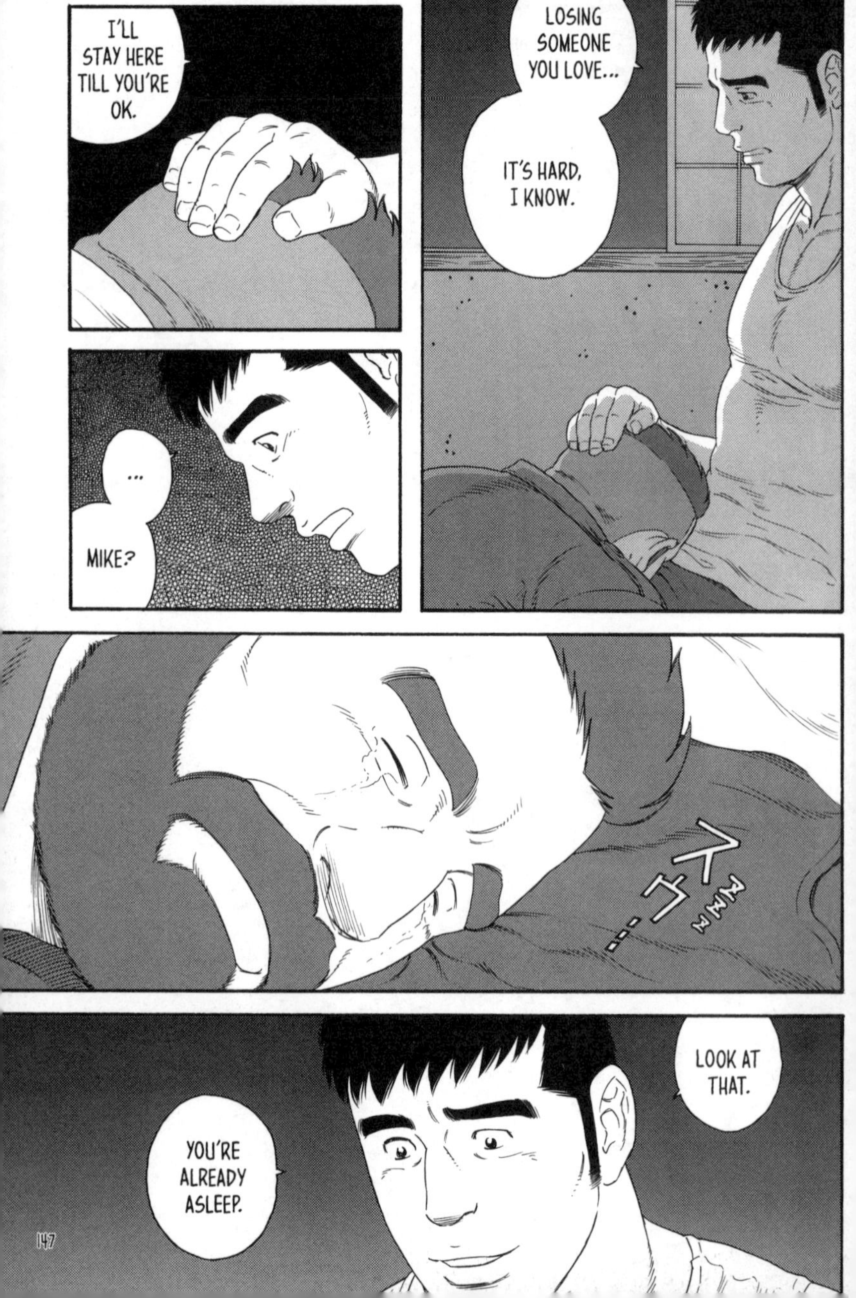
LOSING SOMEONE YOU LOVE...
IT'S HARD, I KNOW.
I'LL STAY HERE TILL YOU'RE OK.
...
MIKE?
LOOK AT THAT.
YOU'RE ALREADY ASLEEP.

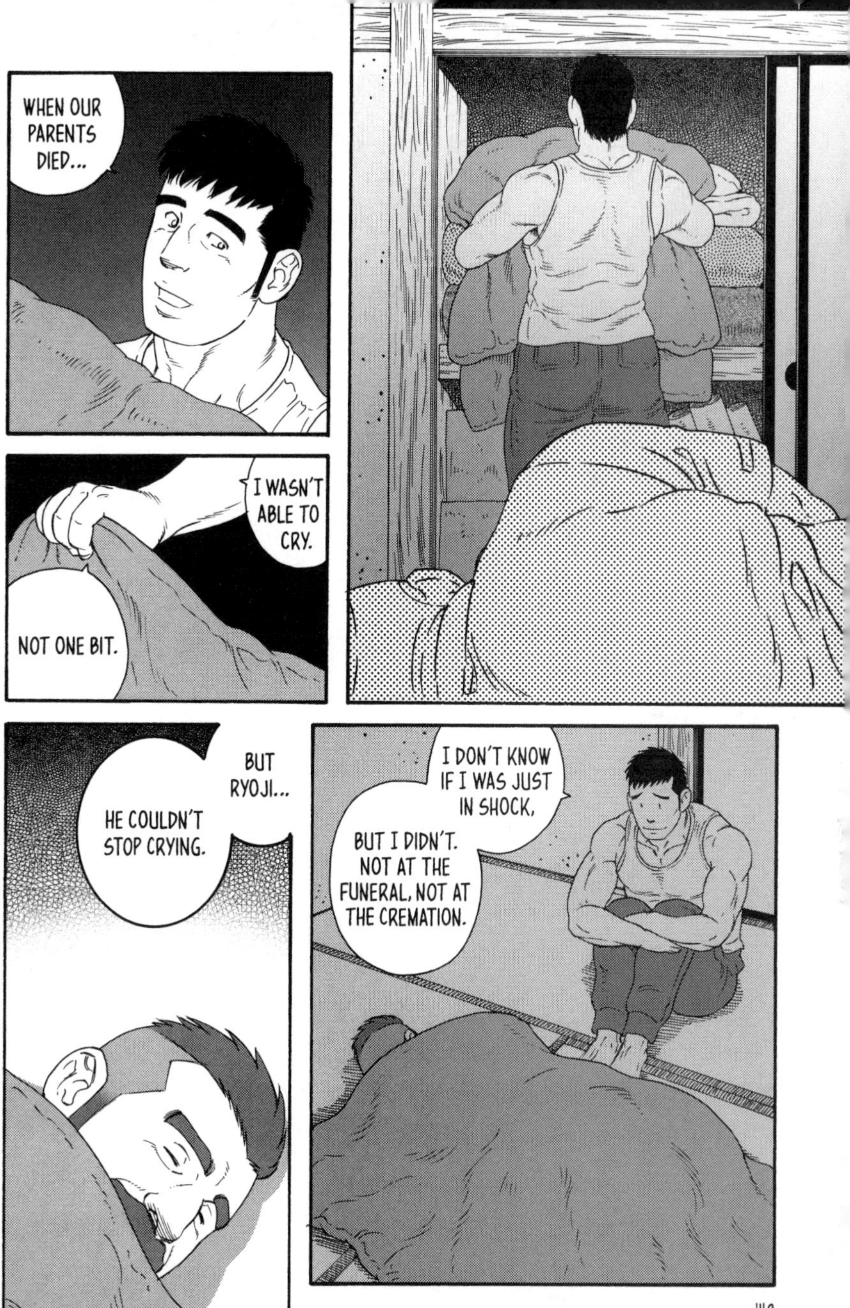
WHEN OUR PARENTS DIED...
I WASN'T ABLE TO CRY.
NOT ONE BIT.
I DON'T KNOW IF I WAS JUST IN SHOCK,
BUT I DIDN'T. NOT AT THE FUNERAL, NOT AT THE CREMATION.
BUT RYOJI...
HE COULDN'T STOP CRYING.

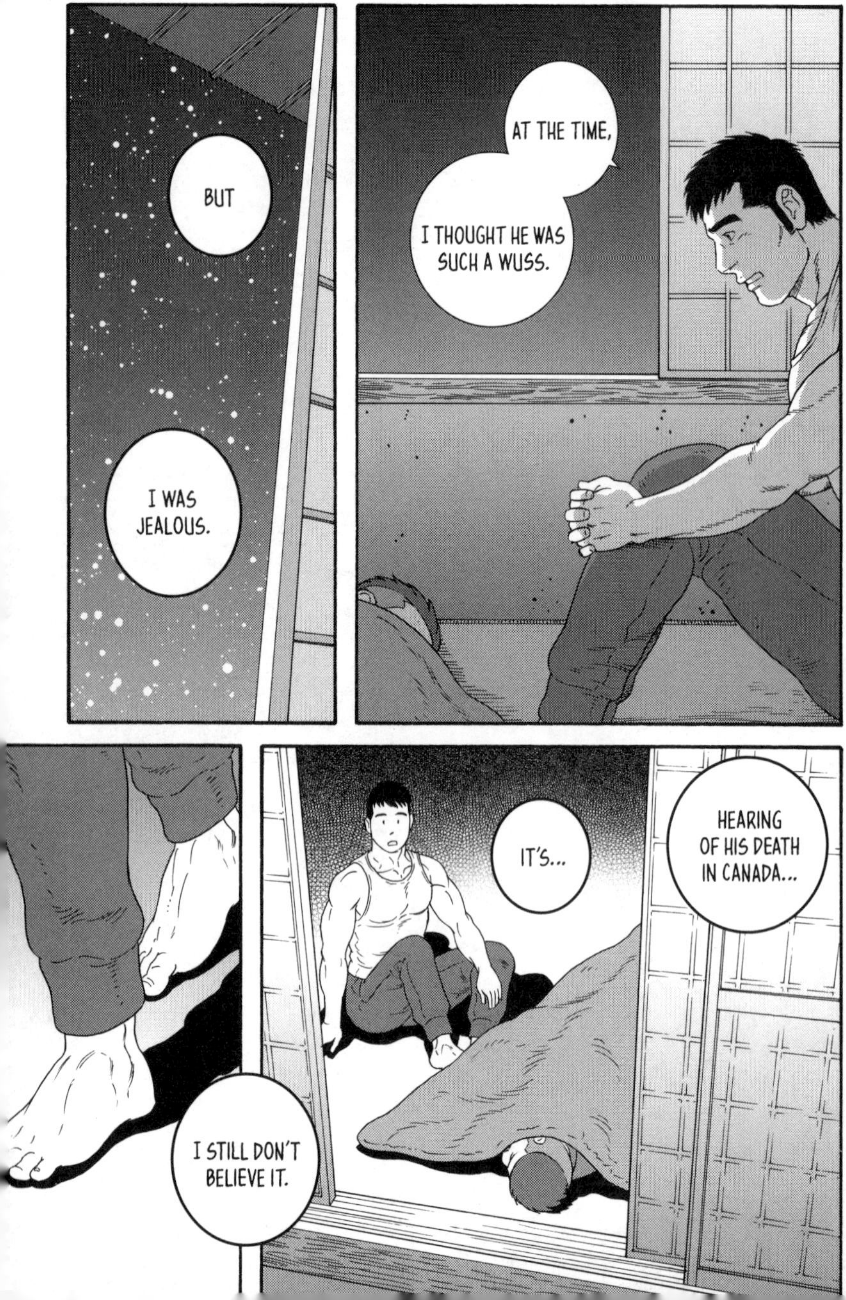
AT THE TIME,
I THOUGHT HE WAS SUCH A WUSS.
BUT
I WAS JEALOUS.
HEARING OF HIS DEATH IN CANADA...
IT'S...
I STILL DON'T BELIEVE IT.

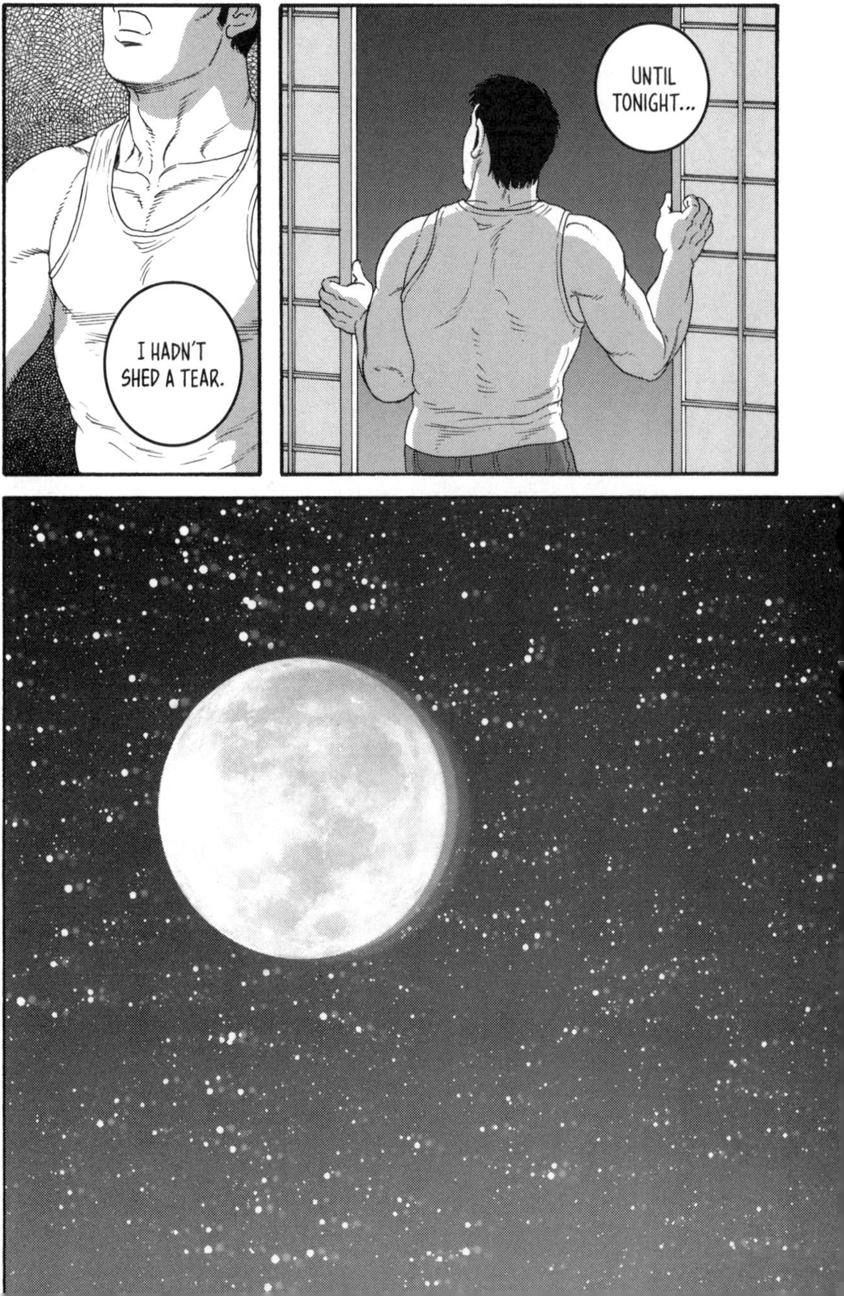
UNTIL TONIGHT...
I HADN'T SHED A TEAR.

CHAPTER SEVEN

MOM

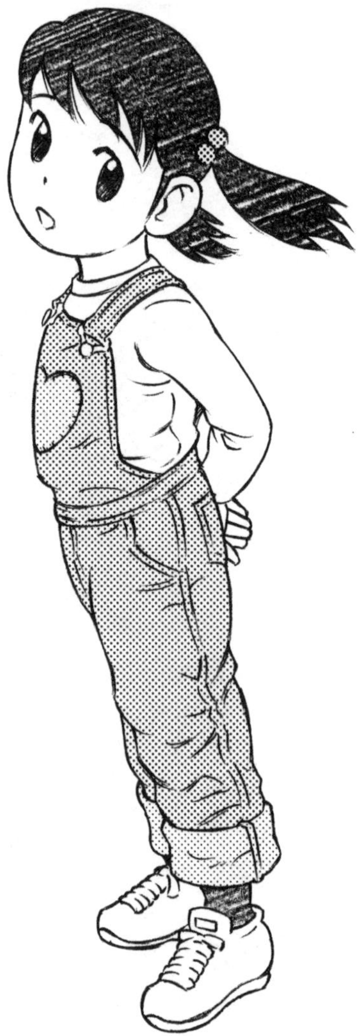

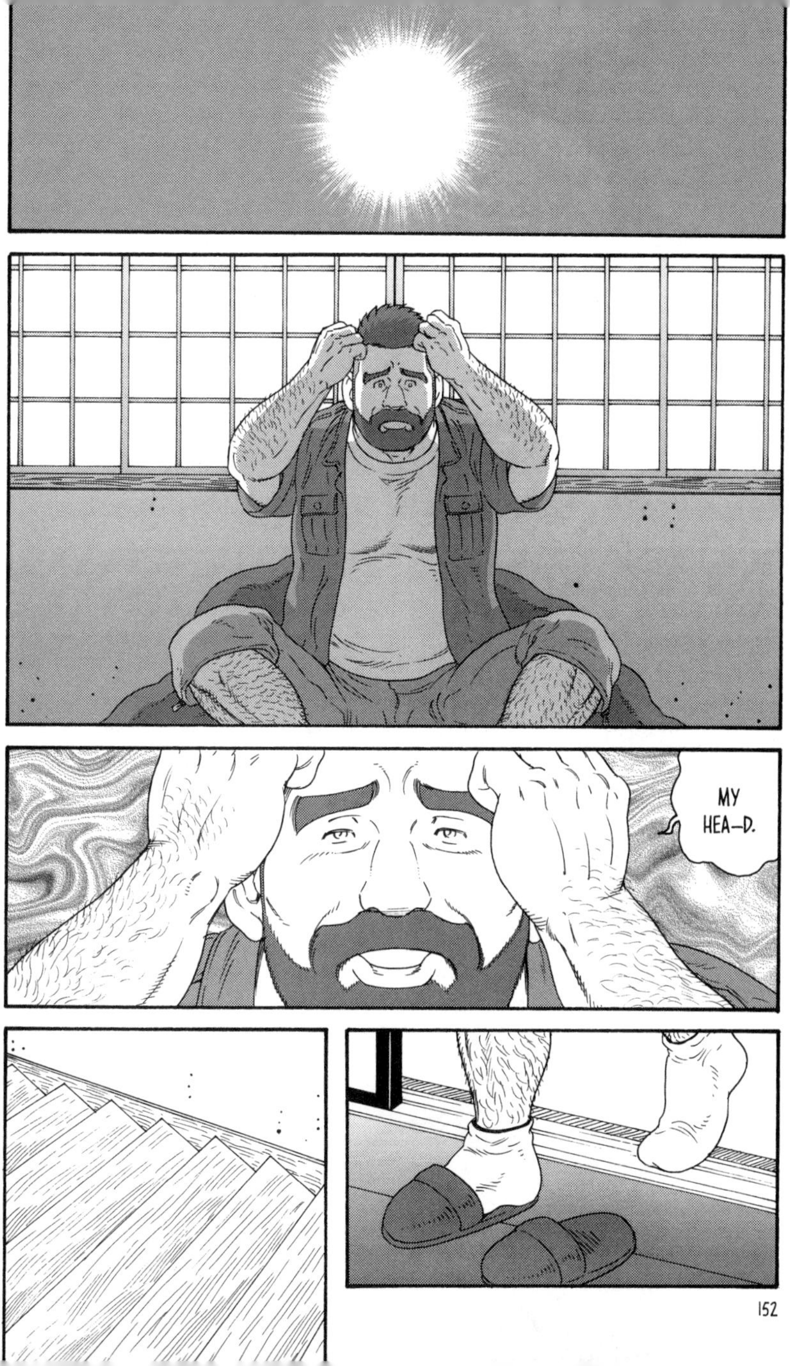
MY HEA—D.

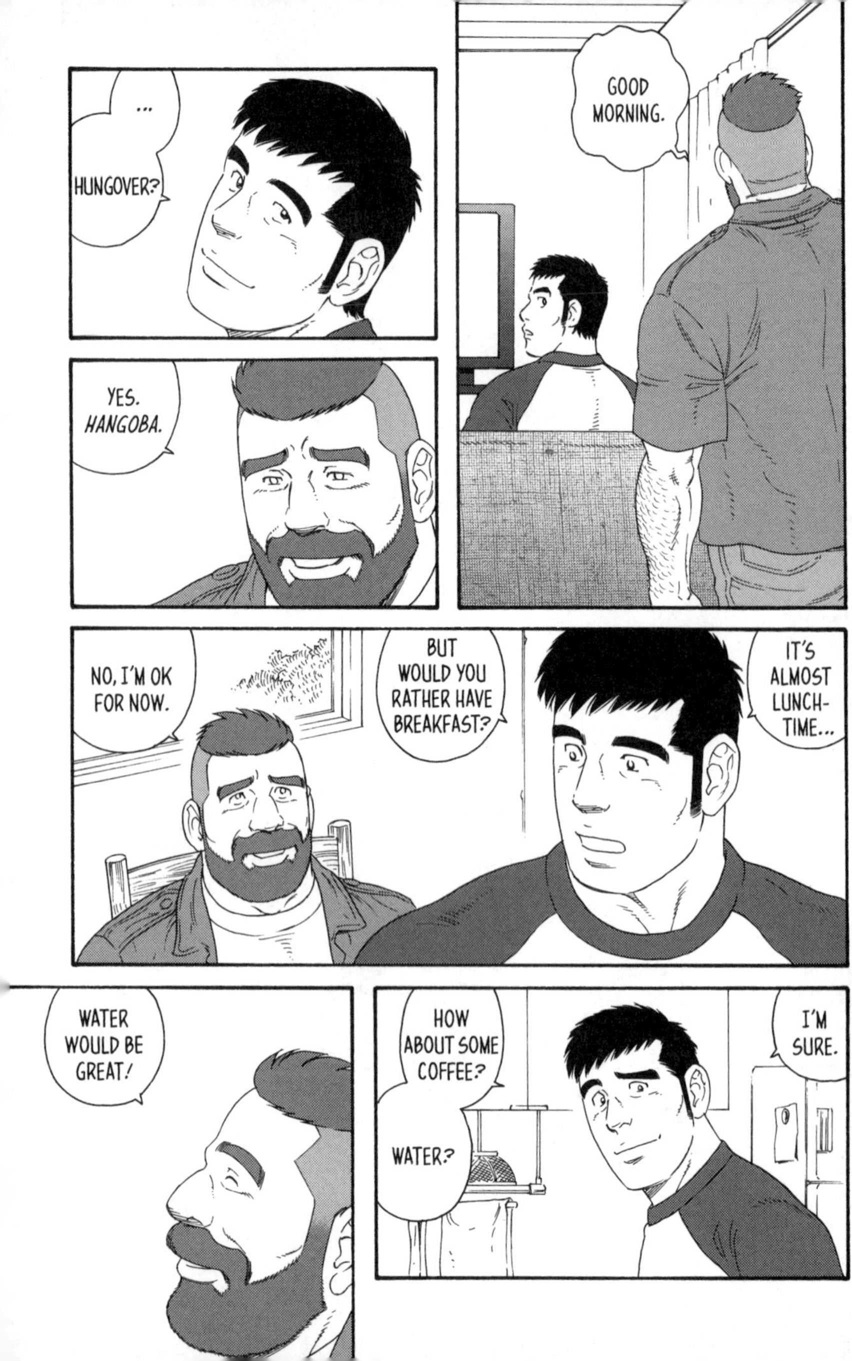
GOOD MORNING.
...
HUNGOVER?
YES. *HANGOBA.*
IT'S ALMOST LUNCH-TIME...
BUT WOULD YOU RATHER HAVE BREAKFAST?
NO, I'M OK FOR NOW.
I'M SURE.
HOW ABOUT SOME COFFEE?
WATER?
WATER WOULD BE GREAT!

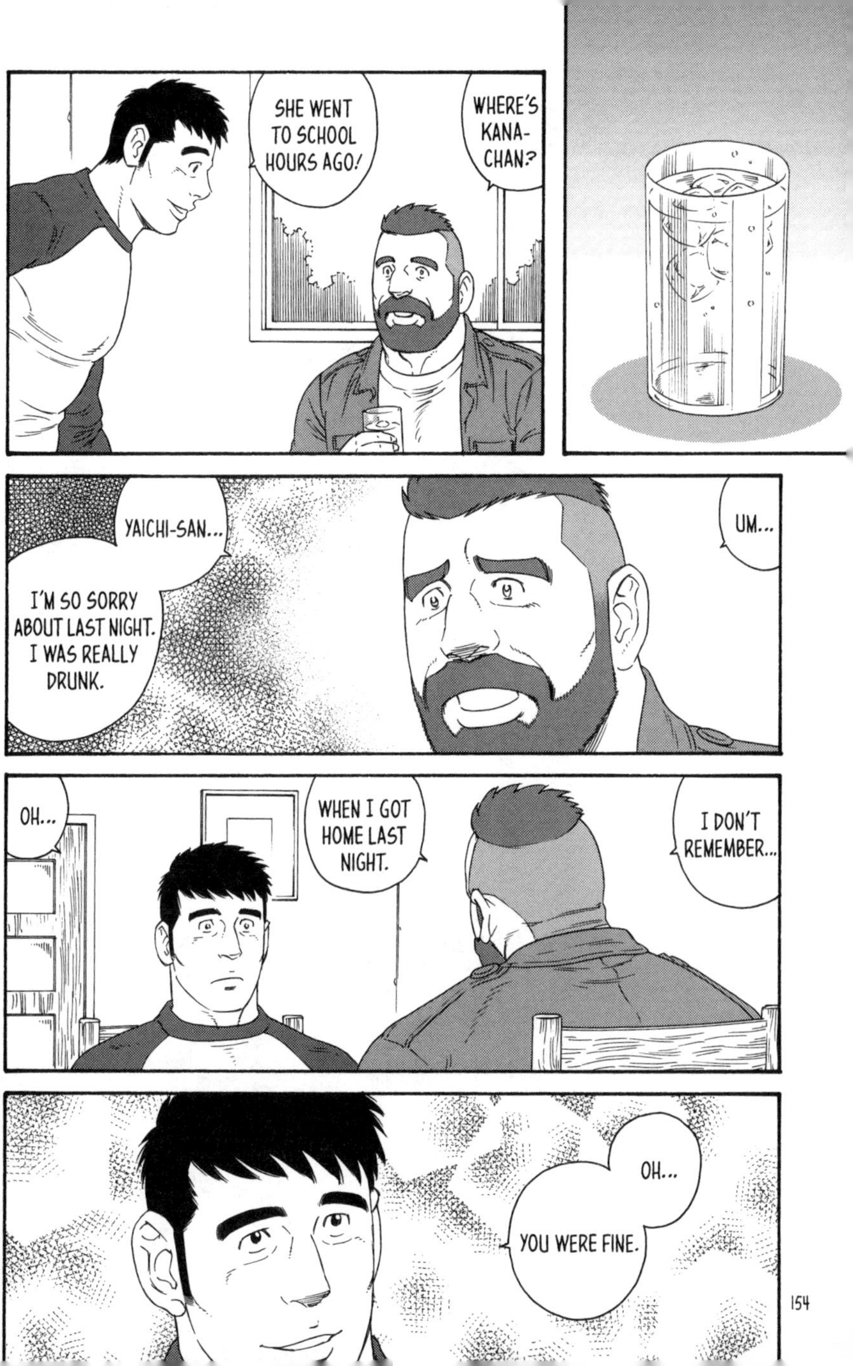
WHERE'S KANA-CHAN?
SHE WENT TO SCHOOL HOURS AGO!
UM...
YAICHI-SAN...
I'M SO SORRY ABOUT LAST NIGHT. I WAS REALLY DRUNK.
I DON'T REMEMBER...
WHEN I GOT HOME LAST NIGHT.
OH...
OH...
YOU WERE FINE.

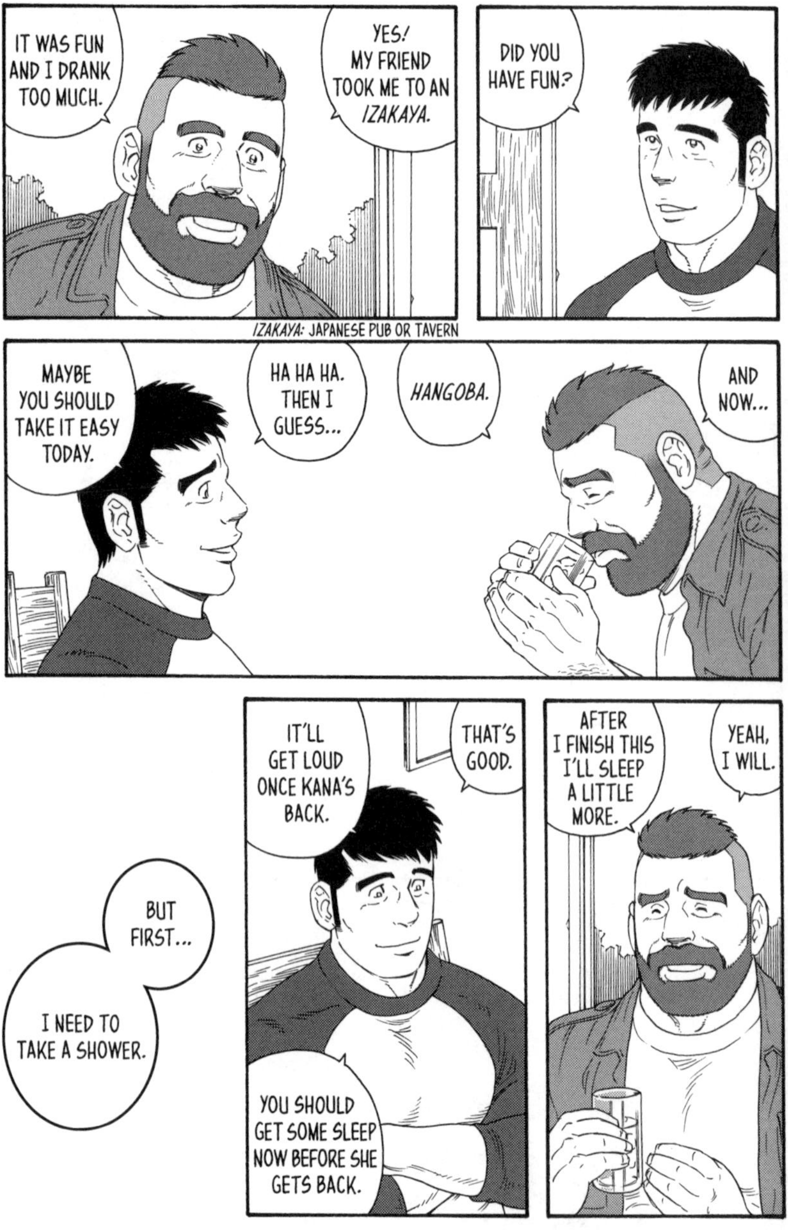
DID YOU HAVE FUN?
YES! MY FRIEND TOOK ME TO AN *IZAKAYA.*
IT WAS FUN AND I DRANK TOO MUCH.
AND NOW...
HANGOBA.
HA HA HA. THEN I GUESS...
MAYBE YOU SHOULD TAKE IT EASY TODAY.
YEAH, I WILL.
AFTER I FINISH THIS I'LL SLEEP A LITTLE MORE.
THAT'S GOOD.
IT'LL GET LOUD ONCE KANA'S BACK.
YOU SHOULD GET SOME SLEEP NOW BEFORE SHE GETS BACK.
BUT FIRST...
I NEED TO TAKE A SHOWER.

IZAKAYA: JAPANESE PUB OR TAVERN

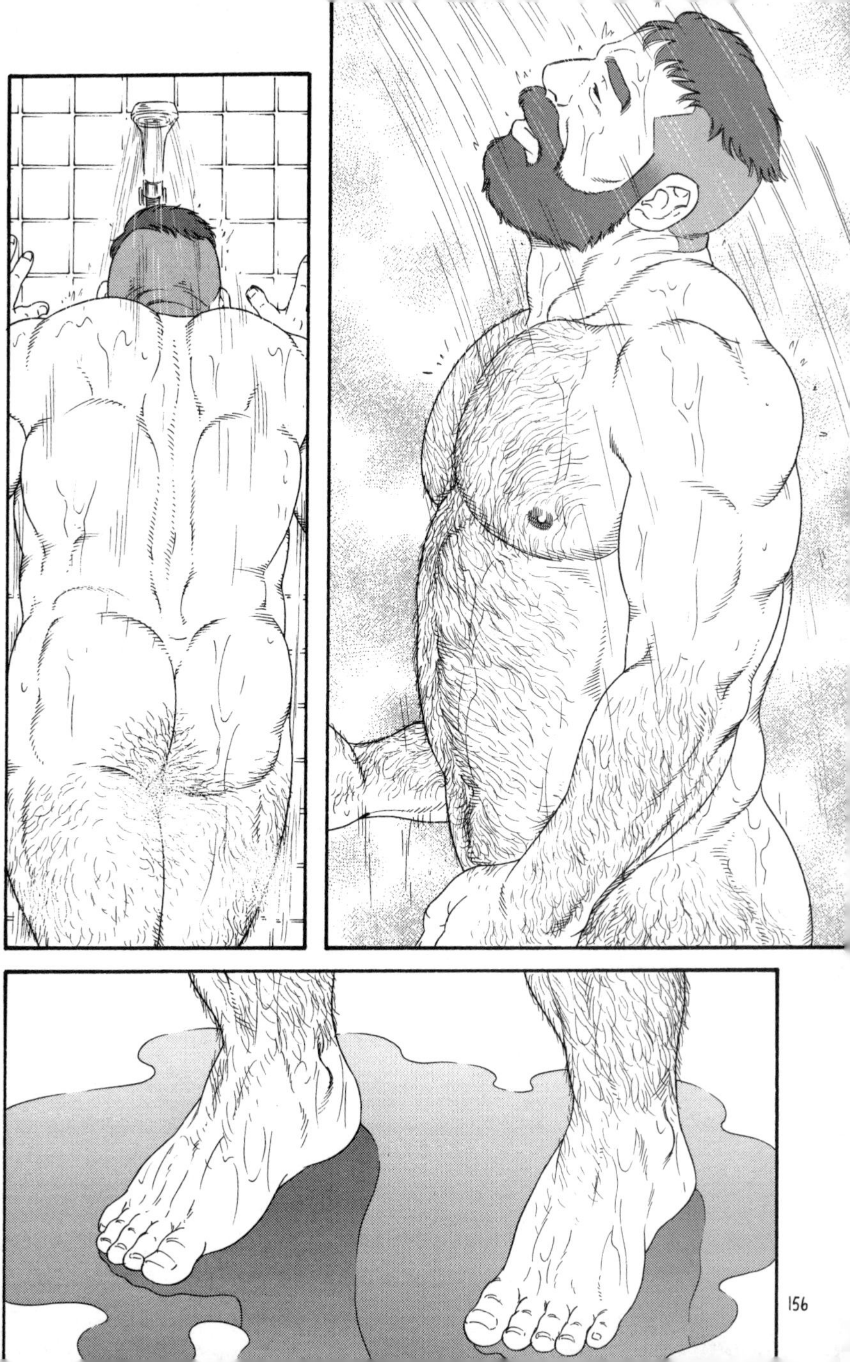

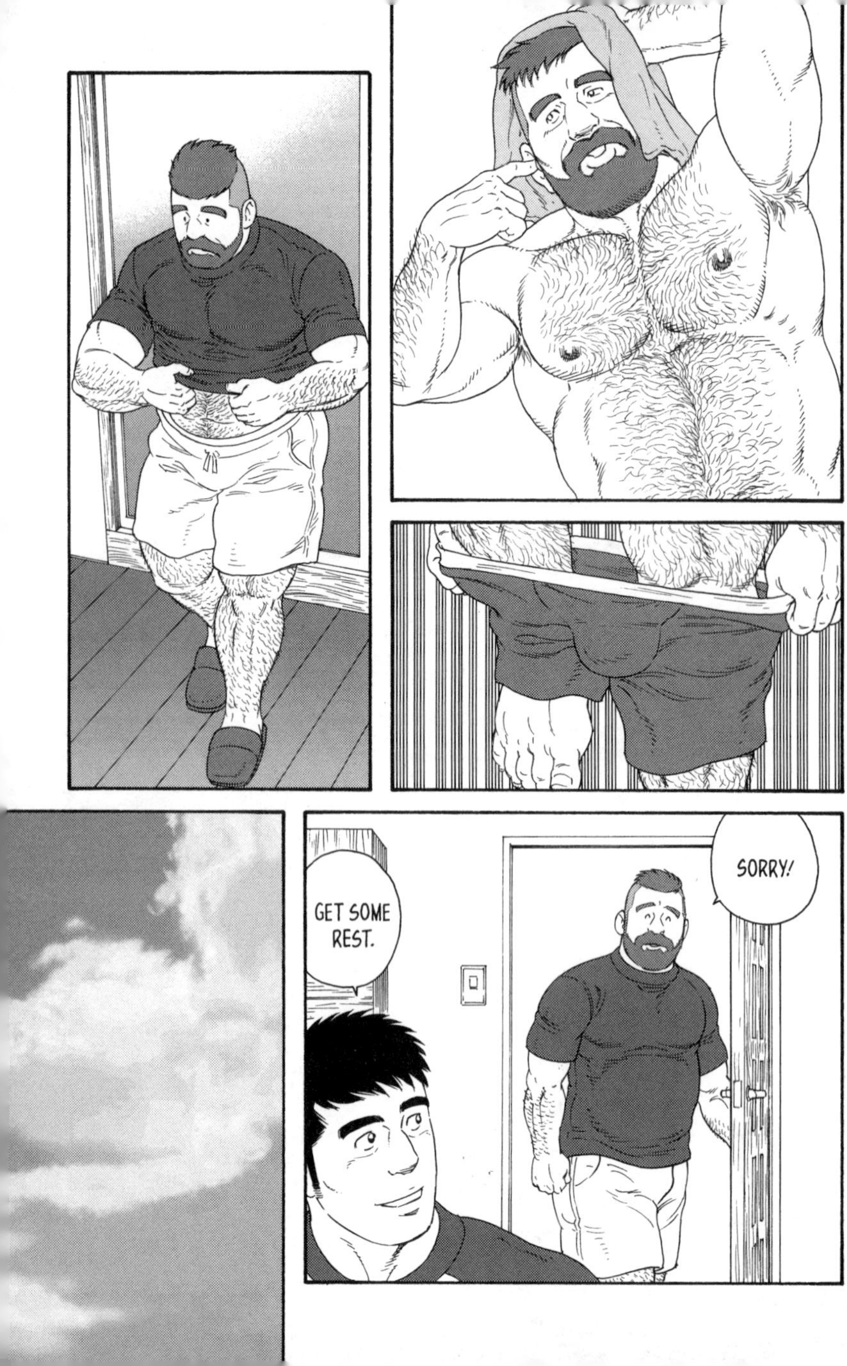
SORRY!
GET SOME REST.

KRRR
SHUT

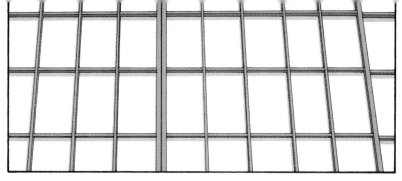

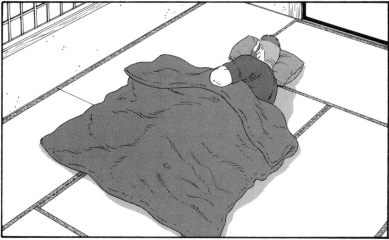

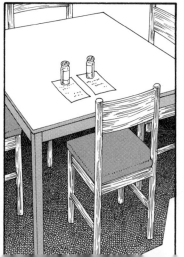

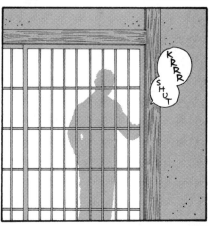

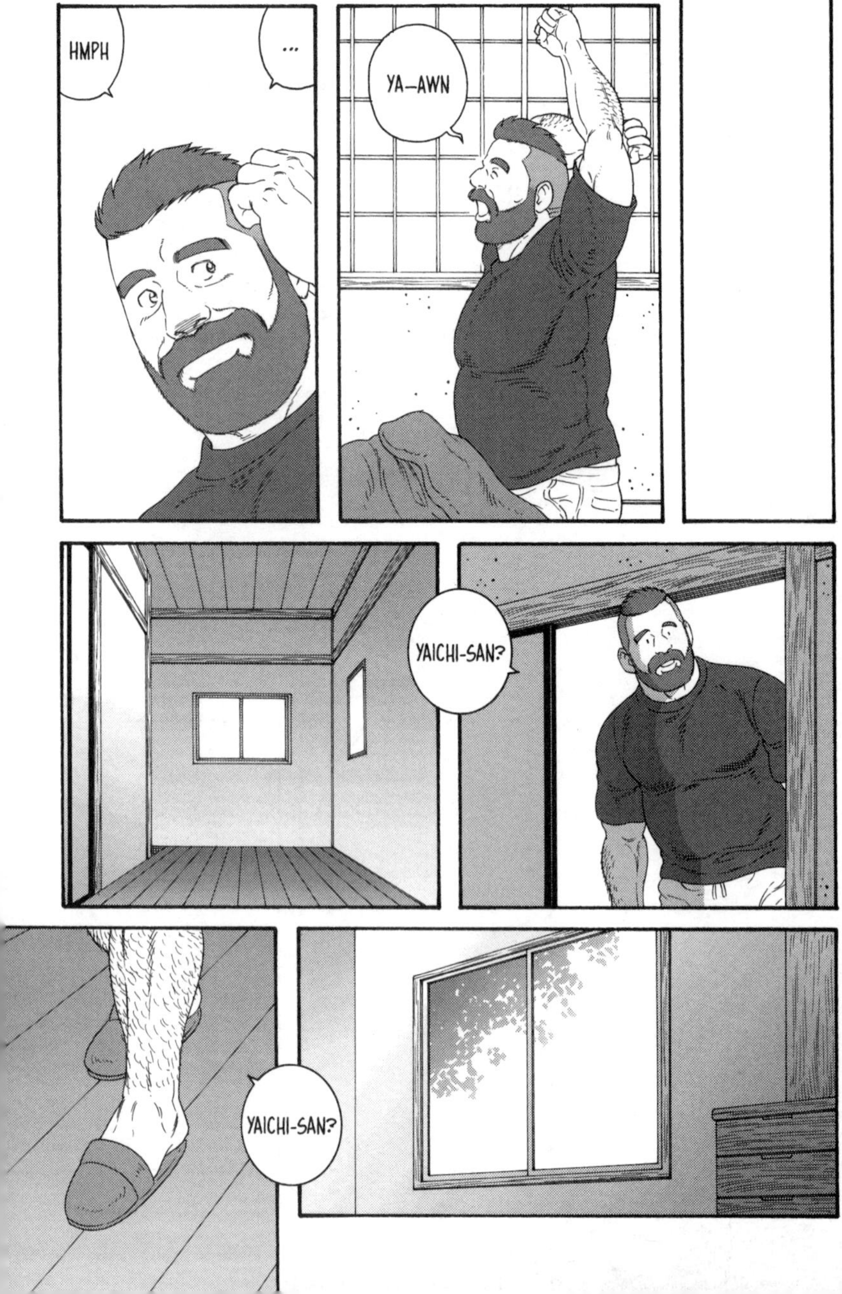
YA—AWN
...
HMPH
YAICHI-SAN?
YAICHI-SAN?

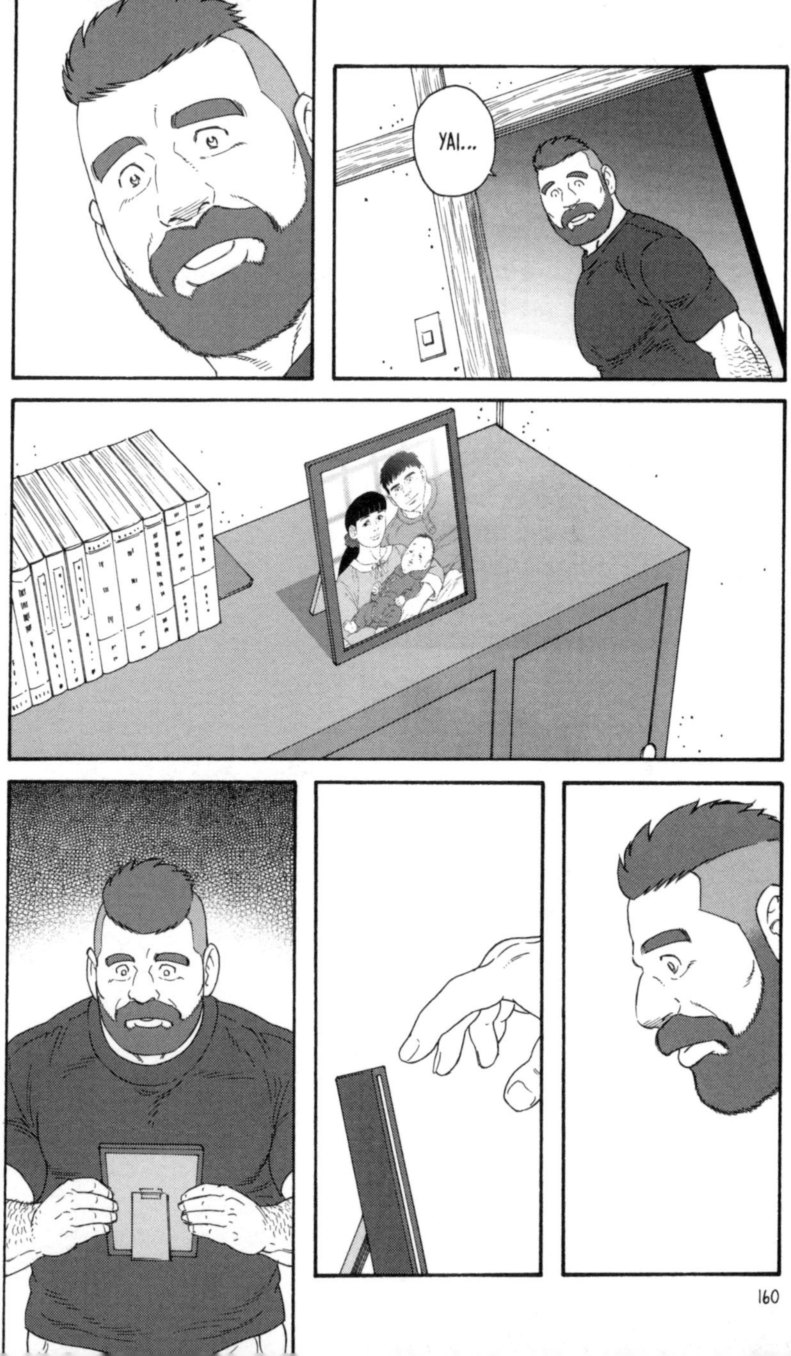
YAI...

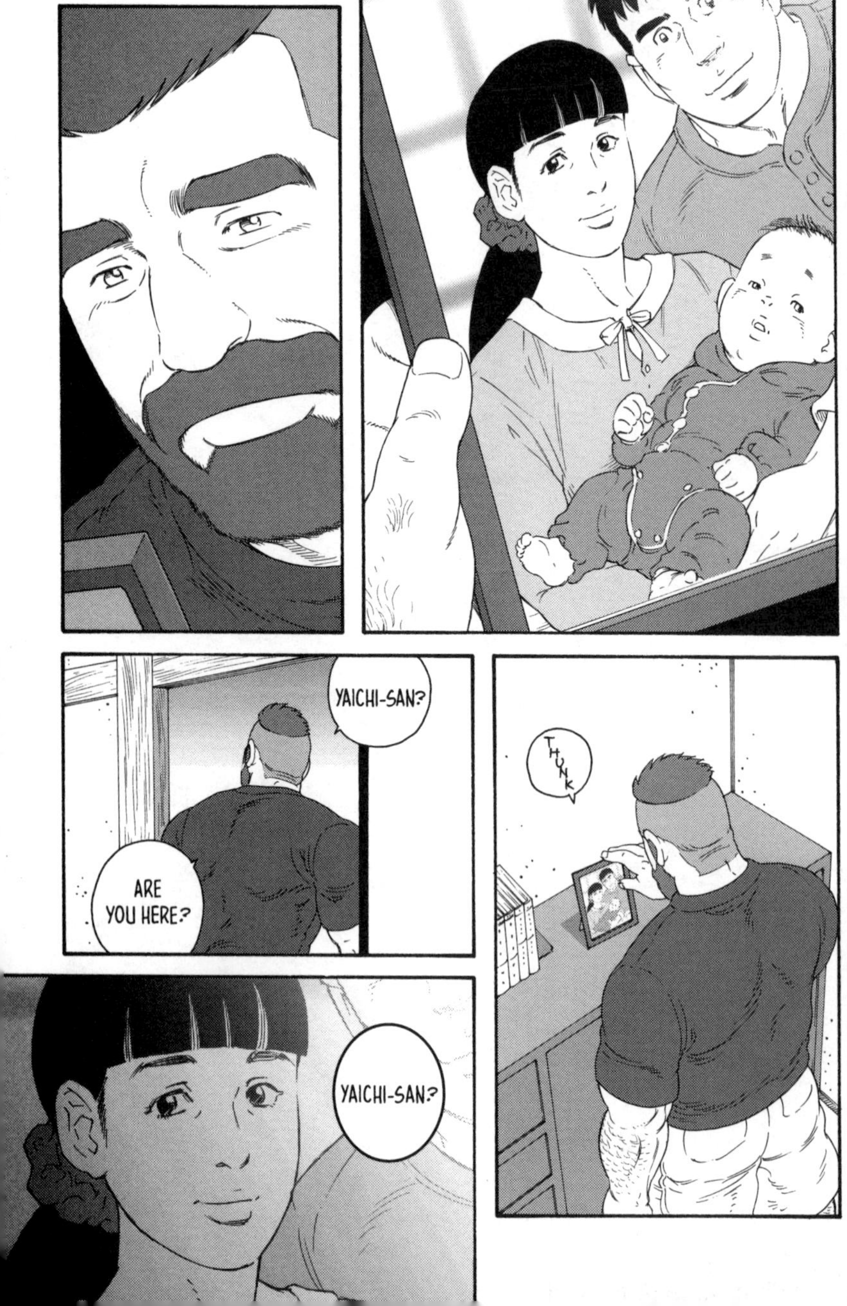
THUNK
YAICHI-SAN?
ARE YOU HERE?
YAICHI-SAN?

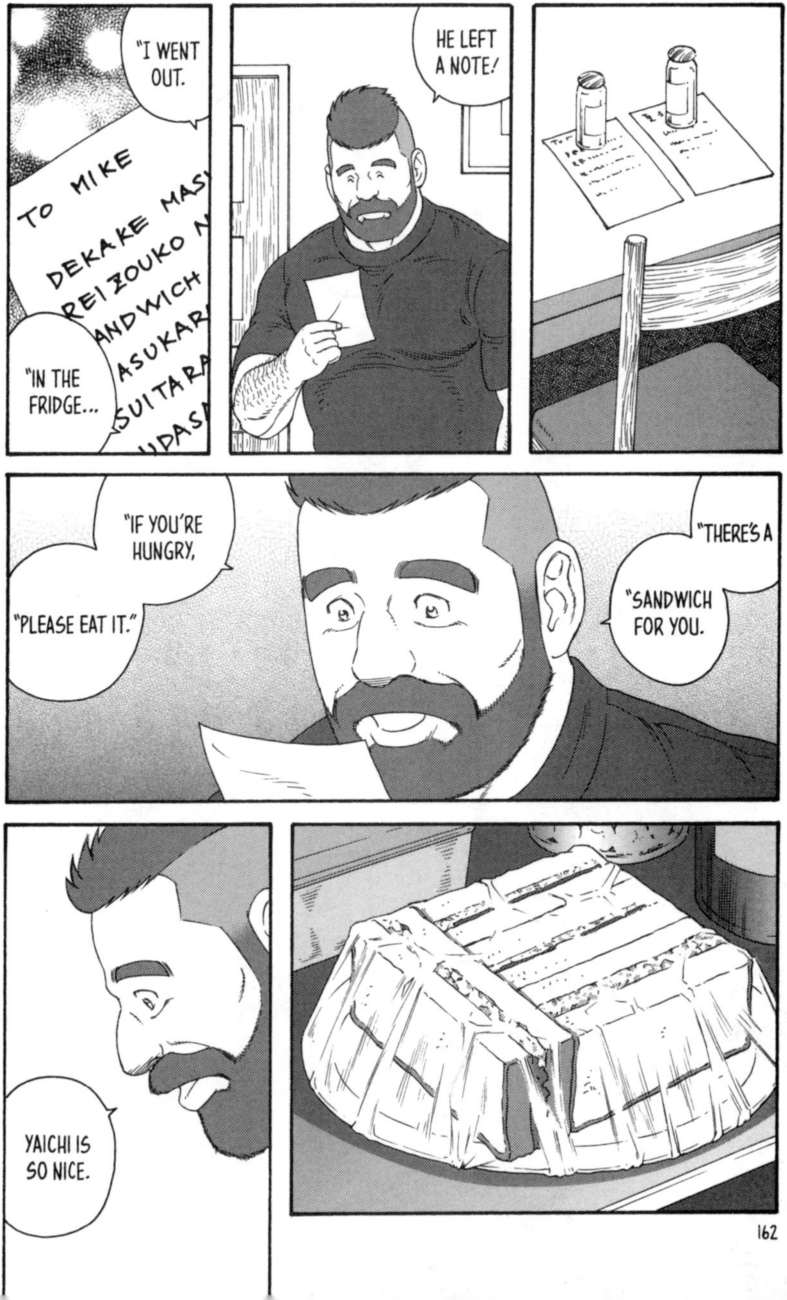
HE LEFT A NOTE!
"I WENT OUT.
TO MIKE
DEKAKE MAS
REIZOUKO N
ANDWICH
ASUKAR
SUITAR
UDAS
"IN THE FRIDGE...
"THERE'S A
"SANDWICH FOR YOU.
"IF YOU'RE HUNGRY,
"PLEASE EAT IT."
YAICHI IS SO NICE.

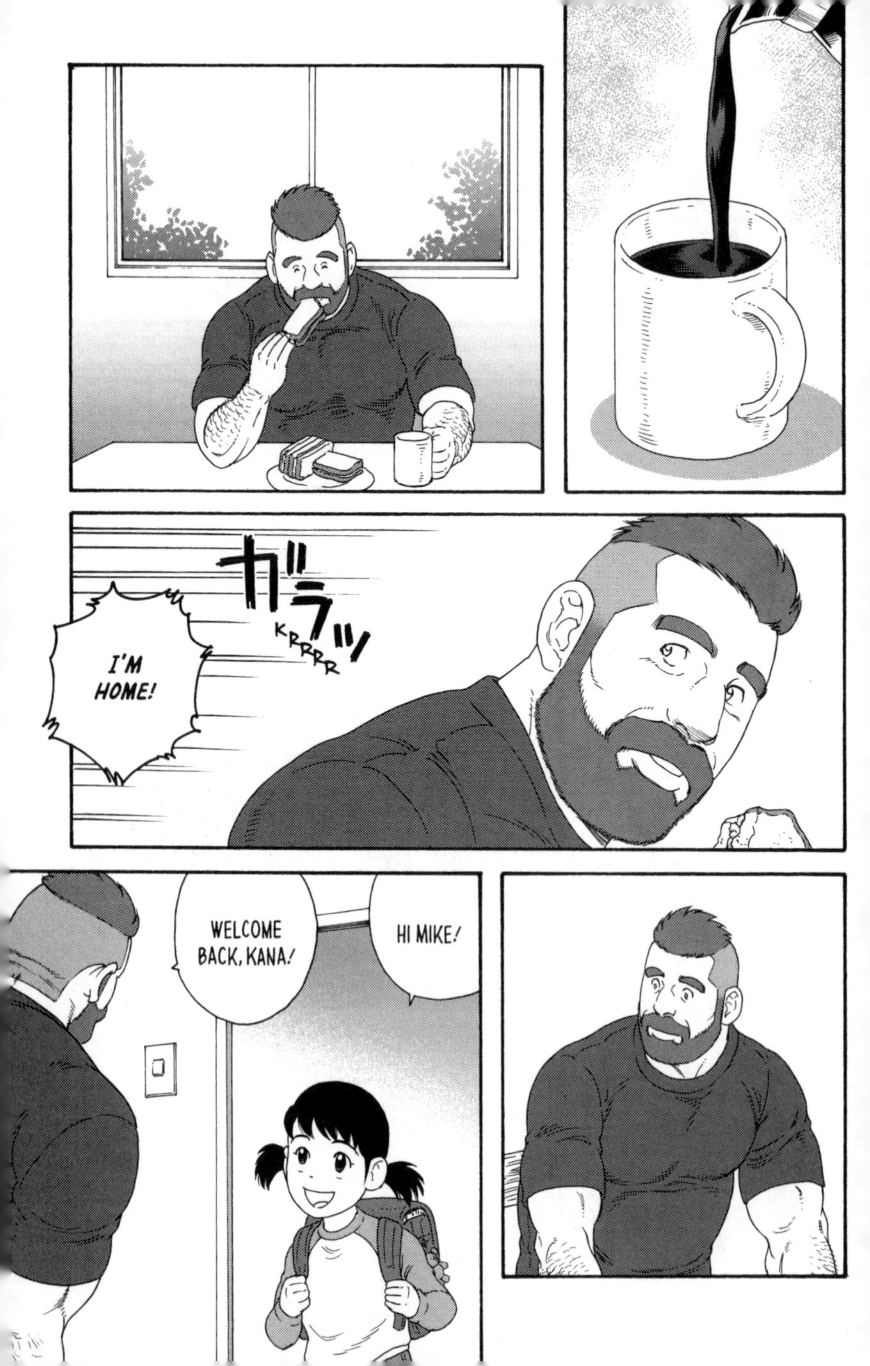
ガラッ
KRRRR
I'M HOME!
HI MIKE!
WELCOME BACK, KANA!

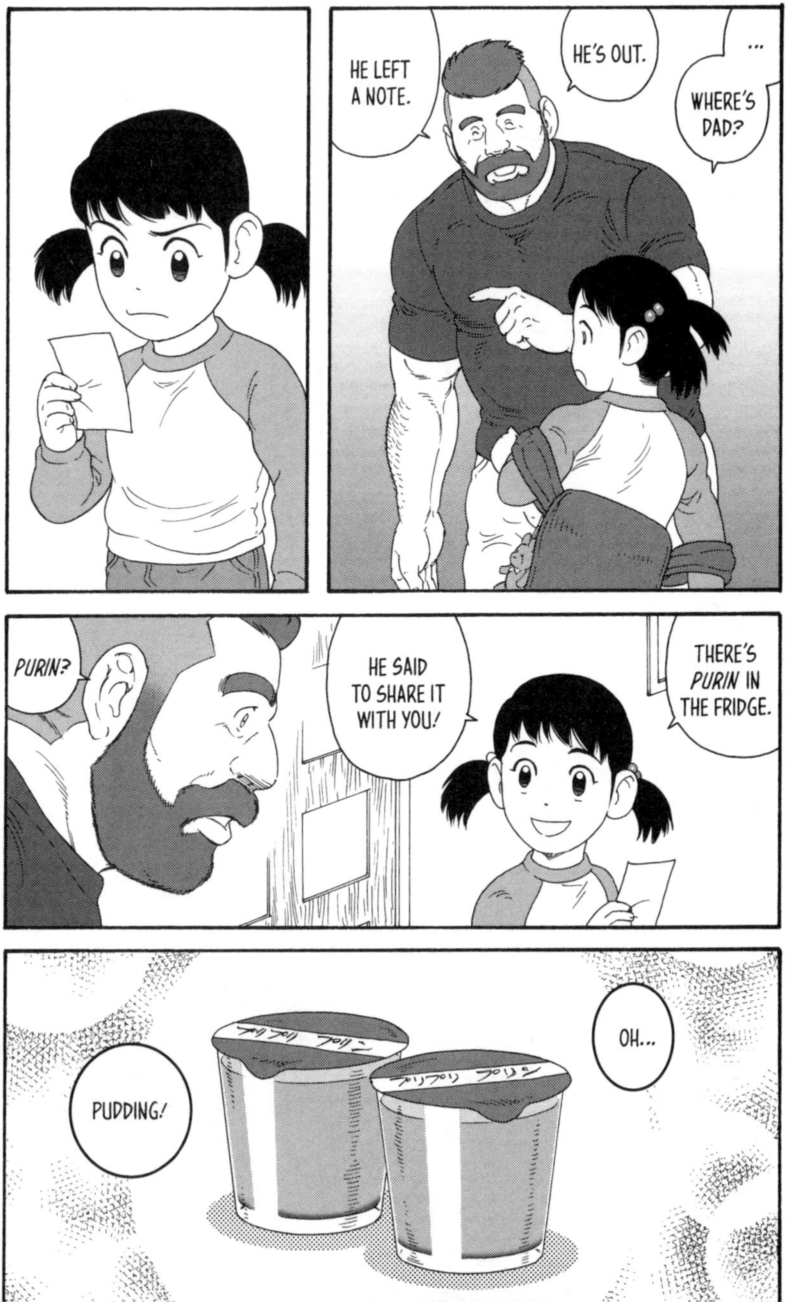
...
WHERE'S DAD?
HE'S OUT.
HE LEFT A NOTE.
THERE'S *PURIN* IN THE FRIDGE.
HE SAID TO SHARE IT WITH YOU!
PURIN?
OH...
プリプリ プリン
プリプリ プリン
PUDDING!

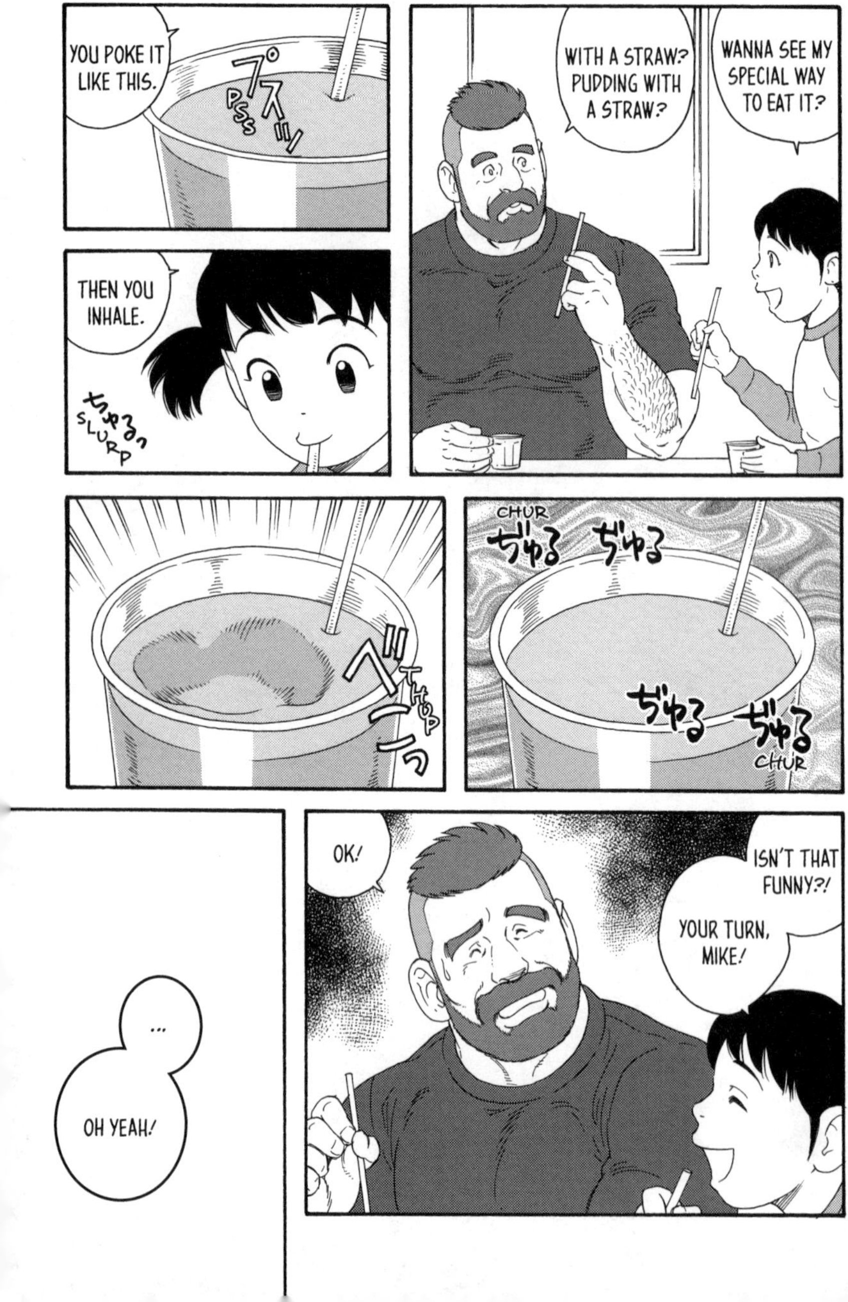
WANNA SEE MY SPECIAL WAY TO EAT IT?
WITH A STRAW? PUDDING WITH A STRAW?
YOU POKE IT LIKE THIS.
プスッ
PSS
THEN YOU INHALE.
ちゅるっ
SLURP
CHUR
ぢゅる ぢゅる
ぢゅる ぢゅる
CHUR
ベーっ
THUP
ISN'T THAT FUNNY?!
YOUR TURN, MIKE!
OK!
...
OH YEAH!

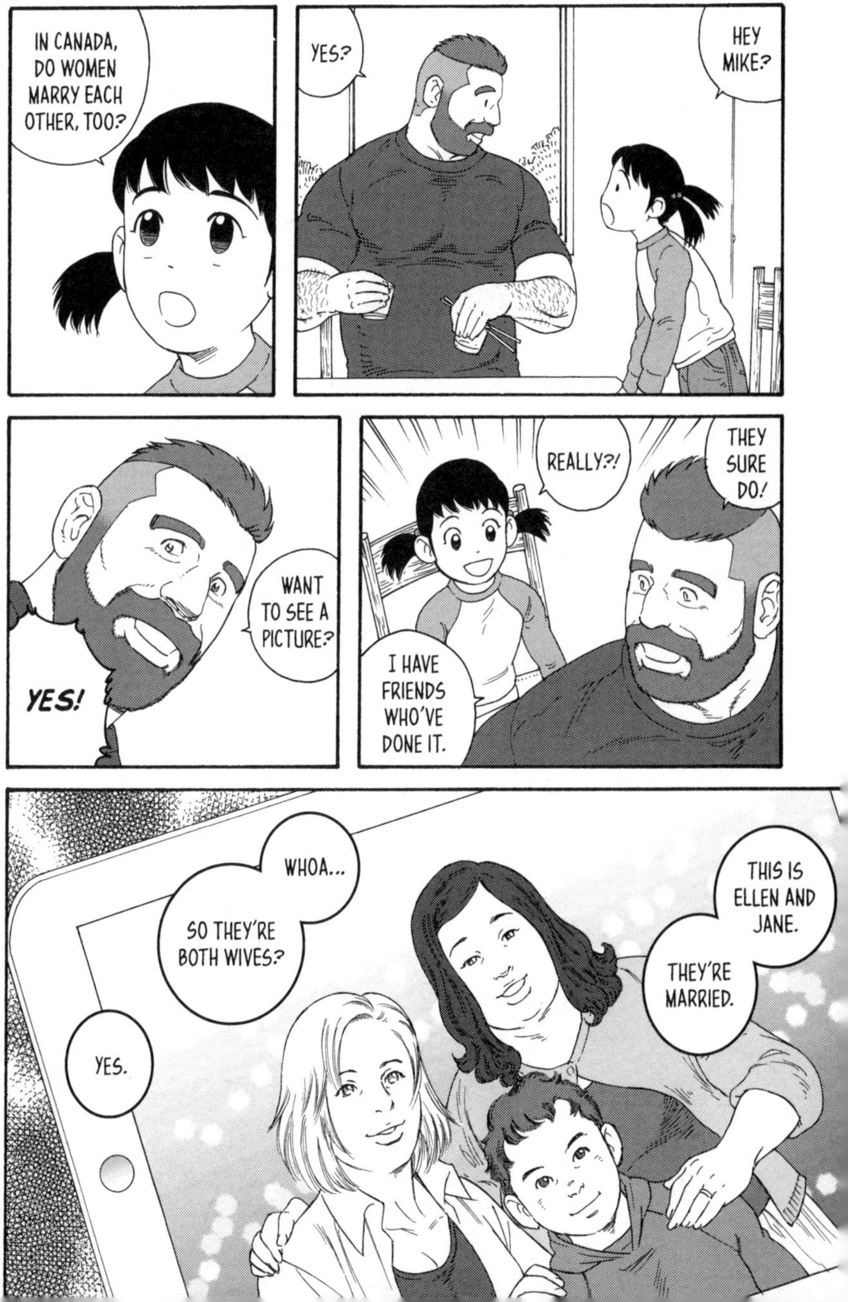
HEY MIKE?
YES?
IN CANADA, DO WOMEN MARRY EACH OTHER, TOO?
THEY SURE DO!
REALLY?!
I HAVE FRIENDS WHO'VE DONE IT.
WANT TO SEE A PICTURE?
YES!
THIS IS ELLEN AND JANE.
THEY'RE MARRIED.
WHOA...
SO THEY'RE BOTH WIVES?
YES.

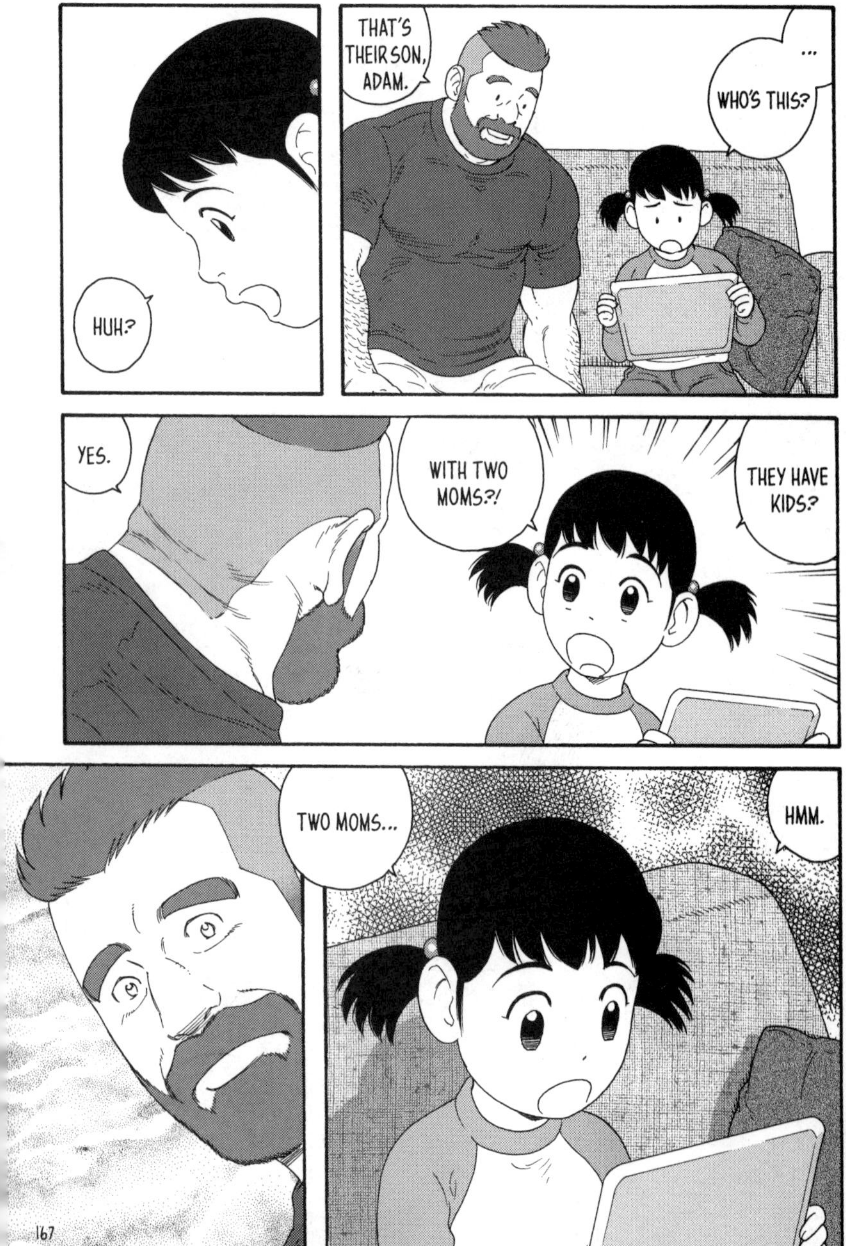
...
WHO'S THIS?
THAT'S THEIR SON, ADAM.
HUH?
THEY HAVE KIDS?
WITH TWO MOMS?!
YES.
HMM.
TWO MOMS...

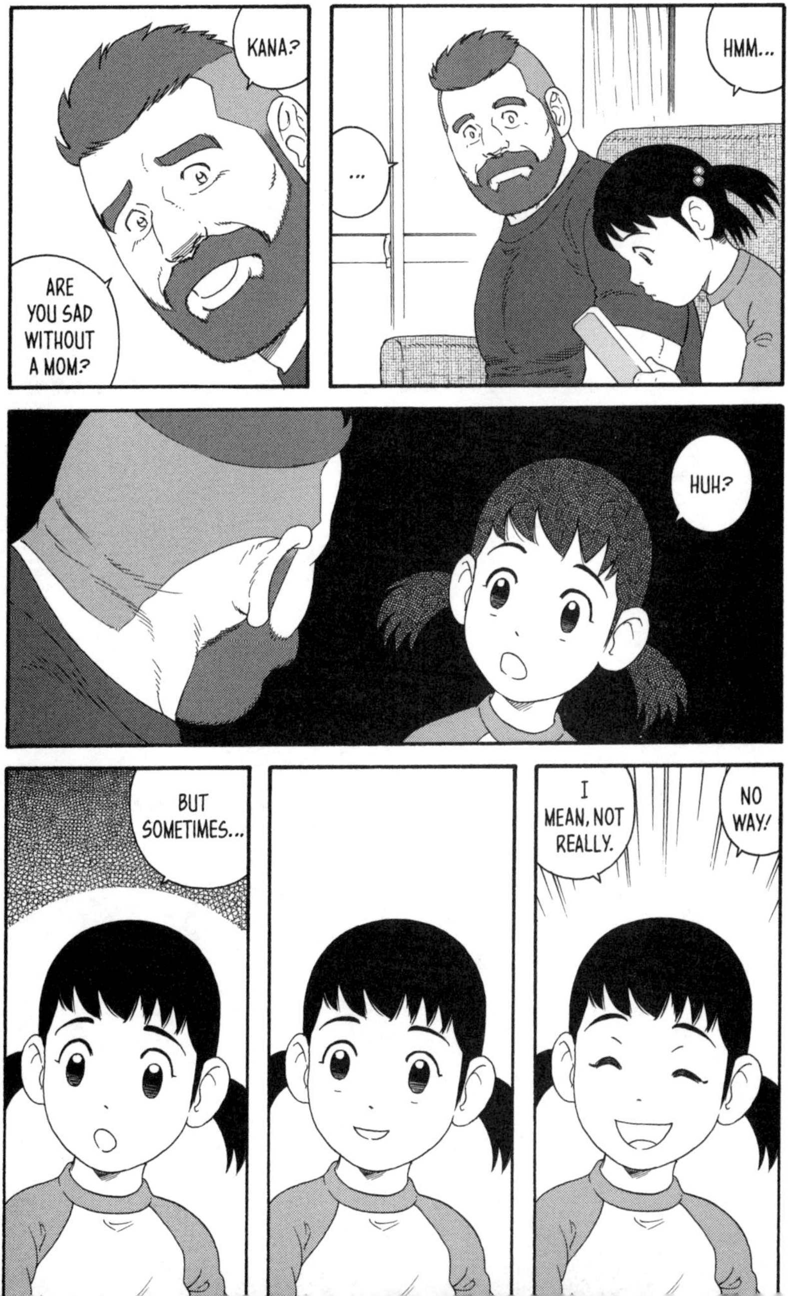
HMM...
...
KANA?
ARE YOU SAD WITHOUT A MOM?
HUH?
NO WAY!
I MEAN, NOT REALLY.
BUT SOMETIMES...

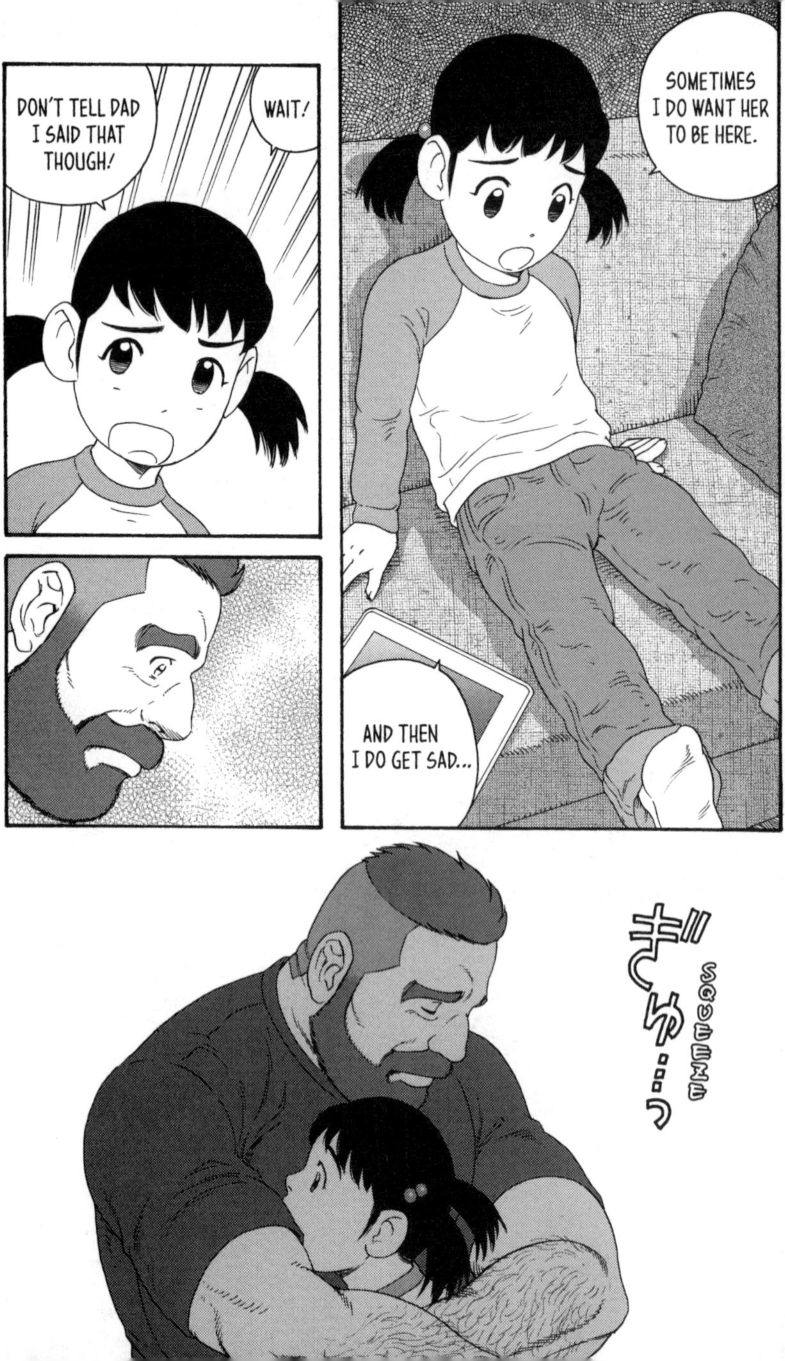
SOMETIMES I DO WANT HER TO BE HERE.
AND THEN I DO GET SAD...
WAIT!
DON'T TELL DAD I SAID THAT THOUGH!
ぎゅっ
SQUEEZE

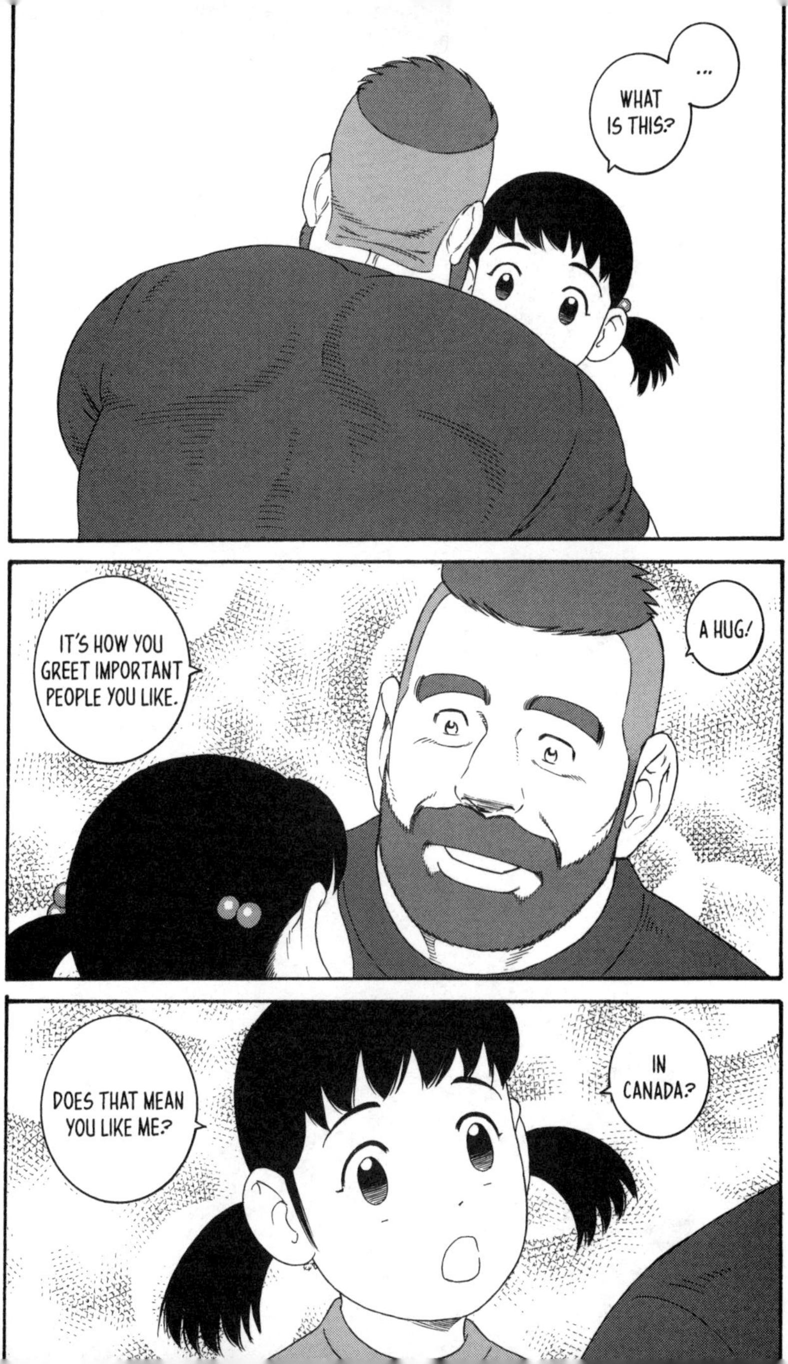
...
WHAT IS THIS?
A HUG!
IT'S HOW YOU GREET IMPORTANT PEOPLE YOU LIKE.
IN CANADA?
DOES THAT MEAN YOU LIKE ME?

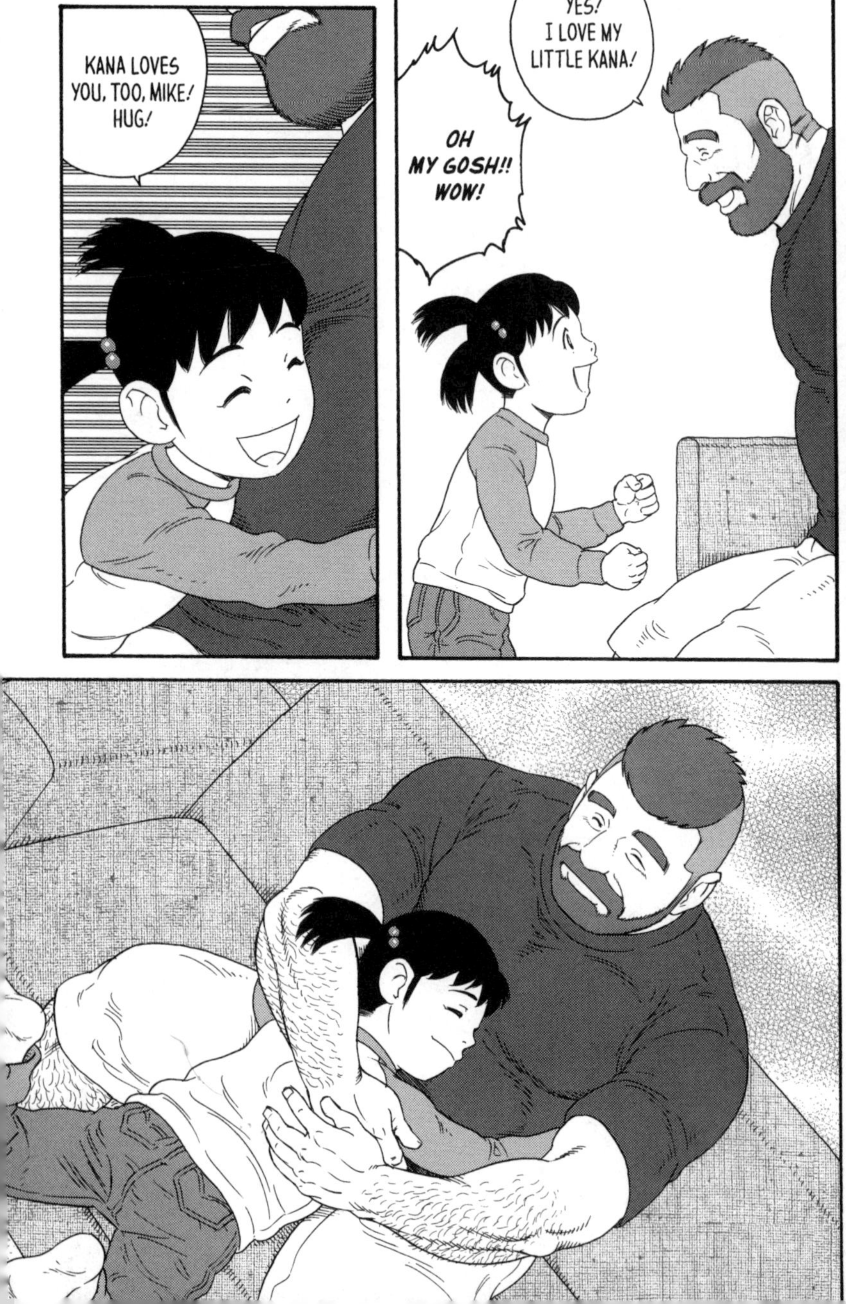
YES! I LOVE MY LITTLE KANA!
OH MY GOSH!! WOW!
KANA LOVES YOU, TOO, MIKE! HUG!

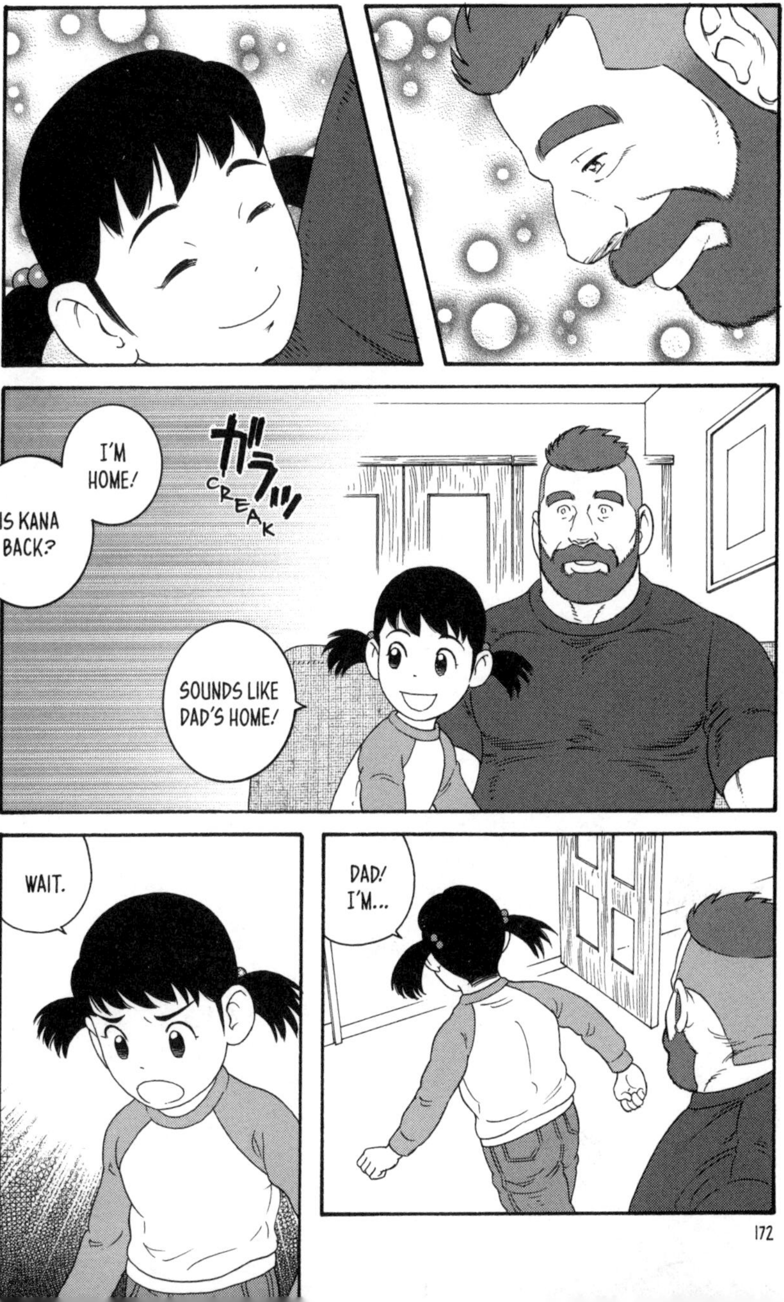
ガラッ
CREAK
I'M HOME! IS KANA BACK?
SOUNDS LIKE DAD'S HOME!
DAD! I'M...
WAIT.

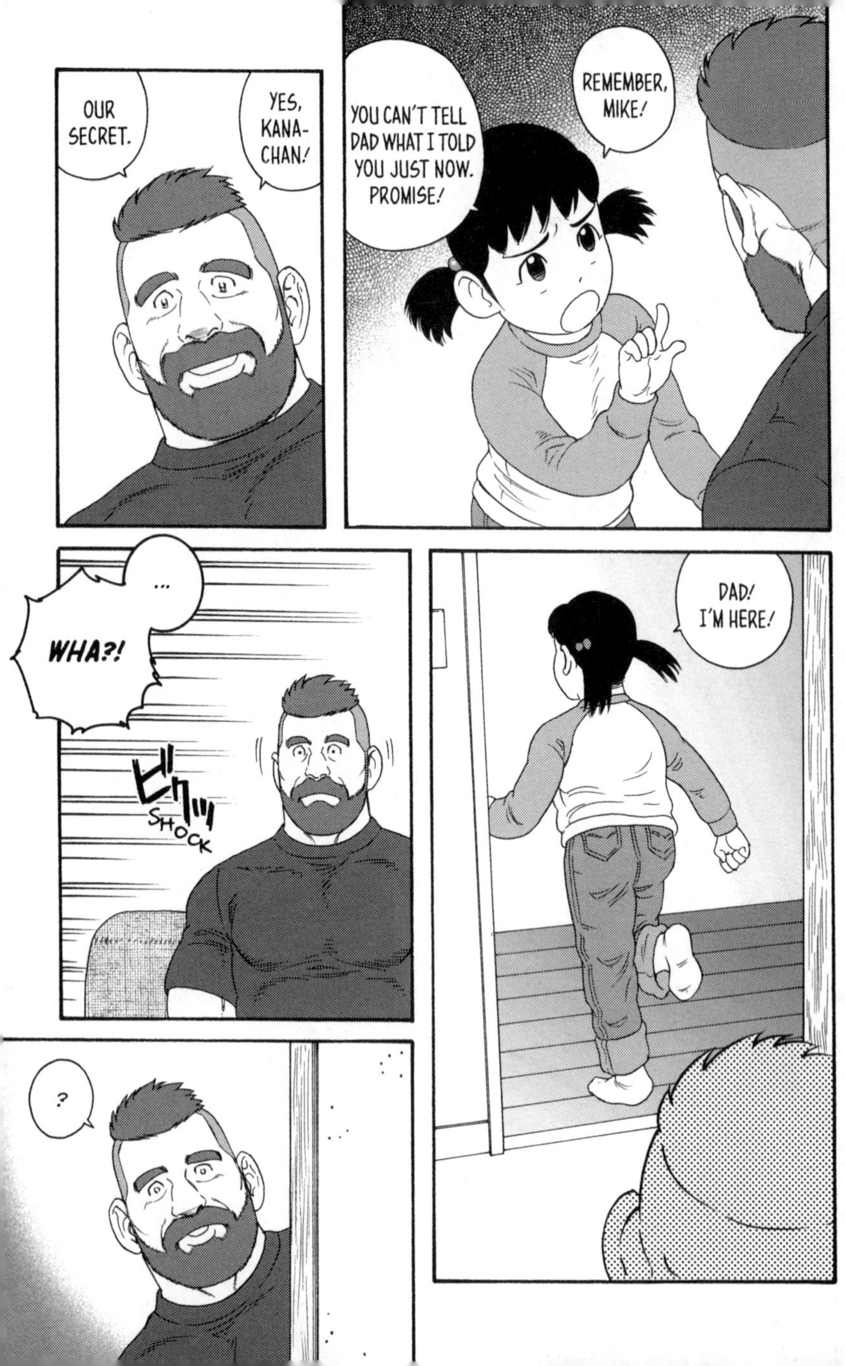
REMEMBER, MIKE!
YOU CAN'T TELL DAD WHAT I TOLD YOU JUST NOW. PROMISE!
YES, KANA-CHAN!
OUR SECRET.
DAD! I'M HERE!
...
WHA?!
ビクッ
SHOCK
?

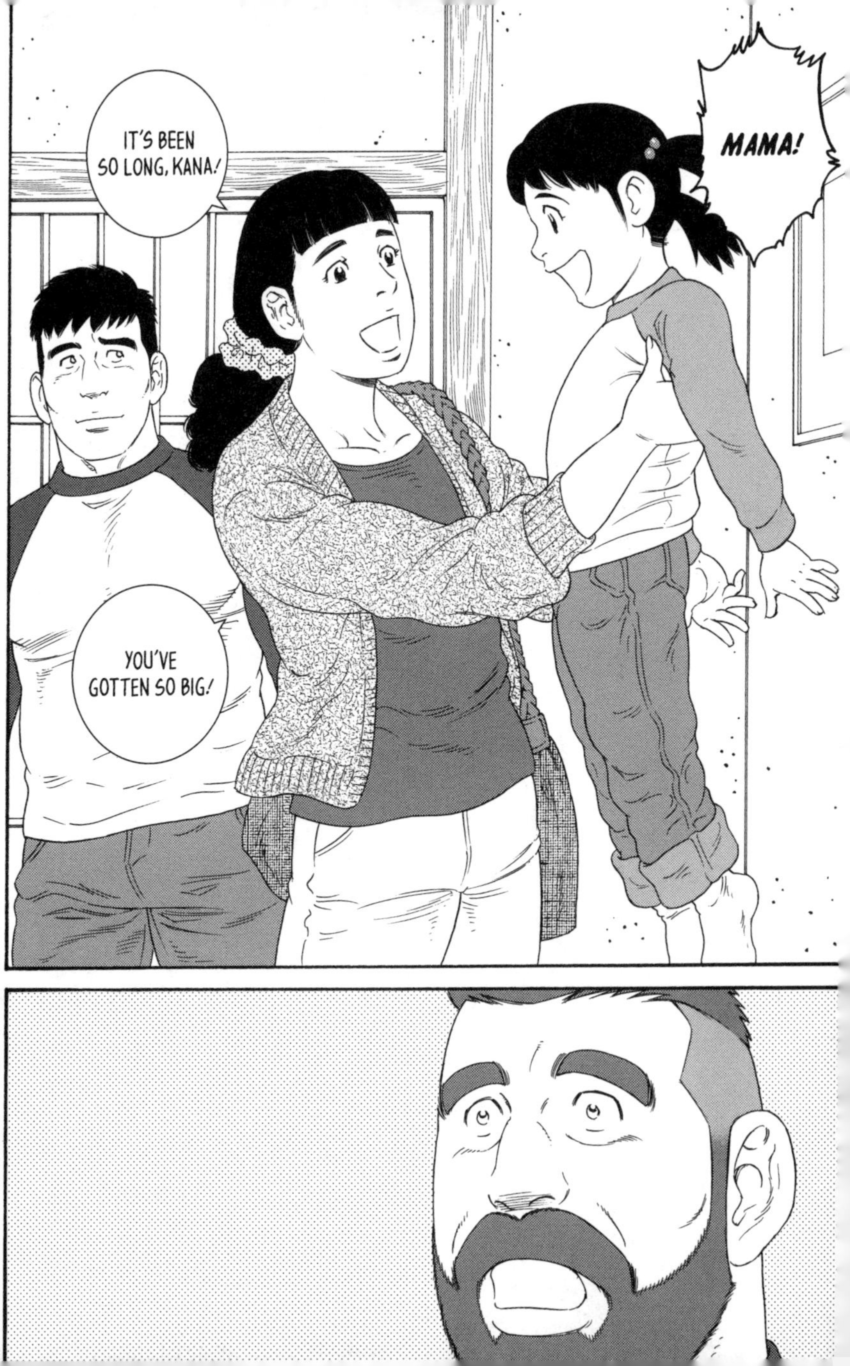
MAMA!
IT'S BEEN SO LONG, KANA!
YOU'VE GOTTEN SO BIG!

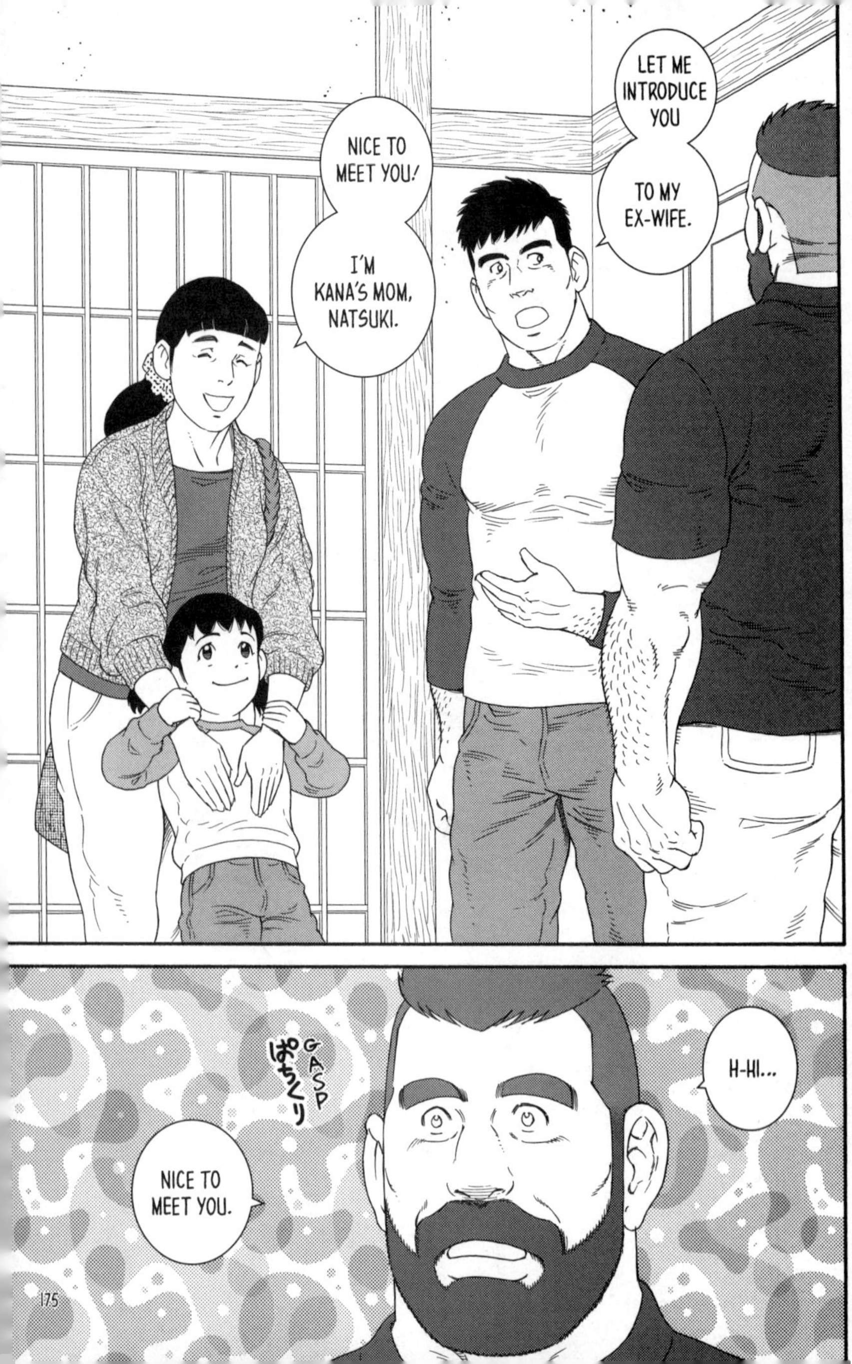
LET ME INTRODUCE YOU
TO MY EX-WIFE.
NICE TO MEET YOU!
I'M KANA'S MOM, NATSUKI.
H-HI...
GASP ぱちくり
NICE TO MEET YOU.

CHAPTER EIGHT

DINING ROOM

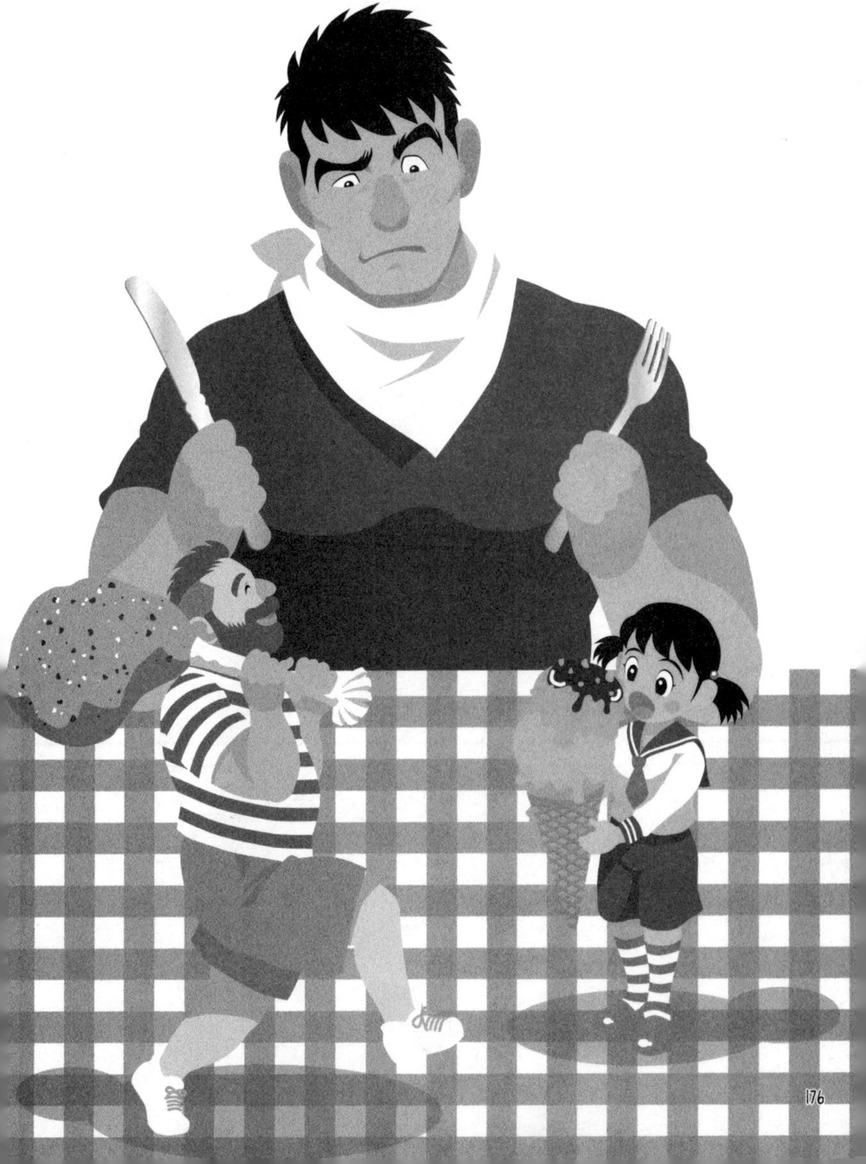

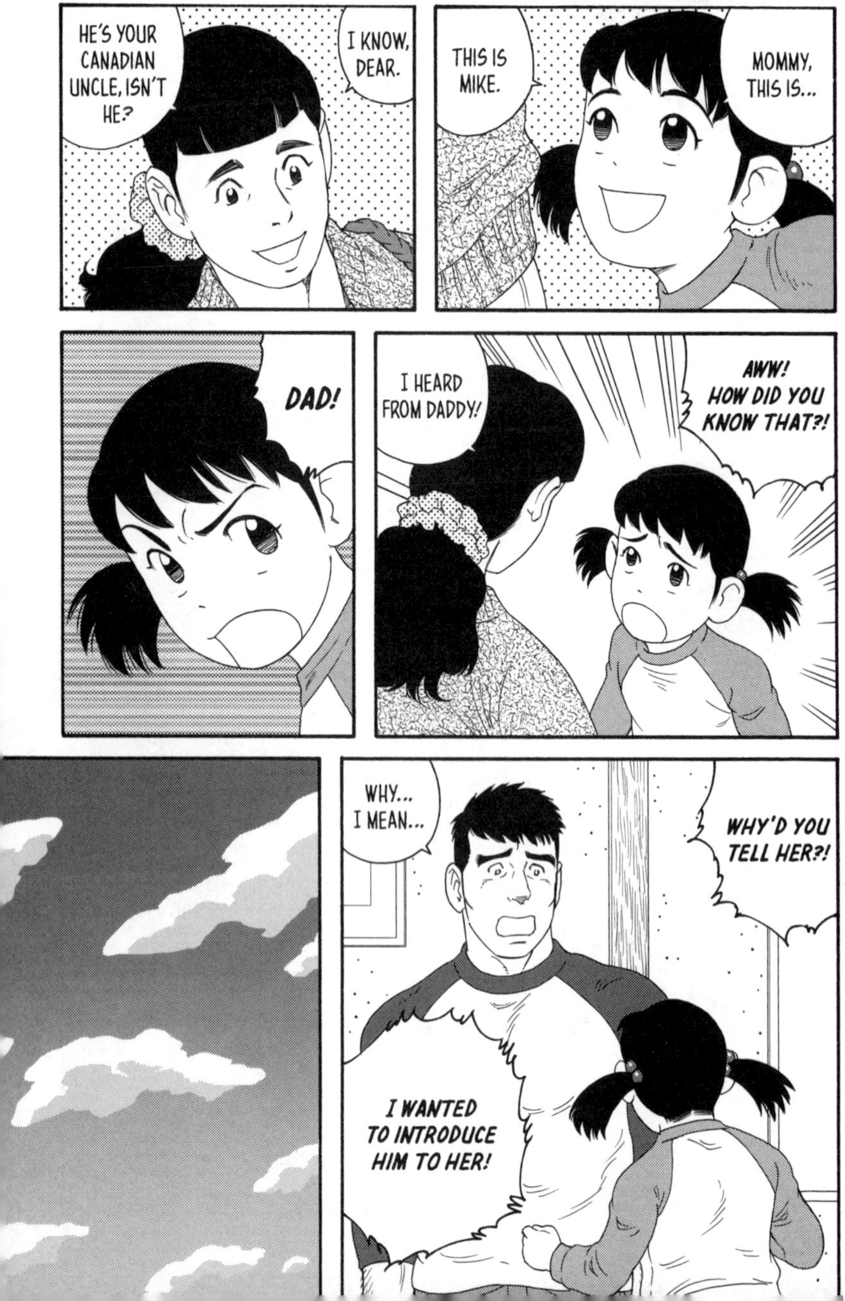
MOMMY, THIS IS...
THIS IS MIKE.
I KNOW, DEAR.
HE'S YOUR CANADIAN UNCLE, ISN'T HE?
AWW! HOW DID YOU KNOW THAT?!
I HEARD FROM DADDY!
DAD!
WHY'D YOU TELL HER?!
WHY... I MEAN...
I WANTED TO INTRODUCE HIM TO HER!

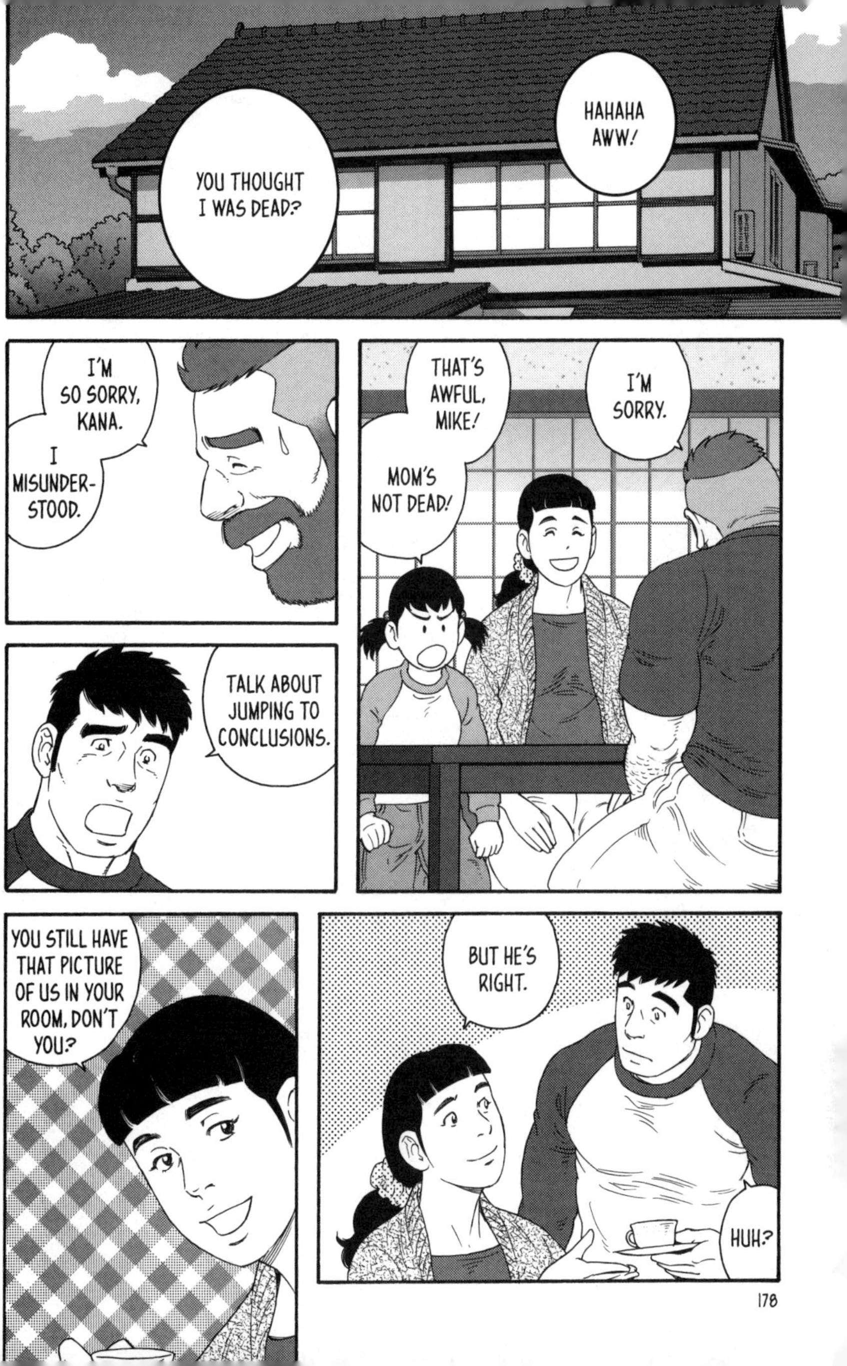
HAHAHA AWW!
YOU THOUGHT I WAS DEAD?
I'M SORRY.
THAT'S AWFUL, MIKE!
MOM'S NOT DEAD!
I'M SO SORRY, KANA.
I MISUNDER-STOOD.
TALK ABOUT JUMPING TO CONCLUSIONS.
BUT HE'S RIGHT.
HUH?
YOU STILL HAVE THAT PICTURE OF US IN YOUR ROOM, DON'T YOU?

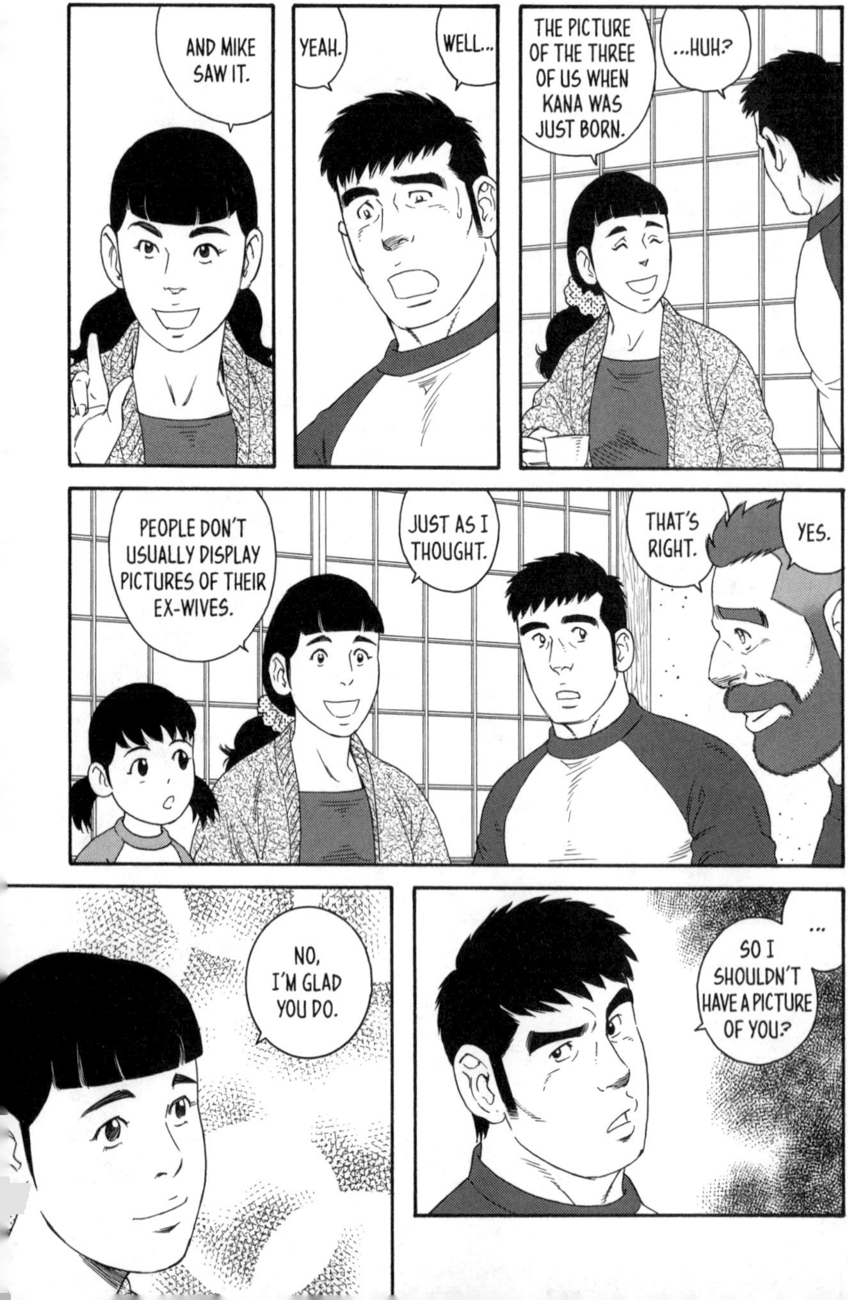
...HUH?
THE PICTURE OF THE THREE OF US WHEN KANA WAS JUST BORN.
WELL...
YEAH.
AND MIKE SAW IT.
YES.
THAT'S RIGHT.
JUST AS I THOUGHT.
PEOPLE DON'T USUALLY DISPLAY PICTURES OF THEIR EX-WIVES.
...
SO I SHOULDN'T HAVE A PICTURE OF YOU?
NO, I'M GLAD YOU DO.

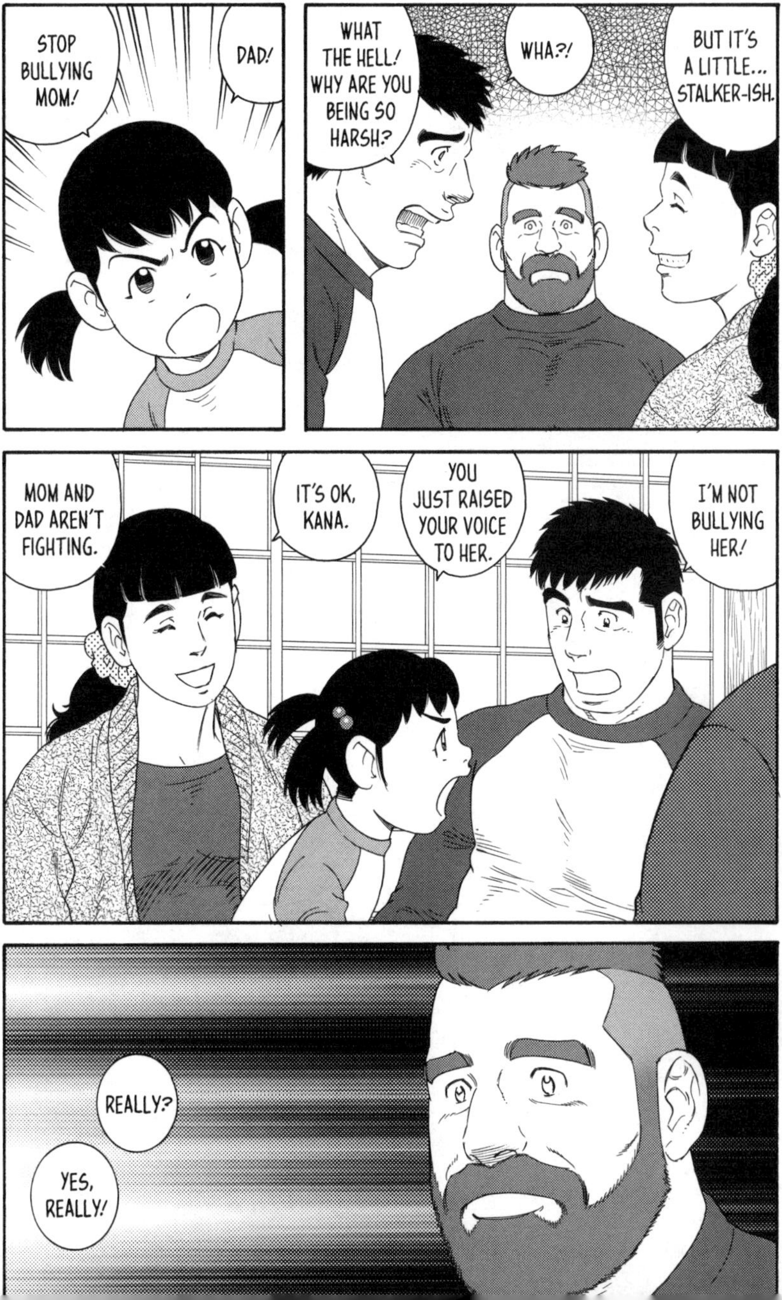
BUT IT'S A LITTLE... STALKER-ISH.
WHA?!
WHAT THE HELL! WHY ARE YOU BEING SO HARSH?
DAD!
STOP BULLYING MOM!
I'M NOT BULLYING HER!
YOU JUST RAISED YOUR VOICE TO HER.
IT'S OK, KANA.
MOM AND DAD AREN'T FIGHTING.
REALLY?
YES, REALLY!

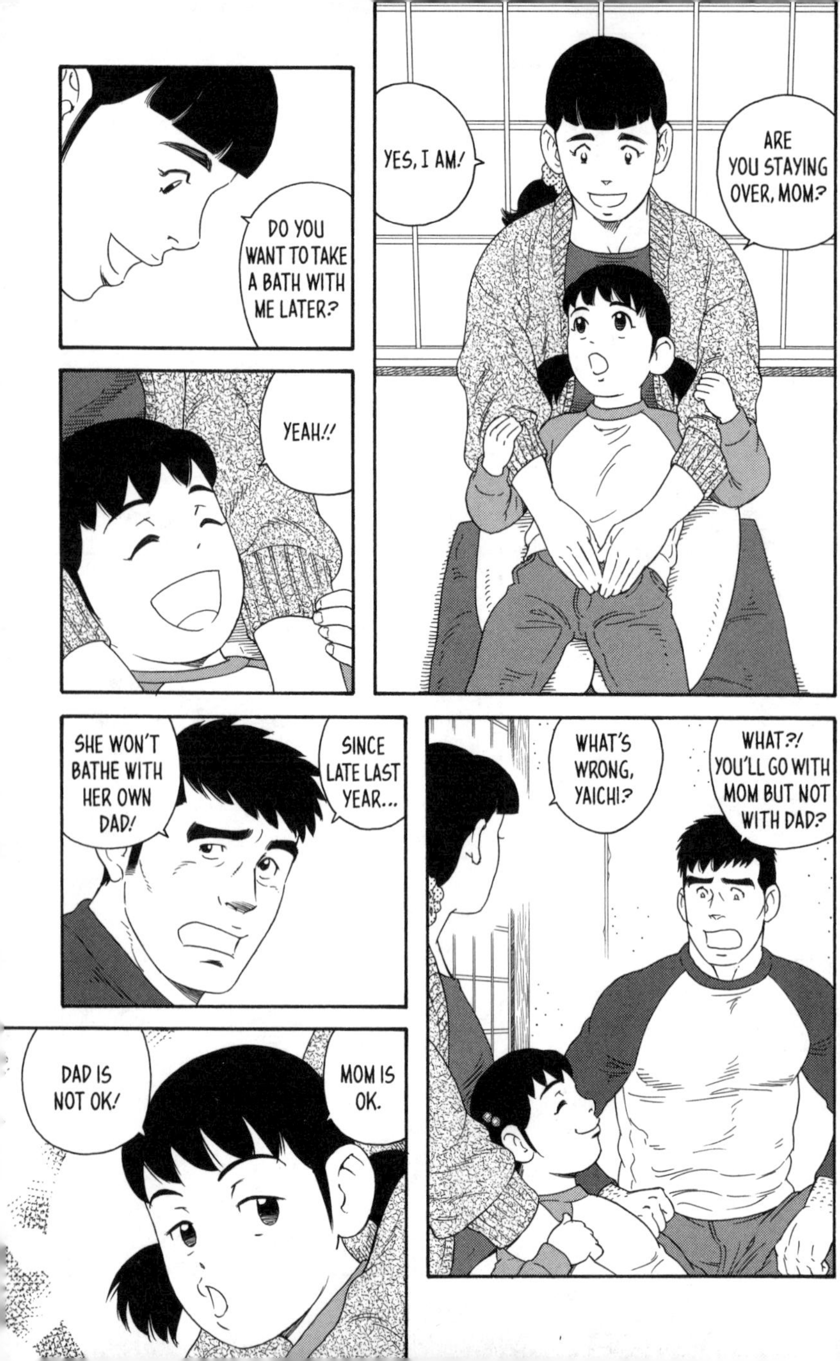
ARE YOU STAYING OVER, MOM?
YES, I AM!
DO YOU WANT TO TAKE A BATH WITH ME LATER?
YEAH!!
WHAT?! YOU'LL GO WITH MOM BUT NOT WITH DAD?
WHAT'S WRONG, YAICHI?
SINCE LATE LAST YEAR...
SHE WON'T BATHE WITH HER OWN DAD!
MOM IS OK.
DAD IS NOT OK!

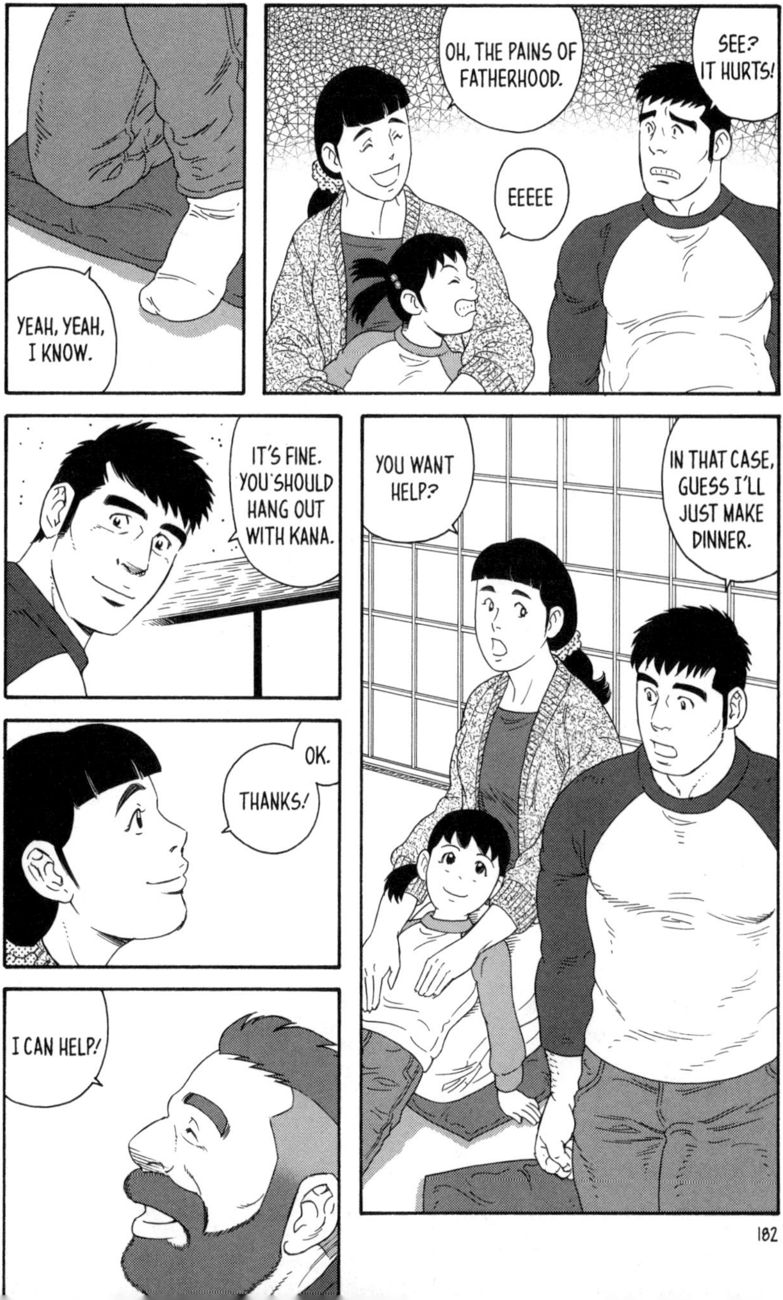
SEE? IT HURTS!
OH, THE PAINS OF FATHERHOOD.
EEEEE
YEAH, YEAH, I KNOW.
IN THAT CASE, GUESS I'LL JUST MAKE DINNER.
YOU WANT HELP?
IT'S FINE. YOU SHOULD HANG OUT WITH KANA.
OK.
THANKS!
I CAN HELP!

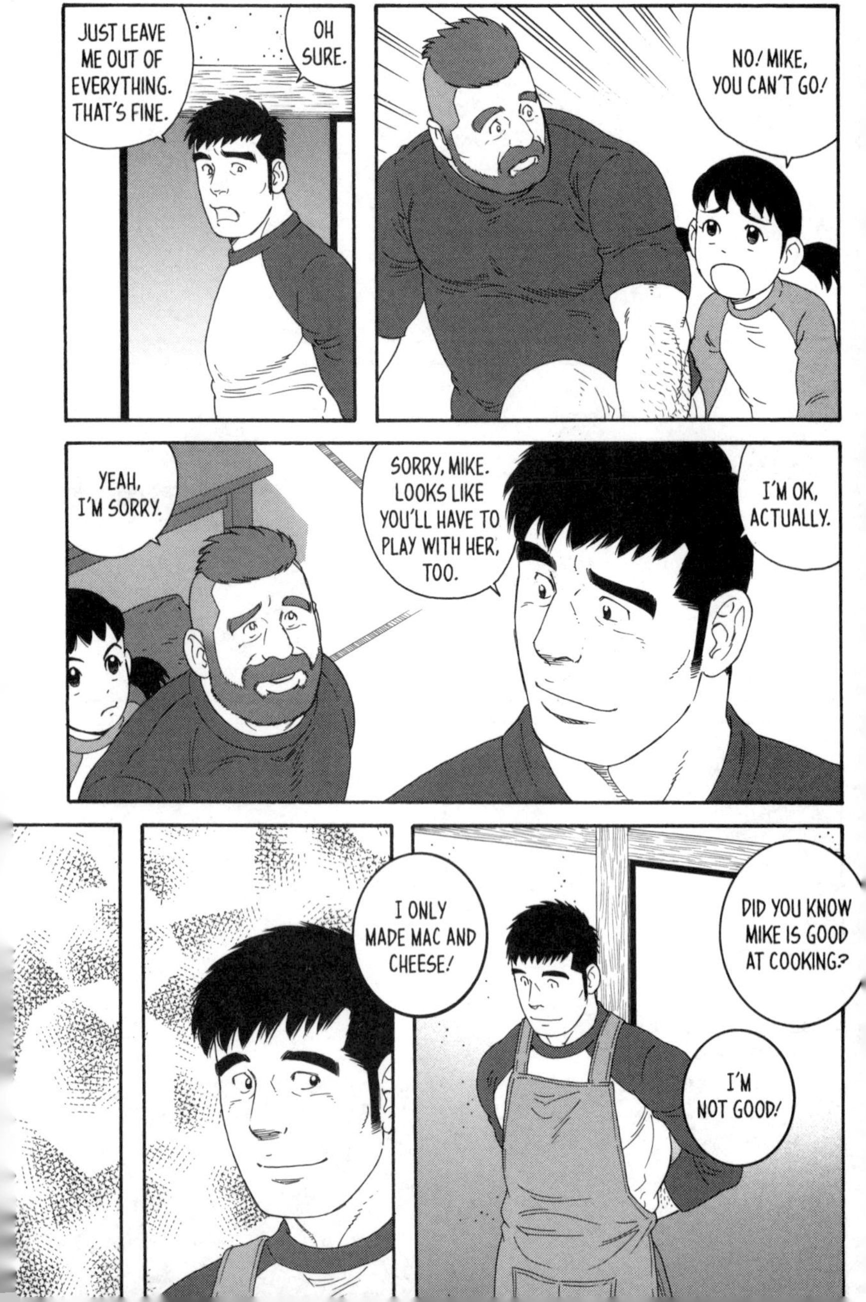
NO! MIKE, YOU CAN'T GO!
OH SURE.
JUST LEAVE ME OUT OF EVERYTHING. THAT'S FINE.
I'M OK, ACTUALLY.
SORRY, MIKE. LOOKS LIKE YOU'LL HAVE TO PLAY WITH HER, TOO.
YEAH, I'M SORRY.
DID YOU KNOW MIKE IS GOOD AT COOKING?
I'M NOT GOOD!
I ONLY MADE MAC AND CHEESE!

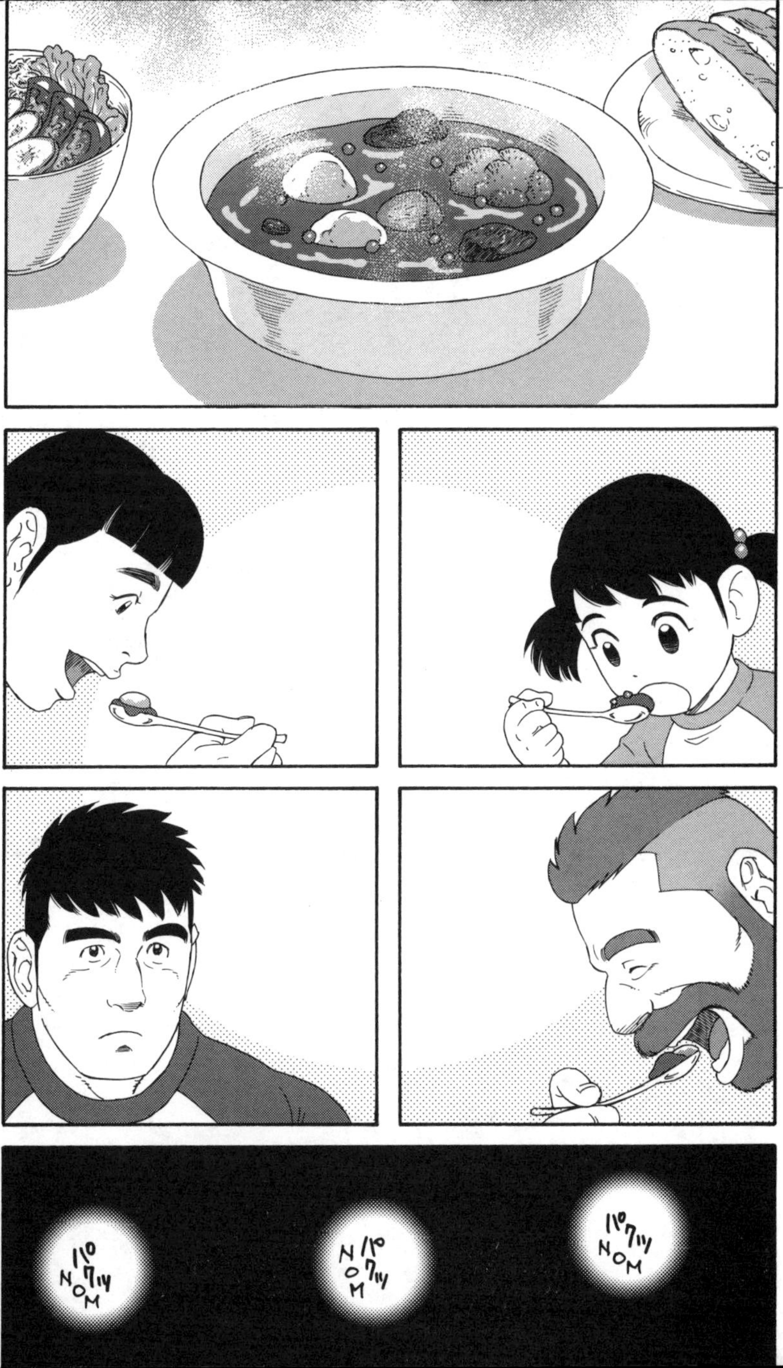
パクッ
NOM
パクッ
NOM
パクッ
NOM

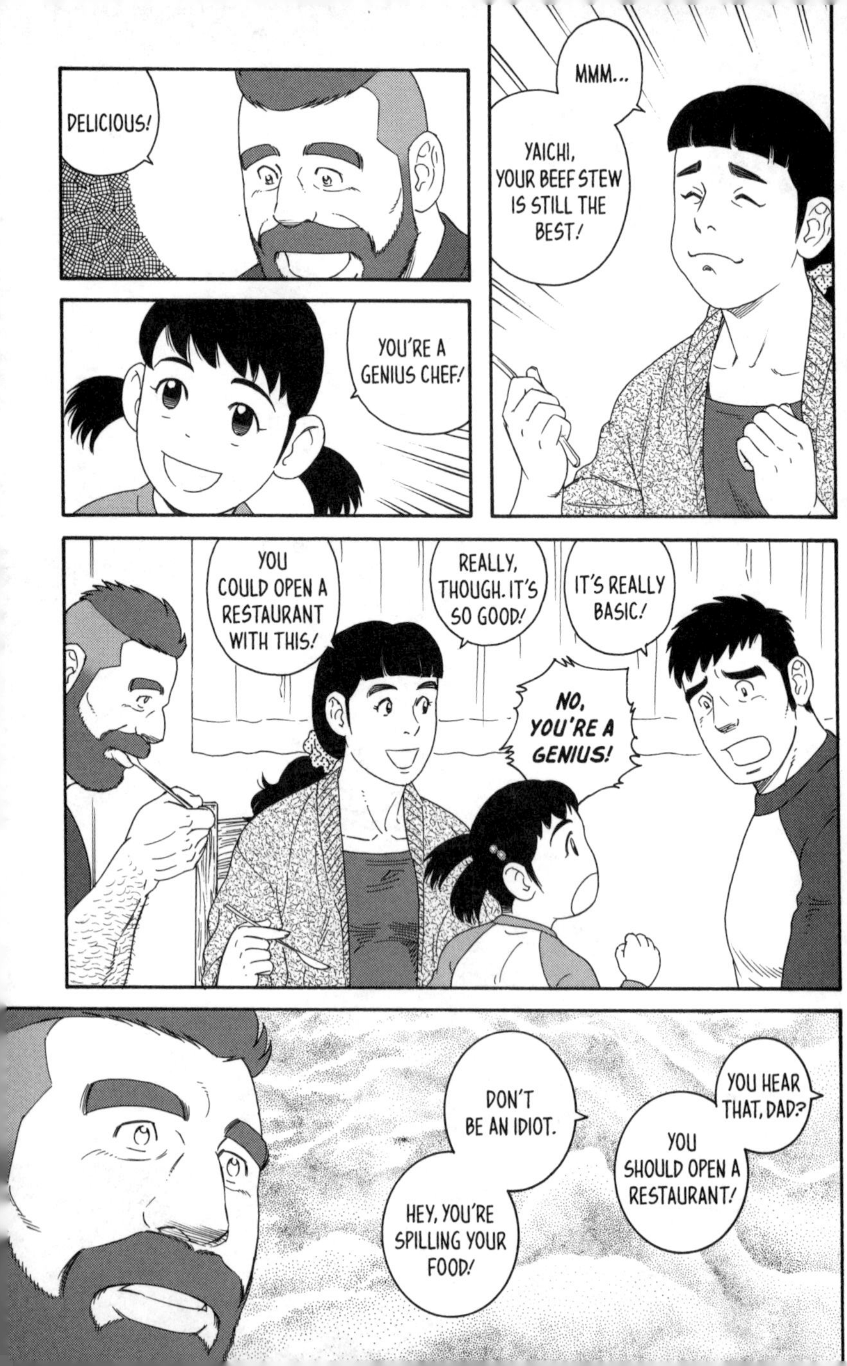
MMM...
YAICHI, YOUR BEEF STEW IS STILL THE BEST!
DELICIOUS!
YOU'RE A GENIUS CHEF!
IT'S REALLY BASIC!
REALLY, THOUGH. IT'S SO GOOD!
YOU COULD OPEN A RESTAURANT WITH THIS!
NO, YOU'RE A GENIUS!
YOU HEAR THAT, DAD?
YOU SHOULD OPEN A RESTAURANT!
DON'T BE AN IDIOT.
HEY, YOU'RE SPILLING YOUR FOOD!

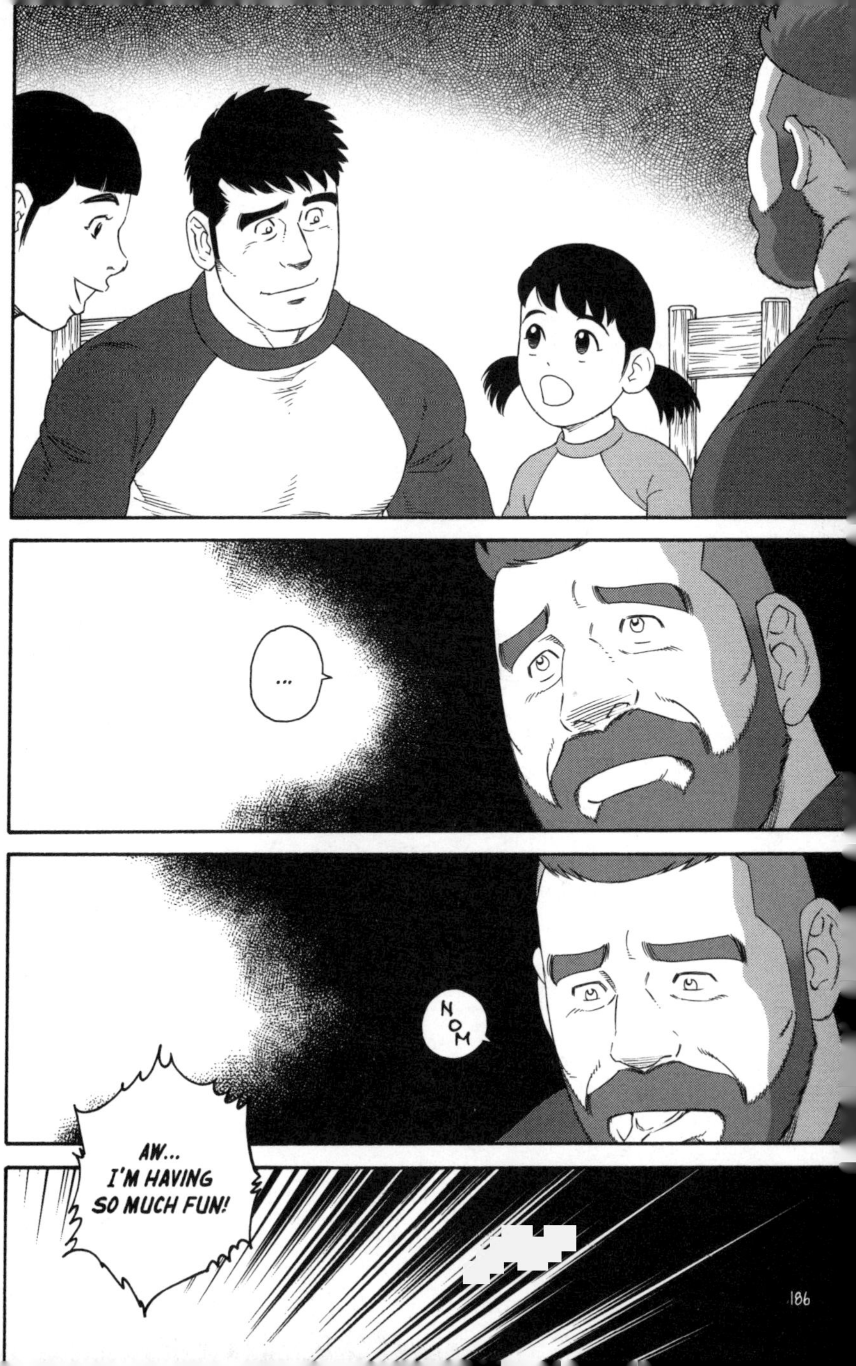
...
NOM
AW... I'M HAVING SO MUCH FUN!

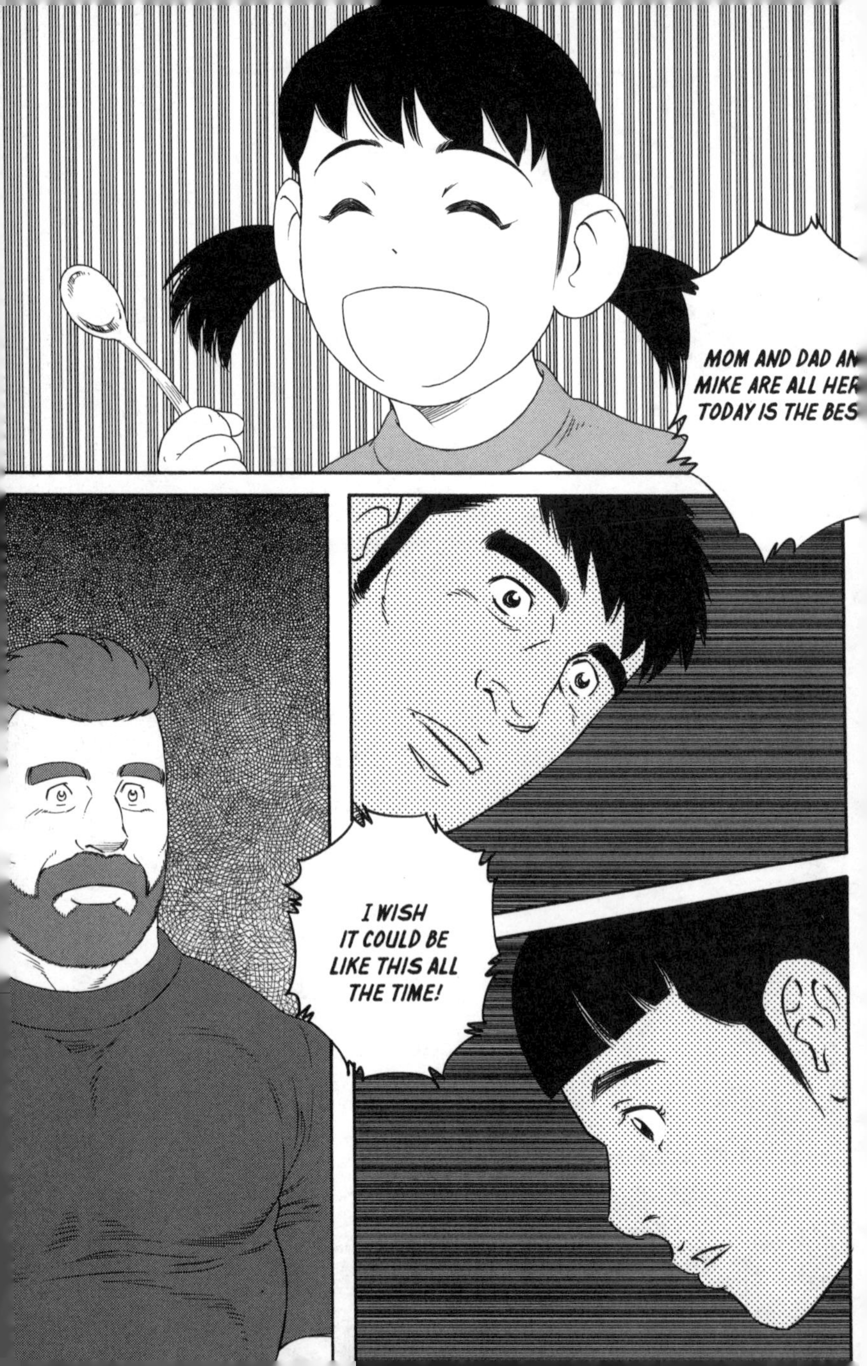
MOM AND DAD AN MIKE ARE ALL HER TODAY IS THE BES
I WISH IT COULD BE LIKE THIS ALL THE TIME!

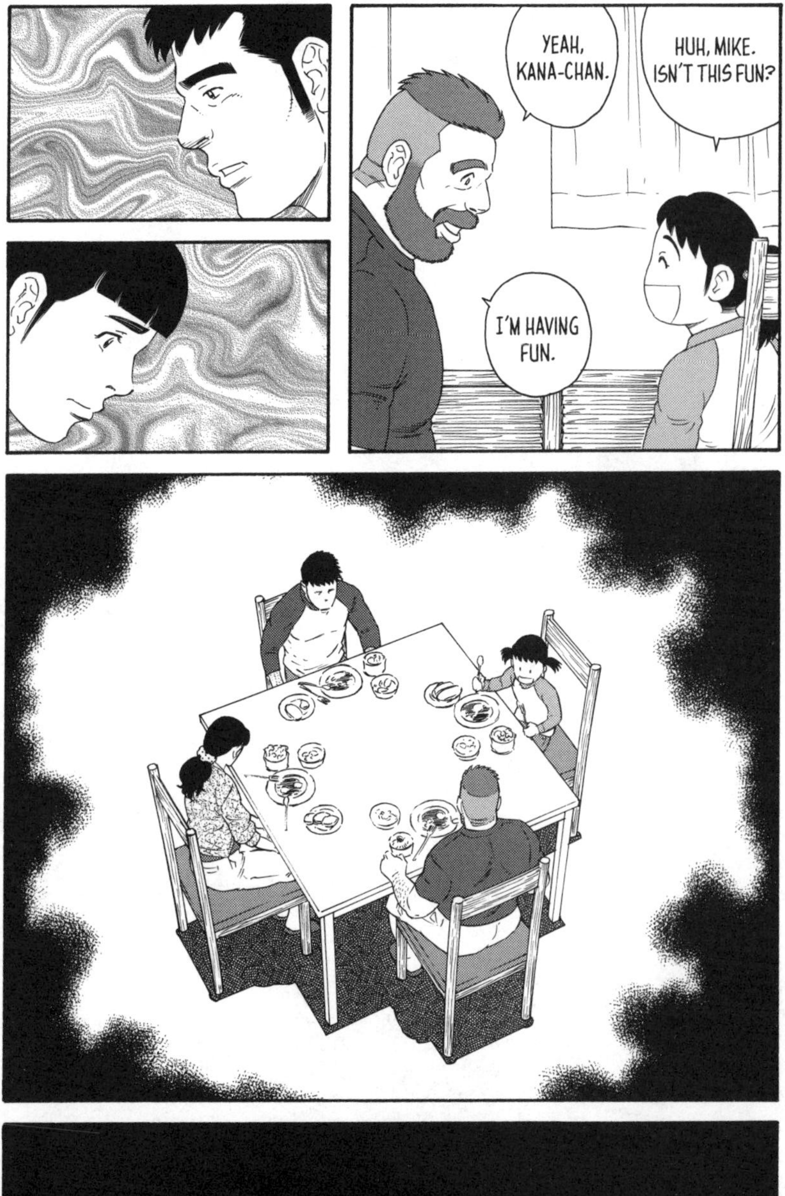
HUH, MIKE. ISN'T THIS FUN?
YEAH, KANA-CHAN.
I'M HAVING FUN.

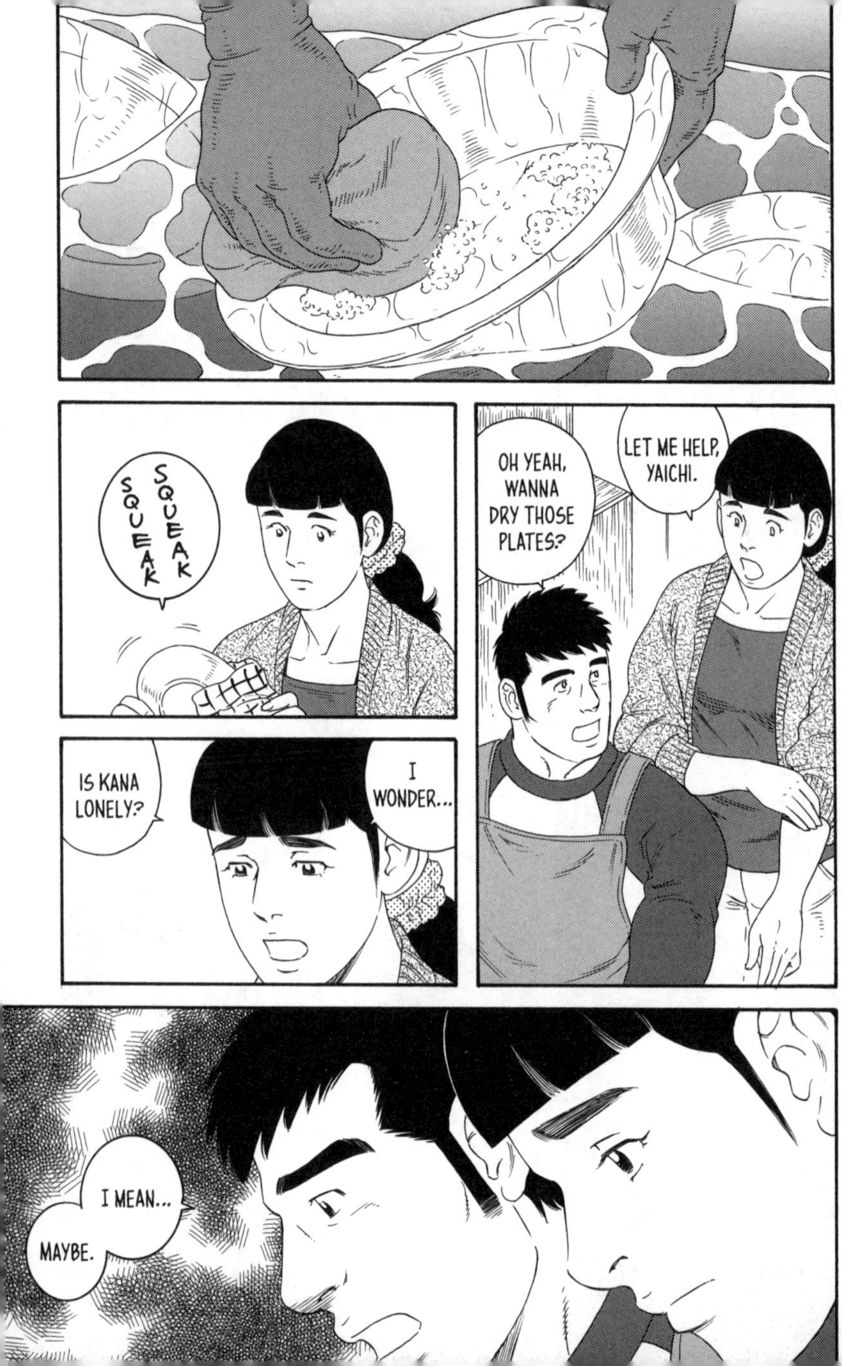
LET ME HELP, YAICHI.
OH YEAH, WANNA DRY THOSE PLATES?
SQUEAK SQUEAK
I WONDER...
IS KANA LONELY?
I MEAN...
MAYBE.

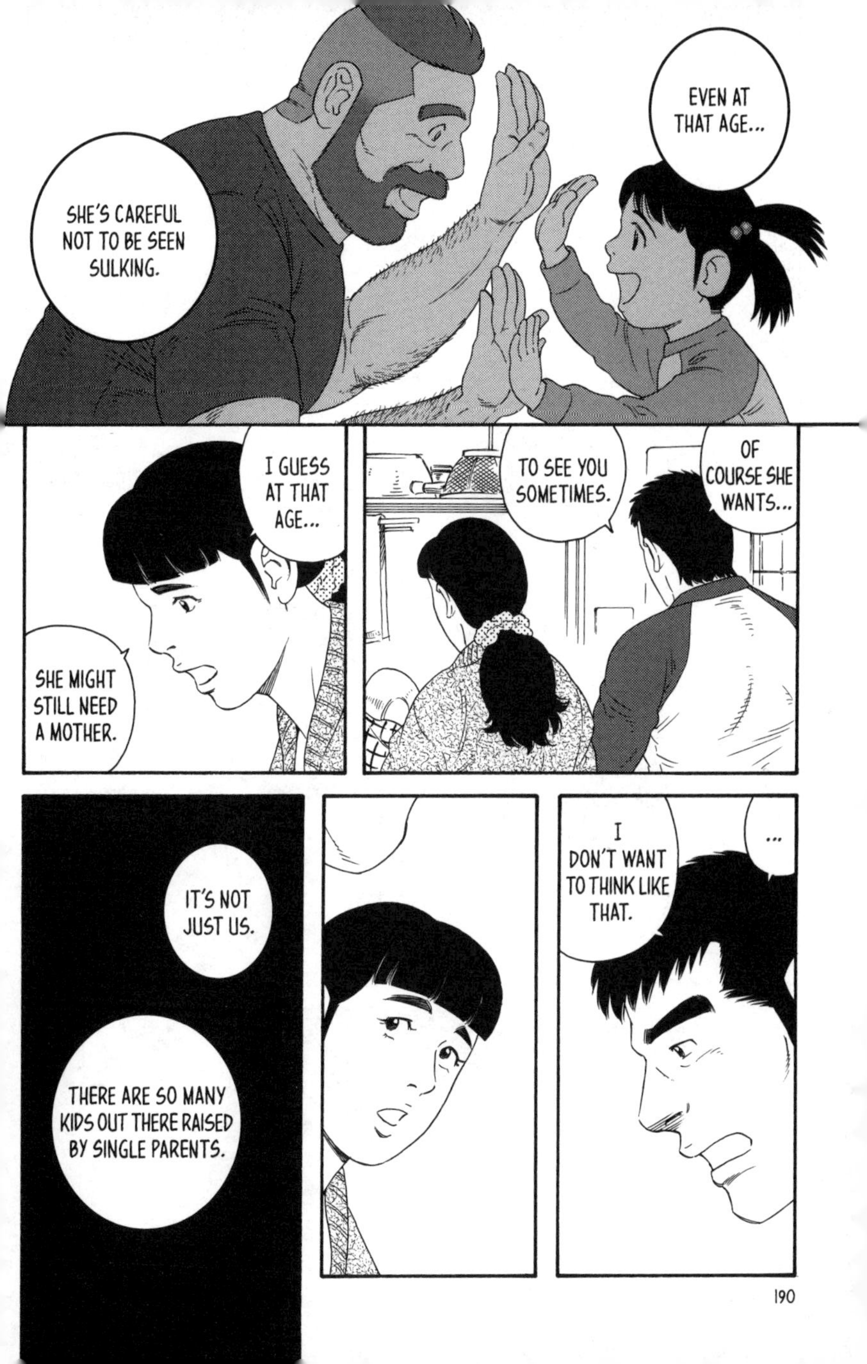
EVEN AT THAT AGE...
SHE'S CAREFUL NOT TO BE SEEN SULKING.
OF COURSE SHE WANTS...
TO SEE YOU SOMETIMES.
I GUESS AT THAT AGE...
SHE MIGHT STILL NEED A MOTHER.
...
I DON'T WANT TO THINK LIKE THAT.
IT'S NOT JUST US.
THERE ARE SO MANY KIDS OUT THERE RAISED BY SINGLE PARENTS.

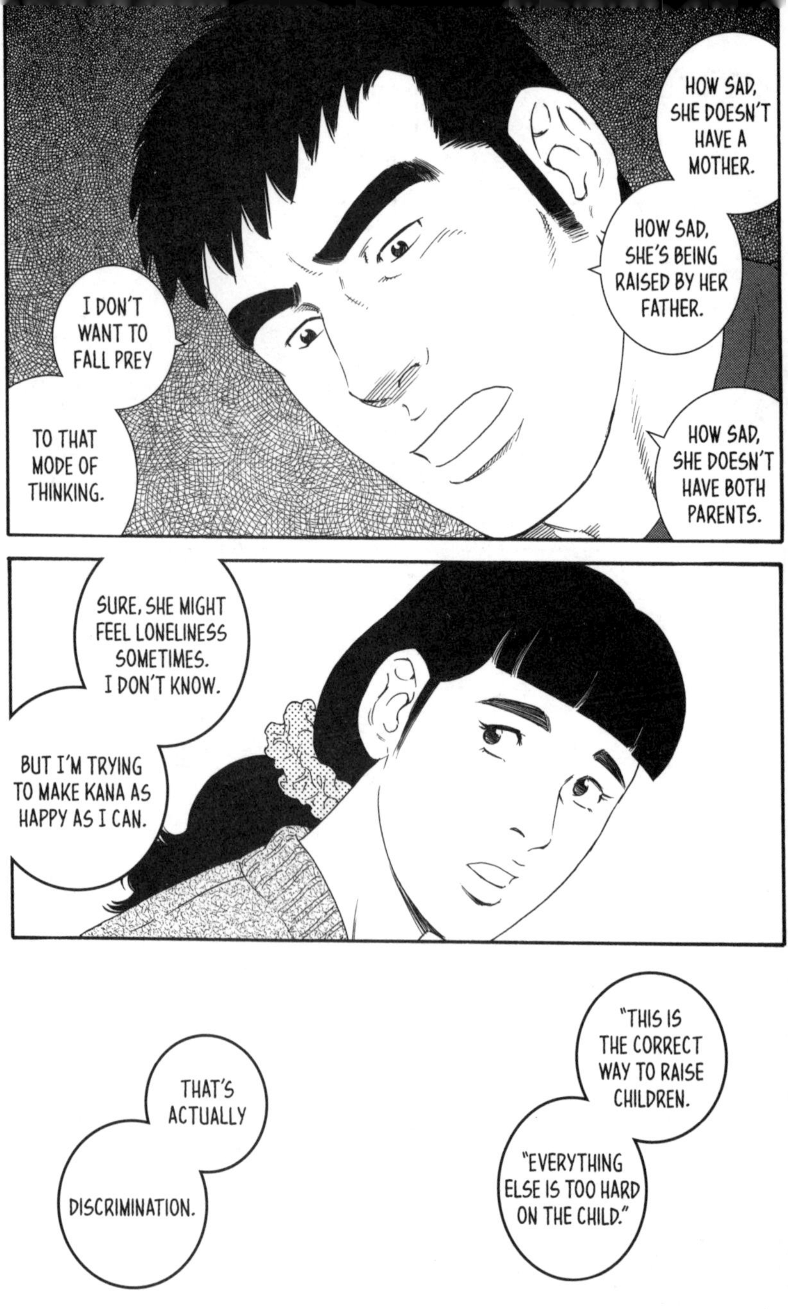
HOW SAD, SHE DOESN'T HAVE A MOTHER.
HOW SAD, SHE'S BEING RAISED BY HER FATHER.
HOW SAD, SHE DOESN'T HAVE BOTH PARENTS.
I DON'T WANT TO FALL PREY
TO THAT MODE OF THINKING.
SURE, SHE MIGHT FEEL LONELINESS SOMETIMES. I DON'T KNOW.
BUT I'M TRYING TO MAKE KANA AS HAPPY AS I CAN.
"THIS IS THE CORRECT WAY TO RAISE CHILDREN.
"EVERYTHING ELSE IS TOO HARD ON THE CHILD."
THAT'S ACTUALLY
DISCRIMINATION.

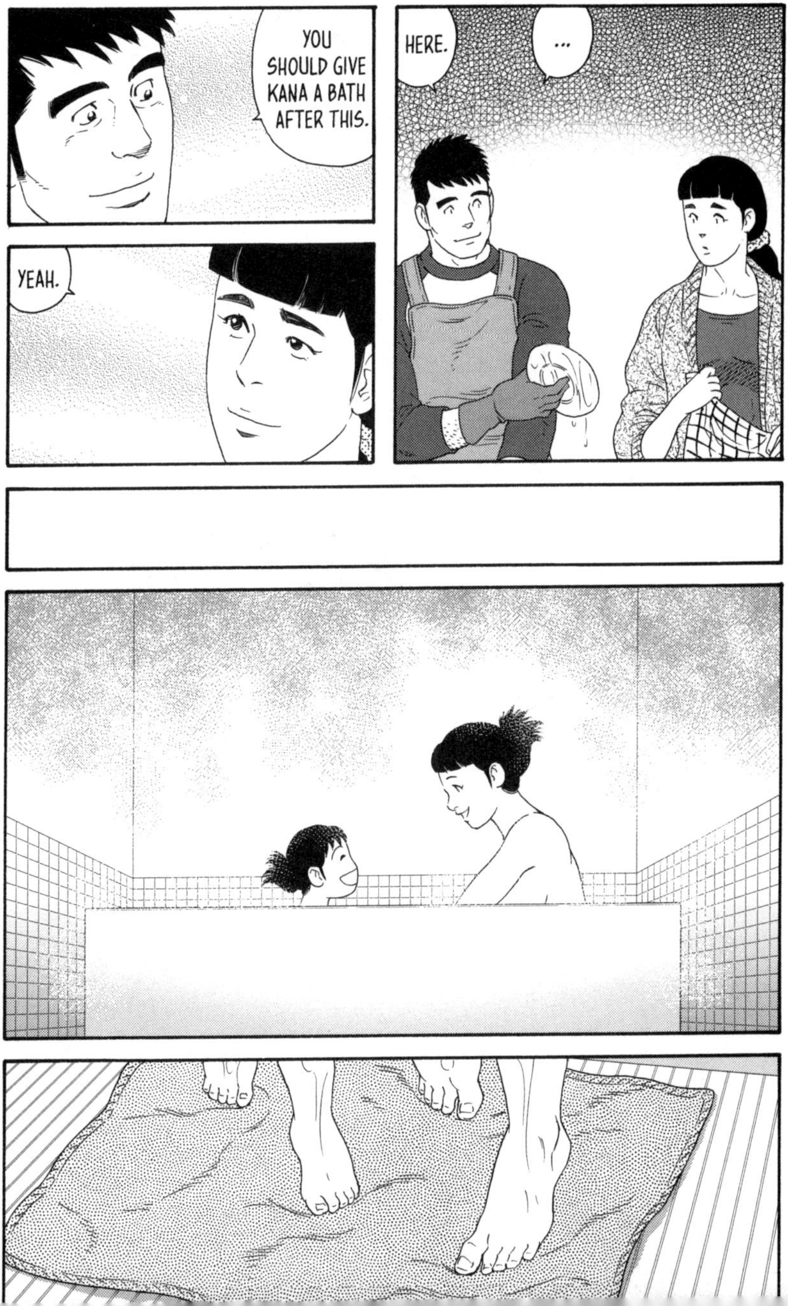
...
HERE.
YOU SHOULD GIVE KANA A BATH AFTER THIS.
YEAH.

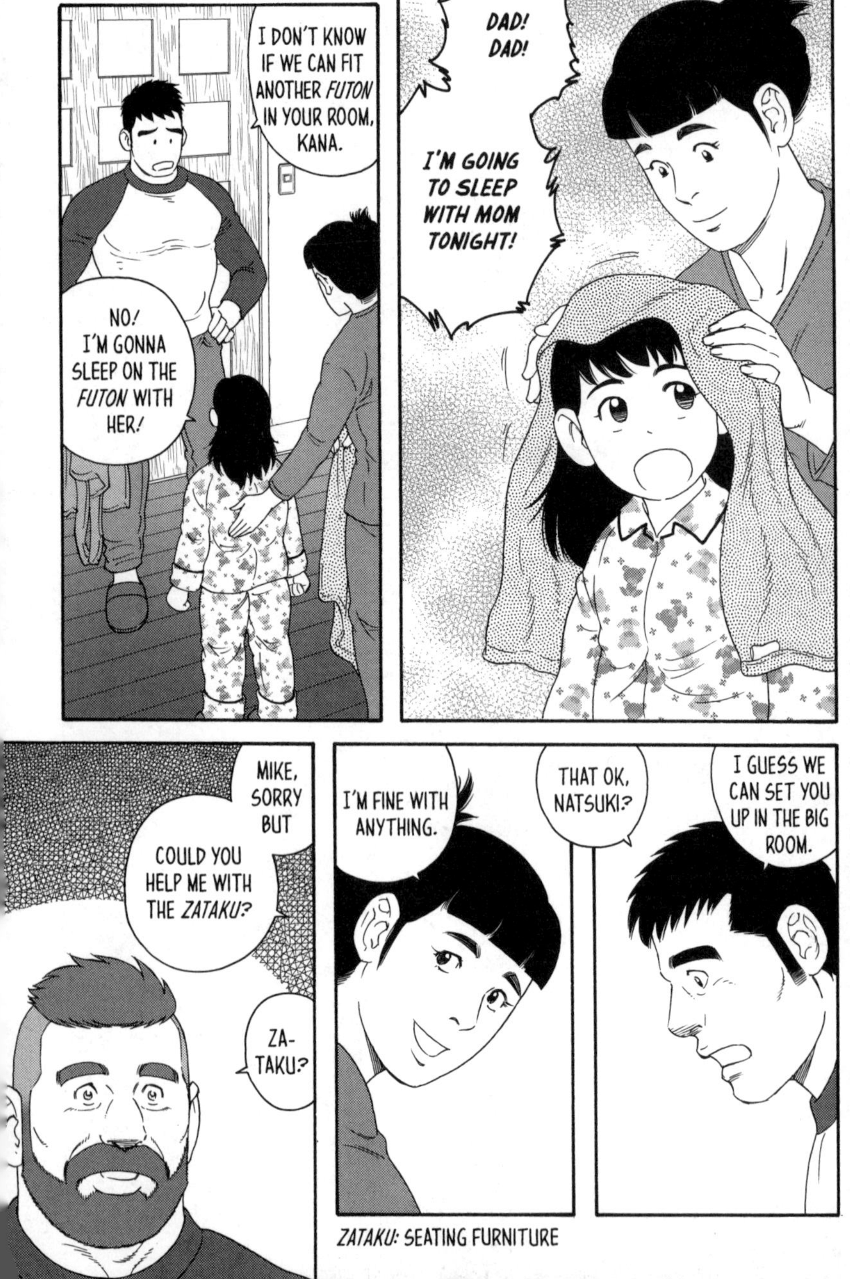
DAD! DAD!
I'M GOING TO SLEEP WITH MOM TONIGHT!
I DON'T KNOW IF WE CAN FIT ANOTHER *FUTON* IN YOUR ROOM, KANA.
NO! I'M GONNA SLEEP ON THE *FUTON* WITH HER!
I GUESS WE CAN SET YOU UP IN THE BIG ROOM.
THAT OK, NATSUKI?
I'M FINE WITH ANYTHING.
MIKE, SORRY BUT
COULD YOU HELP ME WITH THE *ZATAKU*?
ZA-TAKU?

ZATAKU: SEATING FURNITURE

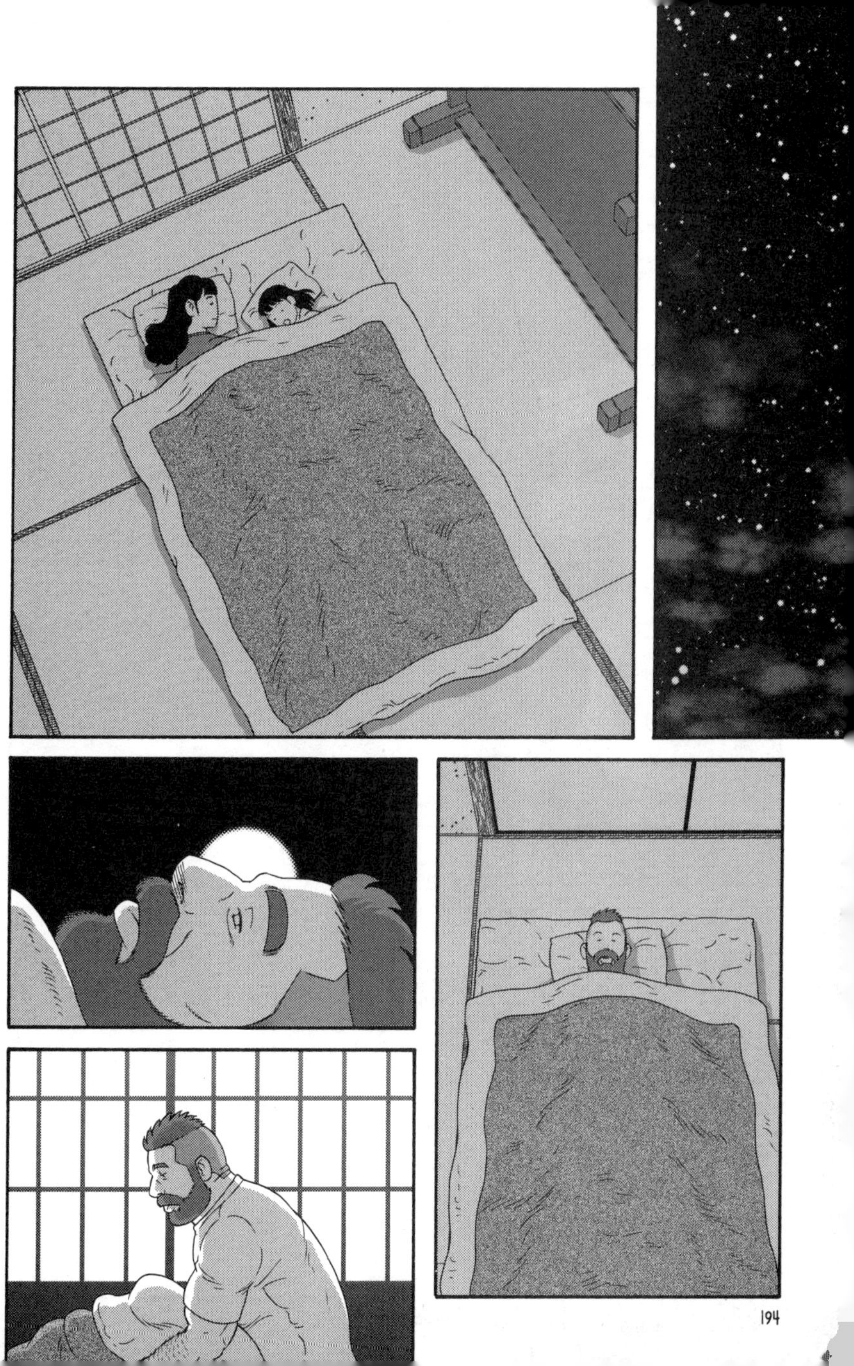

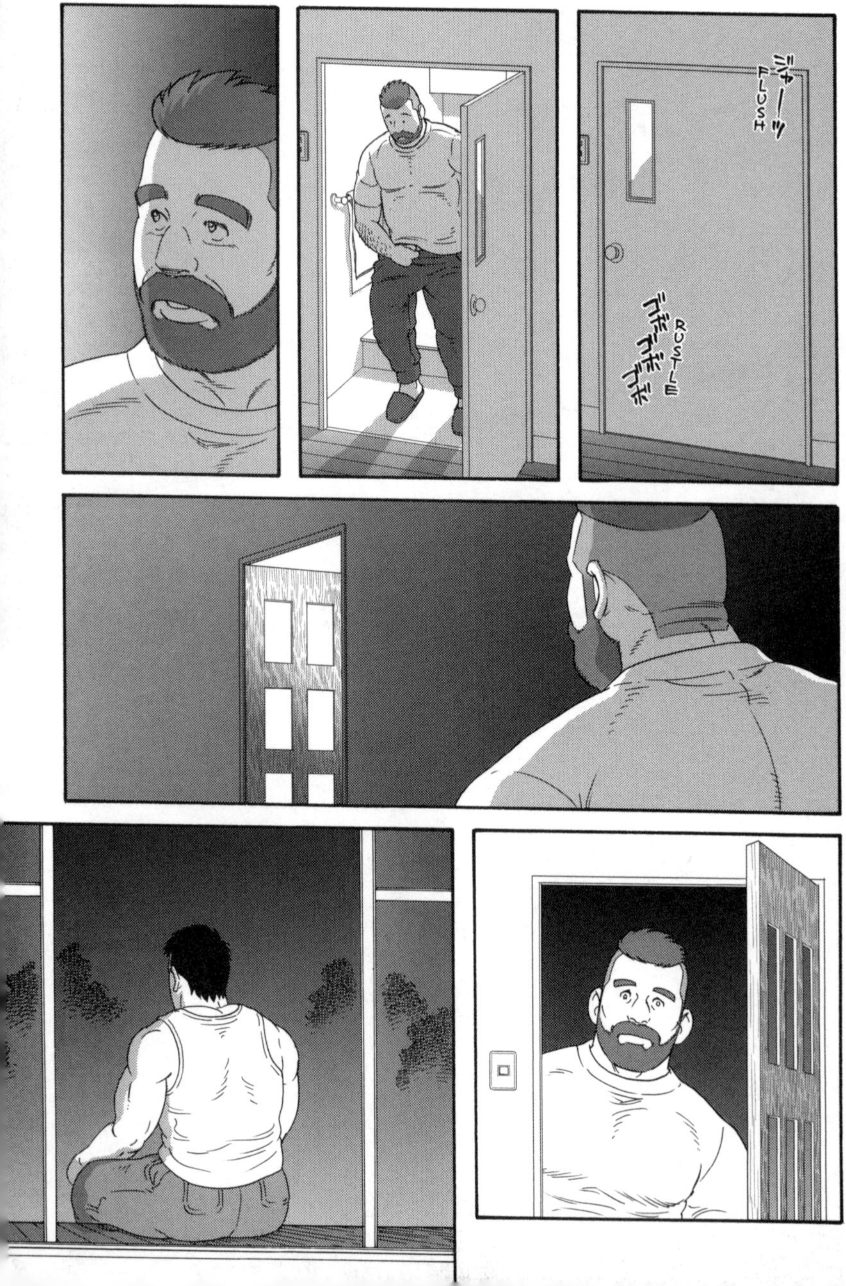
ジャーッ
FLUSH
ゴボゴボゴボ
RUSTLE

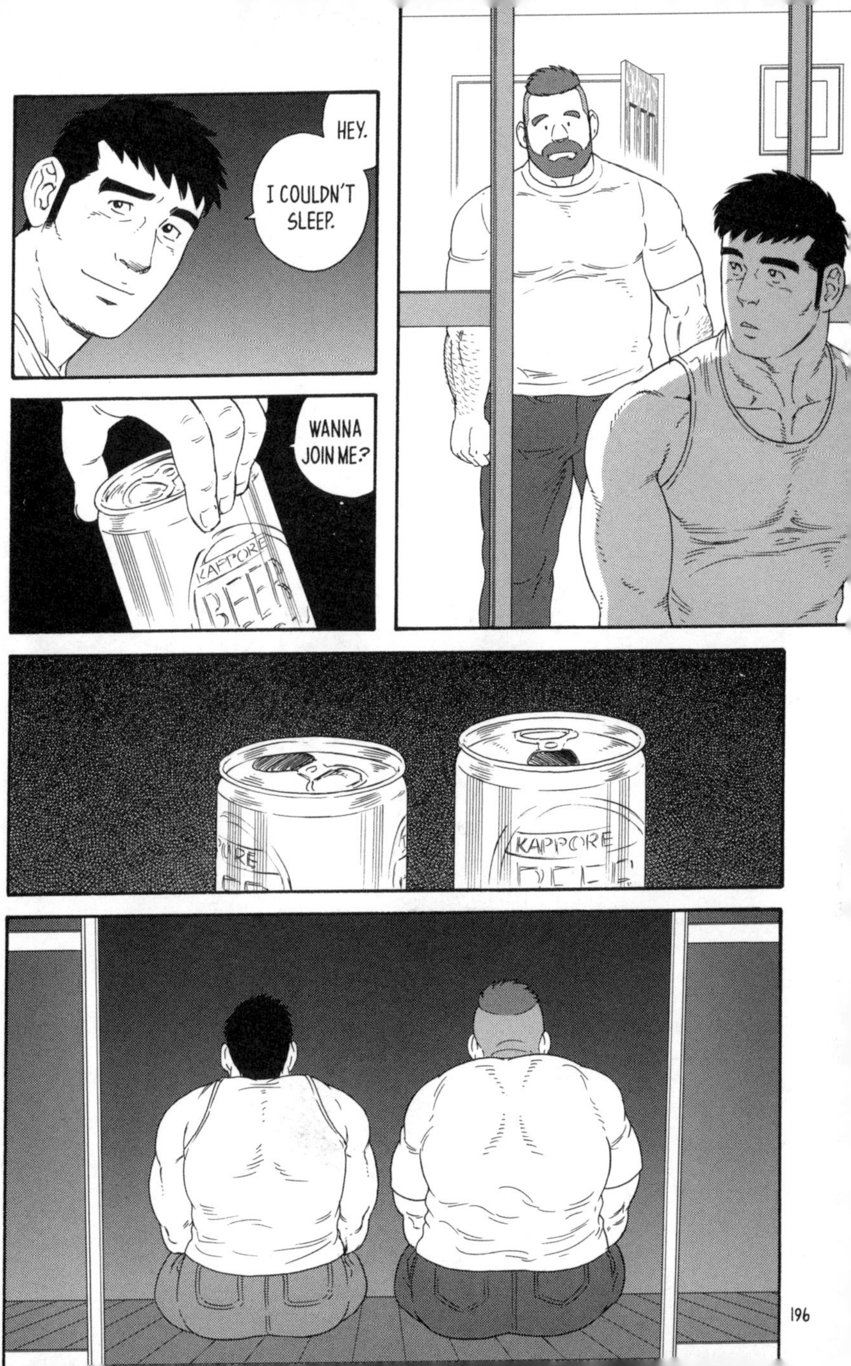
HEY.
I COULDN'T SLEEP.
WANNA JOIN ME?
KAPPORE
KAPPORE

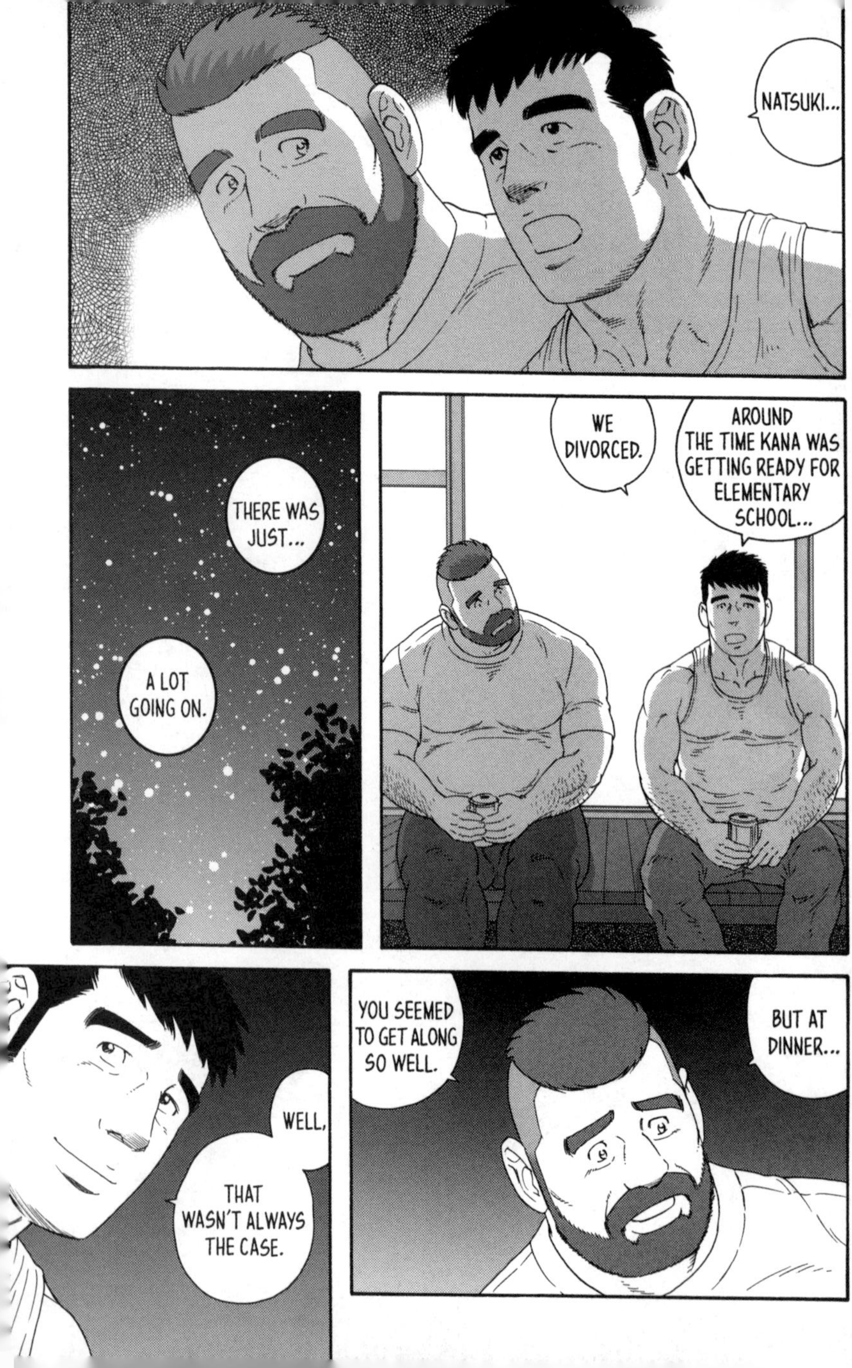
NATSUKI...
AROUND THE TIME KANA WAS GETTING READY FOR ELEMENTARY SCHOOL...
WE DIVORCED.
THERE WAS JUST...
A LOT GOING ON.
BUT AT DINNER...
YOU SEEMED TO GET ALONG SO WELL.
WELL,
THAT WASN'T ALWAYS THE CASE.

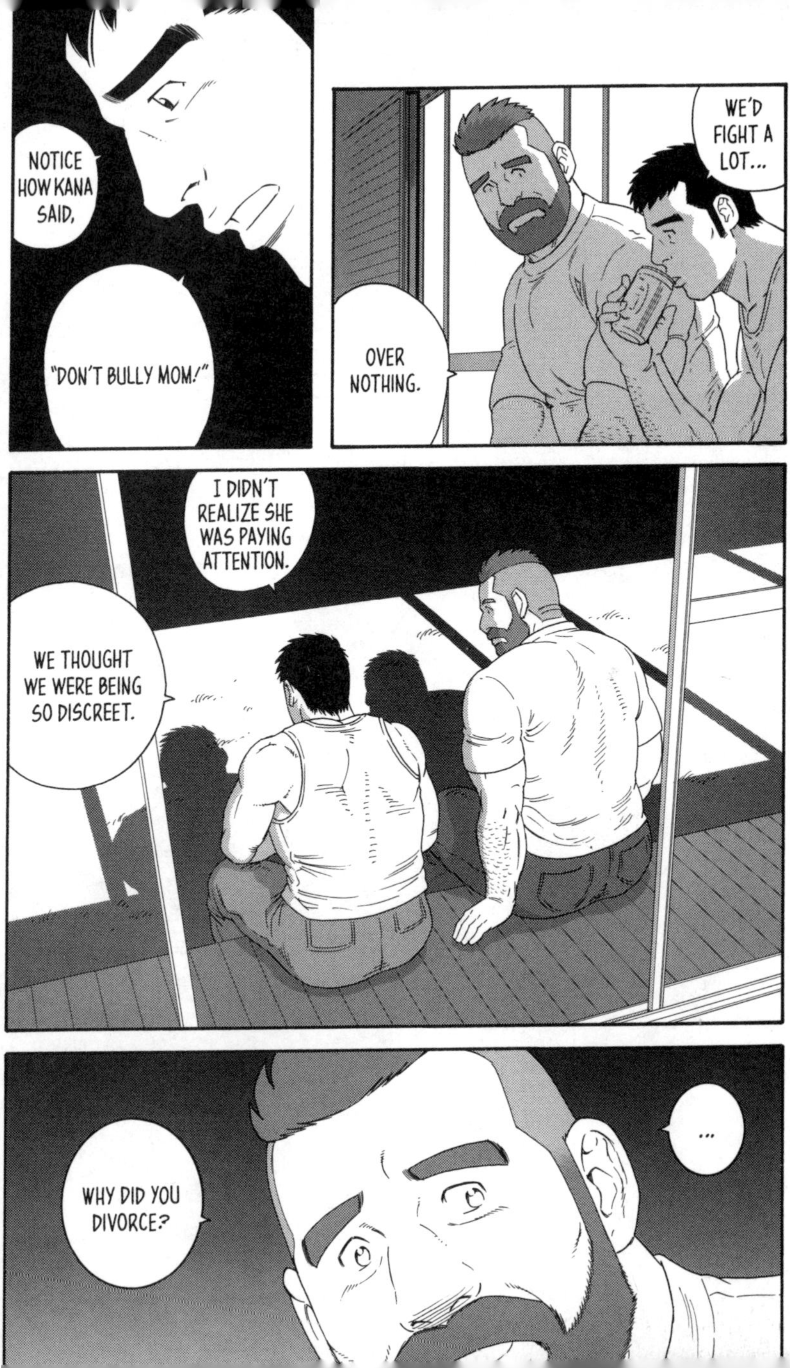
WE'D FIGHT A LOT...
OVER NOTHING.
NOTICE HOW KANA SAID,
"DON'T BULLY MOM!"
I DIDN'T REALIZE SHE WAS PAYING ATTENTION.
WE THOUGHT WE WERE BEING SO DISCREET.
...
WHY DID YOU DIVORCE?

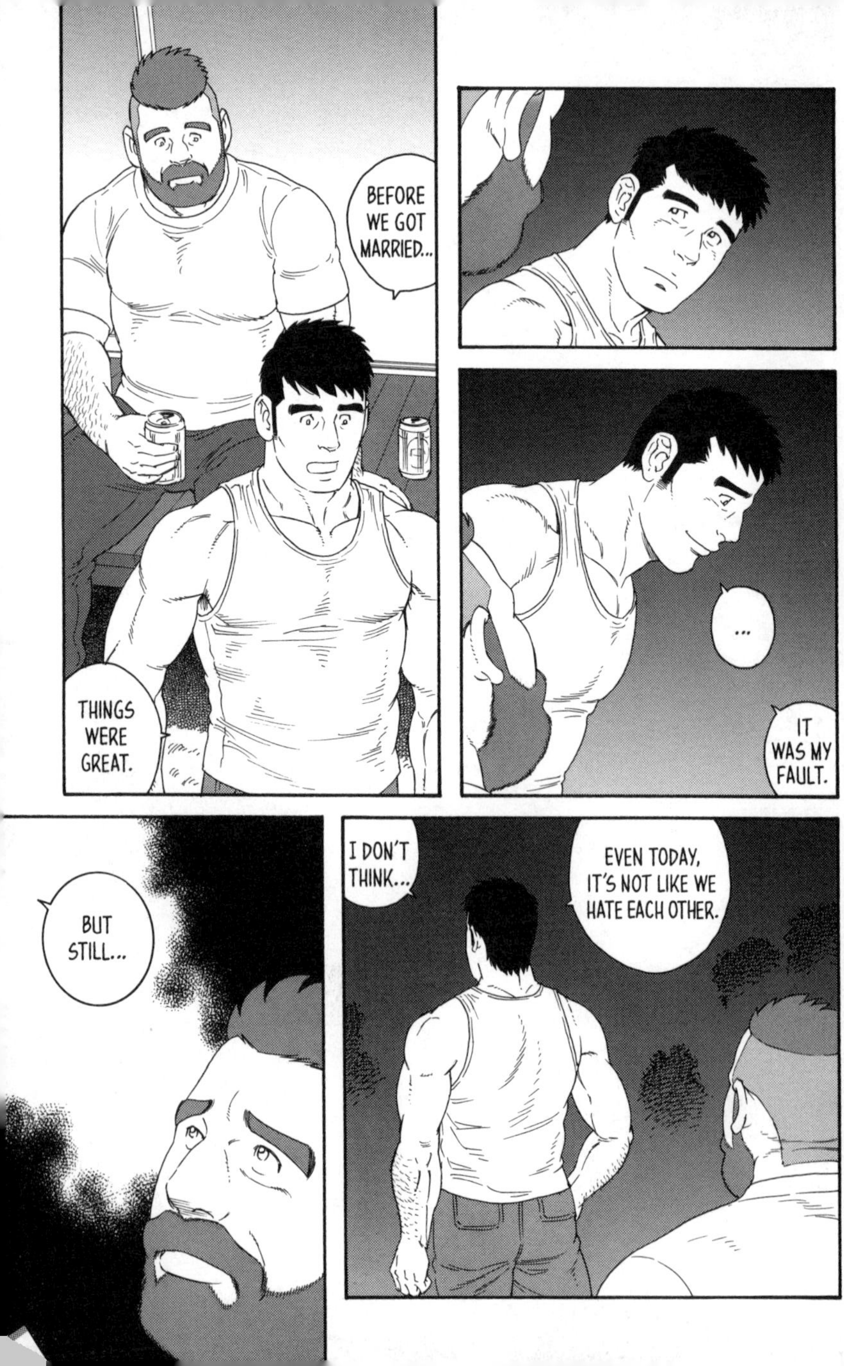
BEFORE WE GOT MARRIED...
THINGS WERE GREAT.
...
IT WAS MY FAULT.
BUT STILL...
I DON'T THINK...
EVEN TODAY, IT'S NOT LIKE WE HATE EACH OTHER.

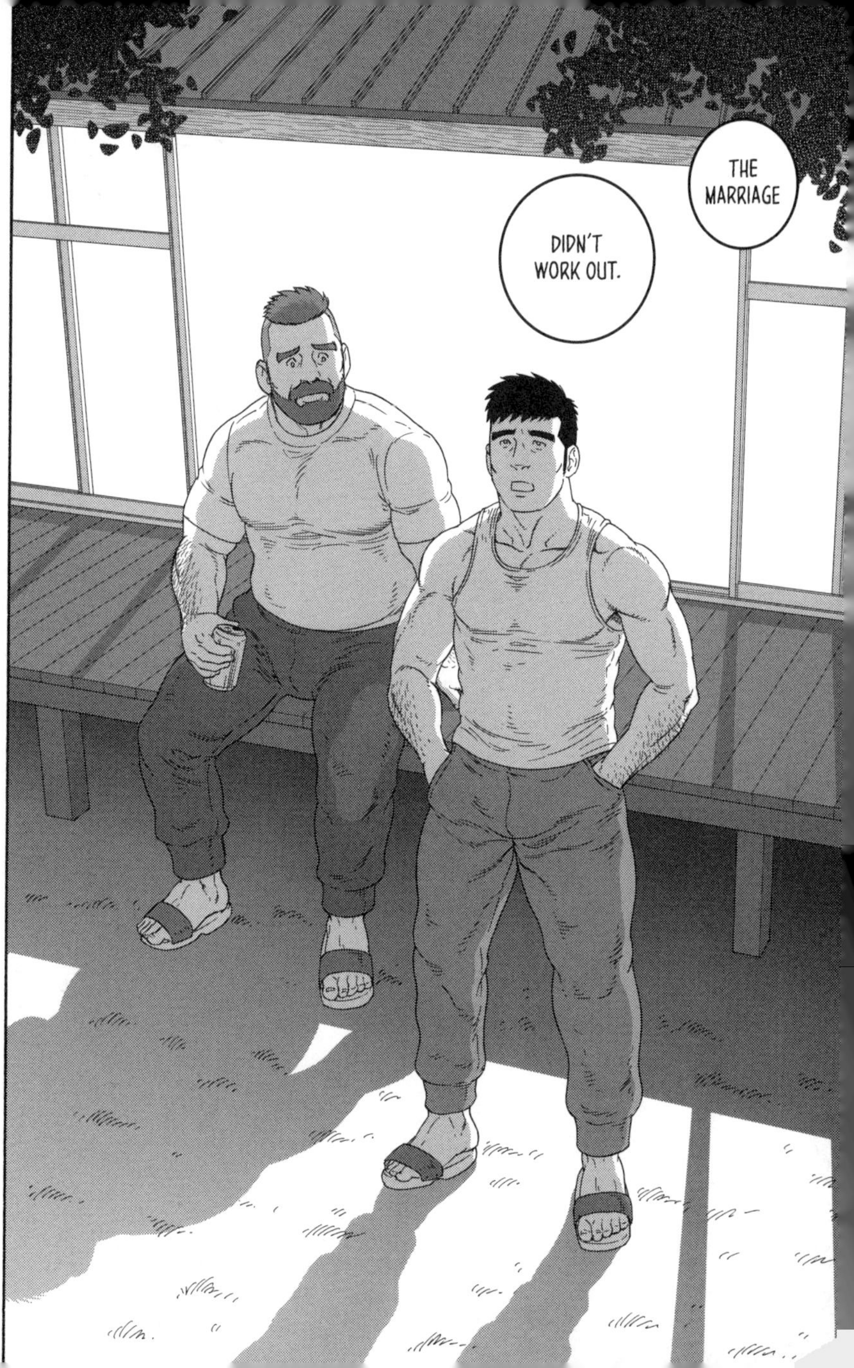
THE MARRIAGE
DIDN'T WORK OUT.

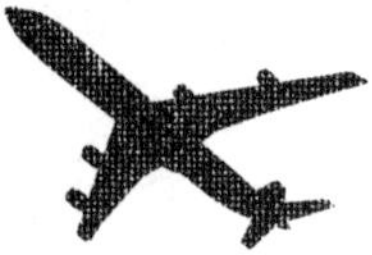

CHAPTER NINE

RETURNING

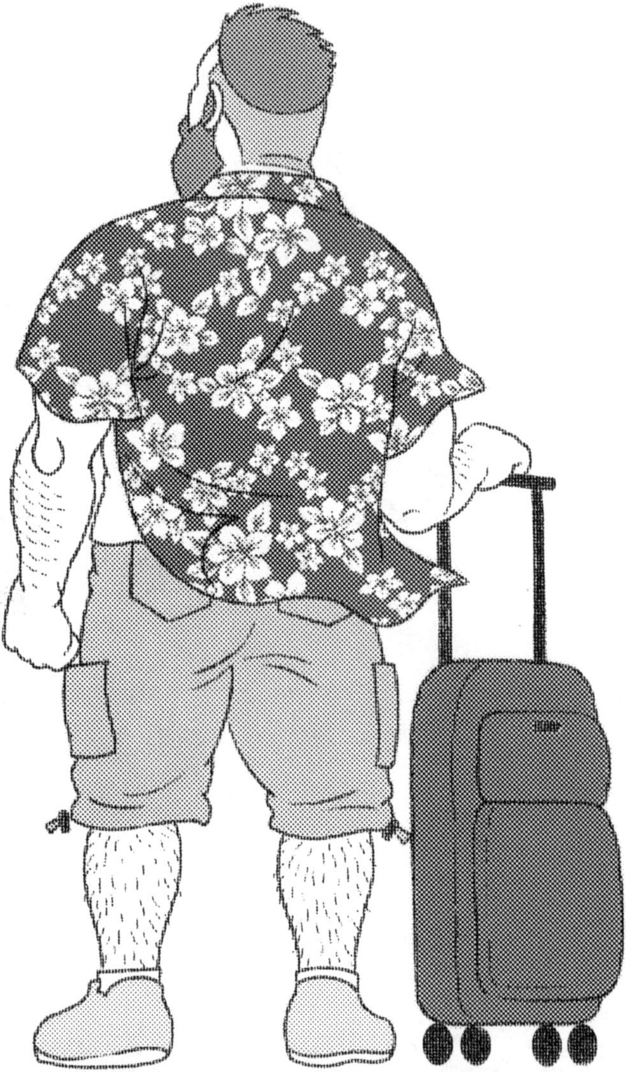

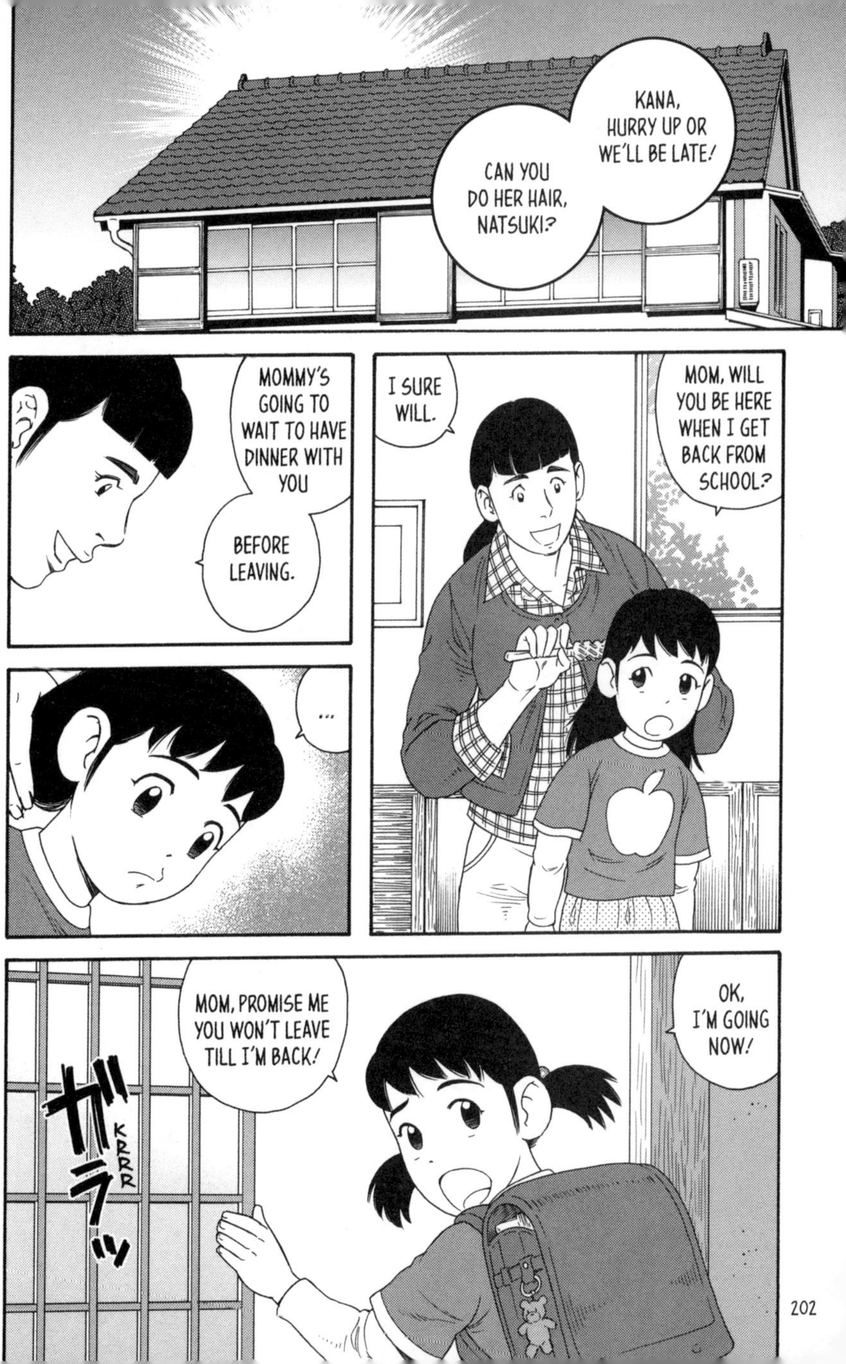
KANA, HURRY UP OR WE'LL BE LATE!
CAN YOU DO HER HAIR, NATSUKI?
MOM, WILL YOU BE HERE WHEN I GET BACK FROM SCHOOL?
I SURE WILL.
MOMMY'S GOING TO WAIT TO HAVE DINNER WITH YOU
BEFORE LEAVING.
...
OK, I'M GOING NOW!
MOM, PROMISE ME YOU WON'T LEAVE TILL I'M BACK!
ガラッ
KRRR

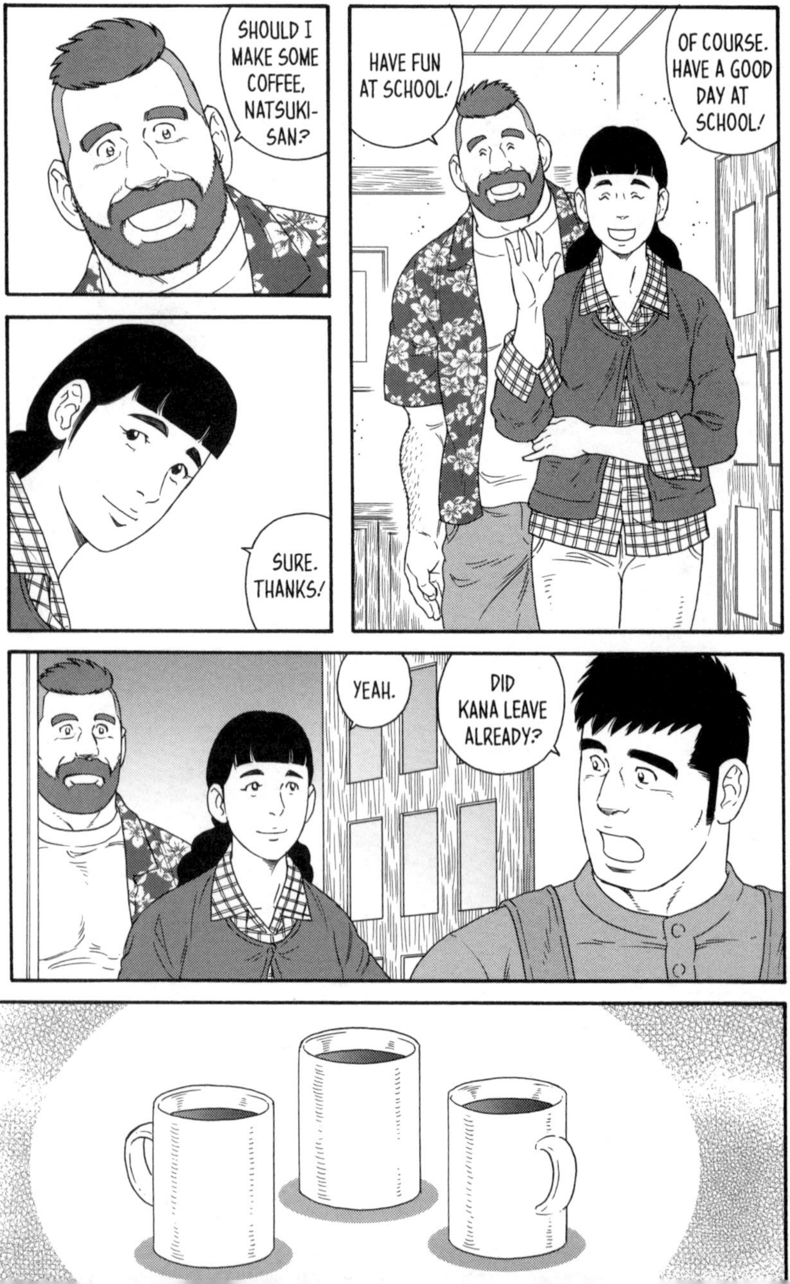
OF COURSE. HAVE A GOOD DAY AT SCHOOL!
HAVE FUN AT SCHOOL!
SHOULD I MAKE SOME COFFEE, NATSUKI-SAN?
SURE. THANKS!
DID KANA LEAVE ALREADY?
YEAH.

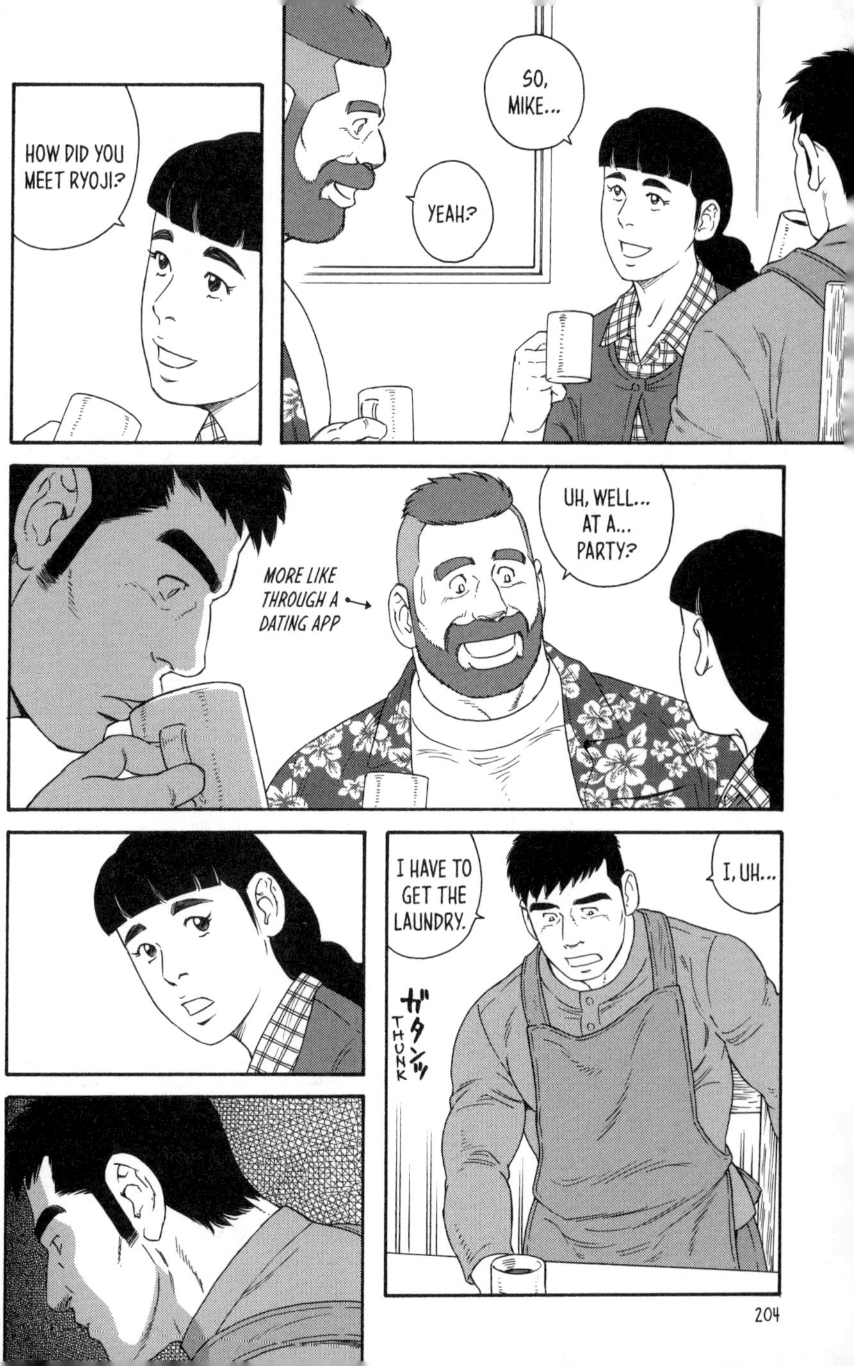
SO, MIKE...
YEAH?
HOW DID YOU MEET RYOJI?
UH, WELL... AT A... PARTY?
MORE LIKE THROUGH A DATING APP
I, UH...
I HAVE TO GET THE LAUNDRY.
ガタンッ
THUNK

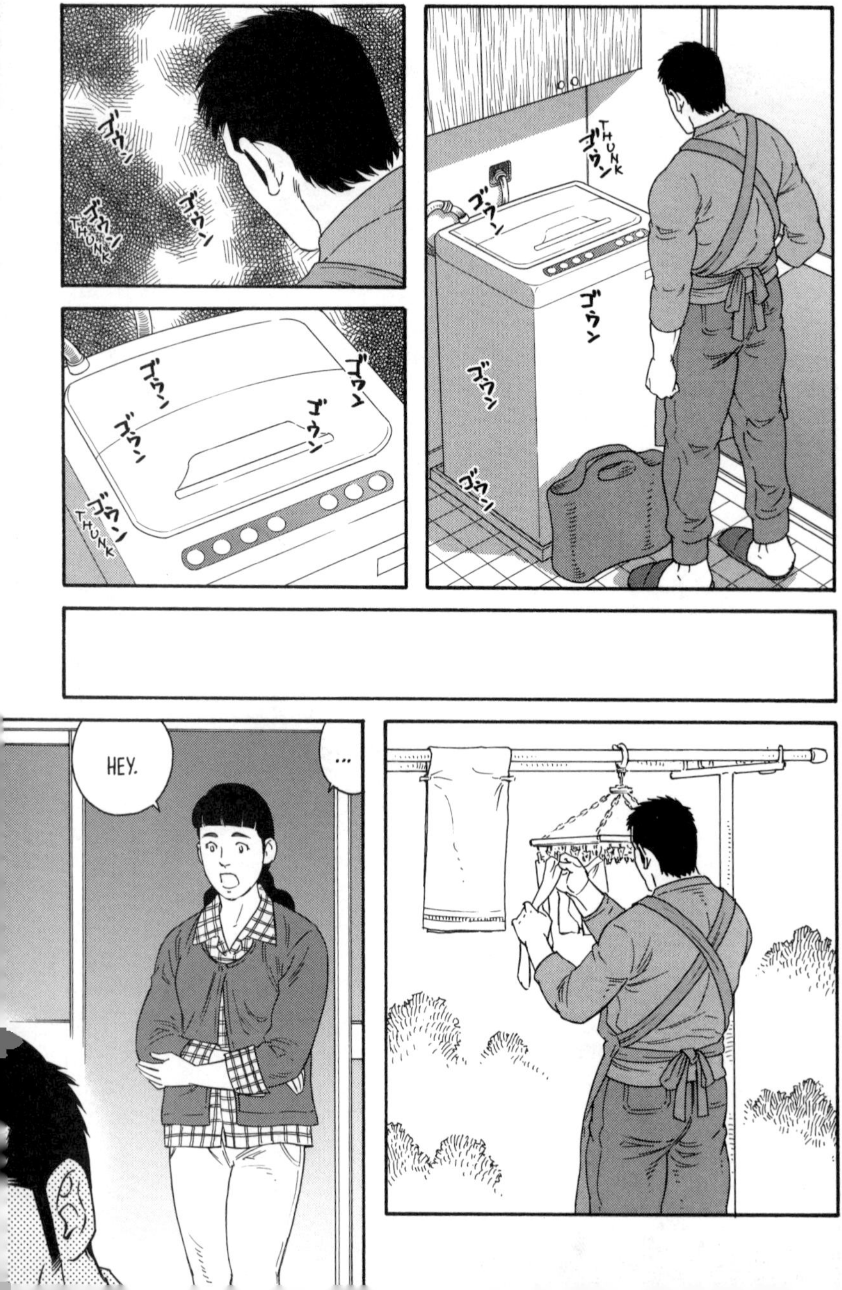
THUNK
ゴウン
ゴウン
ゴウン
ゴウン
ゴウン
ゴウン
ゴウン
ゴウン
THUNK
ゴウン
ゴウン
ゴウン
ゴウン
ゴウン
THUNK
...
HEY.

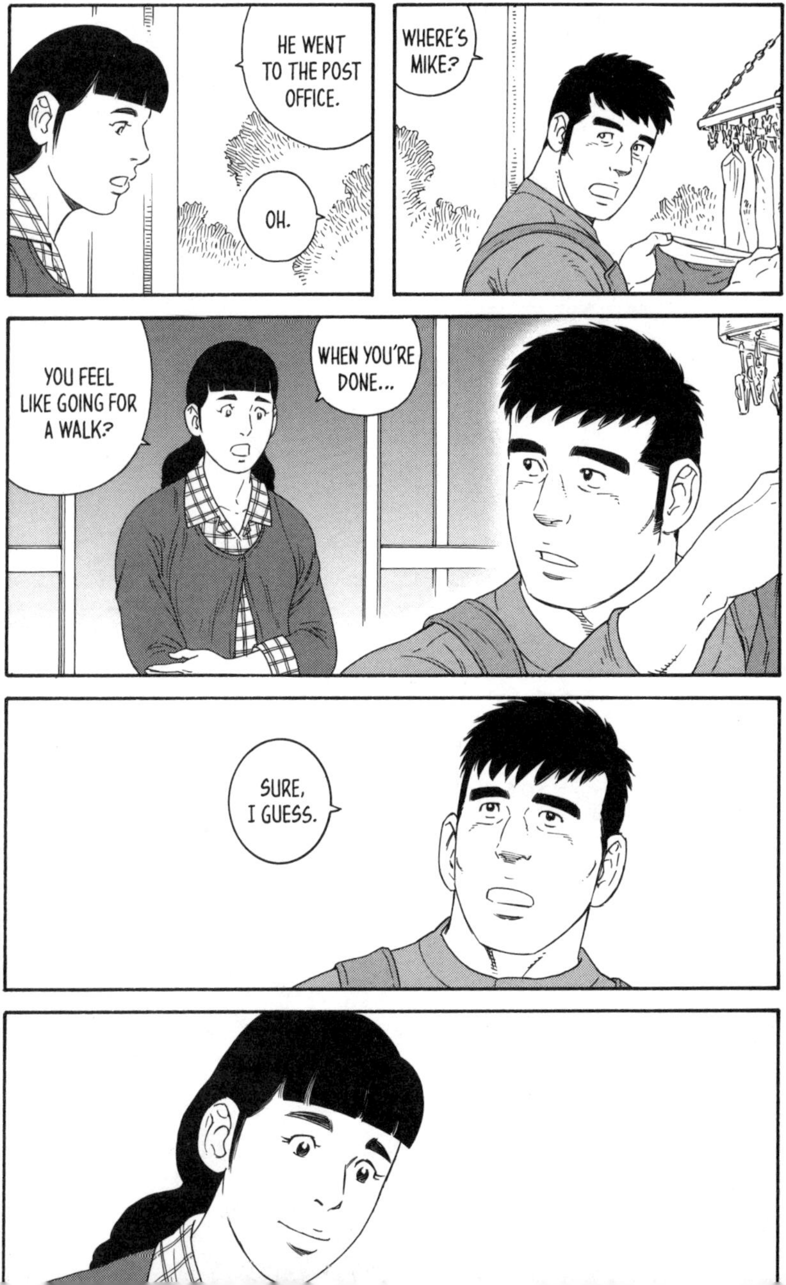
WHERE'S MIKE?
HE WENT TO THE POST OFFICE.
OH.
WHEN YOU'RE DONE...
YOU FEEL LIKE GOING FOR A WALK?
SURE, I GUESS.

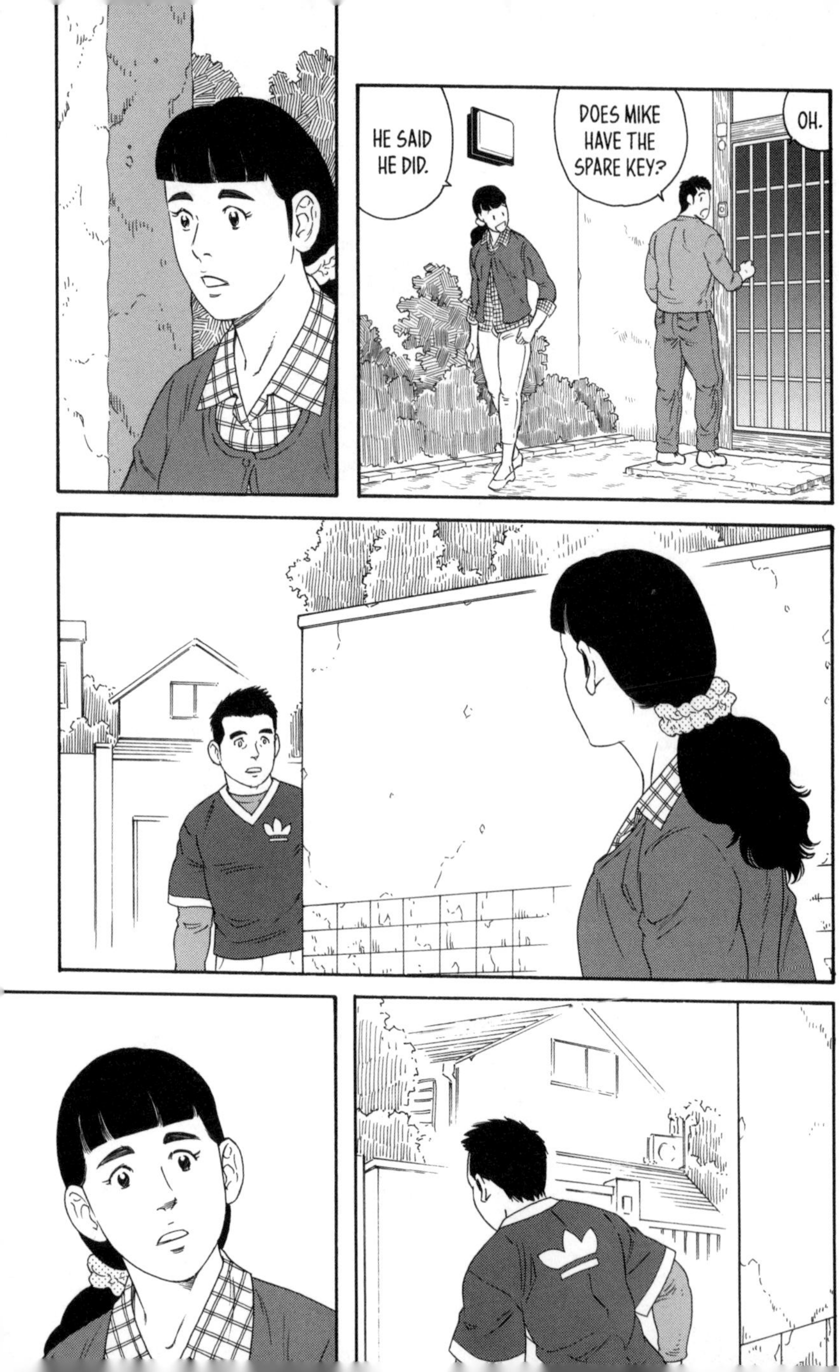
OH.
DOES MIKE HAVE THE SPARE KEY?
HE SAID HE DID.

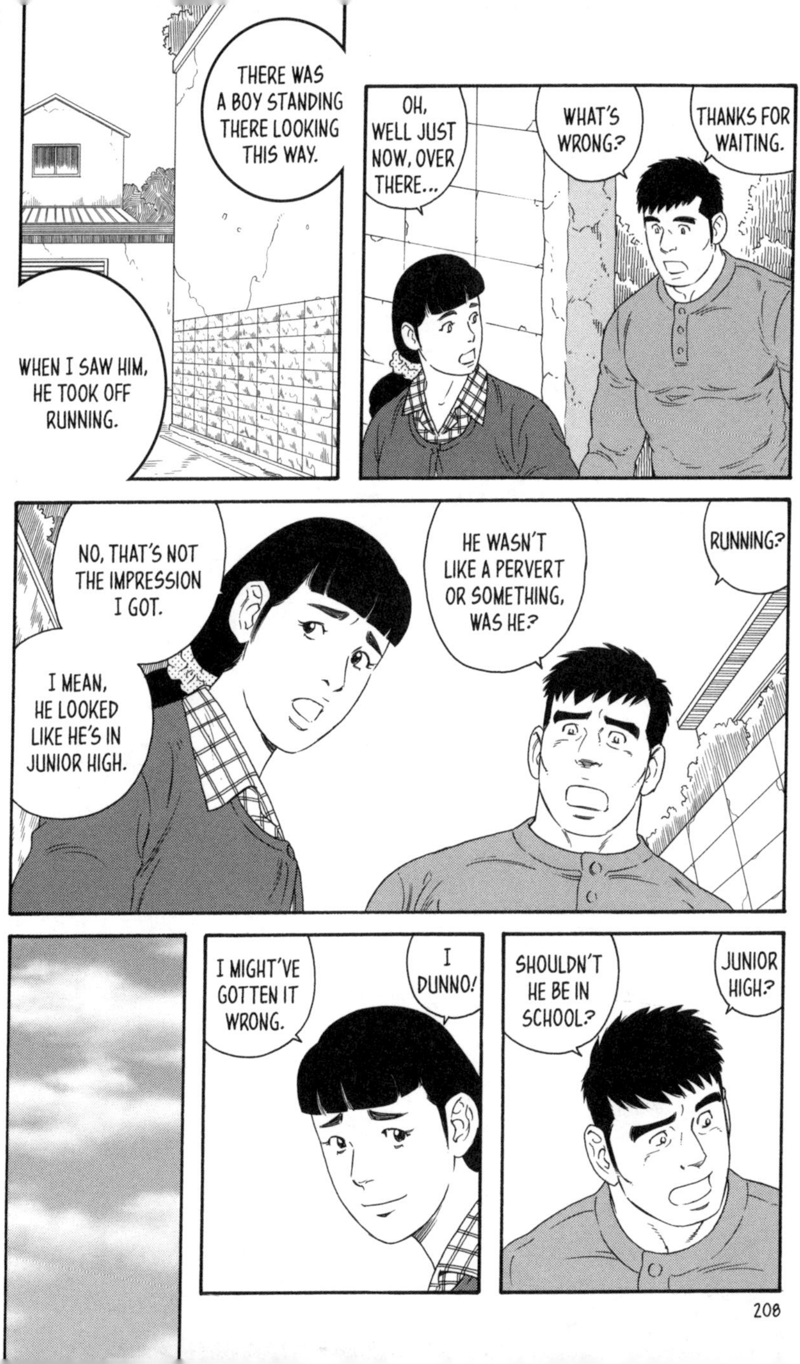
THANKS FOR WAITING.
WHAT'S WRONG?
OH, WELL JUST NOW, OVER THERE...
THERE WAS A BOY STANDING THERE LOOKING THIS WAY.
WHEN I SAW HIM, HE TOOK OFF RUNNING.
RUNNING?
HE WASN'T LIKE A PERVERT OR SOMETHING, WAS HE?
NO, THAT'S NOT THE IMPRESSION I GOT.
I MEAN, HE LOOKED LIKE HE'S IN JUNIOR HIGH.
JUNIOR HIGH?
SHOULDN'T HE BE IN SCHOOL?
I DUNNO!
I MIGHT'VE GOTTEN IT WRONG.

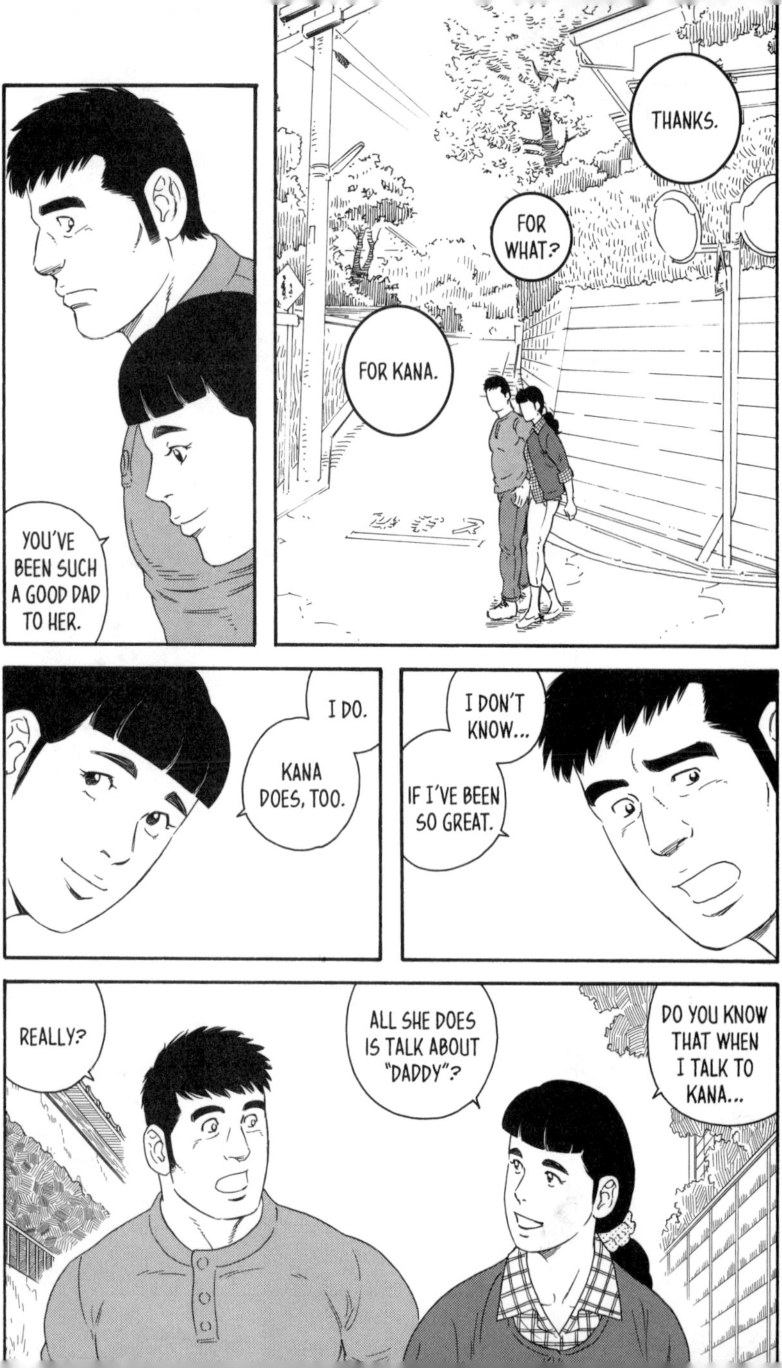
THANKS.
FOR WHAT?
FOR KANA.
YOU'VE BEEN SUCH A GOOD DAD TO HER.
I DON'T KNOW...
IF I'VE BEEN SO GREAT.
I DO.
KANA DOES, TOO.
DO YOU KNOW THAT WHEN I TALK TO KANA...
ALL SHE DOES IS TALK ABOUT "DADDY"?
REALLY?

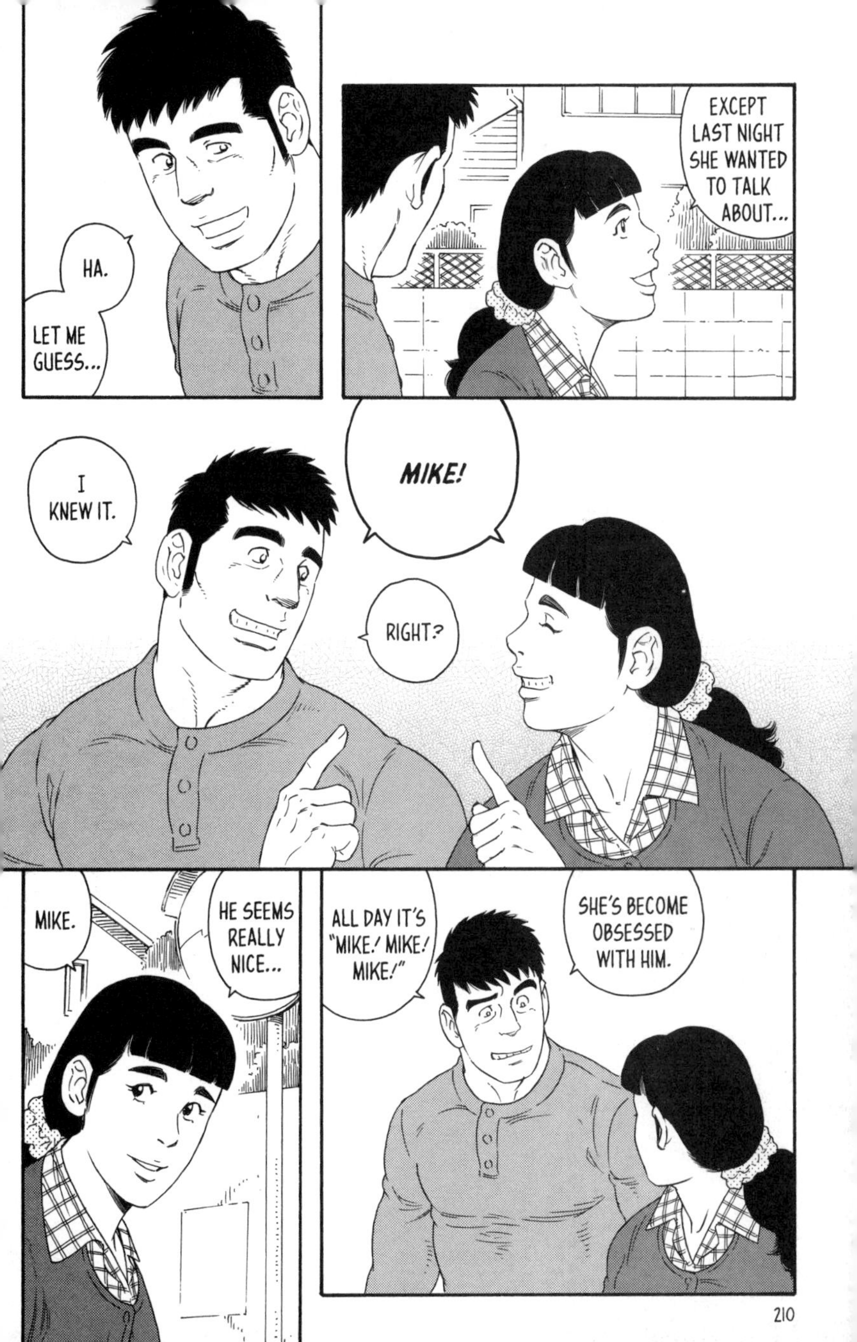
EXCEPT LAST NIGHT SHE WANTED TO TALK ABOUT...
HA.
LET ME GUESS...
MIKE!
I KNEW IT.
RIGHT?
SHE'S BECOME OBSESSED WITH HIM.
ALL DAY IT'S "MIKE! MIKE! MIKE!"
HE SEEMS REALLY NICE...
MIKE.

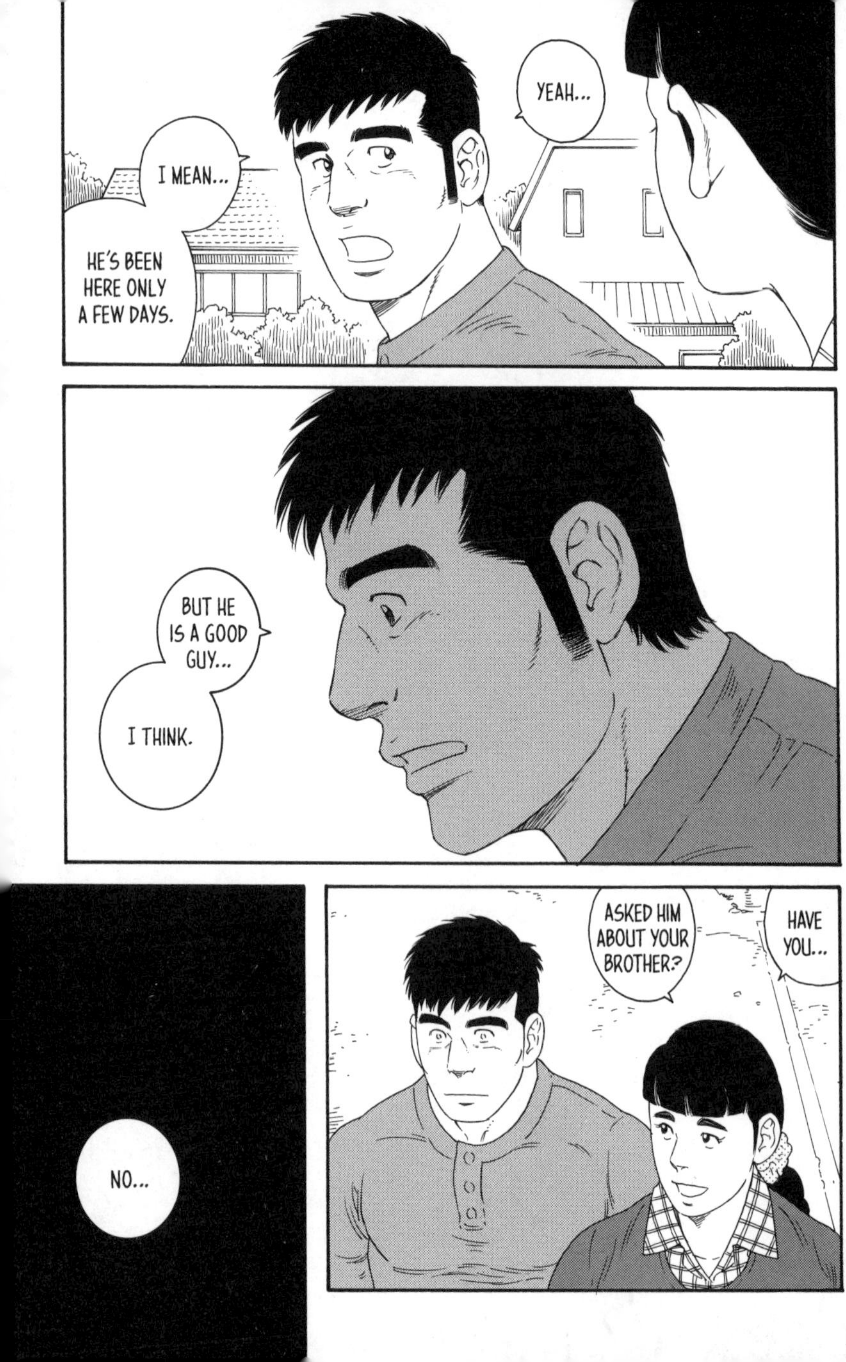
YEAH...
I MEAN...
HE'S BEEN HERE ONLY A FEW DAYS.
BUT HE IS A GOOD GUY...
I THINK.
HAVE YOU...
ASKED HIM ABOUT YOUR BROTHER?
NO...

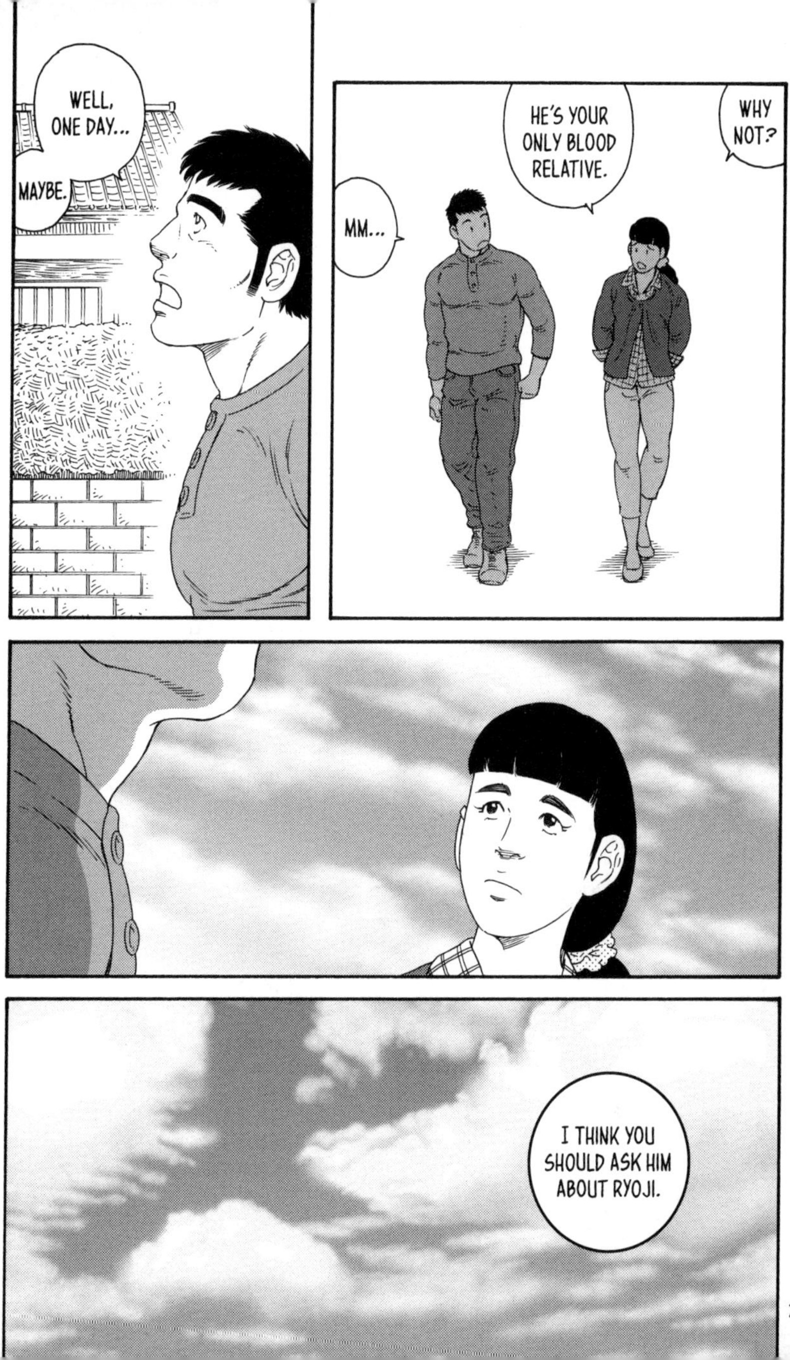
WHY NOT?
HE'S YOUR ONLY BLOOD RELATIVE.
MM...
WELL, ONE DAY...
MAYBE.
I THINK YOU SHOULD ASK HIM ABOUT RYOJI.

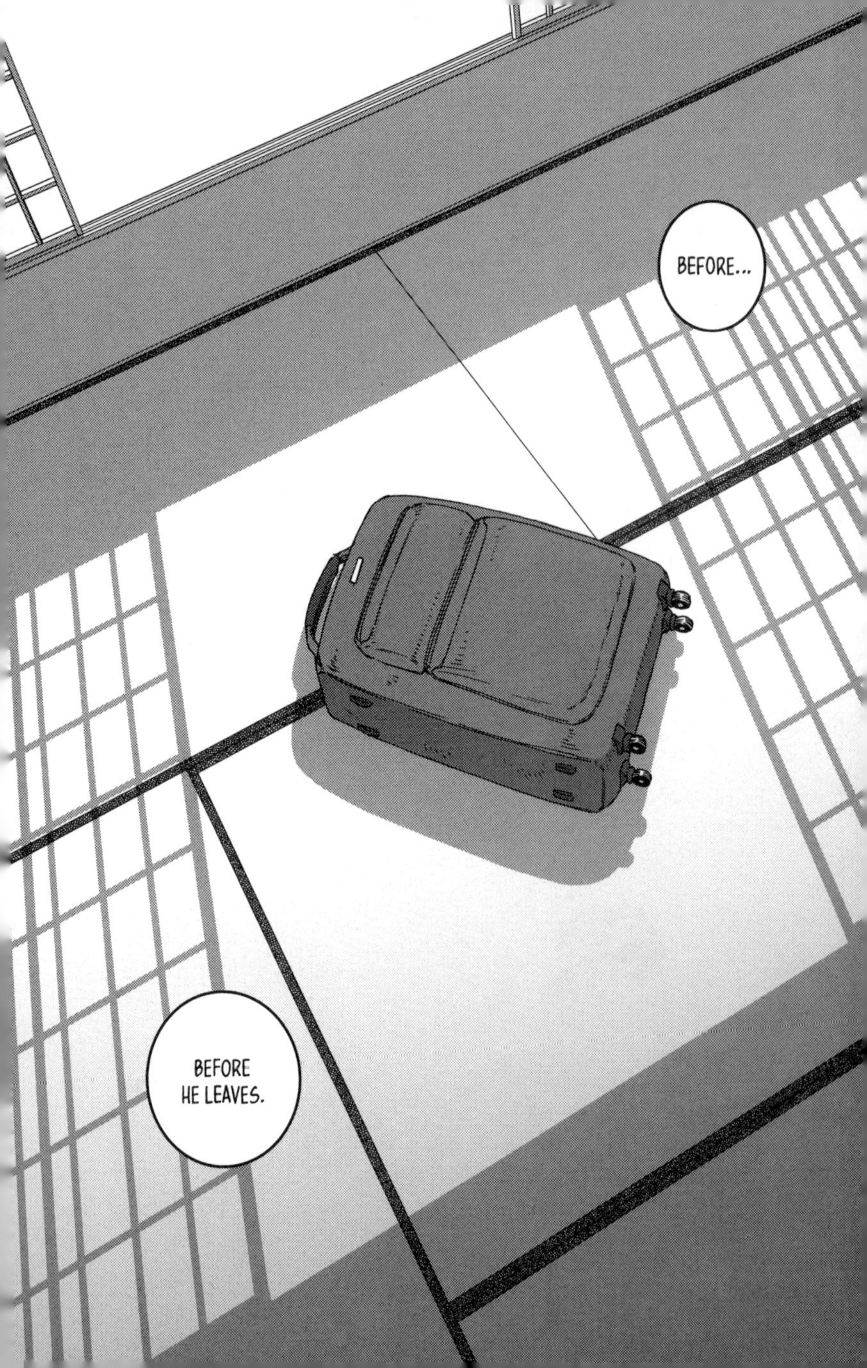
BEFORE...
BEFORE HE LEAVES.

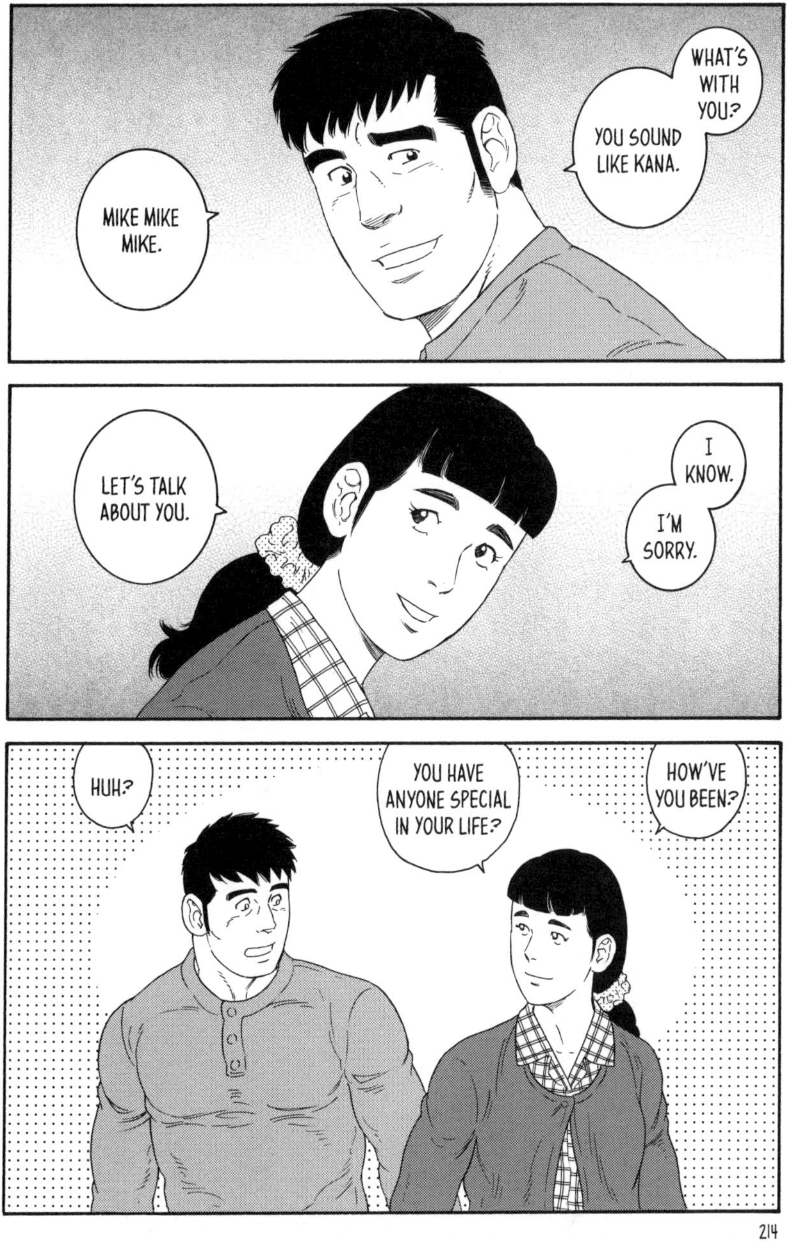
WHAT'S WITH YOU?
YOU SOUND LIKE KANA.
MIKE MIKE MIKE.
I KNOW.
I'M SORRY.
LET'S TALK ABOUT YOU.
HOW'VE YOU BEEN?
YOU HAVE ANYONE SPECIAL IN YOUR LIFE?
HUH?

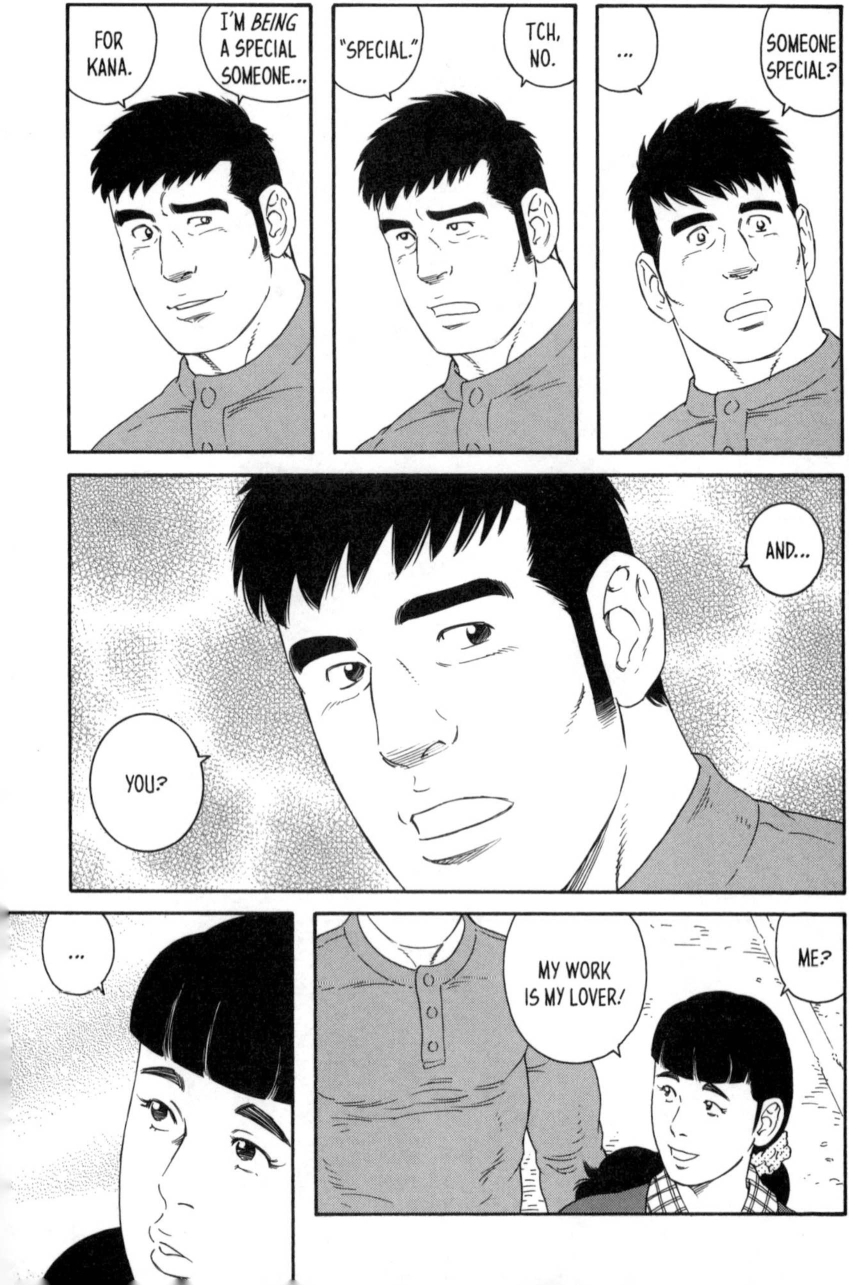
SOMEONE SPECIAL?
...
TCH, NO.
"SPECIAL."
I'M *BEING* A SPECIAL SOMEONE...
FOR KANA.
AND...
YOU?
ME?
MY WORK IS MY LOVER!
...

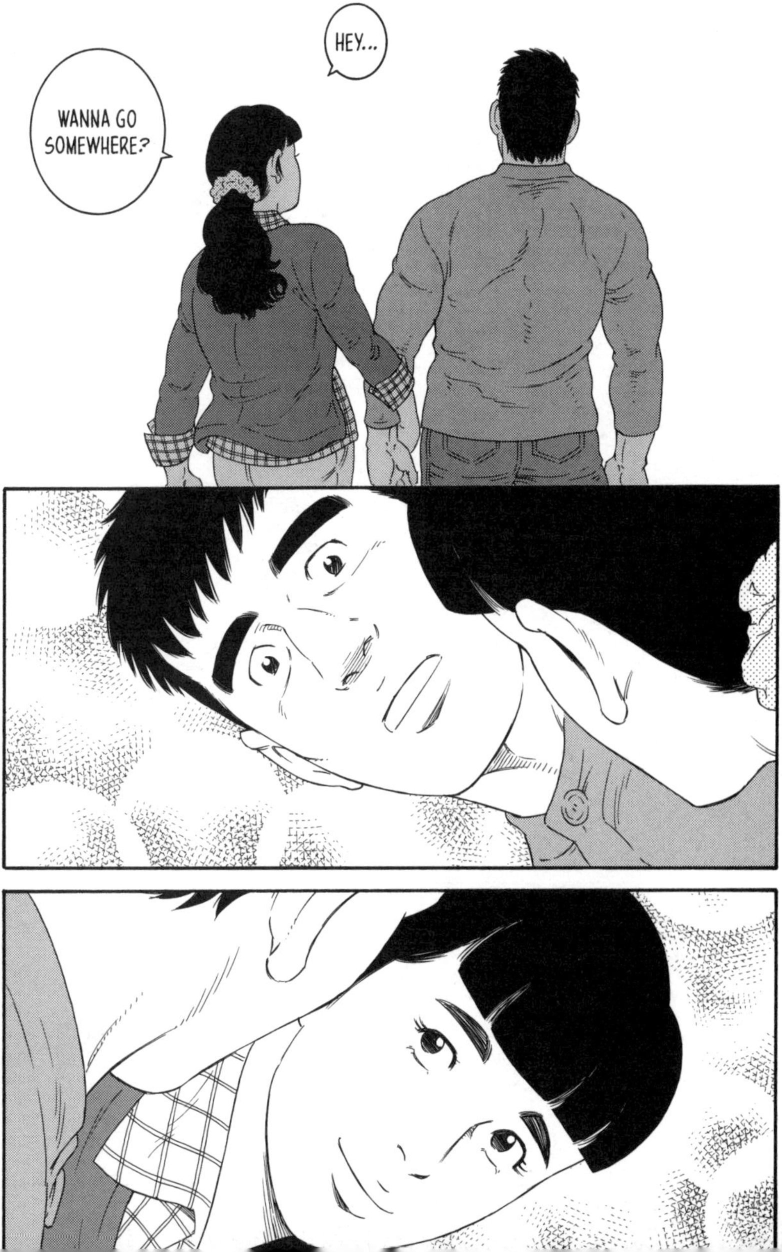
HEY...
WANNA GO SOMEWHERE?

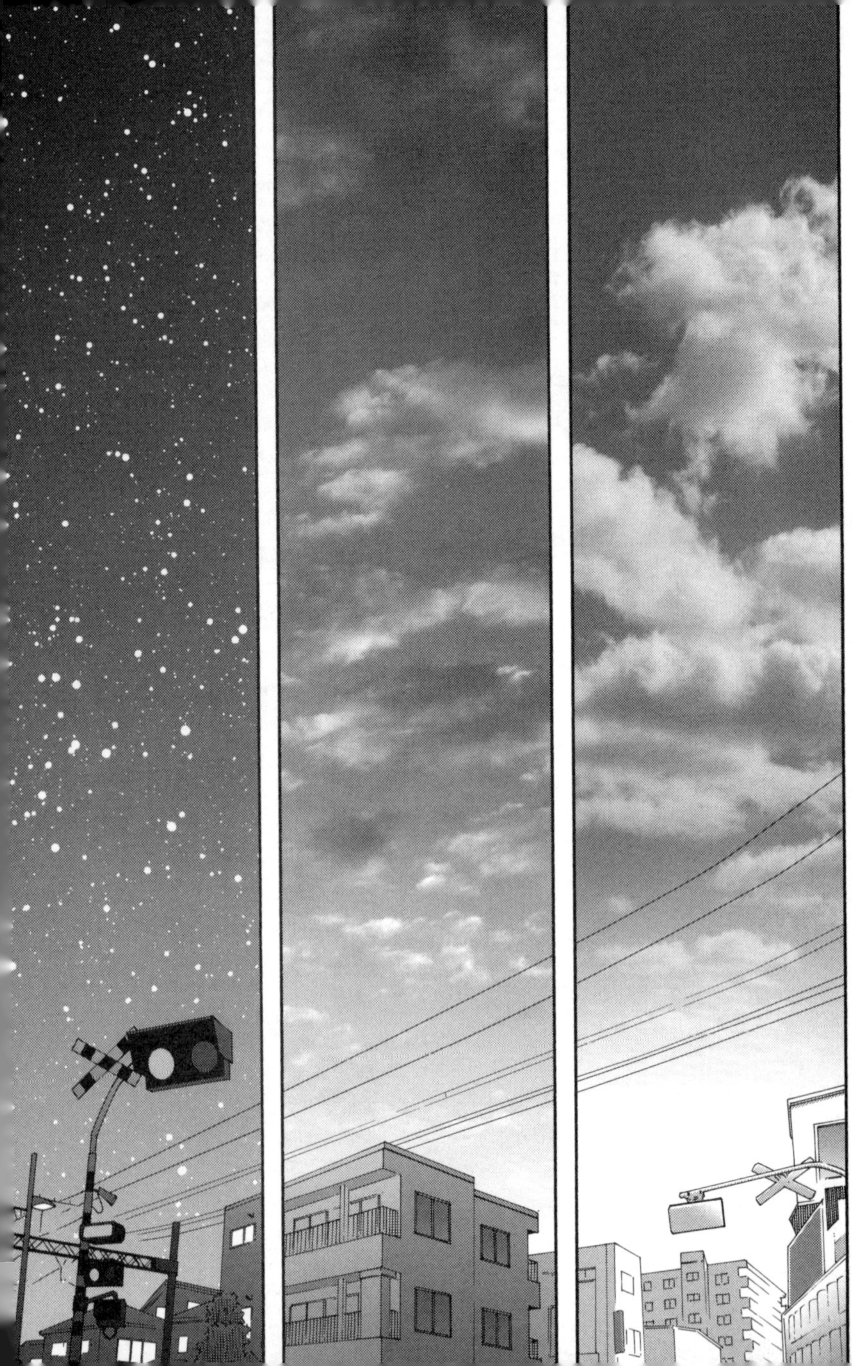

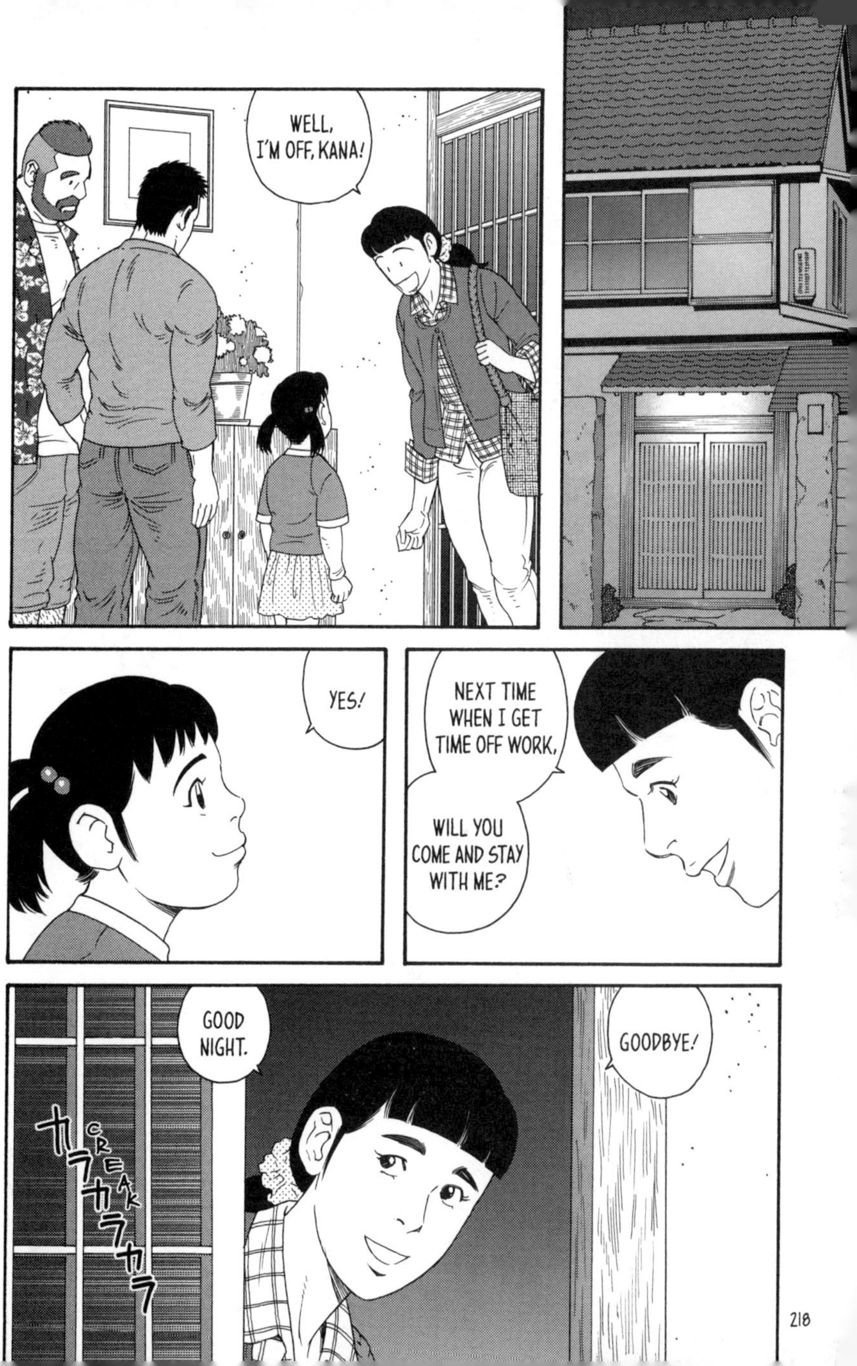
WELL, I'M OFF, KANA!
NEXT TIME WHEN I GET TIME OFF WORK,
WILL YOU COME AND STAY WITH ME?
YES!
GOODBYE!
GOOD NIGHT.
カラカラカラ CREAK

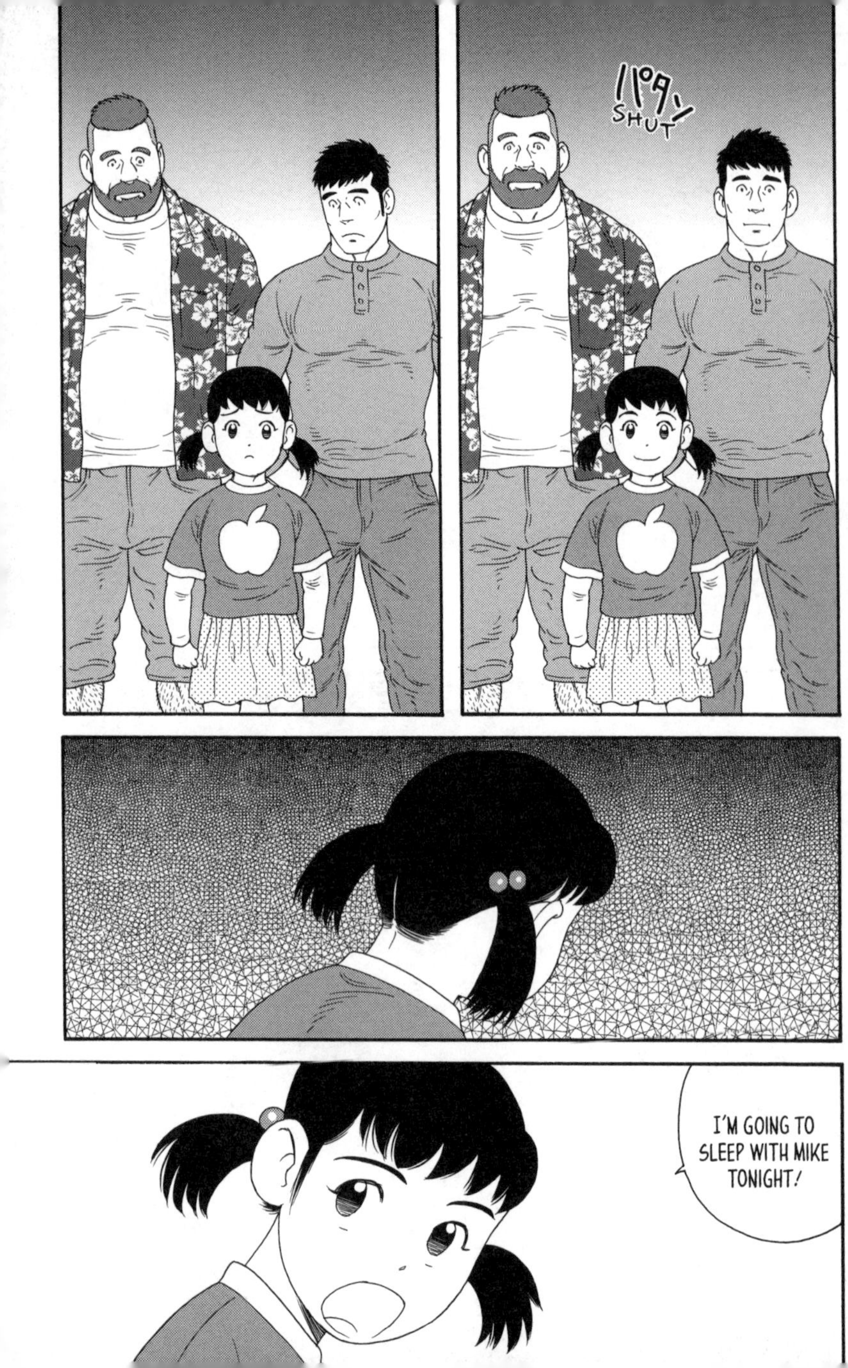
パタン
SHUT
I'M GOING TO SLEEP WITH MIKE TONIGHT!

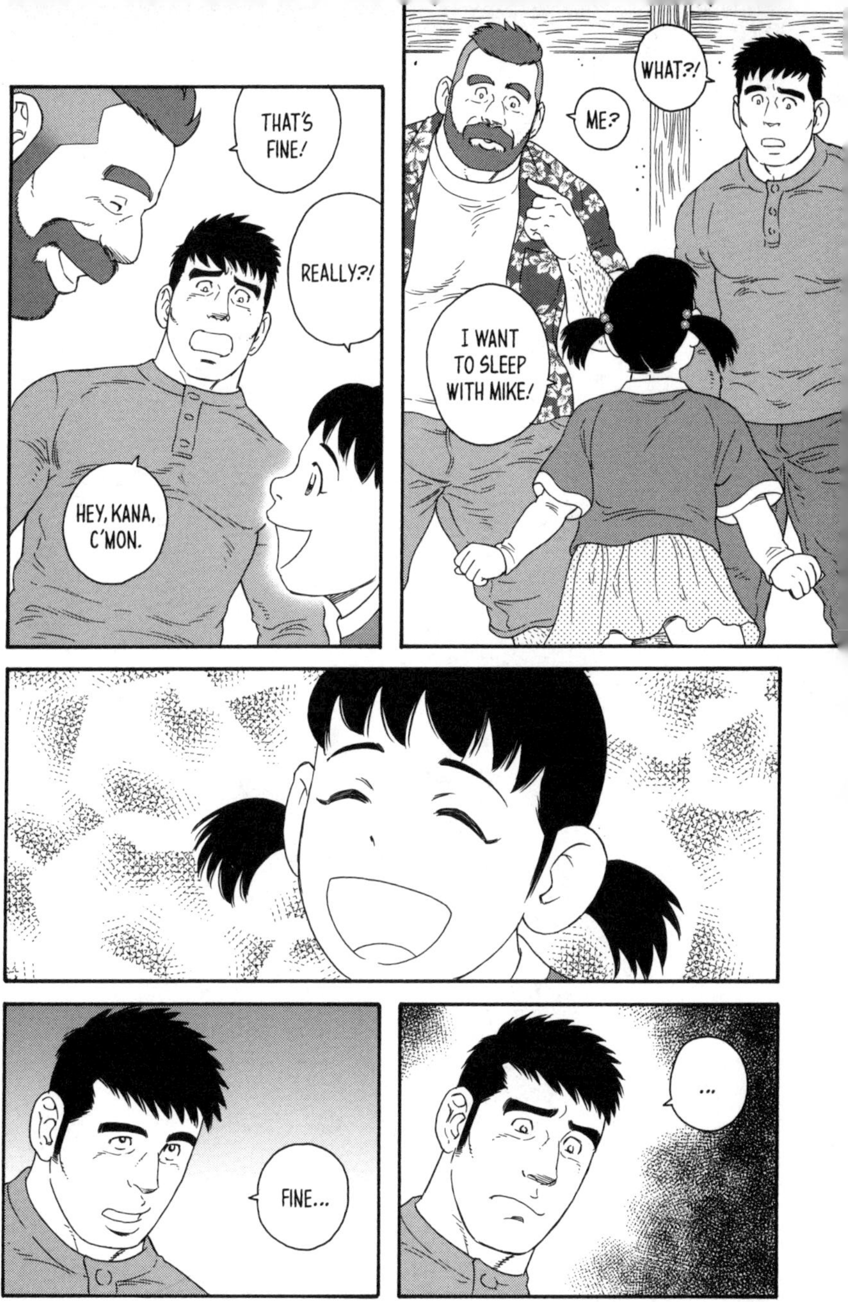
WHAT?!
ME?
I WANT TO SLEEP WITH MIKE!
THAT'S FINE!
REALLY?!
HEY, KANA, C'MON.
...
FINE...

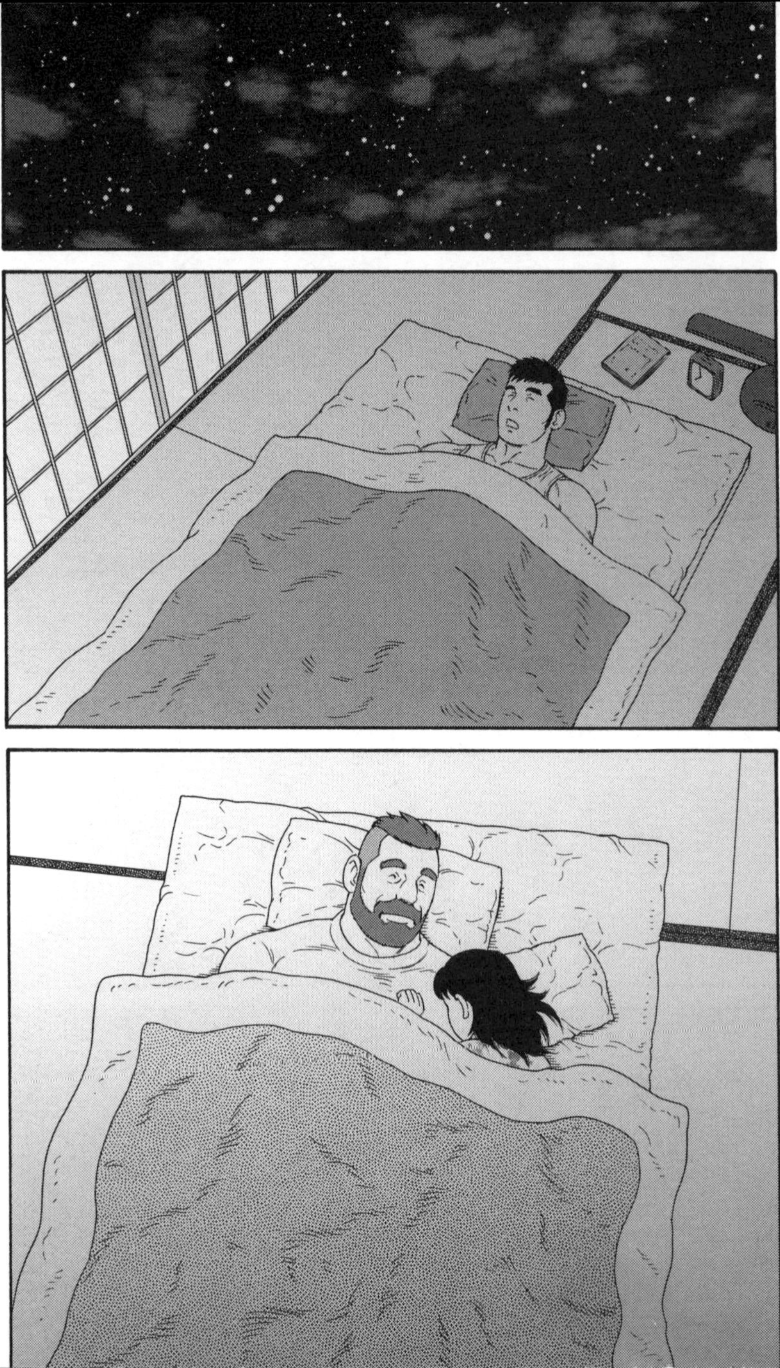

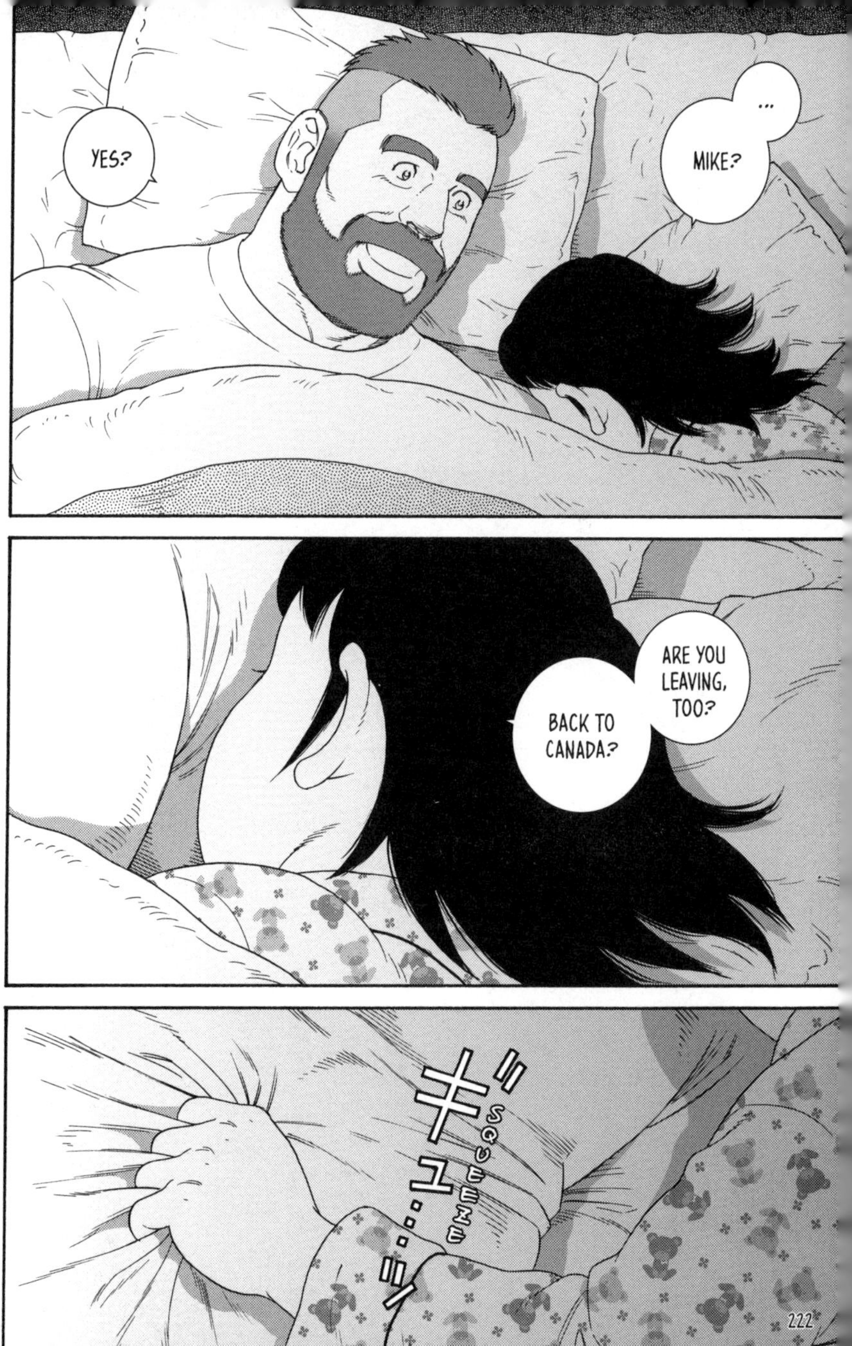
...
MIKE?
YES?
ARE YOU LEAVING, TOO?
BACK TO CANADA?
ギュ…ッ
SQUEEZE

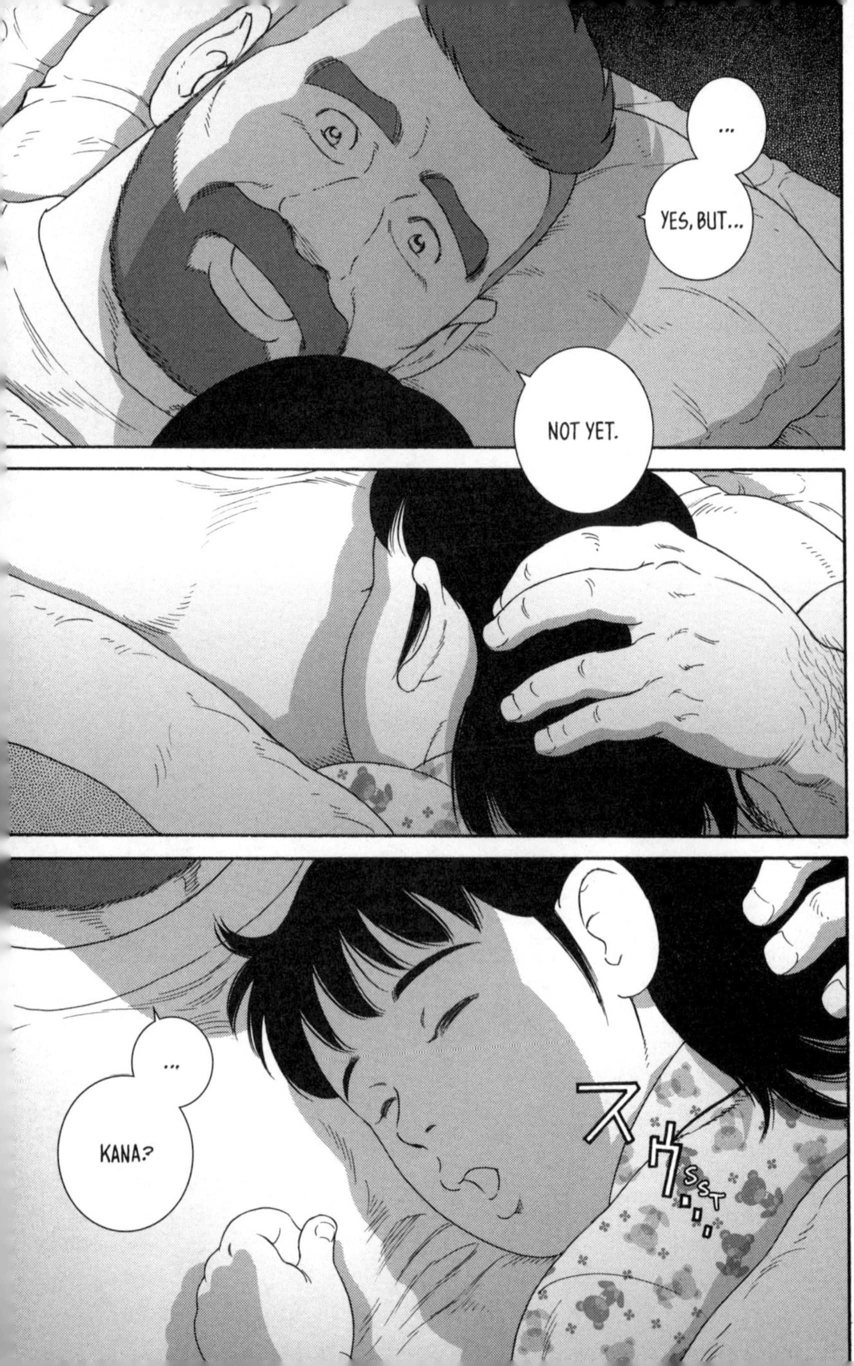
...
YES, BUT...
NOT YET.
...
KANA?
スゥ...
SST

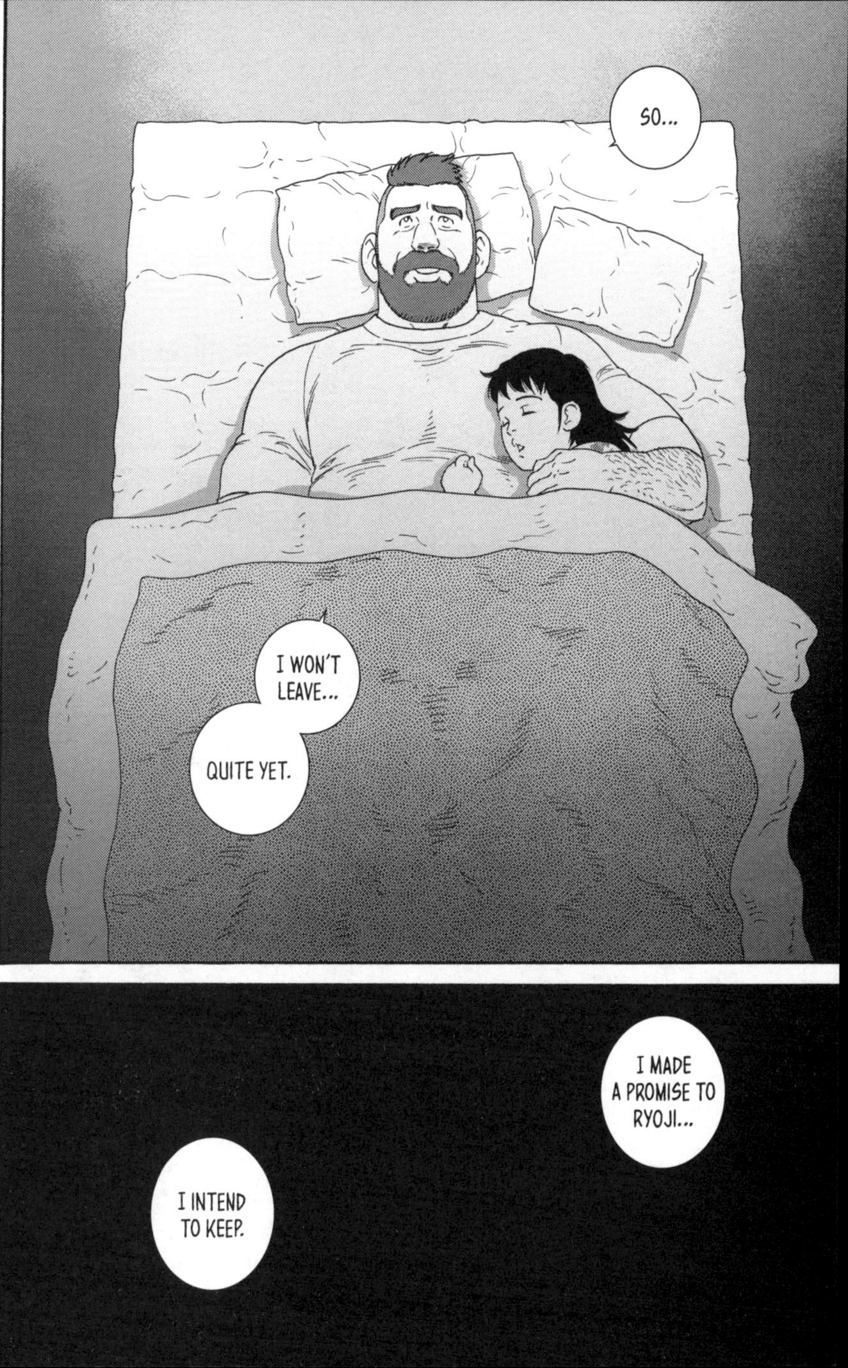
SO...
I WON'T LEAVE...
QUITE YET.
I MADE A PROMISE TO RYOJI...
I INTEND TO KEEP.

CHAPTER TEN
CURRY

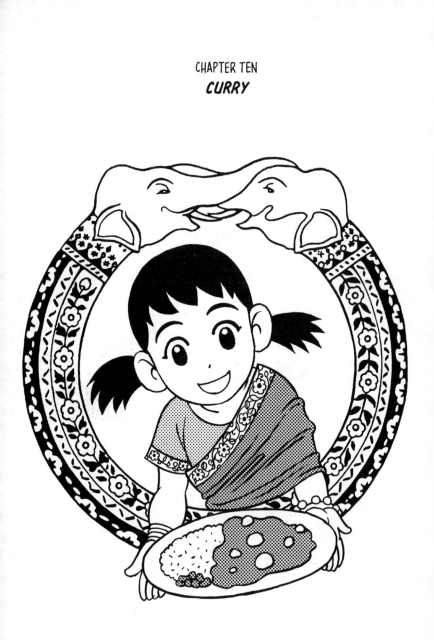

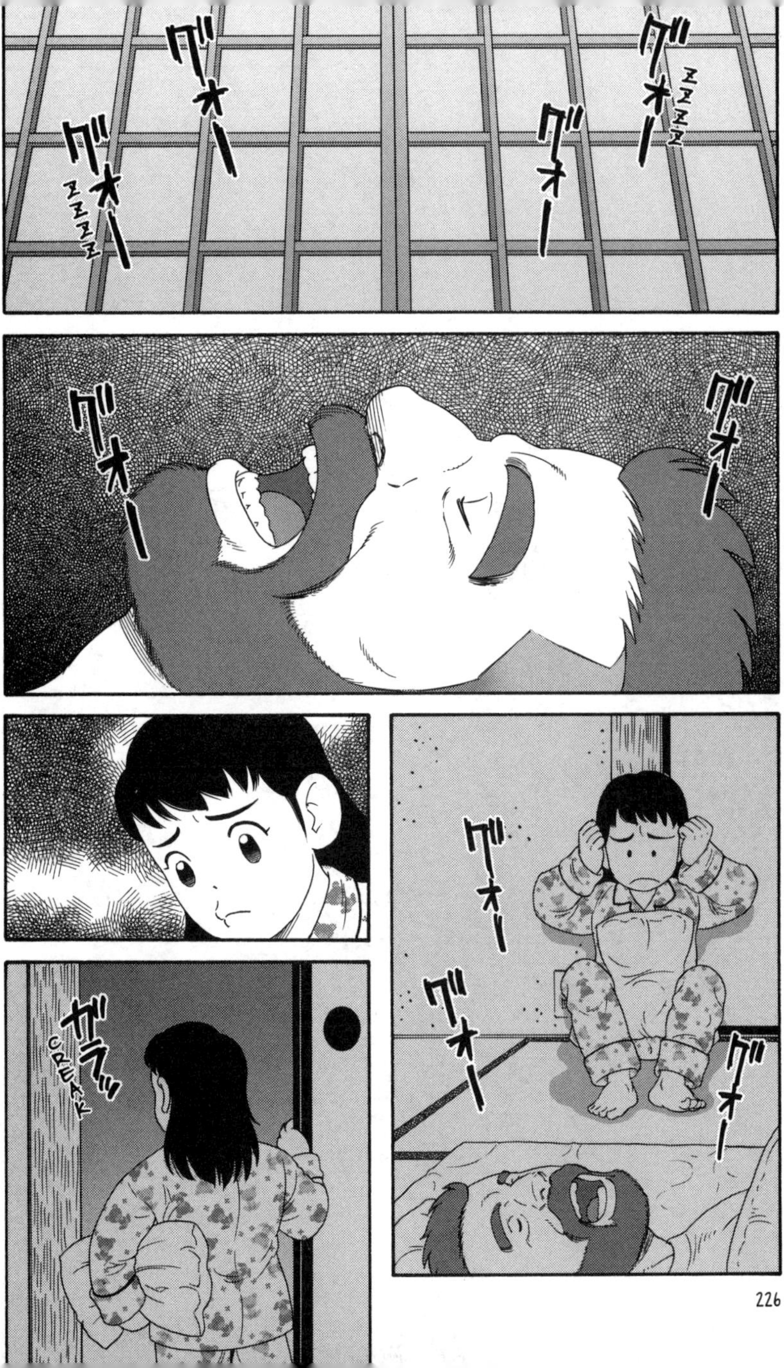
グオー
ZZZZ
グオー
グオー
グオー
ZZZZ
グオー
グオー
グオー
グオー
グオー
ガラッ
CREAK

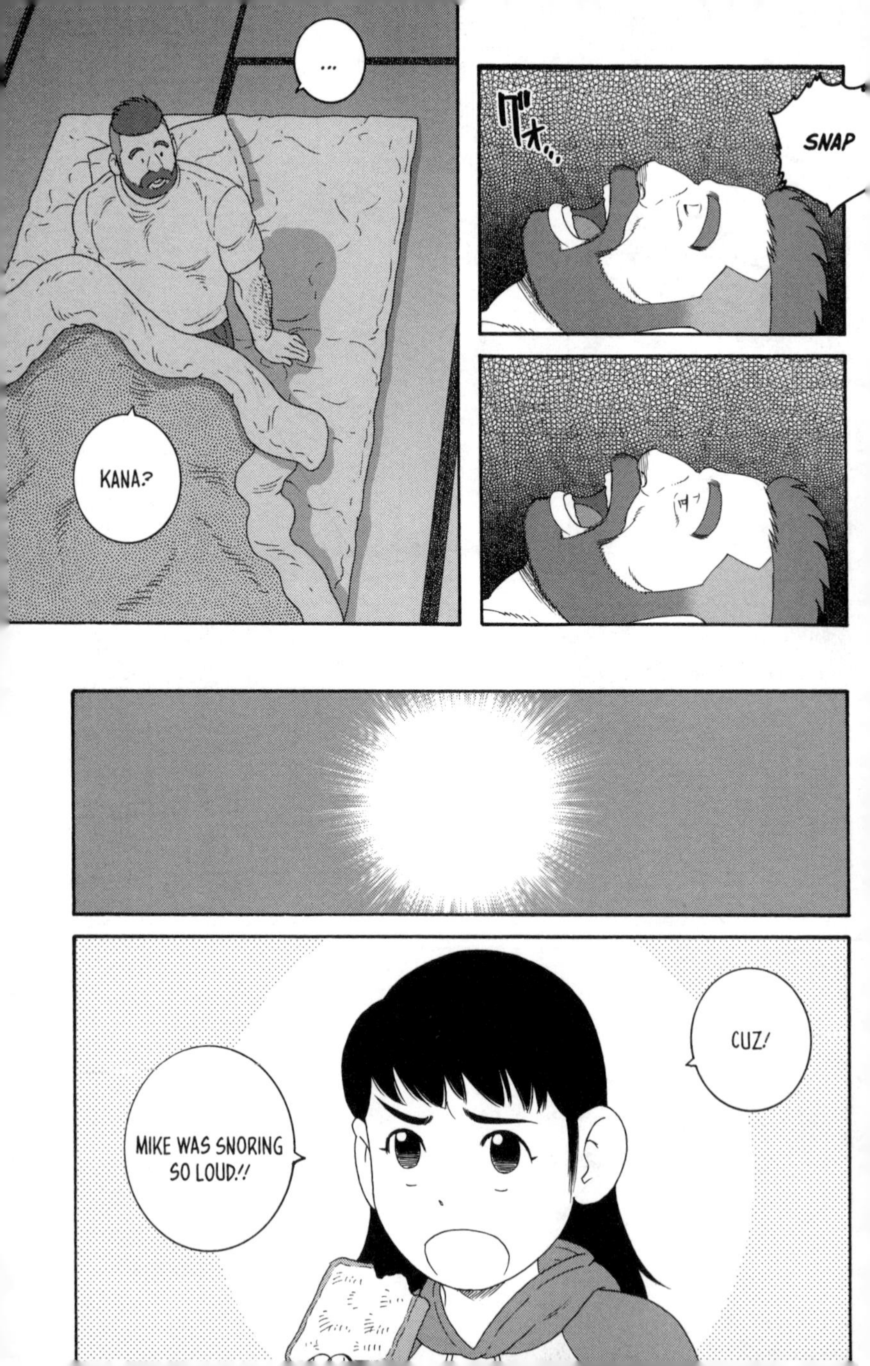
グォ…
SNAP
...
KANA?
CUZ!
MIKE WAS SNORING SO LOUD!!

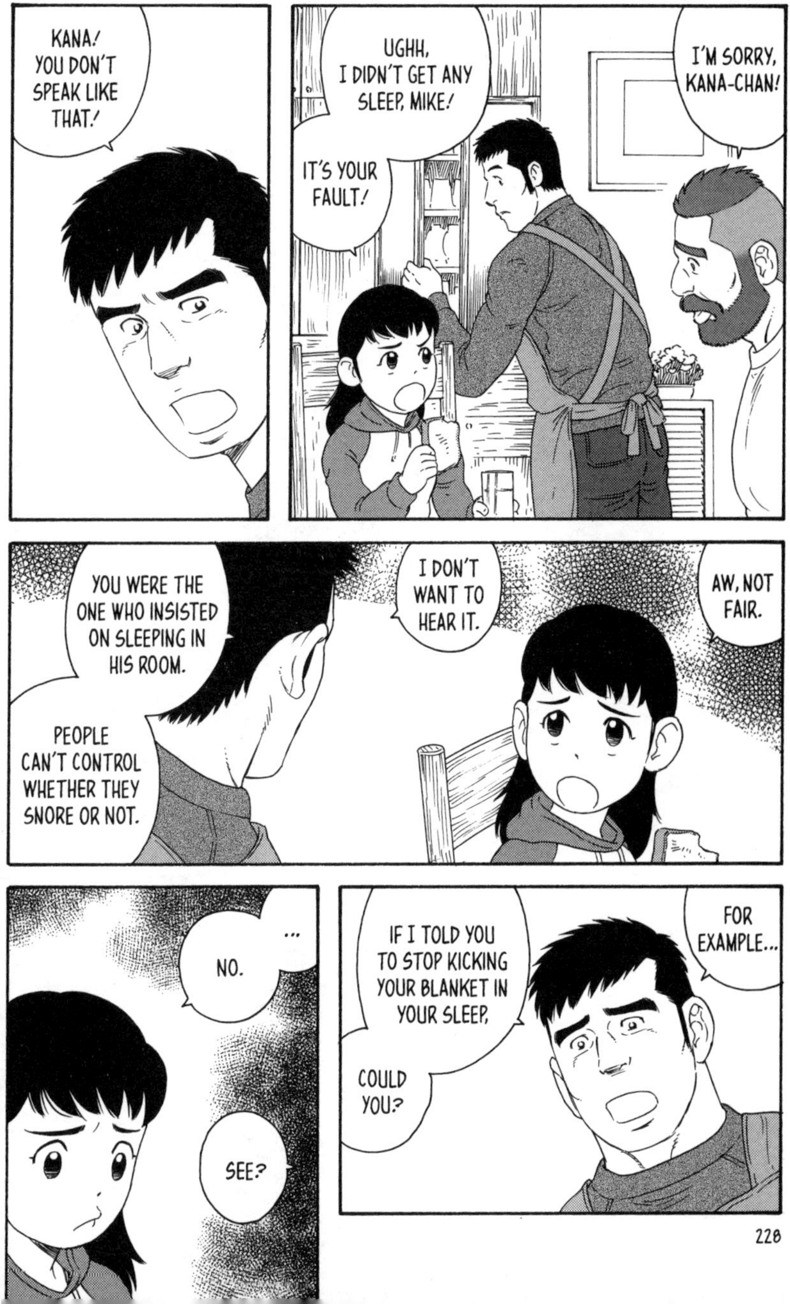
I'M SORRY, KANA-CHAN!
UGHH, I DIDN'T GET ANY SLEEP, MIKE!
IT'S YOUR FAULT!
KANA! YOU DON'T SPEAK LIKE THAT!
AW, NOT FAIR.
I DON'T WANT TO HEAR IT.
YOU WERE THE ONE WHO INSISTED ON SLEEPING IN HIS ROOM.
PEOPLE CAN'T CONTROL WHETHER THEY SNORE OR NOT.
FOR EXAMPLE...
IF I TOLD YOU TO STOP KICKING YOUR BLANKET IN YOUR SLEEP,
COULD YOU?
...
NO.
SEE?

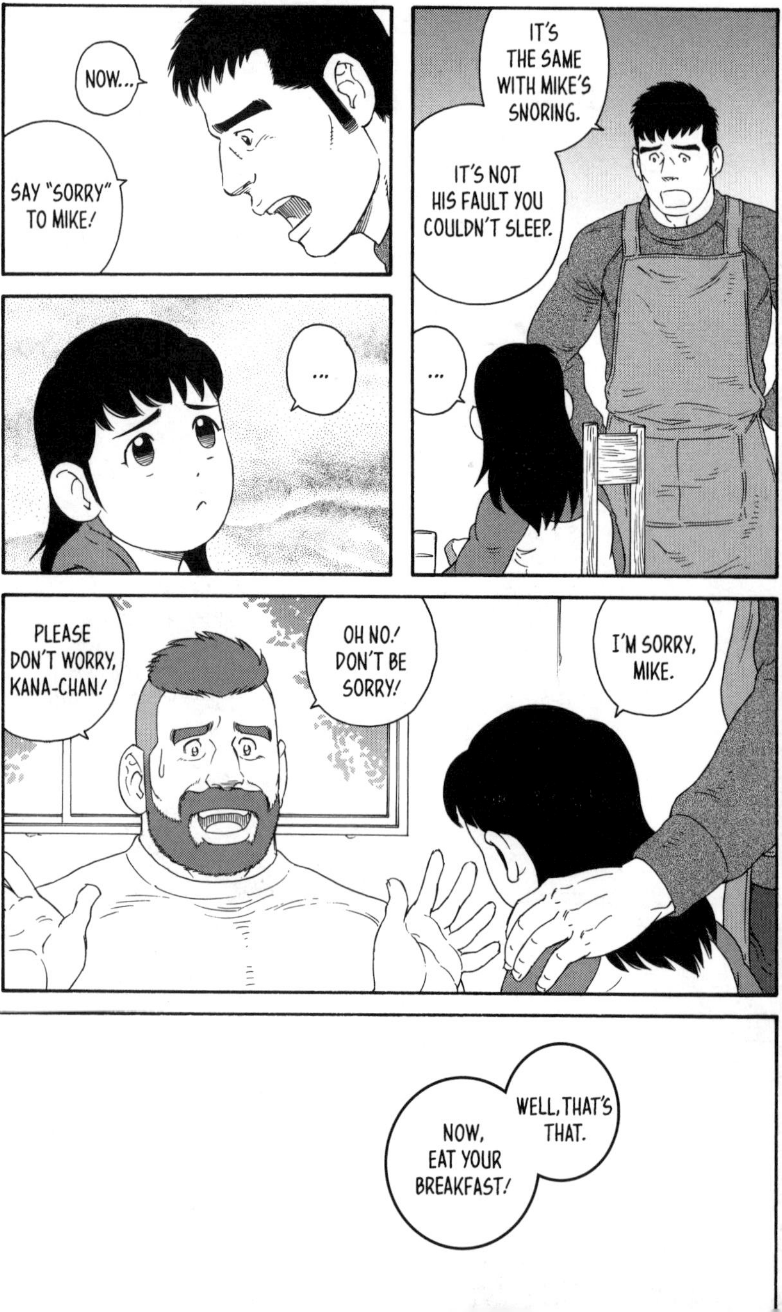
IT'S THE SAME WITH MIKE'S SNORING.
IT'S NOT HIS FAULT YOU COULDN'T SLEEP.
...
NOW...
SAY "SORRY" TO MIKE!
...
I'M SORRY, MIKE.
OH NO! DON'T BE SORRY!
PLEASE DON'T WORRY, KANA-CHAN!
WELL, THAT'S THAT.
NOW, EAT YOUR BREAKFAST!

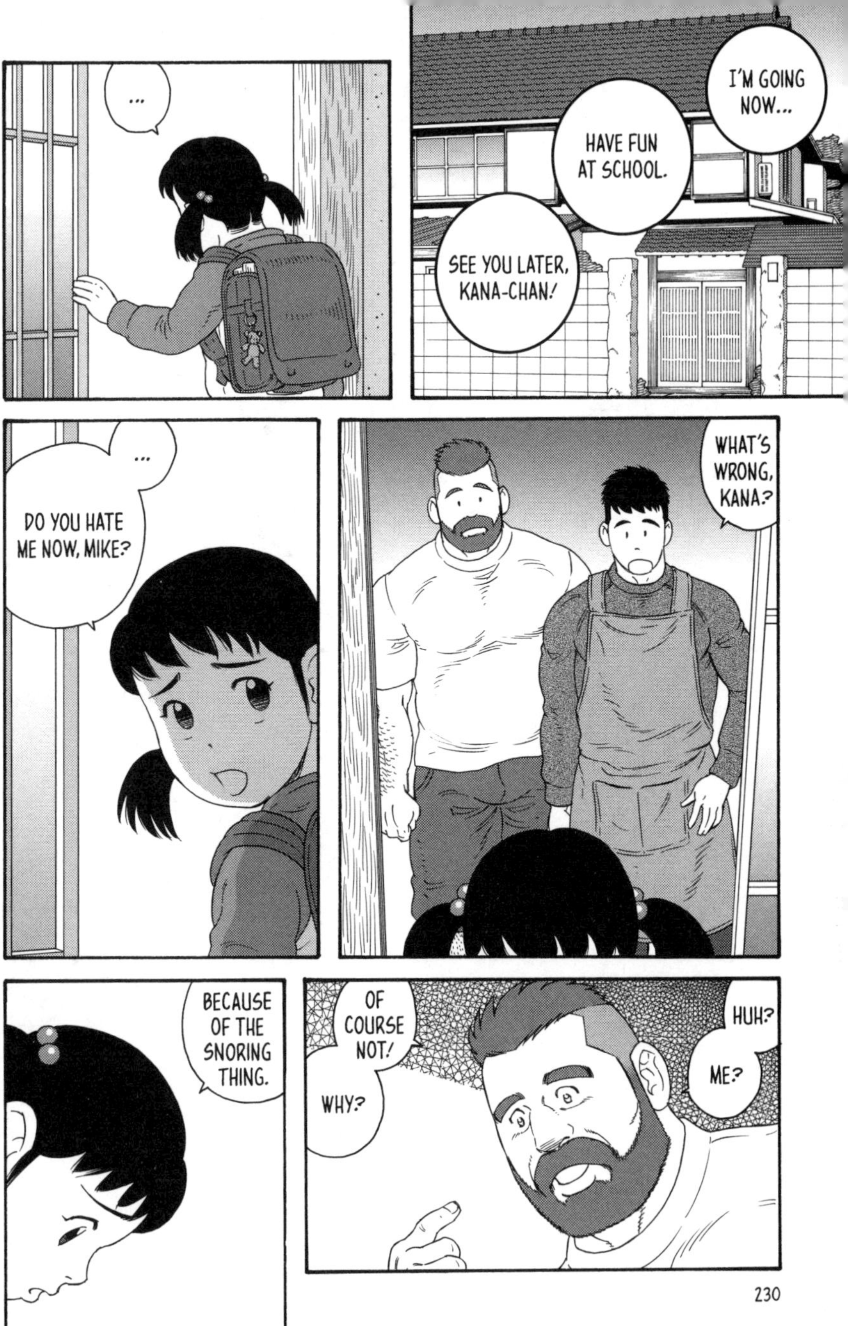
I'M GOING NOW...
HAVE FUN AT SCHOOL.
SEE YOU LATER, KANA-CHAN!
...
WHAT'S WRONG, KANA?
...
DO YOU HATE ME NOW, MIKE?
HUH?
ME?
OF COURSE NOT!
WHY?
BECAUSE OF THE SNORING THING.

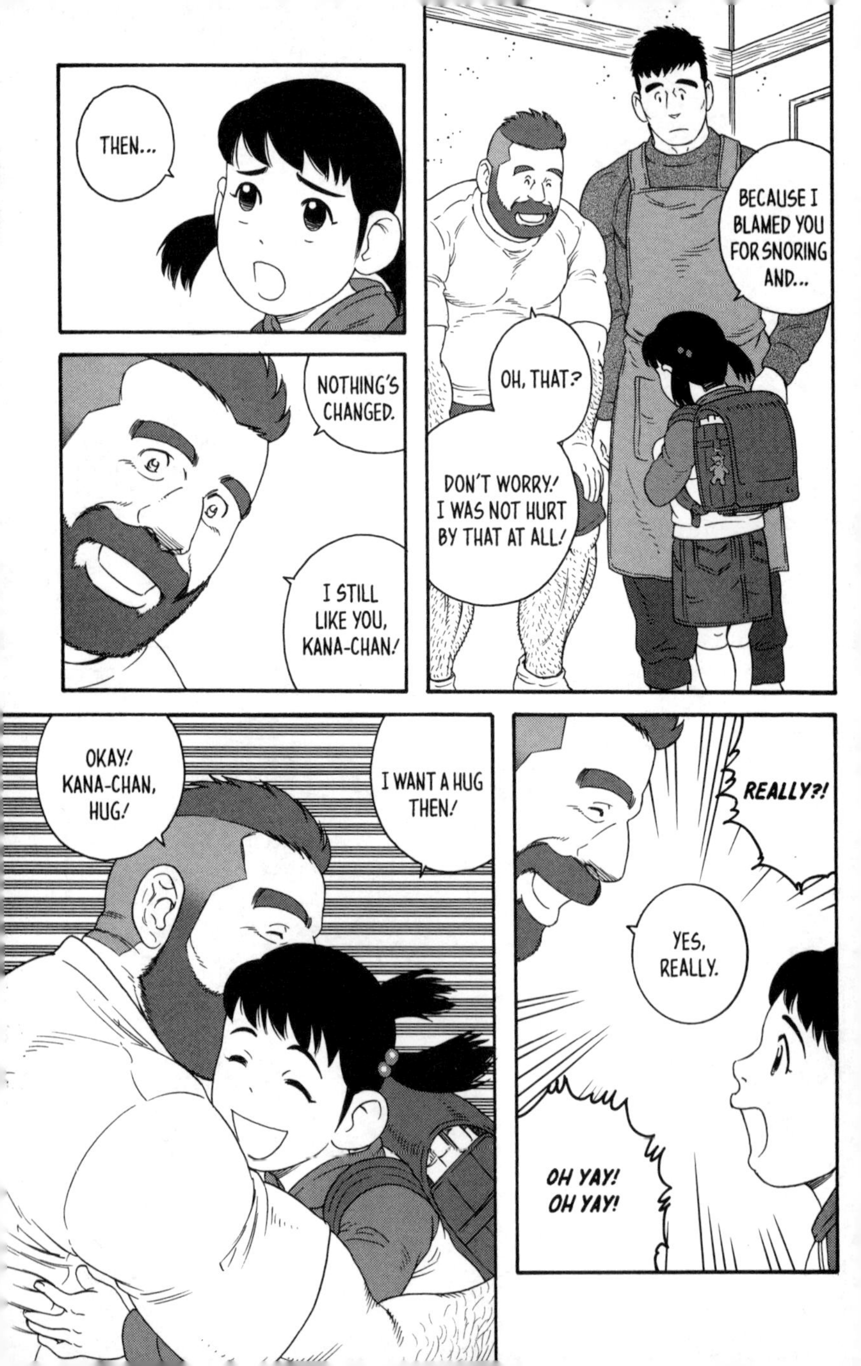
BECAUSE I BLAMED YOU FOR SNORING AND...
OH, THAT?
DON'T WORRY! I WAS NOT HURT BY THAT AT ALL!
THEN...
NOTHING'S CHANGED.
I STILL LIKE YOU, KANA-CHAN!
REALLY?!
YES, REALLY.
OH YAY! OH YAY!
I WANT A HUG THEN!
OKAY! KANA-CHAN, HUG!

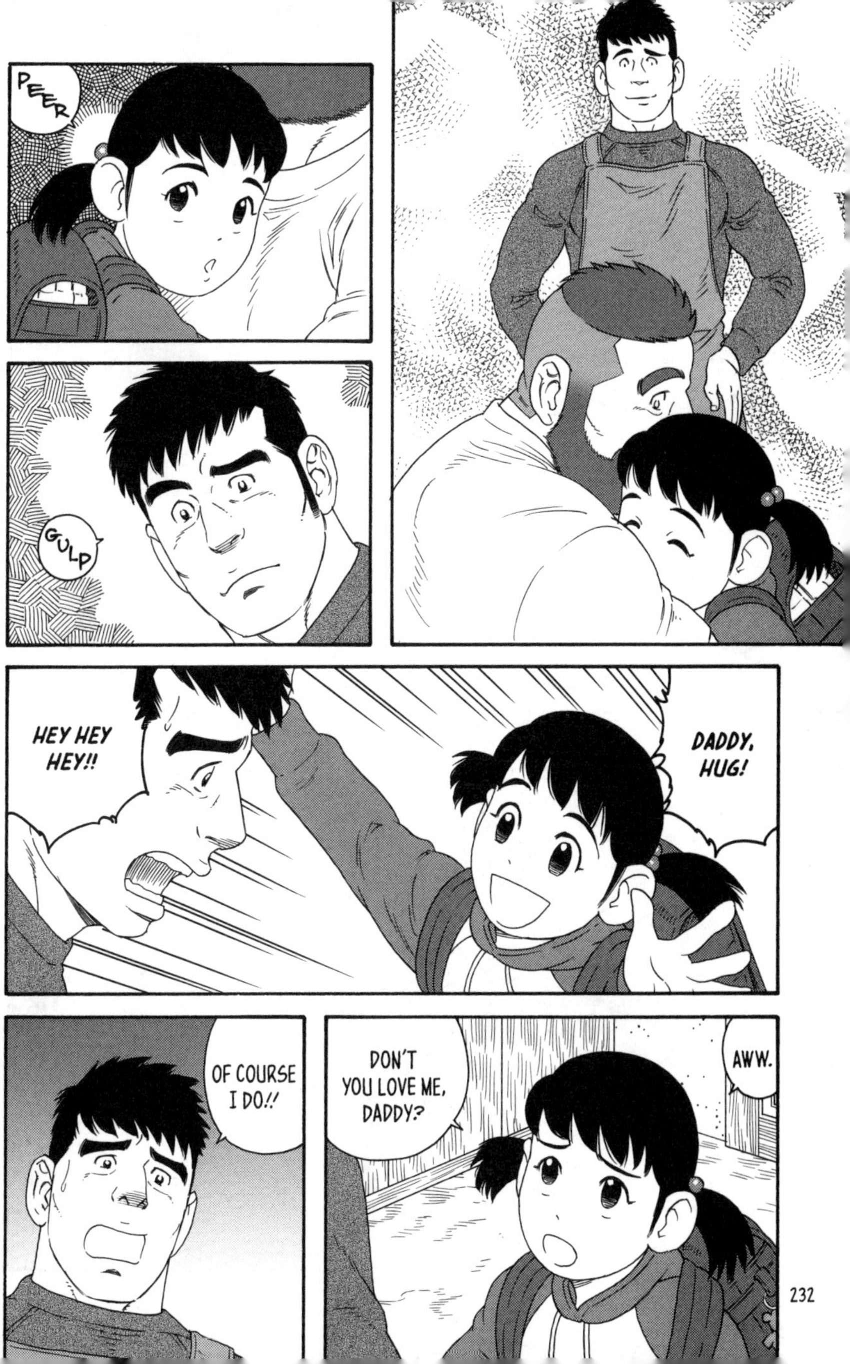
PEEER
GULP
DADDY, HUG!
HEY HEY HEY!!
AWW.
DON'T YOU LOVE ME, DADDY?
OF COURSE I DO!!

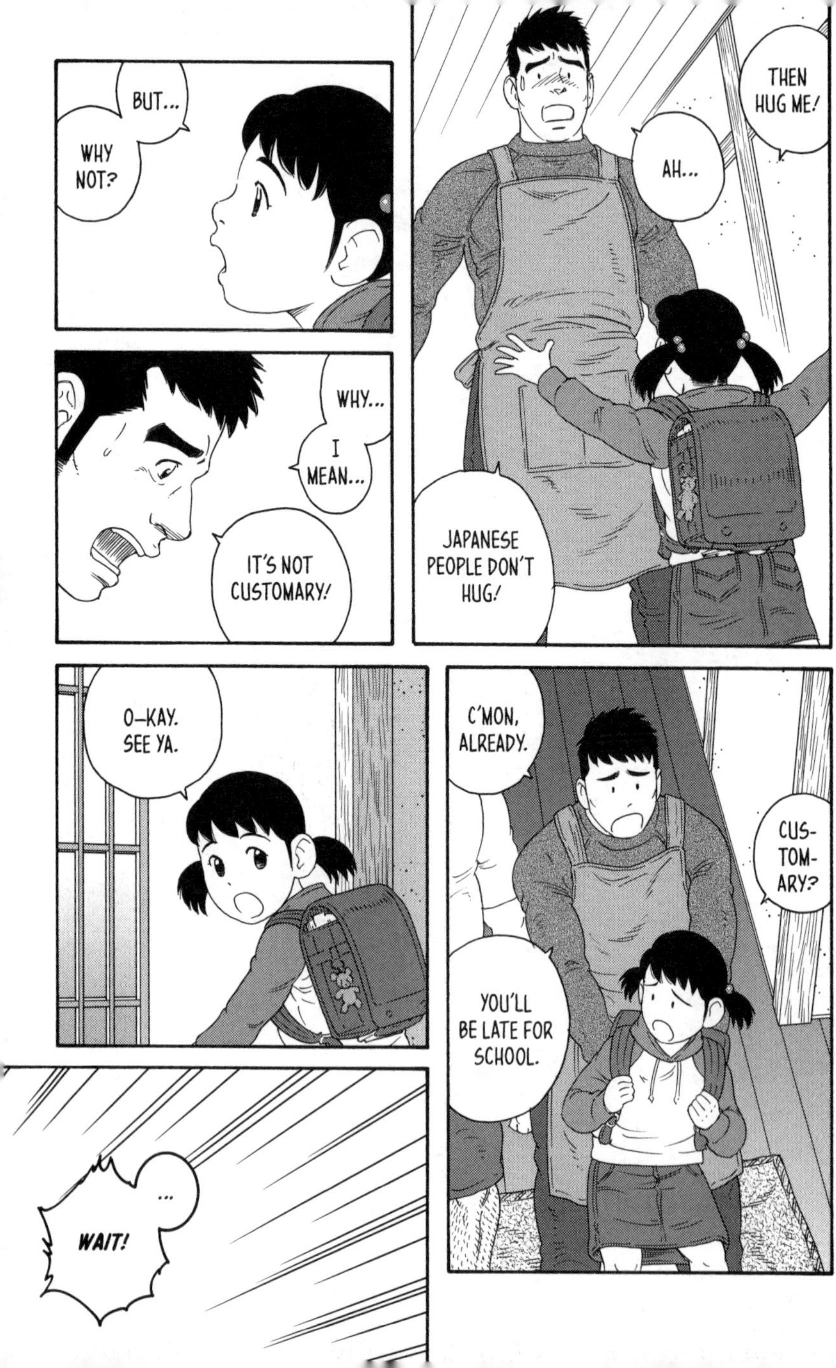
THEN HUG ME!
AH...
JAPANESE PEOPLE DON'T HUG!
BUT...
WHY NOT?
WHY...
I MEAN...
IT'S NOT CUSTOMARY!
CUS-TOM-ARY?
C'MON, ALREADY.
YOU'LL BE LATE FOR SCHOOL.
O-KAY. SEE YA.
...
WAIT!

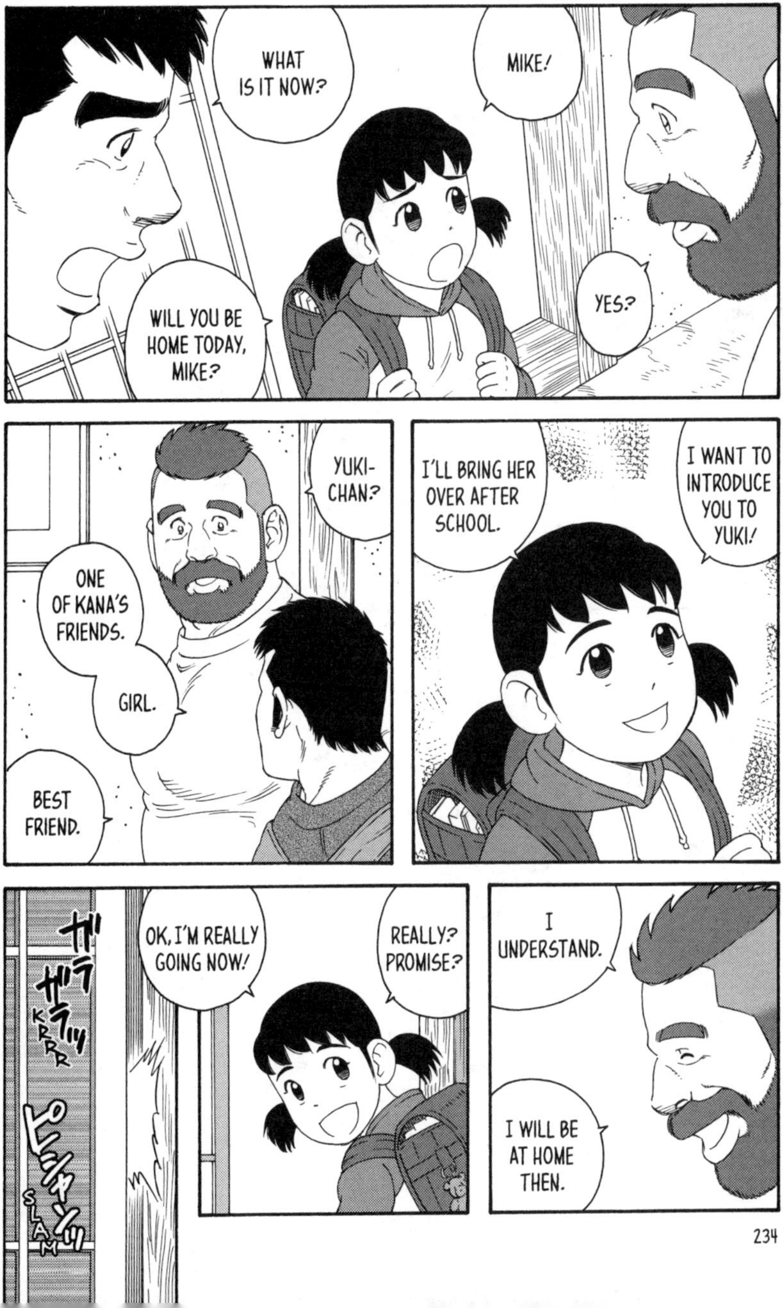
MIKE!
WHAT IS IT NOW?
YES?
WILL YOU BE HOME TODAY, MIKE?
I WANT TO INTRODUCE YOU TO YUKI!
I'LL BRING HER OVER AFTER SCHOOL.
YUKI-CHAN?
ONE OF KANA'S FRIENDS.
GIRL.
BEST FRIEND.
I UNDERSTAND.
I WILL BE AT HOME THEN.
REALLY? PROMISE?
OK, I'M REALLY GOING NOW!
ガラガラッ
KRRR
ピシャンッ
SLAM

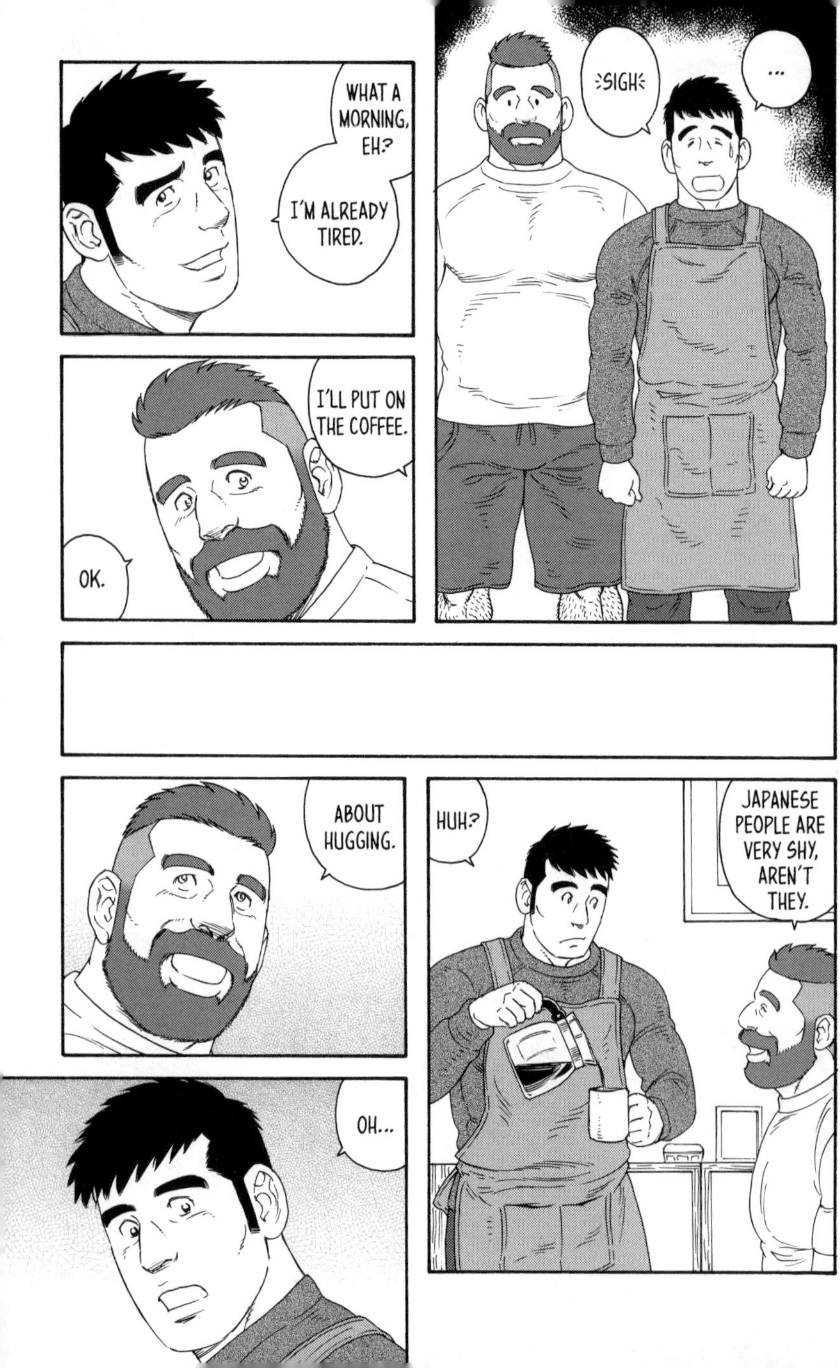
...
SIGH
WHAT A MORNING, EH?
I'M ALREADY TIRED.
I'LL PUT ON THE COFFEE.
OK.
JAPANESE PEOPLE ARE VERY SHY, AREN'T THEY.
HUH?
ABOUT HUGGING.
OH...

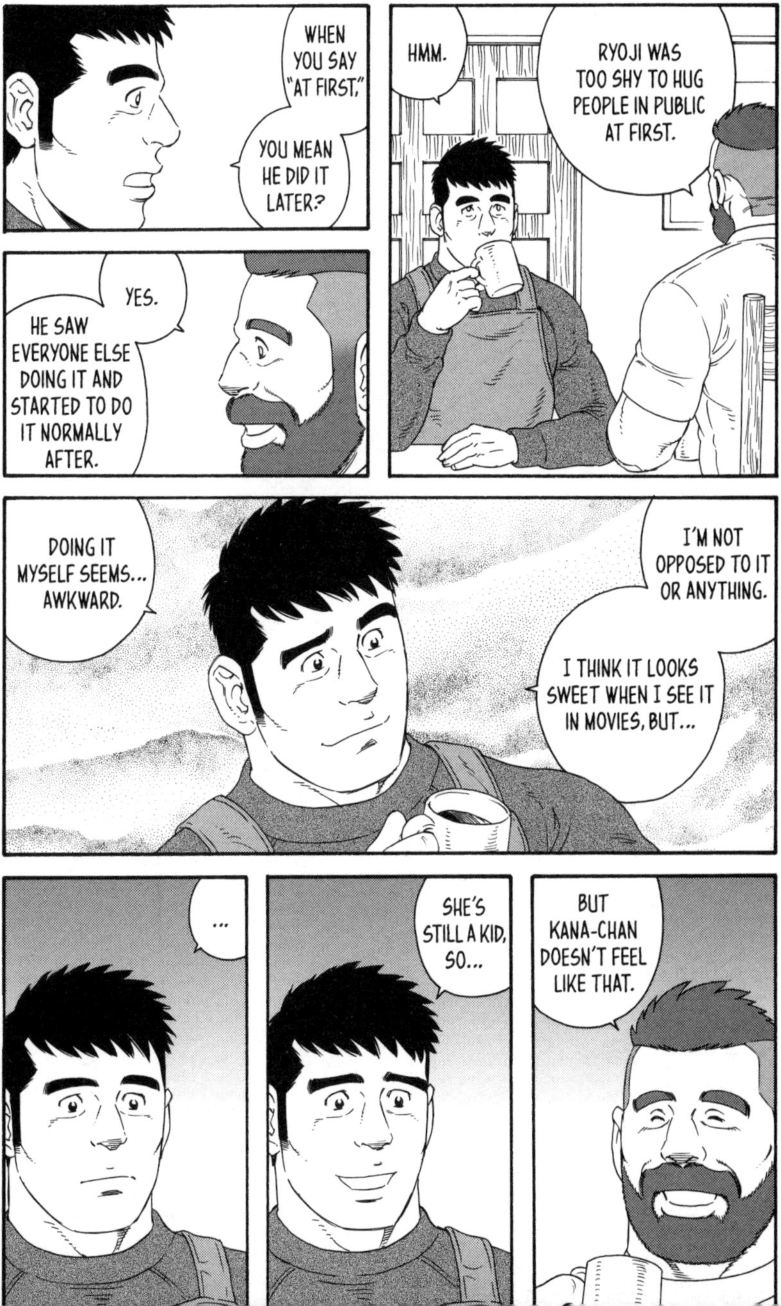
RYOJI WAS TOO SHY TO HUG PEOPLE IN PUBLIC AT FIRST.
HMM.
WHEN YOU SAY "AT FIRST,"
YOU MEAN HE DID IT LATER?
YES.
HE SAW EVERYONE ELSE DOING IT AND STARTED TO DO IT NORMALLY AFTER.
I'M NOT OPPOSED TO IT OR ANYTHING.
I THINK IT LOOKS SWEET WHEN I SEE IT IN MOVIES, BUT...
DOING IT MYSELF SEEMS... AWKWARD.
BUT KANA-CHAN DOESN'T FEEL LIKE THAT.
SHE'S STILL A KID, SO...
...

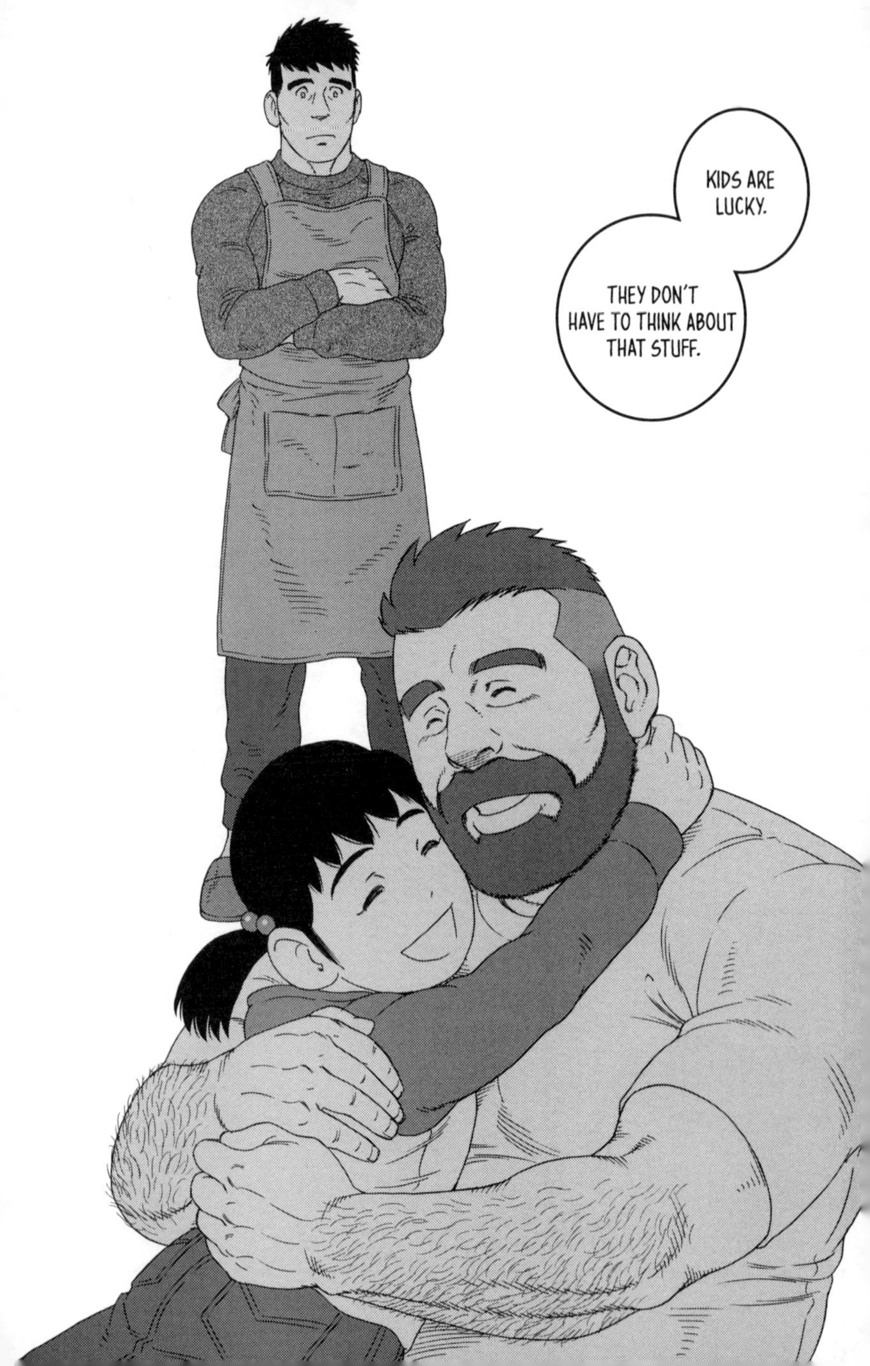
KIDS ARE LUCKY.
THEY DON'T HAVE TO THINK ABOUT THAT STUFF.

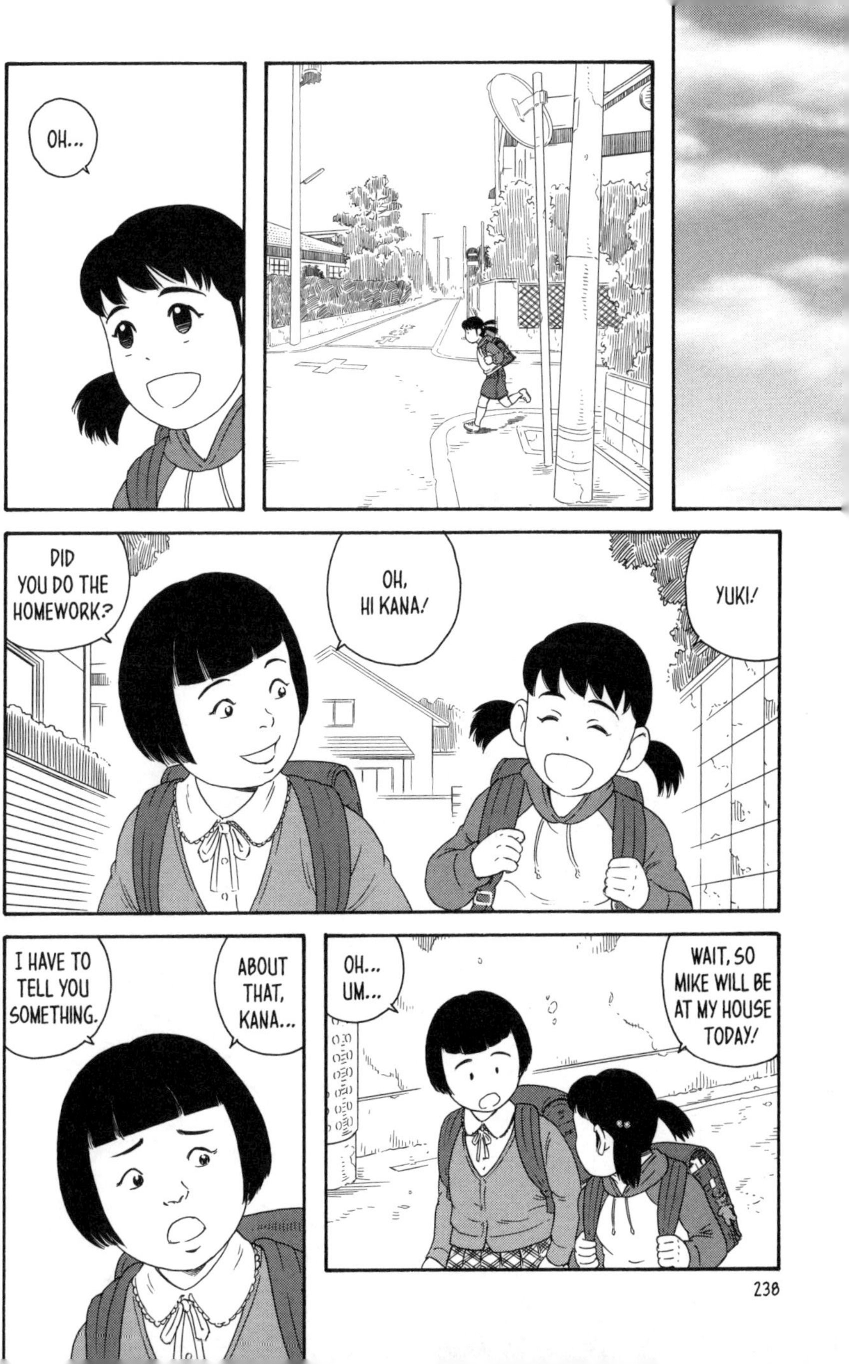
OH...
YUKI!
OH,
HI KANA!
DID
YOU DO THE
HOMEWORK?
WAIT, SO
MIKE WILL BE
AT MY HOUSE
TODAY!
OH...
UM...
ABOUT
THAT,
KANA...
I HAVE TO
TELL YOU
SOMETHING.

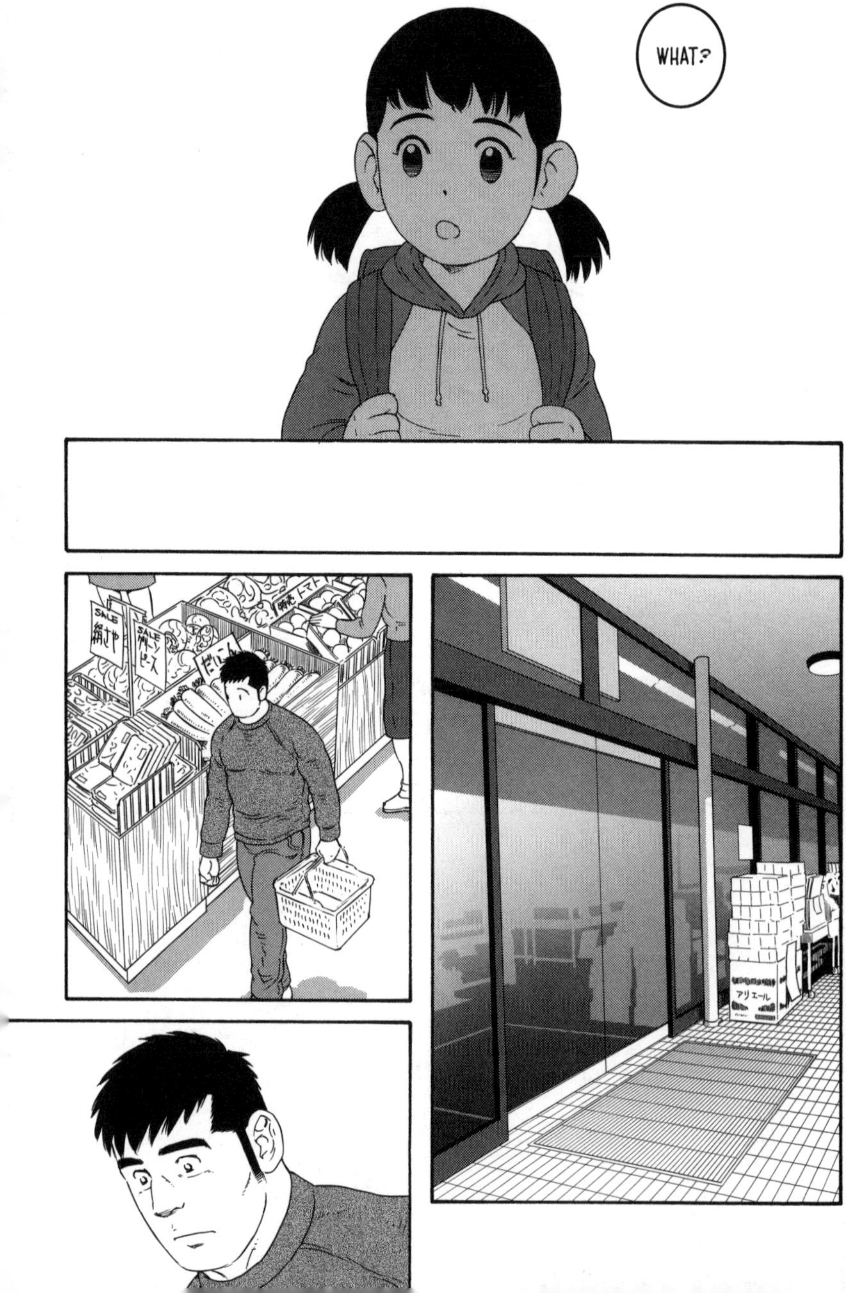
WHAT?
アリエール
トマト

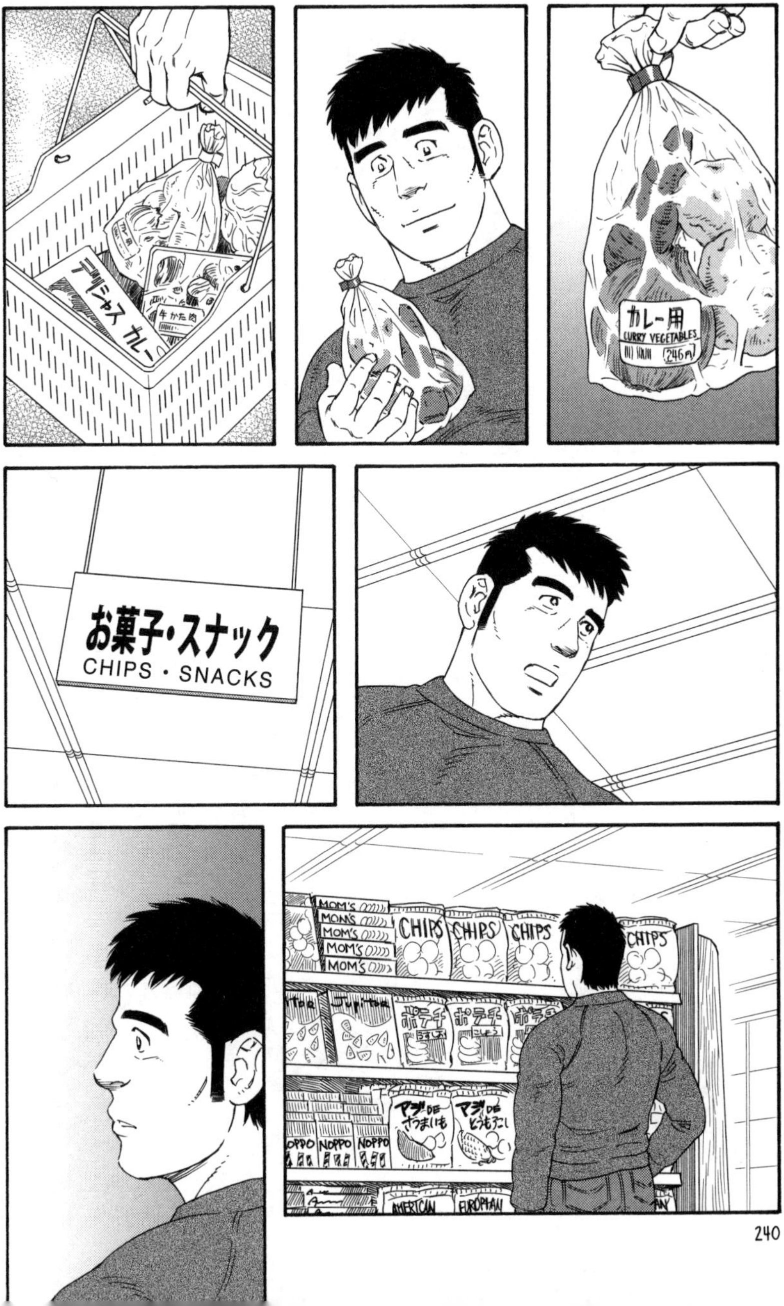
カレー用
CURRY VEGETABLES
246円
デリシャス カレー
牛かた肉
お菓子・スナック
CHIPS・SNACKS
MOM'S
CHIPS
ポテチ
うすしお
こしょう
アジDE さつまいも
アジDE とうもろこし
NOPPO
AMERICAN
EUROPEAN

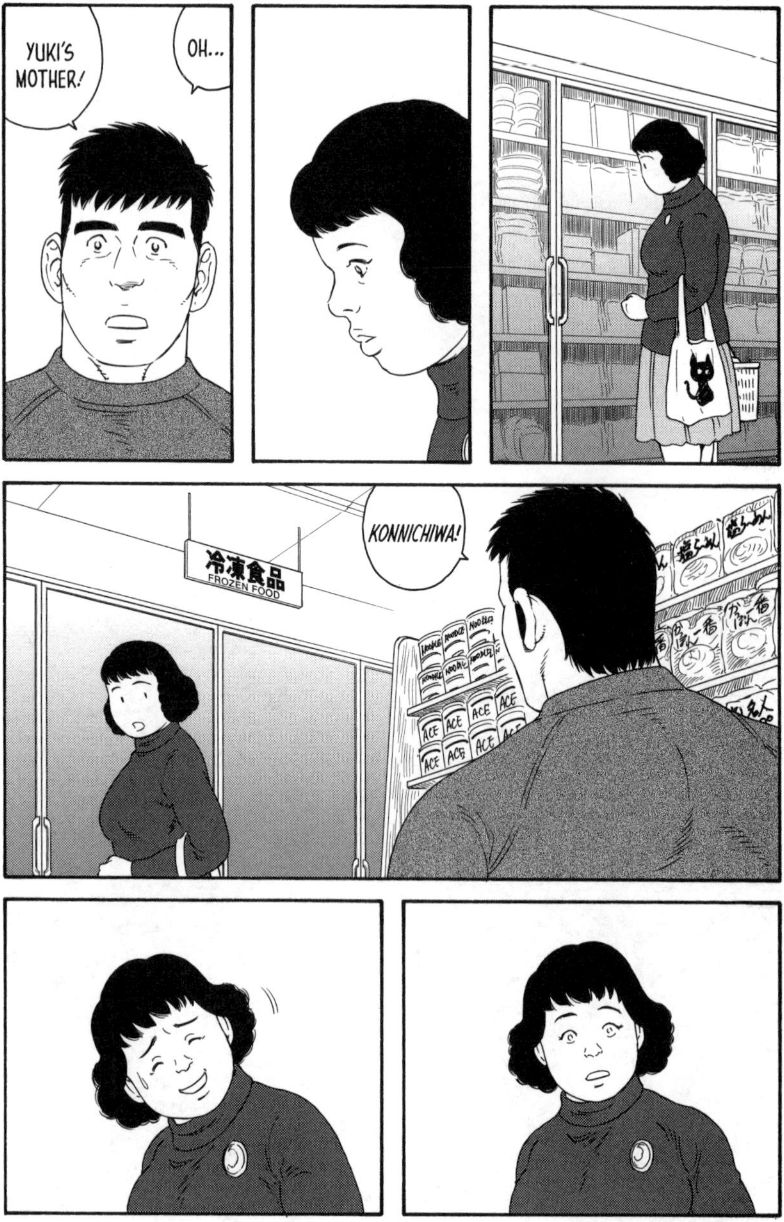
OH...
YUKI'S MOTHER!
KONNICHIWA!
冷凍食品
FROZEN FOOD

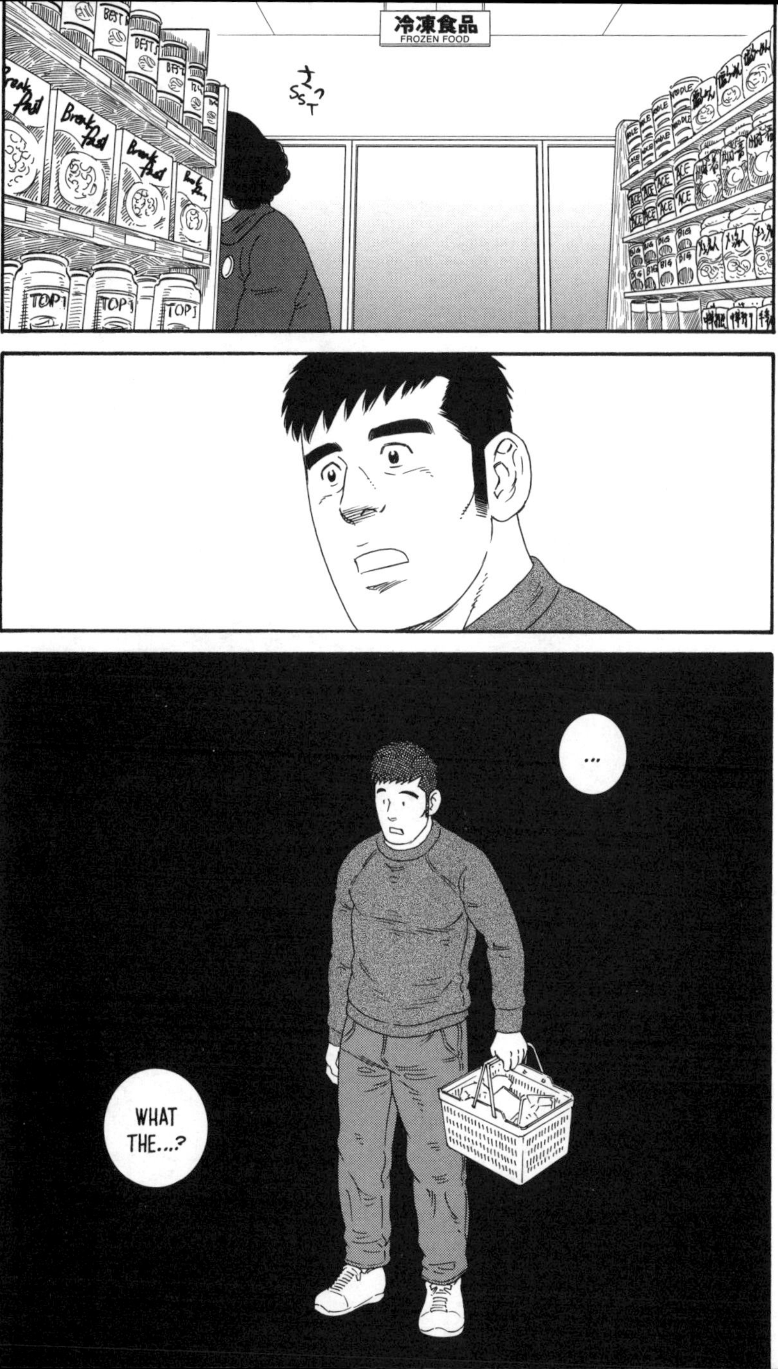
冷凍食品
FROZEN FOOD
SST
...
WHAT THE...?

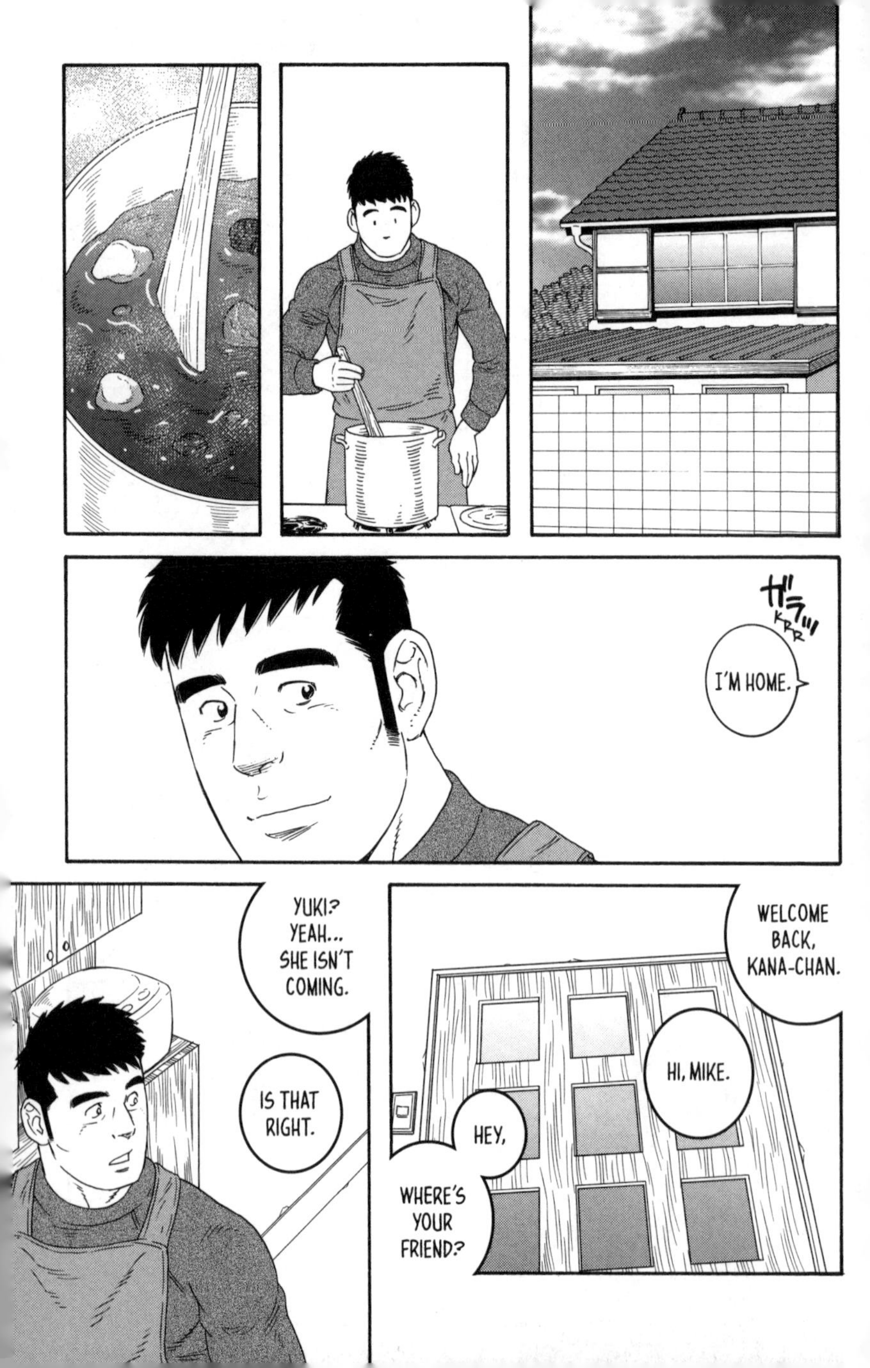
ガラッ
KRR
I'M HOME.
WELCOME BACK, KANA-CHAN.
HI, MIKE.
HEY,
WHERE'S YOUR FRIEND?
YUKI? YEAH... SHE ISN'T COMING.
IS THAT RIGHT.

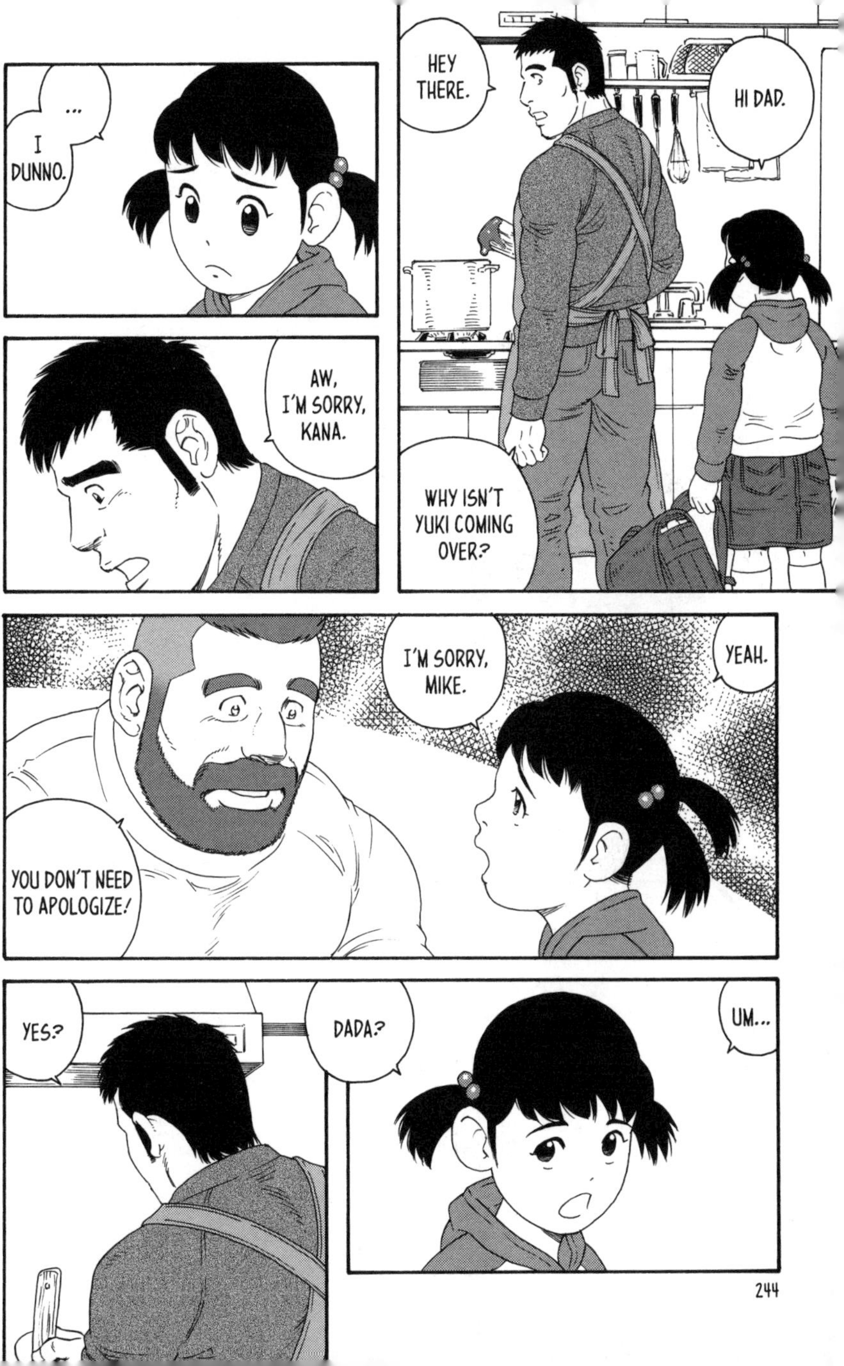
HI DAD.
HEY THERE.
WHY ISN'T YUKI COMING OVER?
... I DUNNO.
AW, I'M SORRY, KANA.
YEAH.
I'M SORRY, MIKE.
YOU DON'T NEED TO APOLOGIZE!
UM...
DADA?
YES?

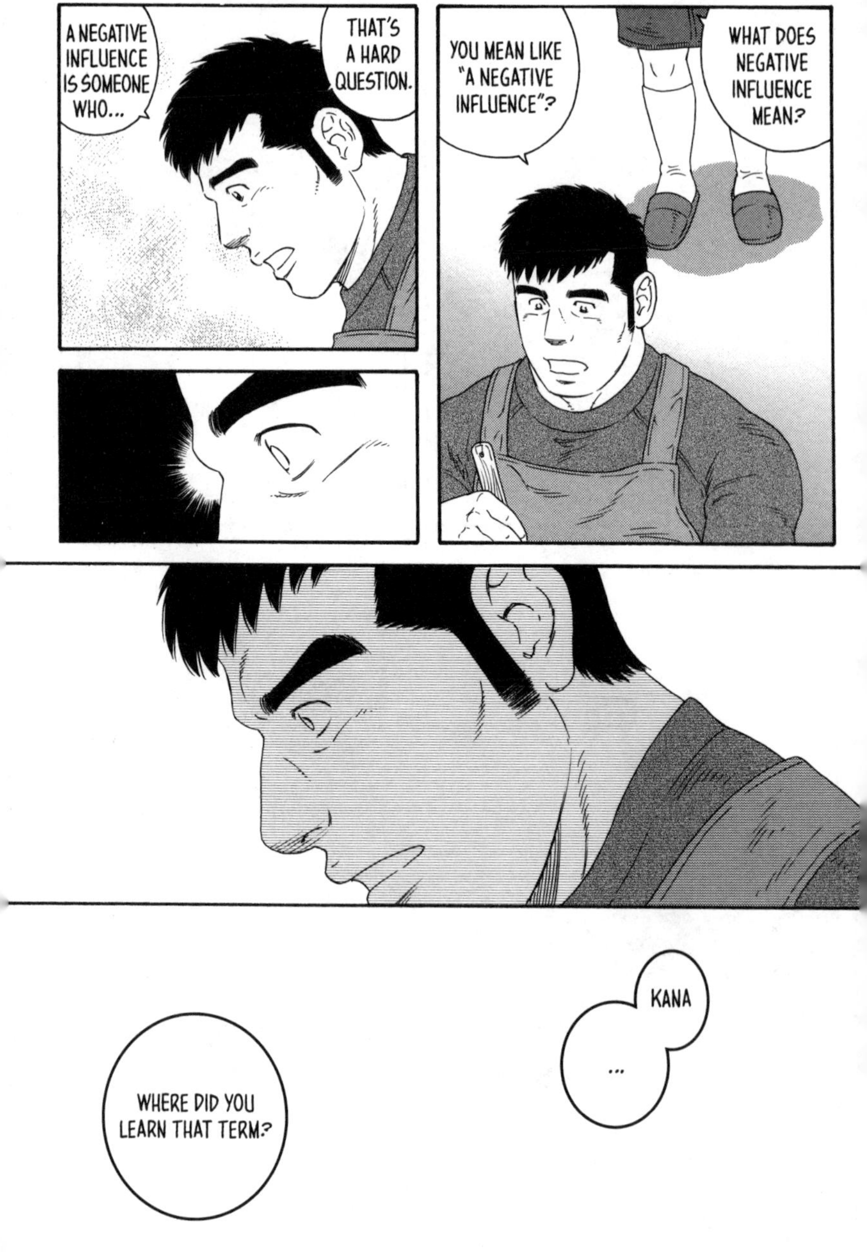
WHAT DOES NEGATIVE INFLUENCE MEAN?
YOU MEAN LIKE "A NEGATIVE INFLUENCE"?
THAT'S A HARD QUESTION.
A NEGATIVE INFLUENCE IS SOMEONE WHO...
KANA
...
WHERE DID YOU LEARN THAT TERM?

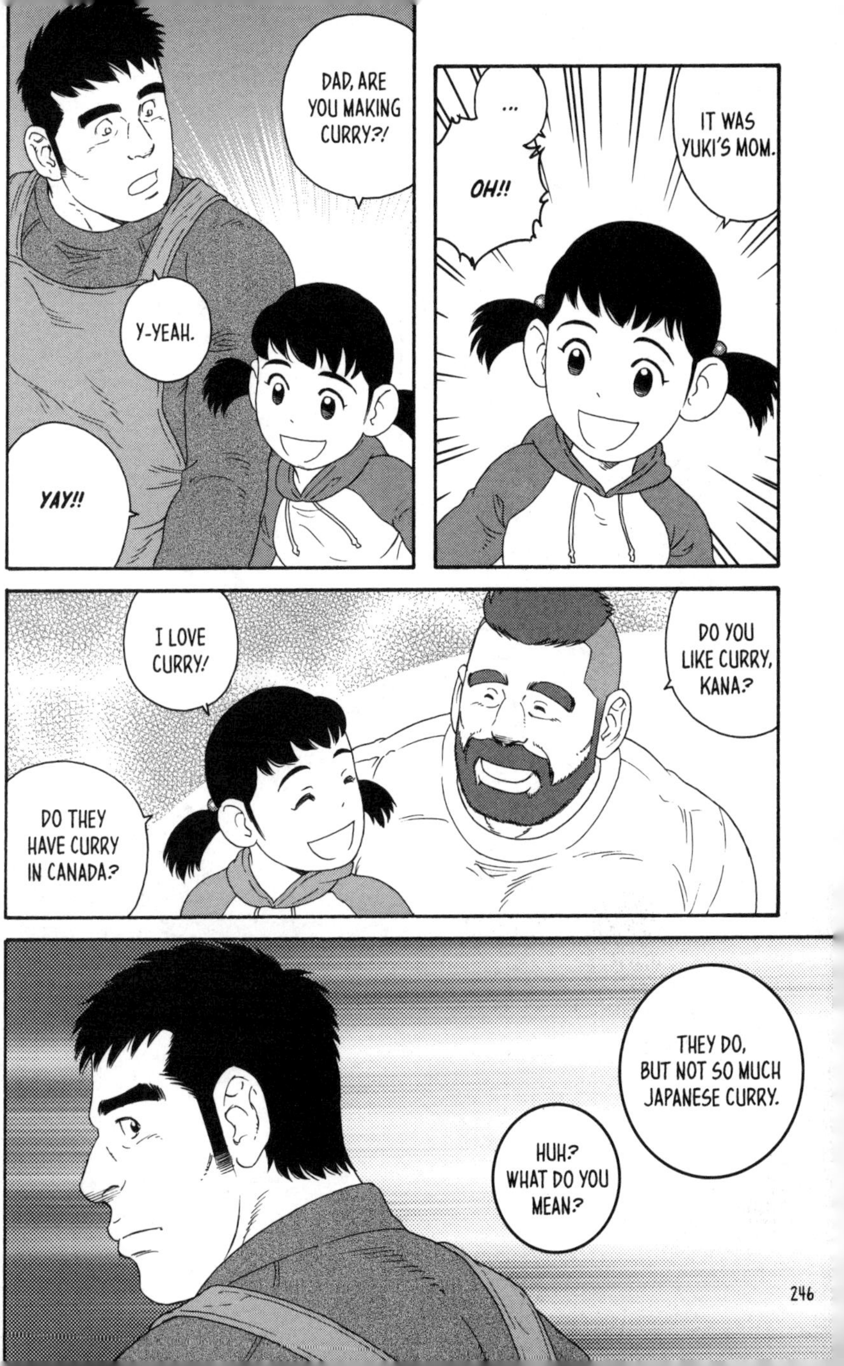
IT WAS YUKI'S MOM.
...
OH!!
DAD, ARE YOU MAKING CURRY?!
Y-YEAH.
YAY!!
DO YOU LIKE CURRY, KANA?
I LOVE CURRY!
DO THEY HAVE CURRY IN CANADA?
THEY DO, BUT NOT SO MUCH JAPANESE CURRY.
HUH? WHAT DO YOU MEAN?

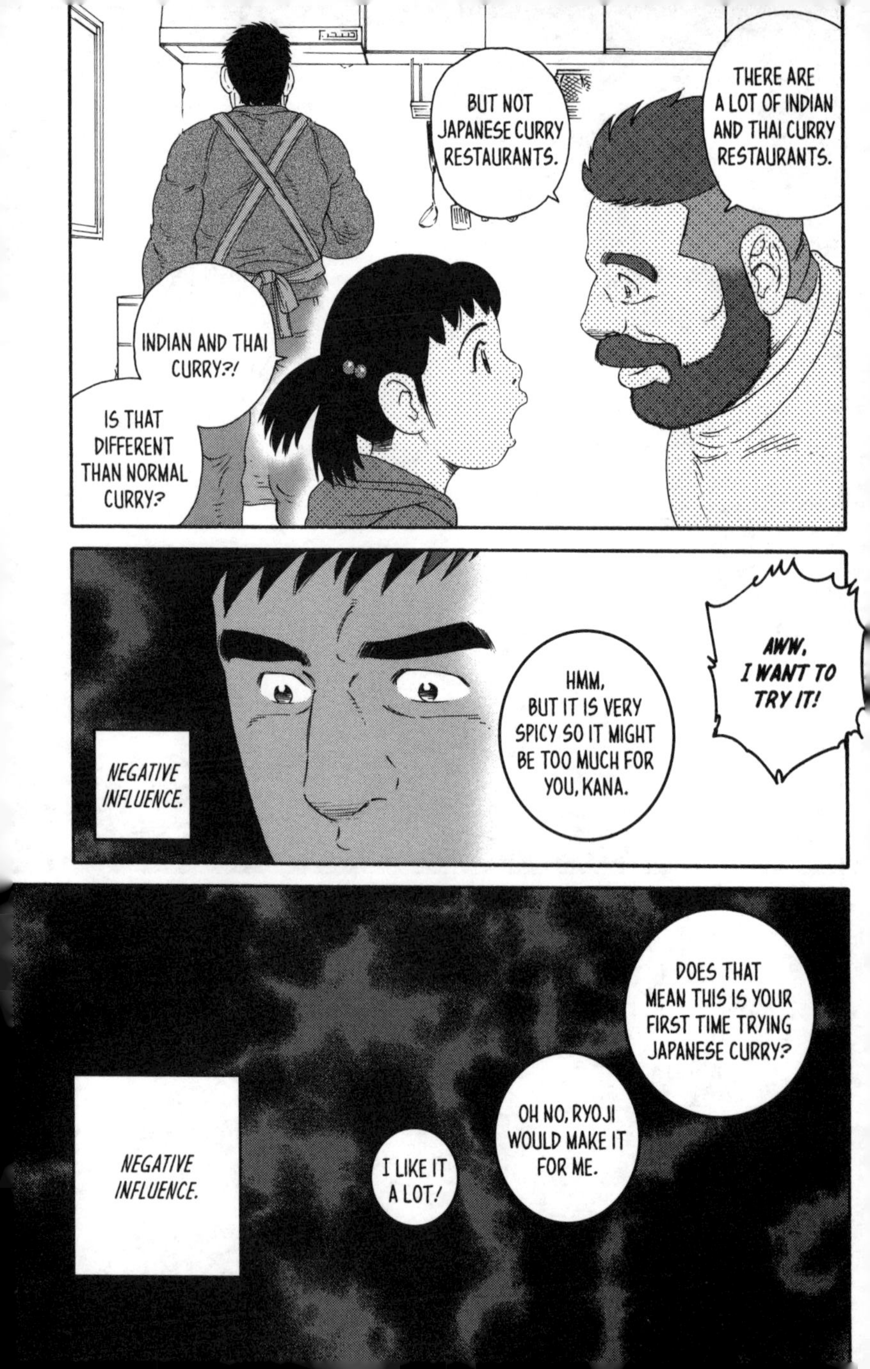
THERE ARE A LOT OF INDIAN AND THAI CURRY RESTAURANTS.
BUT NOT JAPANESE CURRY RESTAURANTS.
INDIAN AND THAI CURRY?!
IS THAT DIFFERENT THAN NORMAL CURRY?
AWW, I WANT TO TRY IT!
HMM, BUT IT IS VERY SPICY SO IT MIGHT BE TOO MUCH FOR YOU, KANA.
NEGATIVE INFLUENCE.
DOES THAT MEAN THIS IS YOUR FIRST TIME TRYING JAPANESE CURRY?
OH NO, RYOJI WOULD MAKE IT FOR ME.
I LIKE IT A LOT!
NEGATIVE INFLUENCE.

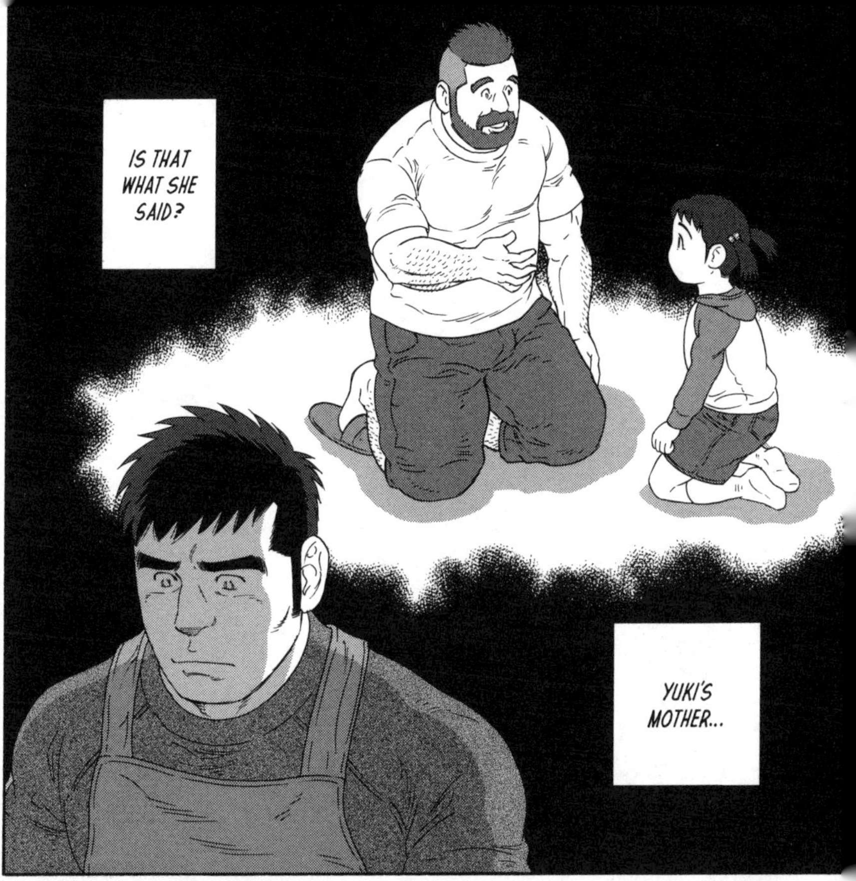
IS THAT WHAT SHE SAID?
YUKI'S MOTHER...
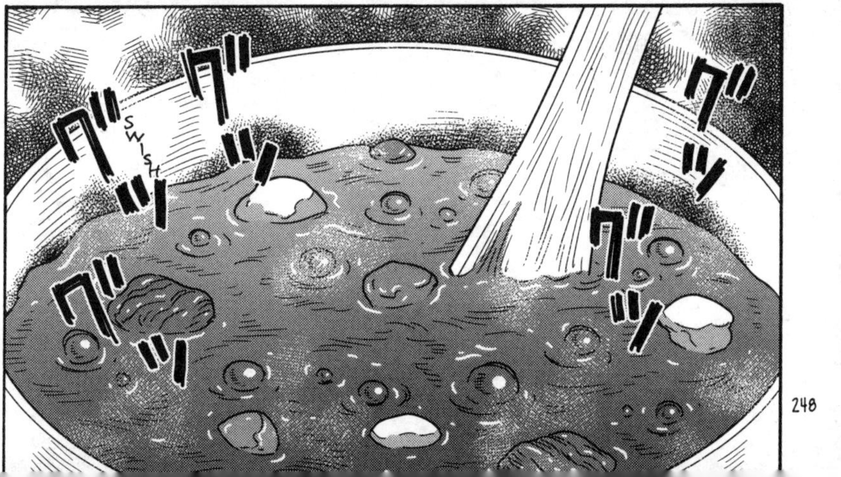
SWISH

CHAPTER ELEVEN

BAD GUYS

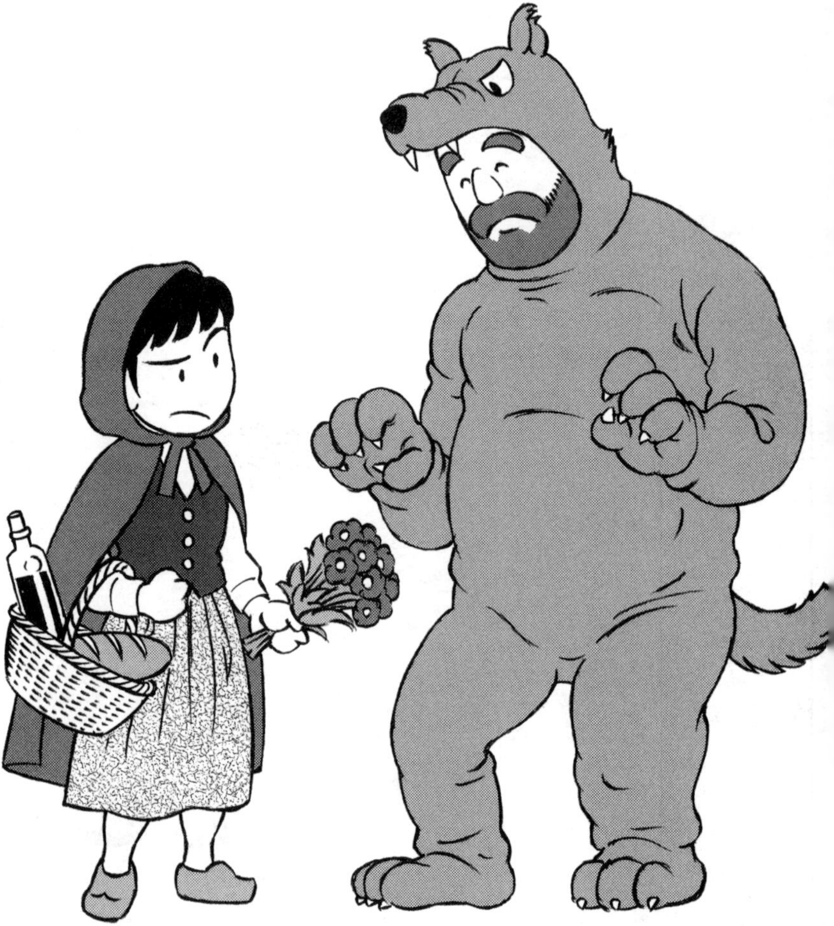

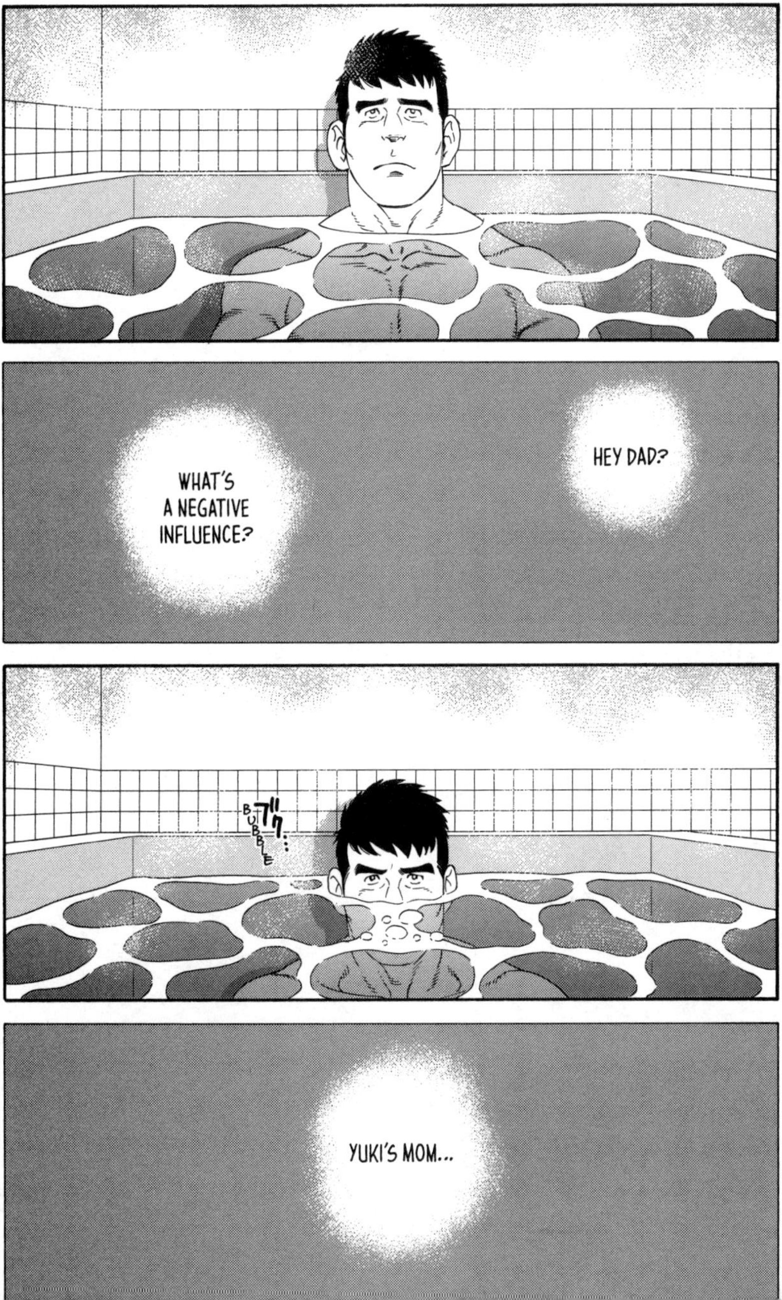
HEY DAD?
WHAT'S A NEGATIVE INFLUENCE?
BUBBLE
YUKI'S MOM...

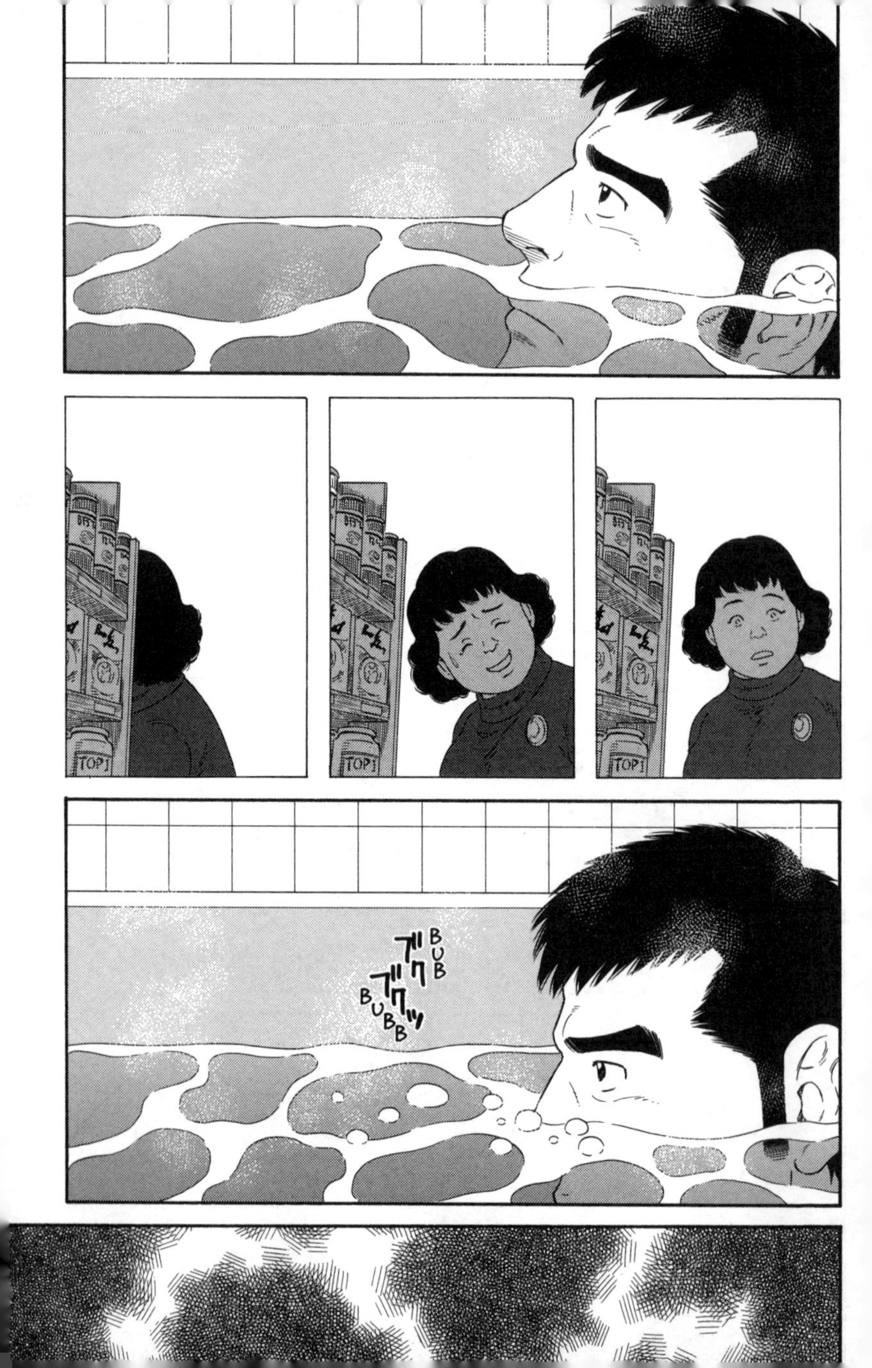
TOP1
ブク BUB
ブクッ BUBB

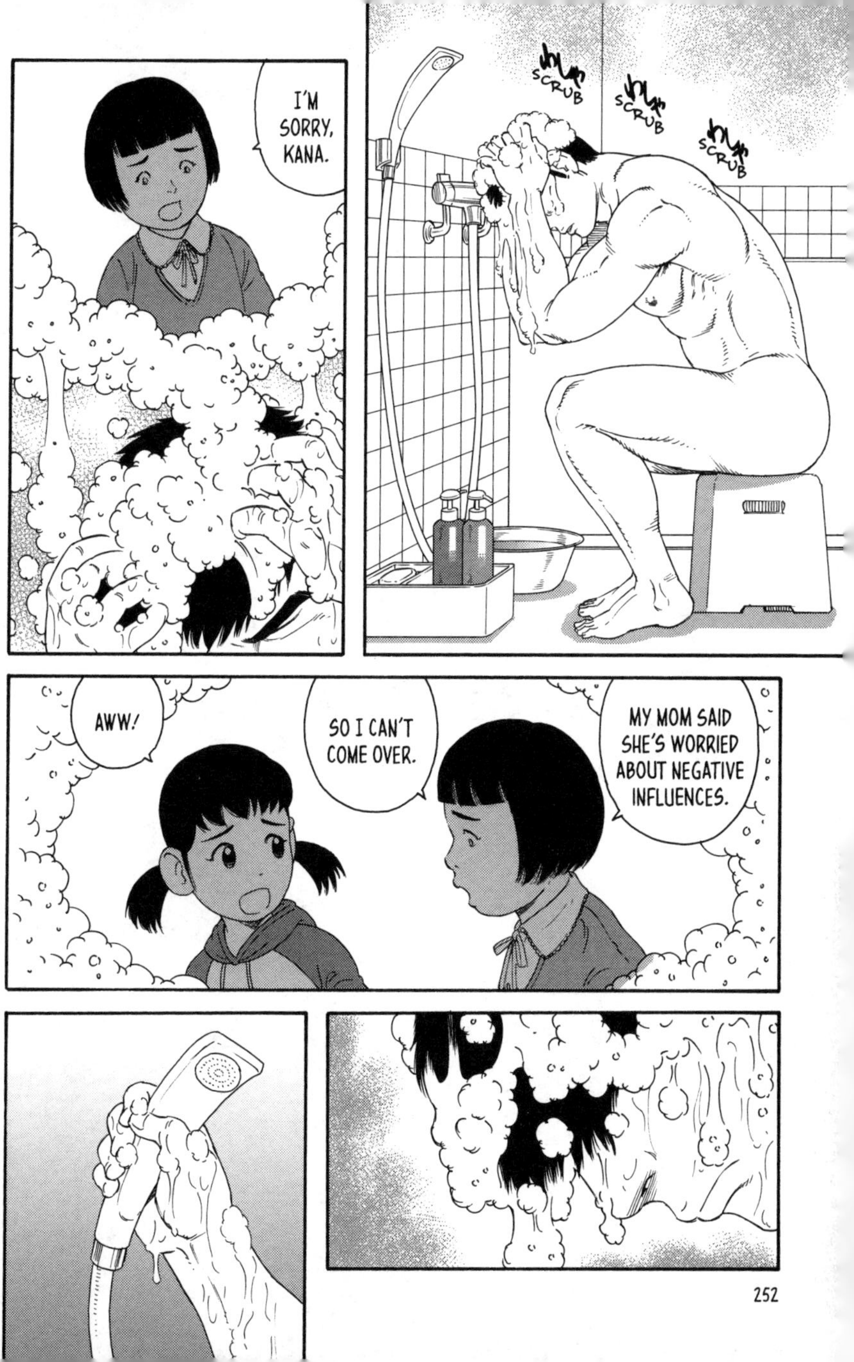
SCRUB
SCRUB
SCRUB
I'M SORRY, KANA.
MY MOM SAID SHE'S WORRIED ABOUT NEGATIVE INFLUENCES.
SO I CAN'T COME OVER.
AWW!

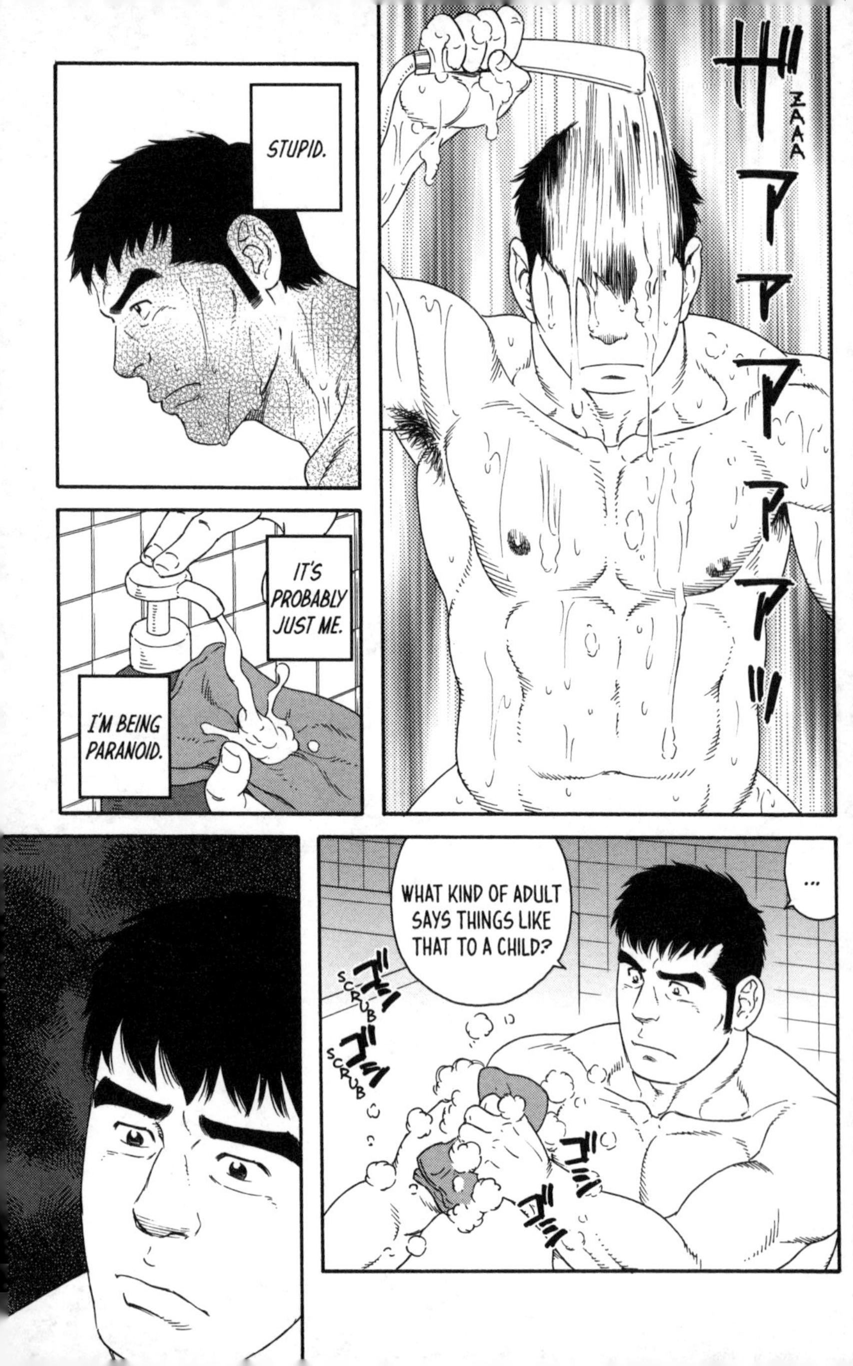
ザァァァァッ
ZAAA
STUPID.
IT'S PROBABLY JUST ME.
I'M BEING PARANOID.
...
WHAT KIND OF ADULT SAYS THINGS LIKE THAT TO A CHILD?
ゴシ
SCRUB
ゴシ
SCRUB
ゴシ
ゴシ

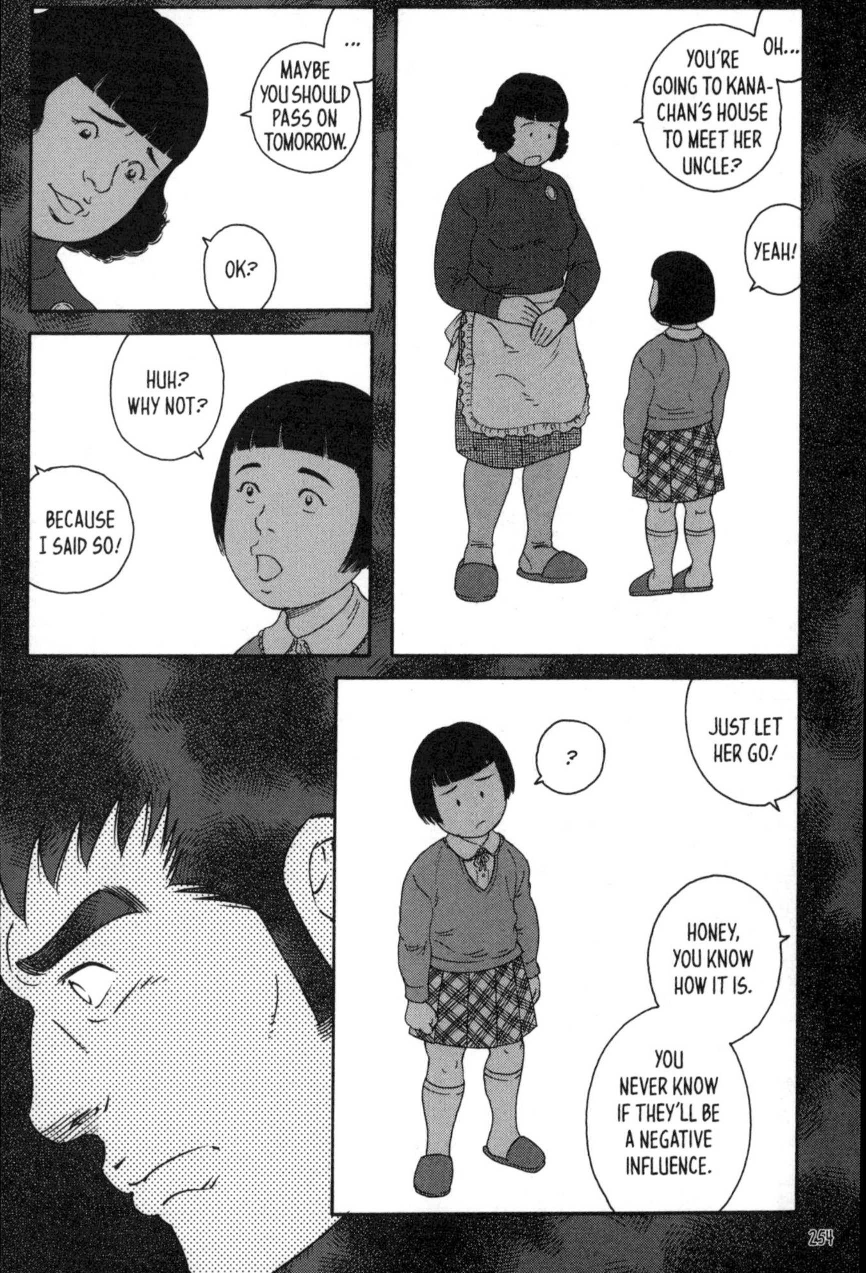
OH...
YOU'RE GOING TO KANA-CHAN'S HOUSE TO MEET HER UNCLE?
YEAH!
...
MAYBE YOU SHOULD PASS ON TOMORROW.
OK?
HUH? WHY NOT?
BECAUSE I SAID SO!
JUST LET HER GO!
?
HONEY, YOU KNOW HOW IT IS.
YOU NEVER KNOW IF THEY'LL BE A NEGATIVE INFLUENCE.

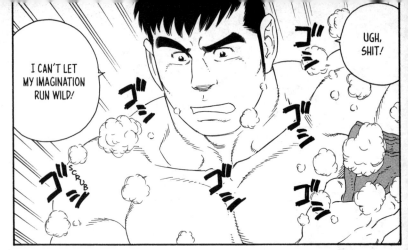

UGH, SHIT!

I CAN'T LET MY IMAGINATION RUN WILD!

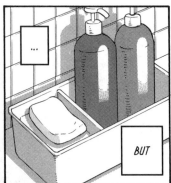

...

BUT

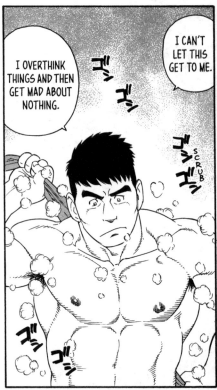

I CAN'T LET THIS GET TO ME.

I OVERTHINK THINGS AND THEN GET MAD ABOUT NOTHING.

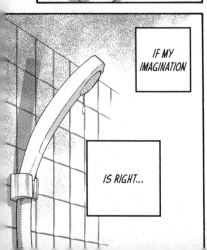

IF MY IMAGINATION

IS RIGHT...

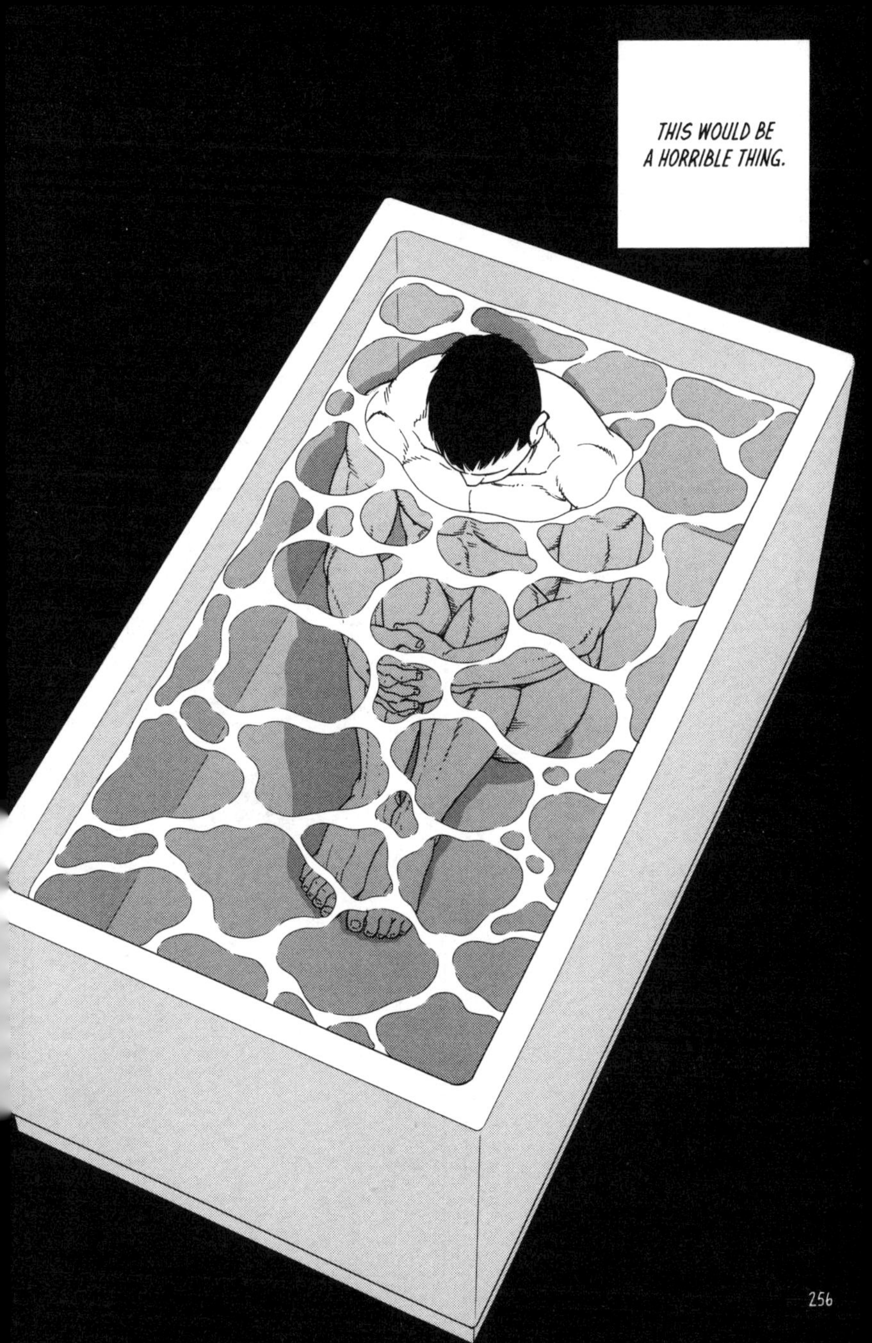
THIS WOULD BE
A HORRIBLE THING.

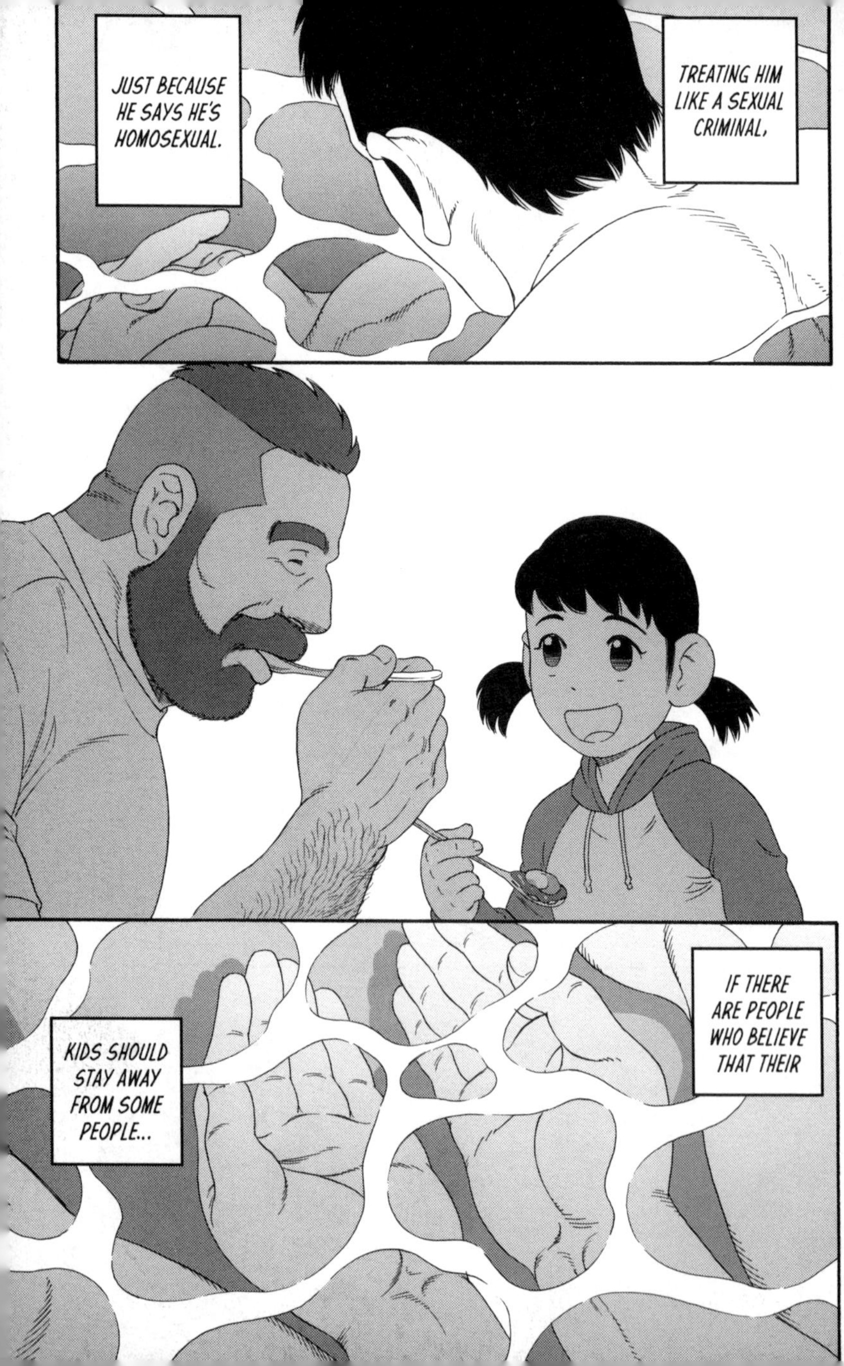
TREATING HIM LIKE A SEXUAL CRIMINAL,
JUST BECAUSE HE SAYS HE'S HOMOSEXUAL.
IF THERE ARE PEOPLE WHO BELIEVE THAT THEIR
KIDS SHOULD STAY AWAY FROM SOME PEOPLE...

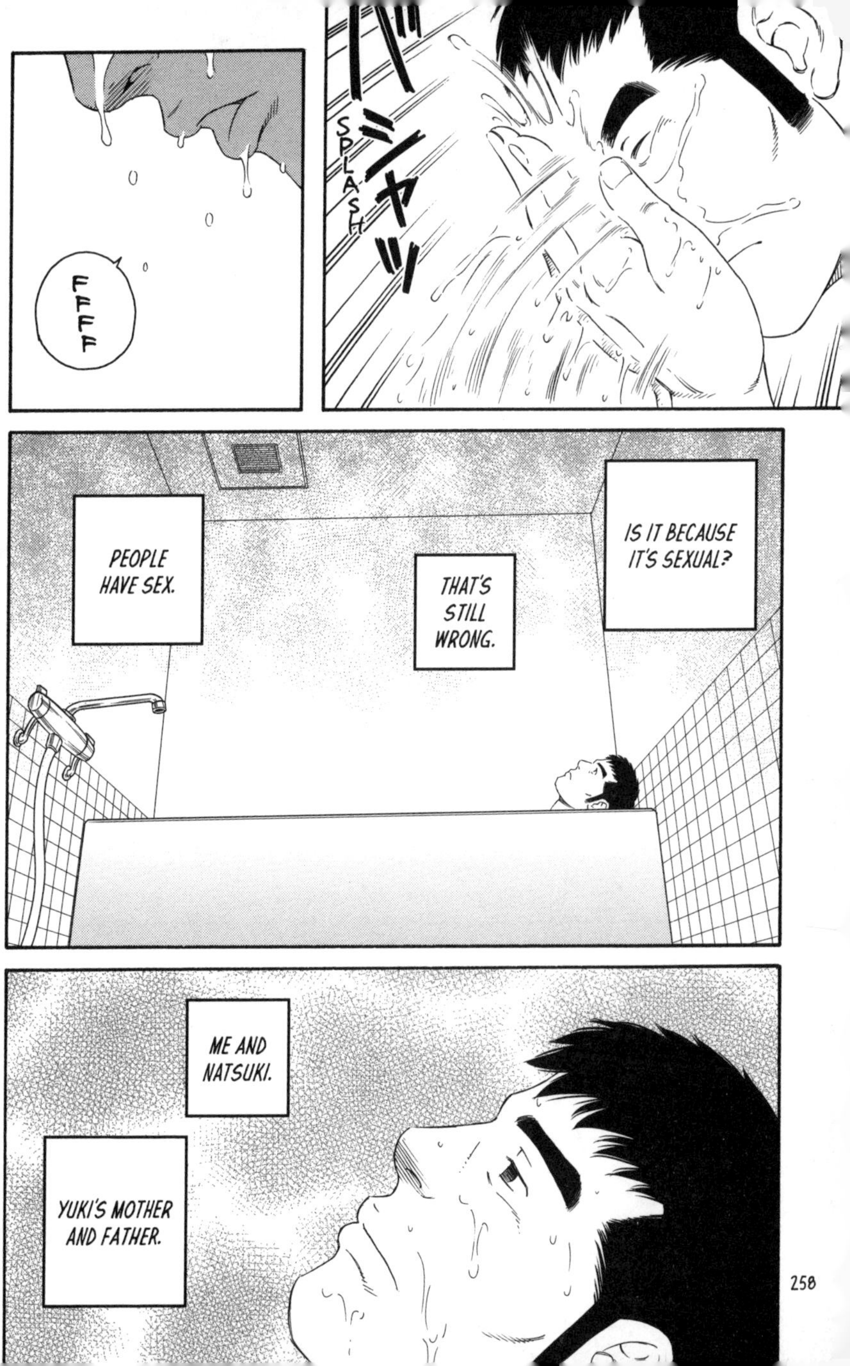
バシャッ
SPLASH
FFFF
IS IT BECAUSE IT'S SEXUAL?
THAT'S STILL WRONG.
PEOPLE HAVE SEX.
ME AND NATSUKI.
YUKI'S MOTHER AND FATHER.

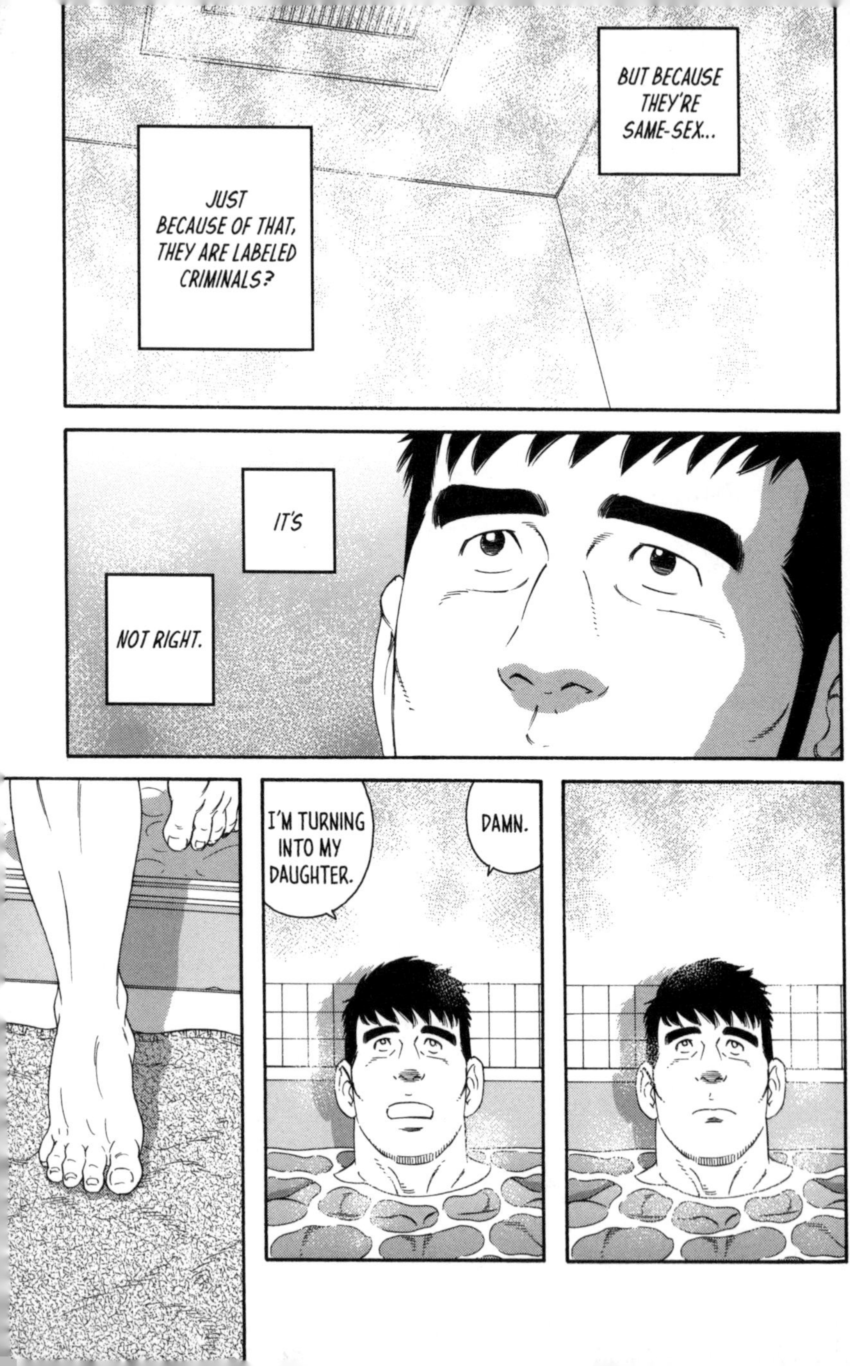
BUT BECAUSE THEY'RE SAME-SEX...
JUST BECAUSE OF THAT, THEY ARE LABELED CRIMINALS?
IT'S
NOT RIGHT.
DAMN.
I'M TURNING INTO MY DAUGHTER.

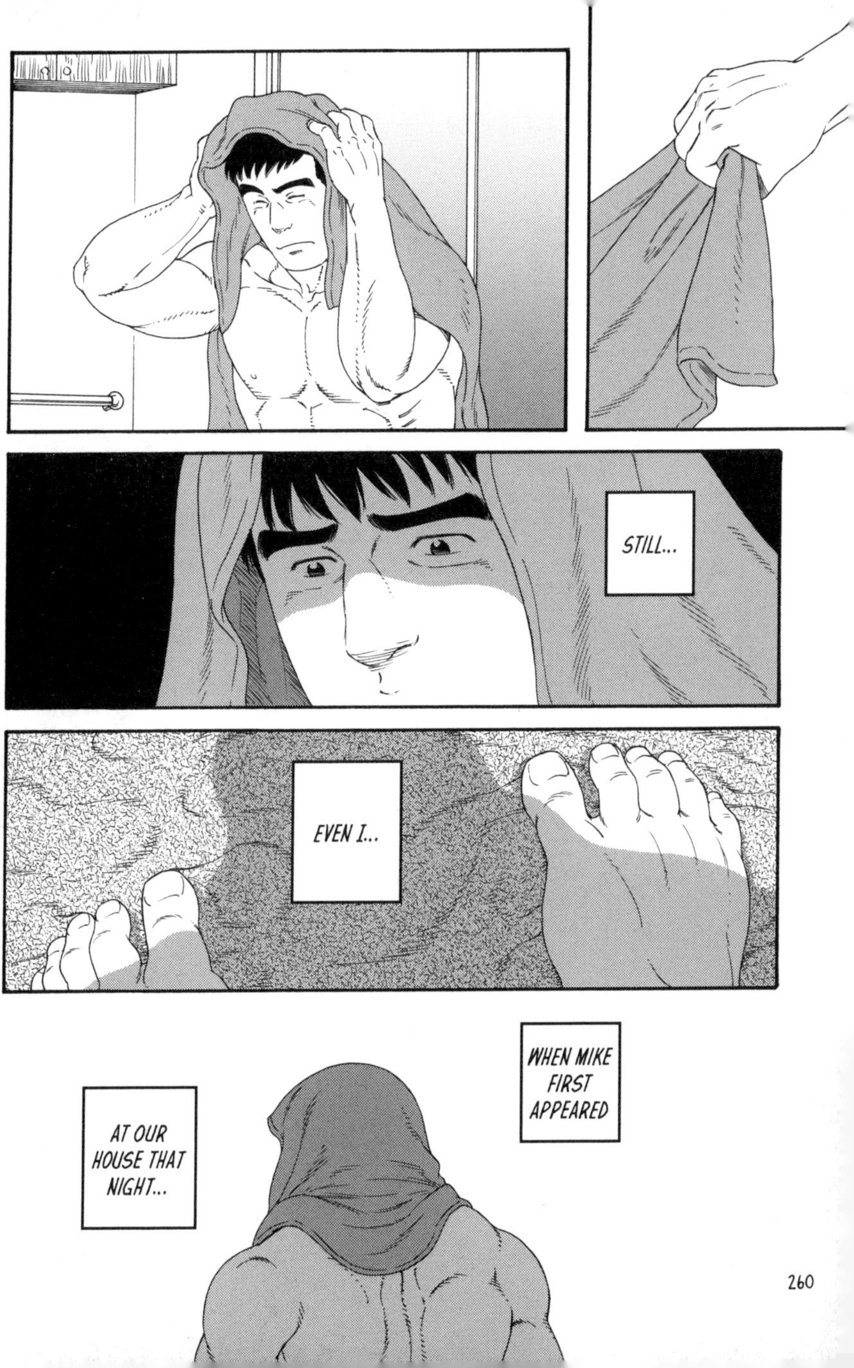
STILL...
EVEN I...
WHEN MIKE FIRST APPEARED
AT OUR HOUSE THAT NIGHT...

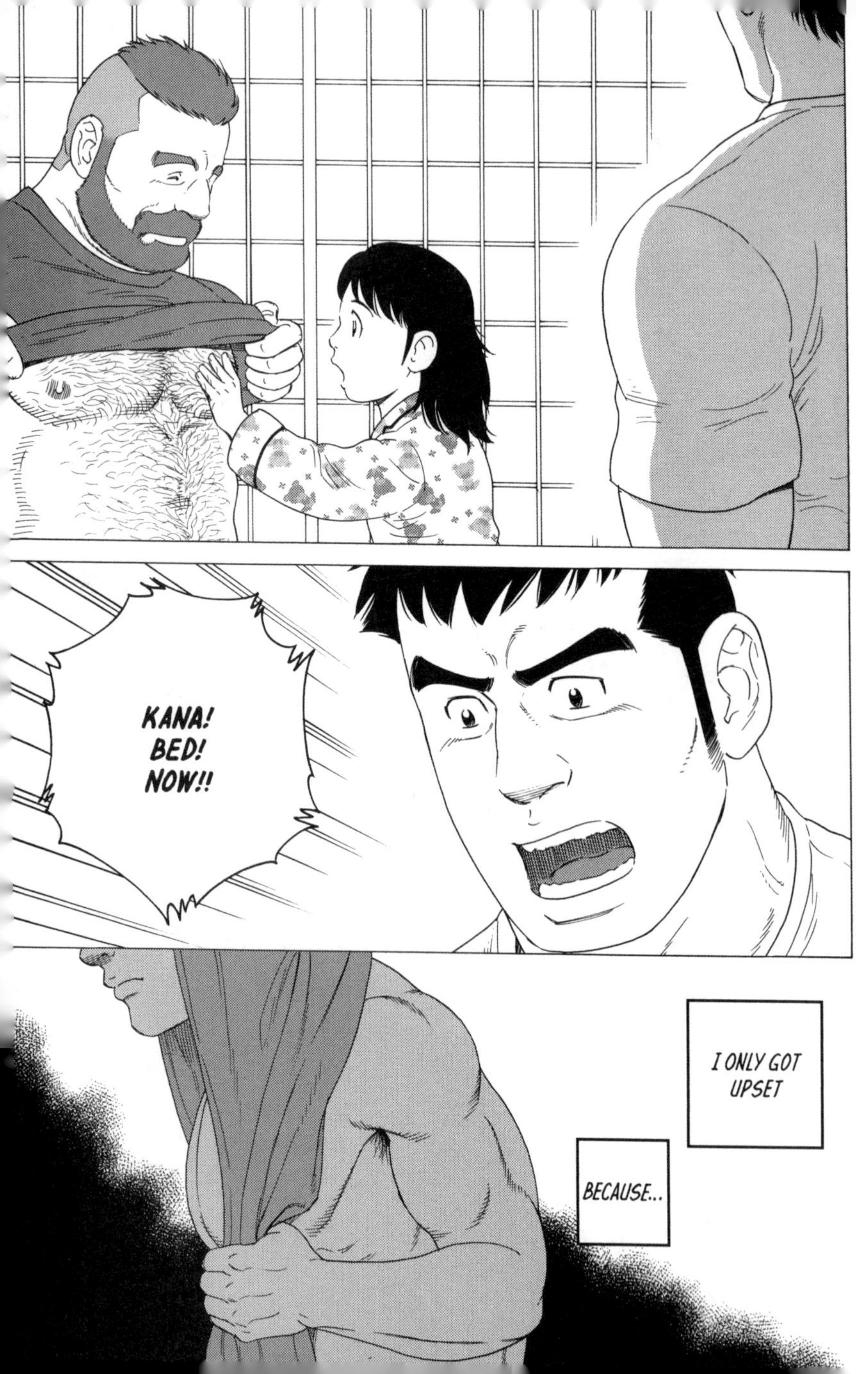
KANA! BED! NOW!!
I ONLY GOT UPSET
BECAUSE...

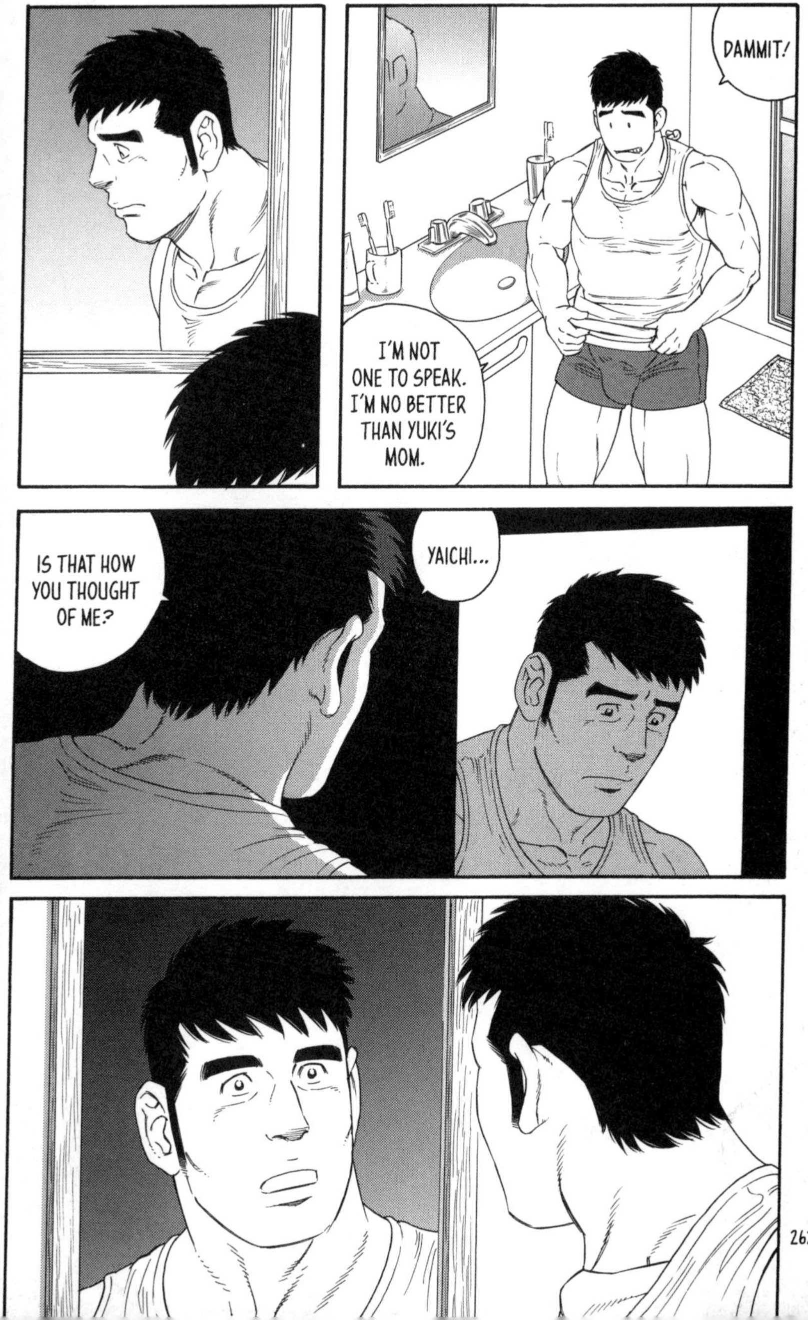
DAMMIT!
I'M NOT ONE TO SPEAK. I'M NO BETTER THAN YUKI'S MOM.
YAICHI...
IS THAT HOW YOU THOUGHT OF ME?

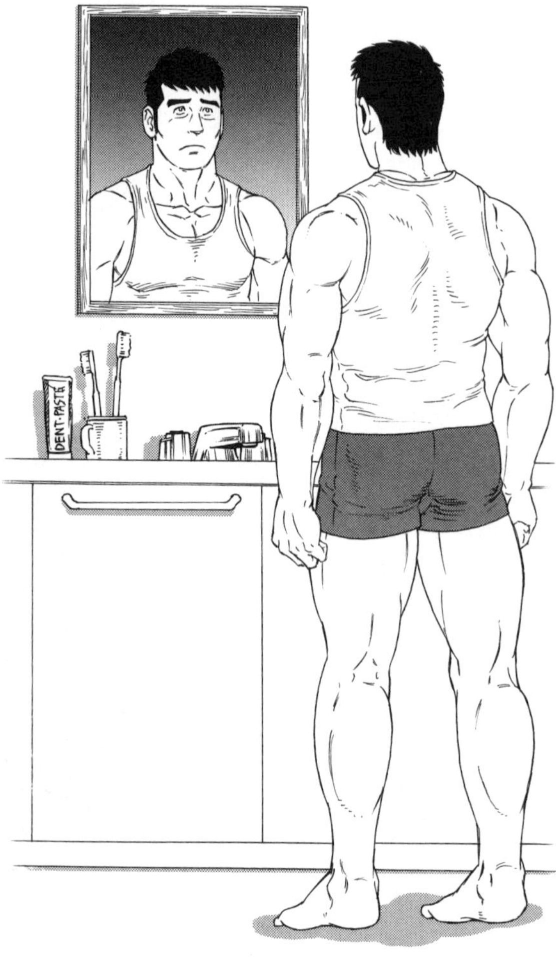
DENT-PASTE

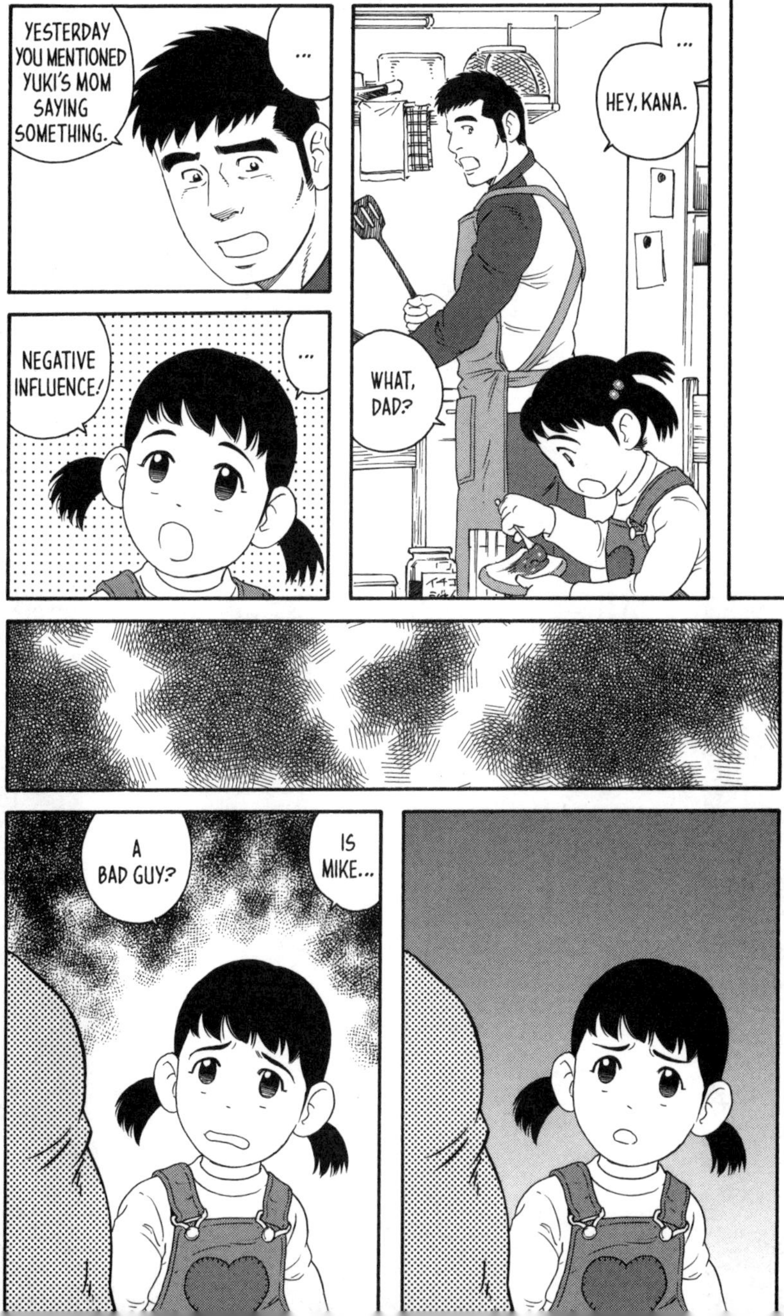
...
HEY, KANA.
WHAT, DAD?
...
YESTERDAY YOU MENTIONED YUKI'S MOM SAYING SOMETHING.
...
NEGATIVE INFLUENCE!
IS MIKE...
A BAD GUY?

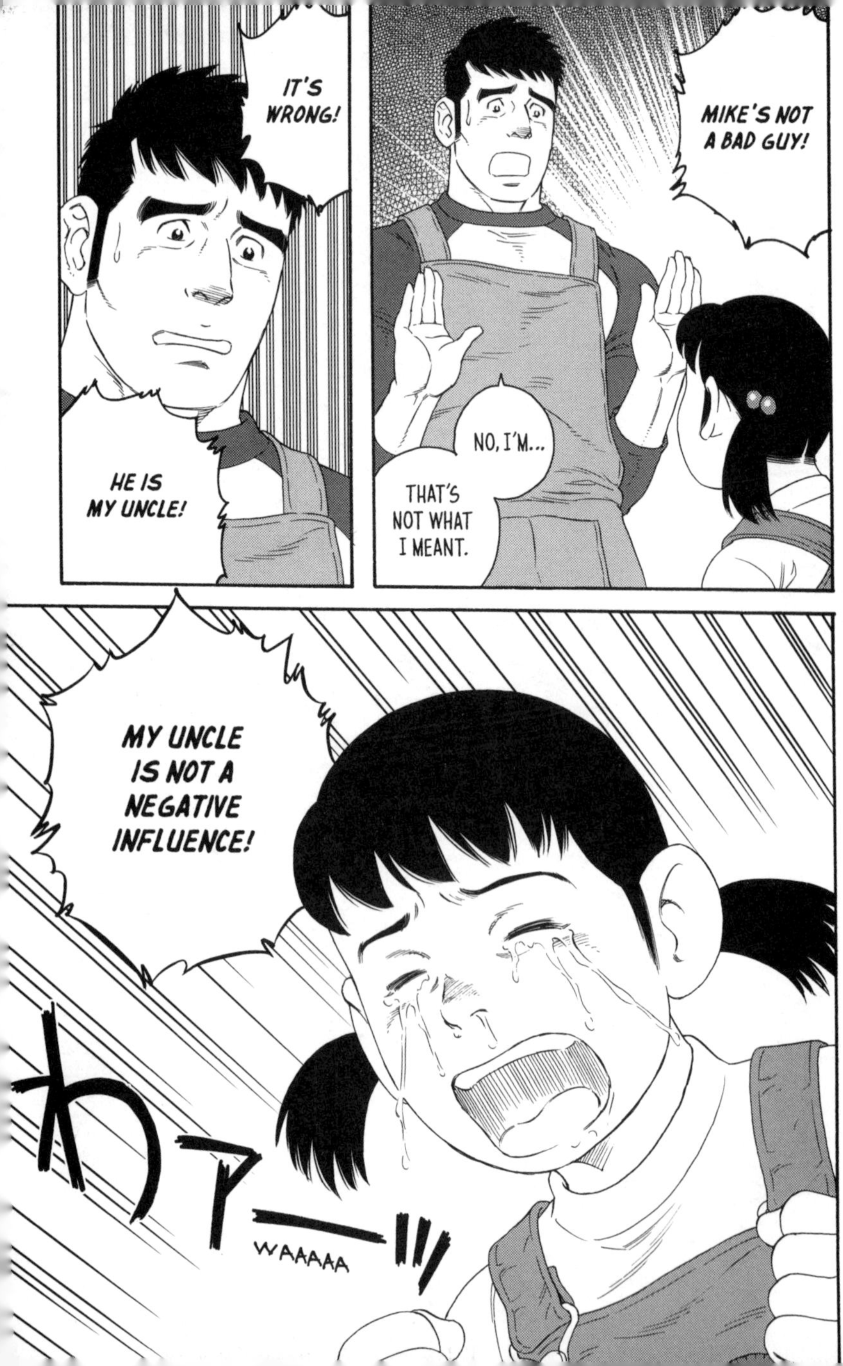
MIKE'S NOT A BAD GUY!
NO, I'M...
THAT'S NOT WHAT I MEANT.
IT'S WRONG!
HE IS MY UNCLE!
MY UNCLE IS NOT A NEGATIVE INFLUENCE!
わァー!!
WAAAAA

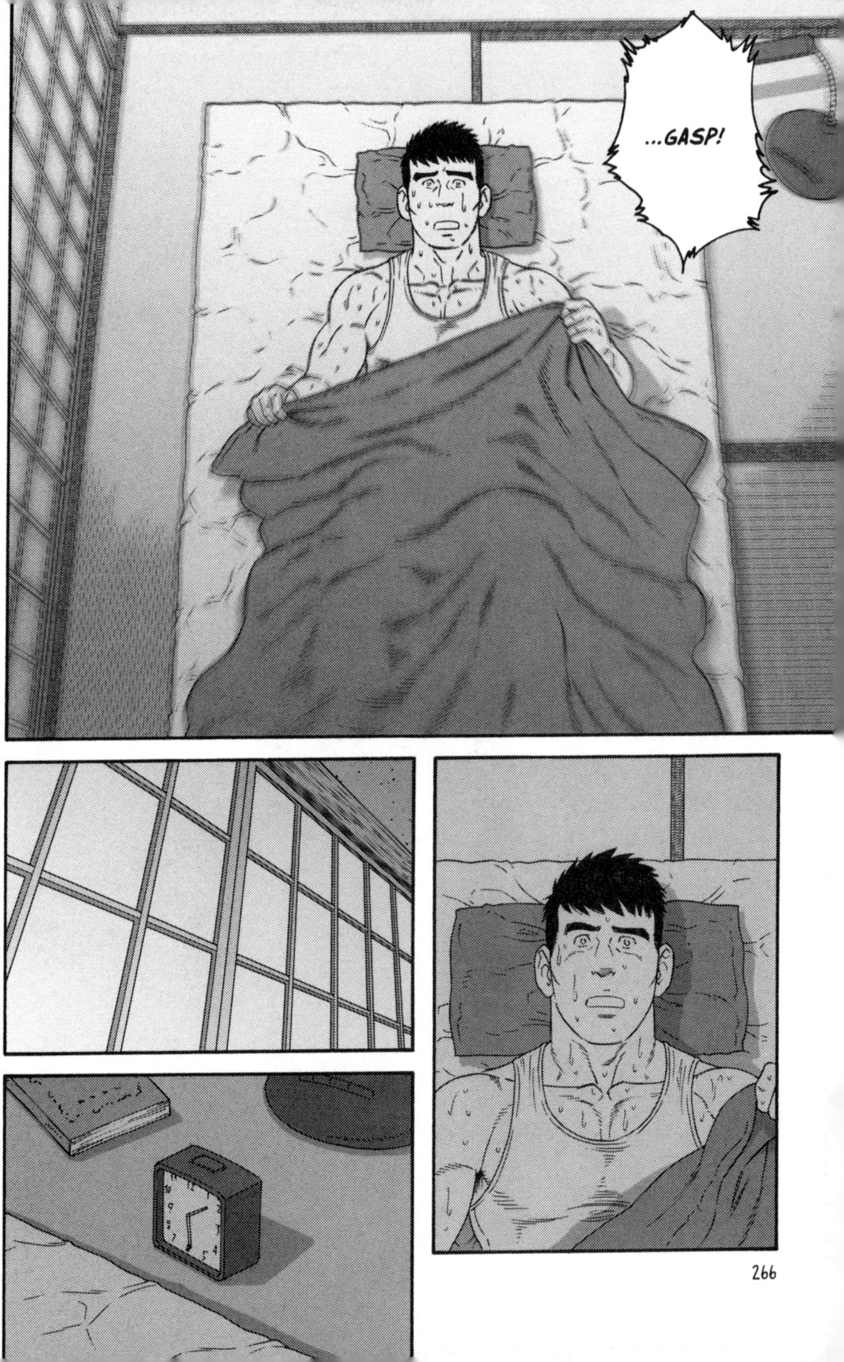
...GASP!

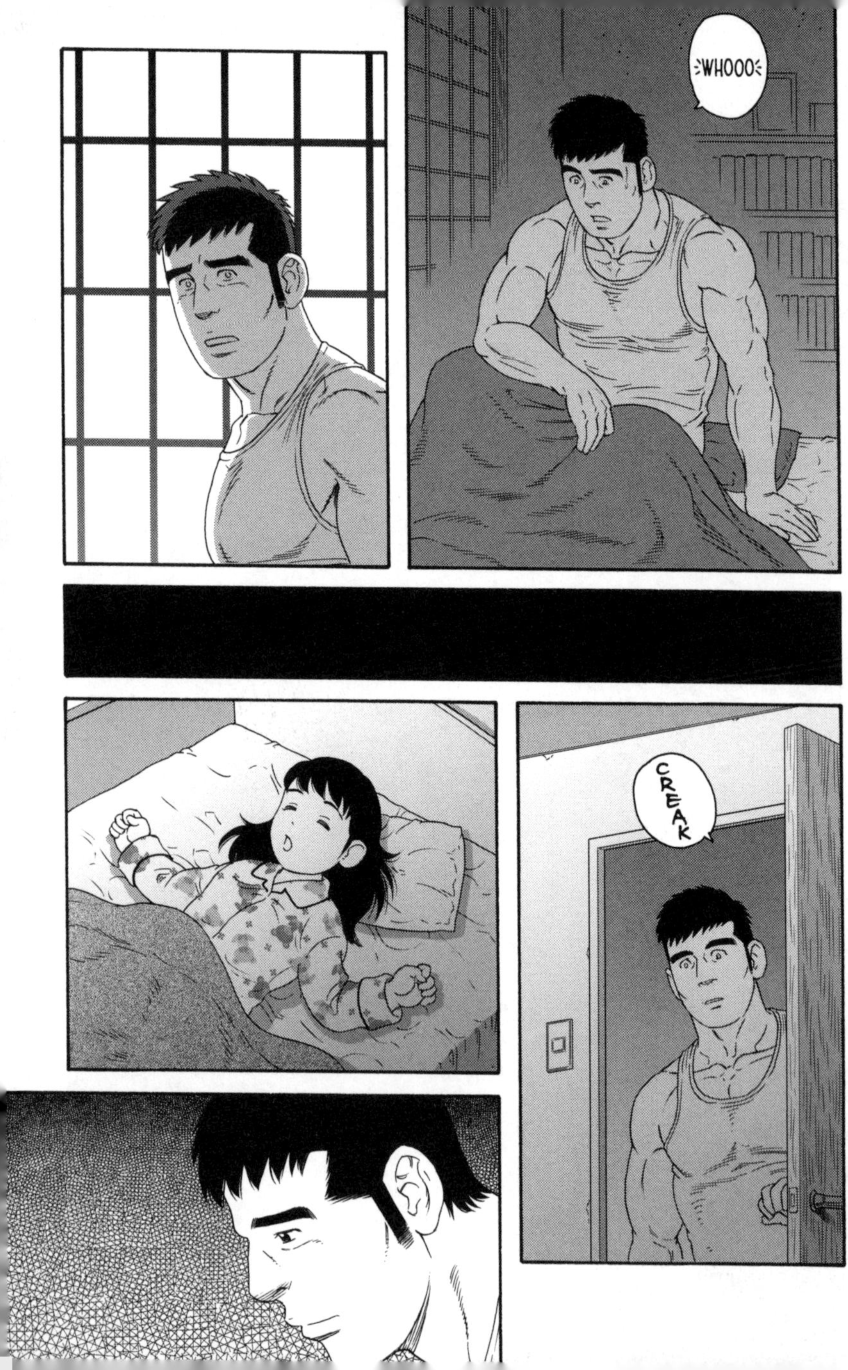
WHOOO
CREAK

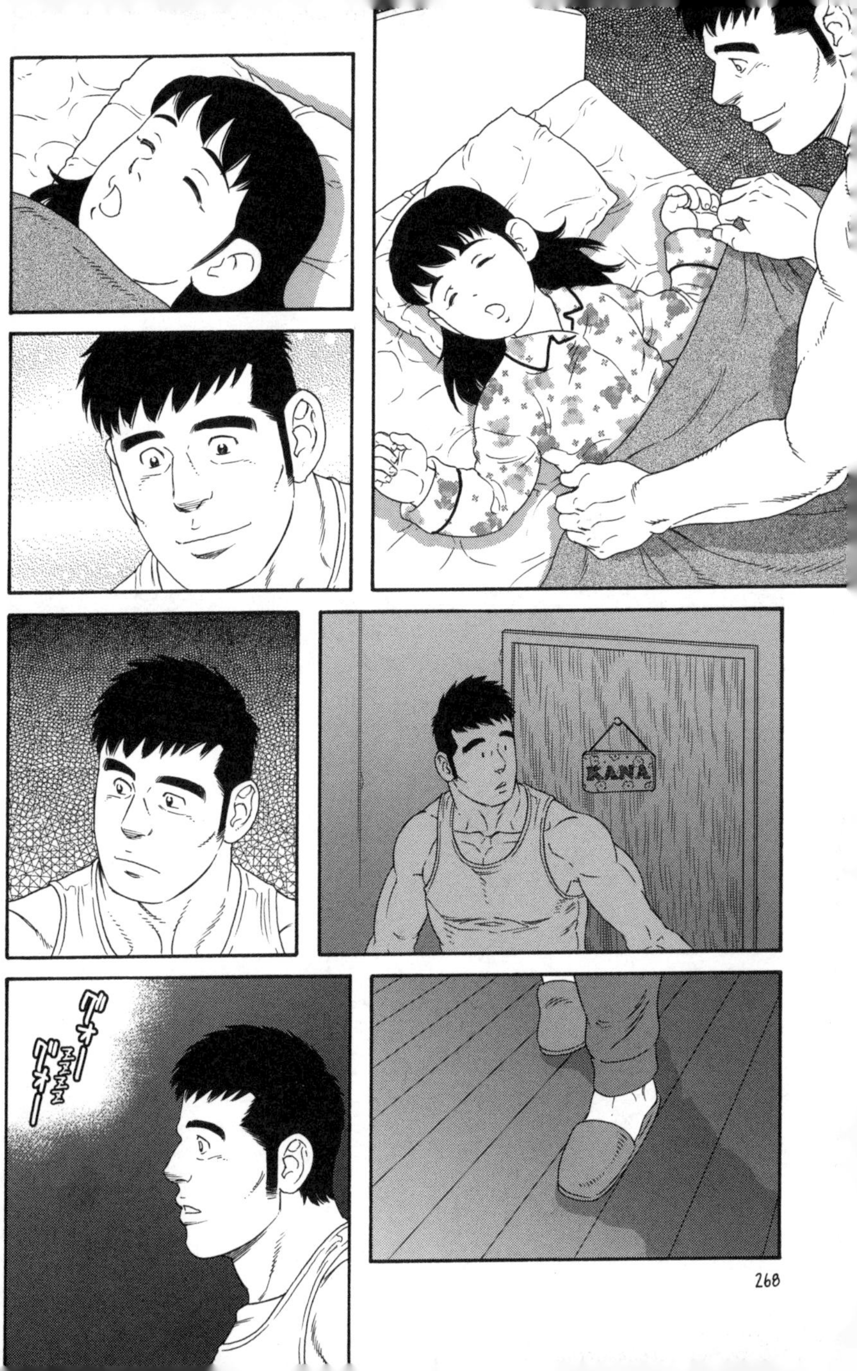
KANA
グオー
ヌヌヌヌ
グオー

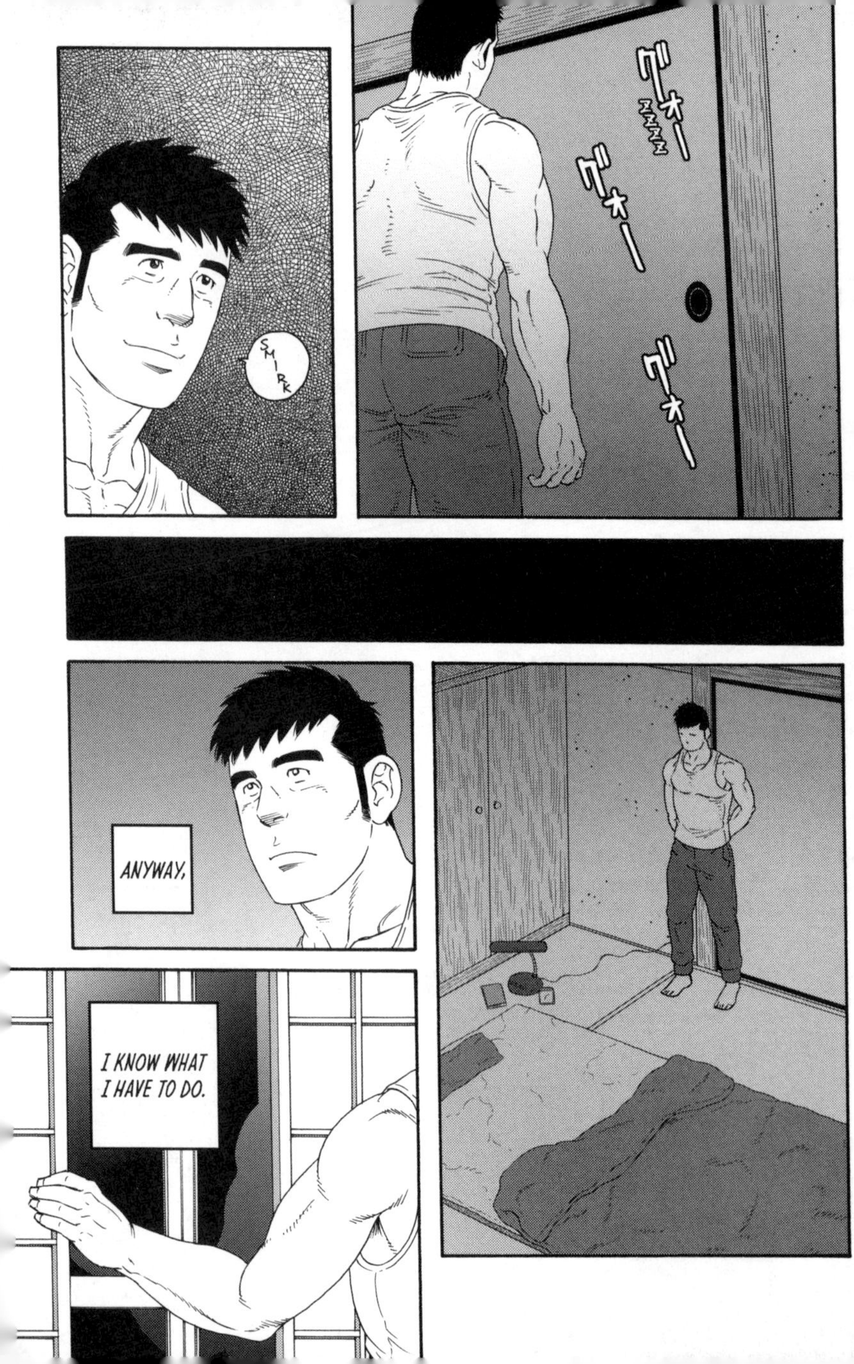

グオー
ZZZZ
グオー
グオー
SMIRK
ANYWAY,
I KNOW WHAT I HAVE TO DO.

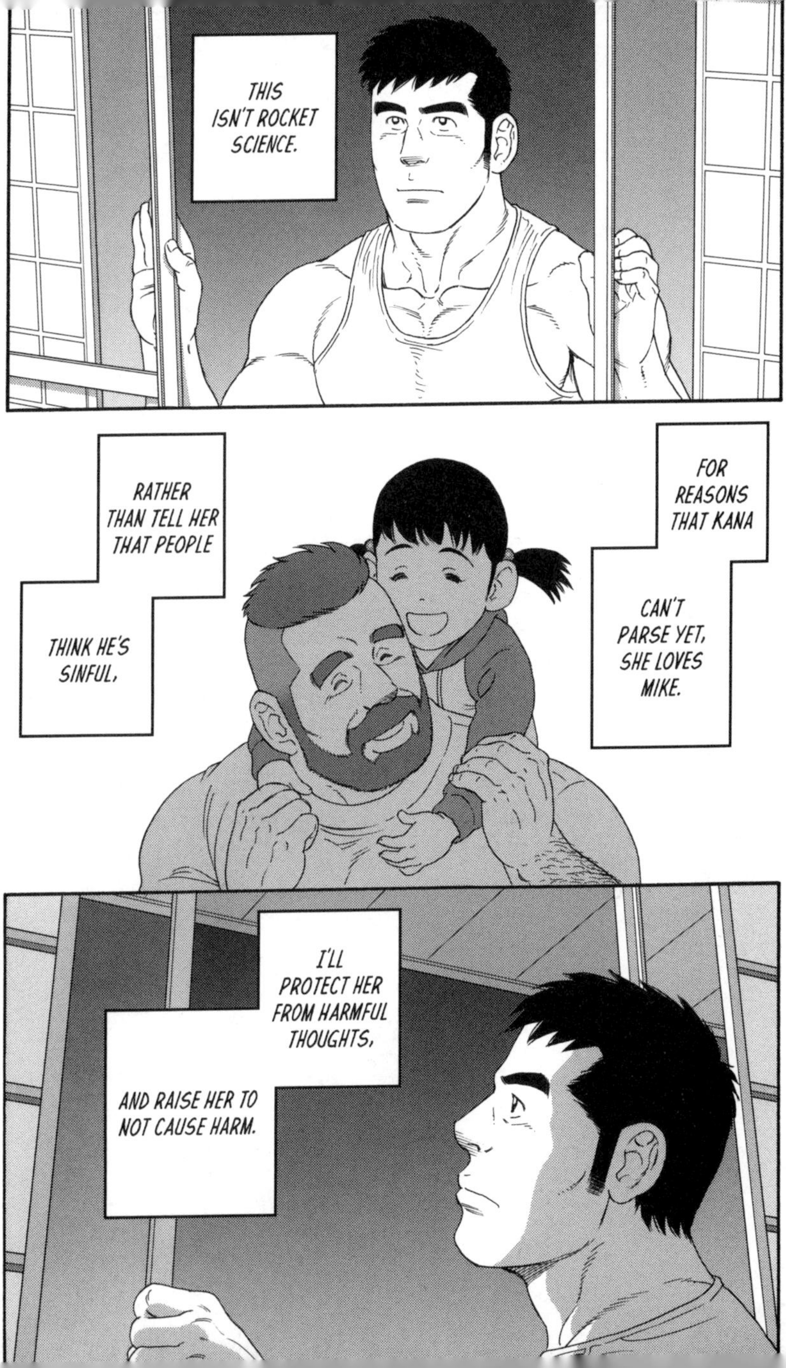
THIS ISN'T ROCKET SCIENCE.
FOR REASONS THAT KANA
CAN'T PARSE YET, SHE LOVES MIKE.
RATHER THAN TELL HER THAT PEOPLE
THINK HE'S SINFUL,
I'LL PROTECT HER FROM HARMFUL THOUGHTS,
AND RAISE HER TO NOT CAUSE HARM.

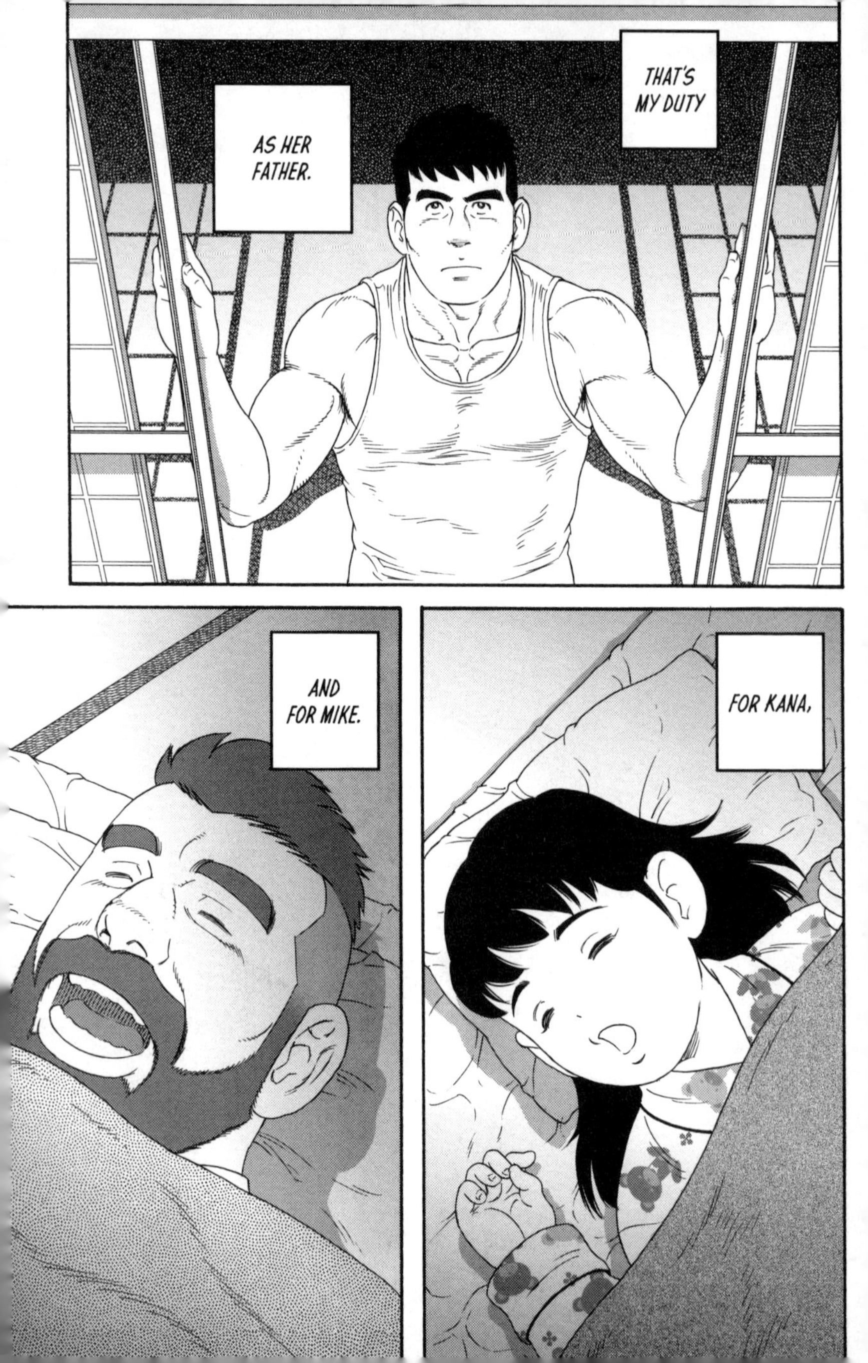
THAT'S MY DUTY
AS HER FATHER.
FOR KANA,
AND FOR MIKE.

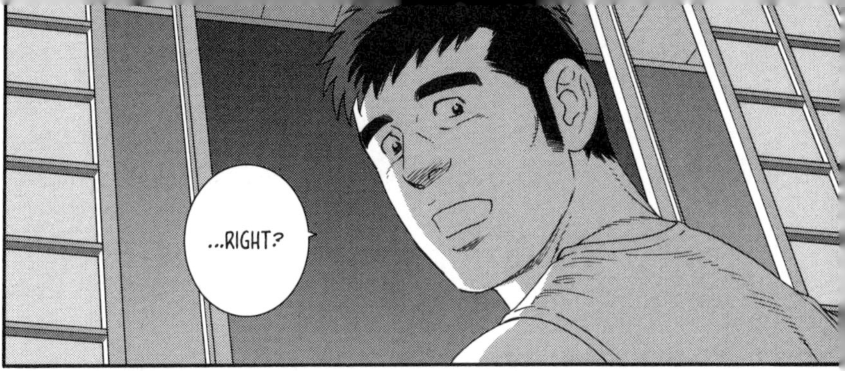
...RIGHT?
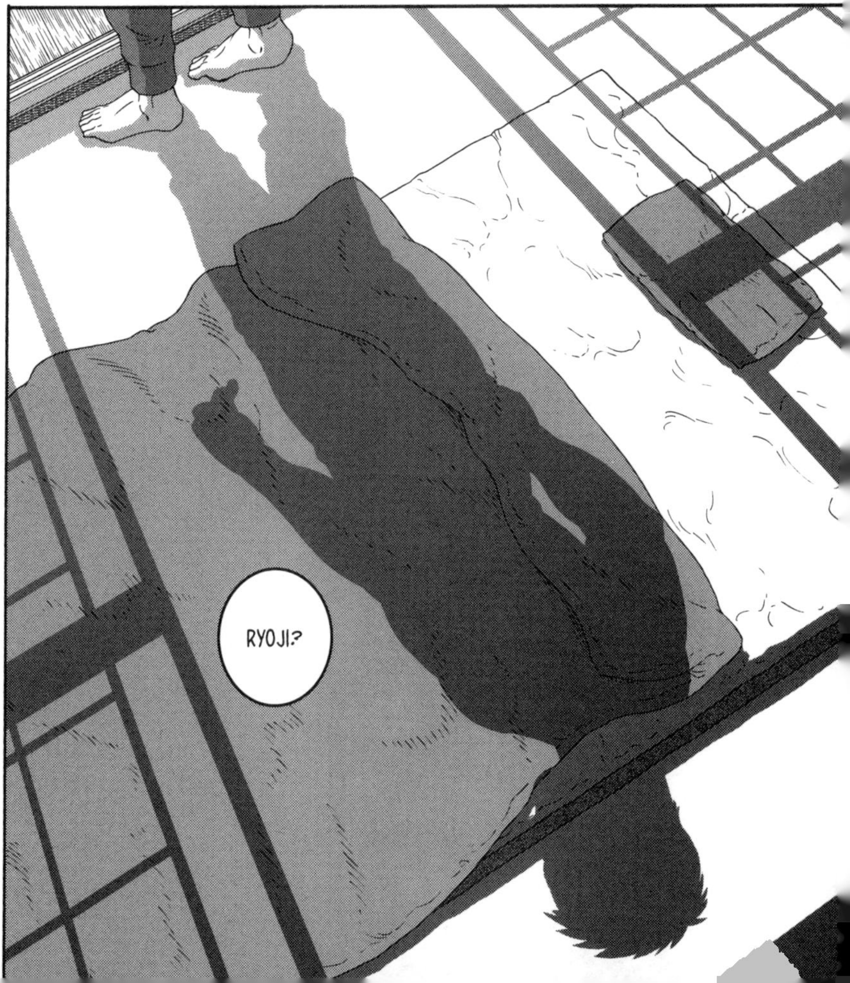
RYOJI?

CHAPTER TWELVE

THE GYM

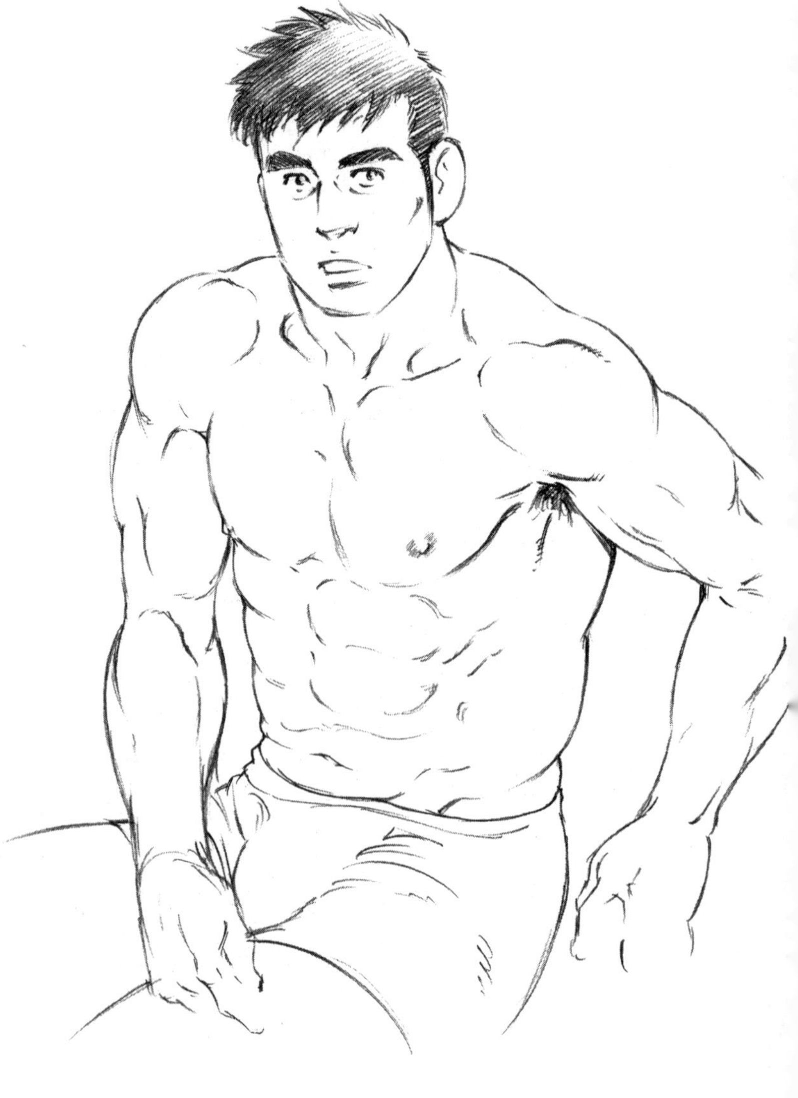

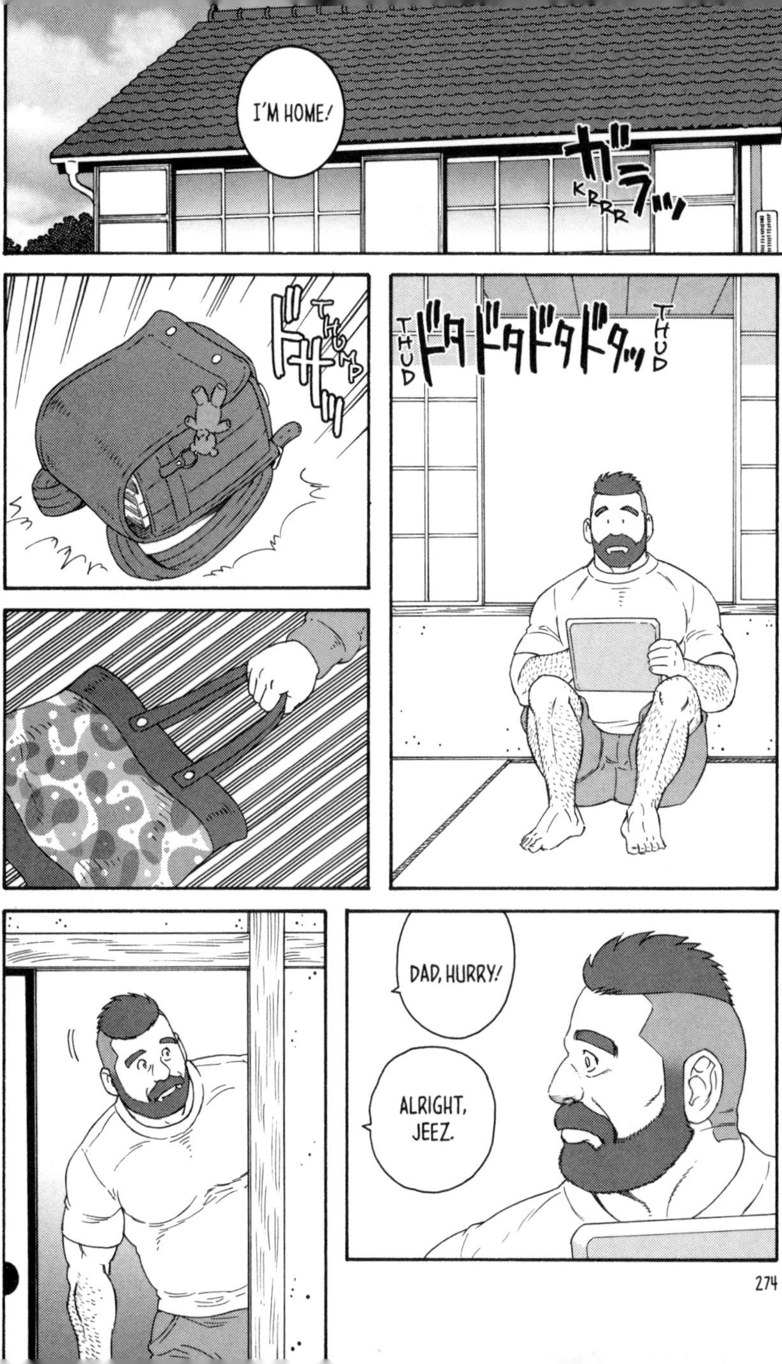
I'M HOME!
ガラッ
KRRR
THUD ドタドタドタドタッ THUD
ドサッ
THUMP
DAD, HURRY!
ALRIGHT, JEEZ.

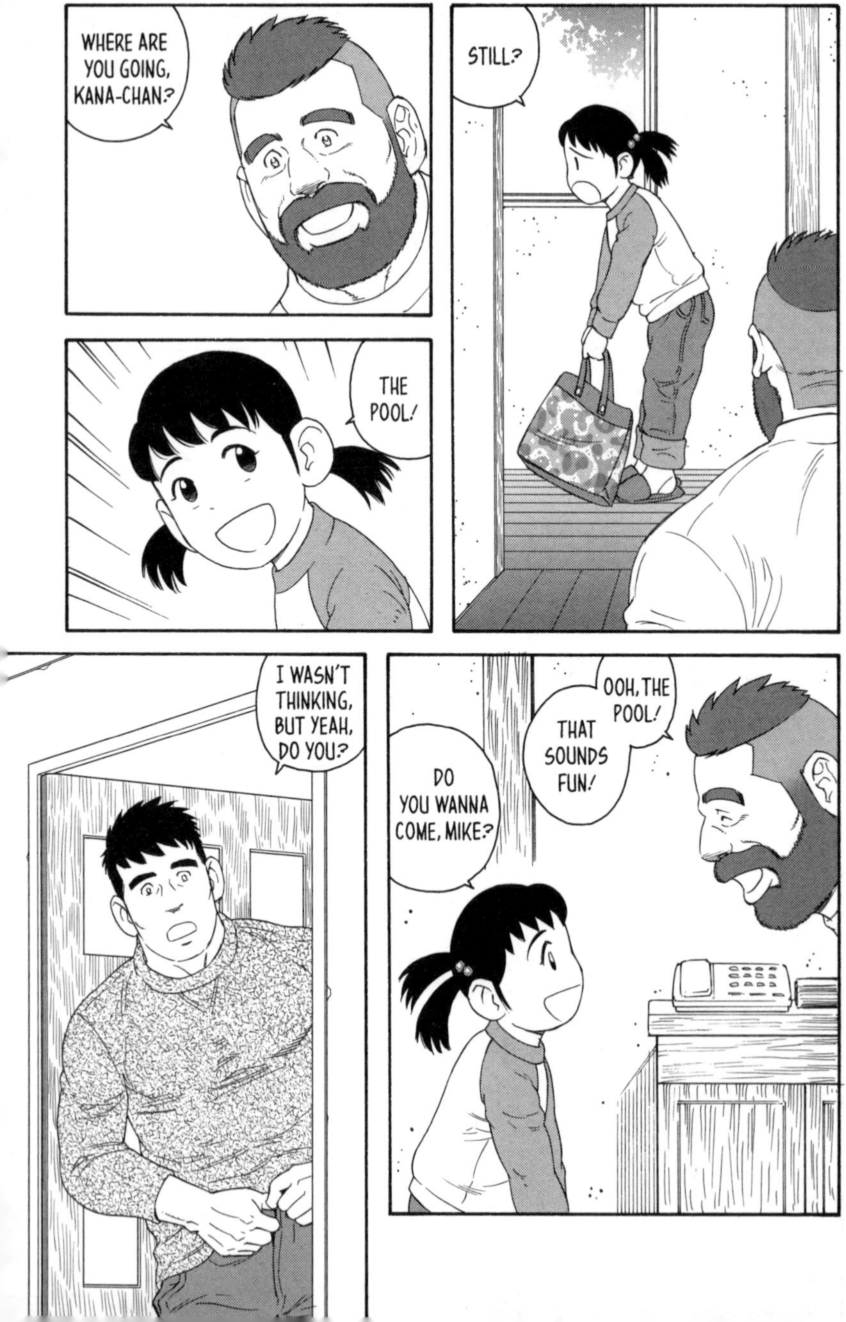
STILL?
WHERE ARE YOU GOING, KANA-CHAN?
THE POOL!
OOH, THE POOL!
THAT SOUNDS FUN!
DO YOU WANNA COME, MIKE?
I WASN'T THINKING, BUT YEAH, DO YOU?

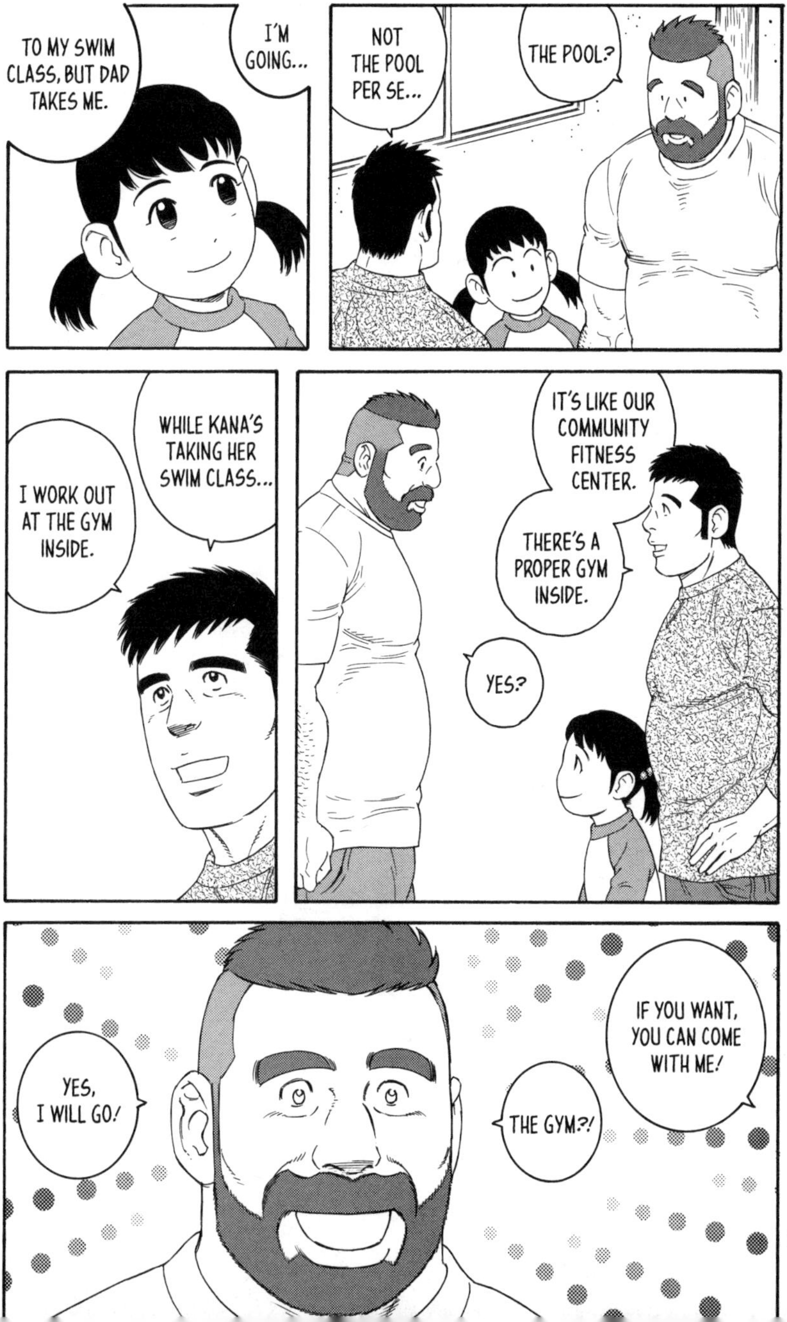
THE POOL?
NOT THE POOL PER SE...
I'M GOING...
TO MY SWIM CLASS, BUT DAD TAKES ME.
IT'S LIKE OUR COMMUNITY FITNESS CENTER.
THERE'S A PROPER GYM INSIDE.
YES?
WHILE KANA'S TAKING HER SWIM CLASS...
I WORK OUT AT THE GYM INSIDE.
IF YOU WANT, YOU CAN COME WITH ME!
THE GYM?!
YES, I WILL GO!

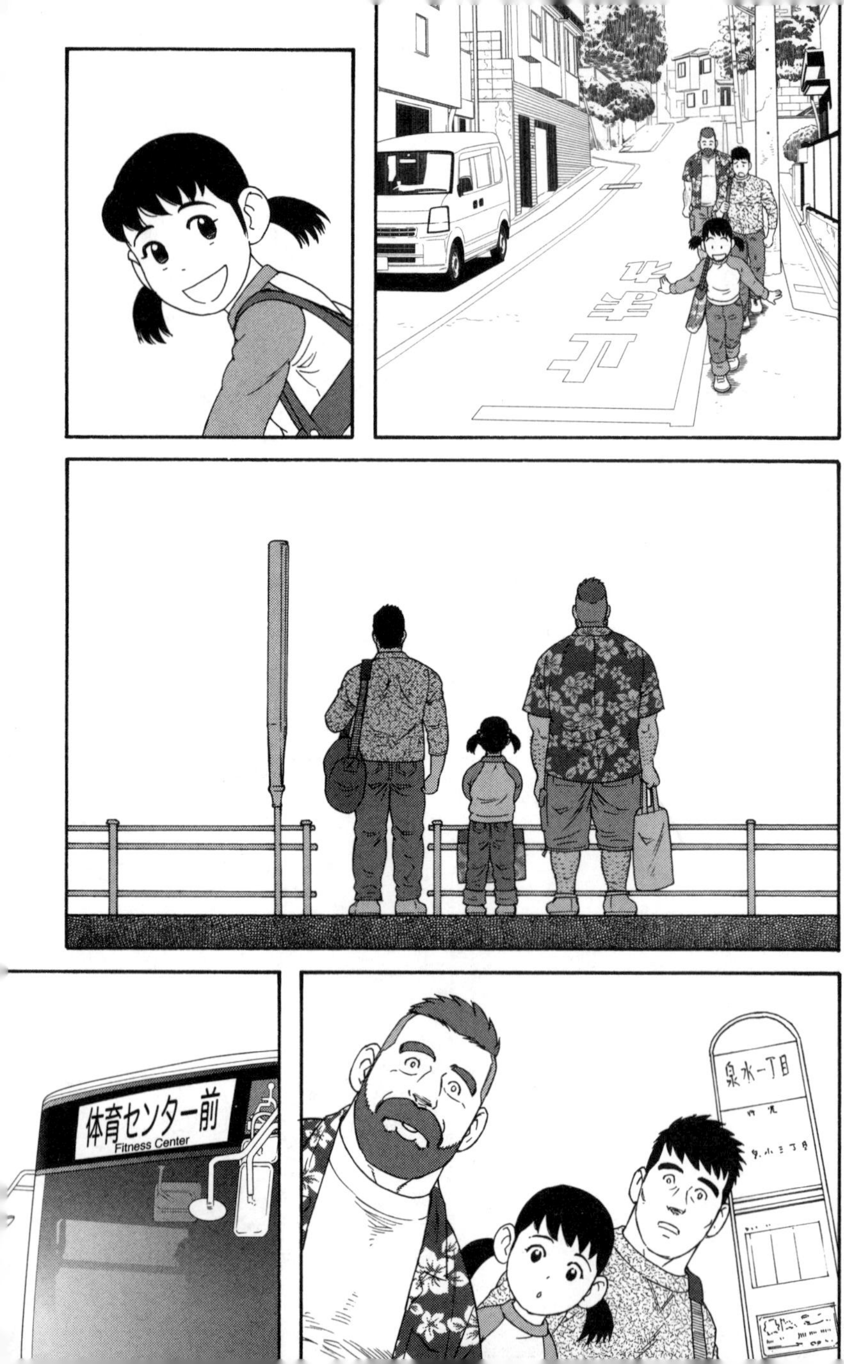
泉水一丁目
体育センター前
Fitness Center

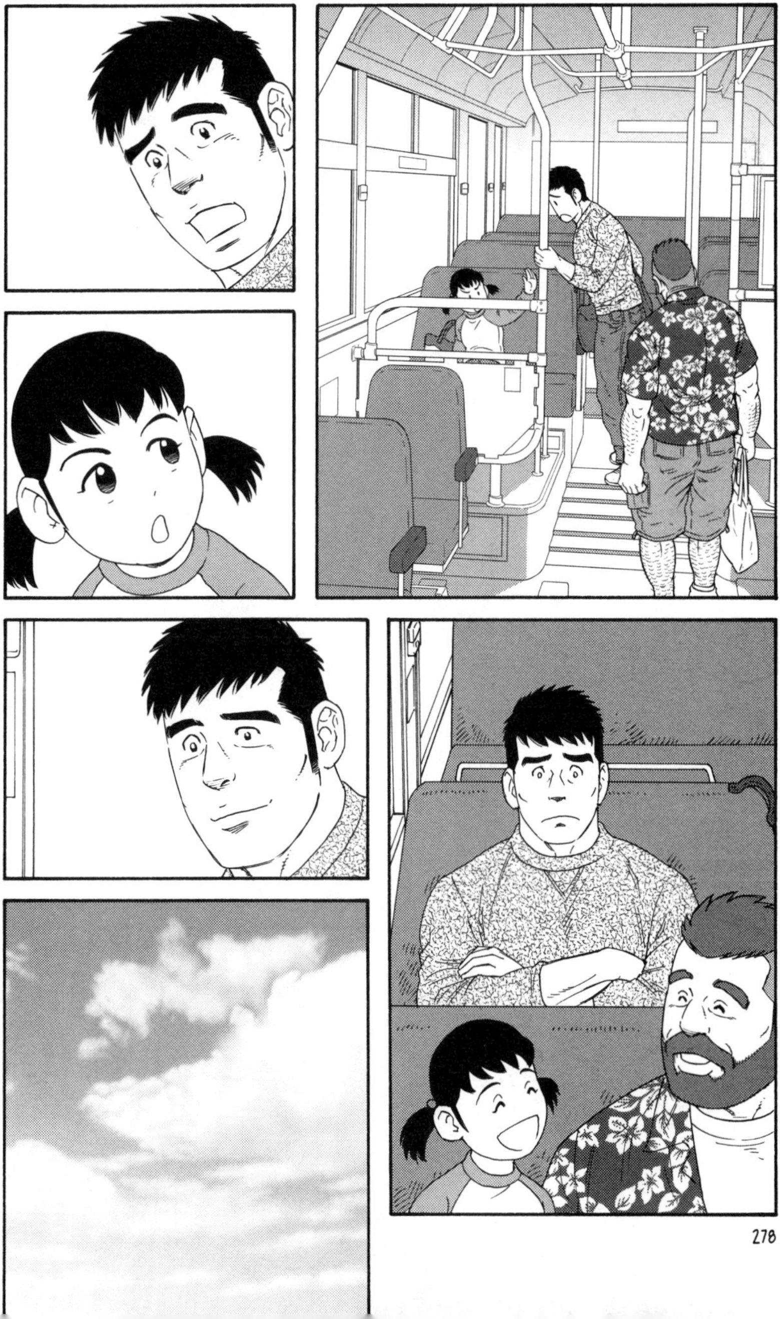

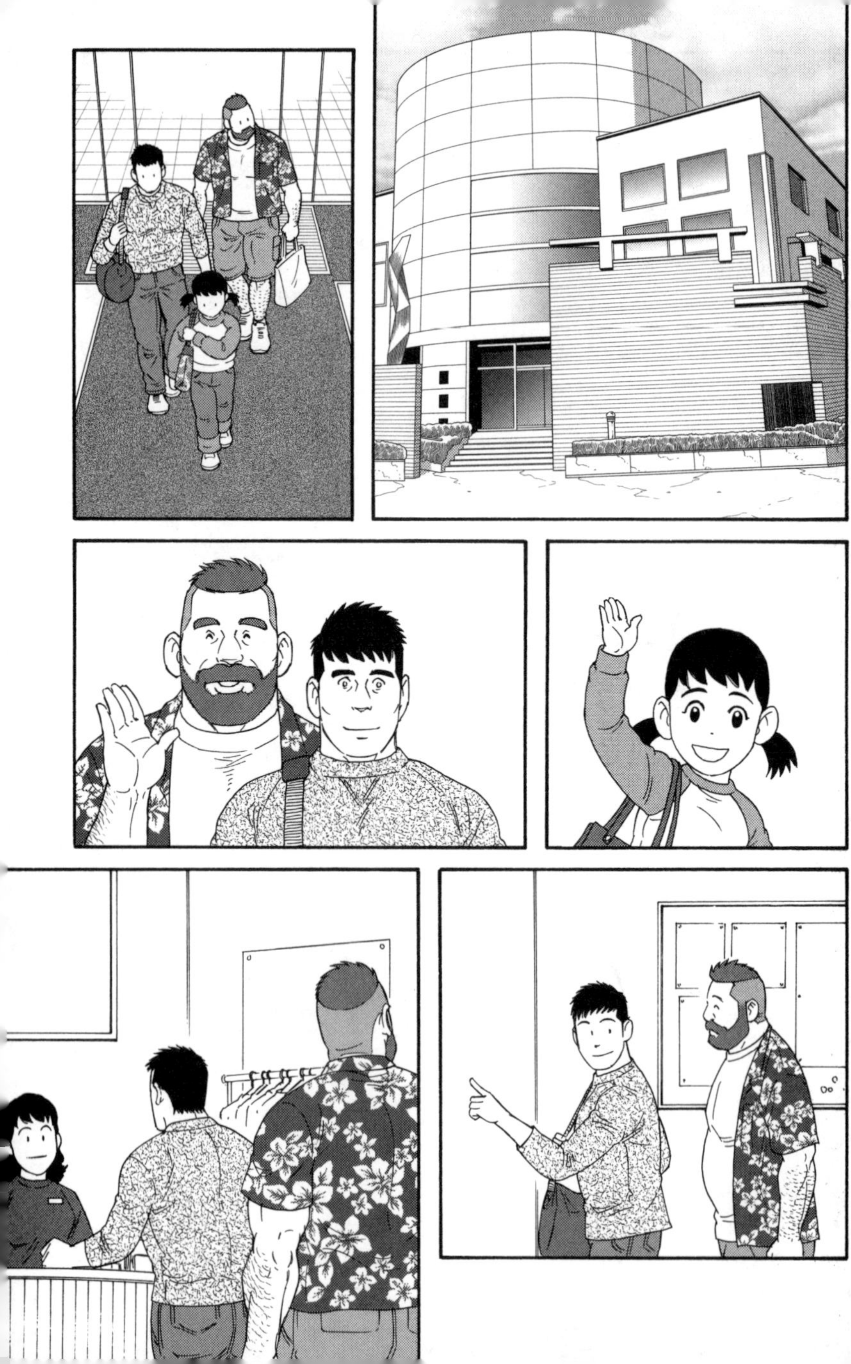

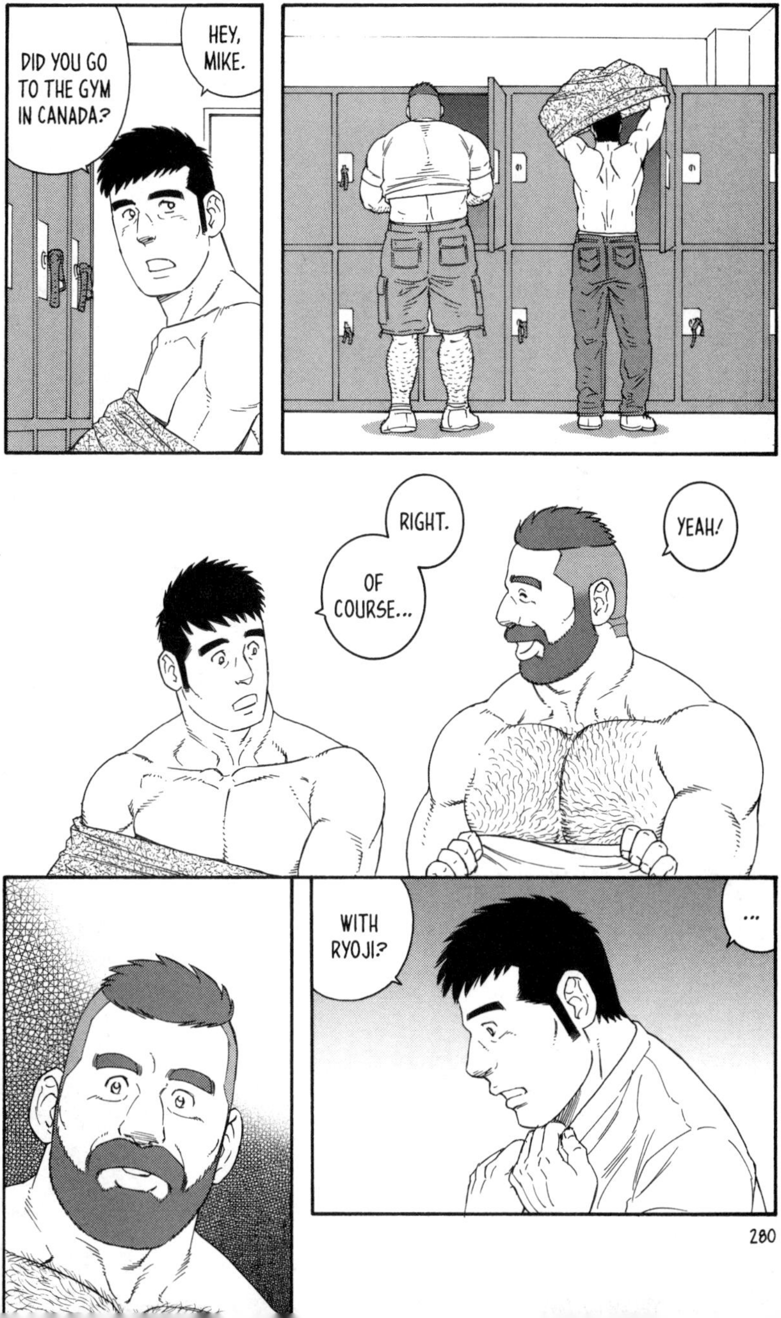
HEY, MIKE.
DID YOU GO TO THE GYM IN CANADA?
YEAH!
RIGHT.
OF COURSE...
...
WITH RYOJI?

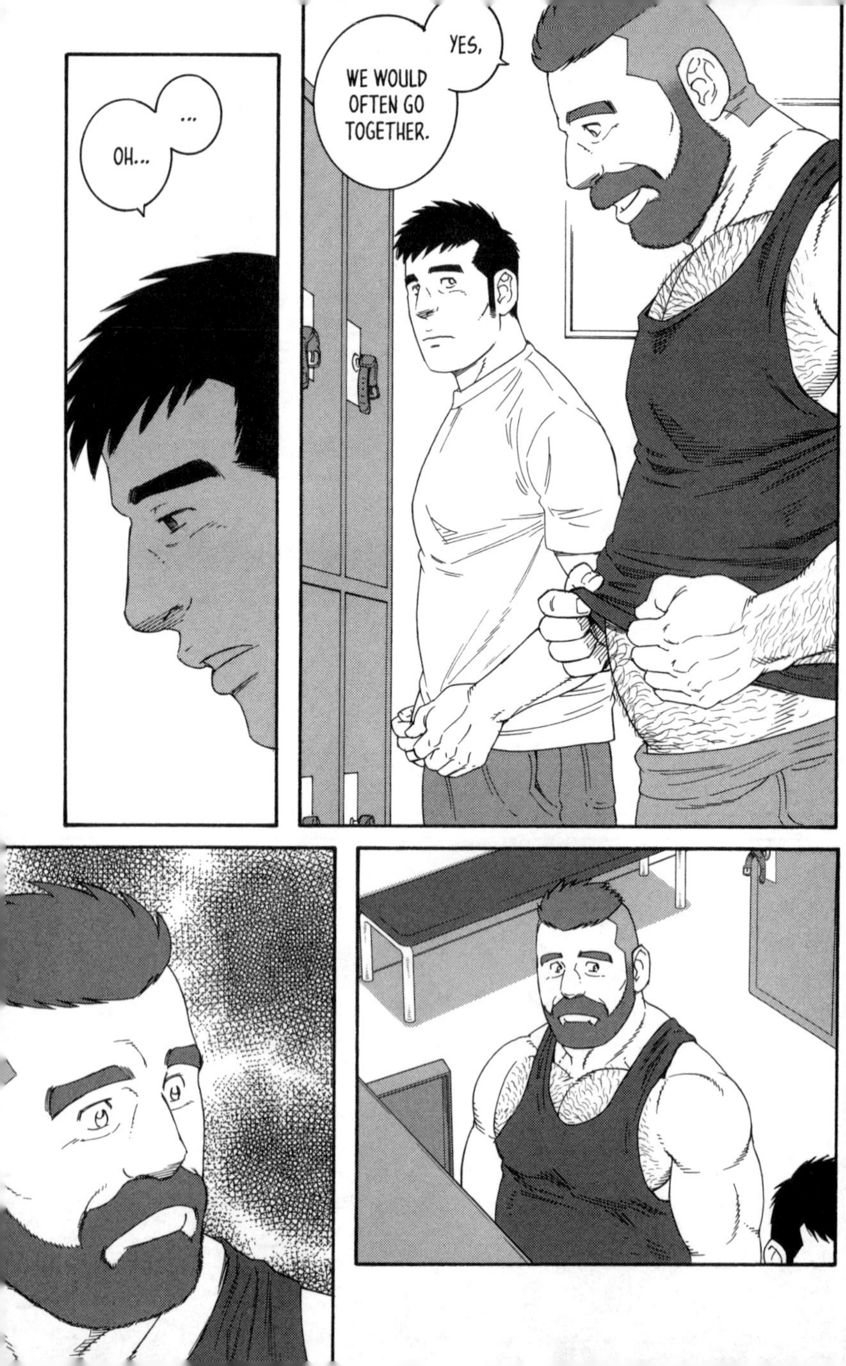
YES,
WE WOULD OFTEN GO TOGETHER.
...
OH...

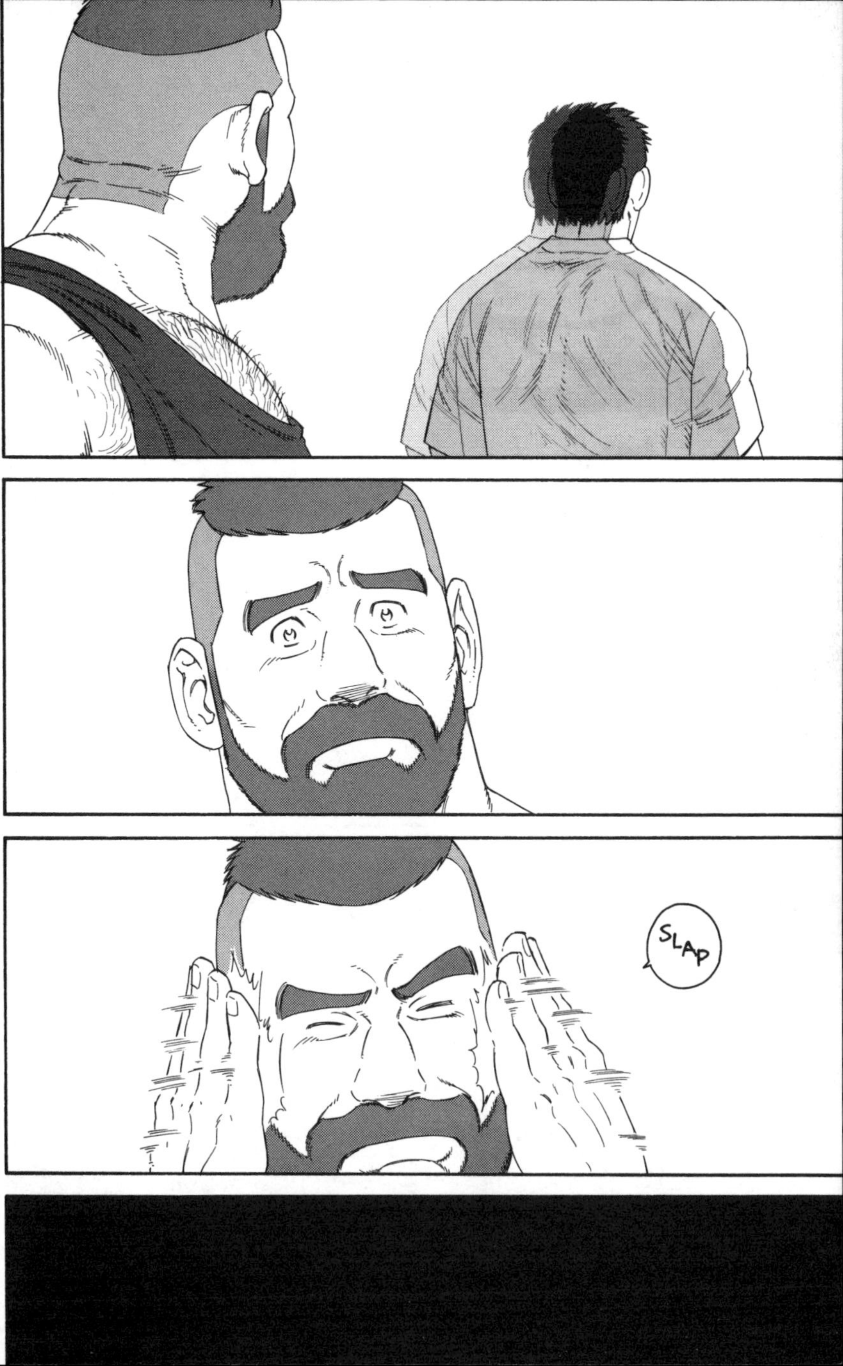
SLAP

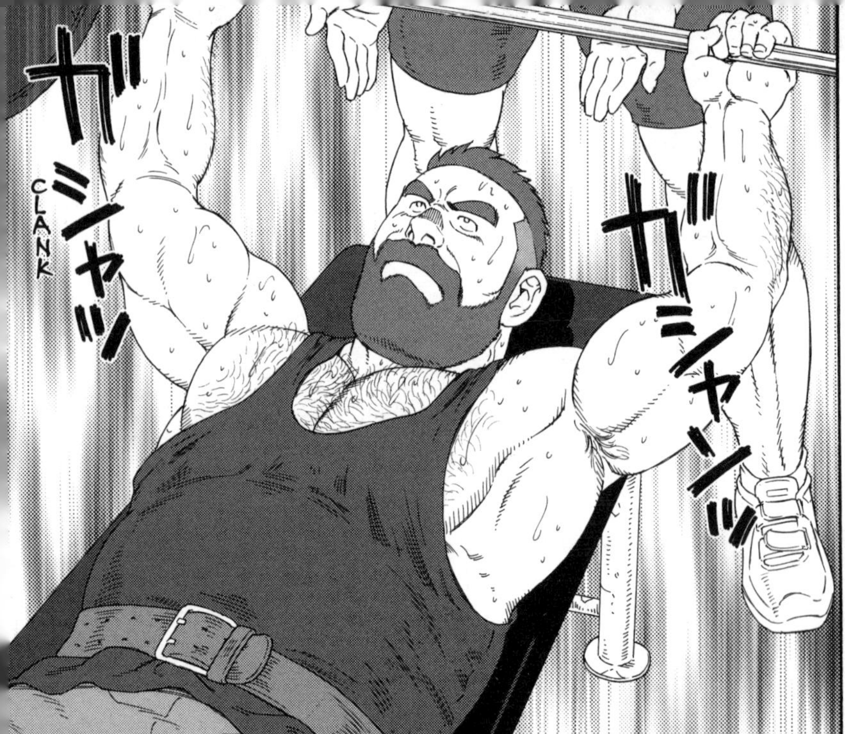
CLANK
CLANK
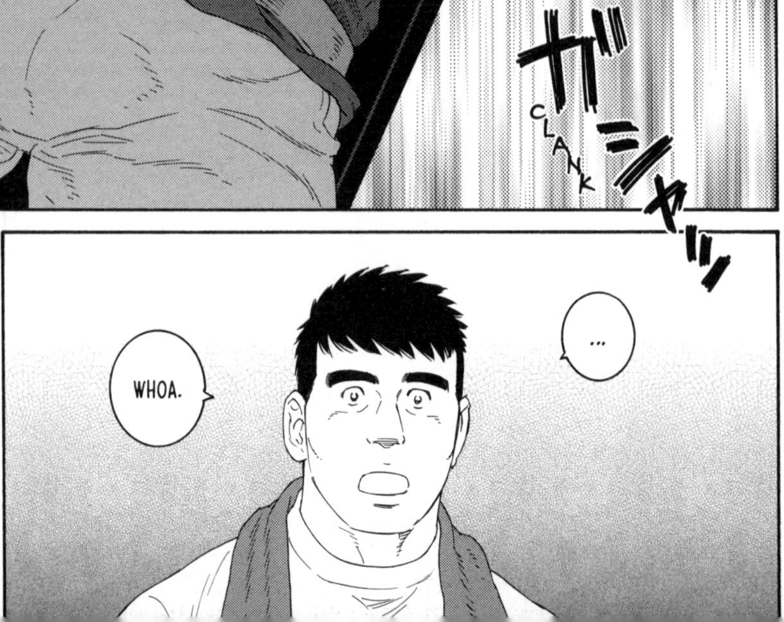
...
WHOA.

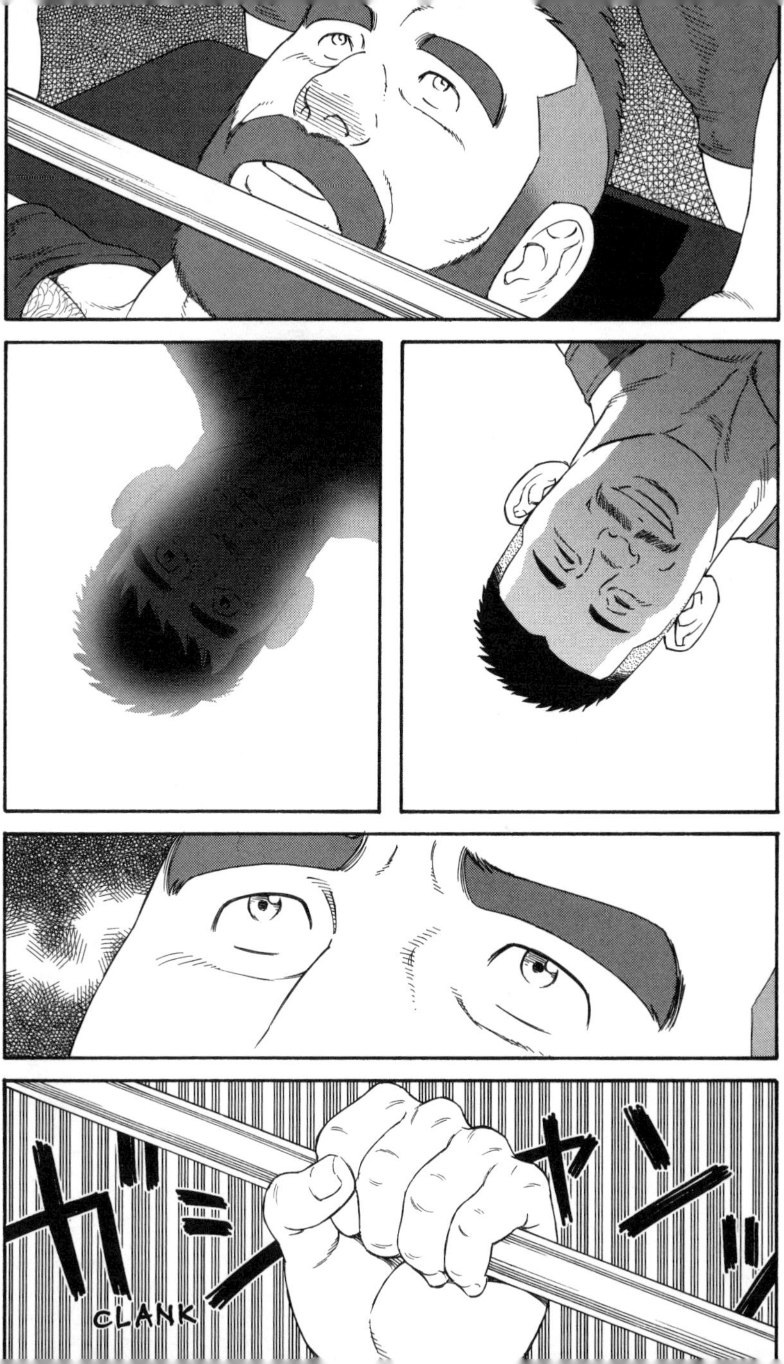
ガシャンッ
CLANK

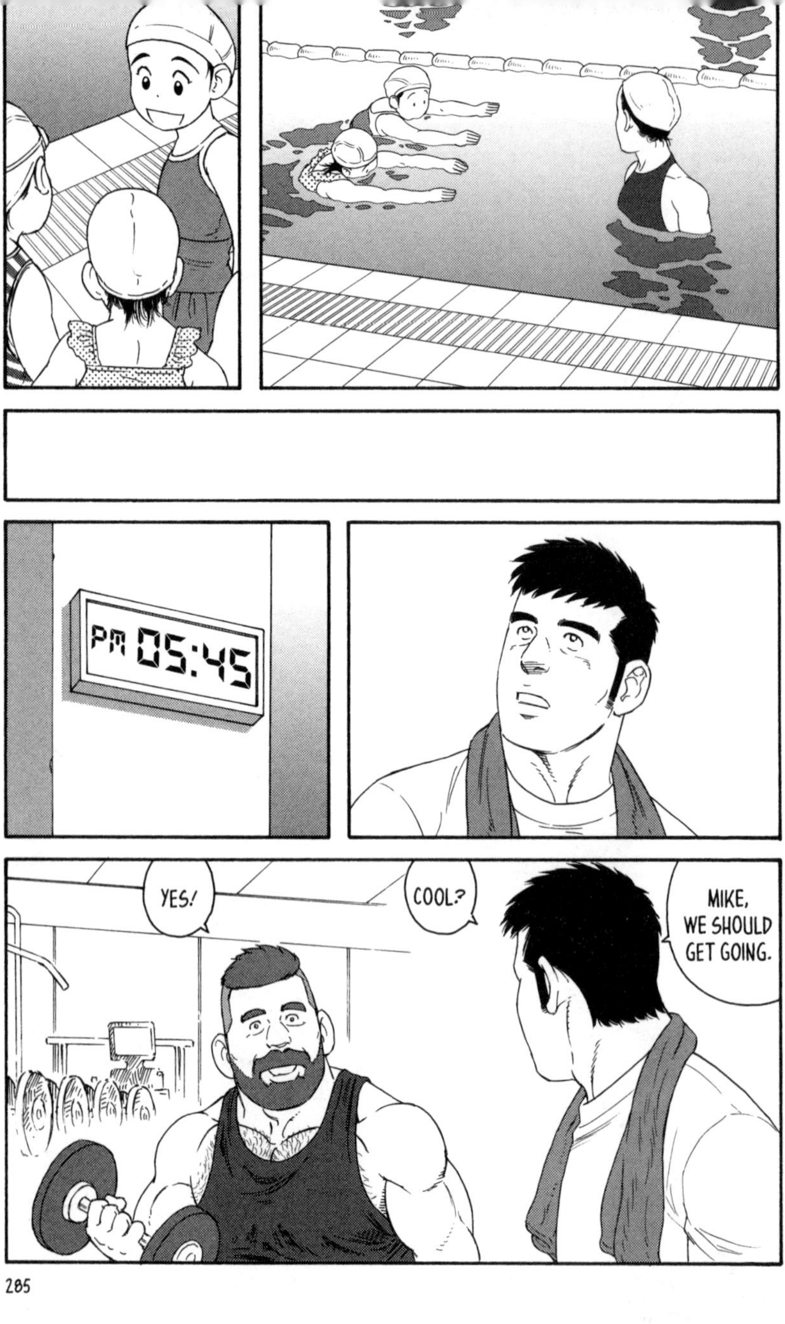
PM 05:45
MIKE, WE SHOULD GET GOING.
COOL?
YES!

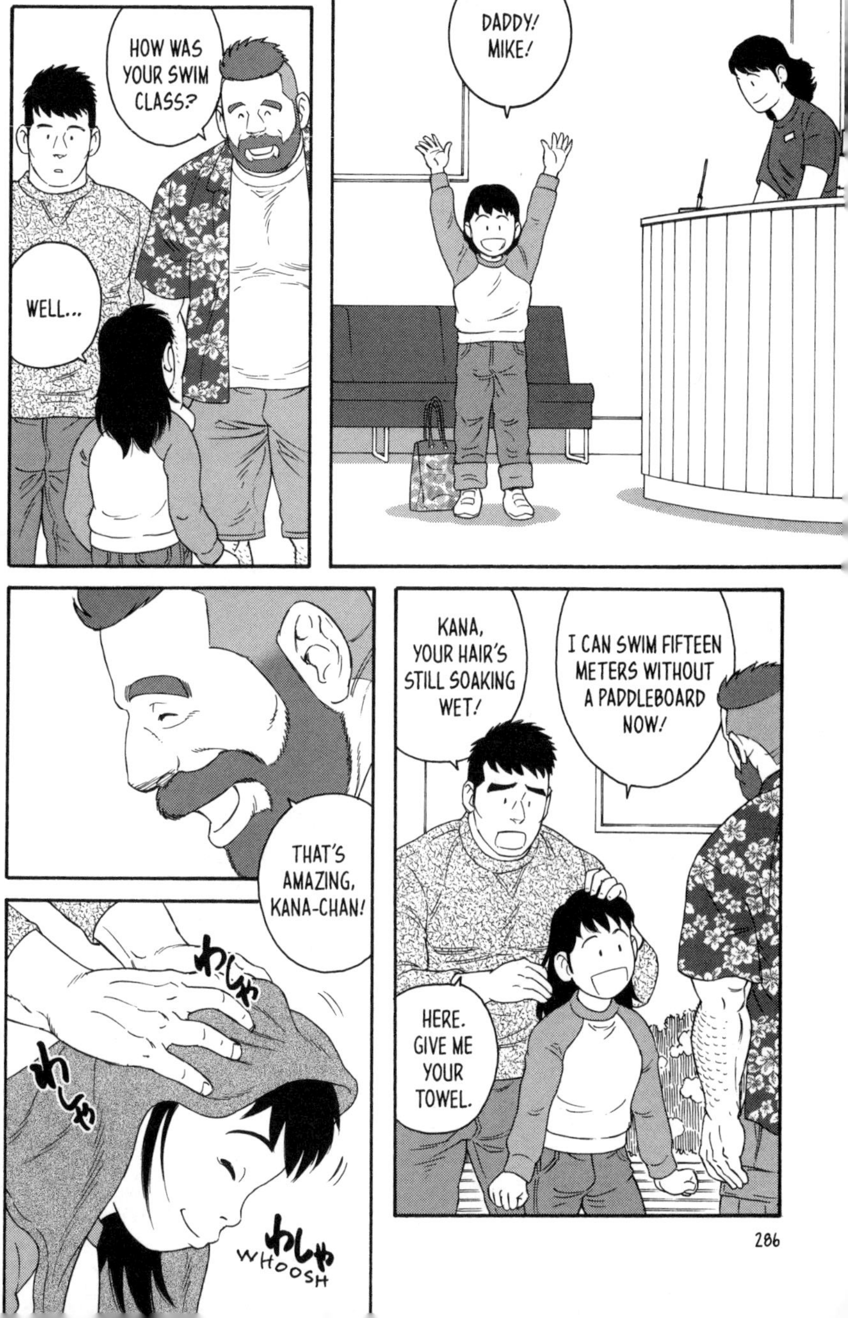
DADDY! MIKE!
HOW WAS YOUR SWIM CLASS?
WELL...
I CAN SWIM FIFTEEN METERS WITHOUT A PADDLEBOARD NOW!
KANA, YOUR HAIR'S STILL SOAKING WET!
HERE. GIVE ME YOUR TOWEL.
THAT'S AMAZING, KANA-CHAN!
わしゃ
わしゃ
わしゃ WHOOSH

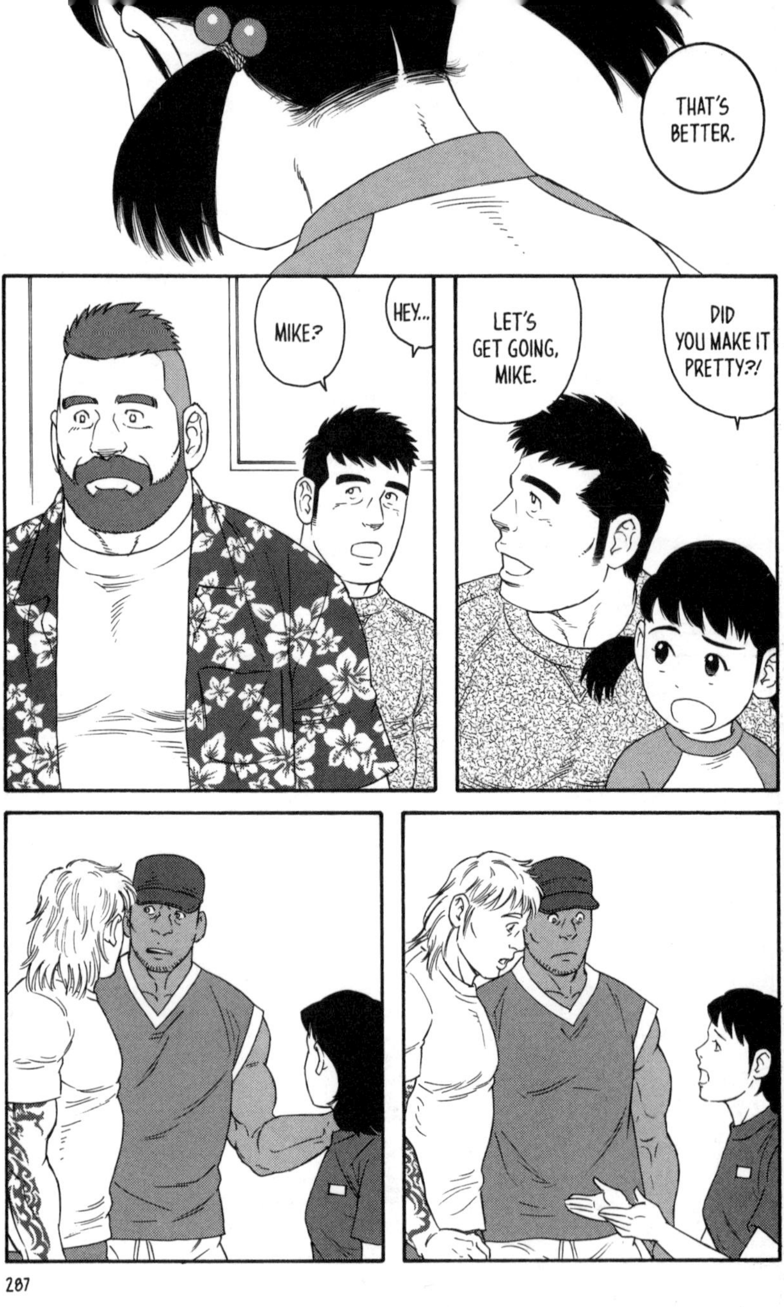
THAT'S BETTER.
DID YOU MAKE IT PRETTY?!
LET'S GET GOING, MIKE.
HEY...
MIKE?

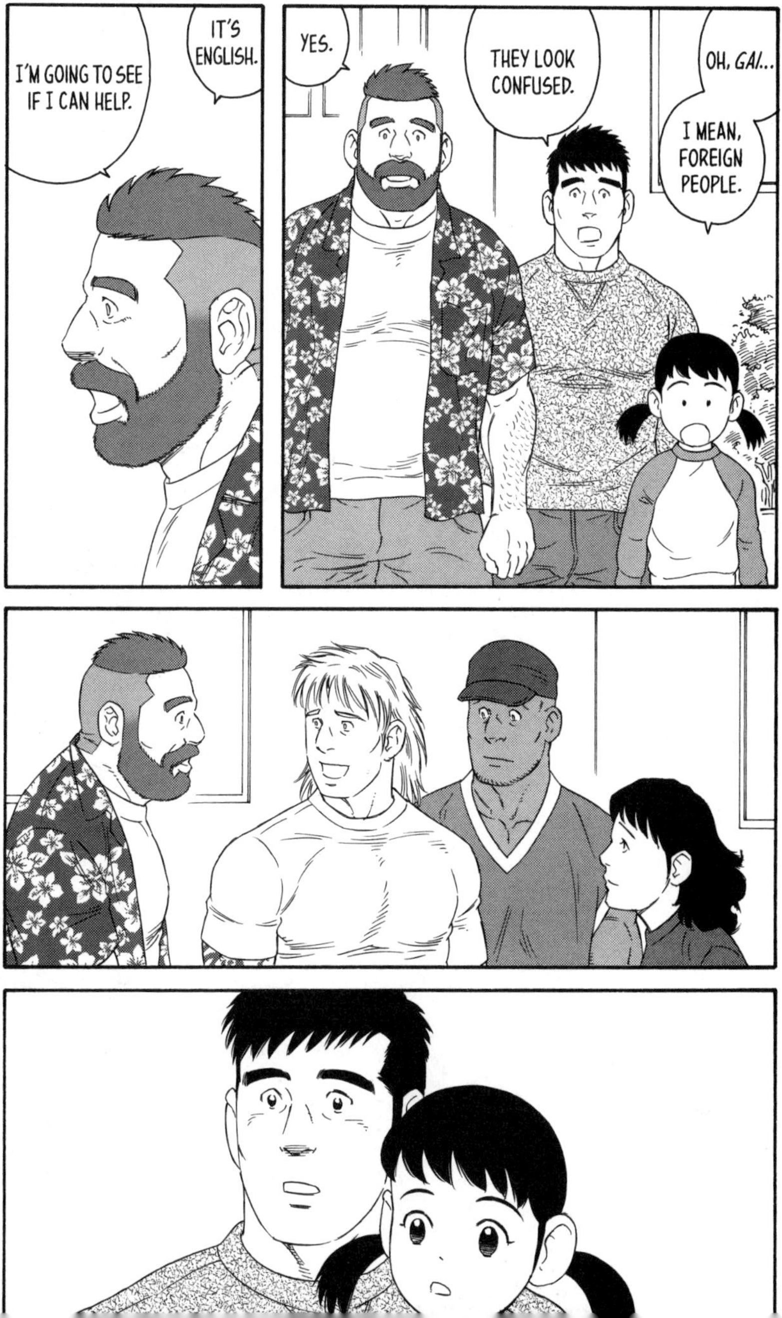
OH, *GAI*...
I MEAN, FOREIGN PEOPLE.
THEY LOOK CONFUSED.
YES.
IT'S ENGLISH.
I'M GOING TO SEE IF I CAN HELP.

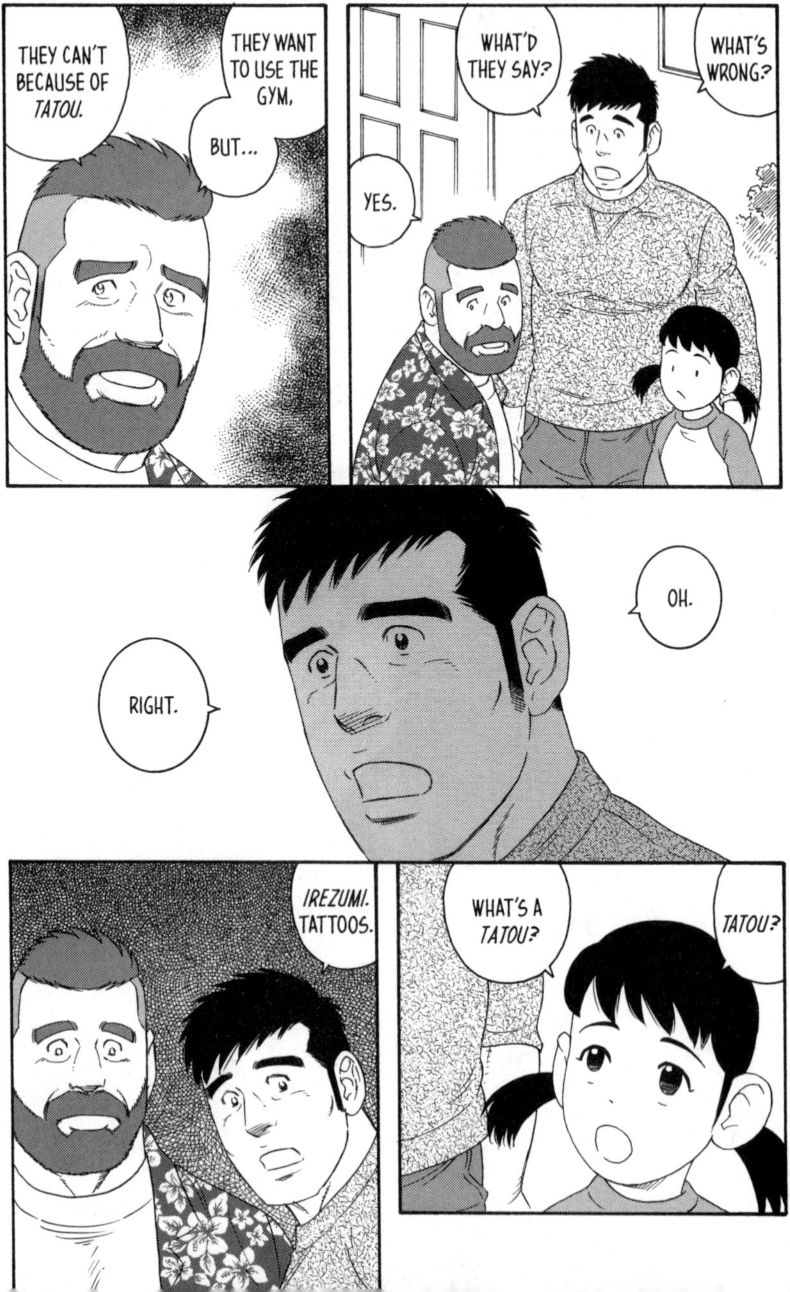
WHAT'S WRONG?
WHAT'D THEY SAY?
YES.
THEY WANT TO USE THE GYM,
BUT...
THEY CAN'T BECAUSE OF *TATOU.*
OH.
RIGHT.
TATOU?
WHAT'S A *TATOU?*
IREZUMI. TATTOOS.

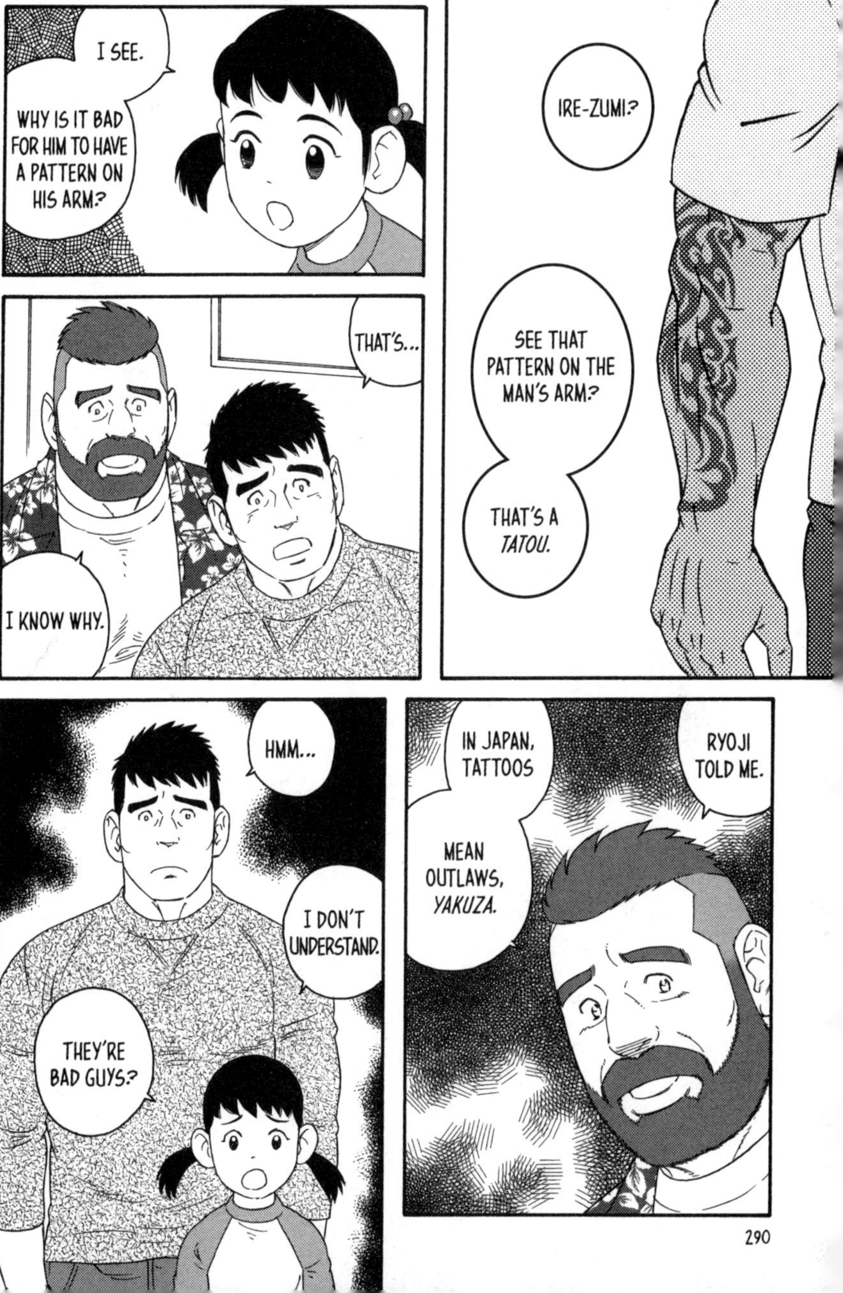
IRE-ZUMI?
SEE THAT PATTERN ON THE MAN'S ARM?
THAT'S A *TATOU.*
I SEE.
WHY IS IT BAD FOR HIM TO HAVE A PATTERN ON HIS ARM?
THAT'S...
I KNOW WHY.
RYOJI TOLD ME.
IN JAPAN, TATTOOS
MEAN OUTLAWS, *YAKUZA.*
HMM...
I DON'T UNDERSTAND.
THEY'RE BAD GUYS?

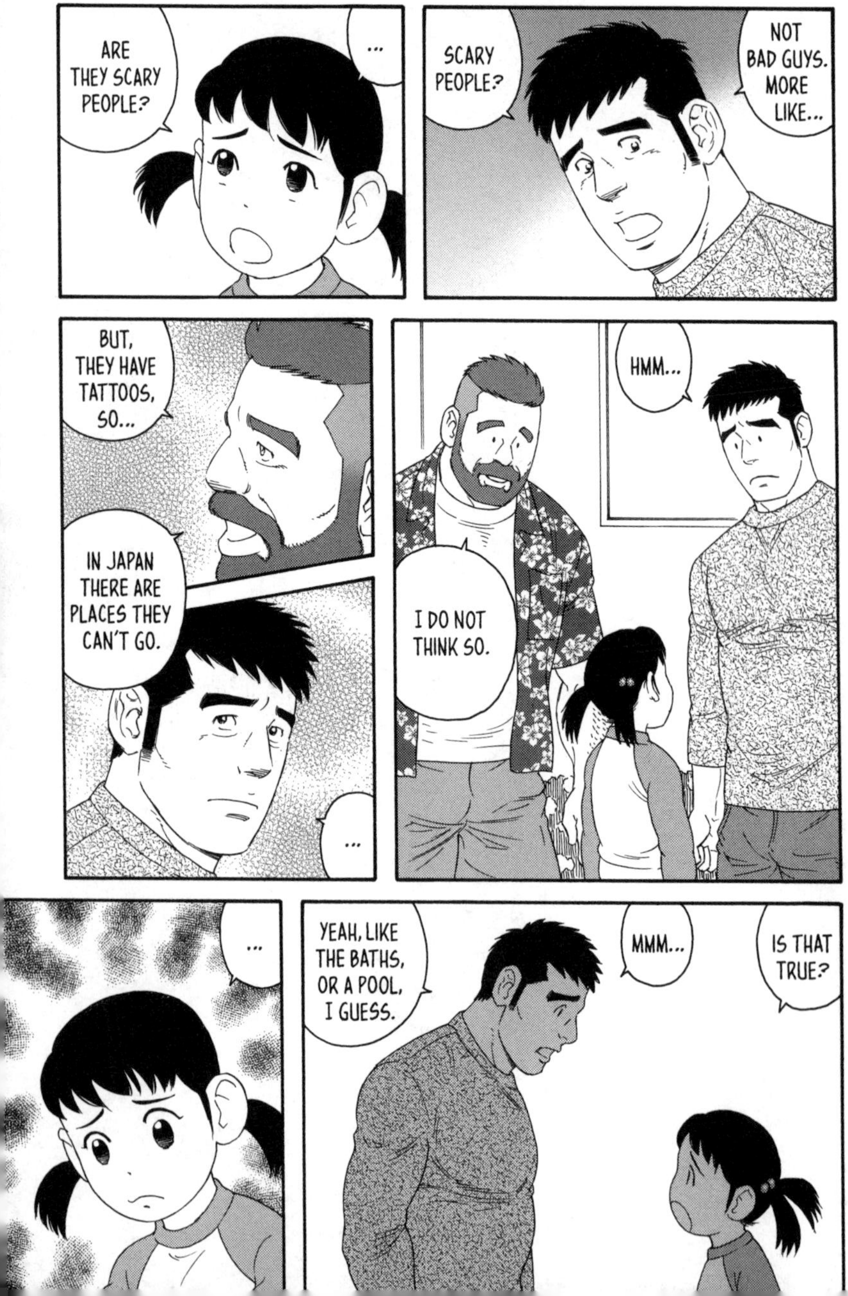
NOT BAD GUYS. MORE LIKE...
SCARY PEOPLE?
...
ARE THEY SCARY PEOPLE?
HMM...
I DO NOT THINK SO.
BUT, THEY HAVE TATTOOS, SO...
IN JAPAN THERE ARE PLACES THEY CAN'T GO.
...
IS THAT TRUE?
MMM...
YEAH, LIKE THE BATHS, OR A POOL, I GUESS.
...

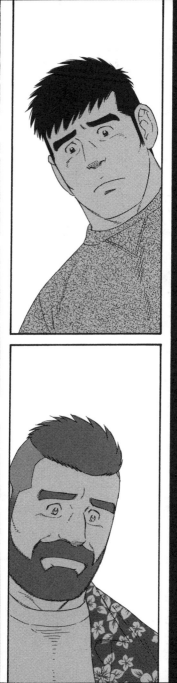

I STILL DON'T UNDERSTAND.

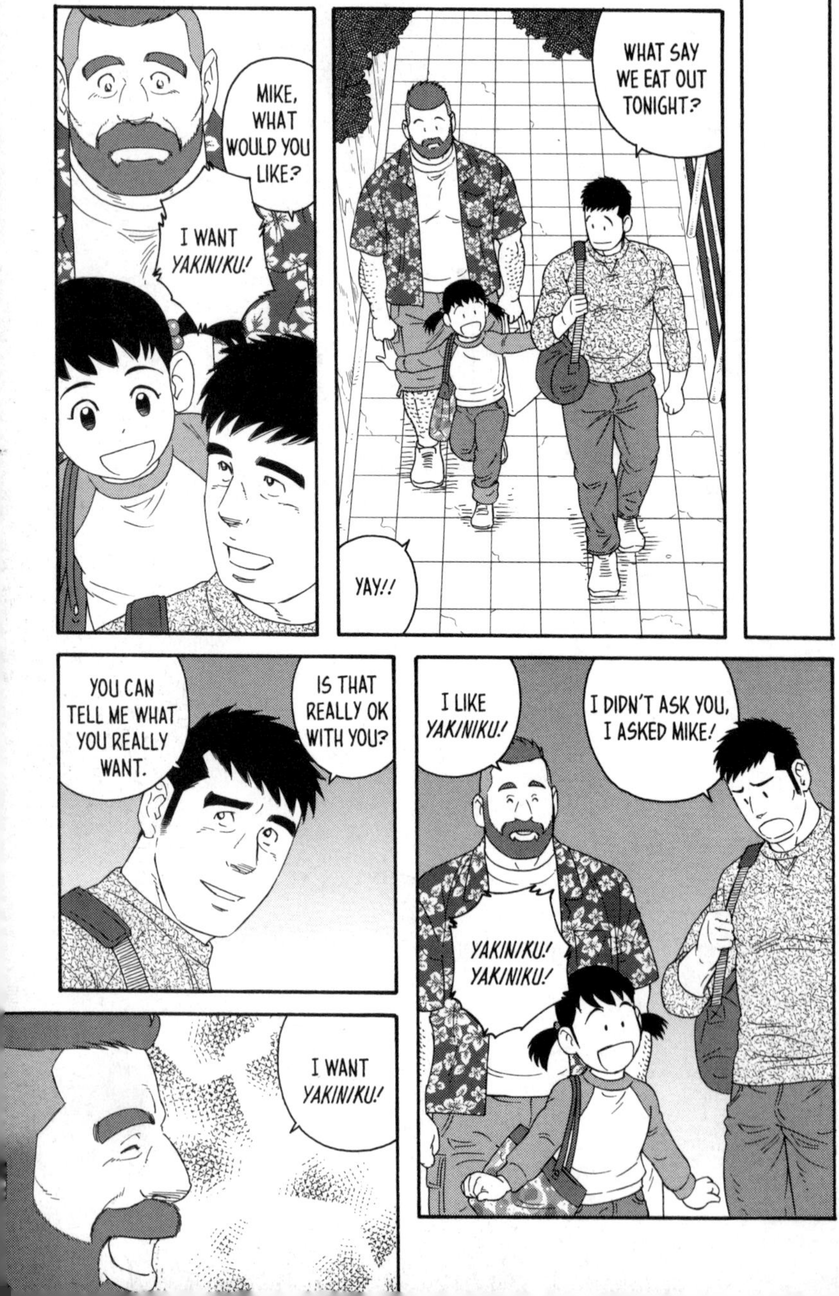
WHAT SAY WE EAT OUT TONIGHT?
YAY!!
MIKE, WHAT WOULD YOU LIKE?
I WANT *YAKINIKU!*
I DIDN'T ASK YOU, I ASKED MIKE!
I LIKE *YAKINIKU!*
YAKINIKU! YAKINIKU!
IS THAT REALLY OK WITH YOU?
YOU CAN TELL ME WHAT YOU REALLY WANT.
I WANT *YAKINIKU!*

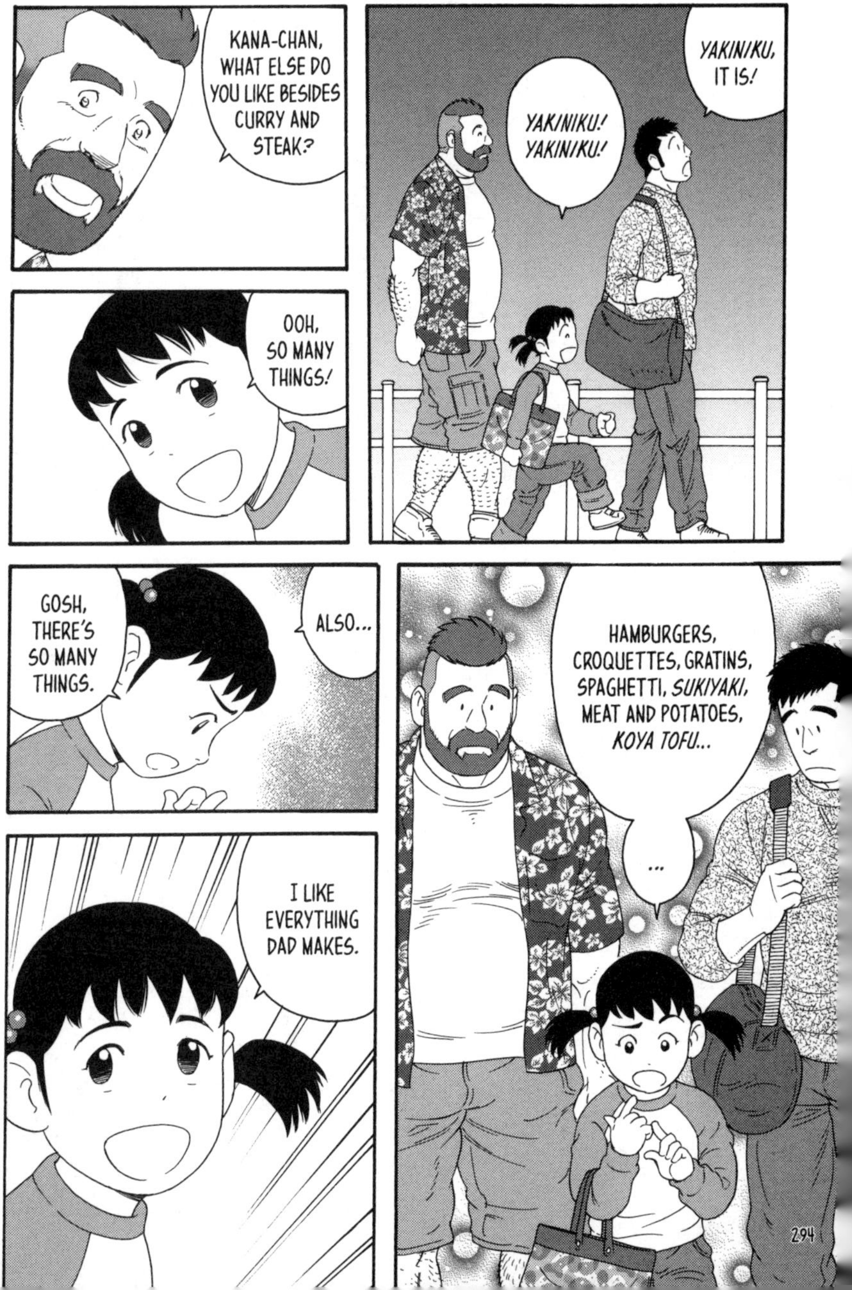
YAKINIKU, IT IS!
YAKINIKU! YAKINIKU!
KANA-CHAN, WHAT ELSE DO YOU LIKE BESIDES CURRY AND STEAK?
OOH, SO MANY THINGS!
HAMBURGERS, CROQUETTES, GRATINS, SPAGHETTI, SUKIYAKI, MEAT AND POTATOES, KOYA TOFU...
...
ALSO...
GOSH, THERE'S SO MANY THINGS.
I LIKE EVERYTHING DAD MAKES.

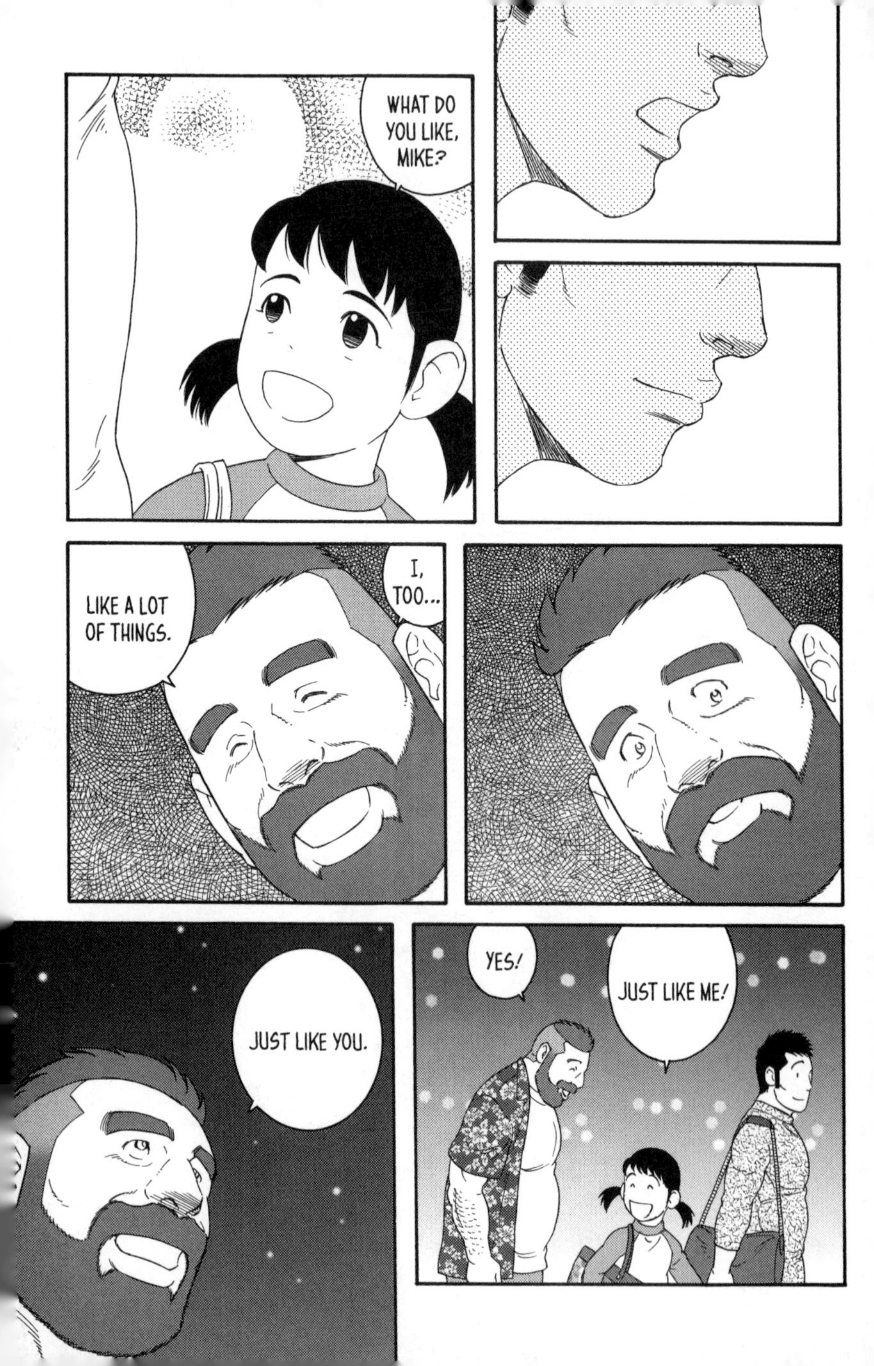
WHAT DO YOU LIKE, MIKE?
I, TOO...
LIKE A LOT OF THINGS.
YES!
JUST LIKE ME!
JUST LIKE YOU.

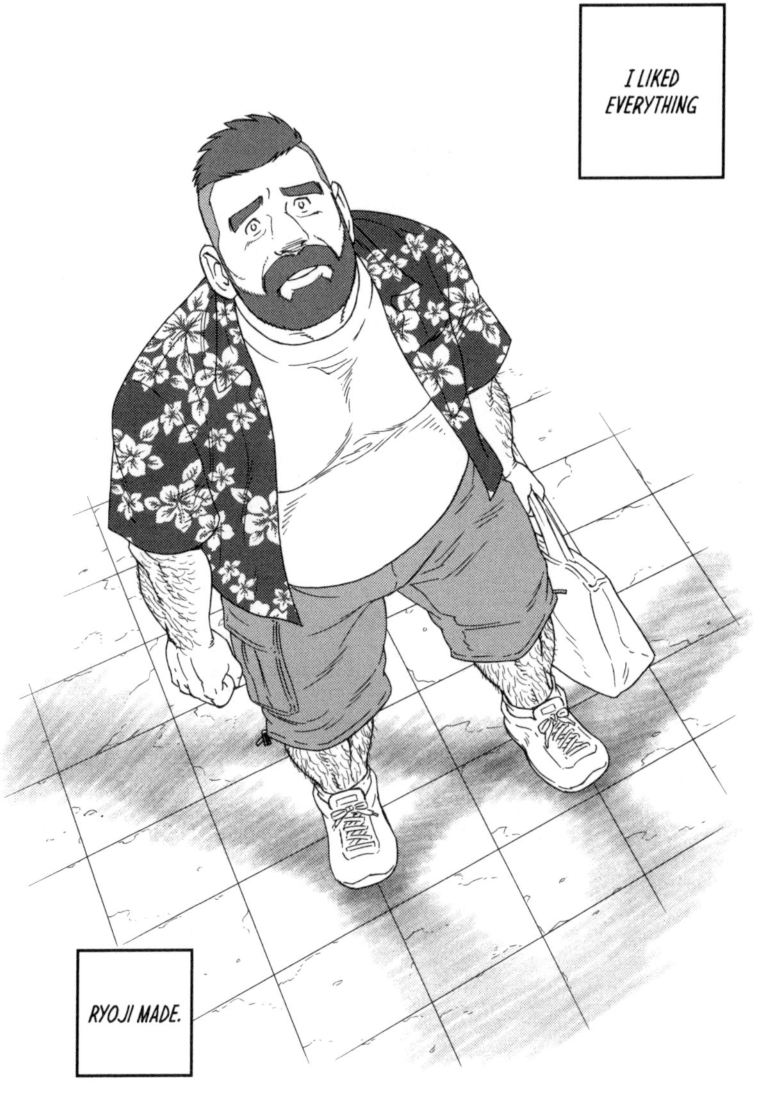
I LIKED EVERYTHING
RYOJI MADE.

CHAPTER THIRTEEN

HOT CHOCOLATE

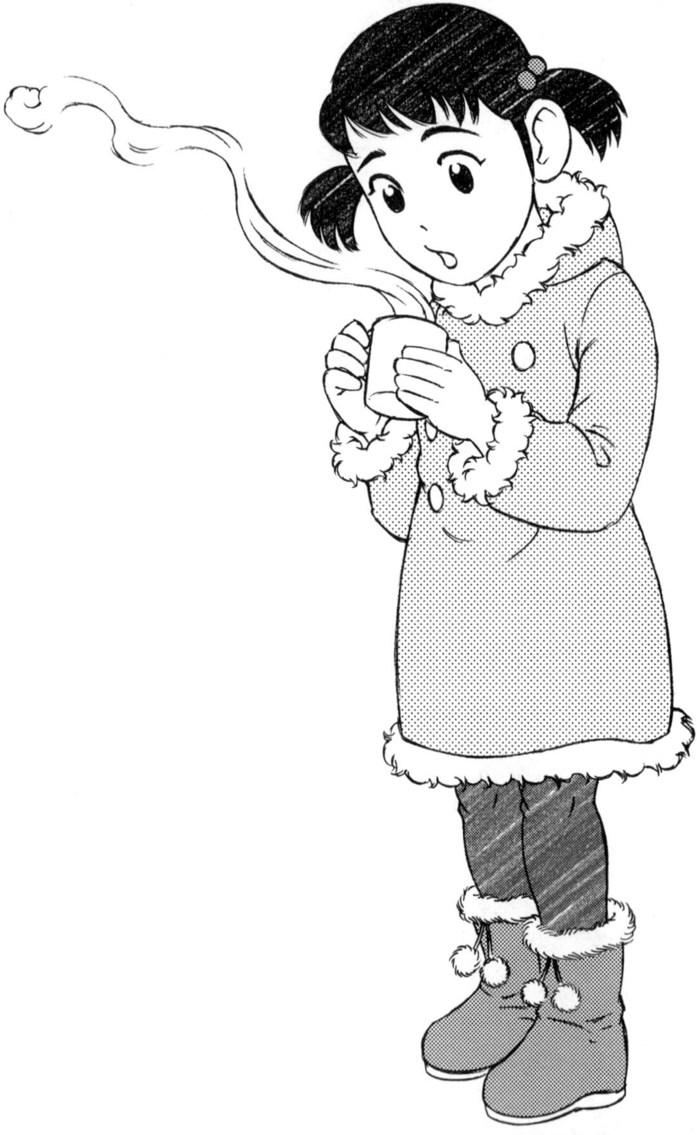

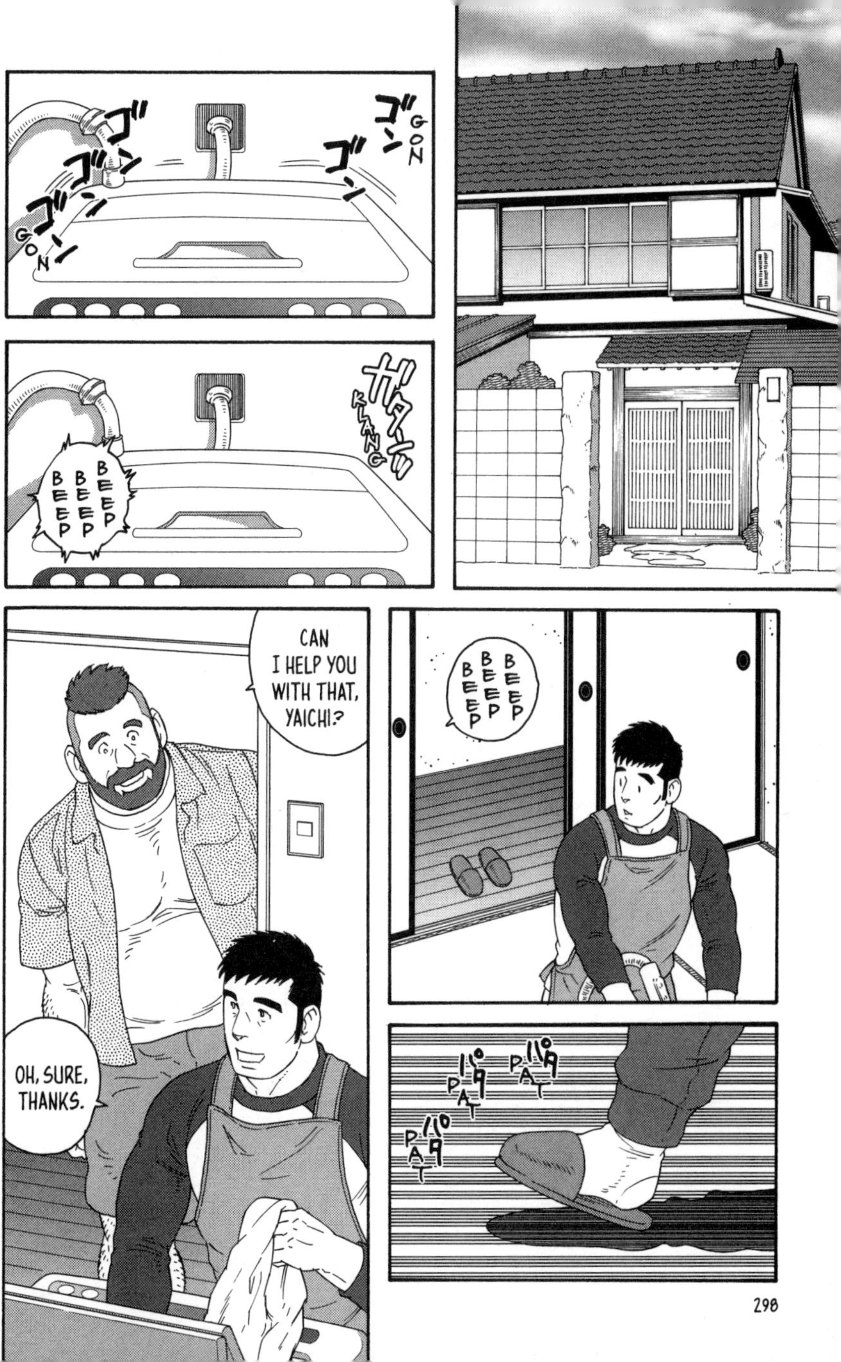
ゴン GON
ゴン ゴン ゴン GON
ガタン KLANG
BEEP BEEP BEEP
BEEP BEEP BEEP
パタ PAT
パタ PAT
パタ PAT
CAN I HELP YOU WITH THAT, YAICHI?
OH, SURE, THANKS.

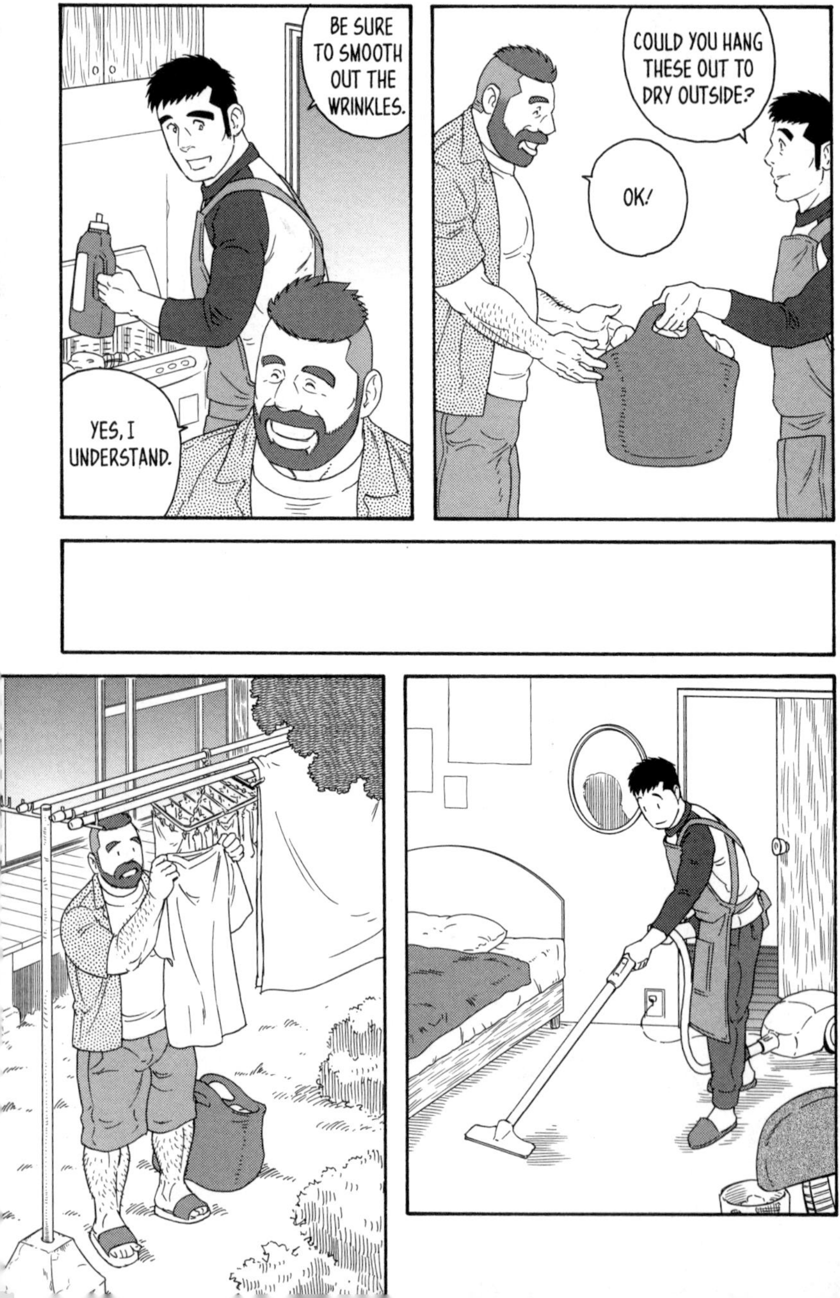
COULD YOU HANG THESE OUT TO DRY OUTSIDE?
OK!
BE SURE TO SMOOTH OUT THE WRINKLES.
YES, I UNDERSTAND.

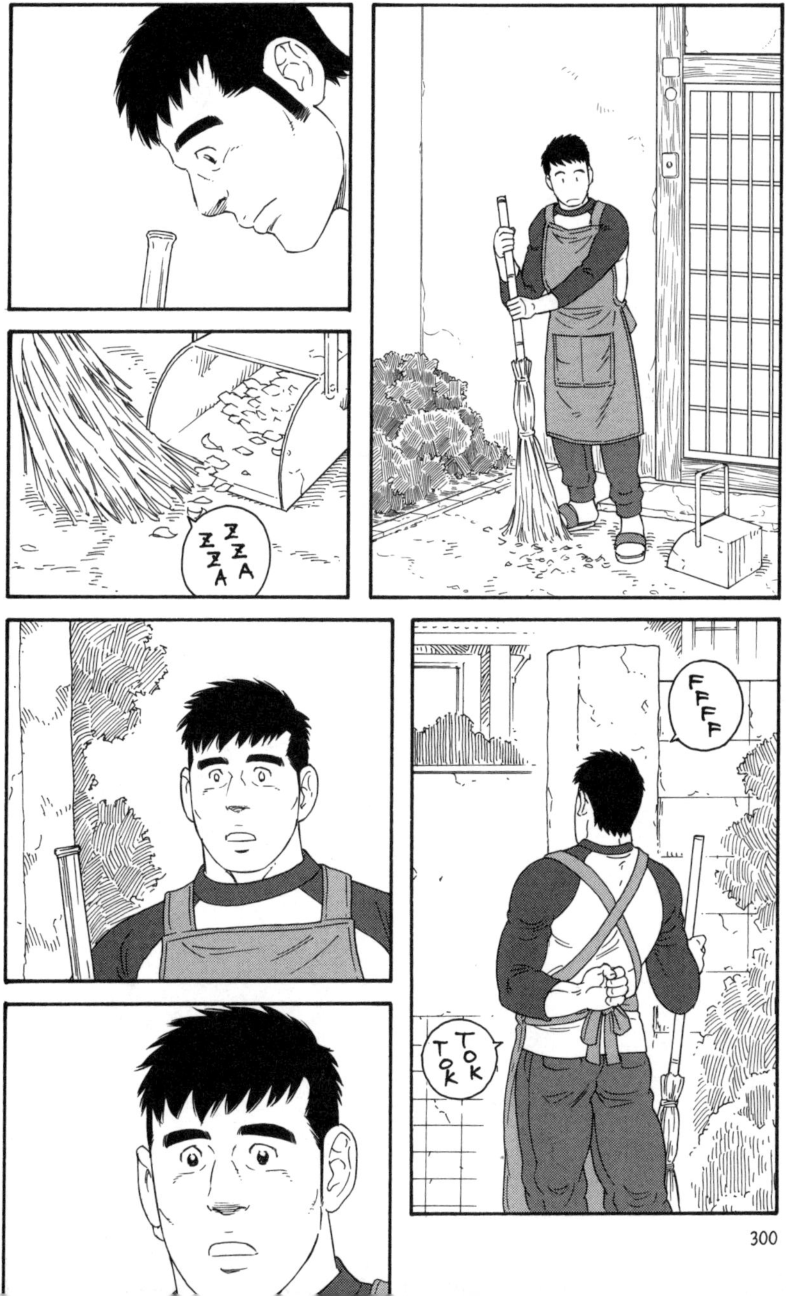
ZZA ZZA
FFFF
TOK TOK

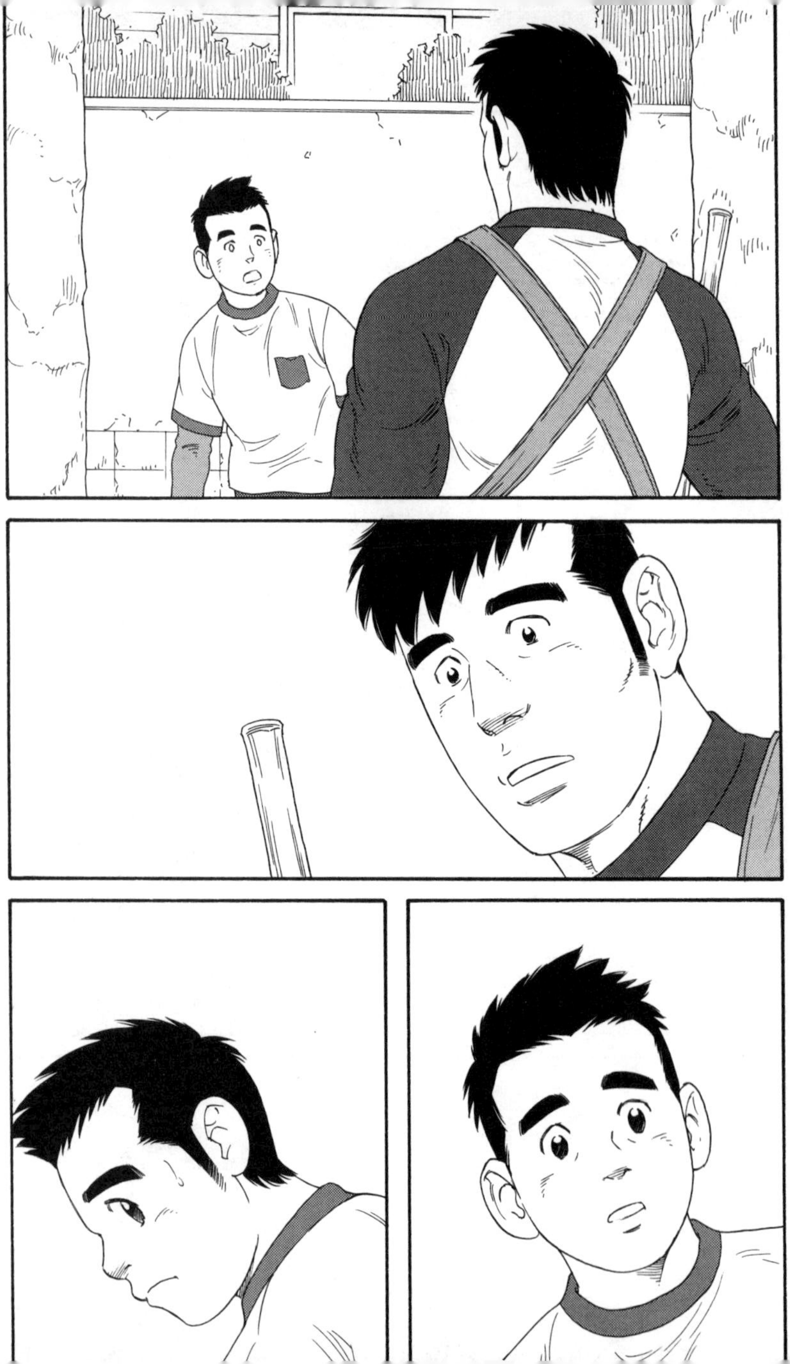

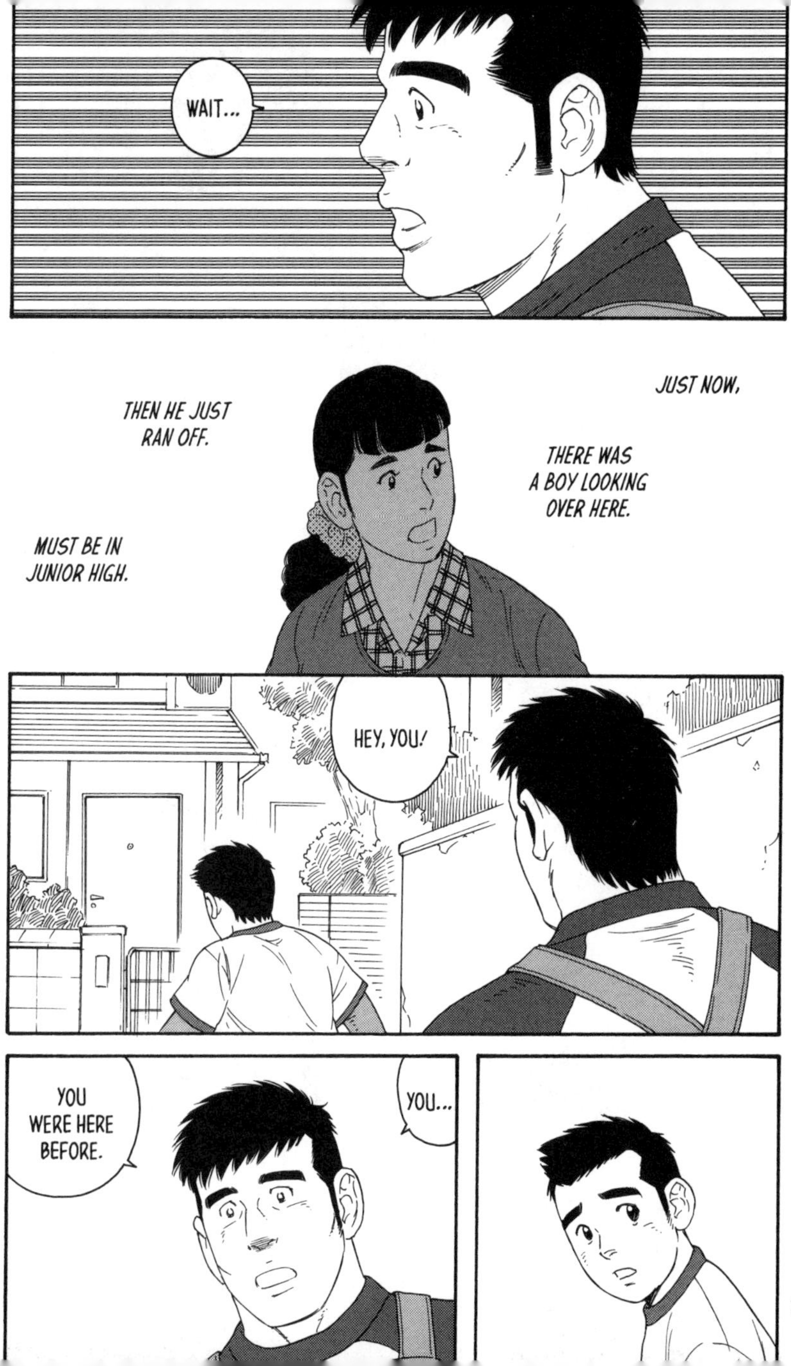
WAIT...
JUST NOW,
THERE WAS A BOY LOOKING OVER HERE.
THEN HE JUST RAN OFF.
MUST BE IN JUNIOR HIGH.
HEY, YOU!
YOU...
YOU WERE HERE BEFORE.

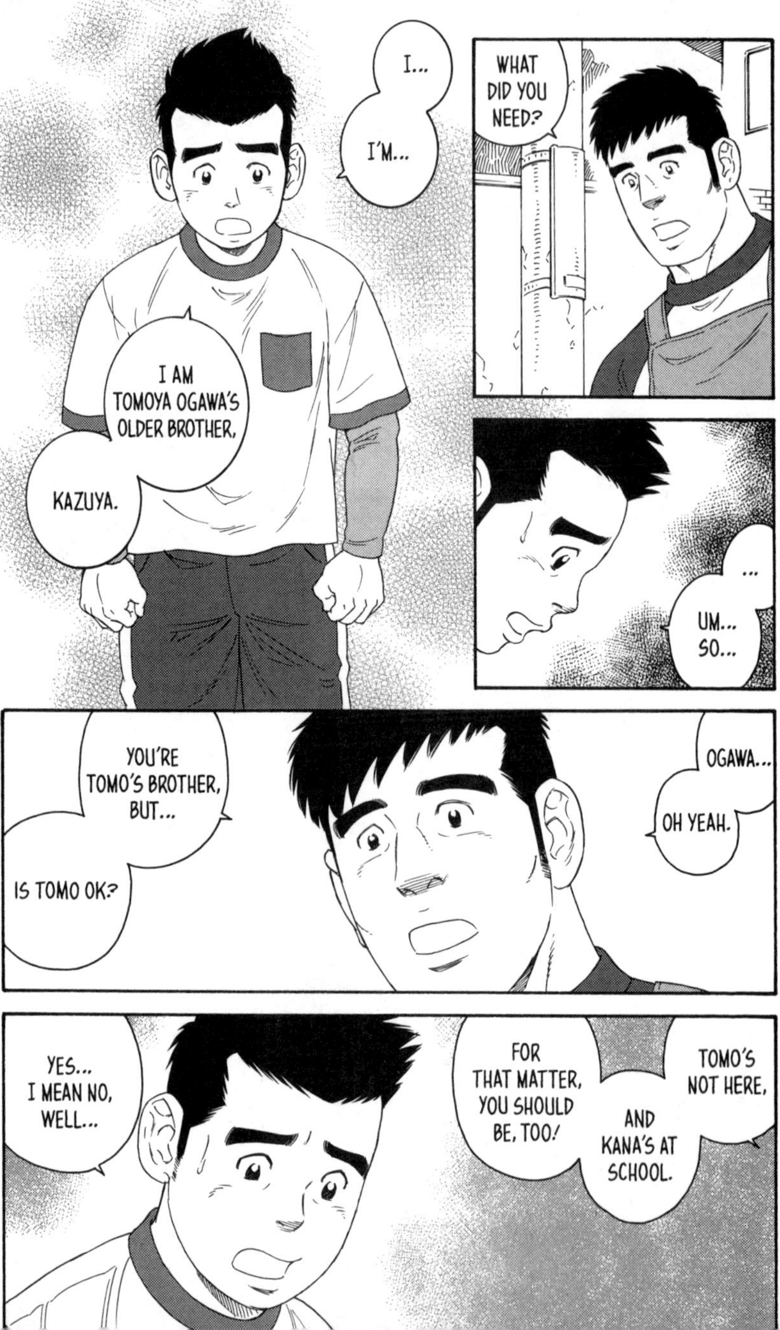
WHAT DID YOU NEED?
...
UM... SO...
I...
I'M...
I AM TOMOYA OGAWA'S OLDER BROTHER,
KAZUYA.
OGAWA...
OH YEAH.
YOU'RE TOMO'S BROTHER, BUT...
IS TOMO OK?
TOMO'S NOT HERE,
AND KANA'S AT SCHOOL.
FOR THAT MATTER, YOU SHOULD BE, TOO!
YES... I MEAN NO, WELL...

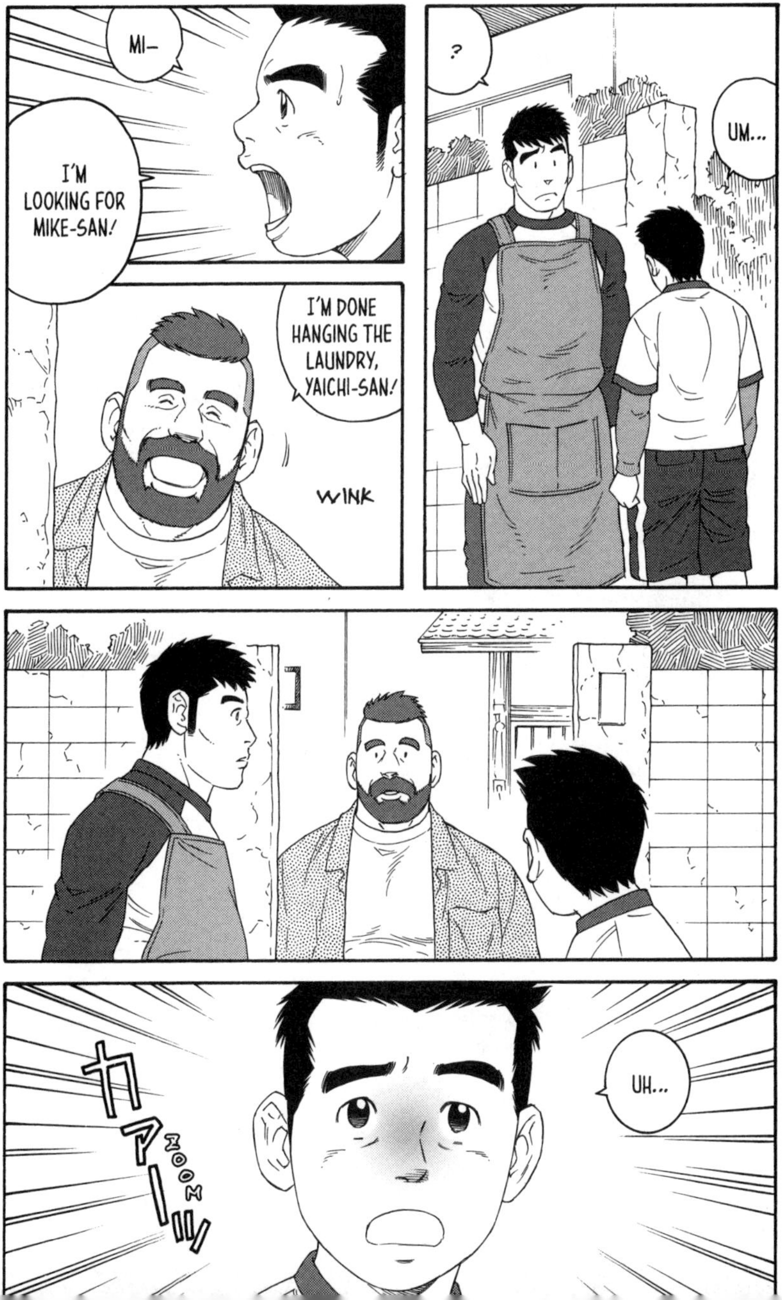
UM...
?
MI–
I'M LOOKING FOR MIKE-SAN!
I'M DONE HANGING THE LAUNDRY, YAICHI-SAN!
WINK
UH...
カァー
ZOOM

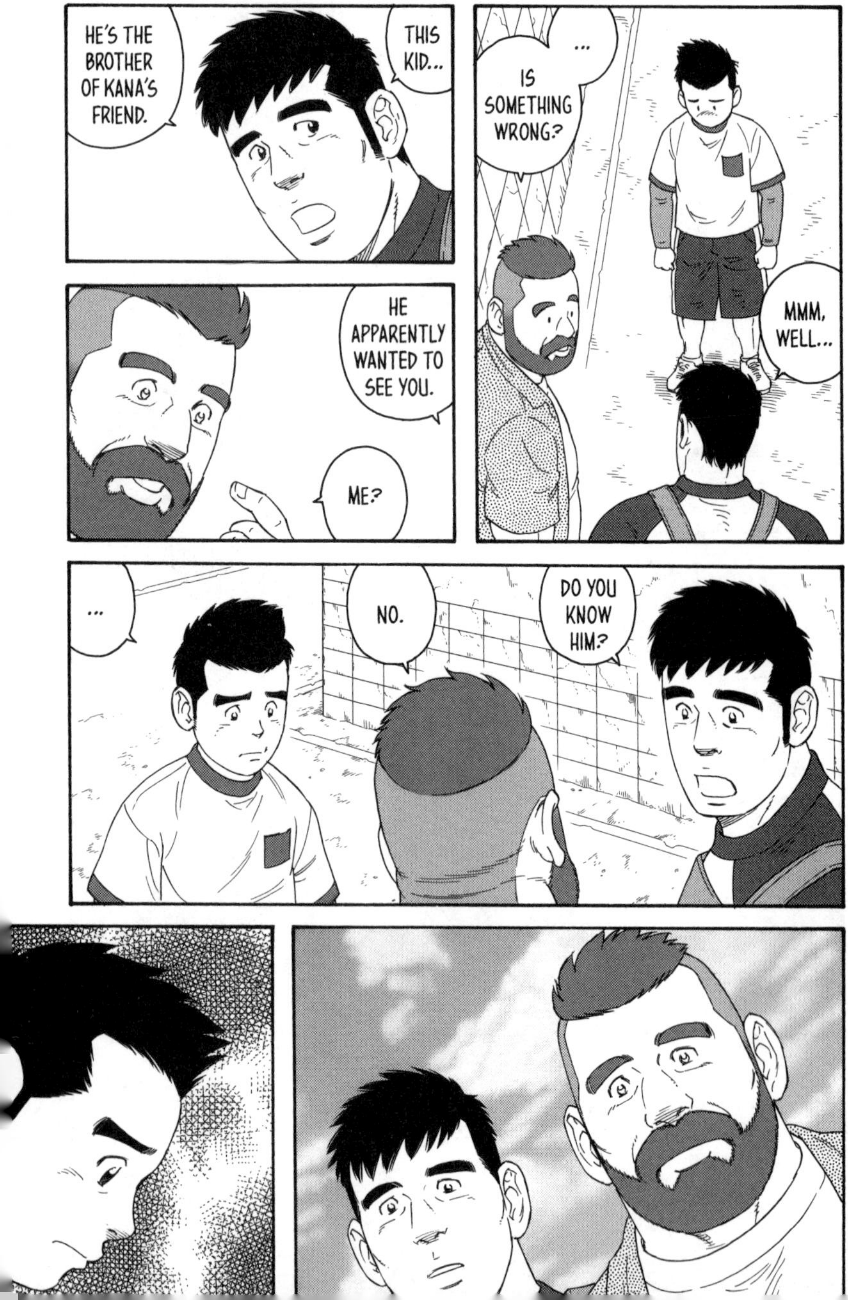
...
IS SOMETHING WRONG?
MMM, WELL...
THIS KID...
HE'S THE BROTHER OF KANA'S FRIEND.
HE APPARENTLY WANTED TO SEE YOU.
ME?
DO YOU KNOW HIM?
NO.
...

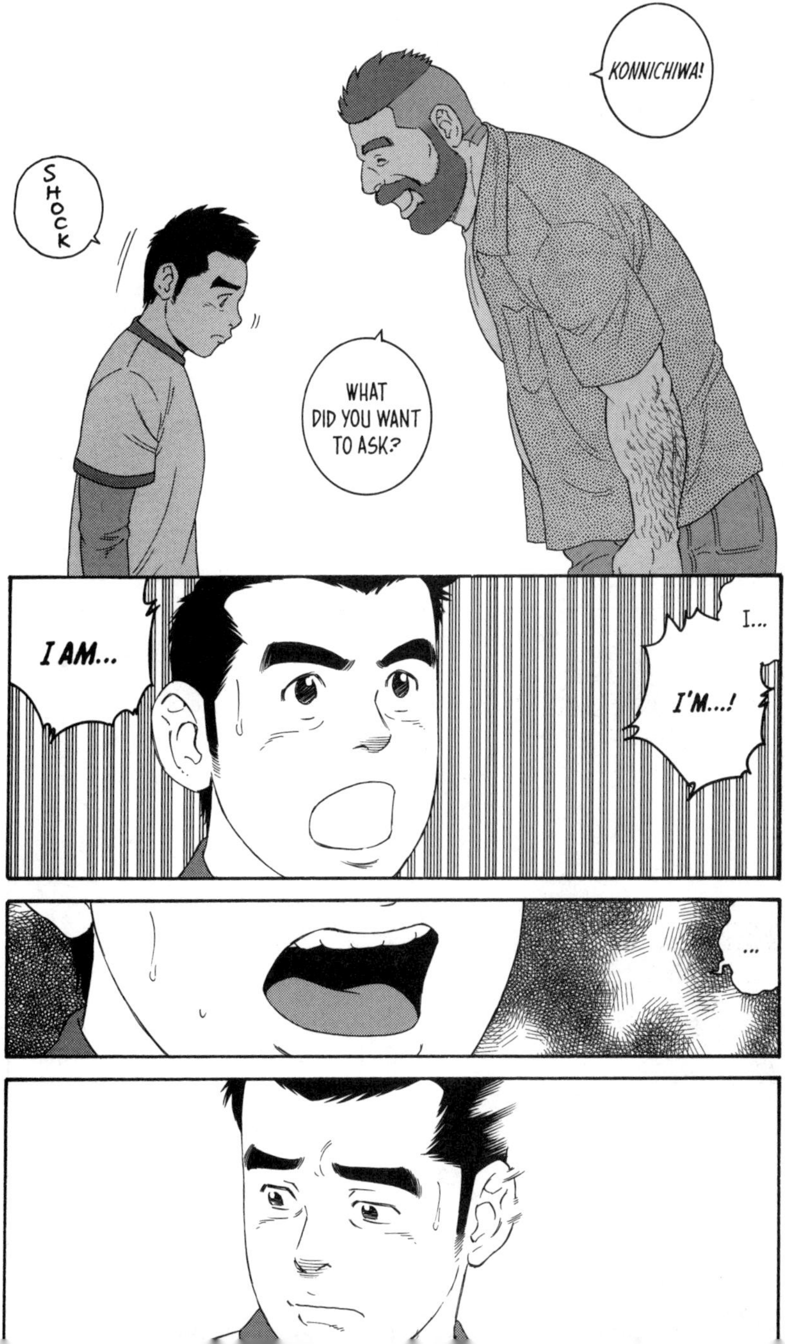
KONNICHIWA!
WHAT DID YOU WANT TO ASK?
SHOCK
I... I'M...!
I AM...
...

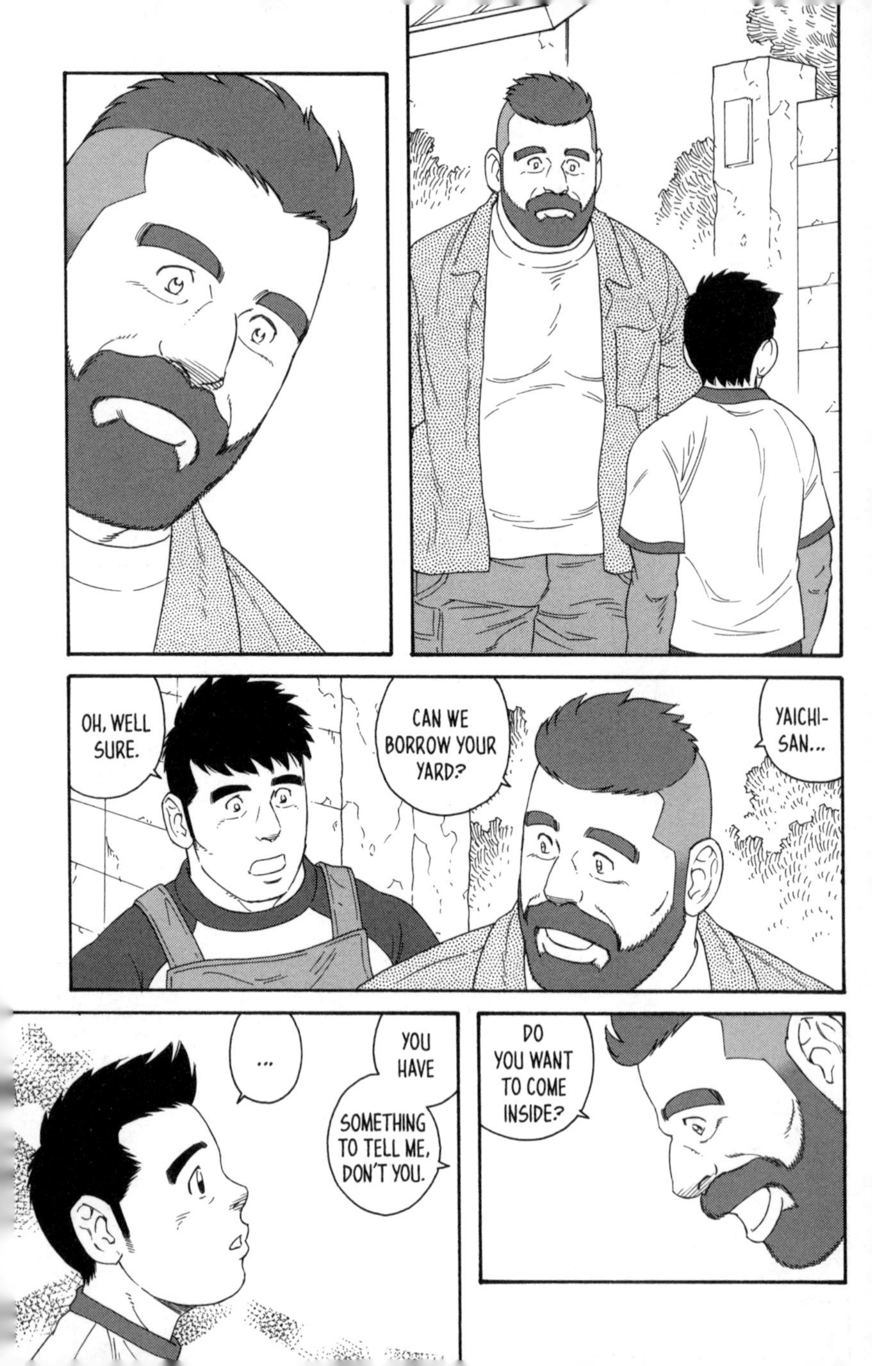
YAICHI-SAN...
CAN WE BORROW YOUR YARD?
OH, WELL SURE.
DO YOU WANT TO COME INSIDE?
YOU HAVE SOMETHING TO TELL ME, DON'T YOU.
...

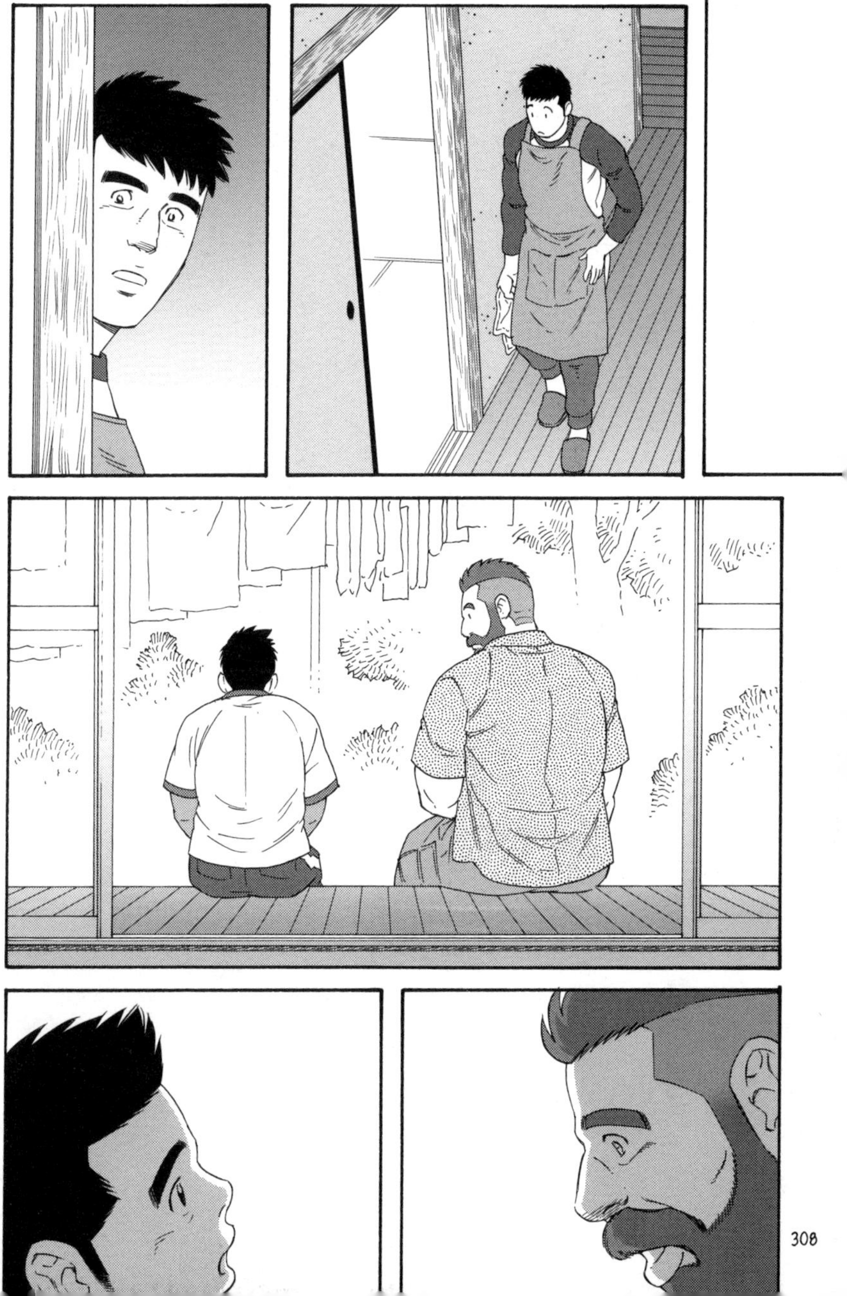

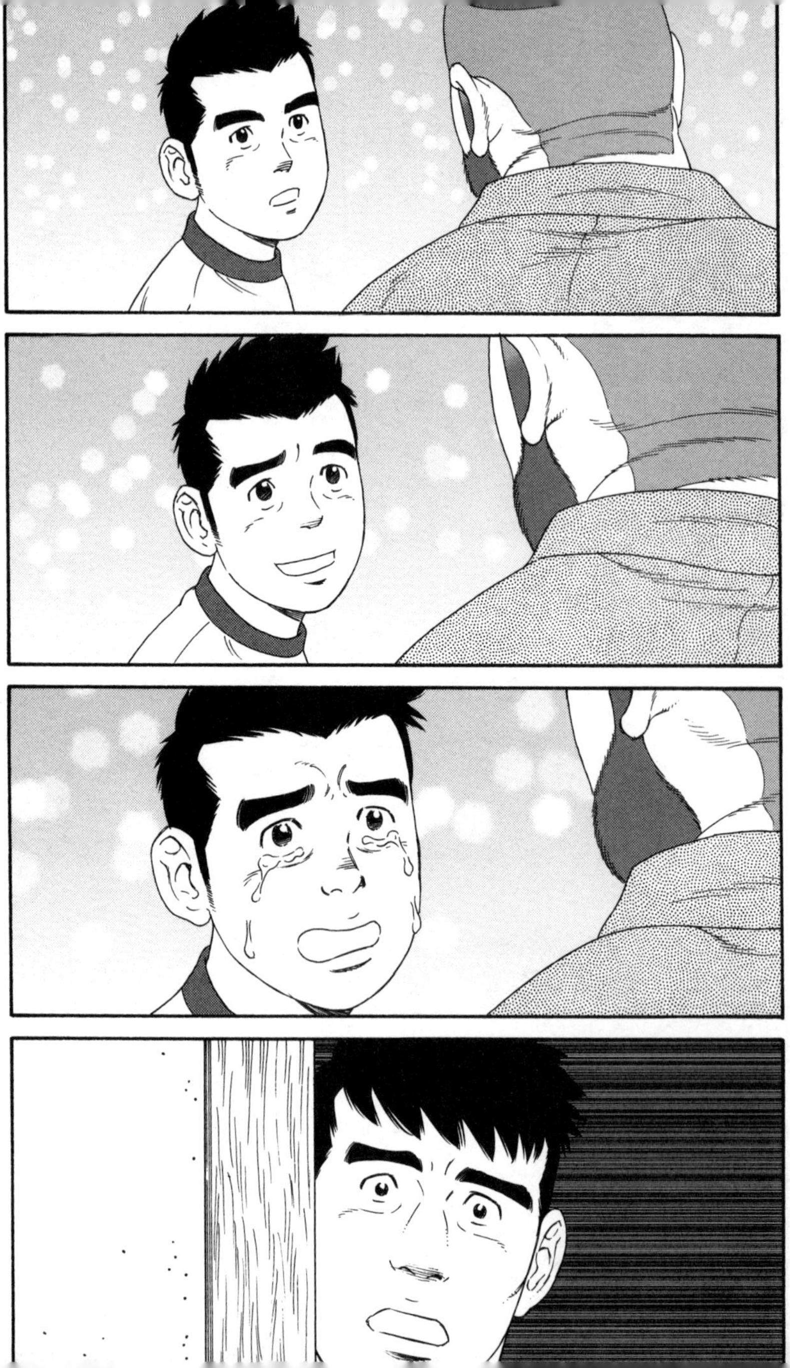

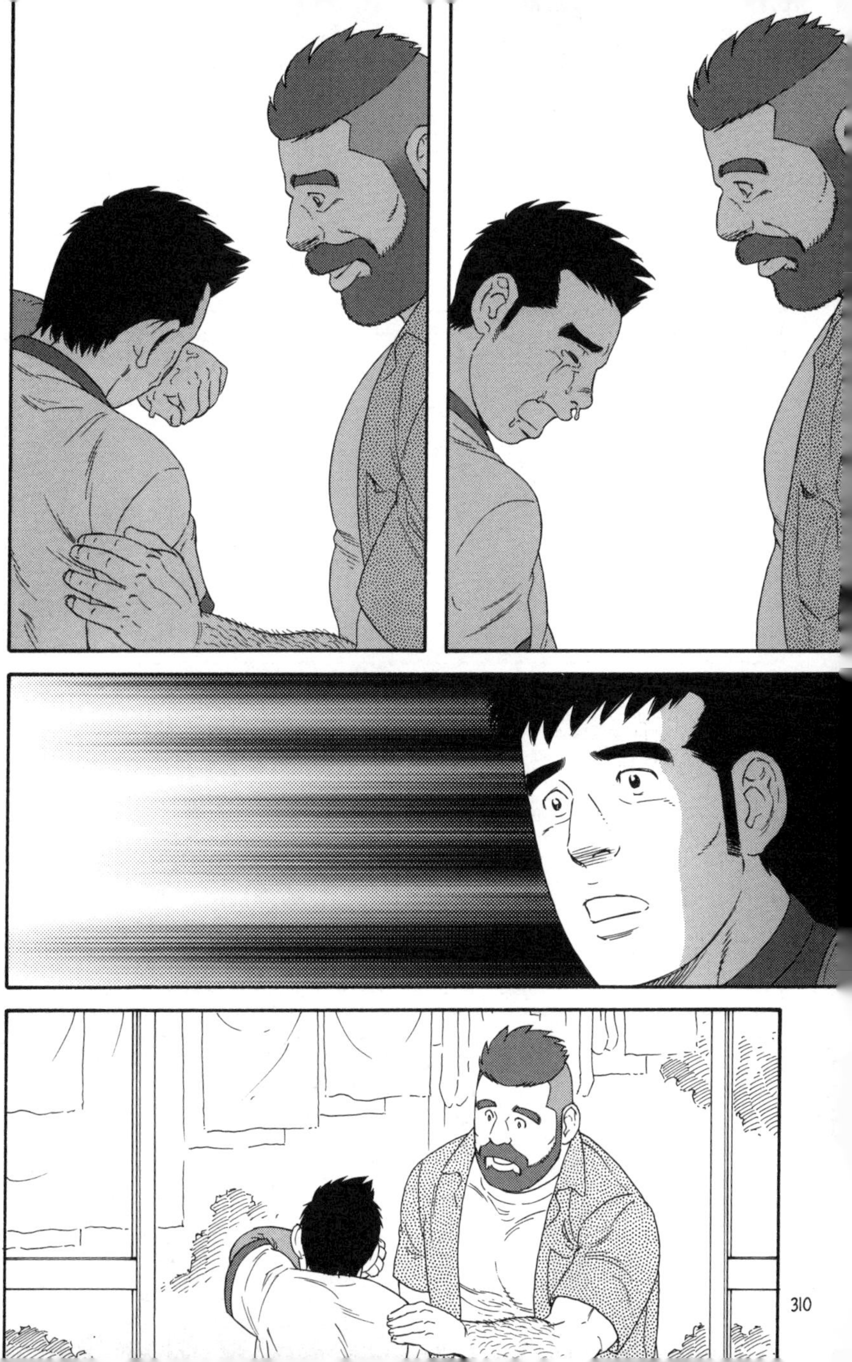

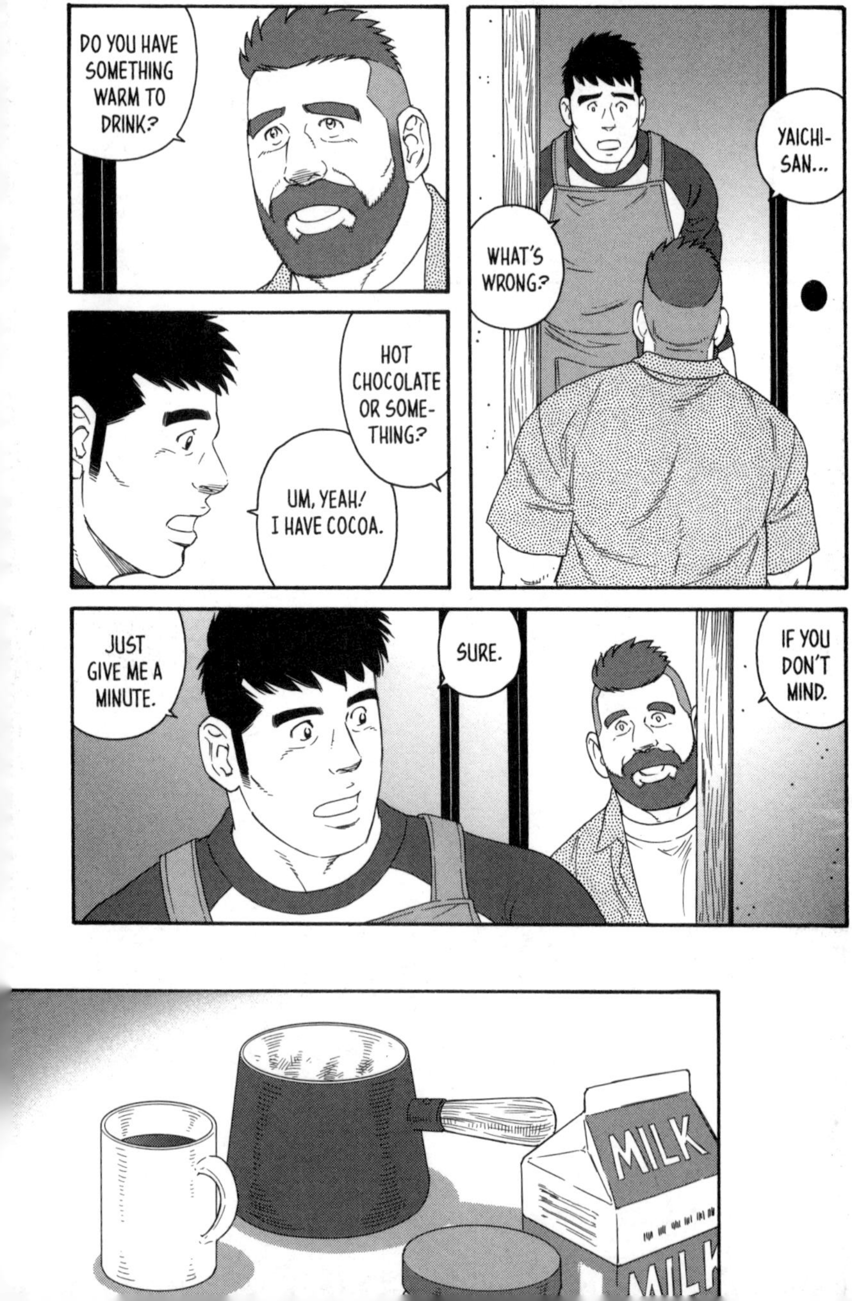
YAICHI-SAN...
WHAT'S WRONG?
DO YOU HAVE SOMETHING WARM TO DRINK?
HOT CHOCOLATE OR SOME-THING?
UM, YEAH! I HAVE COCOA.
IF YOU DON'T MIND.
SURE.
JUST GIVE ME A MINUTE.
MILK

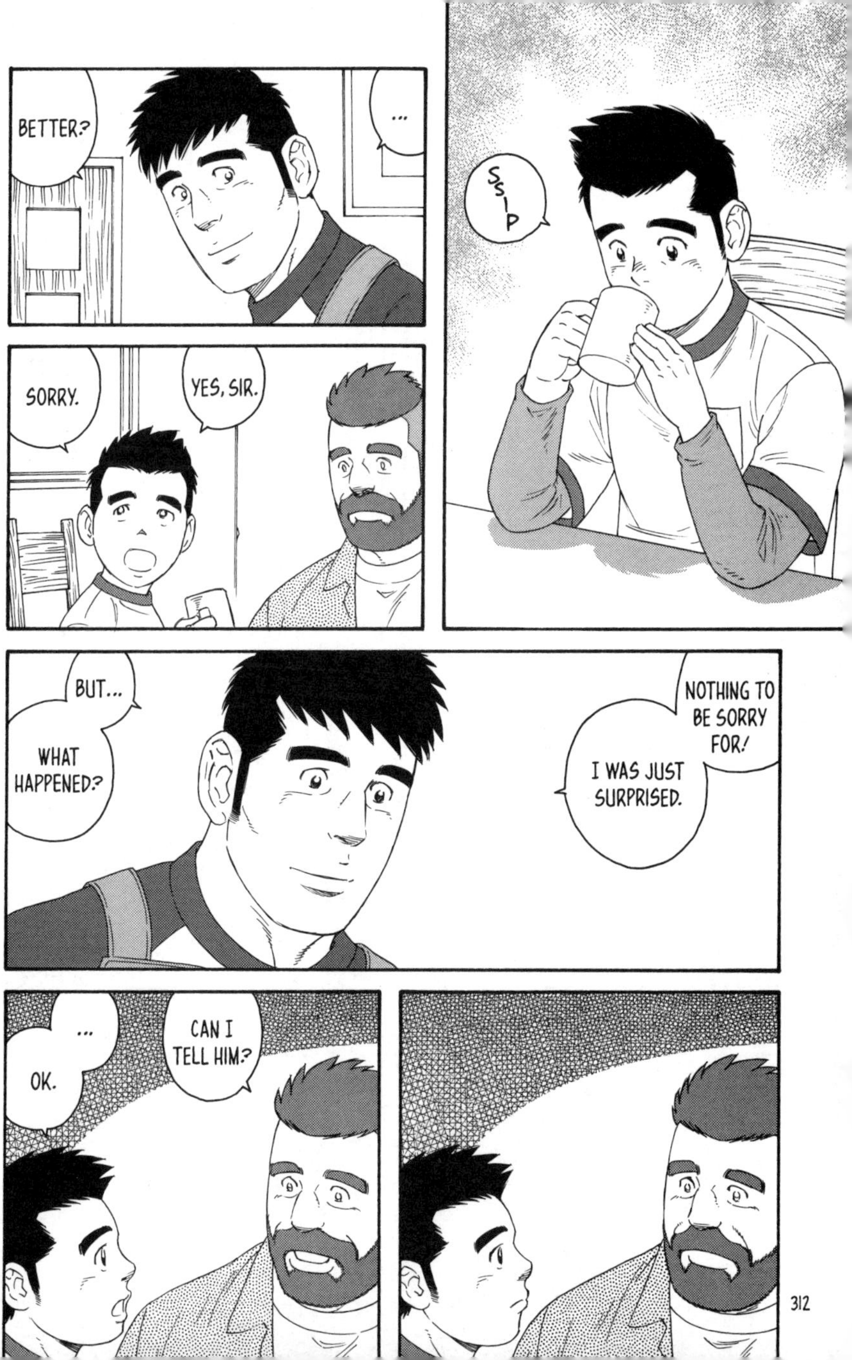
SSIP
...
BETTER?
YES, SIR.
SORRY.
NOTHING TO BE SORRY FOR!
I WAS JUST SURPRISED.
BUT...
WHAT HAPPENED?
CAN I TELL HIM?
...
OK.

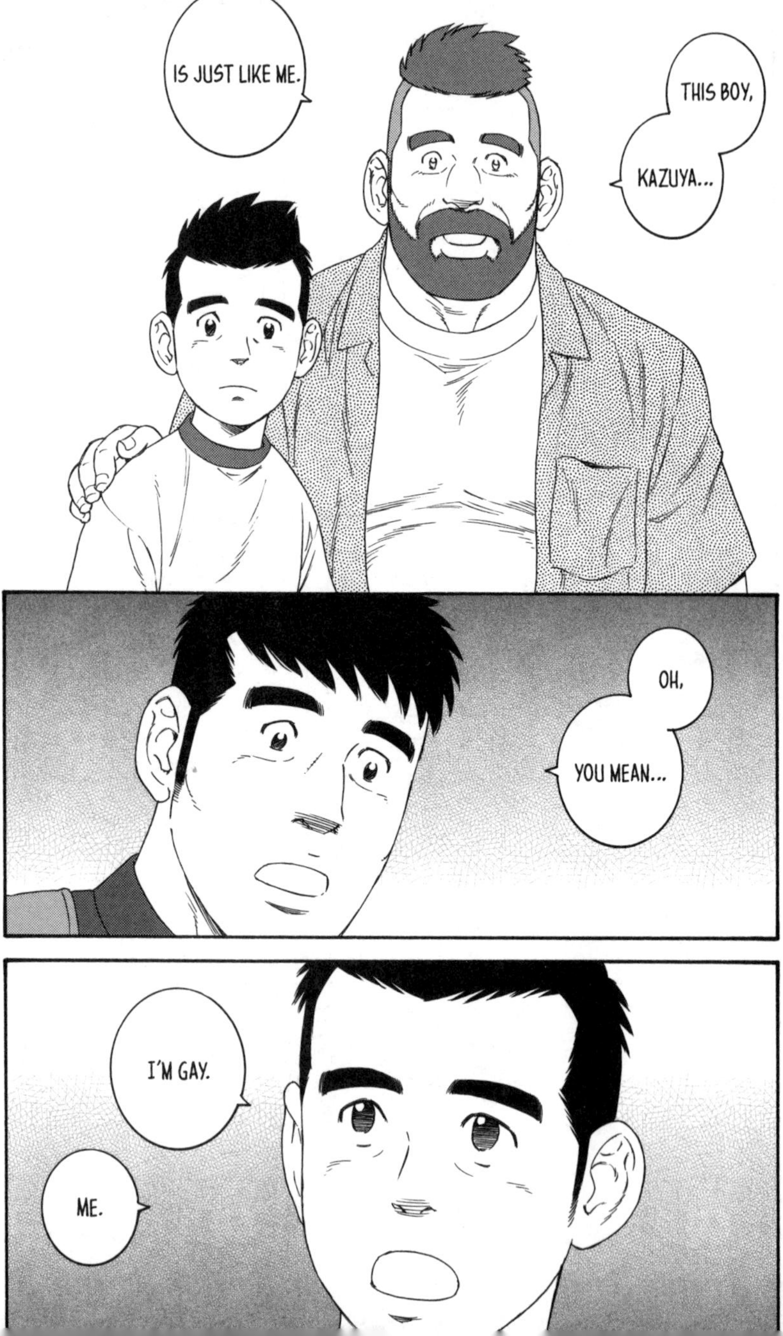
THIS BOY,
KAZUYA...
IS JUST LIKE ME.
OH,
YOU MEAN...
I'M GAY.
ME.

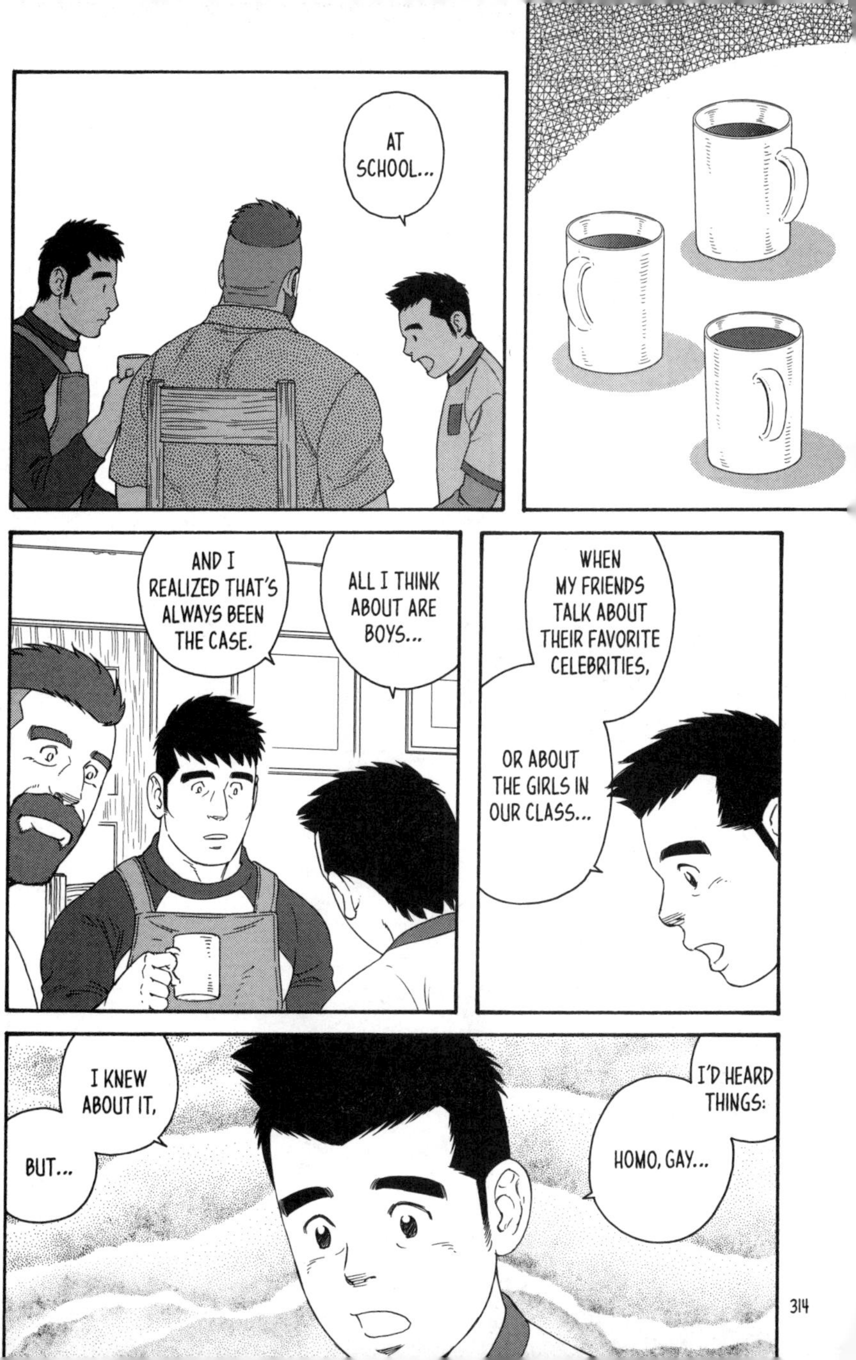
AT SCHOOL...
WHEN MY FRIENDS TALK ABOUT THEIR FAVORITE CELEBRITIES,
OR ABOUT THE GIRLS IN OUR CLASS...
ALL I THINK ABOUT ARE BOYS...
AND I REALIZED THAT'S ALWAYS BEEN THE CASE.
I'D HEARD THINGS:
HOMO, GAY...
I KNEW ABOUT IT,
BUT...

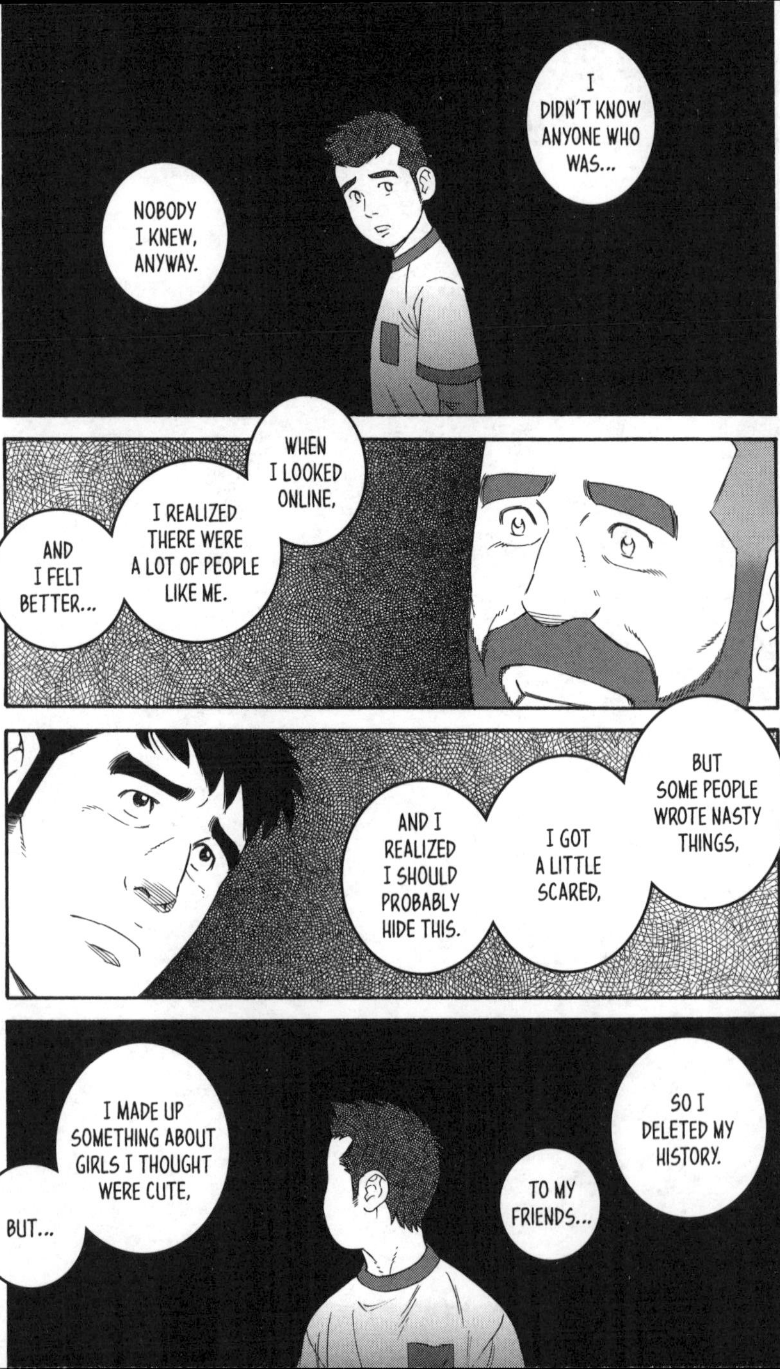
I DIDN'T KNOW ANYONE WHO WAS...
NOBODY I KNEW, ANYWAY.
WHEN I LOOKED ONLINE,
I REALIZED THERE WERE A LOT OF PEOPLE LIKE ME.
AND I FELT BETTER...
BUT SOME PEOPLE WROTE NASTY THINGS,
I GOT A LITTLE SCARED,
AND I REALIZED I SHOULD PROBABLY HIDE THIS.
SO I DELETED MY HISTORY.
TO MY FRIENDS...
I MADE UP SOMETHING ABOUT GIRLS I THOUGHT WERE CUTE,
BUT...

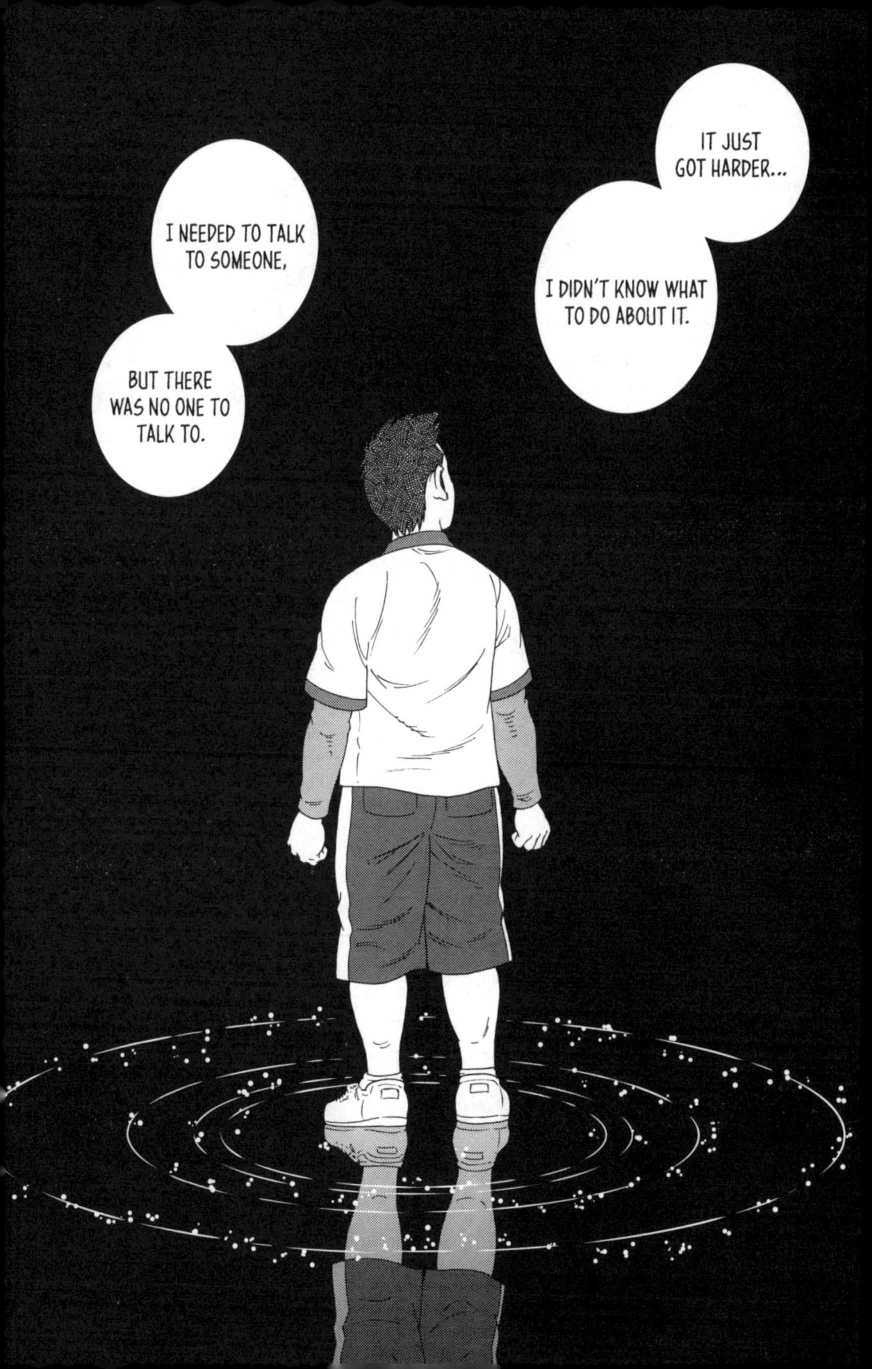

IT JUST GOT HARDER...
I DIDN'T KNOW WHAT TO DO ABOUT IT.
I NEEDED TO TALK TO SOMEONE,
BUT THERE WAS NO ONE TO TALK TO.

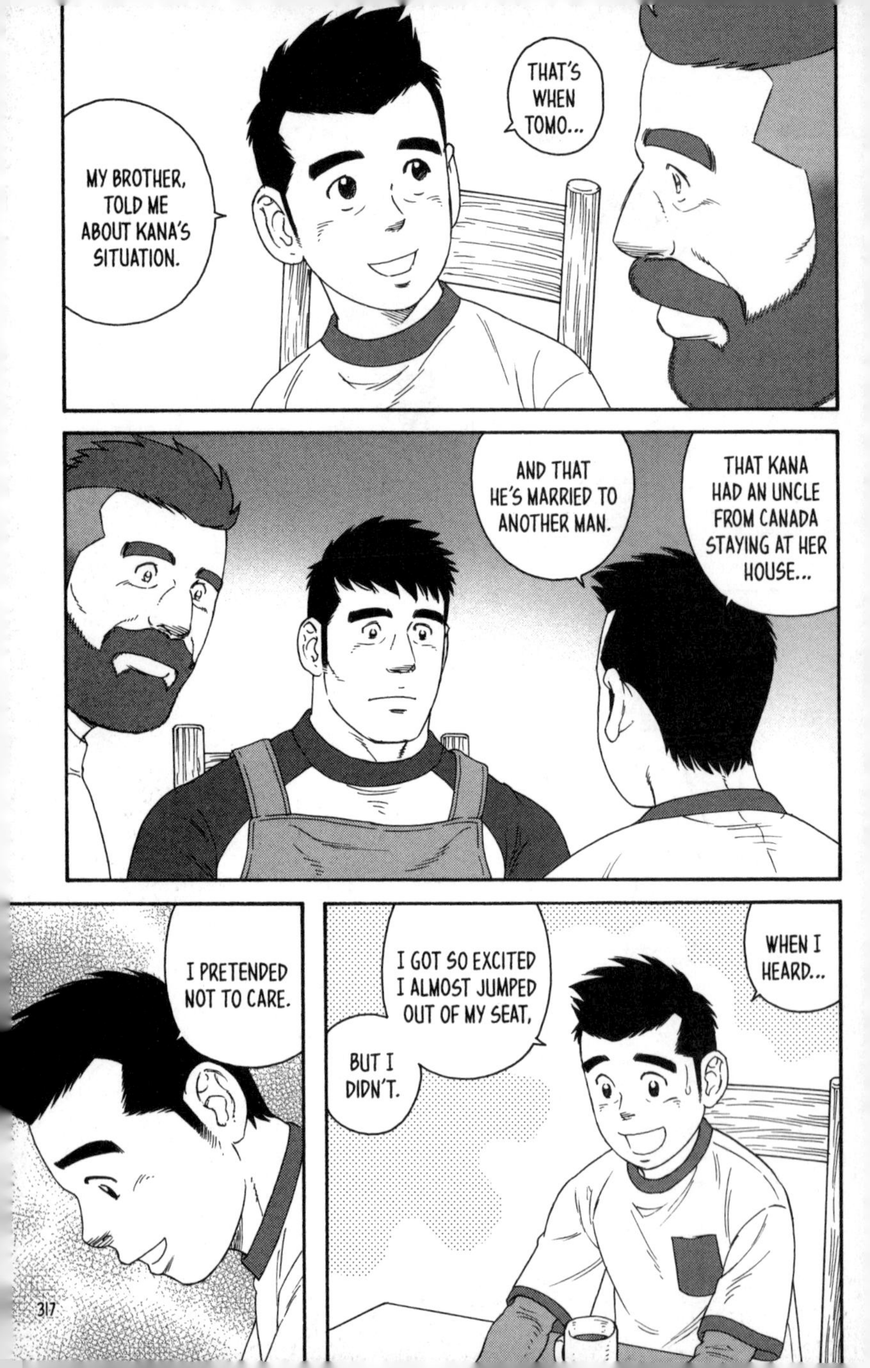
THAT'S WHEN TOMO...
MY BROTHER, TOLD ME ABOUT KANA'S SITUATION.
THAT KANA HAD AN UNCLE FROM CANADA STAYING AT HER HOUSE...
AND THAT HE'S MARRIED TO ANOTHER MAN.
WHEN I HEARD...
I GOT SO EXCITED I ALMOST JUMPED OUT OF MY SEAT,
BUT I DIDN'T.
I PRETENDED NOT TO CARE.

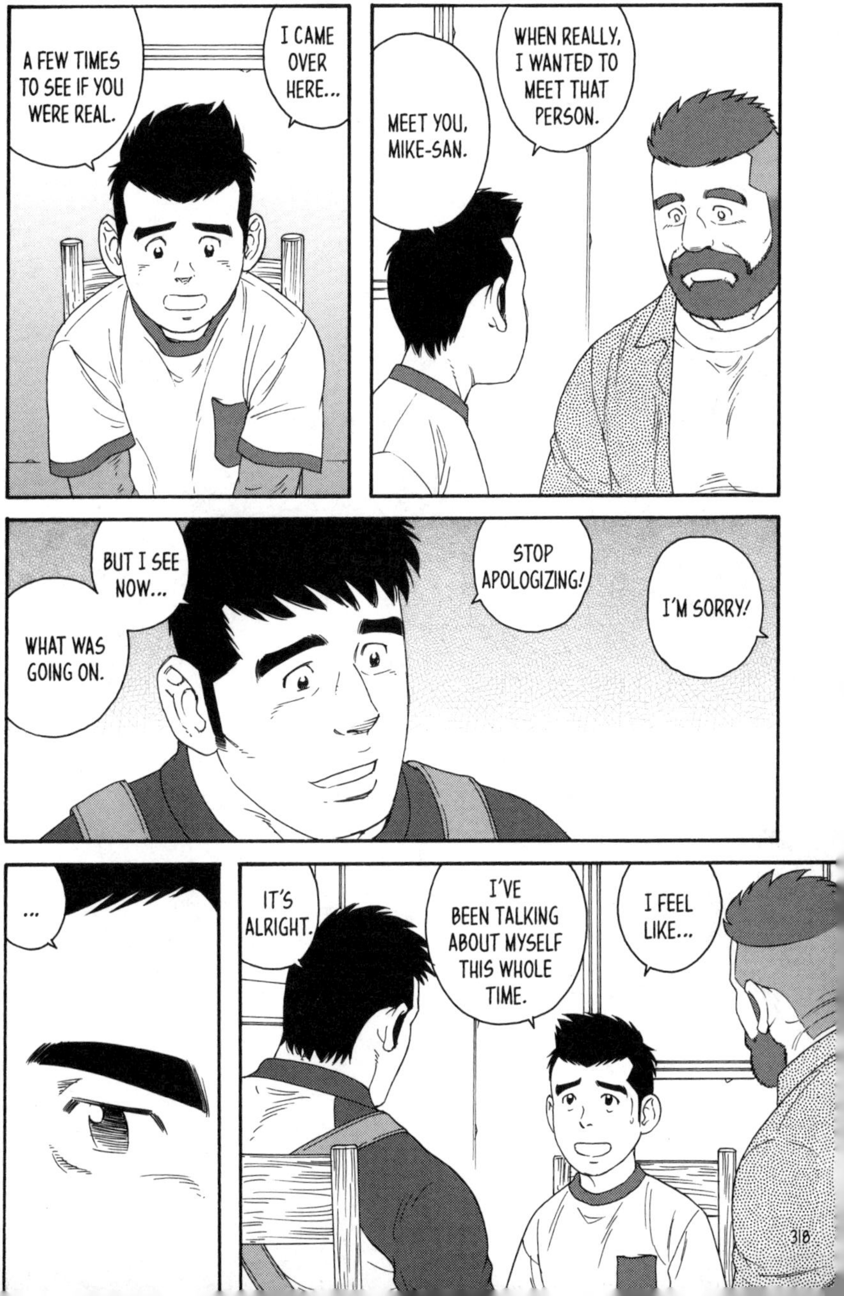
WHEN REALLY, I WANTED TO MEET THAT PERSON.
MEET YOU, MIKE-SAN.
I CAME OVER HERE...
A FEW TIMES TO SEE IF YOU WERE REAL.
I'M SORRY!
STOP APOLOGIZING!
BUT I SEE NOW...
WHAT WAS GOING ON.
I FEEL LIKE...
I'VE BEEN TALKING ABOUT MYSELF THIS WHOLE TIME.
IT'S ALRIGHT.
...

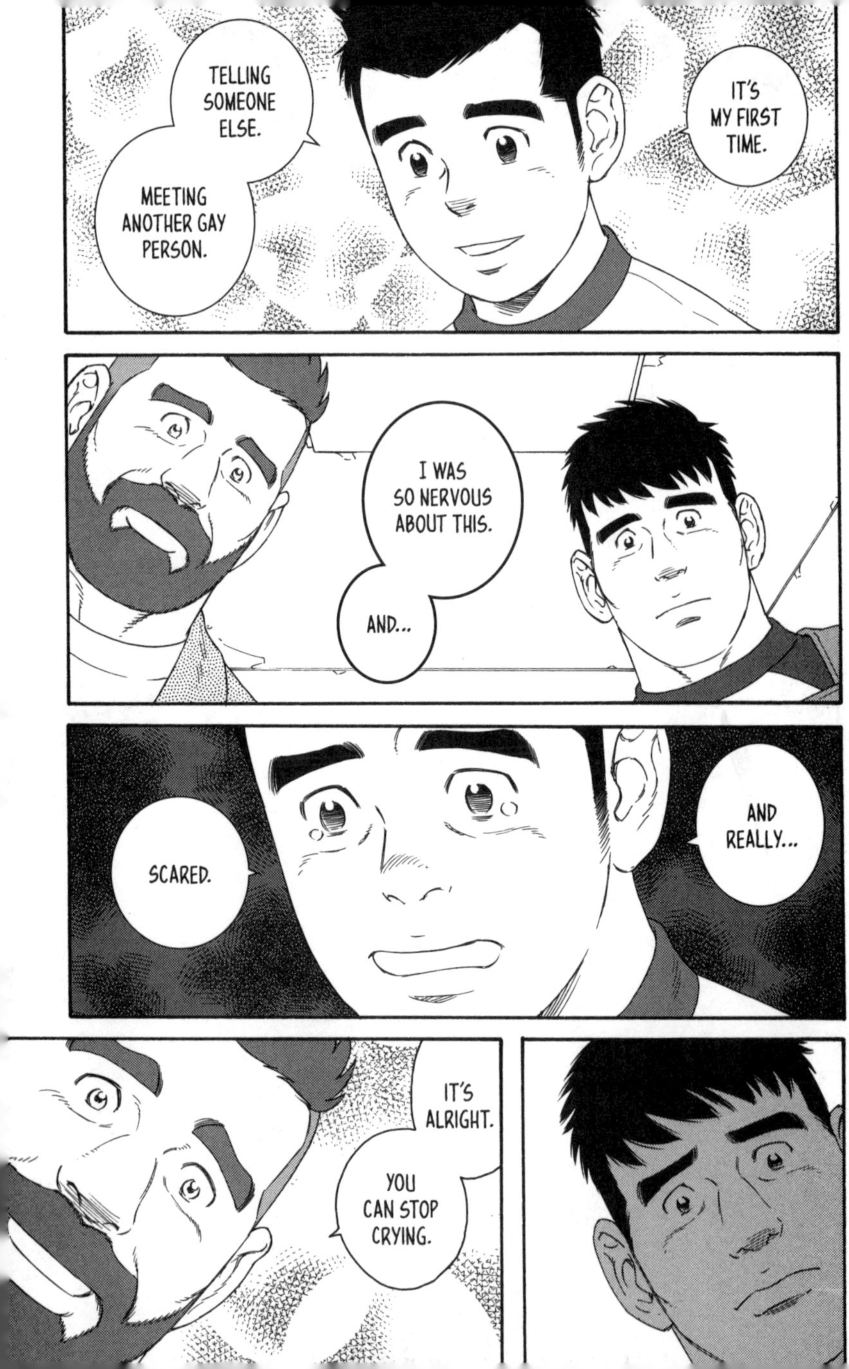
IT'S MY FIRST TIME.
TELLING SOMEONE ELSE.
MEETING ANOTHER GAY PERSON.
I WAS SO NERVOUS ABOUT THIS.
AND...
AND REALLY...
SCARED.
IT'S ALRIGHT.
YOU CAN STOP CRYING.

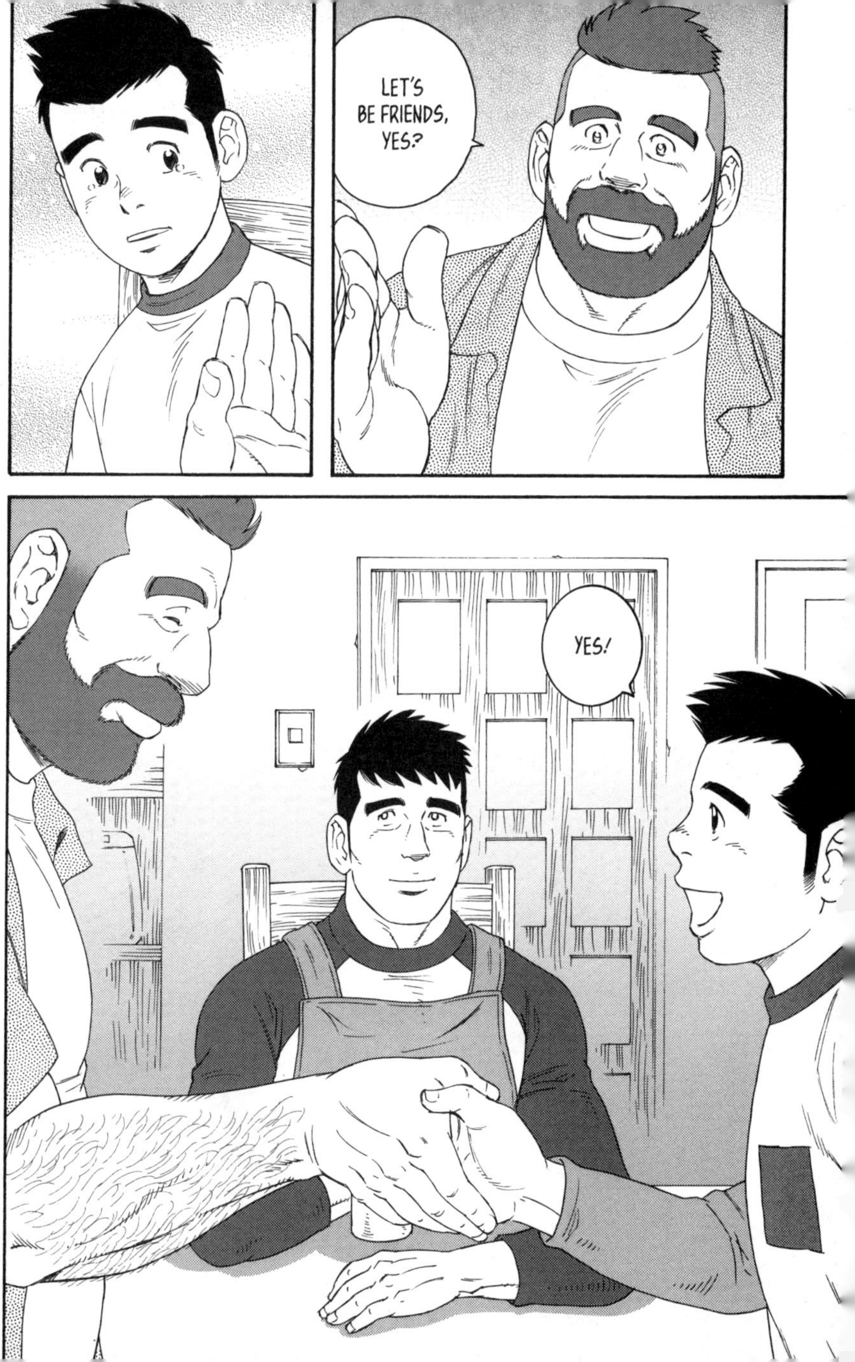
LET'S BE FRIENDS, YES?
YES!

CHAPTER FOURTEEN
RAMEN

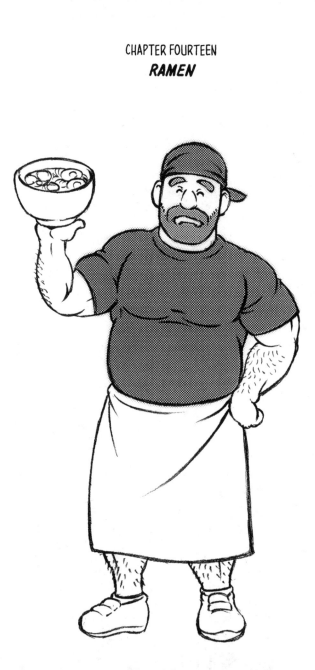

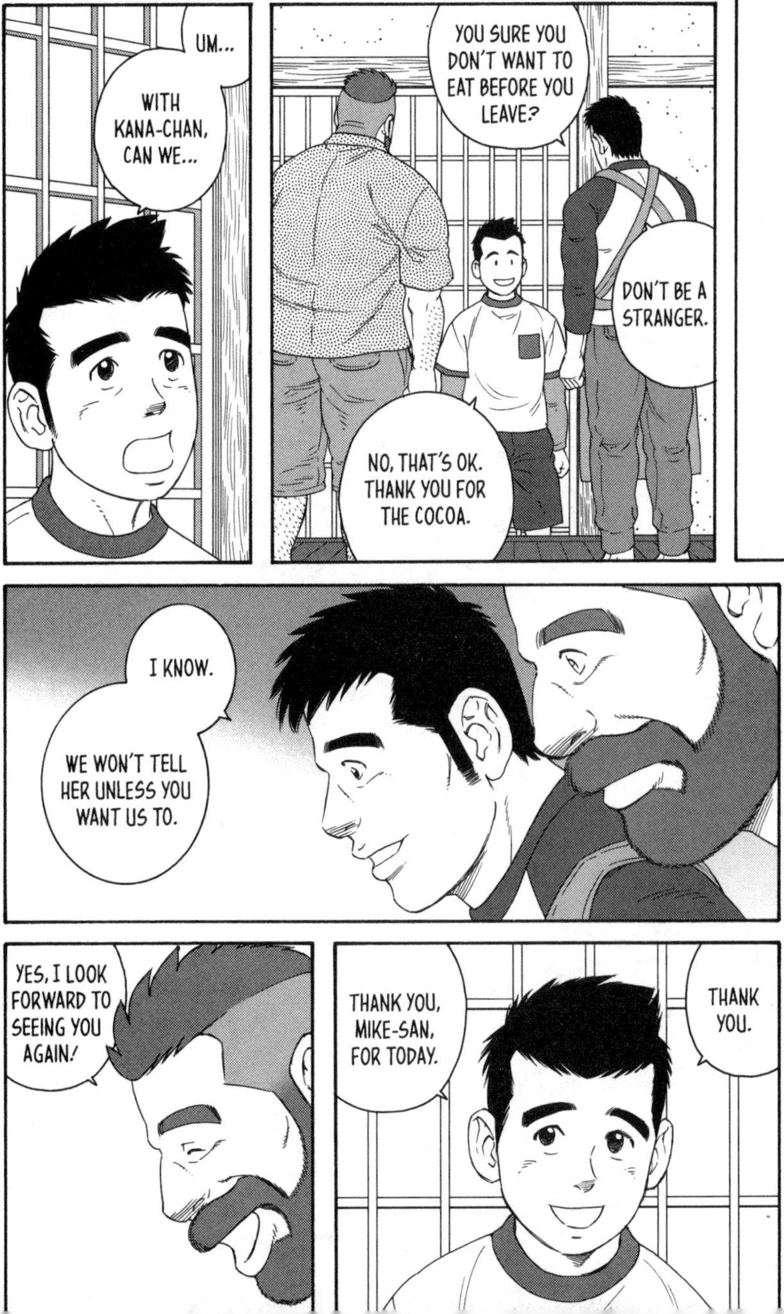
YOU SURE YOU DON'T WANT TO EAT BEFORE YOU LEAVE?
DON'T BE A STRANGER.
NO, THAT'S OK. THANK YOU FOR THE COCOA.
UM...
WITH KANA-CHAN, CAN WE...
I KNOW.
WE WON'T TELL HER UNLESS YOU WANT US TO.
THANK YOU.
THANK YOU, MIKE-SAN, FOR TODAY.
YES, I LOOK FORWARD TO SEEING YOU AGAIN!

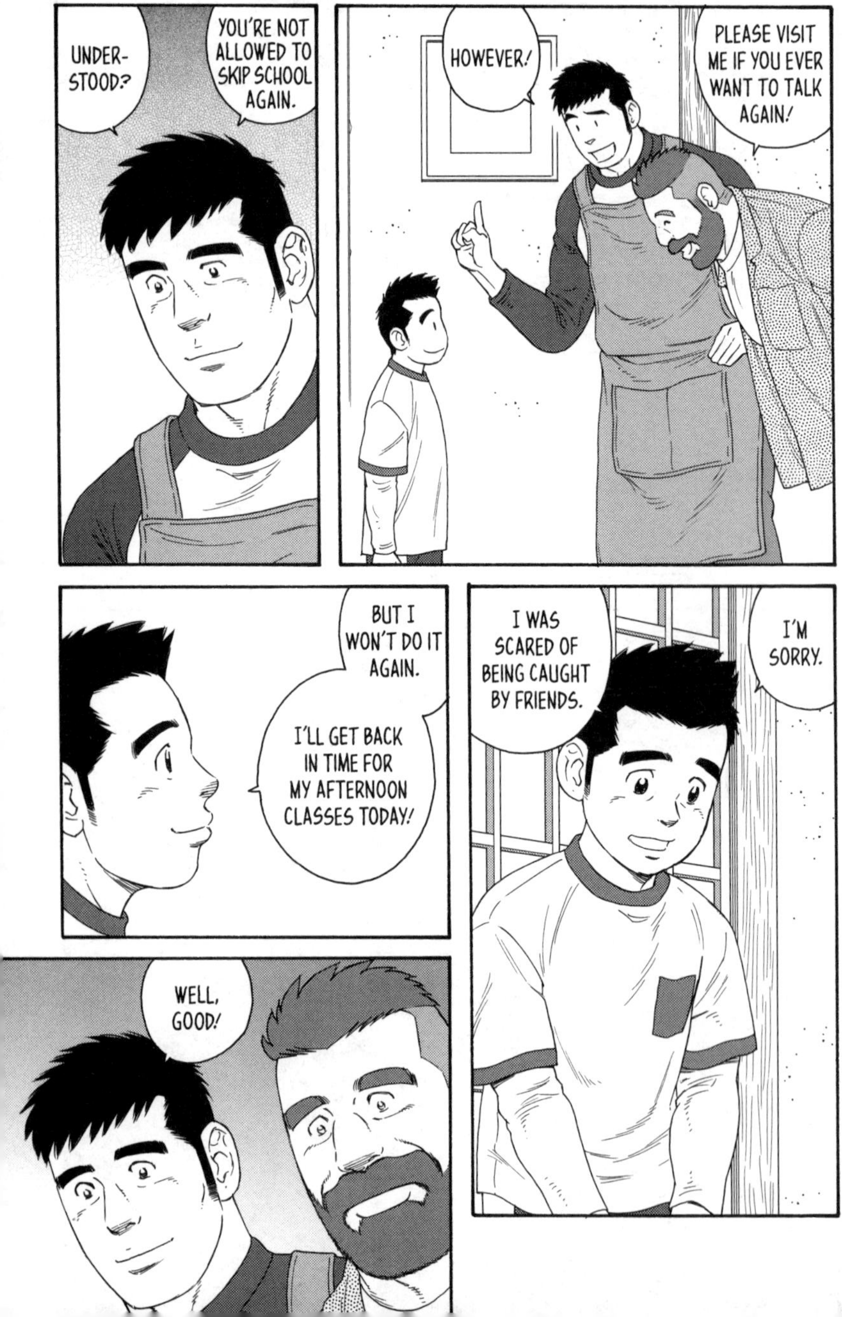
PLEASE VISIT ME IF YOU EVER WANT TO TALK AGAIN!
HOWEVER!
YOU'RE NOT ALLOWED TO SKIP SCHOOL AGAIN.
UNDER-STOOD?
I'M SORRY.
I WAS SCARED OF BEING CAUGHT BY FRIENDS.
BUT I WON'T DO IT AGAIN.
I'LL GET BACK IN TIME FOR MY AFTERNOON CLASSES TODAY!
WELL, GOOD!

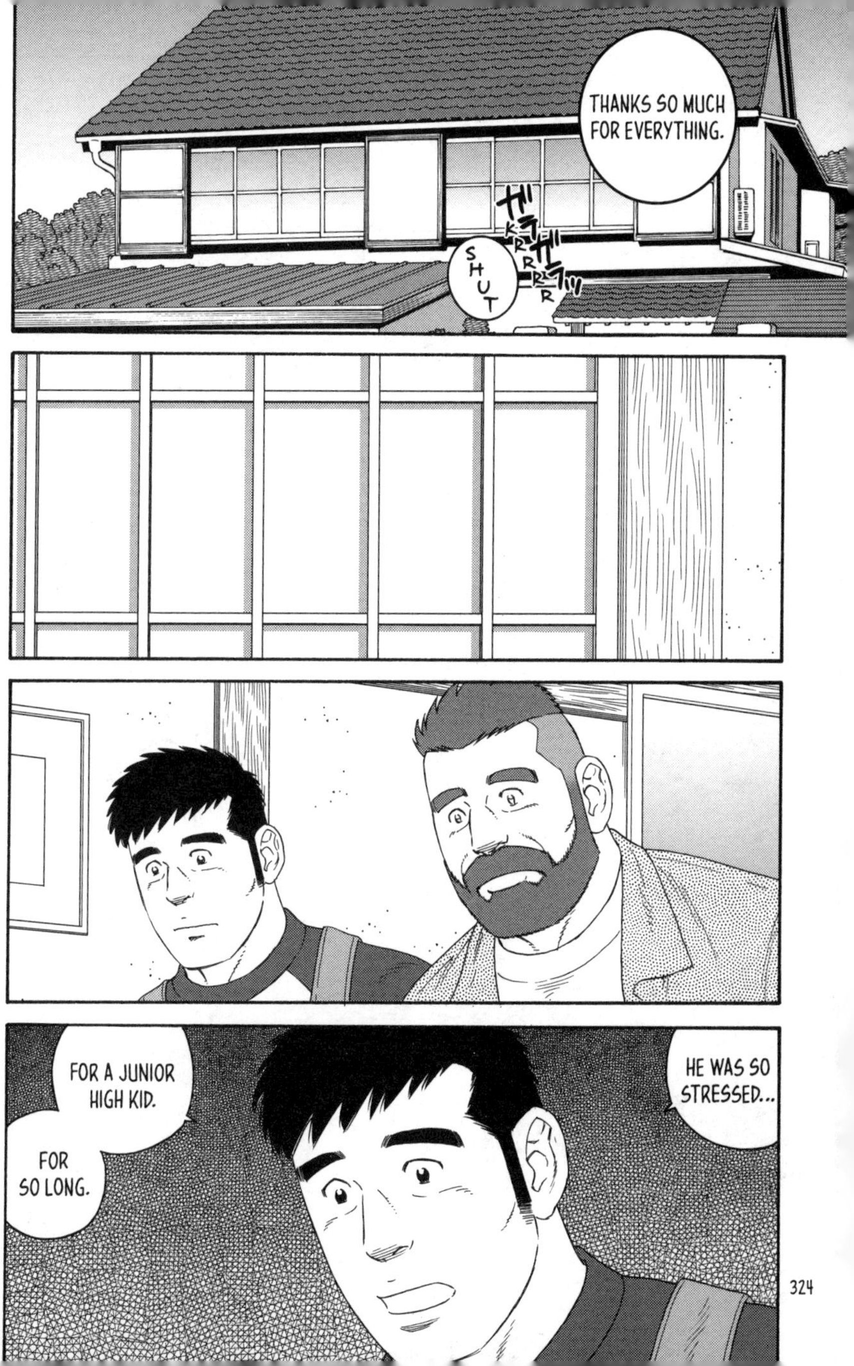
THANKS SO MUCH FOR EVERYTHING.
ガラ
ガラッ
SHUT
HE WAS SO STRESSED...
FOR A JUNIOR HIGH KID.
FOR SO LONG.

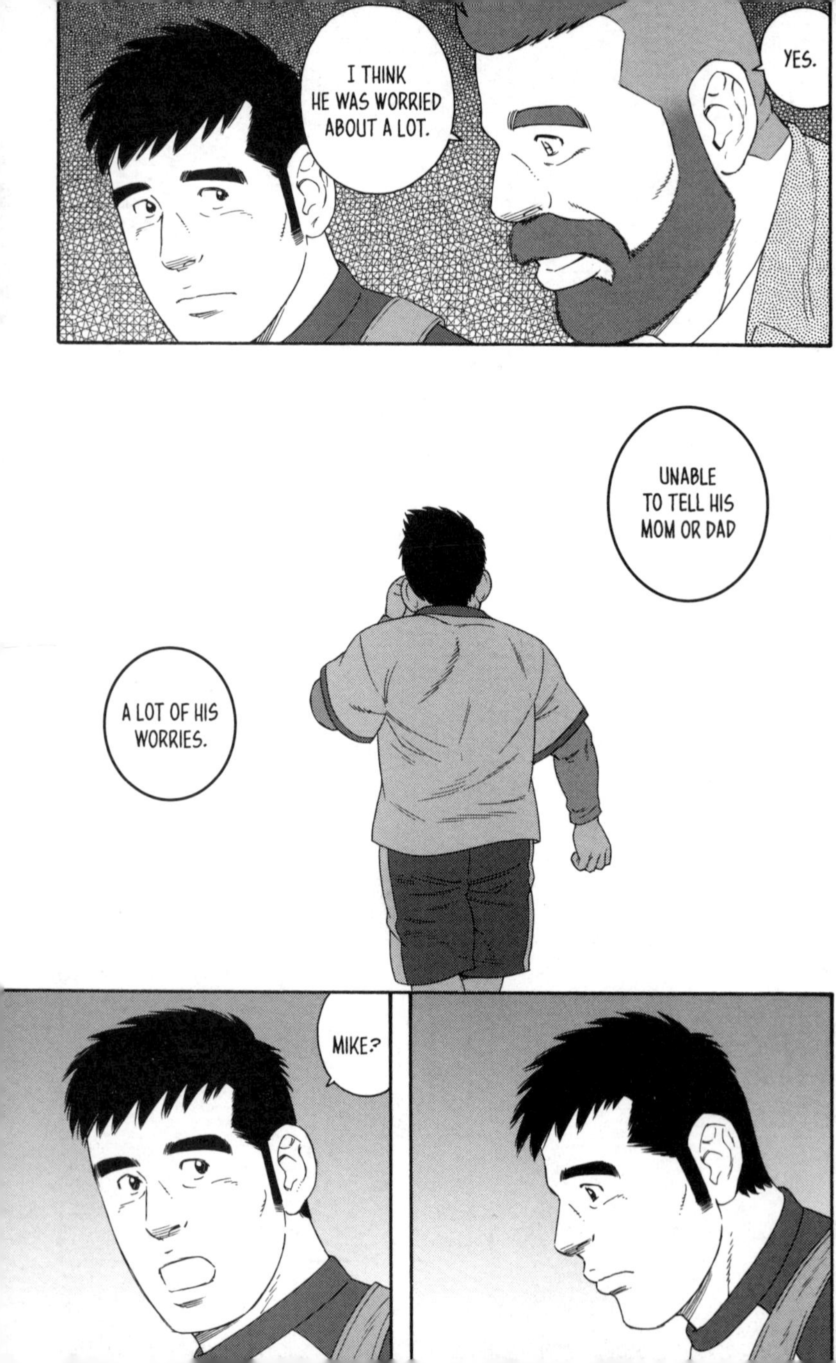
YES.
I THINK HE WAS WORRIED ABOUT A LOT.
UNABLE TO TELL HIS MOM OR DAD
A LOT OF HIS WORRIES.
MIKE?

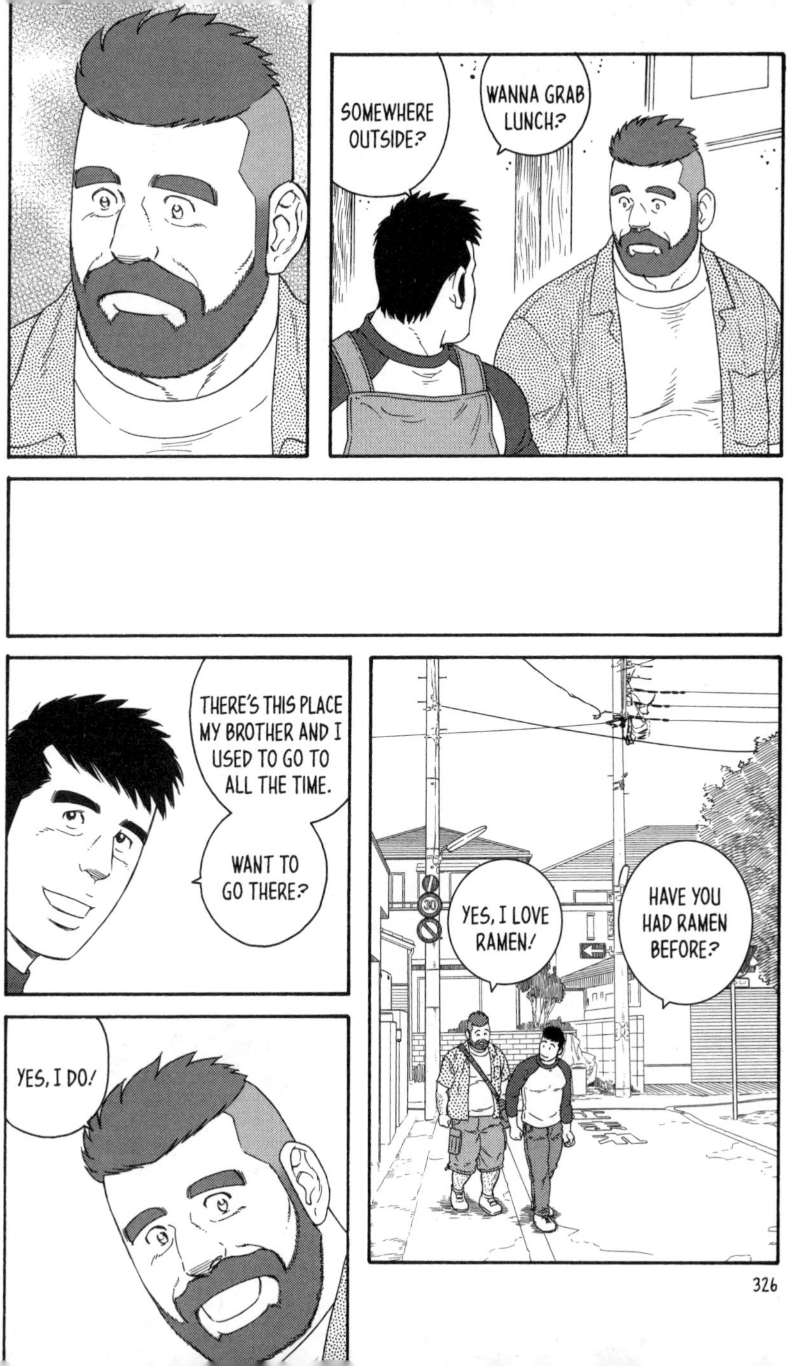
WANNA GRAB LUNCH?
SOMEWHERE OUTSIDE?
HAVE YOU HAD RAMEN BEFORE?
YES, I LOVE RAMEN!
THERE'S THIS PLACE MY BROTHER AND I USED TO GO TO ALL THE TIME.
WANT TO GO THERE?
YES, I DO!

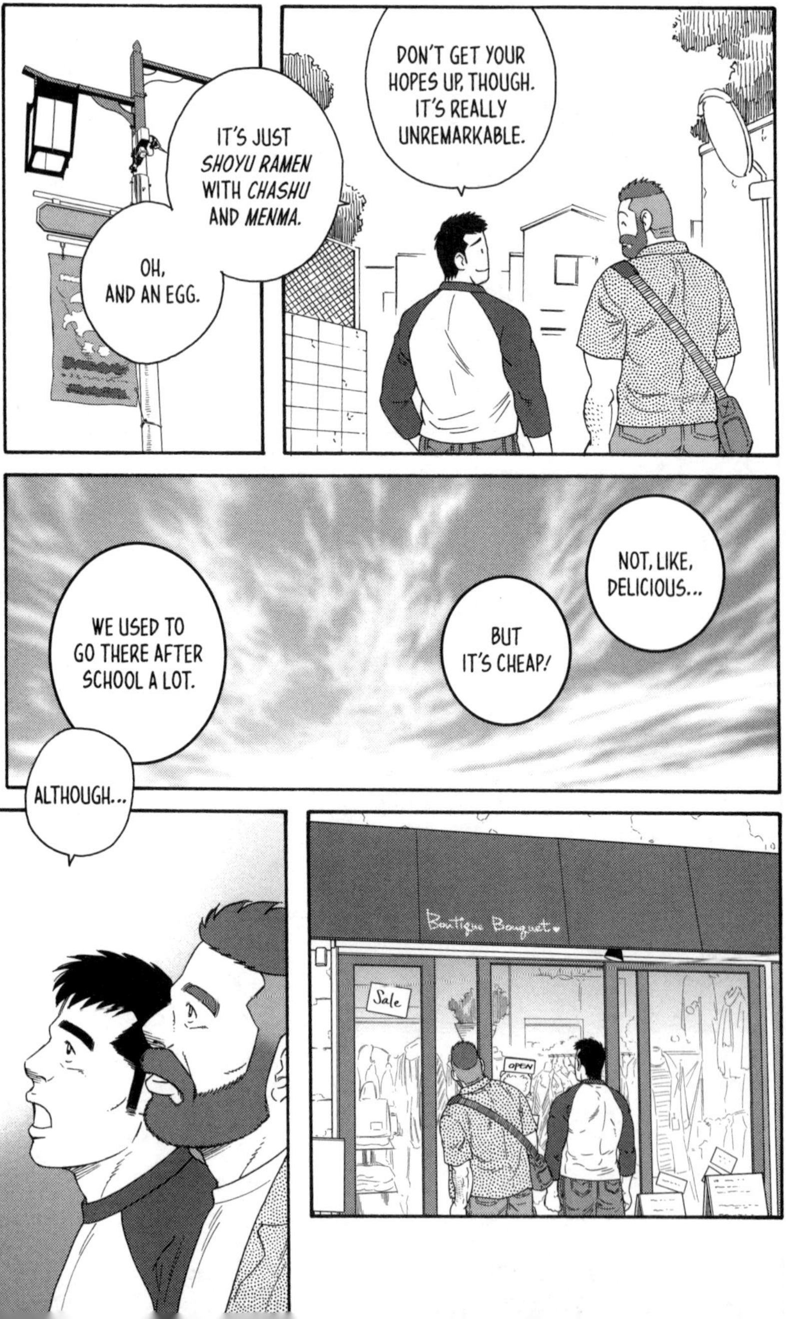
DON'T GET YOUR HOPES UP, THOUGH. IT'S REALLY UNREMARKABLE.
IT'S JUST SHOYU RAMEN WITH CHASHU AND MENMA.
OH, AND AN EGG.
NOT, LIKE, DELICIOUS...
BUT IT'S CHEAP!
WE USED TO GO THERE AFTER SCHOOL A LOT.
ALTHOUGH...
Boutique Bouquet
Sale
OPEN

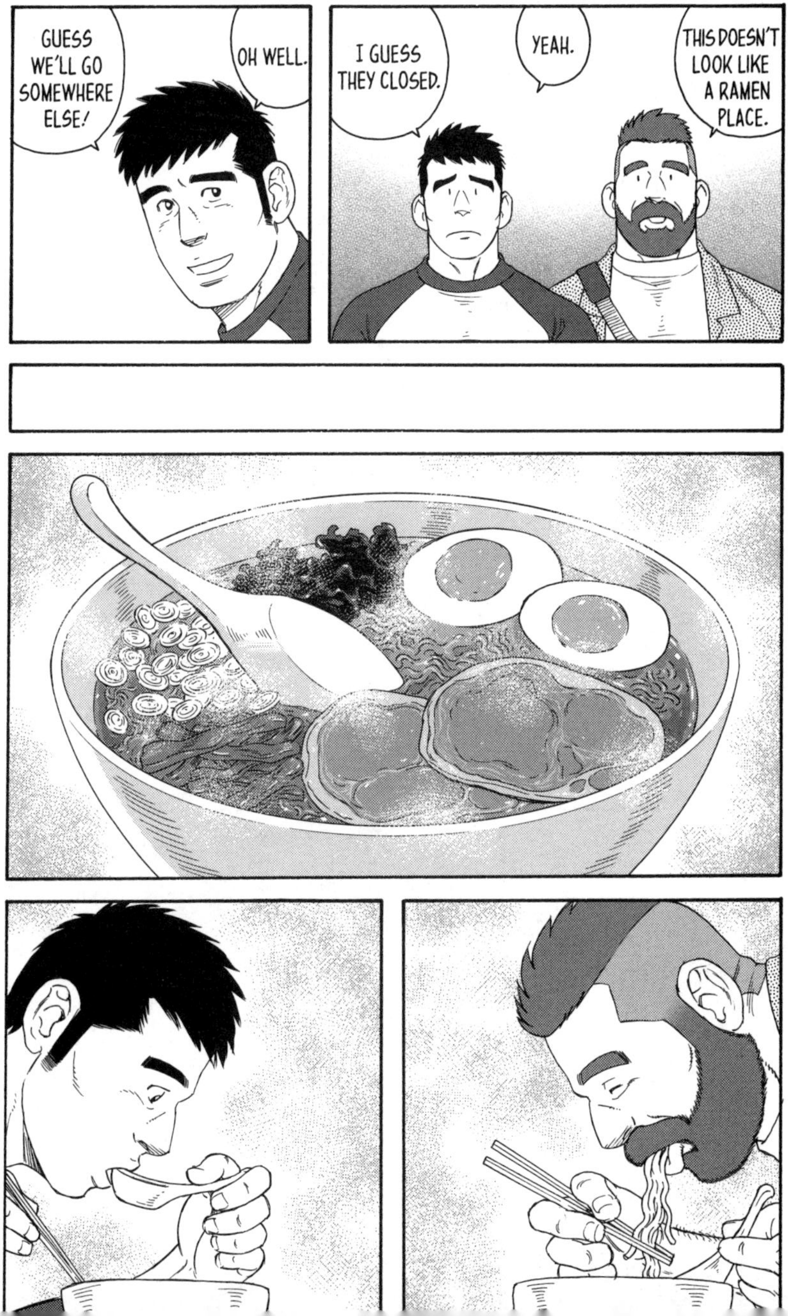
THIS DOESN'T LOOK LIKE A RAMEN PLACE.
YEAH.
I GUESS THEY CLOSED.
OH WELL.
GUESS WE'LL GO SOMEWHERE ELSE!

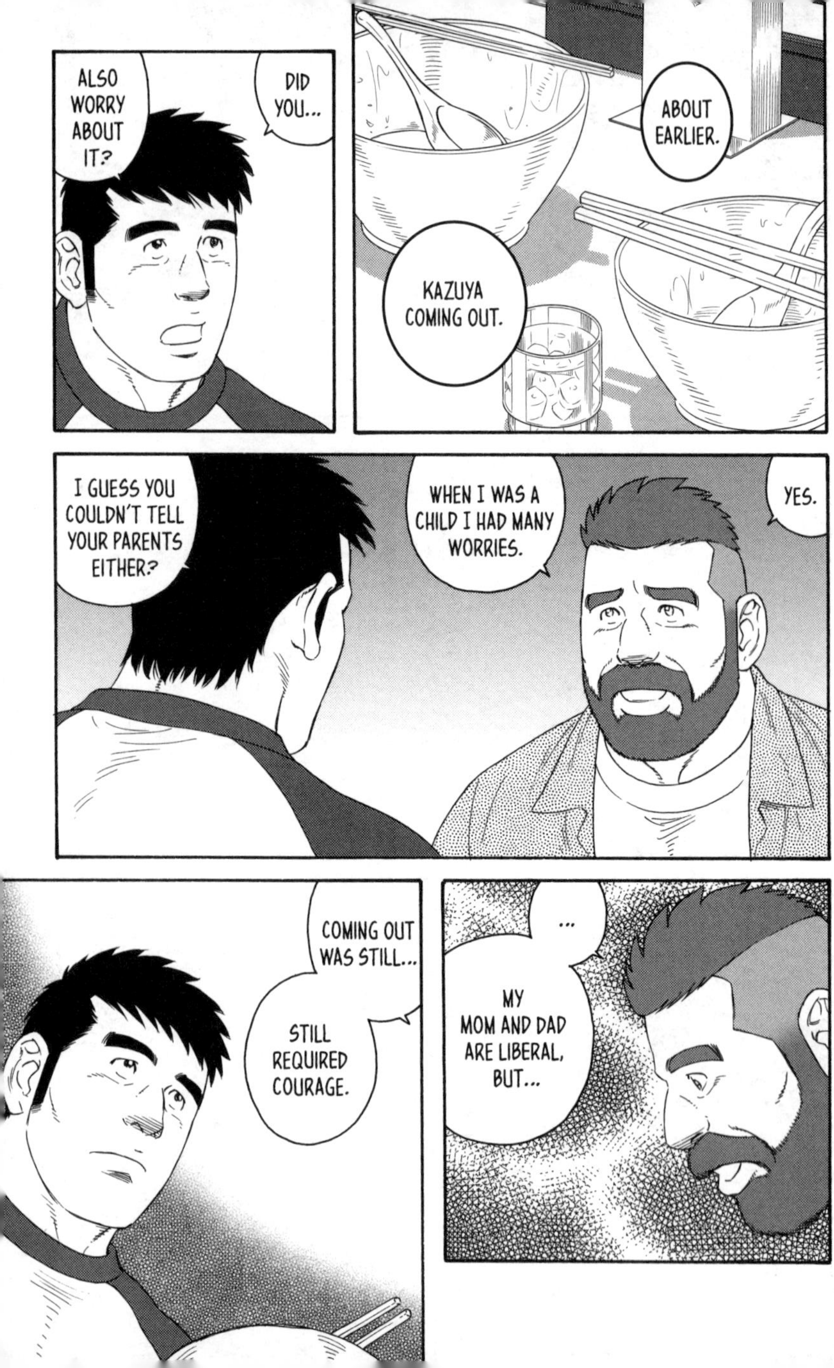
ABOUT EARLIER.
KAZUYA COMING OUT.
DID YOU...
ALSO WORRY ABOUT IT?
YES.
WHEN I WAS A CHILD I HAD MANY WORRIES.
I GUESS YOU COULDN'T TELL YOUR PARENTS EITHER?
...
MY MOM AND DAD ARE LIBERAL, BUT...
COMING OUT WAS STILL...
STILL REQUIRED COURAGE.

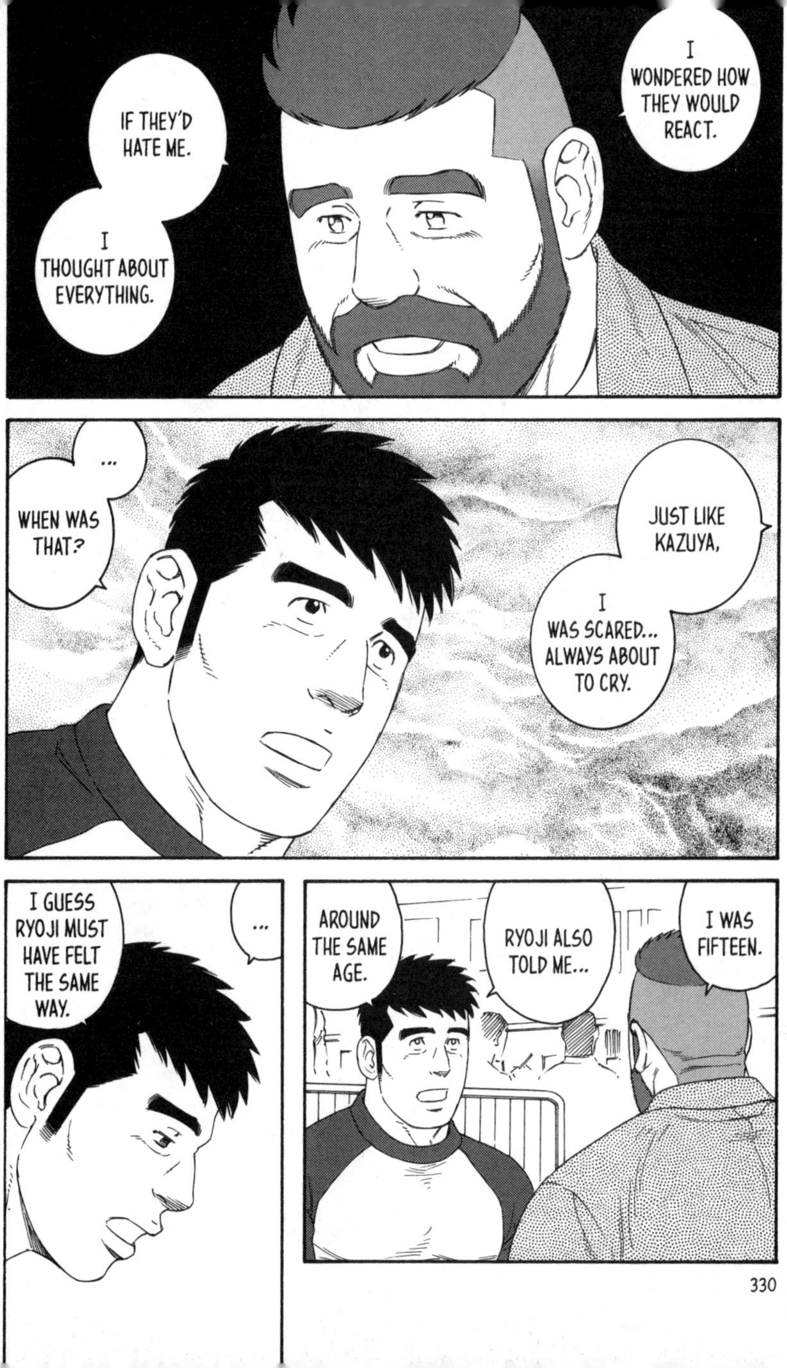
I WONDERED HOW THEY WOULD REACT.
IF THEY'D HATE ME.
I THOUGHT ABOUT EVERYTHING.
JUST LIKE KAZUYA,
I WAS SCARED... ALWAYS ABOUT TO CRY.
...
WHEN WAS THAT?
I WAS FIFTEEN.
RYOJI ALSO TOLD ME...
AROUND THE SAME AGE.
...
I GUESS RYOJI MUST HAVE FELT THE SAME WAY.

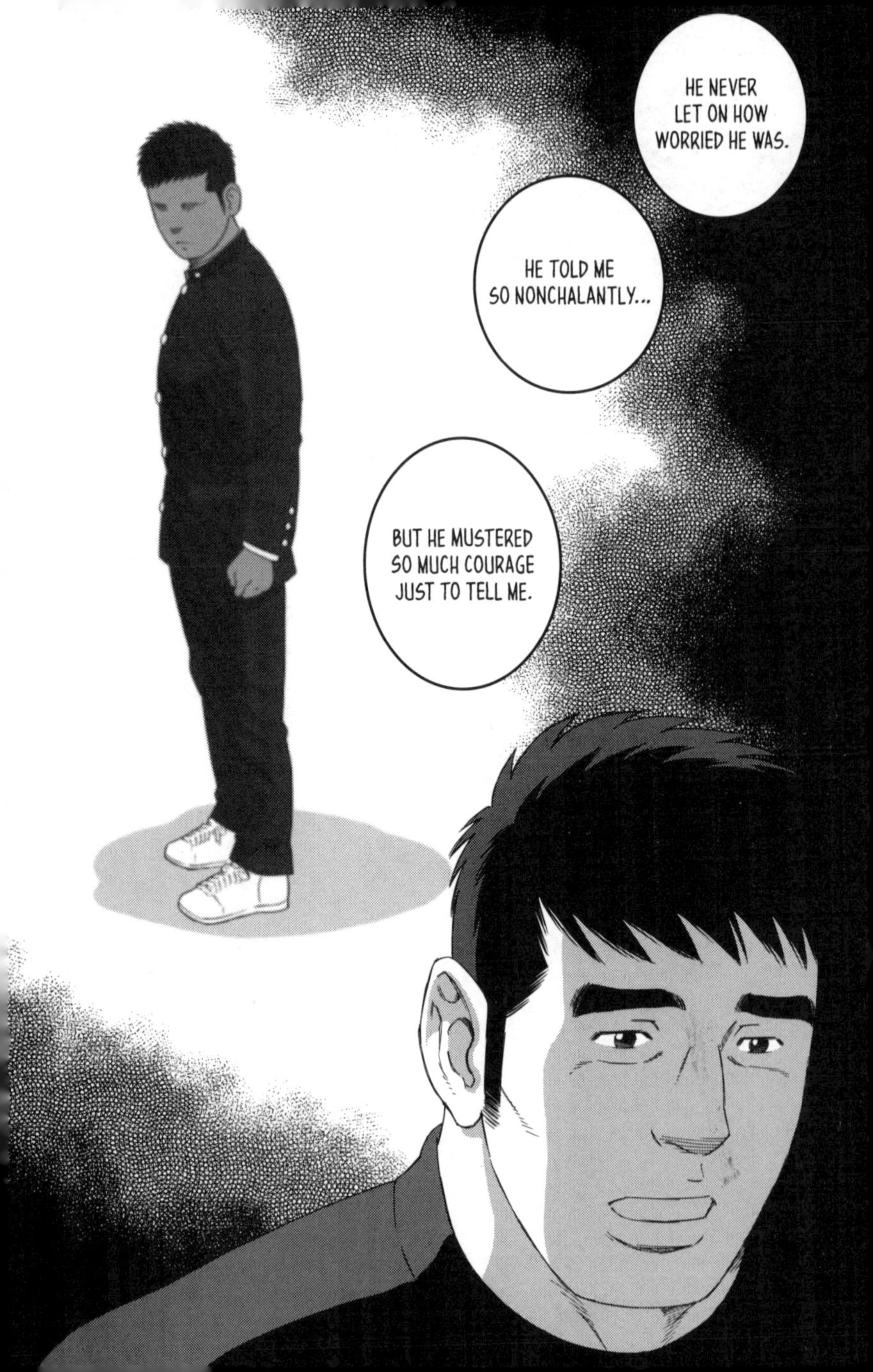
HE NEVER LET ON HOW WORRIED HE WAS.
HE TOLD ME SO NONCHALANTLY...
BUT HE MUSTERED SO MUCH COURAGE JUST TO TELL ME.

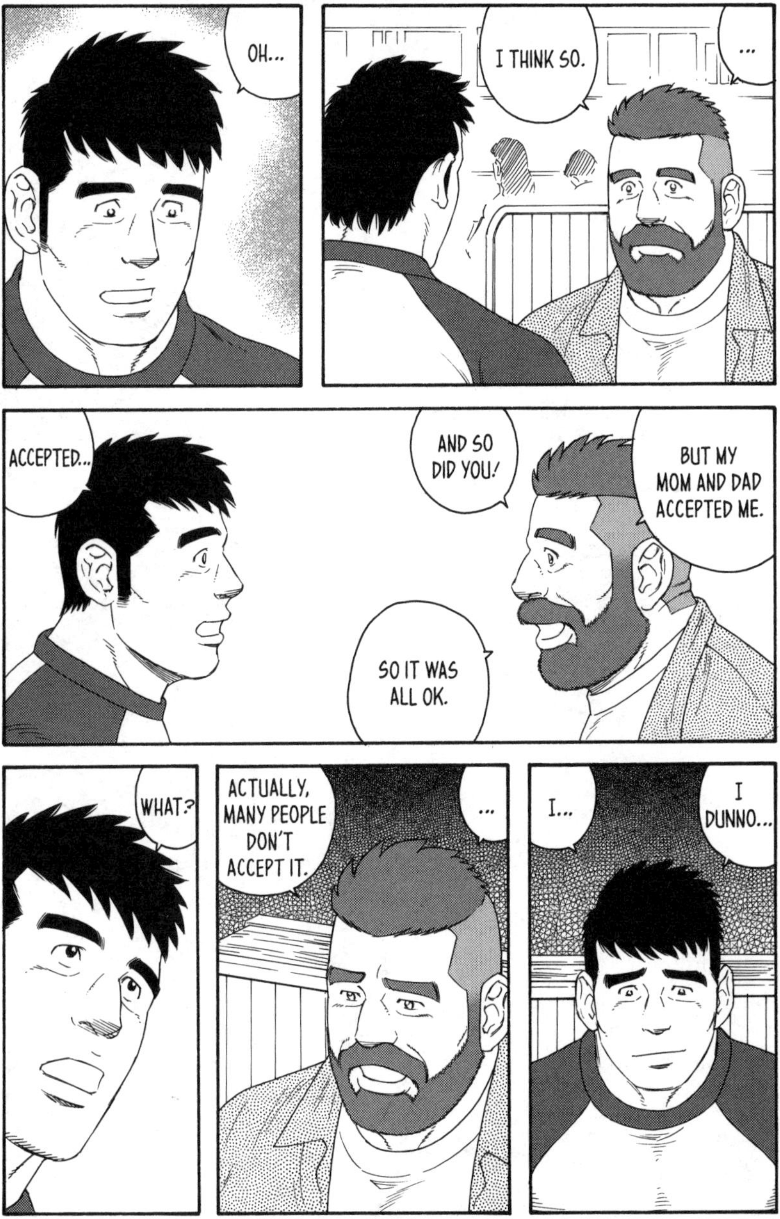
...
I THINK SO.
OH...
BUT MY MOM AND DAD ACCEPTED ME.
AND SO DID YOU!
SO IT WAS ALL OK.
ACCEPTED...
I DUNNO...
I...
...
ACTUALLY, MANY PEOPLE DON'T ACCEPT IT.
WHAT?

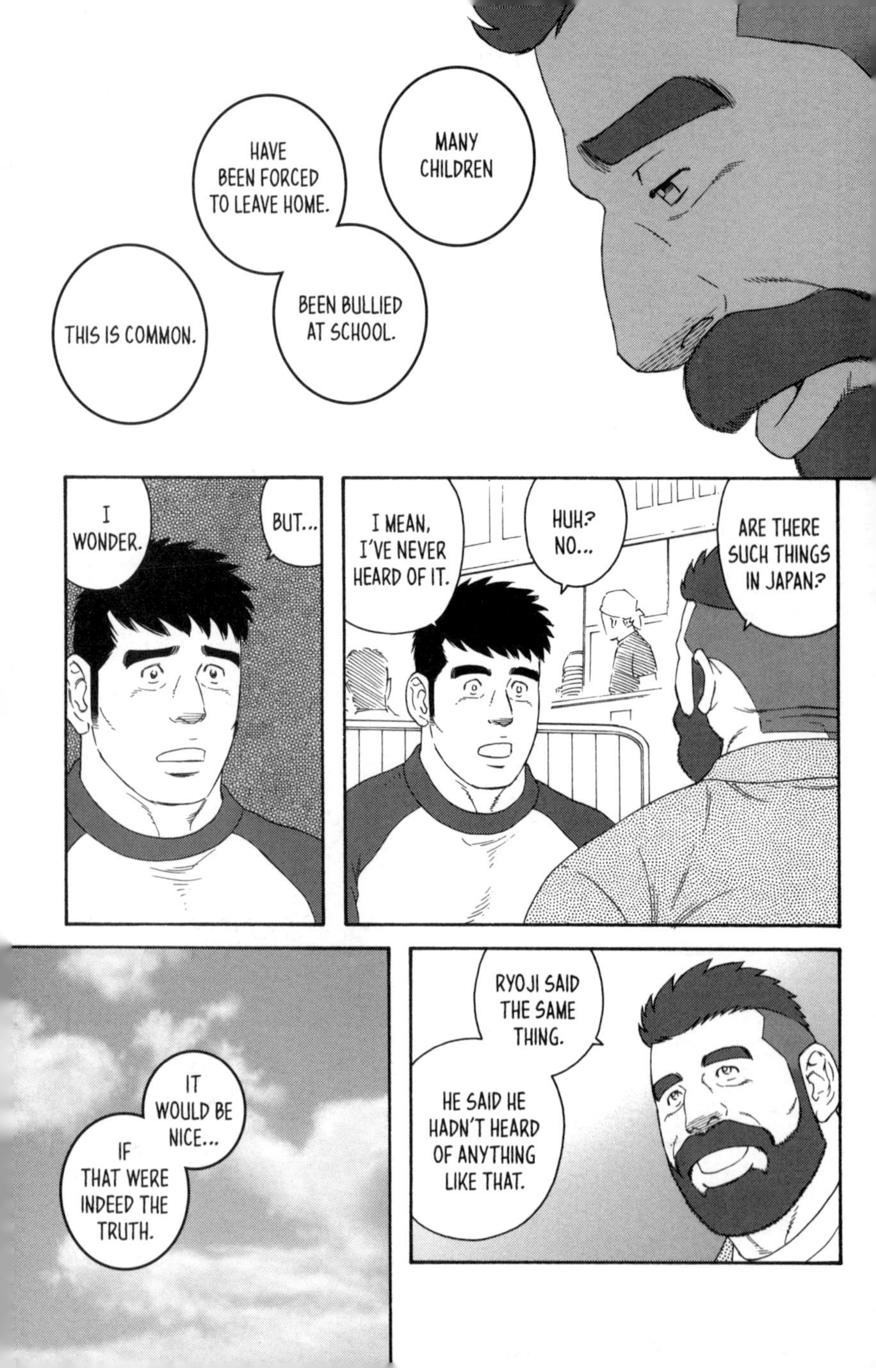
MANY CHILDREN
HAVE BEEN FORCED TO LEAVE HOME.
BEEN BULLIED AT SCHOOL.
THIS IS COMMON.
ARE THERE SUCH THINGS IN JAPAN?
HUH? NO...
I MEAN, I'VE NEVER HEARD OF IT.
BUT...
I WONDER.
RYOJI SAID THE SAME THING.
HE SAID HE HADN'T HEARD OF ANYTHING LIKE THAT.
IT WOULD BE NICE...
IF THAT WERE INDEED THE TRUTH.

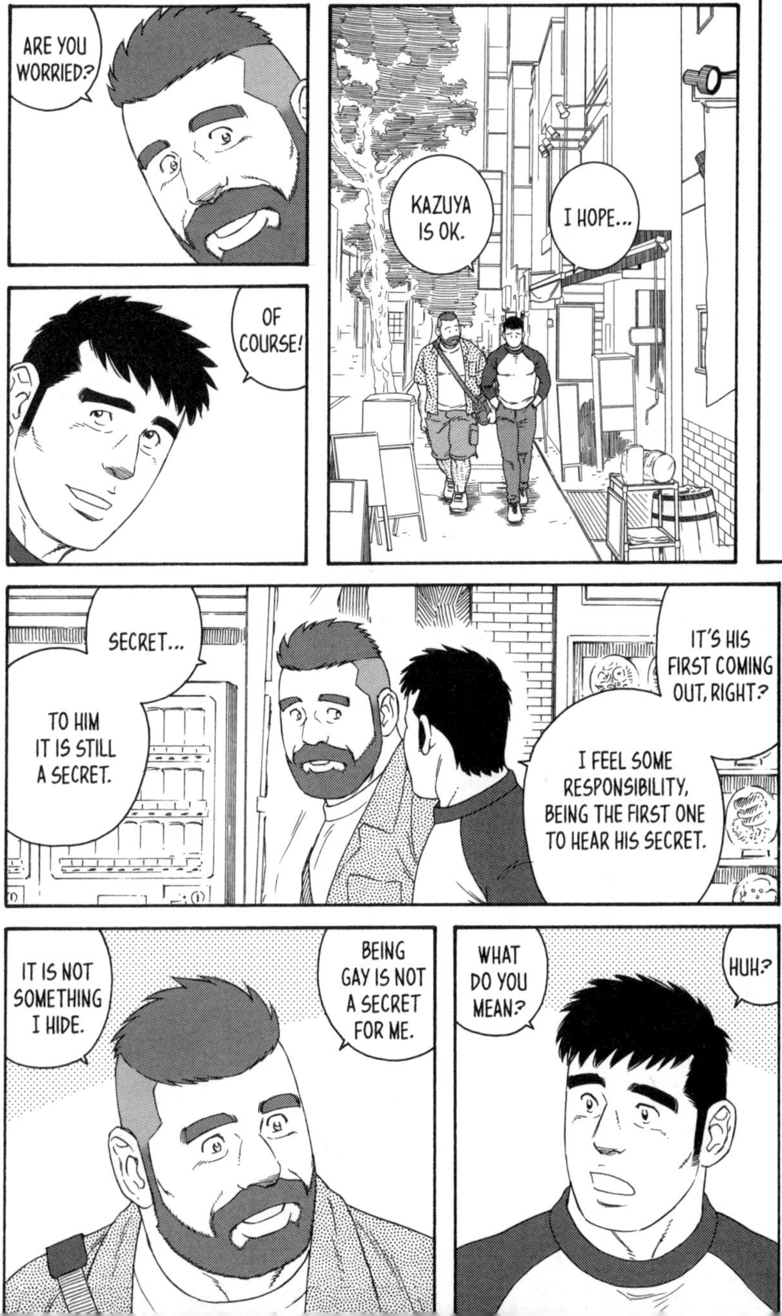
I HOPE...
KAZUYA IS OK.
ARE YOU WORRIED?
OF COURSE!
IT'S HIS FIRST COMING OUT, RIGHT?
I FEEL SOME RESPONSIBILITY, BEING THE FIRST ONE TO HEAR HIS SECRET.
SECRET...
TO HIM IT IS STILL A SECRET.
HUH?
WHAT DO YOU MEAN?
BEING GAY IS NOT A SECRET FOR ME.
IT IS NOT SOMETHING I HIDE.

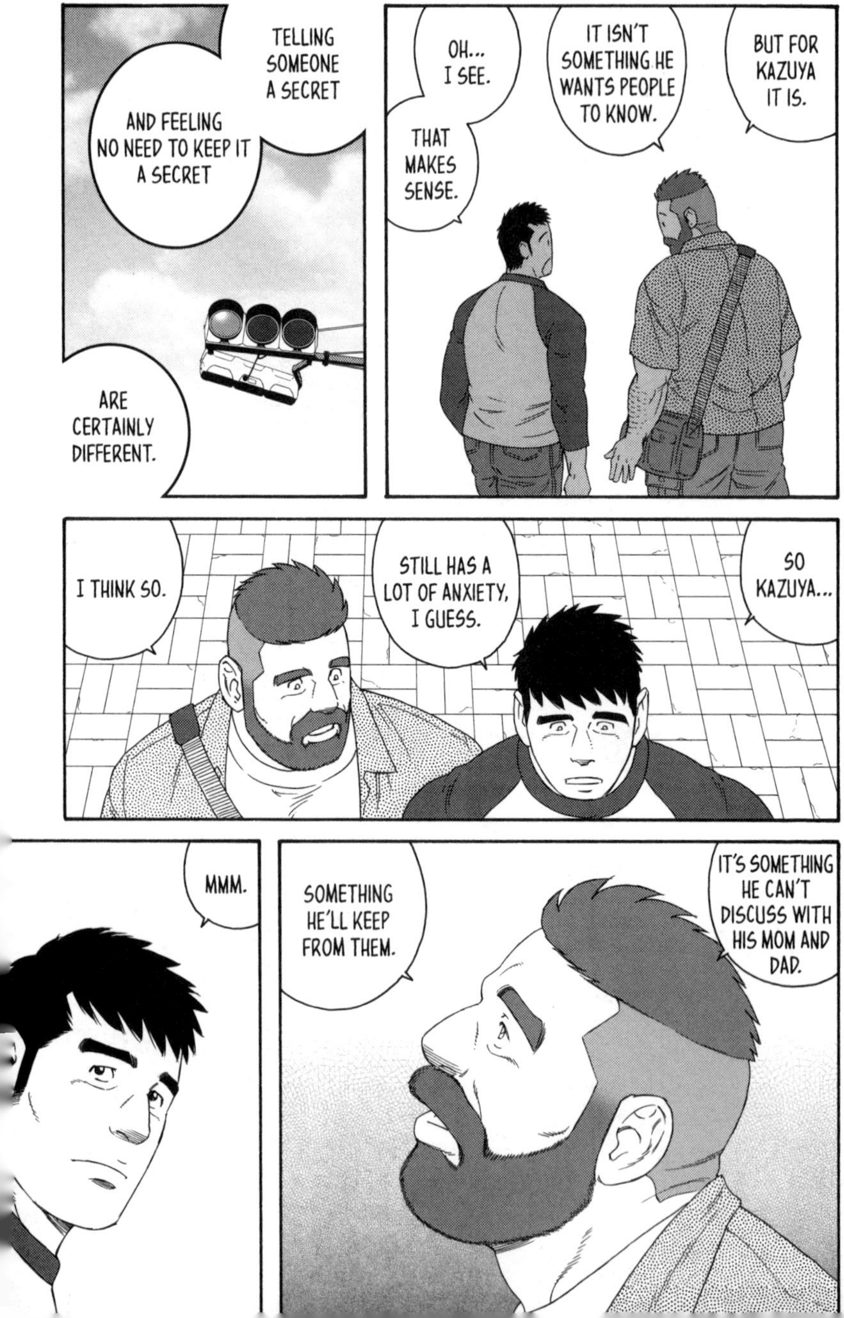
BUT FOR KAZUYA IT IS.
IT ISN'T SOMETHING HE WANTS PEOPLE TO KNOW.
OH... I SEE.
THAT MAKES SENSE.
TELLING SOMEONE A SECRET
AND FEELING NO NEED TO KEEP IT A SECRET
ARE CERTAINLY DIFFERENT.
SO KAZUYA...
STILL HAS A LOT OF ANXIETY, I GUESS.
I THINK SO.
IT'S SOMETHING HE CAN'T DISCUSS WITH HIS MOM AND DAD.
SOMETHING HE'LL KEEP FROM THEM.
MMM.

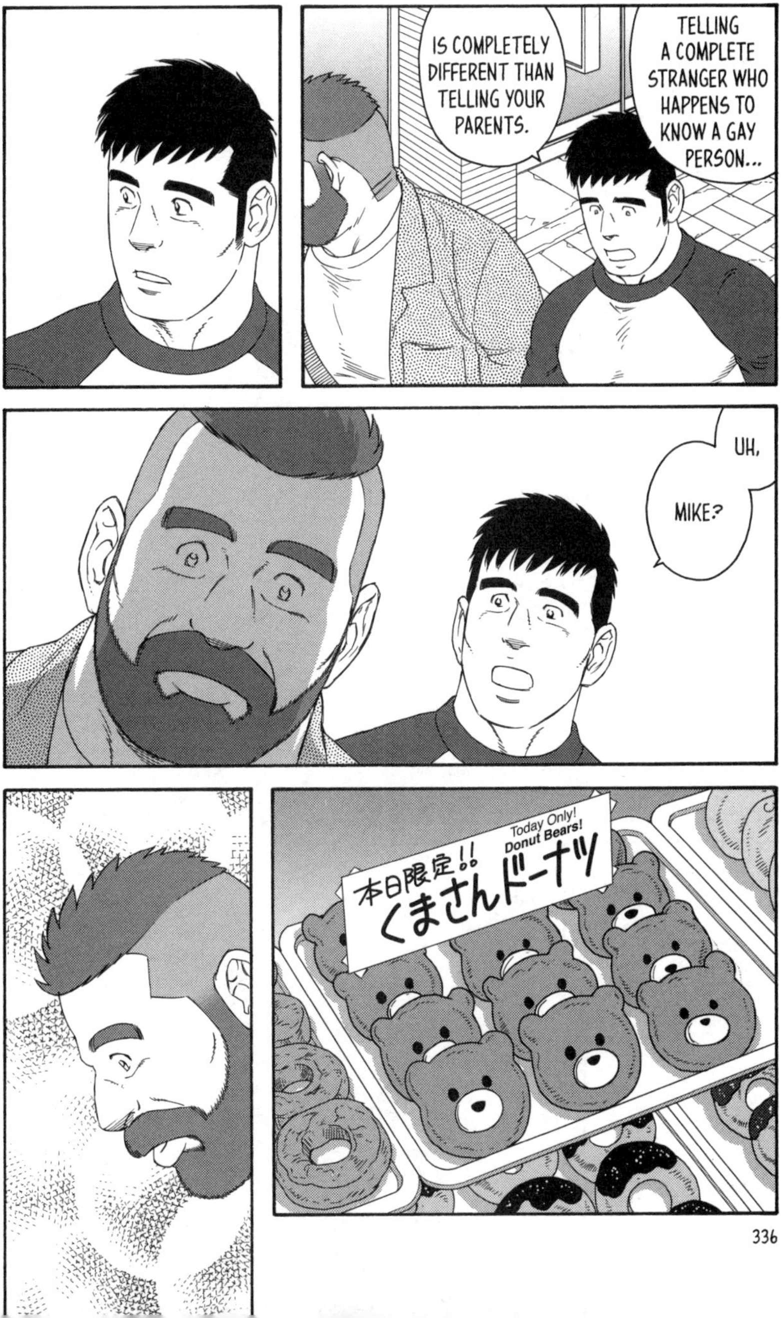
TELLING A COMPLETE STRANGER WHO HAPPENS TO KNOW A GAY PERSON...
IS COMPLETELY DIFFERENT THAN TELLING YOUR PARENTS.
UH,
MIKE?
Today Only! Donut Bears!
本日限定!! くまさんドーナツ

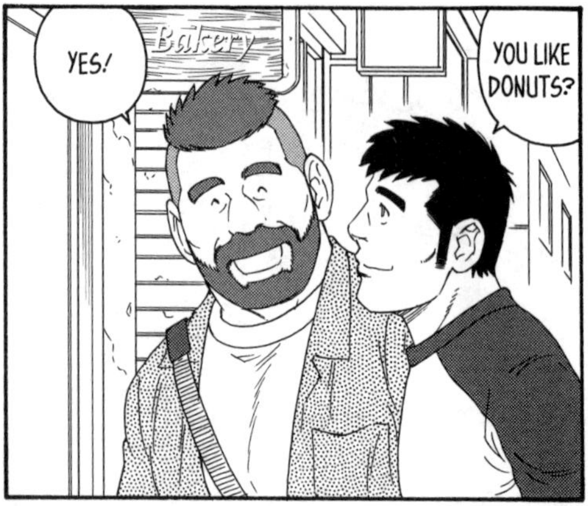
YOU LIKE DONUTS?
Bakery
YES!

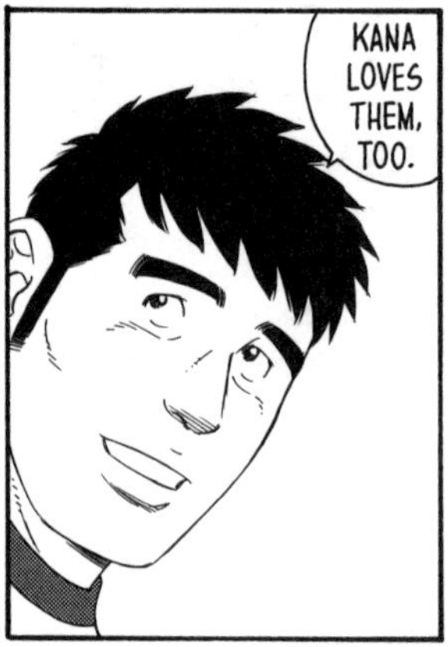
KANA LOVES THEM, TOO.

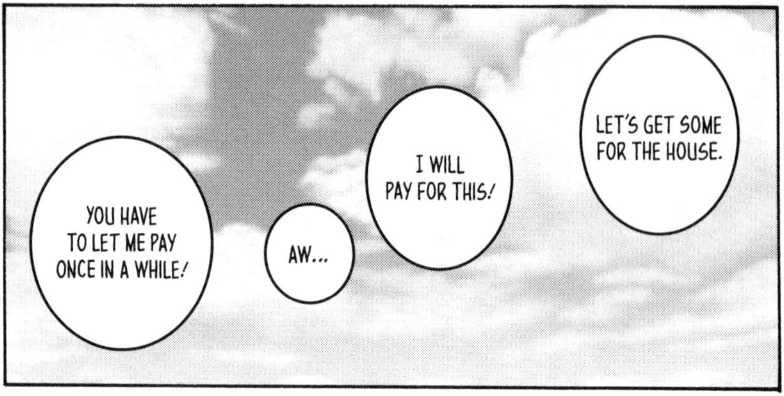
LET'S GET SOME FOR THE HOUSE.
I WILL PAY FOR THIS!
AW...
YOU HAVE TO LET ME PAY ONCE IN A WHILE!

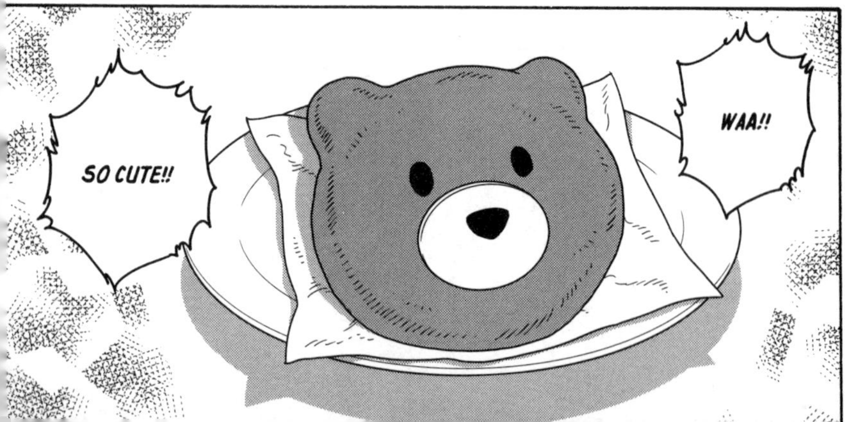
WAA!!
SO CUTE!!

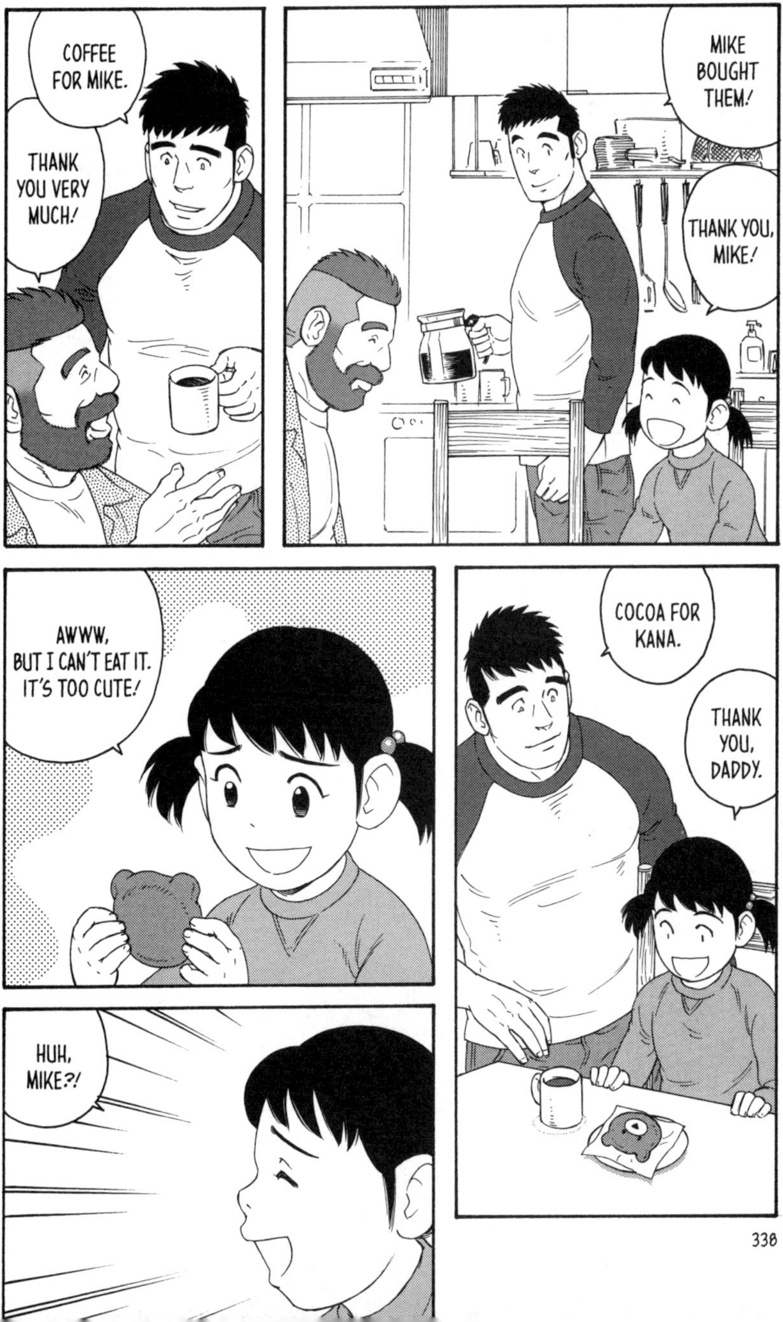
MIKE BOUGHT THEM!
THANK YOU, MIKE!
COFFEE FOR MIKE.
THANK YOU VERY MUCH!
COCOA FOR KANA.
THANK YOU, DADDY.
AWWW, BUT I CAN'T EAT IT. IT'S TOO CUTE!
HUH, MIKE?!

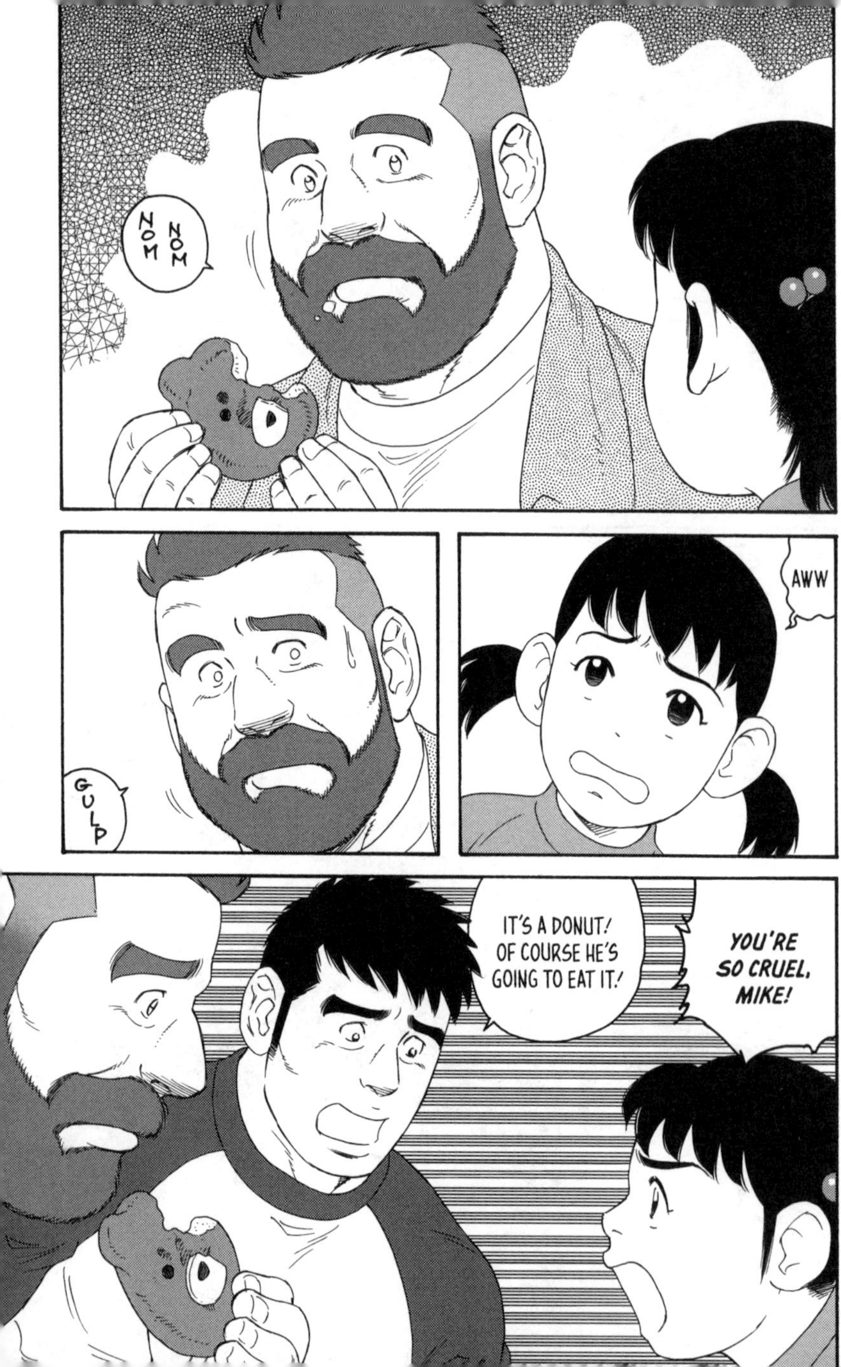
NOM NOM
AWW
GULP
YOU'RE SO CRUEL, MIKE!
IT'S A DONUT! OF COURSE HE'S GOING TO EAT IT!

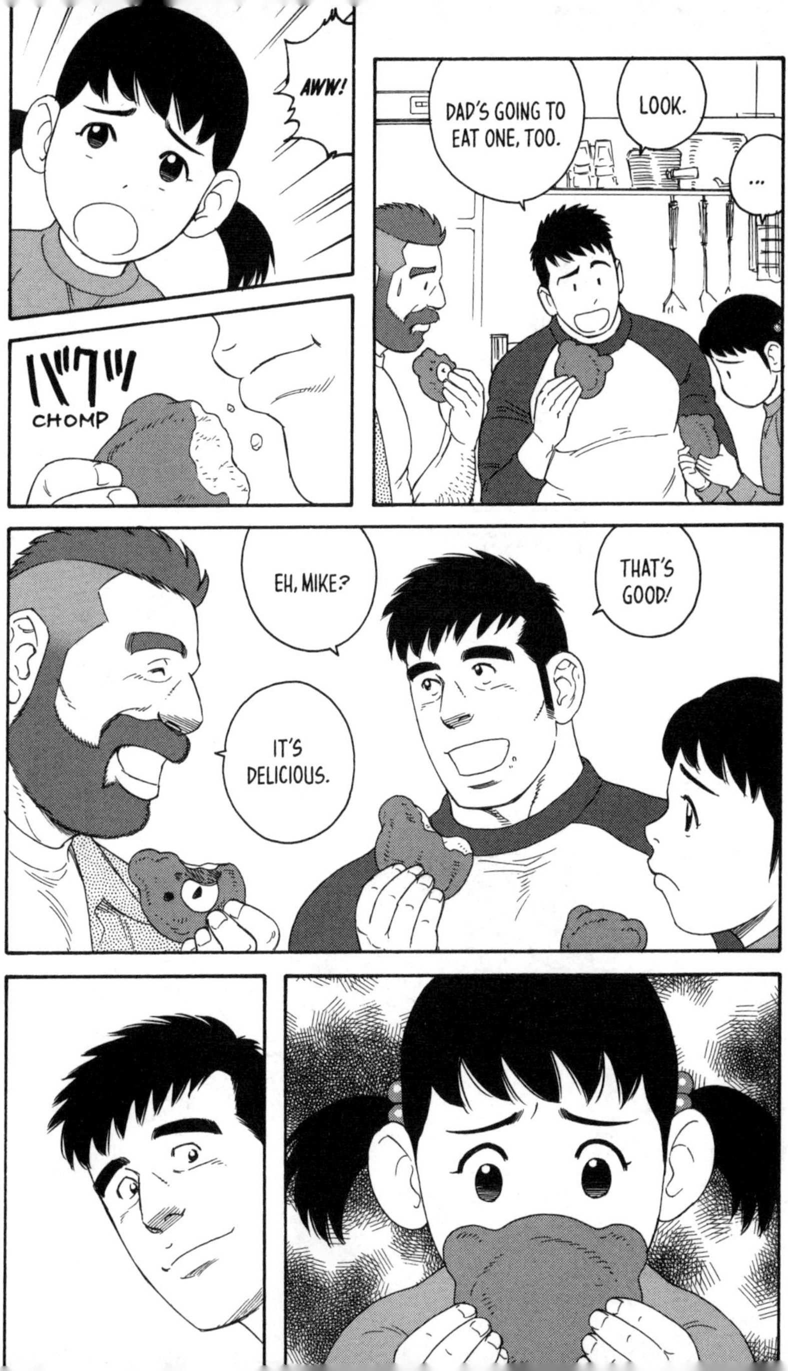

LOOK.
DAD'S GOING TO EAT ONE, TOO.
...
AWW!
バクッ
CHOMP
THAT'S GOOD!
EH, MIKE?
IT'S DELICIOUS.

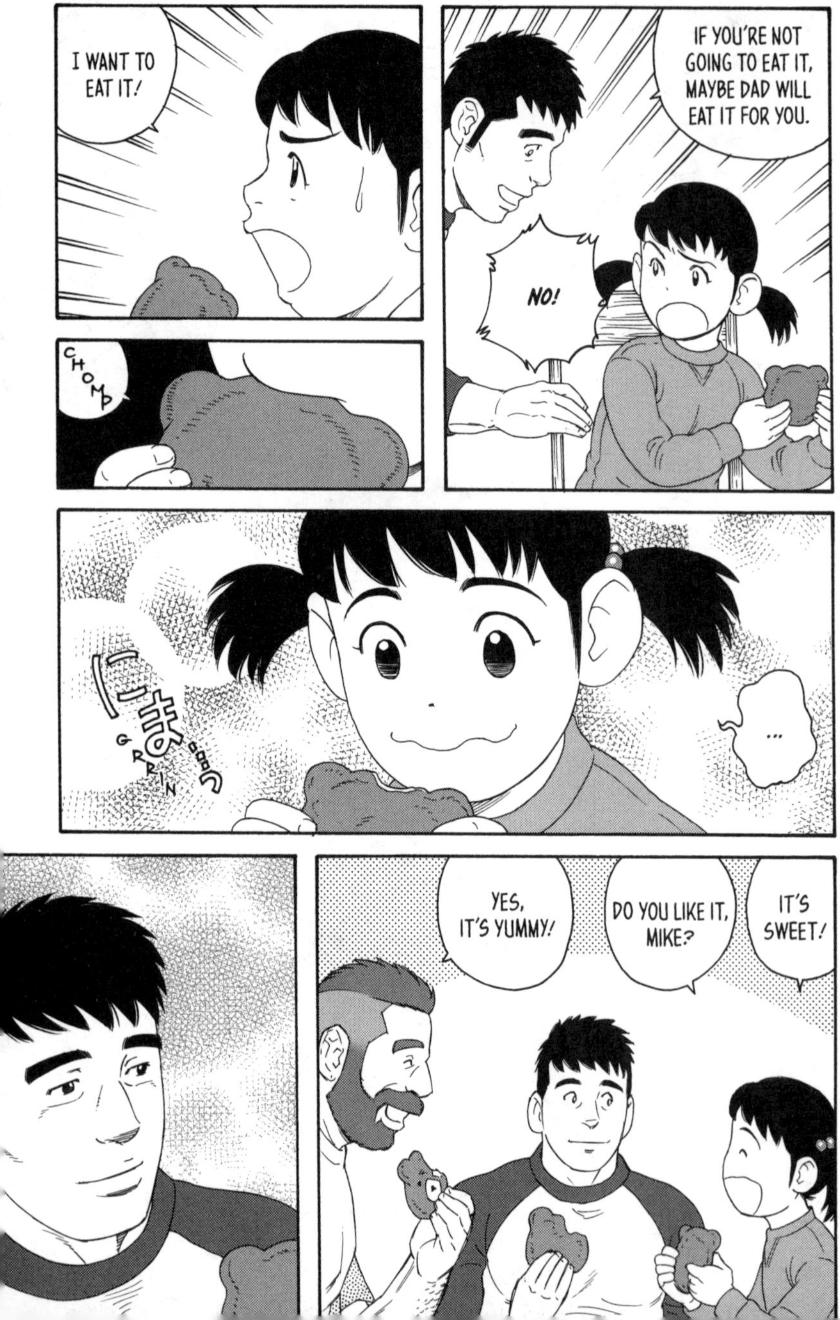
IF YOU'RE NOT GOING TO EAT IT, MAYBE DAD WILL EAT IT FOR YOU.
NO!
I WANT TO EAT IT!
CHOMP
...
にまっ
GRRIN
IT'S SWEET!
DO YOU LIKE IT, MIKE?
YES, IT'S YUMMY!

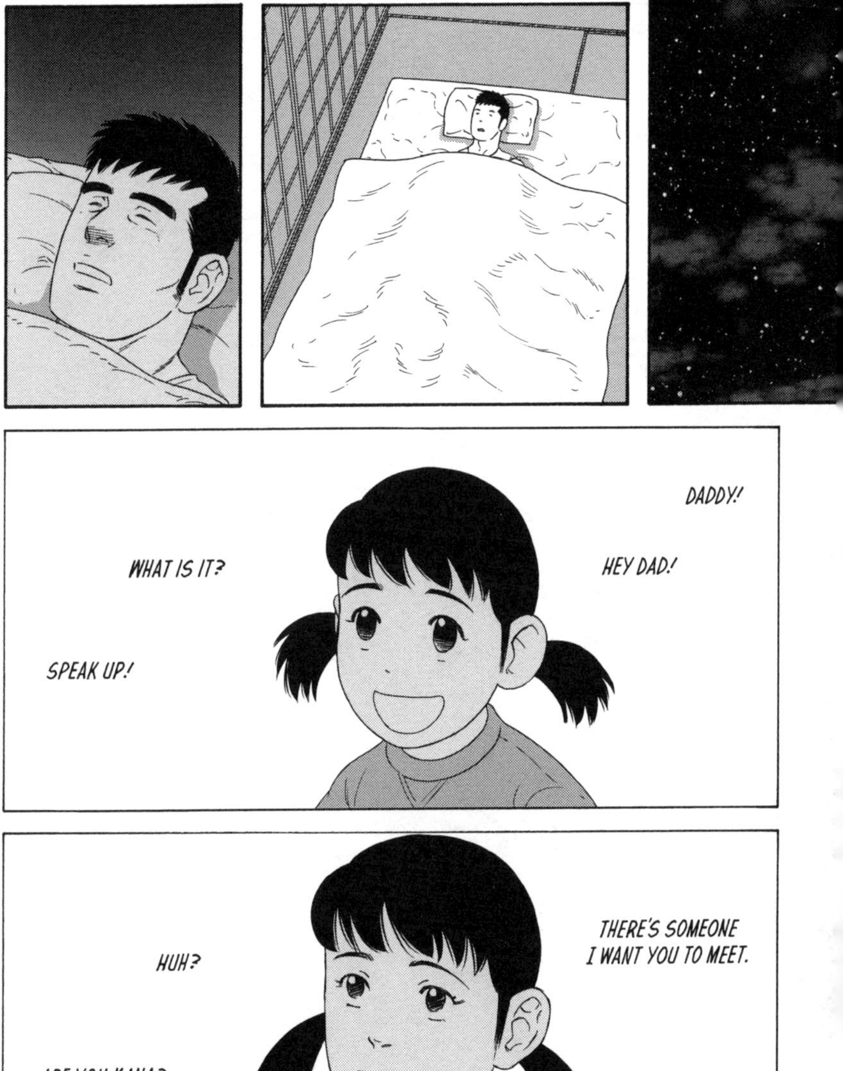
DADDY!
HEY DAD!
WHAT IS IT?
SPEAK UP!
THERE'S SOMEONE I WANT YOU TO MEET.
HUH?
ARE YOU KANA?

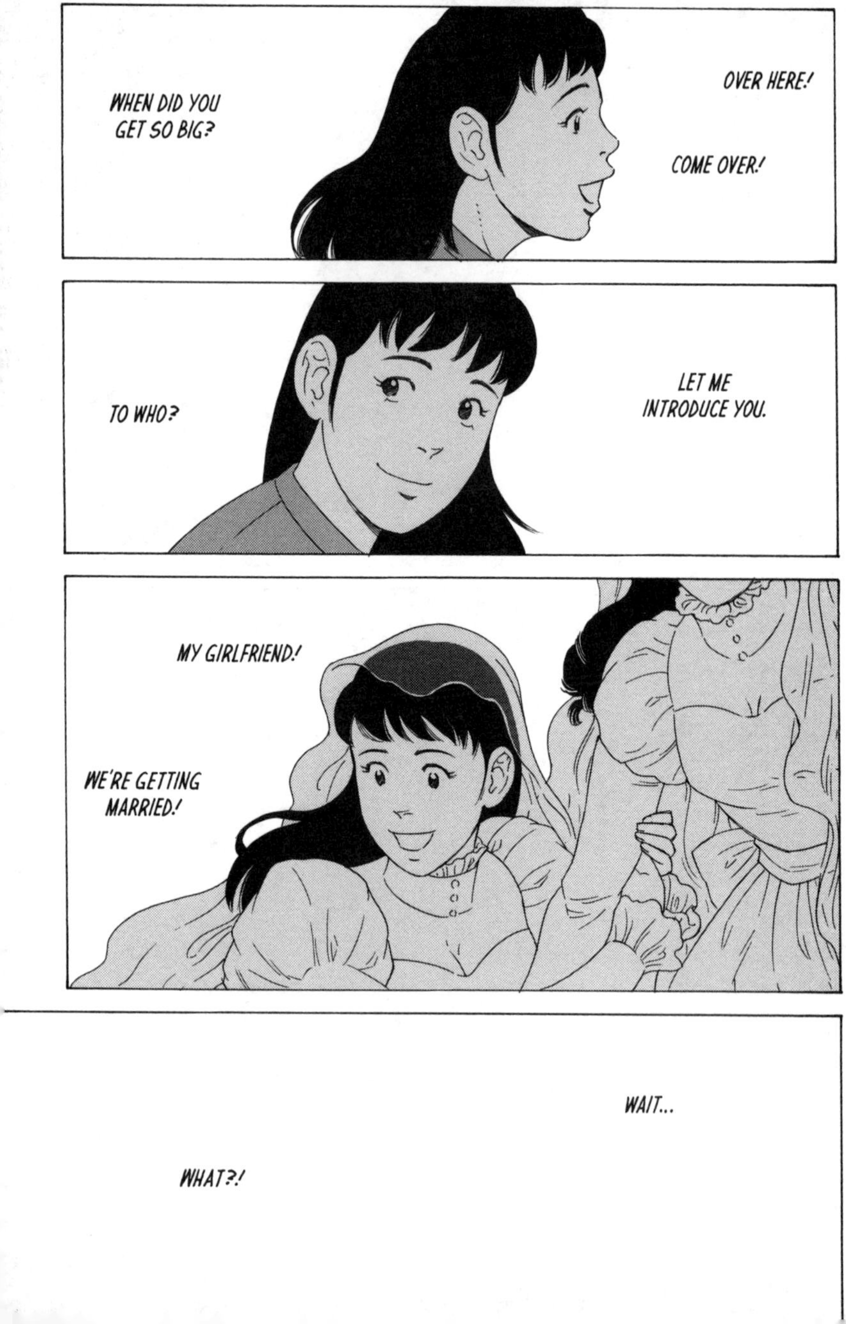
OVER HERE!
COME OVER!
WHEN DID YOU GET SO BIG?
LET ME INTRODUCE YOU.
TO WHO?
MY GIRLFRIEND!
WE'RE GETTING MARRIED!
WAIT...
WHAT?!

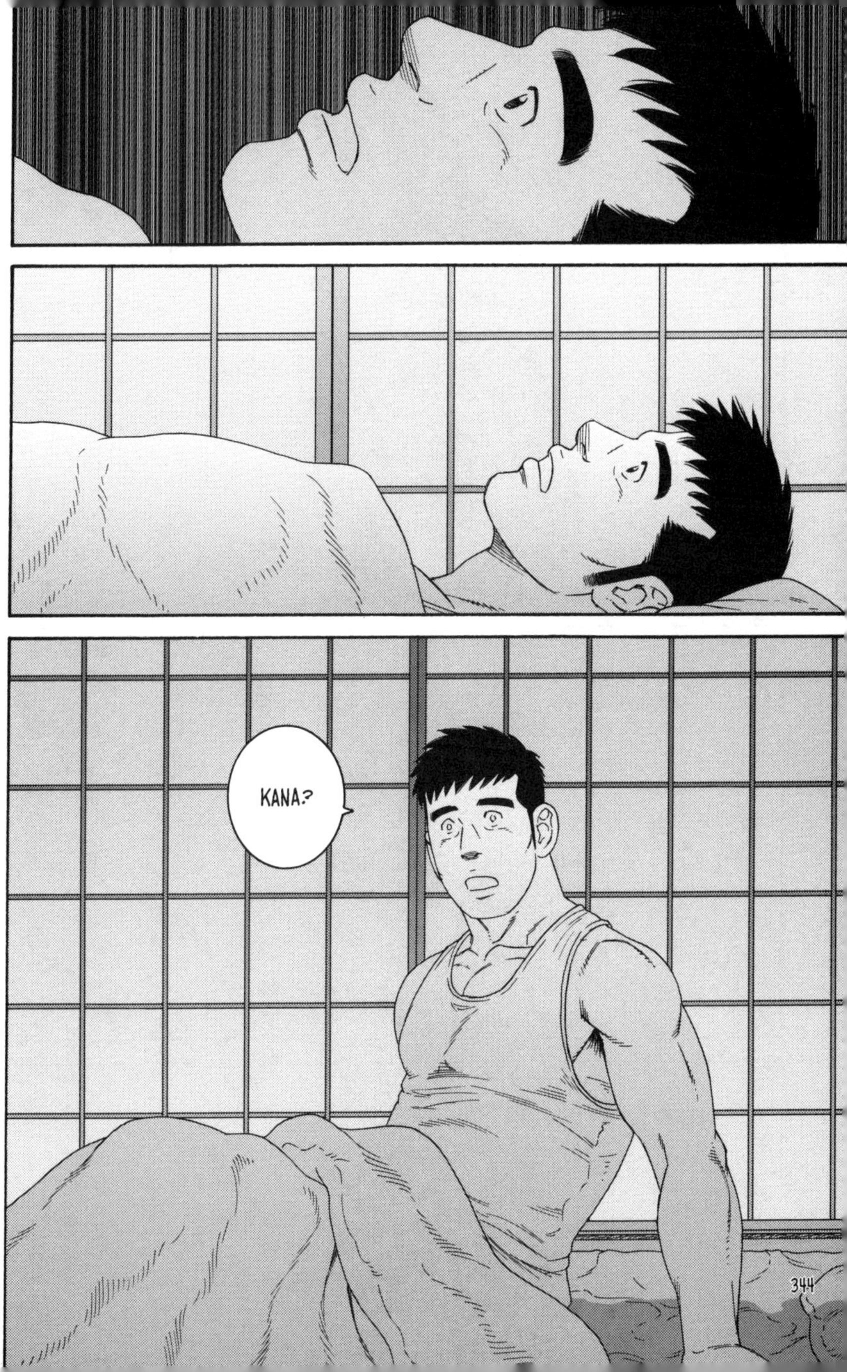
KANA?

PENCILS

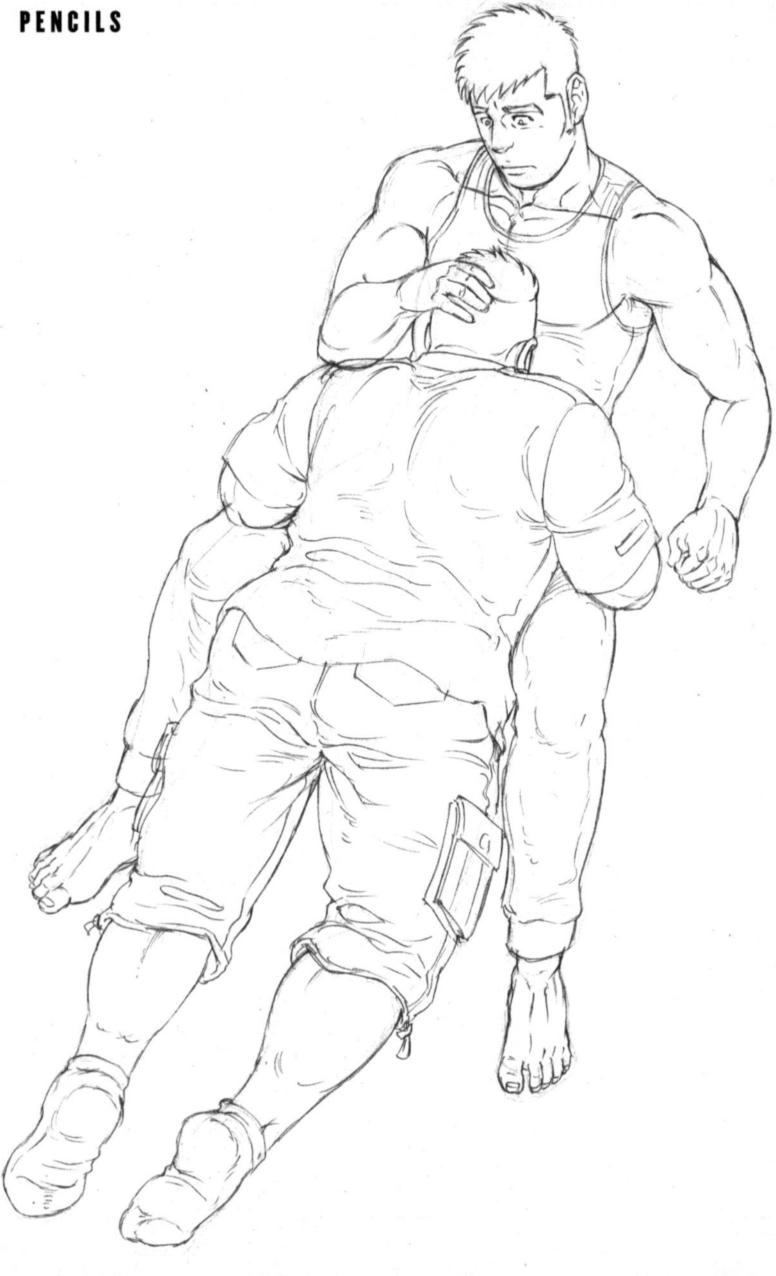

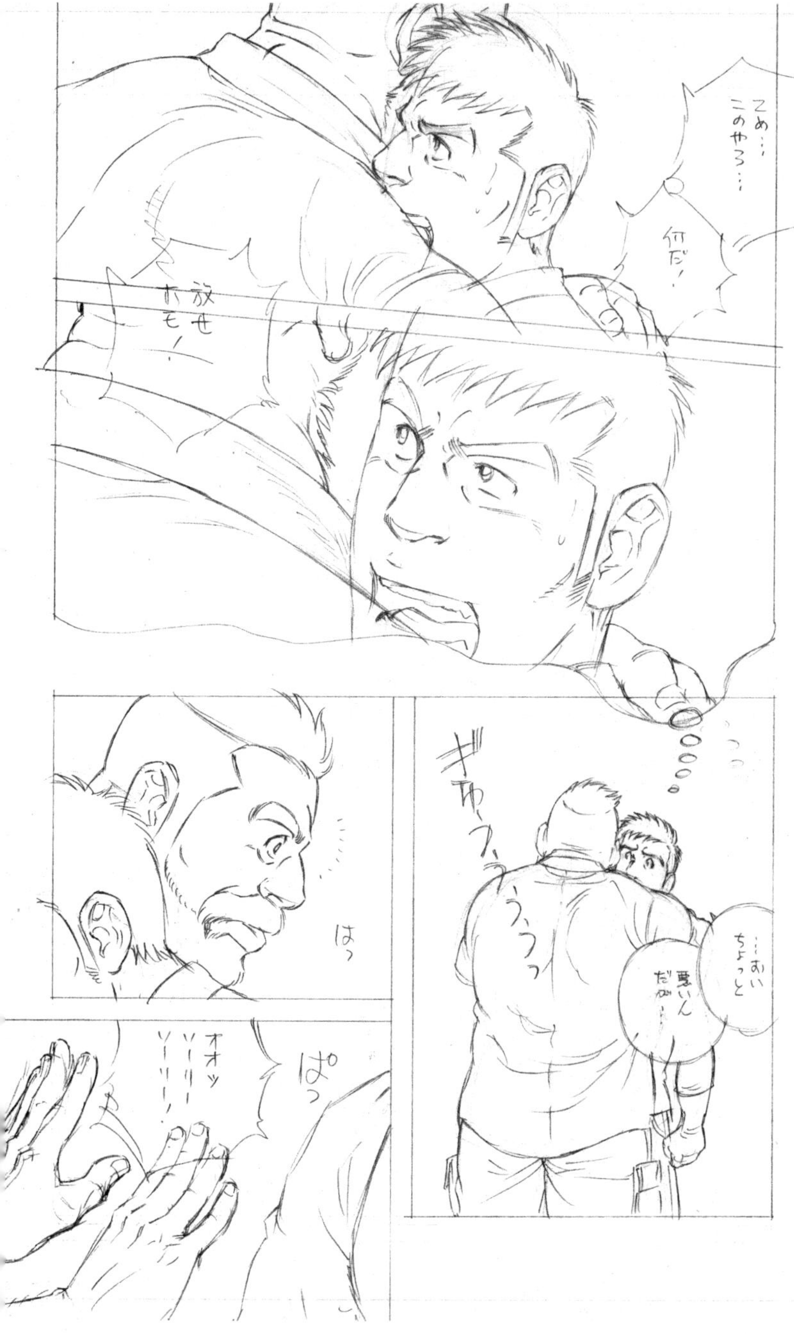
てめ…
このやろ…
何だ！
放せ
おも！
ぎゅーっ
うううっ
…おい
ちょっと
悪いん
だが…
はっ
ぱっ
オオッ
ソーリー
ソーリー！

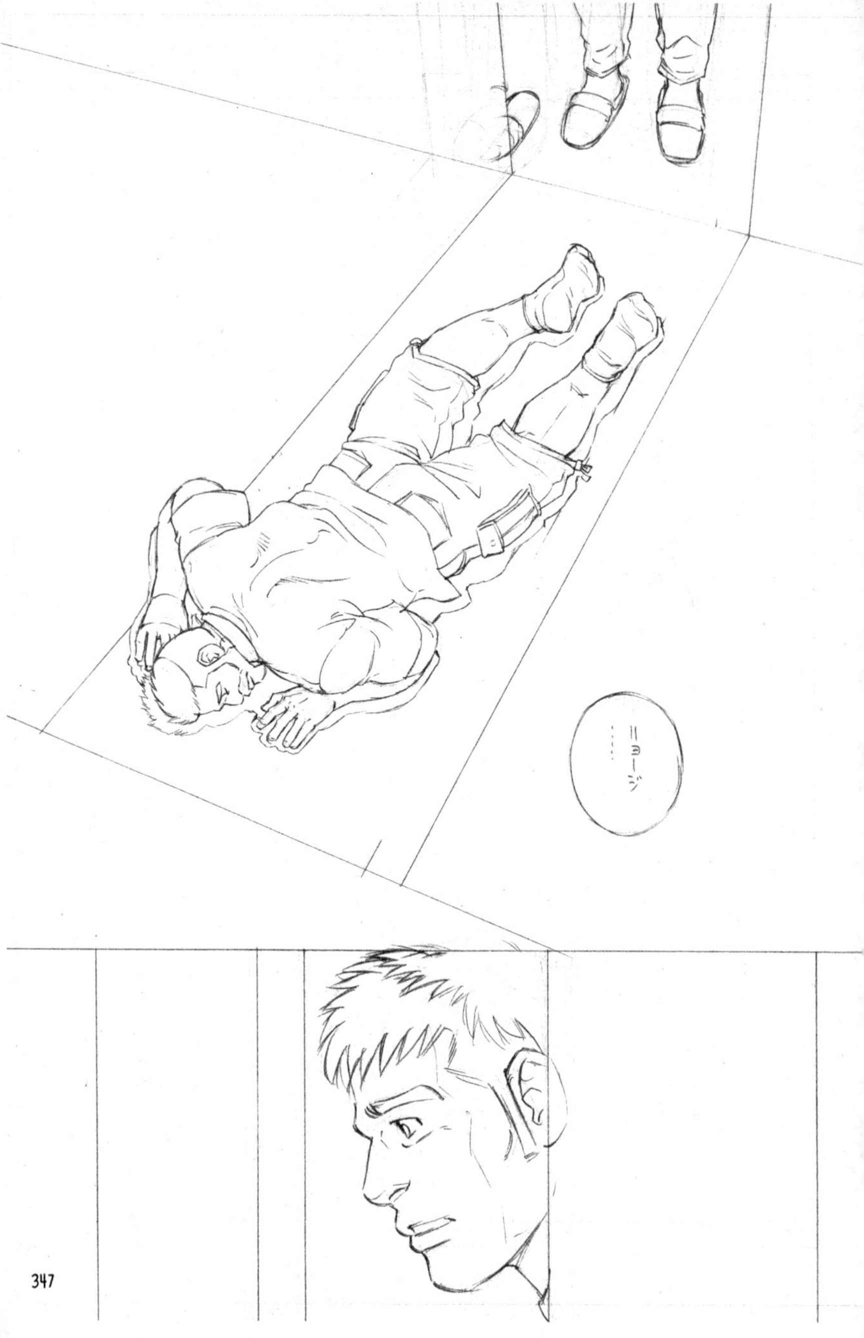
ニョージ……

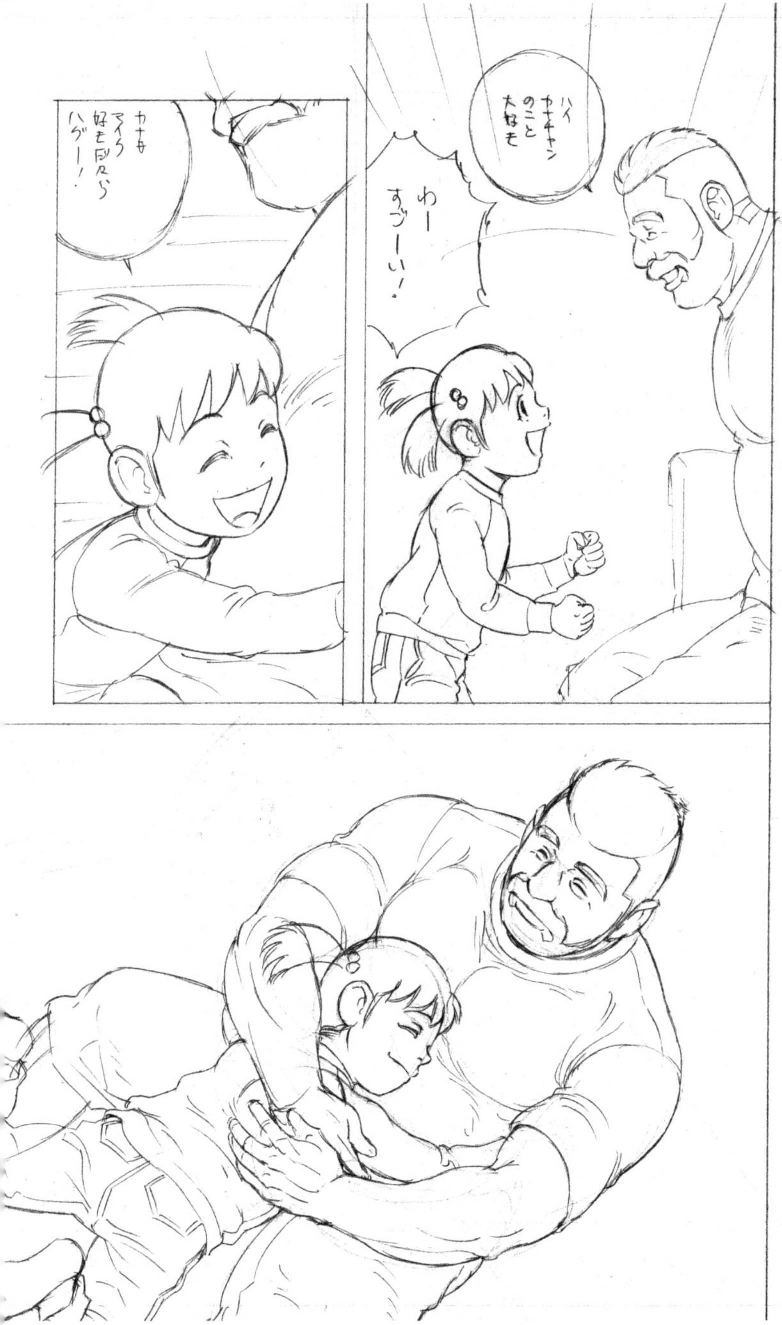
ハイ カナチャンのこと大好きも
わー すごーい！
カナも マイク好きだから ハグー！

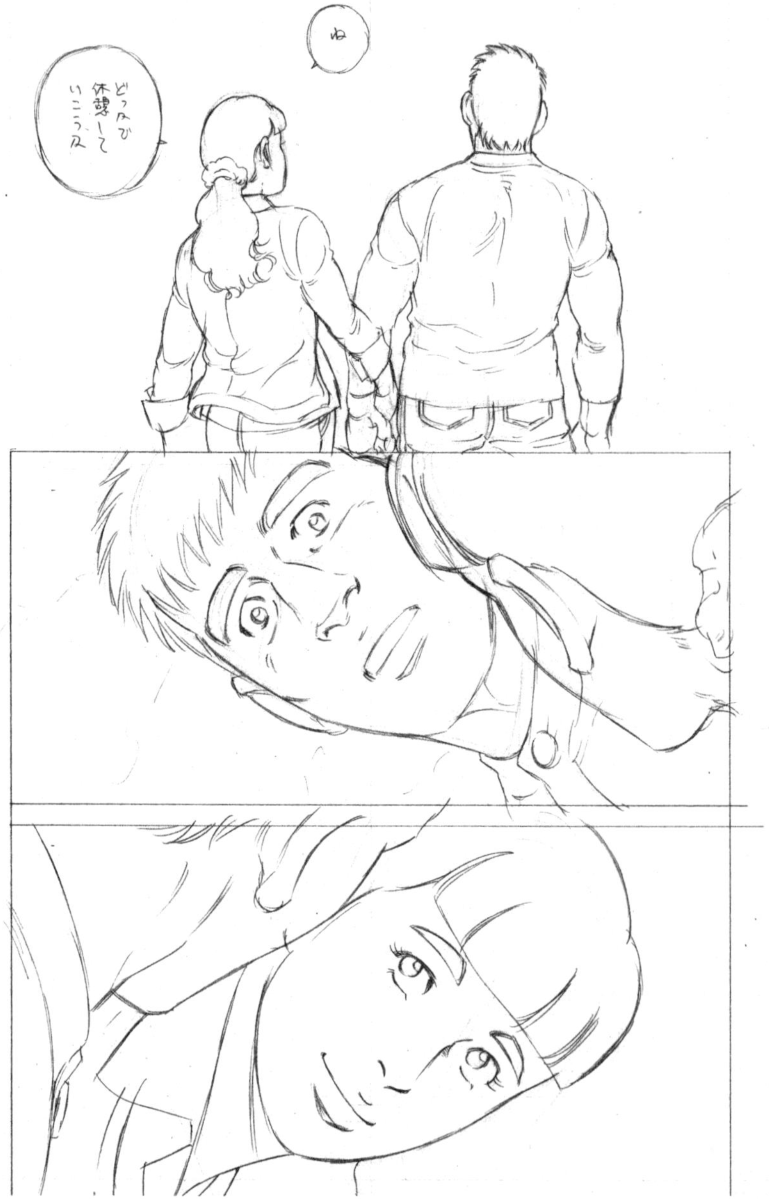
ね
どっかで休憩していこうか

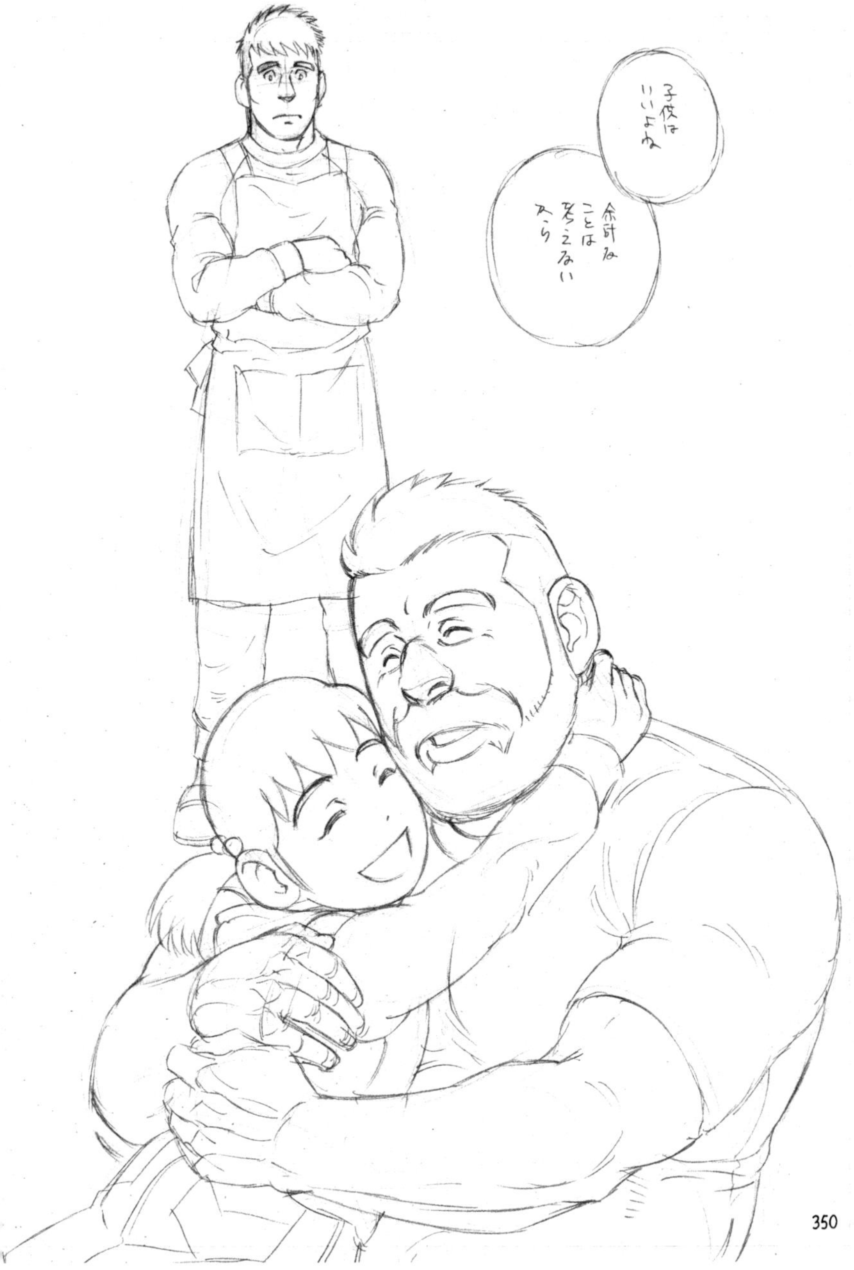
子供はいいよね
余計なことは考えないから

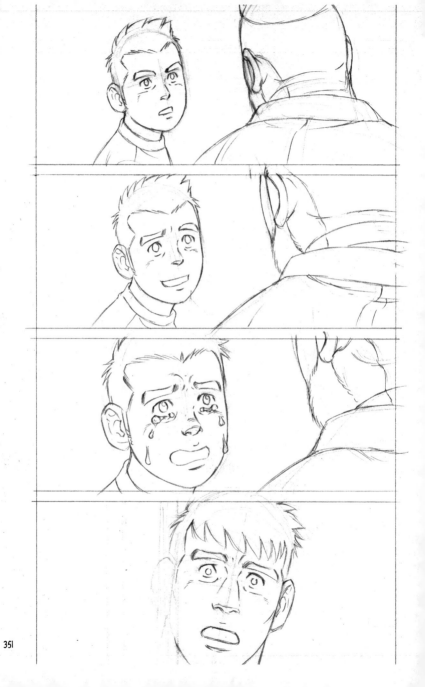

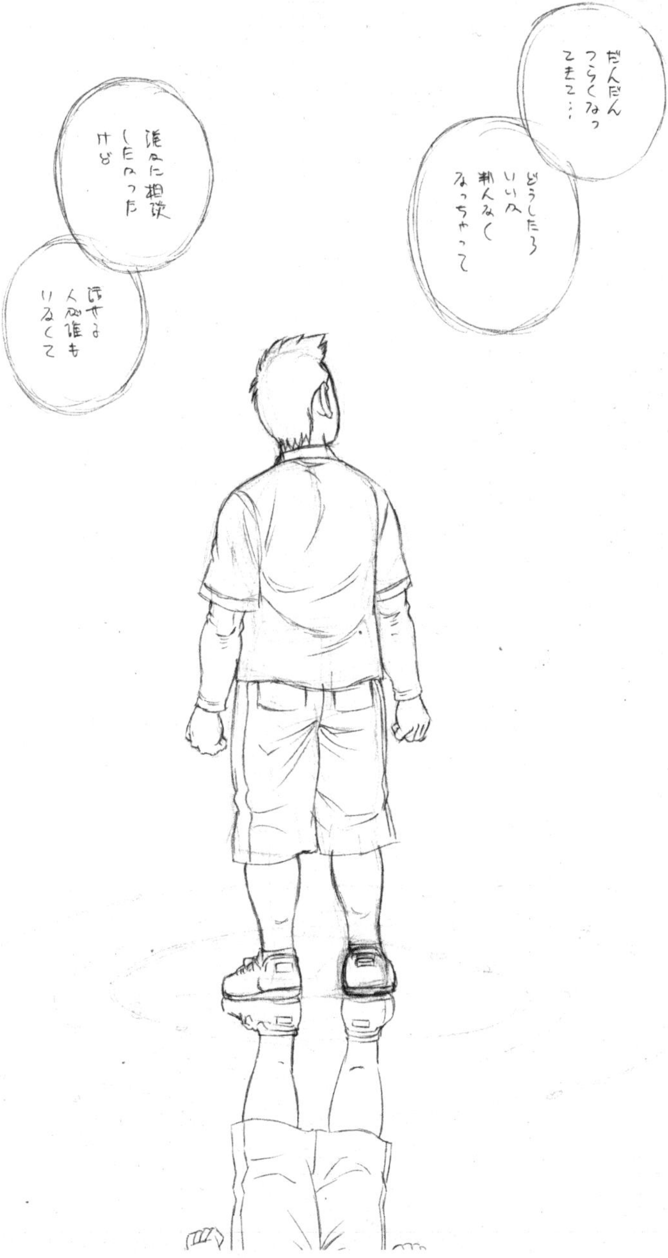
だんだんつらくなってきて…
どうしたらいいか判んなくなっちゃって
誰かに相談したかったけど
話せる人が誰もいなくて

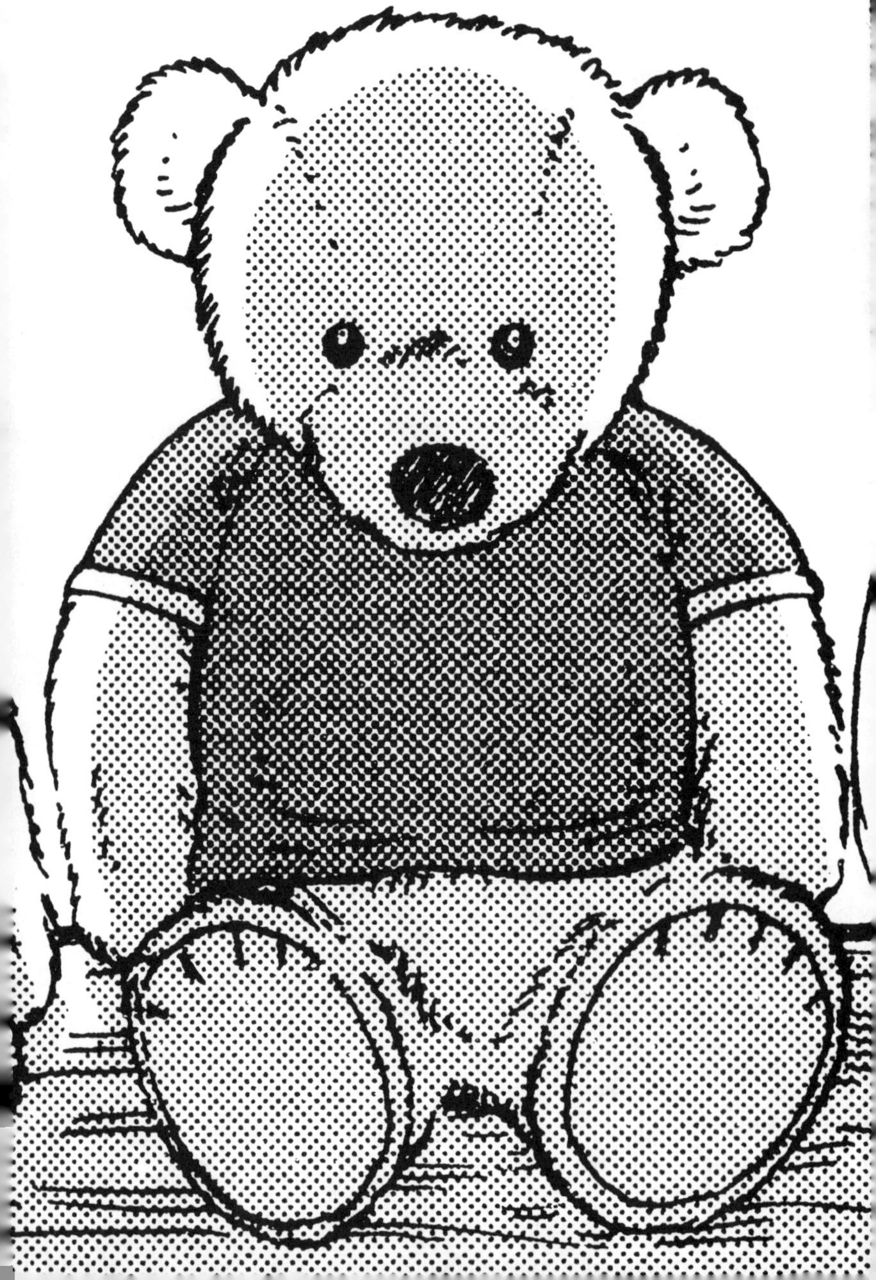

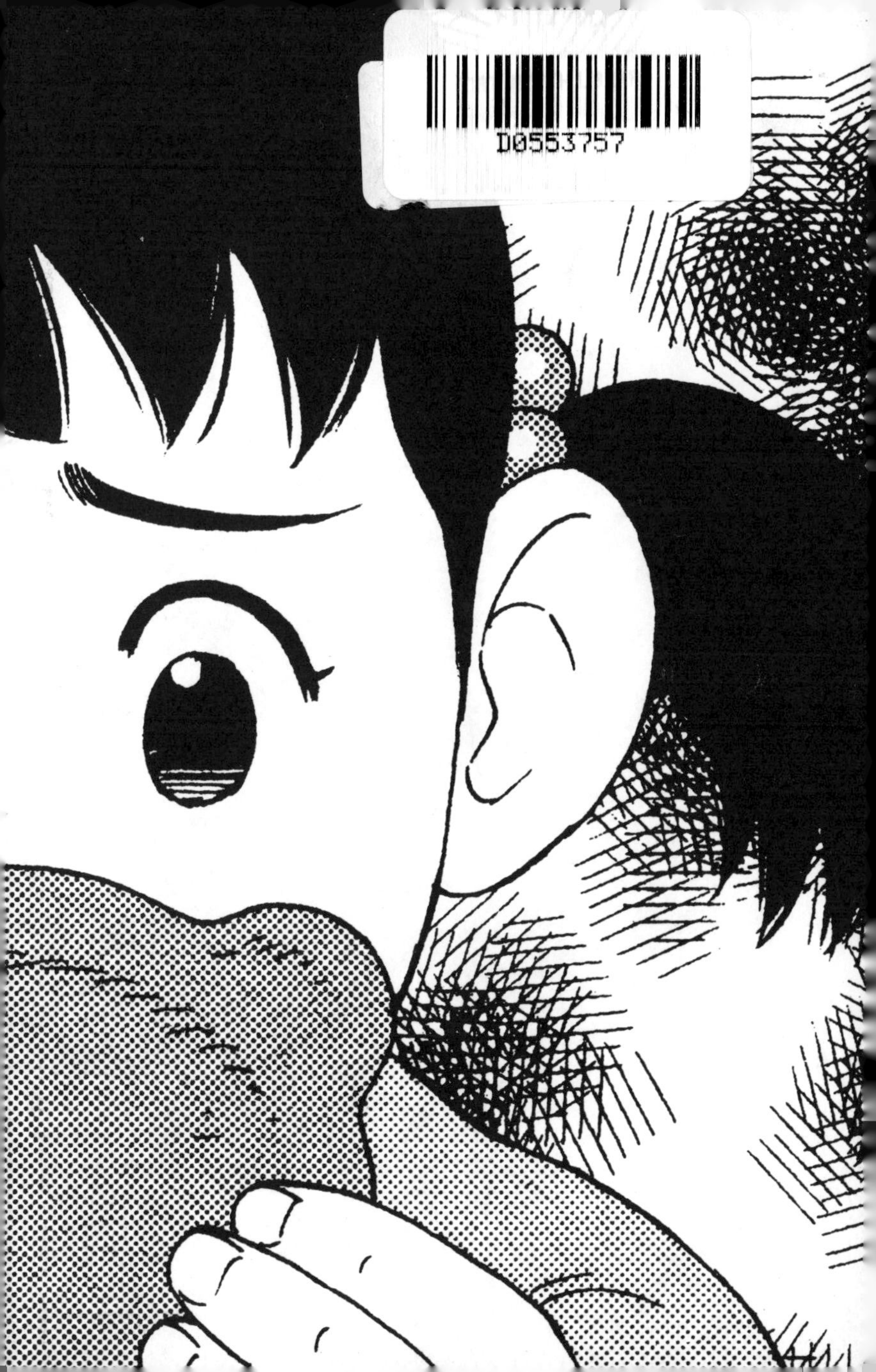